ALSO BY ROBERT LUDLUM

The Bourne Identity

The Matarese Circle

The Holcroft Covenant

The Chancellor Manuscript

The Gemini Contenders

The Rhinemann Exchange

The Matlock Paper

The Osterman Weekend

The Scarlatti Inheritance

ROBERT
LUDLUM

THE
PARSIFAL
MOSAIC

RANDOM HOUSE NEW YORK

All rights reserved under International and Pan-American
Copyright Conventions. Published in the United States by
Random House, Inc., New York, and simultaneously in Canada
by Random House of Canada Limited, Toronto.

Library of Congress Cataloging in Publication Data
Ludlum, Robert, 1927–
The Parsifal mosaic.
I. Title.
PS3562.U26P37   813'.54   81–48276
ISBN 0–394–52111–0   AACR2

Manufactured in the United States of America
9 8 7 6

For Dolores and Charles Ryducha,

two of the finest people I have ever known—

from a grateful brother

Na zdrowie!

BOOK ONE

1

The cold rays of the moon streaked down from the night sky and bounced off the rolling surf, which burst into suspended sprays of white where isolated waves crashed into the rocks of the shoreline. The stretch of beach between the towering boulders of the Costa Brava was the execution ground. It had to be. May God *damn* this goddamned world—it had to be!

He could see her now. And hear her through the sounds of the sea and the breaking surf. She was running wildly, screaming hysterically: *"Pro boha živého! Proč! Co to děláš! Přestaň! Proč! Proč!*

Her blond hair was caught in the moonlight, her racing silhouette given substance by the beam of a powerful flashlight fifty yards behind her. She fell; the gap closed and a staccato burst of gunfire abruptly, insolently split the night air, bullets exploding the sand and the wild grass all around her. She would be dead in a matter of seconds.

His love would be gone.

They were high on the hill overlooking the Moldau, the boats on the river plowing the waters north and south, their wakes furrows. The curling smoke from the factories below diffused in the bright afternoon sky, obscuring the mountains in the distance, and Michael watched, wondering if the winds above Prague would come along and blow the smoke away so the mountains could be seen again. His head was on Jenna's lap, his long legs stretched out, touching the wicker basket she had packed with sandwiches and iced wine. She sat on the grass, her back against the smooth bark of a birch tree; she stroked his hair, her fingers circling his face, gently outlining his lips and cheekbones.

"Mikhail, my darling, I was thinking. Those tweed jackets and dark trousers you wear, and that very proper English which must come from your very proper university, will never remove the Havlíček from Havelock."

"I don't think they were meant to. One's a uniform of sorts, and the other you kind of learn in self-defense." He smiled, touching her hand. "Besides, that university was a long time ago."

"So much was a long time ago, wasn't it? Right down there."

"It happened."

"You were there, my poor darling."

"It's history. I survived."

"Many did not."

The blond woman rose, spinning in the sand, pulling at the wild grass, plunging to her right, for several seconds eluding the beam of light. She headed toward the dirt road above the beach, staying in darkness, crouching, lunging, using the cover of night and the patches of tall grass to conceal her body.

It would not do her any good, thought the tall man in the black sweater at his post between two trees above the road, above the terrible violence that was taking place below, above the panicked woman who would be dead in moments. He had looked down at her once before, not so very long ago. She had not been panicked then; she had been magnificent.

He folded the curtain back slowly, carefully in the dark office, his back pressed against the wall, his face inching toward the window. He could see her below, crossing the floodlit courtyard, the tattoo of her high heels against the cobblestones echoing martially up between the surrounding buildings. The guards were recessed in shadows—outlines of sullen marionettes in their Soviet-style uniforms. Heads turned, signifying appreciative glances directed at the figure striding confidently toward the iron gate in the center of the iron fence enclosing the stone compound that was the core of Prague's secret police. The thoughts behind the glances were clear:

this was no mere secretary working overtime, this was a privileged kurva who took dictation on a commissar's couch till all hours of the night.

But others, too, were watching—from other darkened windows. One break in her confident stride, one instant of hesitation, and a phone would be picked up and orders of detention issued to the gate. Embarrassments, of course, were to be avoided where commissars were concerned, but not if there appeared to be substance behind suspicions. Everything was appearance.

There was no break, no hesitation. She was carrying it off . . . carrying it out! They had done it! Suddenly he felt a jolt of pain in his chest; he knew what it was. Fear. Pure, raw, sickening fear. He was remembering— memories within memories. As he watched her his mind went back to a city in rubble, to the terrible sounds of mass execution. Lidice. And a child —one of many children—scurrying through the billowing gray smoke of burning debris, carrying messages and pockets full of plastic explosives. One break, one hesitation, then . . . history.

She reached the gate. An obsequious guard was permitted to leer. She was magnificent. God, he loved her!

She had reached the shoulder of the road, legs and arms working furiously, digging into the sand and the dirt, clawing for survival. With no wild grass to conceal her, she would be seen; the beam of light would find her, and the end would come quickly.

He watched, suspending emotion, erasing pain, a human litmus accepting impressions without comment. He had to—professionally. He had learned the truth, the stretch of beach on the Costa Brava was confirmation of her guilt, proof of her crimes. The hysterical woman below was a killer, an agent for the infamous Voennaya Kontra Razvedka, the savage branch of the Soviet KGB that spawned terrorism everywhere. That was the truth; it was undeniable. He had seen it all, talked with Washington from Madrid. The rendezvous that night had been ordered by Moscow, the purpose being the delivery by VKR Field Officer Jenna Karas of a schedule of assassinations to a faction of the Baader-Meinhof at an isolated beach called Montebello, north of the town of Blanes. That was the truth.

It did not set him free. Instead, it bound him to another truth, an obligation of his profession. Those who betrayed the living and brokered death had to die. No matter who, no matter . . . Michael Havelock had made the decision, and it was irrevocable. He had set the last phase of the trap himself, for the death of the woman who briefly had given him more happiness than any other person on earth. His love was a killer; to permit her to live would mean the killing of hundreds, perhaps thousands.

What Moscow did not know was that Langley had broken the VKR codes. He himself had sent the last transmission to a boat a half-mile off the Costa Brava shoreline. *KGB confirmation. Officer contact compromised by U.S. Intelligence. Schedules false. Eliminate.* The codes were among the most unbreakable; they would guarantee elimination.

She was rising now. Her slender body rose above the shoulder of sand and dirt. It was going to happen! The woman about to die was his love: they had held each other and there had been quiet talk of a lifetime together, of children, of peace and the splendid comfort of being one— together. Once he had believed it all, but it was not to be.

They were in bed, her head on his chest, her soft blond hair falling across her face. He brushed it aside, lifting up the strands that concealed her eyes, and laughed.

"You're hiding," he said.

"It seems we're always hiding," she replied, smiling sadly. "Except when we wish to be seen by people who should see us. We do nothing that we simply want to. Everything is calculated, Mikhail. Regimented. We live in a movable prison."

"It hasn't been that long, and it won't last forever."

"I suppose not. One day they'll find they don't need us, don't want us any longer, perhaps. Will they let us go, do you think? Or will we disappear?"

"Washington's not Prague. Or Moscow. We'll walk out of our movable prison, me with a gold watch, you with some kind of silent decoration with your papers."

"Are you sure? We know a great deal. Too much, perhaps."

"Our protection lies in what we do know. What I know. They'll always wonder: Did he write it down somewhere? Take care, watch him, be good to him. . . . It's not unusual, really. We'll walk out."

"Always protection," she said, tracing his eyebrows. "You never forget, do you? The early days, the terrible days."

"History. I've forgotten."

"What will we do?"

"Live. I love you."

"Do you think we'll have children? Watch them going off to school; hold them, scold them. Go to hockey-ball games."

"Football . . . or baseball. Not hockey-ball. Yes, I hope so."

"What will you do, Mikhail?"

"Teach, I suppose. At a college somewhere. I've a couple of starched degrees that say I'm qualified. We'll be happy, I know that. I'm counting on it."

"What will you teach?"

He looked at her, touching her face, then his eyes wandered up to the shabby ceiling in the run-down hotel room. "History," he said. And then he reached for her, taking her in his arms.

The beam of light swung across the darkness. It caught her, a bird on fire, trying to rise, trapped by the light that was her darkness. The gunshots followed—terrorists' gunfire for a terrorist. The woman arched backward, the first bullets penetrating the base of her spine, her blond hair cascading behind her. Three shots then came separately, with finality—a marksman's eye delivering a marksman's score; they entered the back of her neck and her skull, propelling her forward over the mound of dirt and sand, her fingers clawing the earth, her blood-streaked face mercifully concealed. A final spasm, and all movement stopped.

His love was dead—for some part of love was a part of whatever they were. He had done what he had to do, just as she had done the same. Each was right, each wrong, ultimately so terribly wrong. He closed his eyes, feeling the unwanted dampness.

Why did it have to be? We are fools. Worse, we are stupid. We do not talk; we die. So men with fluid tongues and facile minds can tell us what is right and wrong—geopolitically, you understand, which means that whatever they say is beyond our puerile understanding.

What will you do, Mikhail?

Teach, I suppose. At a college somewhere . . .

What will you teach?

History . . .

It was all history now. Remembrances of things too painful. Let it be cold history, as the early days were history. They cannot be a part of me any longer. She cannot be a part of me, if she ever was, even in her pretense. Yet I will keep a promise, not to her but to myself. I am finished. I will disappear into another life, a new life. I will go somewhere, teach somewhere. Illuminate the lessons of futility.

He heard the voices and opened his eyes. Below, the killers of the Baader-Meinhof had reached the condemned woman, sprawled out in death, clutching the ground that was her execution place—geopolitically preordained. Had she really been so magnificent a liar? Yes, she had been, for he had seen the truth. Even in her eyes he had seen it.

The two executioners bent down to grab the corpse and drag it away —her once graceful body to be consigned to fire or chained for the deep. He would not interfere; the evidence had to be felt, touched, reflected upon later when the trap was revealed, another lesson taught. Futility— geopolitically required.

A gust of wind suddenly whipped across the open beach; the killers braced themselves, their feet slipping in the sand. The man on the left raised his right hand in an unsuccessful attempt to keep the visored fishing cap on his head; it blew away, rolling toward the dune that was the shoulder of the road. He released his hold on the corpse and ran after it. Havelock watched as the man came closer. There was something about him— About the face? No, it was the hair, seen clearly in the moonlight. It was wavy and dark, but not completely dark; there was a streak of white above his forehead, a sudden intrusion that was startling. He had seen that head of hair, seen that face somewhere before. But where? There were so many memories. Files analyzed, photographs studied—contracts, sources, enemies. Where was this man from? KGB? The dreaded Voennaya? A splinter faction paid by Moscow when not drawing contingency funds from a CIA station chief in Lisbon?

It did not matter. The deadly puppets and the vulnerable pawns no longer concerned Michael Havelock—or Mikhail Havlíček, for that matter. He would route a cable to Washington through the embassy in Madrid in the morning. He was finished, he had nothing more to give. Whatever his superiors wanted in the way of debriefing he would permit. Even going to a clinic; he simply did not care. But they would have no more of his life.

That was history. It had ended on an isolated beach called Montebello on the Costa Brava.

2

Time was the true narcotic for pain. Either the pain disappeared when it ran its course or a person learned to live with it. Havelock understood this, knowing that at this moment in time something of both was applicable. The pain had not disappeared but there was less of it; there were periods when the memories were dulled, the scar tissue sensitive only when prodded. And traveling helped; he had forgotten what it was like to cope with the complexities facing the tourist.

"If you'll note, sir, it's printed here on your ticket. 'Subject to change without notice.'"

"Where?"

"Down here."

"I can't read it."

"I can."

"You've memorized it."

"I'm familiar with it, sir."

And the immigration lines. Followed by customs inspections. The intolerable preceded by the impossible; men and women who countered their own boredom by slamming rubber stamps and savagely attacking defenseless zippers whose manufacturers believed in planned obsolescence.

There was no question about it, he was spoiled. His previous life had had its difficulties and its risks, but they had not included the perils that confronted the traveler at every turn. In his past life, on the other hand, whenever he got to where he was going, there was the movable prison. No, not exactly. There were appointments to keep, sources to contact, informers to pay. Too often at night, in shadows, far away from seeing or being seen.

Now there was none of that. There hadn't been for nearly eight weeks. He walked in daylight, as he was walking now down the Damrak in Amsterdam toward the American Express office. He wondered if the cable would be there. If it was, it would signify the beginning of something. A concrete beginning. A job.

Employment. Strange how the unexpected was so often connected to the routine. It had been three months since that night on the Costa Brava, two months and five days since the end of his debriefing and formal separation from the government. He had come up to Washington from the clinic in Virginia where he had spent twelve days in therapy. (Whatever they had expected to find wasn't there; he could have told them that. He didn't care anymore; couldn't they understand?) He had emerged from the doors of the State Department at four o'clock in the afternoon a free man—also an unemployed, unpensioned citizen with certain resources hardly of the magnitude to be considered an annuity. It had occurred to him as he stood there on the pavement that afternoon that sometime in the future a job had to be found, a job where he could illuminate the lessons of— The lessons. But not for a while; for a while he would do the minimum required of a functioning human being.

He would travel, revisit all those places he had never really visited— in the sunlight. He would read—reread, actually—not codes and schedules and dossiers but all those books he had not read since graduate school. If he was going to illuminate anything for anybody, he had to relearn so much that he had forgotten.

But if there was one thing on his mind at four o'clock that afternoon, it was a fine dinner. After twelve days in therapy, with various chemicals and a restricted diet, he had ached at the thought of a good meal. He had been about to head back to his hotel for a shower and a change of clothes when an accommodating taxi drove down C Street, the sun bouncing off its windows and obscuring any occupants. It stopped at the curb in front of him—at the behest of his signal, Michael had assumed. Instead, a passenger carrying an attaché case stepped out quickly, a harried man late for an appointment, fumbling for his billfold. At first neither Havelock nor the passenger recognized each other; Michael's thoughts were on a restaurant, the other's on paying the driver.

"Havelock?" the passenger inquired suddenly, adjusting his glasses. "It *is* you, isn't it, Michael?"

"Harry? Harry Lewis?"

"You've got it. How are you, M.H.?"

Lewis was one of the few people he ever saw—and he rarely saw Harry —who called him by his initials. It was a minor legacy from graduate school, where he and Lewis had been classmates at Princeton. Michael had gone into government, Lewis into academia. Dr. Harry Lewis was chairman of the political science department at a small, prestigious university in New England, traveling down to D.C. now and then for consultation chores at State. They had run into each other several times when both were in Washington.

"Fine. Still picking up per diems, Harry?"

"A lot fewer than before. Someone taught you people how to read evaluation reports from our more esoteric graduate schools."

"Good Christ, I'm being replaced by a beard in blue jeans with funny cigarettes."

The bespectacled professor was stunned. "You're kidding. You're *out?* I thought you were in for life!"

"The opposite, Harry. Life began between five and seven minutes ago when I wrote out my final signature. And in a couple of hours I'm going to be faced with the first dinner check in years I can't take out of contingency funds."

"What are you going to do, Michael?"

"No thoughts. Don't want any for a while."

The academician paused, taking his change from the taxi driver, then spoke rapidly. "Listen, I'm late for upstairs, but I'm in town overnight. Since I'm on per diem, let me pay for the dinner. Where are you staying? I may have an idea."

No government per diem in the civilized world could have paid for the dinner that night two months and five days ago, but Harry Lewis did have an idea. They had been friends once; they became friends again, and Havelock found it easier to talk with a person who was at least vaguely aware of the work he had done for the government rather than with someone who knew nothing about it. It was always difficult to explain that something could not be explained; Lewis understood. One thing led to another, which in turn led to Harry's idea.

"Have you ever given any thought to getting back to a campus?"

Michael smiled. "How would 'constantly' sound?"

"I know, I know," Lewis pressed, inferring sarcasm. "You fellows—'spooks,' I assume, is the term—get all kinds of offers from the multinationals at damn good money, I'm aware of that. But, M.H., you were one of the best. Your dissertation was picked up by a dozen university presses; you even had your own seminars. Your academic record coupled with your years at State—most of which I realize you can't go into specifically—could make you very attractive to a university administration. We're always saying, 'Let's find someone who's been there, not just a theoretician.' Damn it, Michael, I think you're *it*. Now, I know the money's not—"

"Harry, you misunderstood. I meant it. I *constantly* think about getting back."

It was Harry Lewis's turn to smile. "Then I've got another idea."

A week later Havelock had flown to Boston and driven from there to the brick-and-ivy-and-white-birch campus on the outskirts of Concord, New Hampshire. He spent four days with Harry Lewis and his wife, wandering around, attending various lectures and seminars, and meeting those of the faculty and administration whose support Harry thought might be helpful. Michael's opinions had been sought "casually" over coffee, drinks and dinners; men and women had looked at him as if they considered him a promising candidate. Lewis had done his missionary work well. At the end of the fourth day Harry announced at lunch:

"They like you!"

"Why not?" his wife said. "He's damned likable."

"They're quite excited, actually. It's what I said the other day, M.H. You've *been there*. Sixteen years with the State Department kind of makes you special."

"And?"

"There's the annual administration-trustees conference coming up in eight weeks. That's when the supply-and-demand quotients are studied. Horseflesh. I think you'll be offered a job. Where can I reach you?"

"I'll be traveling. I'll call you."

He had called Harry from London two days ago. The conference was still in progress, but Lewis thought there would be an answer momentarily.

"Cable me AX, Amsterdam," Michael had said. "And thanks, Harry."

He saw the glass doors of the American Express office swing open just ahead. A couple emerged, the man awkwardly balancing the shoulder straps of two cameras while counting money. Havelock stopped, wondering for a moment if he really wanted to go inside. If the cable was there, it would contain either a rejection or an offer. If a rejection, he would simply go on wandering—and there was a certain comfort in that; the floating passivity of not planning had become something of value to him. If an offer, what then? Was he ready for it? Was he prepared to make a decision? Not the kind of decision one made in the field, where it had to be instinctive if one was to survive, but, rather, a decision to commit oneself. Was he capable of a commitment? Where were yesterday's commitments?

He took a deep breath, consciously putting one foot in front of the other, and approached the glass doors.

POSITION AVAILABLE VISITING PROFESSOR OF GOVERNMENT FOR PERIOD OF TWO YEARS. ASSOCIATE STATUS PENDING MUTUAL ACCEPTANCE AT THE END OF THIS TIME. INITIAL SALARY TWENTY-SEVEN-FIVE. WILL NEED YOUR REPLY WITHIN TEN DAYS. DON'T KEEP ME HOLDING MY BREATH.
EVER, HARRY.

Michael folded the cable and put it in his jacket pocket; he did not go back to the counter to write out his own cable to Harry Lewis, Concord, New Hampshire, U.S.A. It would come later. It was enough for the moment to be wanted, to know there was a beginning. It would take several days to absorb the knowledge of his own legitimacy, perhaps several days thereafter to come to grips with it. For in the legitimacy was the possibility of commitment; there was no real beginning without it.

He walked out onto the Damrak, breathing the cold air of Amsterdam, feeling the damp chill floating up from the canal. The sun was setting; briefly blocked by a low-flying cloud, it reemerged, an orange globe hurling its rays through the intercepting vapors. It reminded Havelock of an ocean dawn on the coast of Spain—on the Costa Brava. He had stayed there all night that night, until the sun had forced itself up over the horizon, firing the mists above the water. He had gone down to the shoulder of the road, to the sand and the dirt. . . .

Stop! Don't think about it. That was another life.

Two months and five days ago by sheer chance Harry Lewis had stepped out of a taxi and started to change the world for an old friend. Now, two months and five days later, that change was there to be taken. He would take it, Michael knew, but something was missing: change should be shared, and there was no one to share it with, no one to say, What will you teach?

The tuxedoed waiter at the Dikker en Thijs ground the lip of the flaming brandy glass into the silver receptacle of sugar; the ingredients would follow for café Jamique. It was a ridiculous indulgence, and probably a waste of very good liqueur, but Harry Lewis had insisted they each have one that night in Washington. He would tell Harry that he had repeated the ritual in Amsterdam, although he probably wouldn't have if he had realized how bright the damn flames were and the degree of attention they would draw to his table.

"Thank you, Harry," he said silently once the waiter had left, raising his glass inches off the table to his invisible companion. It was better, after all, not to be completely alone.

He could both feel the approaching presence of a man and see an enlarging darkness in the corner of his eye. A figure dressed in a conservative pinstriped suit was threading his way through the shadows and the candlelight toward the booth. Havelock angled the glass and raised his eyes to the face. The man's name was George; he was the CIA station chief in Amsterdam. They had worked together before, not always pleasantly but professionally.

"That's one way to announce your arrival here," said the intelligence officer, glancing at the waiter's tray table, the silver sugar bowl still on it. "May I sit down?"

"My pleasure. How are you, George?"

"I've been better," said the CIA man, sliding across the seat opposite Michael.

"Sorry to hear that. Care for a drink?"

"That depends."

"On what?"

"Whether I'll stay long enough."

"Aren't we cryptic," said Havelock. "But then you're probably still working."

"I wasn't aware the hours were that clear-cut."

"No, I guess they're not. Am I the reason, George?"

"At the moment, maybe," said the CIA man. "I'm surprised to see you here. I heard you retired."

"You heard correctly."

"Then why are you here?"

"Why not? I'm traveling. I like Amsterdam. You could say I'm spending a lot of accumulated severance pay visiting all those places I rarely got to see in the daytime."

"I could *say* it, but that doesn't mean I believe it."

"Believe, George. It's the truth."

"No screen?" asked the intelligence officer, his eyes leveled at Michael. "I can find out, you know."

"None at all. I'm out, finished, temporarily unemployed. If you check, that's what you'll learn, but I don't think you have to waste channel time to Langley. I'm sure the centrex codes have been altered where I was concerned, all sources and informers in Amsterdam alerted as to my status. I'm off-limits, George. Anyone dealing with me is asking for a short term on the payroll and quite possibly an obscure funeral."

"Those are the *surface* facts," agreed the CIA man.

"They're the only facts. Don't bother looking for anything else; you won't find it."

"All right, say I believe you. You're traveling, spending your severance pay." The agent paused as he leaned forward. "It's going to run out."

"What is?"

"The severance pay."

"Inevitably. At which time I expect I'll find gainful employment. As a matter of fact, this afternoon—"

"Why wait? I might be able to help you there."

"No, you can't, George. I haven't anything to sell."

"Sure, you do. Expertise. A consultant's fee paid out of contingency. No name, no records, untraceable."

"If you're running a test, you're doing it badly."

"No test. I'm willing to pay in order to look better than I am. I wouldn't admit that if I were testing you."

"You might, but you'd be a damn fool. It's third-rate entrapment; it's so awkward you've probably done it for real. None of us want those contingency funds scrutinized too carefully, do we?"

"I may not be in your league, but I'm not third-rate. I need help. We need help."

"That's better. You're appealing to my ego. Much better."

"How about it, Michael. The KGB's all over The Hague. We don't know who they've bought or how far up they go. NATO's compromised."

"We're all compromised, George, and I *can't* help. Because I don't think it makes any difference. We get to square five, pushing them back to four, so they jump over us to seven. Then we buy our way to eight; they block us at nine, and no one reaches square ten. Everyone nods pensively and starts all over again. In the meantime we lament our losses and extol the body count, never admitting that it doesn't make any difference."

"That's a crock of shit! We're not going to be buried by *anyone.*"

"Yes, we are, George. All of us. By 'children yet unborn and unbegot.' Unless they're smarter than we are, which may very well be the case. Christ, I hope so."

"What the hell are you talking about?"

" 'The purple atomic testament of bleeding war.' "

"What!"

"History, George. Let's have that drink."

"No, thanks." The CIA station chief slid back across the seat. "And I think you've had enough," he added, standing up.

"Not yet."

"Go to hell, Havelock." The intelligence officer started to turn away.

"George."

"What?"

"You missed. I was about to say something about this afternoon, but you didn't let me finish."

"So what?"

"So you knew what it was I was going to tell you. When did you intercept the cable? Around noon?"

"Go to hell."

Michael watched as the CIA man returned to his table across the room. He had been dining alone, but Havelock knew he was not alone. Within three minutes the judgment was confirmed. George signed his check— bad form—and walked rapidly through the entrance arch into the lobby. Forty-five seconds later a youngish man from a table on the right side of the room got up to leave, leading a bewildered lady by the elbow. A minute passed, and two men who had been in a booth on the left side rose as one and started for the arch. Through the candlelight, Michael focused on the plates in the booth. Both were piled with food. Bad form.

They had been following him, watching him, employing intercepts. Why? Why couldn't they leave him alone?

So much for Amsterdam.

The noonday sun in Paris was a blinding yellow, its quivering rays bouncing off the river Seine below the bridge. Havelock reached the midpoint of the Pont Royal, his small hotel only blocks away on the Rue du Bac, the route he followed being the most logical one from the Louvre. He knew it was important not to deviate, not to let whoever it was behind him think he suspected his or her presence. He had spotted the taxi, the same taxi, as it made two swift turns in traffic to keep him in sight. Whoever was directing the driver was good; the taxi had stopped for less than two or three seconds at a corner, and then had sped away in the opposite direction. Which meant that whoever was following him was now on foot on the crowded bridge. If contact was the objective, crowds were helpful, and a bridge even more so. People stopped on bridges over the Seine simply to stare absently down at the water; they had been doing so for centuries. Conversations could be had unobtrusively. If contact was the objective, and not surveillance alone.

Michael stopped, leaned against the chest-high stone wall that served as a railing, and lighted a cigarette, his eyes on a *bateau mouche* about to pass under the bridge. That is to say, if anyone was watching him, it would seem as if he were looking at the tourist boat, waving casually at the passengers below. But he was not; pretending to shield his eyes from the sun, he concentrated on the tall figure approaching on his right.

He could distinguish the gray homburg, the velvet-collared overcoat, and the glistening black patent-leather shoes; they were enough. The man was the essence of Parisian wealth and elegance, traveling all over Europe and gracing the salons of the rich. His name was Gravet, and he was considered the most knowledgeable critic of classical art in Paris—which meant the Continent—and only those who had to know knew he also sold far more than his critical expertise. He stopped at the railing seven feet to the right of Havelock, and adjusted his velvet collar; he spoke just loud enough to be heard. "I thought it was you. I've been following you since the Rue Bernard."

"I know. What do you want?"

"The question is, What do *you* want? Why are you in Paris? We were given to understand you were no longer active. Quite frankly, you were to be avoided."

"And reported immediately if I made contact, right?"

"Naturally."

"But you're reversing the process. You've approached me. That's a little foolish, isn't it?"

"A minor risk worth taking," said Gravet, standing erect and glancing about. "We go back a long time, Michael. I don't for a moment believe you're in Paris for your cultural rebirth."

"Neither do I. Who said I was?"

"You were at the Louvre for exactly twenty-seven minutes. Too short a time to absorb anything, and too long to relieve yourself. But quite plausible for meeting someone inside a dark, crowded exhibit—say, at the far end of the third floor."

Havelock began to laugh. "Listen, Gravet—"

"Don't look at me, please! Keep your eyes on the water."

"I went to the Roman collection on the mezzanine. It was filled with a tour from Provence, so I left."

"You were always quick, I admired you for it. And now this ominous alarm: 'He's no longer active. Avoid him.' "

"It happens to be true."

"Whatever this new cover of yours," continued Gravet quickly, dusting the elbows of his coat, "for it to be so radical can only mean you're among very distinguished company. I'm also a broker with a wide range of information. The more distinguished my clients, the better I like it."

"Sorry, I'm not buying. Avoid me."

"Don't be preposterous. You don't know what I have to offer. Incredible things are happening everywhere. Allies become enemies, enemies allies. The Persian Gulf is on fire and all Africa moves in contradictory circles; the Warsaw bloc has lacerations you know nothing about, and Washington pursues a dozen counterproductive strategies matched only by the unbelievable stupidity of the Soviets. I could give you chapter and verse on *their* recent follies. Don't dismiss me, Michael. Pay me. You'll climb even higher."

"Why should I want to climb higher when I've climbed out?"

"Again preposterous. You're a relatively young man; they wouldn't let you go."

"They can watch me, but they can't hold me. All I had to do was give up a pension somewhere down the road."

"Too simple. You all have bank accounts in remote but accessible places, everyone knows that. Diverted contingency funds, covert payments made to nonexistent sources, fees for sudden departures or suddenly required papers. You had your retirement covered by the time you were thirty-five."

"You're exaggerating both my talents and my financial security," said Havelock, smiling.

"Or perhaps a rather lengthy document," the Frenchman went on, as though Michael had not interrupted, "detailing certain covert procedures —solutions, you might say—that must, perforce, describe specific events and personnel. Placed beyond reach of those most interested."

Havelock stopped smiling, but Gravet persisted: "Naturally, that's not *financial* security, but it adds to a sense of well-being, doesn't it?"

"You're wasting your time, I'm not in the market. If you've got something of value, you'll get your price. You know whom to deal with."

"They're frightened second-raters. None of them has your direct avenues to the—centers of determination, shall we say."

"I don't have them anymore."

"I don't believe you. You're the only man here in Europe who talks directly with Anthony Matthias."

"Leave him out of it. And for your information, I haven't spoken with him in months." Suddenly Havelock stood up and turned openly to the Frenchman. "Let's find a taxi and go to the embassy. I know some people over there. I'll introduce you to a first-level attaché and tell him you're selling but I don't have either the resources or the interest to get involved. Okay?"

"You know I can't do that! And, *please*—" Gravet did not have to finish the request.

"All right, all right." Michael returned to the wall with the river below. "Then give me a number or a place of contact. I'll phone it in and you can listen."

"Why are you doing this? Why the charade?"

"Because it's not a charade. As you said, we go back a long time. I'll do you the favor and maybe you'll be convinced. Maybe you'll convince others, if they ask. Even if they don't ask. How about it?"

The Frenchman turned his head while leaning over the wall and stared at Havelock. "No, thank you, Michael. As with all manner of Satans, better a second-rater I've dealt with than one I haven't. For what it's worth, I think I believe you. You would not reveal a source like me, even to a first-level attaché. I'm down too deep, too respectable; you might need me. Yes, I do believe you."

"Make my life easier. Don't keep it a secret."

"What about your opposite numbers in the KGB? Will they be convinced?"

"I'm sure of it. Their moles probably got word to Dzerzhinsky Square before I signed the separation papers."

"They'll suspect a ploy."

"All the more reason to leave me alone. Why bite into poisoned bait?"

"They have chemicals. You all have chemicals."

"I can't tell them anything they don't know, and what I do know has already been changed. That's the funny thing: my enemies have nothing to fear from me. The few names they might learn aren't worth the price. There'd be reprisals."

"You've inflicted a great many wounds. There's pride, vengeance; it's the human condition."

"Not applicable. In those areas we're even, and again I'm not worth it because there's no practical result. Nobody kills unless there's a reason. None of us wants to be responsible for the fallout. Crazy, isn't it? Almost Victorian. When we're finished, we're out. Maybe we'll all get together in a large black strategy room in hell and have a few drinks, but while we're here, we're out. That's the irony, the futility, Gravet. When we're out we don't care anymore. We don't have any reason to hate. Or to kill."

"Nicely phrased, my friend. You've obviously thought about these things."

"I've had a lot of time recently."

"And there are those who are extremely *interested* in your recent observations, your conclusions—your role in life, as it were. But then, it's to be expected. They're such a manic-depressive people. Morose, then jubilant; filled with violence one minute, songs of the earth and sadness the next. And often quite paranoid; the darker aspects of classicism, I think. The slashing diagonals of Delacroix in a multiracial national psyche, so far-reaching, so contradictory. So suspicious—so Soviet."

Havelock stopped breathing; he returned Gravet's stare. "Why did you do it?"

"There was no harm. Had I learned otherwise, who knows what I would have told them? But since I *do* believe you, I explain why I had to test you."

"Moscow thinks I'm still in?"

"I shall render the judgment that you are not. Whether they accept it or not is another matter."

"Why won't they?" asked Havelock, his eyes on the water below.

"I have no idea. . . . I shall miss you, Michael. You were always civilized. Difficult but civilized. Then again, you're not a native-born American, are you? You're really European."

"I'm American," said Havelock quietly. "Really."

"You've done well by America, I'll say that. If you change your mind —or it's changed for you—get in touch with me. We can always do business."

"It's not likely, but thanks."

"That's not an outright rejection, either."

"I'm being polite."

"Civilized. *Au revoir*, Mikhail. . . . I prefer the name you were born with."

Havelock turned his head slowly and watched Gravet walk with studied grace down the pavement of the Pont Royal toward the entrance of the bridge. The Frenchman had accepted a blind interrogation from people he found loathsome; he must have been paid very well. But why?

The CIA was in Amsterdam and the CIA did not believe him. The KGB was in Paris and the KGB did not believe him, either. *Why?*

So much for Paris. How far would they go to keep him under a micro-scope?

The Arethusa Delphi was one of those small hotels near the Syntagma Square in Athens that never let the traveler forget he is in Greece. The rooms were white on white on shimmering white. Walls, furniture and space-dividing ornamental beads were relieved only by garish plastic-framed oil paintings depicting the antiquities: temples, agoras and oracles romanticized by postcard artists. Each room had a pair of narrow double doors that opened onto a miniature balcony—large enough for two small chairs and a Lilliputian table—on which guests could have black morning coffee. Throughout the lobby and in the elevators one never escaped the rhythmic pounding of Greek folk music, strings and cymbals at *prestissimo greco*.

Havelock led the olive-skinned woman out of the elevator, and as the doors closed, both stood for a moment in mock anticipation. The music was gone; they sighed in relief.

"Zorba took a break." Michael gestured to the left toward his room.

"The rest of the world must think we are nervous wrecks," said the woman, laughing, touching her dark hair and smoothing out the long white dress that complemented her skin and accentuated her breasts and tapered body. Her English was heavily accented, cultivated on those Mediterranean islands that are the playgrounds of the Mediterranean rich. She was a high-priced courtesan whose favors were sought after by the princes of commerce and inheritance, a good-natured whore with a decent wit and a quick laugh, a woman who knew her time of pleasure-giving was limited. "You rescued me," she said, squeezing Havelock's arm as they walked down the corridor.

"I kidnapped you."

"Often interchangeable terms," she replied, laughing again.

It had been a little of both. Michael had run across a man on the Marathonos with whom he had worked in the Thermaikos sector five years ago. A dinner party was being held that night at a café on Syntagma Square; since it was convenient, Havelock accepted the invitation. The woman was there, the escort of a considerably older, boorish businessman. The ouzo and the *prestissimo greco* had done its damage. Havelock and the woman had been seated next to each other; legs and hands touched, they exchanged looks: comparisons were obvious. Michael and the island courtesan had slipped away.

"I think I'm going to face an angry Athenian tomorrow," said Havelock, opening the door of his room, leading the woman inside.

"Don't be silly," she protested. "He's not a gentleman. He's from Epidaurus; there are no gentlemen in Epidaurus. He's an aging bull of a peasant who made money under the colonels. One of the nastier consequences of their regime."

"When in Athens," said Michael, going to the bureau where there was a bottle of prized Scotch and glasses, "stay away from Epidaurians." He poured drinks.

"Have you been to Athens often?"

"A few times."

"What did you do? What line of work?"

"I bought things. Sold things." Havelock carried the drinks back across the room. What he saw was what he wanted to see, although he had not expected to see it so quickly. The woman had removed her thin silk cape and draped it on a chair. She then proceeded to unbutton her gown from the top, the swelling of her breasts provocative, inviting.

"You didn't buy me," she said, taking the drink with her free hand. "I came of my own free will. *Efharistou,* Michael Havelock. Do I say your name right?"

"Very nicely."

She touched his glass with hers, the sound gentle as she stepped closer. She reached up and placed her fingers on his lips, then his cheek, and finally around the back of his neck, drawing his face to hers. They kissed, her lips parting, the soft swollen flesh and moisture of her mouth arousing him; she pressed her body against his, pulling his left hand to the breast beneath her half-open gown. She leaned back, breathing deeply.

"Where is your bathroom? I'll get into something—less."

"Over there."

"Why don't *you?* Get into something less, that is. We'll meet at the bed. I'm really rather anxious. You're very, *very* attractive, and I'm—very anxious."

She picked up her cape from the chair and walked casually, sensually toward the door beyond the bed. She went inside, glancing back over her shoulder, her eyes telling him things that probably were not true, but were nevertheless exciting for the night. The practiced whore, whatever her reasons were, would perform, and he wanted, needed, the release of that performance.

Michael stripped himself down to his shorts, carried his drink to the bed, and tore away the spread and the blanket. He climbed under the sheet and reached for a cigarette, turning his body away from the wall.

"Dobriy vyehchyer, priyatel."

At the sound of the deep male voice, Havelock spun around on the bed, instinctively reaching for a weapon—a weapon that was not there. Standing in the frame of the bathroom door was a balding man whose face Michael recognized from dozens of photographs going back years. He was from Moscow, one of the most powerful men in the Soviet KGB. In his hand was a gun, a large, black Graz-Burya automatic. There was a click; the hammer snapped into firing position.

3

"You may leave now," said the Russian to the woman concealed behind him. She slid past, glancing at Havelock, then rushed to the door and let herself out.

"You're Rostov. Pyotr Rostov. Director of External Strategies. KGB. Moscow."

"Your face and name are also known to me. And your dossier."

"You went to a lot of trouble, *priyatel*," said Michael, using the Russian word for friend, its meaning, however, denied by his cold delivery. He shook his head, trying to clear it of a sickening mist, the effect of the ouzo and Scotch. "You could have stopped me on the street and invited me for a drink. You wouldn't have learned any more or any less, and very little that's valuable. Unless this is a *kazn gariah.*"

"No execution, Havlíček."

"Havelock."

"Son of Havlíček."

"You'd do well not to remind me."

"The gun is in my hand, not yours." Rostov eased the hammer of his automatic back into its recess, the weapon still leveled at Michael's head. "But that's in the distant past and has no connection with me. Your recent activities, however, are very much my concern. Our concern, if you will."

"Then your moles aren't earning their money."

"They file reports with irritating frequency, if only to justify it. But are they accurate?"

"If they told you I was finished, they were accurate."

" 'Finished'? A word with such finality, yet subject to interpretation, no? Finished with what? Finished with one phase, on to another?"

"Finished with anything that might concern you."

"Out of sanction?" asked the KGB officer, rounding the border of the doorframe and leaning against the wall, his Graz-Burya steady, leveled now at Havelock's throat. "No longer employed by your government in any official capacity? It's difficult to accept. It must have been a blow to your dear friend Anthony Matthias."

Michael studied the Russian's face, lowering his eyes to the huge gun aimed at him. "A Frenchman mentioned Matthias the other day. I'll tell you what I told him, although I don't know why I should. You paid him to bring up Matthias's name."

"Gravet? He despises us. He's civilized toward us only when he's walking through the galleries of the Kremlin or the Hermitage in Leningrad. He might tell us anything."

"Why did you use him, then?"

"Because he's fond of you. It's far easier to spot a lie when the liar is referring to someone he likes."

"Then you believed him."

"Or you convinced him and our people had no choice. Tell *me*. How did the brilliant and charismatic American Secretary of State react to his *krajan*'s resignation?"

"I have no idea, but I assume he understood. It's exactly what I told Gravet. I haven't seen Matthias or spoken to him in months. He's got enough problems; there's no reason why those of an old student should be added."

"But you were far more than a student. His family knew your family in Prague. You became what you are—"

"*Were,*" interrupted Havelock.

"—because of *Anton* Matthias."

"It was a long time ago."

Rostov was silent; he lowered his weapon slightly, then spoke. "Very well, a long time ago. What about now? No one's irreplaceable, but you're a valuable man. Knowledgeable, productive."

"Value and productivity are generally associated with commitment. I don't have it anymore. Let's say I lost it."

"Am I to infer you could be tempted?" The KGB man lowered the weapon further. "In the direction of another commitment?"

"You know better than that. Outside of personal revulsions that go back a couple of decades, we've got a mole or two in the Dzerzhinsky. I've no intention of being marked 'beyond salvage.' "

"A hypocritical term. It implies compassion on the part of your executioners."

"It says it."

"Not well." Rostov raised his automatic, thrusting it forward slowly. "We have no such problems with verbal rationales. A traitor is a traitor. I could take you in, you know."

"Not easily." Michael remained still, his eyes locked with the Russian's. "There are corridors and elevators, lobbies to pass through and streets to cross; there's risk. You could lose. Everything. Because I have nothing to lose but a cell at the Lubyanka."

"A room, not a cell. We're not barbarians."

"Sorry. A room. The same kind of room we have reserved in Virginia for someone like you—and we're both wasting money. When people like you and me get out with our heads still on, everything's altered. The Amytals and the Pentothals are invitations to traps."

"There are still the moles."

"I don't know who they are any more than you did when you were in the field—for those same reasons, those same rooms. None of us do on either side. We only know the current codes, words that take us where we have to go. Whatever ones I had are meaningless now."

"In all sincerity are you trying to convince me a man of your experience is of no value to us?"

"I didn't say that," interrupted Havelock. "I'm simply suggesting that you weigh the risks. Also something else, which, frankly, you pulled off with reasonable success two years ago. We took a man of yours who was finished, ready for a farm in Grasnov. We got him out through Riga into Finland and flew him to a room in Fairfax, Virginia. He was injected with everything from scopolamine to triple Amytal, and we learned a lot. Strategies were aborted, whole networks restructured, confusion the order of the day. Then we learned something else: everything he told us was a lie. His head was programmed like a computer disk; valuable men became useless, time was lost. Say you got me to the Lubyanka—which I don't think you could—how do you know I'm not our answer to what you did to us?"

"Because you would not expose the possibility." Rostov pulled the gun back, but did not lower it.

"Really? It strikes me as a pretty good blanket. I mean, you'd never know, would you? On the other hand, we've developed a serum—which I know nothing about except that it's injected at the base of the skull—that voids the programming. Something to do with neutralizing the lobus occipitalis, whatever the hell that is. From here on we can make a determination."

"Such an admission astonishes me."

"Why should it? Maybe I'm just saving our respective directors a lot of aggravation; that could be my objective. Or maybe none of it's true; maybe there is no serum, no protection, and I'm making it all up. That's also a possibility."

The Russian smiled. *"Khvatit!* You *are* out! You amuse us both with logic that could serve you. You're on your way to that farm in your own Grasnov."

"That's what I've been trying to tell you. Am I worth the risk?"

"Let's find out." Suddenly the Russian flipped his automatic, barrel up; he slapped it back in the palm of his hand and threw it to Havelock on the bed. Michael caught the weapon in midair.

"What am I supposed to do with this?"

"What do you want to do with it?"

"Nothing. Assuming the first three shells are rubber capsules filled with dye, I'd only soil your clothes." Havelock pressed the magazine release; the clip dropped to the bed. "It's not a very good test, anyway. Say the firing pin works and this thing makes any noise at all, twenty *khruschei* could break in here and blow me out of the park."

"The firing pin works and there's no one outside in the hallway. The Arethusa Delphi is very much in Washington's camp; it's watched and I'm not so foolish as to parade our personnel. I think you know that. It's why you're here."

"What are you trying to prove?"

The Russian smiled again and shrugged. "I'm not really sure. A brief something in the eyes, perhaps. When a man's under a hostile gun and that gun is suddenly his, there is an instant compulsion to eliminate the prior threat—assuming the hostility is returned. It's in the eyes; no amount of control can disguise it—if the enmity is active."

"What was in my eyes?"

"Absolute indifference. Weariness, if you will."

"I'm not sure you're right, but I admire your courage. It's more than I've got. The firing pin really works?"

"Yes."

"No capsules?"

The Russian shook his head, his expression conveying quiet amusement. "No bullets. That is to say, no powder in the shells." Rostov raised his left hand and, with his right, pulled back the sleeve of his overcoat. Strapped to the flat of his wrist, extending up toward his elbow, was a thin barrel, the trigger mechanism apparently activated by the bending of his arm. *"Snotvornoye,"* he said, touching the taut, springlike wires. "What you call narcotic darts. You would have slept peacefully for the better part of tomorrow while a doctor insisted that your odd fever be studied at the hospital. We'd have gotten you out, flown you up to Salonika and over the Dardanelles into Sevastopol." The Russian unsnapped a strap above his wrist and removed the weapon.

Havelock studied the KGB man, not a little perplexed. "You really could have taken me."

"Until the attempt is made, one never knows. I might have missed the first shot, and you're younger, stronger than I; you could have attacked, broken my neck. But the odds were on my side."

"I'd say completely. Why didn't you play them?"

"Because you're right. We *don't* want you. The risks *are* too great—not those you spoke of, but others. I simply had to know the truth and I'm now convinced. You are no longer in the service of your government."

"What risks?"

"They're unknown to us, but they are there. Anything you can't understand in this business is a risk, but I don't have to tell you that."

"Tell me *something.* I just got a pardon; I'd like to know why."

"Very well." The Soviet intelligence officer hesitated; he walked aimlessly toward the double doors that led to the miniature balcony and opened one several inches. Then he closed it and turned to Havelock. "I should tell you first that I'm not here on orders from Dzerzhinsky Square, or even with its blessings. To be frank, my aging superiors in the KGB believe I'm in Athens on an unrelated matter. You can either accept that or not."

"Give me a reason to or not. Someone must know. You *jedratele* don't do anything solo."

"Specifically, two others. A close associate in Moscow and a dedicated man—a mole, to be sure—out of Washington."

"You mean Langley?"

The Russian shook his head. He replied softly, "The White House."

"I'm impressed. So two ranking *kontrolyorya* of the KGB and a Soviet mole within walking distance of the Oval Office decide they want to talk to me, but they don't want to take me. They can fly me into Sevastopol and from there to a room at the Lubyanka, where any talking we did would be far more productive—from their point of view—but they won't do that. Instead, the spokesman for these three—a man I know only from photographs and by reputation—tells me there are risks associated with me that he can't define but knows that they exist, and because of them I'm given the option of talking or not—about what I haven't the vaguest idea. Is that a fair reading?"

"You have the Slavic propensity for going right to the core of a subject."

"I don't see any ancestral connection. It's common sense. You spoke, I listened; that's what you said—or what you're about to say. Basic logic."

Rostov stepped away from the balcony doors, his expression pensive. "I'm afraid that's the one factor that's missing. The logic."

"Now we're talking about something else."

"Yes, we are."

"What?"

"You. The Costa Brava."

Havelock paused. The anger was in his eyes, but it was controlled. "Go on."

"The woman. She's why you retired, isn't she?"

"This conversation is terminated," said Havelock abruptly. "Get out of here."

"Please." The Russian raised both hands, a gesture of truce, perhaps a plea. "I think you should listen to me."

"I don't think so. There's nothing you could say that would remotely interest me. The Voennaya is to be congratulated; it was a hell of a job. They won, she won. And then she lost. It's finished, and there's nothing further to say about it."

"There is."

"Not to me."

"The VKR are maniacs," said the Russian quietly, urgently. "I don't have to tell you that. You and I are enemies, and neither would pretend otherwise, but we acknowledge certain rules between us. We're not salivating dogs, we're professionals. There's a fundamental respect each has for the other, perhaps grounded in fear, although not necessarily. Grant me that, *priyatel.*"

Their eyes were level, penetrating. Havelock nodded. "I know you from the files, just as you know me. You weren't part of it."

"Wasted death is still death, still a waste. Unnecessary and provocative death a very dangerous waste. It can be hurled back tenfold in fury at the instigator."

"Tell that to the Voennaya. There was no waste as far as they were concerned. Only necessity."

"Butchers!" snapped Rostov, his voice guttural. "Who can tell them anything? They're descendants of the old OGPU slaughterhouses, inheritors of the mad assassin Yagoda. They're also up to their throats in paranoid fantasies going back half a century when Yagoda gunned down the quieter, more reasonable men, hating their lack of fanaticism, equating that lack with treason against the revolution. Do you *know* the VKR?"

"Enough so as to stand far back and hope to hell you can control it."

"I wish I could answer confidently in the affirmative. It's as if a band of your screaming right-wing zealots had been given official status as a subdivision of the Central Intelligence Agency."

"We have checks and balances—sometimes. If such a subdivision came to be—and it could—it would be continuously scrutinized, openly criticized. Funds would be watched closely, methods studied; ultimately the group would be thrown out."

"You've had your lapses, your various un-American activities committees, your McCarthys, the Huston plans, purges in the irresponsible press. Careers have been destroyed, lives degraded. Yes, you've had your share of lapses."

"Always short-lived. We have no gulags, no 'rehabilitation' programs in a Lubyanka. And that irresponsible press has a way of becoming responsible now and then. It threw out a regime of arrogant hot shots. The Kremlin's wilder ones stay in place."

"We both have our lapses, then. But we're so much younger; youth is allowed mistakes."

"And there's nothing," interrupted Michael, "to compare with the VKR's *paminyatchik* operation. That wouldn't be tolerated or funded by the worst Congress or administration in history."

"Another paranoid fantasy!" cried the KGB officer, adding derisively, "The *paminyatchiki!* Even the word is a corruption, meaningless! A discredited strategy mounted decades ago! You can't honestly believe it still flourishes."

"Perhaps less than the Voennaya does. Obviously more than you do— if you're not lying."

"Oh, *come*, Havelock! Russian infants sent to the United States, growing up with old-line, no doubt pathetically senile, Marxists so as to become entrenched Soviet agents? Insanity! Be reasonable. It's psychologically unsound—if not disastrous—to say nothing of certain inevitable comparisons. We'd lose the majority to blue jeans, rock music and fast automobiles. We'd be idiots."

"Now you're lying. They exist. You know it and we know it."

Rostov shrugged. "A question of numbers, then. And value, I might add. How many can be left? Fifty, a hundred, two hundred at the outside? Sad, amateurishly conspiratorial creatures wandering around a few cities, meeting in cellars to exchange nonsense, uncertain of their own values, the very reasons for being where they are. Very little credence is given these so-called travelers, take my word for it."

"But you haven't pulled them out."

"Where would we put them? Few even speak the Russian language; they're a large embarrassment. Attrition, *priyatel*, that's the answer. And dismissing them with lip service, as you Americans say."

"The Voennaya doesn't dismiss them."

"I told you, the men of the VKR pursue misguided fantasies."

"I wonder if you believe that," said Michael, studying the Russian. "Not all those families were pathetic and senile, not all the travelers amateurs."

"If there is currently—or in the recent past—any movement of consequence on the part of the *paminyatchiki*, we are not aware of it," said Rostov firmly.

"And if there is and you're not aware of it, that would be something of consequence, wouldn't it?"

The Russian stood motionless; he spoke, his voice low and pensive. "The VKR is incredibly secretive. It would be something of consequence."

"Then maybe I've given you something to think about. Call it a parting gift from a retired enemy."

"I look for no such gifts," said Rostov coldly. "They're as gratuitous as your presence here in Athens."

"Since you don't approve, go back to Moscow and fight your own fights. Your infrastructure doesn't concern me any longer. And unless you've got another comic-book weapon up your other sleeve, I suggest you leave."

"That's just it, *pyehshkah.* Yes, *pyehshkah.* Pawn. It is as you say—an infrastructure. Separate sections, indeed, but one entity. There is first the KGB; all else follows. A man—or a woman—may gravitate to the Voennaya, may even excel in its deepest operations, but first he or she must have sprung from the KGB. At the very minimum there *has* to be a Dzerzhinsky dossier *somewhere.* With foreign recruits it's, as you would say, a double imperative. Internal protection, of course."

Havelock sat forward on the bed, confusion joining the anger in his eyes. "Say what you're trying to say and say it quickly. There's a smell about you, *priyatel!*"

"I suspect there is about all of us, Mikhail Havlíček. Our nostrils never quite adjust, do they? Perversely, they become sensitive—to variations of that basic odor. Like animals."

"Say it."

"There is no listing for a Jenna Karasova or the Anglicized Karas in any branch or division of the KGB."

Havelock stared at the Russian, then suddenly he spun off the bed, gripping the sheet and whipping it into the air, obscuring the Russian's vision. He lunged forward, hammering Rostov against the wall beyond the balcony doors. He twisted the KGB man clockwise by the wrist and smashed his head into the frame of a cheap oil painting as he whipped his right arm around Rostov's neck in a hammerlock. "I could kill you for that," he whispered, breathless, the muscles of his jaw pulsating against Rostov's bald head. "You said I might break your neck. I could do it right *now!*"

"You could," said the Russian, choking. "And you'd be cut down. Either in this room or on the street outside."

"I thought you didn't have anyone in the hotel!"

"I lied. There are three men, two dressed as waiters down the hallway by the elevators, one inside the staircase. There's no final protection for you here in Athens. My people are out there—on the street as well— every doorway covered. My instructions are clear: I'm to emerge from a specific exit at a specific time. Any deviations from either will result in your death. The room will be stormed; the cordon around the Arethusa is unbreakable. I'm not an idiot."

"Maybe not, but as you said, you're an *animal!*" He released the Russian and hurled him across the room. "Go back to Moscow and tell them the bait's too obvious, the stench too rotten! I'm not taking it, *priyatel.* Get out of here!"

"No bait," protested Rostov, regaining his balance and holding his throat. "Your own argument: what could you really tell us that would be worth the risks, or the reprisals, perhaps? *Or* the uncertainties? You're finished. Without programming, you could lead us into a hundred traps —a theory that has crossed our minds, incidentally. You talk freely and we act on what you say, but what you tell us is no longer operative. Through you we go after strategies—not simple codes and ciphers, but supposedly long-term vital strategies—that Washington has aborted without telling *you.* In the process we reveal our personnel. Surely you're aware of this. You talk of logic? Heed your own words."

Havelock stared at the Soviet officer, his breathing audible, anger and bewilderment compounding the emotional strain. Even the shadow of a possibility that an error had been made at Costa Brava was more than he could face. *But there was no error.* A Baader-Meinhof defector had set off the revealing chain of events. The evidence had been sent to Madrid, and he had pored over it, sifting every fragment for a shred to the contrary. There was nothing; there was everything. Even Anthony Matthias— *Anton* Matthias, friend, mentor, surrogate father—had demanded in-depth verification; it had been returned: Positive.

"No! The proof was there! *She* was there! I saw for myself! I said I had to see for myself and they agreed!"

" 'They'? Who is 'they'?"

"You know as well as I do! Men like you! The inside shell—strategists! You didn't look hard enough. You're *wrong!*"

The Russian moved his head slowly in circles, his left hand massaging his throat; he spoke softly. "I won't deny that the possibility exists—as I said, the VKR is maniacally secretive, *especially* in Moscow—but that possibility is remote. . . . We were astonished. An unusually productive decoy conduit is led into a terrorist trap by her own people, who then proceed to hold the KGB responsible for her death by claiming she was one of us. The result of this manipulation is the neutering of the woman's constant companion, her lover, a deep-cover, multilingual field agent of exceptional talent. Disillusion and disgust overwhelm him; he takes himself out. We are amazed; we search the dossier vaults, including the most inaccessible. She is *nowhere*. Jenna Karas—Karasova—was never a part of us." Rostov paused, his eyes conveying his awareness: Michael Havelock was a dangerously provoked panther about to spring, about to strike. The Russian continued, his voice flat: "We are grateful; we profit by your elimination, but we ask ourselves why? Why was this done? Is it a trick? If so, for what purpose? Who gains? On the surface we do, but again, why? *How?*"

"Ask the VKR!" shouted Michael contemptuously. "They didn't plan it this way, but that's the way it happened. I'm the bonus! Ask *them!*"

"We did," said the Russian. "A section director, saner than most, who, because of his relative sanity, is frightened of his peers. He told us that he personally was not familiar with the Karas woman or the specifics at Costa Brava, but since the field personnel raised no questions, he assumed no questions *should* be raised. As he pointed out, the results were favorable: two condors shot down, both talented, one exceptional. The Voennaya was pleased to take credit."

"Why shouldn't they? I was out, and she could be justified. A sacrifice by any name is still the same. It's expendable for a purpose. He said it; he acknowledged it."

"He did not acknowledge it and he was saying something quite different. I told you, he's a frightened man. Only my rank persuaded him to go as far as he did."

"You're reaching."

"I listened. As you listened to me a few moments ago. He was telling us that he hadn't the vaguest idea what had happened or why."

"He *personally* didn't know," said Havelock angrily. "The people in the field knew. *She* knew!"

"A tenuous rationalization. His office is responsible for all activities in the southwest Mediterranean sector. The territory includes the Costa Brava. An emergency rendezvous—especially one ostensibly involving the Baader-Meinhof—would certainly be cleared by him." Rostov paused briefly, then added quietly, "Under normal circumstances."

"A not so tenuous rationalization?" asked Michael.

"I leave myself the narrowest margin for error. An extremely remote possibility."

"It's the one I accept!" Havelock shouted again, suddenly disturbed at his own outburst.

"You want to accept it. Perhaps you have to."

"The VKR more often than not gets its orders directly from the policy rooms of the Kremlin. It's no secret. If you're not lying, you were passed over."

"To be sure, and the thought frightens me more than I can tell you. But as much as I'm forced to acknowledge your professional accomplishments, *priyatel*, I do not think the policy makers in the Kremlin are concerned with the likes of you and me. They have more weighty matters, global matters. And, to the point, they have no expertise where we're concerned."

"They do with Baader-Meinhof! *And* the PLO, *and* the Brigate Rosse, *and* a couple of dozen 'red armies' blowing things up all over the goddamn place! *That's* policy!"

"Only for maniacs."

"Which is exactly what we're talking about! Maniacs!" Michael paused, the obvious striking him. "We broke the VKR codes. They were authentic; I've seen too many variations not to know. *I* set up the contact. She *responded.* I sent the final transmission to the men in the boat offshore. *They* responded! Explain that!"

"I can't."

"Then get *out!*"

The KGB officer looked at his watch. "I must, in any event. Time is up."

"Yes, it is."

"We're at an impasse," said the Russian.

"I'm not."

"No, I don't think you are, and that compounds the risk about you. You know what you know and I know what I know. Impasse, whether you like it or not."

"Your time's up, remember?"

"I'm not forgetting. I don't care to be caught in the cross fire. I'll leave now." Rostov went to the door and turned, his hand on the knob. "Several minutes ago you said the bait was too obvious, the stench too rotten. Tell that to Washington, *priyatel.* We're not taking it either."

"Get *out!*"

The door closed, and Havelock stood motionless for nearly a minute, picturing the Russian's eyes. They had held too much truth in them. Over the years Michael had learned to discern the truth, especially in his enemies. Rostov had not been lying; he had spoken the truth as he believed it to be. Which meant that this powerful strategist for the KGB was being manipulated by his own people in Moscow. Pyotr Rostov was a blind probe—an influential intelligence officer sent out with information he is convinced his superiors do not have in order to make contact with the enemy and turn an American agent, recruiting him for the Soviets. The higher up the officer, the more credible his story—as long as he spoke the truth as he saw it, truth that was perceived as such by his enemy.

Michael walked to the bedside table, where he had left the glass of whisky a half hour ago. He picked it up, drained the Scotch, and looked down at the bed. He smiled to himself, thinking how the evening had veered from where it had been heading thirty minutes ago. The whore had performed, but not in any way he might have expected. The sensuous courtesan from the playgrounds of the rich had been a setup. When were the setups going to stop? Amsterdam. Paris. Athens.

Perhaps they would not stop until he did. Perhaps as long as he kept moving the would-be trappers would keep moving with him, watching him, cornering him, waiting for him to commit whatever crimes their imaginations led them to believe he would commit. It was in the movement itself that they found the ominous substance for their suspicions. No man wandered aimlessly after a lifetime of wandering under orders. If he kept it up, it had to mean he was following other orders, different orders; otherwise he'd stay put. Somewhere.

Perhaps it was time he stopped. Maybe his odyssey of recovery had about run its course; there was a cable to be sent, a commitment to be made. A beginning. A nearly forgotten friend had become a friend again, and that man had offered him a new life, where the old life could be buried, where there were roots to cultivate, relationships to create, things to teach.

What will you teach, Mikhail?

Leave me alone! You are no part of me—you never were!

He would send the cable to Harry Lewis in the morning, then rent a car and drive northwest to the ferry for the Adriatic port of Kérkira, where he would catch the boat to Brindisi in Italy. He had done it before under God knows what name or with what objective. He would do it now as Michael Havelock, visiting professor of government. From Brindisi he would take the circuitous train routes across Italy into Rome, a city he enjoyed immensely. He would stay in Rome for a week or two; it would be the last stop on his odyssey, the place where he would put to rest all thoughts of a life that was over.

There were things to do in Concord, New Hampshire, U.S.A. He would assume his duties as visiting professor in something less than three months; in the meantime there were practicalities to be dealt with: lectures to be sketched out under the guidance of knowledgeable associates; curricula to study and evaluate, determining where his contributions might best be directed. A short visit, perhaps, with Matthias, who would certainly have insights to offer. No matter how pressed for time, Matthias would *take* the time, because, above all men, Anton would be happiest for him: his old student had returned to the campus. It was where it had all begun.

So many things to do.

He needed a place to live: a house, furniture, pots and pans and books, a chair to sit in, a bed to sleep in. Choices. He had not thought about such things ever before. He thought about them now and felt the excitement growing inside him.

He went to the bureau, uncapped the Scotch and poured himself a drink. *"Přiteli,"* he said softly, for no particular reason, as he looked at his face in the mirror. Suddenly he stared at his eyes and, in terror, slammed the glass down with such force that it shattered; blood spread slowly over his hand. His eyes would not let him go! And he understood. Had his own eyes seen the truth that night on the Costa Brava?

"Stop it!" he screamed, whether silently or out loud, he could not tell. *"It's over!"*

Dr. Harry Lewis sat at his desk in his book-lined study, the cablegram in his hand. He listened for the sound of his wife's voice. It came.

"See you later, dear," she called from the hallway beyond. The front door opened and closed. She was out of the house.

Lewis picked up his telephone and dialed the area code 202. Washington, D.C. The seven digits that followed had been committed to memory, never written down. Nor would they be recorded on a bill, having bypassed the computers electronically.

"Yes?" asked the male voice on the other end of the line.

"Birchtree," said Harry.

"Go ahead, Birchtree. You're being taped."

"He's accepted. The cable came from Athens."

"Is there any change in dates?"

"No. He'll be here a month before the trimester starts."

"Did he say where he was going from Athens?"

"No."

"We'll watch the airports. Thank you, Birchtree."

The Rome Havelock had come to visit was not the Rome in which he cared to stay. Strikes were everywhere, the chaos compounded by volatile Italian tempers that erupted on every street corner, every picket line, in the parks and around the fountains. Mail had been strewn in gutters, adding to the uncollected garbage; taxis were scarce—practically nonexistent—and most of the restaurants had been closed because of the lack of deliveries. The *poliziotti*, having taken sufficient abuse, were on a work stoppage, snarling further the normal insanity of Rome's traffic, and since the telephones were part of the government's postal service, they functioned on a level below normal, which made them damn near impossible. The city was full of a kind of hysteria, which was aggravated by yet another stern papal decree—from a foreigner, a *polacco!*—that was at odds with every progressive step since Vatican II. *Giovanni Ventitreesimo! Dove sei?*

It was his second night, and Michael had left his *pensione* on the Via Due Macelli over two hours before, walking nearly the mile to the Via Flaminia Vecchia in hopes of finding a favorite restaurant open. It was not, and no amount of patience brought forth a taxi to bring him back to the Spanish Steps.

Reaching the north end of the Via Veneto, he was heading toward the side street that would eliminate the crowds in the gaudy carnival that was the Veneto when he saw it—a poster in the lighted window of a travel agency proclaiming the glories of Venice.

Why not? Why the hell not? The floating passivity of not planning included sudden changes in plans. He looked at his watch; it was barely eight-thirty, probably too late to get out to the airport and chance a reservation on a plane, but if he remembered correctly—and he did—the trains kept running until midnight out of Rome. Why not a train? The lazy, circuitous trip from Brindisi by rail, passing through countrysides that had not changed in centuries, had been startlingly beautiful. He could pack his single suitcase in minutes, walk to the train station in twenty. Surely the money he was willing to pay would get him accommodations; if not, he could always return to the Via Due Macelli. He had paid for a week in advance.

Forty-five minutes later Havelock passed through the huge portals of the massive Ostia Railroad Station, built by Mussolini in the halcyon days of trumpets and drums and marching boots and trains that ran on time.

Italian was not Michael's best language, but he could read it well enough: *Biglietto per Venezia. Prima classe.* The line was short and his luck held. The famed *Freccia della Laguna* was leaving in eight minutes, and if the signore wished to pay the premium scale, he could have the finest accommodations by way of his own compartment. He so wished, and as the clerk stamped his ornate ticket, he was told that the *Freccia* was leaving from *binario trentasei,* a dual platform several football fields away from the counter.

"Fate presto, signore! Non perdete tempo! Fate in fretta!"

Michael walked rapidly into the mass of rushing humanity, threading his way as fast as possible toward dual Track 36. As usual—as he recalled from memories past—the giant dome was filled with crowds. Screeching arrivals and wailing departures were joined in counterpoint; screamed epithets punctuated the deafening roar, because the porters, too, were obviously on strike. It took nearly five hectic minutes to shoulder his way through the huge stone arch and emerge on the double-track platform. It was, if possible, more chaotic than the station itself. A crowded train had arrived from the north as the *Freccia della Laguna* was about to depart. Freight dollies collided with hordes of embarking and disembarking passengers. It was a scene from a lower circle of Dante, screaming pandemonium.

Suddenly, across the platform, through the milling crowds, he caught sight of the back of a woman's head, the brim of a soft hat shadowing her face. She was stepping out of the incoming train from the north, and had turned to talk to a conductor. It had happened before: the same color or cut of the hair, the shape of a neck. A scarf, or a hat or a raincoat like those she had worn. It had happened before. Too often.

Then the woman turned; pain seared Havelock's eyes and temples and surged downward—hot knives stabbing his chest. The face across the platform, seen sporadically through the weaving, colliding crowds, was no illusion. It was *she.*

Their eyes locked. Hers widened in raw fear; her face froze. Then she whipped her head away and plunged into the crowds in front of her.

Michael pressed his eyelids shut, then opened them, trying to rid himself of the pain and the shock and the sudden trembling that immobilized him. He dropped his suitcase; he had to *move,* run, race after this living corpse from the Costa Brava! She was alive! This woman he had loved, this apparition who had betrayed that love and had died for it, was *alive!*

Like a crazed animal, he parted the bodies in his path, screaming her name, ordering her to stop, commanding the crowds to stop her. He raced up the ramp and through the massive stone archway oblivious to the shrieking, furious passengers he pummeled and left in his wake, unaware of the slaps and punches and body blocks hurled at him, unconscious of the hands that ripped his clothing.

She was nowhere to be seen in the station crowds.

What in the name of God had *happened?*

Jenna Karas was alive!

4

With the terrifying impact of a bolt of lightning the sight of Jenna Karas had thrown him back into the shadow world he had left behind. She was alive! He had to keep moving; he had to find her. He ran blindly through the crowds, separating arms and gesturing hands and protesting shoulders. First to one exit, then to another, and a third and a fourth. He stopped to question what few police he found, picking the words from a blurred Italian lexicon somewhere in his mind. He shouted her description, ending each distorted phrase with *"Aiuto!"*—only to be met with shrugs and looks of disapproval.

He kept running. A staircase—a door—an elevator. He thrust 2,000 lire on a woman heading into the ladies' room; 5,000 to a freight hand. He pleaded with three conductors leaving the station carrying satchels, which meant they were going home.

Nothing. She was nowhere.

Havelock leaned over a trash can, the sweat rolling down his face and neck, his hands scraped and bleeding. He thought for a moment that he would vomit into the garbage; he had passed over the edge of hysteria. He had to pull himself back; he had to get hold of himself. And the only way to do so was to keep moving, slower and slower, but to keep moving, let the pounding in his chest decelerate, find a part of his mind so he could think. He vaguely remembered his suitcase; the possibility that it was still there was remote, but looking for it was something to do. He started back through the crowds, body aching, perceptions numbed, buffeted by the gesticulating hordes around him, as if he were in a dark tunnel filled with shadows and swirling winds. He had no idea how long it took for him to pass through the arch and walk down the ramp to the near-deserted platform. The *Freccia* had left, and the clean-up crews were invading the cars of the stationary train from the north—the train that had carried Jenna Karas.

There it was, crushed but still intact, straps broken, clothes protruding, yet oddly whole. His suitcase was wedged in the narrow space between the edge of the platform and the filthy, flat side of the third car. He knelt down and pulled it out of its jammed recess, sliding up first one side and then the other as the leather squeaked abrasively. The suitcase was suddenly freed; he lost his balance and fell on the concrete, still holding on to the half-destroyed handle. A man in overalls pushing a wide broom approached. Michael got to his feet awkwardly, aware that the maintenance crewman had stopped, his broom motionless, his eyes conveying both amusement and disgust. The man thought he was drunk.

The handle broke; held by a single clasp, the suitcase abruptly tilted downward. Havelock yanked it up and clutched it in his arms; he started down the platform toward the ramp, knowing his walk was trancelike.

How many minutes later, or which particular exit he used, he would never know, but he was out on the street, the suitcase held against his chest, walking unsteadily past a row of lighted storefronts. He was conscious of the fact that people kept glancing at him, at his torn clothes and the crushed suitcase, its contents spilling out. The swirling mists were beginning to break up, the cold night air diffusing them. He had to find his sanity by concentrating on the little things: he would wash his face, change his clothes, have a cigarette, replace the suitcase.

F. MARTINELLI *Valigeria.* The neon letters glowed impressively in deep red above the wide storefront window filled with accessories for the traveler. It was one of those shops near the Ostia Station that cater to the wealthy foreigner and the self-indulgent Italian. The merchandise was expensive replicas of ordinary objects turned into luxuries by way of sterling silver and polished brass.

Havelock stood for a moment, breathing deeply, holding on to the suitcase as if it were somehow an object that would carry him, a plank in a wild sea—without it he would drown. He walked inside; mercifully, it was near closing time, and the shop was devoid of customers.

The manager emerged from behind the middle counter, looking alarmed. He hesitated, then stepped back as if to retreat quickly. Havelock spoke rapidly in barely passable Italian. "I was caught in an insane crowd on the platform. I'm afraid I fell. I'll need to buy a few things—a number of things, actually. I'm expected at the Hassler fairly soon."

At the mention of Rome's most exclusive hotel, the manager at once turned sympathetic, even brotherly.

"Animali!" he exclaimed, gesturing to his God. "How perfectly dreadful for you, signore! Here, let me help you—"

"I'll need a new piece of luggage. Soft, very good leather, if you have it."

"Naturalmente."

"I realize it's an imposition, but could I possibly wash up somewhere? I'd hate to greet the Contessa the way I look now."

"This way, signore! A thousand apologies! I speak for all Rome! This way—"

While Michael washed and changed clothes in the back room, he focused his thoughts—as they came to him—on the brief visits he and Jenna Karas had made to Rome. There had been two. On the first they had passed through for a single night; the second was much longer, very official—three or four days, if he remembered correctly. They had been awaiting orders from Washington, having traveled as a Yugoslav couple through the Balkan countries in order to gather information on the sudden expansion in border defenses. There had been a man, an army intelligence officer not easily forgotten; he had been Havelock's D.C. conduit. What made the man memorable was his cover; he was posing as the only first-level black attaché at the embassy.

Their first conference had not been without humor—black humor. Michael and Jenna were to meet the attaché at an out-of-the-way restaurant west of the Palatine. They had waited in the crowded stand-up bar, preferring that the conduit select a table, and were oblivious to the tall black soldier ordering a vodka martini on their right. After several minutes the man smiled and said, "I'm jes' Rastus in the *catasta di legna*, Massa Havelock. Do you think we might sit down?"

His name was Lawrence Brown. Lieutenant Colonel Lawrence B. Brown—the middle initial was for his real name, Baylor.

"So help me God," the colonel had told them over after-dinner drinks that night, "the fellows in G-two felt there was more 'concrete association' —that's what they called it—by using Brown in the cover. It went under the heading of 'psy-acceptance,' can you believe it? Hell, I suppose it's better than Attaché Coffee-Face."

Baylor was a man he could talk to . . . if Baylor would agree to talk to him. And where? It would not be anywhere near the embassy; the United States government had several terrible things to explain to a retired field agent.

It took over twenty minutes on the manager's phone—while the manager repacked Michael's clothing in an outrageously priced new suitcase —before Havelock reached the embassy switchboard. Senior Attaché Brown was currently attending a reception on the first floor.

"Tell him it's urgent," said Michael. "My name is . . . Baylor."

Lawrence Baylor was reluctant to the point of turning Havelock down. Anything a retired intelligence officer had to say would best be said at the embassy. For any number of reasons.

"Suppose I told you I just came out of retirement. I may not be on your payroll—or anyone else's—but I'm very much back in. I'd suggest you don't blow this, Colonel."

"There's a café on the Via Pancrazio, La Ruota del Pavone. Do you know it?"

"I'll find it."

"Forty-five minutes."

"I'll be there. Waiting."

Havelock watched from a table in the darkest corner of the café as the army officer ordered a carafe of wine from the bar and began walking across the dimly lit room. Baylor's mahogany face was taut, stern; he was not comfortable, and when he reached the table, he did not offer his hand. He sat down opposite Michael, exhaled slowly, and attempted a grim smile.

"Nice to see you," he said with little conviction.

"Thank you."

"And unless you've got something to say we want to hear, you're putting me in a pretty rough spot, buddy. I hope you know that."

"I've got something that'll blow your mind," said Havelock, his voice involuntarily a whisper. The trembling had returned; he gripped his wrist to control it. "It's blown mine."

The colonel studied Michael, his eyes dropping to Havelock's hands. "You're stretched, I can see that. What is it?"

"She's *alive*. I *saw* her!"

Baylor was silent, immobile. His eyes roamed Michael's face, noting the marks of recent scrapes and bruises on Havelock's skin. It was obvious that he had made the connection. "Are you referring to the Costa Brava?" he asked finally.

"You know damn well I am!" said Michael angrily. "My abrupt retirement and the circumstances thereof have been flashed to every goddamned station and post we've got. It's why you just said what you did. 'Beware the screwed-up talent,' Washington tells you. 'He might do anything, say anything, think he has scores to settle.' "

"It's happened."

"Not to me. I don't have any scores to think about because I'm not interested in the ballgame. I'm rational. I saw what I saw. And she saw me! She acknowledged me! She *ran!*"

"Emotional stress is first cousin to hysteria," said the colonel quietly. "A man can see a lot of things that aren't there in that condition. And you had a jolt."

"Past tense, not currently applicable. I was out. I accepted the fact and the reasons—"

"Come *on*, buddy," insisted the soldier. "You don't throw away sixteen years of involvement."

"*I* did."

"You were here in Rome with her. Memories get activated, twisted. As I said, it happens."

"Again, negative. Nothing was activated, nothing twisted. I *saw*—"

"You even called *me*," interrupted Baylor sharply. "The three of us spent a couple of evenings together. A few drinks, a few laughs. Association; you reached me."

"There was no one else. My cover was D-squared: you were my only contact here in Rome! I can walk into the embassy now, I couldn't then."

"Then let's go," said the colonel quickly.

"No way! Besides, that's not the point. *You* are. You fielded orders to me from Washington seven months ago, and now you're going to send an emergency flag back to those same people. Tell them what I've told you, what I saw. You haven't got a choice."

"I've got an opinion. I'm relaying what a former talent said while in a state of extreme anxiety."

"Fine! Good! Then try this. Five days ago in Athens I nearly killed a man we both know from the Dzerzhinsky files for telling me Costa Brava wasn't a Soviet exercise. That she wasn't any part of the KGB, much less the VKR. I didn't kill him because I thought it was a probe, a *blind* probe —that man was telling the *truth*, as he knew the truth. I sent a message back to Moscow. The bait was too obvious, the smell too rotten."

"I suppose that was charitable of you, considering your record."

"Oh, no, the charity started with *him.* You see, he could have taken me. I could have found myself in Sevastopol on my way to Dzerzhinsky Square without even knowing I'd left Athens."

"He was that good? That well connected?"

"So much so, he was self-effacing. But he didn't take me. I wasn't booked on the Dardanelles airlift. He didn't want me."

"Why not?"

"Because he was convinced *I* was the bait. Pretty fair irony, isn't it? There was no room at the Lubyanka. I was turned out. Instead, he gave me his own message for Washington: Dzerzhinsky wouldn't touch me." Havelock paused. "And now *this.*"

The colonel narrowed his eyes pensively, and, with both hands, turned his glass on the table. "I don't have your expertise, but say you actually did see what you say you saw."

"I did. Accept it."

"No concessions, but say it's possible. It could still be a lure. They've got you under a glass, know your plans, your itinerary. Their computers pick up a woman reasonably similar in appearance, and with a little cosmetic surgery they've got a double sufficient for short distances. 'Beware the screwed-up talent.' You never know when he thinks he has 'scores to settle.' Especially if he's given some time to stew, to get worked up."

"What I saw was in her *eyes!* But even if you won't accept that, there's something else; it voids the strategy, and every point can be checked. Two hours ago I didn't know I'd be inside that station; ten minutes before I saw her I didn't know I'd be on that platform, and neither could anyone else. I came here yesterday and took a room in a *pensione* on the Due Macelli for a week, paid in advance. At eight-thirty tonight I saw a poster in a window and decided to go to Venice. I didn't speak to anyone." Michael reached into his pocket, took out his ticket for the *Freccia della Laguna* and placed it in front of Lawrence Baylor. "The *Freccia* was scheduled to leave at nine-thirty-five. The time of purchase is stamped across the top of this. Read it!"

"Twenty-one, twenty-seven," said the army officer, reading. "Twenty-seven past nine. Eight minutes before the train left."

"All verifiable. Now look at me and tell me I'm lying. And while you're at it, explain how that setup could have been mounted given the time span *and* the fact that she was on an incoming train!"

"I can't. *If* she—"

"She was talking to a conductor seconds before she got off. I'm sure I can find him."

Baylor was silent again; he stared at Havelock, then spoke softly. "Don't bother. I'll send the flag." He paused, adding, "Along with qualified support. Whatever you saw, you're not lying. Where can I reach you?"

"Sorry, I'll reach you."

"They'll want to talk to you, probably in a hurry."

"I'll be in touch."

"Why the static?"

"Something Rostov said in Athens."

"*Rostov?* Pyotr Rostov?" The colonel's eyes widened. "You don't go much higher in the Dzerzhinsky."

"There's higher."

"He'll do. What did he say? What did he tell you?"

"That our nostrils never quite adjust. Instead, they develop a kind of sensitivity—to variations of the basic rotten smell. Like animals."

"I expected something less abstract," said Baylor, annoyed.

"Really? From where I stand, it sounds concrete as hell. The Costa Brava trap was engineered in Washington, the evidence compiled by the inner shell in one of those white, sterile offices on the top floor of State."

"I understood you were in control," interrupted Baylor.

"The last phase. I insisted on it."

"Then you—"

"I acted on everything that was given to me. And now I want to know *why* it was given to me. Why I saw what I did tonight."

"*If* you saw—"

"She's *alive.* I want to know why! How!"

"I still don't understand."

"Costa Brava was meant for *me.* Someone wanted me out. Not dead, but out. Comfortably removed from those temptations that often afflict men like me."

"Scores to settle?" asked the colonel. "The Agee syndrome? The Snepp complex? I didn't know you were infected."

"I've had my quota of shocks, my share of questions. Someone wanted those questions buried and *she* went along. Why?"

"Two assumptions I'm not willing to concede are facts. And if you intended to bare a few shocks not in the national interest, I imagine—and I'm speaking hypothetically in the extreme, of course—there are other methods of . . . burying them."

"Dispatch? Call me dead?"

"I didn't say we'd kill you. We don't live in that kind of country." The colonel paused, then added, "On the other hand, why not?"

"For the same reason others haven't met with odd accidents that prearranged pathologists might label something else. Self-protection is ingrained in our job, brother. It's another syndrome; it's called the Nuremberg. Those shocks, instead of being buried, might surface. Sealed depositions to be opened by unnamed attorneys in the event of questionable et ceteras."

"*Jesus,* you said that? You went that far?"

"Strangely enough, I never did. Not seriously. I simply got angry. The rest was assumed."

"What kind of world do you people live in?"

"The same one you do—only, we've been around a little longer, a little deeper. And that's why I won't tell you where you can reach me. My nostrils have picked up a sickening odor from the Potomac." Havelock leaned forward, his voice harsh, low, nearly a whisper again. "I know that girl. For her to do what she did, something had to have been done to her, held over her. Something obscene. I want to know what it was and why."

"Assuming—" Baylor began slowly, "assuming you're right, and I don't for an instant concede that you are, what makes you think they'll tell you?"

"It was all so sudden," said Michael, leaning back, his body rigid, his voice now floating as if in a painful dream. "It was a Tuesday and we were in Barcelona. We'd been there for a week; something was going to happen in the sector, that's all Washington told us. Then word came from Madrid: a Four Zero communication had been flown in by courier, contents restricted to the embassy, Eyes Only. Mine only. There's no Cons Op station in Madrid, no one cleared to relay the information, so I flew in Wednesday morning, signed for that goddamned steel container, and opened it in a room guarded by three marines. Everything was there, everything she'd done, all the information she'd transmitted—information she could have gotten only from me. The trap was there, too, myself in control if I so wished—and I so wished. They knew it was the only way I'd be convinced. On Friday I was back in Barcelona, and by Sunday it was over . . . and I *was* convinced. Five days and the walls came tumbling down. No trumpets, just flashlights and screams and loud ugly noises intruding on the surf. Five days . . . so sudden, so swift, everything at a crescendo. It was the only way it could have been done."

"You haven't answered my question," Baylor interrupted quietly. "If you're right, what makes you think they'll tell you?"

Havelock leveled his eyes at the soldier. "Because they're afraid. It comes down to the why. The questions, the shocks; which one was it?"

"What are you talking about?"

"The decision to remove me wasn't made gradually, Colonel. Something triggered it. They don't force a man out the way I was forced out because of accumulated differences. Talent's expensive; proven field talent too difficult to replace. Accommodations can be made, explanations offered, agreements reached. All these are tried before they let the talent go. But no one tried with me."

"Can you be more specific?" the officer pressed, again annoyed.

"I wish I could be. It's something I know, or they *think* I know. Something I could have written down. And it's a bomb."

"Do you?" Baylor asked coldly, professionally. "Have such a piece of information?"

"I'll find it," replied Havelock, suddenly pushing back his chair, prepared to leave. "You tell them that. Just as I'll find her, tell them that, too. It won't be easy because she's not with them anymore. She got away; she's gone under. I also saw that in her eyes. But I'll find her."

"Maybe—" Baylor said urgently, "maybe if everything you say proves out, they'd be willing to help."

"They'd better be," said Michael getting to his feet, and looking down at the soldier-conduit. "I'll need all the help I can get. In the meantime I want this whole goddamned thing spelled out—chapter and verse, to quote an old source of mine. Because if it isn't, I'm going to start telling tales out of school. When and from where none of you will know, but the words will be there loud and clear. And somewhere among them will be that bomb."

"Don't do anything stupid!"

"Don't mistake me, I don't want to. But what was done to her, to me —to *us*—just wasn't fair, Colonel. I'm back in. Solo. I'll be in touch."

Havelock turned and walked swiftly out of the café into the Via Pancrazio.

He reached the Via Galvani on his way back to the railroad station, where he had deposited his newly acquired suitcase in a coin locker. Suddenly the painful irony struck him. It had been a suitcase in a coin locker at an airport in Barcelona that had condemned Jenna Karas. The defector from the Baader-Meinhof—in exchange for the quiet cancellation of a death sentence pronounced in absentia—had led them to it. The German terrorist had told Madrid that *das Fräulein Karas* kept secret, updated field records within her reach at all times. It was a Voennaya custom dictated by the strange relationship the violent and clandestine branch of Soviet intelligence had with the rest of the KGB. Certain field personnel on long-range deep-cover operations had access to their own files in the event that their superiors in Moscow suddenly were not accessible. Self-protection sometimes assumed odd forms; no one had questioned it.

No one had questioned. Not even he.

Someone makes contact with her and gives her a key, stating a location. A room or a locker, even a bank. The material is there, including new objectives as they are developed.

A man had stopped her one afternoon two days before Michael left for Madrid. In a café on the Paseo Isabel. A drunk. He had shaken her hand, then kissed it. Four days later Michael had found a key in Jenna's purse. On Sunday, two days later, she was dead.

There had been a key, but whose key was it? He had seen photocopies verified by Langley of every item in that suitcase. But whose suitcase was it? If not hers, how did three sets of fingerprints confirmed to be hers get inside? And if the prints were hers, why did she permit it?

What had they done to her? What had they done to a blond woman on the Costa Brava who had screamed in Czech and whose spine and neck and head had been pierced with bullets? What kind of people were they who could put human beings on strings and blow them up as calmly as one might explode mannequins in a horror show? That woman had died; he had seen too much death to be mistaken. It was no charade, as the elegant Gravet might have put it.

Yet it was all a charade. They were all puppets. But on what stage and for whose benefit were they performing?

He hurried faster on the Via Galvani; the Via della Mamorata was in sight. He was only blocks now from the massive railroad station; he would begin there. At least, he had an idea; whether it made sense or not the next half hour would tell.

He passed a garishly lighted newsstand where tabloids competed with glossy magazines. Capped teeth and outsized breasts battled for attention with mutilated bodies and graphic descriptions of rape and mayhem. And then he saw the famous face staring up at him from the cover of the international edition of *Time*. The clear eyes behind the horn-rimmed glasses shone as they always did, full of high intelligence—cold at first glance, yet somehow warmer the longer one looked at them, softened, perhaps by an understanding few on this earth possessed. There he was, the high cheekbones and the aquiline nose, the generous lips from which such extraordinary words poured forth.

"A man for all seasons, all peoples." That was the simple caption beneath the photograph. No name, no title; none was necessary. The world knew the American Secretary of State, heard his reasoned, deliberate voice and understood. This *was* a man for all; he transcended borders and languages and national insanities. There were those who believed—and Michael was one of them—that either the world would listen to Anthony Matthias or it would be blown to hell in a mushroom cloud.

Anton Matthias. Friend, mentor, surrogate father. Where Costa Brava was concerned, he, too, had been a puppet. *Who would dare?*

As Havelock put several lira notes down on the counter and picked up the magazine, he remembered vividly the handwritten note Anton had insisted the strategists in Washington include with the Four Zero file flown to Madrid. From their few brief conversations in Georgetown, Matthias had grasped the depth of his feelings for the woman assigned to him for the past eight months. At last, perhaps, he was ready to get out and find the peace that had eluded him all these years. The statesman had made gentle fun of the situation; when a fellow Czech past forty and in Michael's line of work decided to concentrate on one woman, Slavic tradition and contemporary fiction suffered irreparable blows.

But there had been no such levity in Matthias's note.

Můj milý synu

The attached pains my heart as it will yours. You who suffered so much in the early days, and have given of yourself so brilliantly and selflessly to our adopted country in these later ones, must again know pain. I have demanded and received a complete verification of these findings. If you wish to remove yourself from the scene, you may, of course, do so. Do not feel bound by the attached recommendations. There is only so much a nation can ask, and you have given with honor and more. Perhaps now the angers we spoke of years ago, the furies that propelled you into this terrible life, have subsided, permitting you to return to another world that needs the labors of your mind. I pray so.

Tvůj,
Anton M.

Havelock forced the note from his mind; it served only to aggravate the incomprehensible. Verification: *Positive.* He opened the magazine to the article on Matthias. There was nothing new, merely a recap of his more recent accomplishments in the area of arms negotiations. It ended with the observation that the Secretary of State was off for a well-deserved vacation at an unnamed location. Michael smiled; he knew where it was. A cabin in the Shenandoah Valley. It was entirely possible that before the night was over he would use a dozen codes to reach that mountain cabin. But not until he found out what had happened. For Anton Matthias had been touched by it too.

The crowds inside the giant dome of the Ostia had thinned out, the last of the trains leaving Rome having departed or being about to depart. Havelock pulled his suitcase from the locker and looked around for a sign; it had to be somewhere. It could well be a waste of time, but he did not think so; at least it was a place to start. He had told the intelligence officer–attaché in the café on the Via Pancrazio: "She was talking to a conductor seconds before she got off. I'm sure I can find him."

Michael reasoned that someone running did not casually strike up a conversation with a conductor for the sake of conviviality; too much was on that someone's mind. And in every city there were those sections where men and women who wished to disappear could do so, where cash was the only currency, mouths were kept shut, and hotel registries rarely reflected accurate identities. Jenna Karas might know the names of districts, even streets, but she did not—had not known—Rome itself. A city on strike might just possibly convince someone running that it was urgent to ask a question or a direction of someone who might have the answer.

There was the sign on the wall, an arrow pointing to the office complex: AMMINISTRATORE DELLA STAZIONE.

Thirty-five minutes later, having convinced a night manager that it was imperative and in both his and the conductor's financial interest that the conductor be found, he had the address of the man assigned to cars *tre, quattro,* and *cinque* for the incoming train on *binario trentasei* at eight-thirty that evening. As the rail system was government service, a photograph was attached to the employment sheet. It was the same man he had seen talking to Jenna Karas. Among his qualifications was a proficiency in English. *Livello primario.*

He climbed the worn stone steps of the apartment building to the fifth floor, found the name "Mascolo" on the door and knocked. The red-faced conductor was dressed in loose trousers held up by wide suspenders over an undershirt. His breath reeked of cheap wine, and his eyes were not entirely focused. Havelock took a 10,000-lire note from his pocket.

"Who can remember one passenger among thousands?" protested the man, seated opposite Michael at the kitchen table.

"I'm sure *you* can," said Havelock, removing another bill. *"Think.* She was probably one of the last people you spoke to on that train. Slender, medium height, a wide-brimmed hat—you were in the vestibule."

"Sì! Naturalmente. Una bella ragazza! I remember!" The conductor took the money and drank some wine; he belched and continued. "She asked me if I knew where she could make connections for Civitavecchia."

"Civitavecchia? That's a town north of here, isn't it?"

"Sì. A seaport on the Tyrrhenian."

"Did you know?"

"There are very few trains between Rome and Civitavecchia, signore, and certainly not at that hour. It is at best a stop for freight, not passengers."

"What did you tell her?"

"Just that. She appeared reasonably well dressed, so I suggested she negotiate a taxi for a flat rate. If she could find one. Rome is a *manicomio!"*

Havelock nodded thanks, placed another bill on the table and went to the door. He glanced at his watch; it was twenty past one in the morning. Civitavecchia. A seaport on the Tyrrhenian. Ships heading out to sea on a given day invariably left with the early light. At dawn.

He had roughly three hours to reach Civitavecchia, search the waterfront, find a pier, find a ship—find an unlisted passenger.

5

He raced out of the marble lobby of the hotel in Bernini Circle and rushed blindly up through the winding streets until he reached the Via Veneto. The desk clerk at the hotel had not been able to help him but not for lack of trying; spurred by the thick folds of lire, he futilely punched the telephone bar and screamed numbers at the sleepy switchboard operator. The night clerk's contacts were limited; he could not raise a rented car.

Havelock stopped for breath, studying the lights on the Veneto. The hour was too late for the full array, but several cafés and the Excelsior Hotel were illuminated. Someone had to help him—he had to get to Civitavecchia! *He had to find her. He could not lose her.* Not again, not *ever* again! He had to reach her and hold her and tell her that terrible things had been done to them, tell her over and over again until she saw the truth in his eyes and heard that truth in his voice; and saw the love he felt so deeply, and understood the unendurable guilt that never left him —for he had killed that love.

He began running again, first into the Excelsior, where no amount of money interested an arrogant clerk.

"You've got to help me!"

"You are not even a guest, signore," said the man, glancing to his left.

Slowly Michael angled his head. Across the lobby two policemen were watching the scene. They conferred; obviously, the night operation at the Excelsior was under open official scrutiny. Peddlers of capsules and pills, white powder and syringes, were working the world-famous boulevard. One of the uniformed men stepped forward. Havelock turned and walked rapidly to the entrance, once again running into the half-deserted street, toward the nearest profusion of light.

The tired maître d' of the Café de Paris told him he was a *capo zuccone*. Who would have an automobile to rent to a stranger at this hour? The American manager of a third-rate version of a Third Avenue bar told him to "pound sand."

Again the winding streets, again the sweat drenching his hairline, rolling down his cheeks. The Hassler—the Villa Medici! He had used the name of the elegant hotel in the luggage shop by the Ostia. . . .

The night concierge at the Hassler's Villa Medici was accustomed to the vagaries of Rome's wealthiest hotel guests. Arrangements were made for Michael to rent a Fiat, one of the Hassler's staff vehicles. The price was exorbitant, but with it came a map of Rome and its environs, the most direct route to Civitavecchia marked in red.

He reached the port city at three-fifteen and by three-forty-five he had driven up and down the waterfront, studying it until he decided where to park the car and start his search for Jenna Karas.

It was a section common to most waterfronts where the floodlights washing the piers remained on all night and activity never stopped; where groupings of dockworkers and deckhands mingled like slow-moving automatons, crisscrossing each other—men and machinery meshed in volatile conflict—loading the cargo holds and preparing the massive boilers and outdated engines of the larger vessels soon to head out into deep water. Where cafés and coffeehouses lined the mist-laden alleys, punctuated by the diffused light of the streetlamps—places of refuge serving the harshest whisky and the most glutinous food.

To the north and south were the smaller piers, halyards and masts swaying in silhouette against the moonlight; filthy marinas for the fishing boats and the trawlers that ventured no more than forty kilometers out to those watery places that decades of experience and tradition told the captains were where the catches were most plentiful. These piers did not begin to stir until the early light was closer, faint sprays of yellowish white inching their way over the southwest horizon, pushing the night sky upward. Only then did groaning, dull-eyed men walk down the wooden planks toward oily gunwales and the interminable, blinding day ahead. Jenna Karas would not be in these places where the boats cast off at dawn only to return home when the sun went down. She would be somewhere in that complex of larger piers, where ships looked to the tides and the charts and sailed to other ports, other countries.

She was somewhere in this stretch of the waterfront where swirling pockets of mist rolled off the sea and across the docks, through intersecting pools of floodlights and the hammering tattoo of nocturnal labors. She would be hidden—not visible to those who should not see her: *controllori* of the piers, paid by the state and the shipping companies to be on the lookout for material and human contraband. Keep her out of sight; the moment will come when she can be taken on board, after a *capo operaio* has inspected a hold and signed the papers that state the ship in question is free to depart, free from the taint of transgressing the laws of land and sea. Then she can walk swiftly out of the shadows and down a pier, *controllori* and *operai* themselves out of sight, their duties finished.

Which pier? Which ship? *Where are you, Jenna?*

There were three freighters, all medium tonnage, berthed alongside each other at three of the four major cargo docks. The fourth housed two smaller vessels—barge class—with conveyor equipment and thick piping machinery transporting and pumping bulk cargo up into the open holds. She would be taken aboard one of the freighters; the immediate thing to learn was the departure time of each.

He parked the Fiat on a side street that intersected the *viale* fronting the four piers. He walked across the wide avenue, dodging several vans and trucks, to the first pier on the left, to the gate manned by a uniformed guard, a civil servant of questionable civility. He was unpleasant, and the nuisance of having to piece together Havelock's barely fluent Italian added to his hostility.

"What do you want to know for?" asked the guard, filling the doorway of the gatehouse. "What's it to you?"

"I'm trying to find someone who may have booked passage," said Michael, hoping the words he used were close enough to his meaning.

"Passaggio? Biglietto? Who buys a ticket on a Portuguese freighter?"

Havelock saw his opening; he leaned closer, glancing about as he spoke. "This is the ship, then. Forgive my poor use of your language, *Signor Controllore.* It's unforgivable. Actually, I'm with the embassy of Portugal in Rome. In my way an—inspector, as you are. We were told there may be certain irregularities with this vessel. Any cooperation from you could be duly conveyed to your superiors."

The human ego when tied to opportunity was not affected by the lowliness of a civil service rating. The hostile guard was abruptly pleasant, moving aside to admit the *straniero importante.*

"*Scusatemi, signore!* I did not understand. We who patrol these holes of corruption must cooperate with one another, no? And, in truth, a word to my superiors—in Rome, of course."

"Of course. Not here."

"Of course. Not here. They are brutes down here. Come in, come in. It must be chilly for you."

The *Miguel Cristóvão* was scheduled to leave port at 5:00 A.M. Its captain was a man named Aliandro, who had been in the wheelhouse of the *Cristóvão* for the past twelve years, a skipper who knew every island, every shoal in the western Mediterranean, it was said.

The two other freighters were of Italian registry. The guards at the gates were wearily cooperative, perfectly willing to give whatever information the oddly spoken foreigner requested. What he wished to know he could read in any newspaper under *Navi Informazione–Civitavecchia,* the pages of which were usually torn out and tacked to the walls of the various cafés around the waterfront. They helped when crewmen got drunk and forgot their schedules.

The *Isola d'Elba* was leaving at five-thirty, the *Santa Teresa* twenty minutes later, at five-fifty.

Havelock started to walk away from the third gate. He looked at his watch; it was eight minutes past four. So little time.

Jenna! Where are you?

He heard the sound of a bell behind him. It was sudden, abrasive, echoing in its own vibrations, an outside bell meant to be heard above the shouts and machinery of the piers. Alarmed, he turned quickly. The guard had stepped inside the glass cubicle that was his gatehouse and was answering the telephone. The verbal flow of attentive *Sì* emphasized the fact that whoever was on the other end of the line was issuing orders that were to be thoroughly understood.

Telephones and guards at checkpoints were sources of concern to Michael. For a moment he was not sure whether or not to run. The answer was given instantly. The guard hung up the phone and stuck his head out the door. "You! You want to know so much about this stinking tub, here's something else! The *Teresa* stays put. She doesn't sail until six godforsaken trucks get here from Torino, which could be eight hours from now. The unions will make those bastards pay, let me tell you! Then they'll fine the crew for being drunk! They're *all* bastards!"

The *Teresa* was out of the running, for a while at least. He could concentrate on the *Elba* and the *Cristóvão*. If Jenna was to be smuggled aboard the *Teresa,* he had hours, but not if it was one of the other two. If either was the case, he still had only minutes. He had to spend them wisely but swiftly, wasting as few as possible. There was no time for the subtleties of move and countermove, for circling the grounds of inquiry and selecting targets cautiously, being aware of whoever might be watching him. There was time only for money—if takers could be found. And force—if those same takers tripped themselves on lies that meant they knew the truth.

Havelock walked quickly back to the second gate, where the *Isola d'Elba* was berthed, altering his story only slightly for the weary guard. He wished to speak to a few of the vessel's crew, those who might be on shore awaiting the ship's call. Would the cooperative civil servant, having shaken a hand with several thousand lire folded in the palm, know which of the waterfront cafés were favored by the *Elba*'s crew?

"They stick together, no, signore? When fights break out, seamen want their friends around, even those they hate on board. Try Il Pinguino. Or perhaps La Carrozza di Mare. The whisky's cheaper at the first, but the food makes one vomit. It's better at La Carrozza."

The once hostile, now obsequious guard at the gate of the *Cristóvão* was more than cooperative; he was effusively friendly.

"There is a café on the Via Maggio where, it is said, many things pass hands."

"Would the *Cristóvão*'s men be there?"

"Some, perhaps. The Portuguese do not mix well, of course. No one trusts them— Not *you,* signore! I refer only to the garbage of the sea. The same everywhere. Not *you,* may God forgive me!"

"The name, please?"

"Il Tritone."

It took less than twelve minutes to disqualify Il Tritone. Michael walked through the heavy doors, beneath the crude bas-relief of a naked creature half man and half fish, into the raucous squalor of the waterfront bar. The smoke was thick, the stench of stale whisky thicker. Men shouted between the tables; others lurched, and not a few had collapsed, their heads resting on folded arms, small pools of alcohol surrounding hands and nostrils and bearded cheeks.

Havelock chose the oldest-looking man behind the bar and approached him first. "Are there any here from the *Cristóvão?*"

"Portoghese?"

"Sì."

"A few—over there, I think."

Michael looked through the smoke and the weaving bodies to a table across the room. There were four men. "What about the *Isola d'Elba?*" he asked, turning back to the bartender.

"Porci!" replied the man. "Pigs! They come in here, I throw them out! Scum!"

"They must be something," said Havelock, scanning the Tritone's clientele, his throat trembling at the thought of Jenna among such men.

"You want crew from the *Elba,* go to Il Pinguino. Over there, they don't care."

Michael took out a 10,000-lire note, and placed it in front of the bartender. "Do you speak Portuguese? Enough to be understood?"

"Down here, if one cares to make a living one must be understood in half a dozen tongues." The man slipped the money into his apron pocket, adding, "They no doubt speak Italian, probably better than you, signore. So let us speak in English. What do you wish me to do?"

"There's an empty table back there," said Havelock, relieved, changing languages, and gesturing with his head toward the left rear corner of the café. "I'm going over and sit down. You go to those men and tell them I want to see them—one at a time. If you think they won't understand me, come over with each and be my interpreter."

"Interprete?"

"Sì."

"Bone."

One by one the four Portuguese sailors came to the table, each bewildered, two proficient in Italian, one in English, one needing the services of the *interprete.* To each, Michael said the same words:

"I'm looking for a woman. It's a minor matter, nothing to be concerned about; call it an affair of the heart. She's an impetuous woman; we've all known them, haven't we? But now she may have gone too far for her own good. I'm told she has a friend on the *Cristóvão.* She may have been around the pier, asking questions, looking for transport. She's an attractive woman, average height, blond hair, probably wearing a raincoat and a wide-brimmed hat. Have you seen anyone like that? If you have, there could be a lot more money in your pocket than there is now."

And with each man he gave an explanation for his summons that the sailor could take back to his companions, along with 5,000 lire: "Whatever you tell me remains between us. For my good more than yours. When you go back to your table, you can say the same thing I'm telling everyone. I want rough sex with someone leaving Civitavecchia, but I'm not going to take it from any son of a bitch who won't leave his papers down at a hotel desk. Released by me. Got it?"

Only with the third man did the bartender, who insisted on being present at each interview, caution Havelock firmly. "This one will leave his papers at a desk," he said.

"Then he's not my type."

"*Bene!*"

"*Grazie.*"

"*Prego.*"

Nothing. No such woman had been seen or heard of on the *Cristóvão* pier. The four Portuguese crewmen resumed their drinking.

Havelock thanked the perplexed older man beside him, and pressed another bill into his apron pocket. "Which way to Il Pinguino?" he asked.

"The *Elba* crew?"

"That's right."

"I'll go with you," said the bartender, removing his apron and the money in its pocket.

"Why?"

"You sound like a decent man. Also stupid. You walk into Il Pinguino asking questions, your money's for everyone. All it takes is one sailor with a quiet knife."

"I can take care of myself."

"You are not only stupid, you are *very* stupid. I own Il Tritone; they respect me at Il Pinguino. You'll be safer with me. You pass money too quickly."

"I'm in a hurry."

"*Presto!* Let's get on with it. It's a bad morning here. Not like the old days when men knew that half a chestful was enough. You taste it in your throat, you know. These assholes mix up comfort with wanting no memory. *Vieni!*"

The café five blocks away brought back memories, remembrances of a life he had thought was over—he had been in too many such places in that other life. If Il Tritone catered to the garbage of humanity, Il Pinguino took the dregs and considered it *clientela scelta.* The smoke was thicker, the shouting louder; men did not lurch, they lunged at nothing and everything, intent only on the violence in their minds. These were men who found amusement in the sudden exposure of another's weakness or a semblance of weakness—which they construed as an absence of manhood—and then attacked.

They had nothing else. They challenged the shadows of their own deepest fears.

The owner of Il Tritone was greeted by his counterpart within seconds of ushering Havelock through the door. The Pinguino's *proprietario* matched his establishment, having few teeth and arms that hung like huge, hairy cheeses. He was not as large as Michael's newfound friend, but there was a sense of violence about him that made one think of a boar that could be quickly stirred to anger.

The greetings between the two men were spoken rapidly, perfunctorily. But there was respect, as Il Tritone's owner had said there would be, and the arrangements were made swiftly, with a minimum of explanation.

"The American looks for a woman. It is a *malinteso,* and not our business," said the owner of Il Tritone. "She may be sailing with the *Elba,* and one of these thieves may have seen her. He's willing to pay."

"He'd better hurry," replied the sullen boar. "The oilers left an hour ago; they're sweating piss-green by now. The second mate will be here any minute to gather up the rest of the deck."

"How many are there?"

"Eight, ten, who knows? I count lire, not faces."

"Have one of your people go around and ask quietly, find them, and tell me who they are. Clear a table for my companion. I'll bring each one to him."

"You give orders as though the Pinguino were the Tritone."

"Because I would accord you the same courtesy, even as my tongue thickened as yours does now. One never knows. You could need my help tomorrow. . . . Each pig from the *Elba* is worth ten thousand lire to you."

"*Bene.*" The Pinguino's owner walked away toward the bar.

"Do not give these men any excuse for talking to you as you did the *Portoghese,*" said Michael's companion. "For them it was good thinking, but not for these. There's no time, and in their drunkenness they could find the wrong meaning. Bottles are broken easily in here."

"Then what am I going to say? I've got to separate them, give each a reason for talking to me alone. I can't go up to all of them at once. One may know something, but he's not going to tell me in front of the others."

"Agreed. So tell each you trust only *him.* The others—you were told —are *not* to be trusted. You spoke with them only for appearance, because your business concerns the *Elba.* It will be enough."

"I'm a stranger. Who would tell me something like that?"

"A man who knows his clientele—the one you paid. The owner of Il Pinguino." The owner of Il Tritone grinned. "By the time they reach port again, he'll be covered with stink. He'll need the *carabinieri* every night."

Separately, warily, in varying phases of stupor, the remaining crew of the *Elba* sat down and listened to Havelock's increasingly fluent Italian as he repeated the same question. And with each he studied the man's face, the eyes, looking for a reaction, a glint of recognition, a brief straying of a glance that covered a lie. With the sixth man he thought he found it; it was in the lips—a sudden stretching unrelated to the sagging muscle tone induced by whisky, and in the clouded eyes, dulled further by an instinctive desire not to listen. The man knew something.

"You've seen her, *haven't* you?" said Michael, losing control, speaking in English.

"*Ascolta,*" interrupted the owner of Il Tritone. "*In italiano, signore.*"

"Sorry." Havelock repeated the question, which was more an accusation, in Italian.

The sailor responded with a shrug, shifted his position, and started to get up. Michael reached over quickly and clamped his hand on the seaman's arm. The response was now ugly; the sailor squinted his rheumy, red-veined eyes, his mouth like that of an angry dog, lips parted, stained yellow teeth showing. In seconds he would lunge—drunkenly, to be sure, but nevertheless, attack was imminent.

"*Lascialo,*" ordered the owner of Il Tritone, then spoke rapidly under his breath in English. "Show him money. Quickly! This pig will grab your throat, and they'll be all over us and you will learn nothing. You are right. He's seen her."

Havelock released the man's arm, reached into his pocket and took out the thick pack of awkwardly small lire notes. He separated two bills and placed them in front of the sailor; they totaled 40,000 lire, a day's pay on board ship.

"As you can see," he said in Italian, "there's more here. You can't take it from me, but I can give it to you. On the other hand, you can walk away and not tell me anything." Michael paused, leaned back in the chair, staring at the man, his expression hostile. "But I can make trouble for you. And I will."

"*In che modo?*" The crewman was as angry as he was bewildered, his eyes darting between Havelock's face, the money, and the owner of Il Tritone, who sat impassively, his rigid posture showing that he was aware of the danger in Michael's tactic.

"How?" Havelock leaned forward, his fingers pulling the lire toward him, as though retrieving two vital cards in a game of baccarat. "I'll go over to the *Elba* and find your captain. Whatever I say to him about you he's not going to like."

"*Che cosa?* What? . . . What can you say to him *in riguardo a me* that he would *credere?*" The sailor's sudden use of English words was unexpected. He turned to the owner of Il Tritone. "Perhaps this pig will grab *your* throat, old man. I need no help from others. For you or this *ricco americano.*" The man unzipped his coarse wool jacket; the handle of a knife protruded from a scabbard strapped to his belt; his head swayed from the effects of the whisky. A very thin line was about to be crossed.

Abruptly, Michael settled back in his chair and laughed quietly. It was a genuine laugh, in no way hostile or challenging, further confusing the seaman. "*Bene!*" said Michael, suddenly leaning forward again, removing two more 5,000-lire notes from the loose packet of bills. "I wanted to find out if you had balls, and you told me. Good! A man without balls doesn't know what he sees. He makes things up because he's afraid, or because he sees money." Havelock gripped the man's hand at the wrist, forcing the palm open. It was a strong if friendly grip, indicating a strength the sailor had to acknowledge. "Here! Fifty thousand lire. There's no quarrel between us. Where did you see her?"

The abrupt changes of mood were beyond the man's comprehension. He was reluctant to forgo the challenge, but the combination of the money, the grip and the infectious laugh made him retreat. "Are you . . . go to my captain?" he asked in English, eyes swimming.

"What for? You just told me. It has nothing to do with him. Why bring that *farabutto* into it? Let him earn his own money. Where did you see her?"

"On the street. *Ragazza bionda. Bella. Cappello a larga tesa.*"

"Blond, attractive . . . wide hat! *Where?* Who was she with? A mate, a ship's officer? *Un ufficiale?*"

"Not the *Elba.* The next ship. *Nave mercantile.*"

"There are only two. The *Cristóvão* and the *Teresa.* Which one?"

The man glanced around, head bobbing, eyes only half focused. "She was talking to two men . . . one a *capitano.*"

"Which *one?*"

"*A destra,*" whispered the sailor, pulling the back of his hand across his wet lips.

"On the right?" asked Michael quickly. "The *Santa Teresa?*"

The seaman now rubbed his chin and blinked; he was afraid, his eyes suddenly focused to the left of the table. He shrugged, crushing the money in his right hand, as he pushed back his chair. *"Non so niente. Una puttana del capitano."*

"Mercantile italiano?" pressed Havelock. "The Italian freighter? The *Santa Teresa?"*

The sailor stood up, his face white. *"Sì. . . . No! Destra . . . sinistra!"* The man's eyes were now riveted somewhere across the room; Michael angled his head unobtrusively. Three men at a table against the wall were watching the crewman from the *Elba. "Il capitano. Un marinaio superiore! Il migliore!"* cried the seaman hoarsely. "I know nothing else, signore!" He lurched away, shouldering a path through the bodies gathered at the bar toward the alley door.

"You play dangerously," commented the owner of Il Tritone. "It could have gone either way."

"With a mule—drunk or otherwise—nothing's ever replaced the carrot and the whip," said Havelock, his head still turned slightly, his concentration still on the three men at the table across the room.

"You could have had blood on your stomach and have learned nothing at all."

"But I *did* learn something."

"Not a great deal. A freighter on the right, on the left. Which?"

"He said on the right first."

"Coming off the pier, or going on to it?"

"From his immediate point of view. Going on. *Destra.* The *Santa Teresa.* She'll be put on board the *Teresa,* which means I have time to find her before she's given the signal. She's somewhere within sight of the dock."

"I'm not so sure," said Il Tritone's owner, shaking his head. "Our mule was specific. The captain was *un marinaio superiore. Migliore.* The best, a great seaman. The captain of the *Teresa* is a tired merchantman. He never sails past Marseilles."

"Who are those men at the table over there?" asked Michael, his question barely audible through the din. "Don't turn your head, just shift your eyes. Who are they?"

"I do not know them by name."

"What does that mean?"

"Italiano," said the owner of Il Tritone, his voice flat.

"The *Santa Teresa,"* said Havelock, removing a number of bills and putting the rest of the money back into his pocket. "You've been a great help," he said. "I owe the *proprietario*. The rest is for you."

"*Grazie.*"

"*Prego.*"

"I will see you down the alley to the waterfront. I still do not like it. We don't know those men are from the *Teresa*. Something is not *in equilibrio.*"

"The percentages say otherwise. It's the *Teresa*. Let's go."

Outside the noisy café the narrow thoroughfare was comparatively silent; naked light bulbs shone weakly, enveloped in mist above intermittent doorways, and centuries-old smooth cobblestones muffled the sound of footsteps. At the end of the alley the wide avenue that fronted the piers could be seen in the glow of the streetlamps; until one reached it the alley itself was a gauntlet of shadows. One walked cautiously, alert to the spaces of black silence.

"*Ecco!*" whispered the Italian, his eyes up ahead. "Someone's in that doorway. On the left. Do you have a weapon?"

"No. I haven't had time—"

"Then *quickly!*" The owner of Il Tritone suddenly broke into a run, passing the doorway as a figure lurched out—a stocky man with arms raised, hands poised for interception. But there was no gun in those hands, no weapon but the thick hands themselves.

Havelock took several rapid strides toward the prowler, then spun into the shadows on the opposite side of the alley. The man lunged; Michael spun around again and, grabbing his assailant's coat, hammered his right foot up into the man's midsection. He pivoted a third time, now yanking the man off the ground, and hurled him into the wall. As the man fell, Havelock sprang downward, his left knee sinking into the man's stomach, his right hand gripping the face and clawing at the eyes.

"*Basta! Por favor! Se Deus quiser!*" choked the prowler, holding his groin, saliva dribbling from his mouth. The language was Portuguese, the man one of the crew of the *Cristóvão*. Michael yanked him up against the wall, into the dim light; he was the seaman who had spoken a few words of English at the table in Il Tritone.

"If you're going into theft with assault and battery, you're not doing it very well!"

"No, senhor! I wish only to talk, but I cannot be seen! You pay me, I'll tell you things, but not where I can be seen with you!"

"Go on."

"You pay!"

Havelock clamped the sailor's neck against the brick with his forearm, reached into his pocket and took out his money. Shoving his knee into the man's chest and freeing his hand, he removed two bills. "Twenty thousand lire," he said. "Talk!"

"It's worth more. Much more, senhor! You will see."

"I can take it back if it's not. . . . Thirty thousand, that's it. Go *on!*"

"The woman goes aboard the *Cristóvão . . . sete . . .* seven *minutos* before we sail. It is arranged. She comes out the east warehouse door. She is guarded now; you cannot reach her. But she must walk forty meters to the cargo boarding plank."

Michael released him and added another note to the three in the seaman's hand. "Get out of here," he said. "I never saw you."

"You must *swear* to it, senhor!" cried the man, scrambling to his feet.

"Sworn. Now get out."

Suddenly voices were heard at the end of the alley; two men came running out of the light.

"*Americano! Americano!*" It was the owner of Il Tritone; he had returned with help. As the Portuguese started to race away they grabbed him.

"Let him go!" yelled Havelock. "It's all right! Let him go!"

Sixty seconds later Michael explained to the owner of Il Tritone. "It's not the *Teresa.* It's the *Cristóvão.*"

"It's what was missing!" cried the Italian. "The knowledgeable *capitano,* the great seaman. It was there and I did not see it. Aliandro. João Aliandro! The finest captain in the Mediterranean. He could work his ship into any dangerous coastline, dropping off cargo wherever he wished, wherever the rocks and shoals called for no observers on shore. You have found your woman, signore."

He crouched in the shadows of a stationary crane, the open spaces of the machinery allowing him unobstructed sight lines. The freighter's cargo had been loaded; the teams of stevedores dispersed, swearing as they went their various ways across the wide avenue and down the narrow alleys into cafés. Except for the four-man cast-off crew the pier was deserted, and even those men were barely visible, standing motionless by the huge pilings, two men to a line, fore and aft.

A hundred yards behind him was the entrance gate, the obsequious guard inside his glass booth, his figure a gray silhouette in the rolling early-morning fog. Diagonally to the left in front of the crane some eighty-odd feet away was the ribbed, weather-beaten gangplank that went up to the *Cristóvão's* forward deck. It was the last physical connection to the ship to be hauled on board before the giant hawsers were slipped off the pilings, freeing the behemoth for the open water.

On the right, no more than sixty feet from the crane, was the door to the pier's warehouse office; it was locked, and all lights were off inside. And beyond that door was Jenna Karas, a fugitive from her own and others' betrayal—his love, who had turned on that love for reasons only she could tell him. . . . In moments now, the door would open and she would have to walk from that door to the gangplank, then up the cracked wooden causeway to the deck. Once on board, she would be free; giant lines would be thrown over the pier, whistles would blow, and the gangplank would be whipped in the air, sucked up on deck and stowed. But until then she was not free; she was human contraband in open transit, crossing territory where no one would dare protect her. Inside the warehouse office she could be protected; an intruder breaking in could be shot for the act itself. But not in the open; men would not risk being caught smuggling human flesh on board ships. The prison sentences were long; a few thousand lire was not worth that risk.

A hundred and forty-odd feet, then, was the span she had to cross in order to disappear. Again. Not in death, but in an enigma.

Michael looked at his watch; it was four-fifty-two, the second hand approaching the minute mark—seven minutes before the *Cristóvão* was scheduled to blare its bass-toned departure signal, followed by sharper, higher sounds that warned all vessels of its imminent thrust out of its secure haven, the rules of the sea instantly in force. High up on the deck, fore and midships, a few men wandered aimlessly, pinpointed by the erratic glow of their cigarettes. Except for those on the rope winches and the gangplank detail, there was nothing for them to do but smoke and drink coffee and hope their heads would clear without excessive pain. From inside the massive black hull, the muffled roar of the turbines was heard; behind the fires the coarse, muted meshing of giant gear wheels signified the approaching command to engage the mammoth screws in third-torque speed. Oily, dark waters churned around the curve of the *Cristóvão's* stern.

The warehouse door opened, and Havelock felt a massive jolt in his chest as the blond woman stepped out of the darkness into the lesser darkness of the swirling mists and shadows. The living corpse from the

Costa Brava entered the wall-less tunnel that would take her aboard the *Cristóvão,* lead her to an unknown coastline in an unknown country, and escape. From him. *Why?*

The hammering in his chest was intolerable, the pain in his eyes excruciating; he had to endure both for seconds longer. Once Jenna reached the midpoint of the pier, in sight of the gate, and the guard and the alarms he could raise, Michael would intercept her. Not an instant sooner.

She was there! *Now.*

He lunged from behind the crane and raced forward, not caring about the sound of his footsteps, intent only on reaching her.

"Jenna! For God's sake, *Jenna!*"

He grabbed her shoulders; the woman spun around in terror.

His breath exploded from his throat. The face that was turned up to him was an old face, an ugly face, the pockmarked face of a waterfront whore. The eyes that stared at him were the wide, dark eyes of a rodent, outlined with thick, running borders of cheap mascara; the lips were blood-red and cracked, the teeth stained and chipped.

"Who are you?" His scream was the scream of a madman. *"Liar! Liar!* Why are you *lying!* Why are you *here!* Why *aren't* you here! *Liar!"*

Mists not of the sea blurred his mind, crosscurrents of insanity. He was beyond reason, knowing only that his hands had become claws, then fists —scraping, hammering—*kill the rodent, kill the impostor! Kill, kill!*

Other screams, other shouts, commands and countercommands filled the roaring caverns of his consciousness. There was no beginning, no end, only a furious core of frenzy.

Then he felt blows, but did not feel pain. Men were all around him, then above him; fists and heavy boots struck him. Repeatedly. Everywhere.

And then the darkness came. And silence.

Above the pier, on the second floor of the warehouse office, a figure stood at the window looking down at the scene of violence below. She breathed deeply, her fingers stretched across her lips, tears welling in her clear brown eyes. Absently Jenna Karas pulled her hand away from her face and pressed it against the side of her head, against the long blond hair that fell beneath the wide-brimmed hat.

"Why did you do it, Mikhail?" she whispered softly to herself. "Why do you want to kill me?"

6

He opened his eyes, aware of the sickening stench of cheap whisky, feeling the dampness about his chest and throat—his shirt, jacket and trousers had been drenched. In front of him were gradations of darkness, shadows of gray and black interrupted by tiny, dancing specks of light that bobbed and weaved in the farthest darkness. There was dull pain everywhere, centered in his stomach, rising through his neck to his head, which felt swollen and numb. He had been beaten severely and dragged to the end of the pier—the far right end, beyond the warehouse, if his blurred orientation was anywhere near accurate—and left to regain consciousness, or, conceivably, to roll over the edge to a watery death.

But he had not been killed; that told him something. Slowly he moved his right hand to his left wrist; his watch was there. He stretched his legs and reached into his pocket; his money, too, was intact. He had not been robbed; that told him something else.

He had spoken with too many men, and too many others had seen him in those strange conversations. They had been his protection. Murder was murder, and regardless of what Il Tritone's owner had said, a "quiet knife" on the waterfront was a subject for investigation, as was assault and robbery when the victim was a wealthy foreigner. No one wanted too many questions asked on the piers; cool heads had ordered him left as he was, which meant they had been paid to implement other orders, higher orders. Otherwise something would have been stolen—a watch, a few thousand lire; this was the waterfront.

Nothing. An inquisitive, wealthy foreigner had gone berserk, attacking a blond whore on the pier, and men had protected her. No investigation was called for, as long as the *ricco americano maledetto* had his property intact, if not his senses.

A setup. A professionally executed snare, the trappers exonerated once the trap had sprung shut. The whole night, the morning, had been a setup! He rolled over to his left; the southeast ocean was a line of fire beyond the horizon. Dawn had come, and the *Cristóvão* was one of a dozen small silhouettes on the water, obscure shapes diffusedly defined by the blinking lights, signals to other silhouettes.

Slowly Havelock got to his knees, pressing them against the wet planks beneath him, pushing himself up painfully with his hands. Once on his feet he turned around, again slowly, testing his legs and ankles, moving his shoulders, arching his neck, then his back. There was nothing broken, but the machine was badly bruised; it would not respond to quick commands, and he hoped he would not have to issue any.

The guard. Had the ego-stroked civil servant been part of the act? Had he been told to confront the foreigner with hostility at first, then turn to obsequiousness, thus pulling the mark in for the trap? It was effective strategy; he should have seen through it. Neither of the other two guards had been difficult, each perfectly willing to tell him whatever he wanted to know, the man at the gate of the *Teresa*'s pier even going so far as to inform him of the freighter's delayed schedule.

The owner of Il Tritone? The sailor from the *Cristóvão* in a narrow, dark alley? Were they, too, part of it? Had the coincidence of logical progression led him to those men on the waterfront who had been waiting for him? Yet, how could they have been waiting? Four hours ago Civitavecchia was a vaguely remembered name on a map; it had held no meaning for him. There had been no reason for him to come to Civitavecchia, no way for an unknown message to be telegraphed. Yet it had been; he had to accept that without knowing how or why. There was so much beyond his understanding, a maddening mosaic with too many pieces missing.

Anything you can't understand in this business is a risk, but I don't have to tell you that. Rostov. Athens.

A decoy—a blond, pockmarked whore—had been paraded through the predawn mist to pull him out and force him to act. But *why?* What had they expected him to do? He had made it plain what he intended to do. So what was learned, what clarified? What was the point? Was she trying to kill him? Was that what Costa Brava was all about?

Jenna, why are you doing this? What happened to you? To us?

He walked unsteadily, stopping to brace his legs as his balance went out of control. Reaching the edge of the warehouse, he propelled himself along the wall past darkened windows and the huge loading doors until he came to the corner of the building. Beyond was the deserted pier, the wash of intersecting floodlights swollen with pockets of rolling fog. He peered around the steel molding, squinting to focus on the glass cubicle that was the guard's post. As before, the figure inside was barely visible, but he was there; Michael could see the stationary glow of a cigarette in the center of the middle pane.

The glow moved to the right; the guard had gotten off his stool and was sliding the door of the booth open. A second figure could be seen walking through the mist from the wide avenue fronting the row of piers. He was a medium-sized man in an overcoat, wearing a hat, the brim angled as a stroller's might be on the Via Veneto. The clothes were not the clothes of the waterfront; they belonged in the city streets. The man approached the glass booth, stopped by the door, and spoke with the guard. Both then looked toward the end of the pier, at the warehouse; the guard gestured and Michael knew they were talking about him. The man nodded, turned and raised his hand; within seconds his summons was obeyed. Two other men came into view, both large, both wearing clothes more suited to the waterfront than those of the man who commanded them.

Havelock leaned his head against the edge of steel, a deep, despairing sense of futility mingling with his pain. Exhaustion overwhelmed him. He was no match for such men; he could barely raise his arms, nor his feet. Since he had no other weapons, it meant he had no weapons at all.

Where was Jenna? Had she gone aboard the *Cristóvão* after the decoy had fulfilled its function? It was a logical— No, it wasn't! The commotion would have centered too much attention on the freighter and would have roused unfriendly or unpaid officials too easily. The ship itself had been a decoy, the blond whore the lure. Jenna was boarding one of the other two!

Michael turned away from the wall and hobbled across the wet planks toward the edge of the pier. He wiped his eyes, staring through the heavy mist. Involuntarily he gasped, the pain in his stomach was so acute. The *Elba* was gone! He had been pulled to the wrong pier, duped into an uncontrollable situation while Jenna went on board the *Elba*. Was the captain of the *Elba,* like the skipper of the *Cristóvão,* a master navigator? Would he—could he—maneuver his awkward ship close enough to an unpatrolled shoreline so that a small boat might ferry his contraband to a beach?

One man had the answer. A man in an overcoat and an angled hat, clothes worn on the waterfront by someone who did not haul and fork-lift but, instead, bought and sold. That man would know; he had negotiated Jenna's passage.

Havelock lurched back to the corner of the warehouse wall. He had to reach that man; he had to get by two others coming for him. If only he had a weapon, *any* kind of weapon. He looked around in the faintly lessening darkness. Nothing. Not even a loose board or a slat from a broken crate.

The water. The drop was long, but he could manage it. If he could get to the far end of the pier before he was seen, it would be presumed he had plunged over while unconscious. How many seconds did he have? He inched his face to the edge and peered around the molding into the wash of the floodlights, prepared to push himself away and run.

He did not run. The two men were no longer walking toward him. They had stopped, both standing motionless inside the fenced gate. Why? Why was he being left where he was without further interference?

Suddenly, from out of the impenetrable mist several piers away came an ear-shattering screech of a ship's klaxon. Then another, followed by a prolonged bass chord that vibrated throughout the harbor. It was the *Santa Teresa!* It was his answer! The two men had been summoned not to punish him further, but to restrict him to the first pier. There was no delayed schedule for the *Teresa;* that, too, was part of the setup. She was sailing on time, and Jenna was *on board.* As the ship's clock ran down, there was only one thing left for the negotiator to do: keep the disabled hunter in place.

Fiercely he told himself he had to get to that pier, stop her, stop the freighter from casting off, for once the giant lines were slipped off the pilings there was nothing he could do, no way to reach her. She would disappear into one of a dozen countries, a hundred cities—nothing left, not for him, not any longer. Without her he didn't want to go on!

He wished he knew what the blaring signals meant, how much time

he had. He could only estimate. There had been two blasts from the
Cristóvão; moments later the blond decoy had emerged from the shadows
of the warehouse door. Seven minutes. Yet there had been no bass chord
following the high-pitched whistles. Did its absence signify less time or
more? He probed his memory, racing over scores of assignments that had
taken him to waterfronts everywhere.

He remembered; more accurately, he *thought* he remembered as a
blurred recent memory struggled to surface. The high-pitched shrieks
were for ships in the distance, the vibrating lower tones for those nearer
by—a rule of thumb for the sea, and the docks. And while he was being
beaten, the outer vibrations of a low, grinding chord had fused with his
own screams of protest and fury. The bass-toned whistle had followed
shortly after the shrieks—prelude to imminent departure. Seven minutes
—less one, more likely two, perhaps three.

He had only minutes. Six, five—four, no more than that. The *Teresa's*
pier was several hundred yards away; in his condition it would take at least
two minutes to get there, and that would happen only if he could get past
the two jacketed men who had been called to stop him. Four minutes at
the outside, two minimum. Jesus! *How?* He looked around again, trying
to control his panic, aware that every second reduced his chances.

A stocky black object was silhouetted between two pilings ten yards
away; he had not noticed it before because it was a stationary part of the
dock. He studied it now. It was a barrel, an ordinary barrel, undoubtedly
punctured during loading or unloading procedures, and now used as a
receptacle for coffee cups, trash, predawn fires; they were on piers everywhere. He ran to it, gripped it, rocked it. It swung free; he lowered it to
its side and rolled it back toward the wall. Time elapsed: thirty, perhaps
forty seconds. Time remaining: between one and a half and three-plus
minutes. The tactic that came into focus was a desperate one, but it was
the only one that was possible. He could not get past those men unless
they came to him, unless the fog and the translucent, brightening darkness worked for him and against them. There was no time to think about
the guard and the man in the overcoat.

He crouched in the shadows, against the wall, both hands on the sides
of the filthy barrel. He took a deep breath and screamed as loud as he
could, knowing the scream would echo throughout the deserted pier.

"*Aiuto! Presto! Sanguino! Muoio!*"

He stopped, listening. In the distance he heard the shouts; they were
questions, then commands. He screamed again: "*Aiuto!*"

Silence.

Then racing footsteps. Nearer . . . drawing nearer.

Now! He shoved the barrel with all the strength he could muster. It clanked as it rolled laterally over the planks, through the fog, toward the edge of the pier.

The two men rounded the corner of the warehouse in the misty light; the barrel reached the edge of the dock. It struck one of the pilings. Oh, *Christ!* Then it spun and plunged over. The sound of the splash below was loud; the two men shouted at each other and raced to the edge.

Now!

Havelock rose to his feet and ran out of the shadows, his hands extended, shoulders and arms battering rams. He forced his unsteady legs to respond, each racing step painful but calculated, sure. He made contact. First the man on the right, pummeling him with both outstretched hands; then the Italian on his left, crashing his shoulder into the small of the man's back.

A deafening blast from the *Teresa*'s funnels covered the screams of the two men as they plummeted into the water below. Michael swung to his left and hobbled back toward the corner of the warehouse; he would go out onto the deserted pier and face the once obsequious guard and the elegantly dressed man. Time elapsed: another minute. Less than three remained at most.

He ran unsteadily out onto the vast expanse of the pier with its fog-laden pools of floodlights and immobile machinery. Pitching his voice at the edge of hysteria, he shouted in broken Italian: "Help me! Help *them!* It's *crazy!* I'm hurt. Two men came to help me. As they drew near there were gunshots! *Three gunshots!* From the next pier. I could hardly hear them because of the freighter, but I did hear them! *Gunshots!* Quickly! They're wounded. One dead, I think! Oh, *Christ*, hurry!"

The exchange between the two men was verbal chaos. As Havelock staggered erratically toward the gate he could see that the guard's automatic was drawn, but it was not the same guard; he was shorter, stockier, older. The guard's broad face was full of resentment, in contrast to that of the civilian—in his mid-thirties, tanned, suave—which was cold and without expression. The man in the overcoat was ordering the guard to investigate; the guard was shouting that he would not leave his post, not for 20,000 lire! The *capo regime* could look into his own garbage; *he* was no frightened *bambino* of the docks. The *capo* could buy a few hours of his time, his disappearance, but not more!

A setup. From the beginning, a charade.

"Andate voi stessi!" yelled the guard.

Swearing, the civilian started toward the warehouse and broke into a run, then abruptly slowing his pace he cautiously approached the corner of the building.

The guard was now in front of the glass booth, his gun leveled at Michael. "You! Walk to the fence," he shouted in Italian. "Raise your hands above you and grab the wire as high as you can! Do not turn around! I'll fire into your head if you do!"

Barely two minutes left; if it was going to work, it would happen now.

"Oh, *Jesus!"* Havelock screamed as he gripped his chest and fell.

The guard rushed forward; Michael remained motionless in a fetal position, dead weight on the damp, hard surface. "Get up!" commanded the uniformed man. "Get to your feet!"

The guard reached down and grabbed Havelock's shoulder. It was the movement Michael had been waiting for. He spun off the ground, clasping the weapon above his head, and gripped the wrist at his shoulder, wrenching it clockwise as he rose and hammering his knee into the falling guard's throat. The gun barrel was in his hand; he swung it down, crashing it into the base of the Italian's skull. The man collapsed. Havelock dragged him into the shadows of the booth, then raced out of the open gate, jamming the weapon into his jacket pocket.

A prolonged, belching sound came from the distance, followed by four hysterically pitched screeches. The *Teresa* was about to slip away from its berth! Michael felt a sickening sense of futility sweeping over him as he ran breathlessly down the wide avenue, his legs barely able to carry him, his feet swerving, slapping the pavement. When he reached the *Teresa's* pier, the guard—the same guard—was inside his glass booth, once again on the telephone, nodding his outsized head, his dull eyes accepting other lies.

There was now a chain stretched across the open gate—only an official hindrance, not a prohibition. Havelock grabbed the hook and yanked it out of its cemented base; the chain curled snakelike into the air and clattered to the ground.

"Che cosa? Fermati!"

Michael raced—his legs in agony—down the long stretch of the pier, through the circular pools of floodlights, past immobile machinery, toward the freighter outlined in the swirling mists at the end of the dock. His right leg collapsed; his hands broke the fall but not the impact, his right shoulder sliding across the moist surface. He grabbed his leg, forcing himself up, and propelled himself along the planks until he could work up the momentum to run again.

Gasping for air as he ran, he finally reached the end of the pier.

The futility was complete: the freighter *Santa Teresa* was floating thirty feet beyond the pilings; the giant hawsers slithered over the dark waters as they were hauled in by men who looked down at him through the shadows.

"Jenna!" he screamed. "Jenna! *Jenna!*"

He fell to the wet wood of the pier, arms and legs throbbing, chest in spasms, his head splitting as if cracked open with an ax. He . . . had . . . lost her. . . . A small boat could drop her off at any of a thousand unpatrolled stretches of coastline in the Mediterranean; she was gone. The only person on earth he cared about was gone forever. Nothing was his, and he was nothing.

He heard the shouts behind him, then the hammering of racing feet. And as he heard the sounds he was reminded of other sounds, other feet . . . another pier. From where the *Cristóvão* had sailed!

There was a man in an overcoat who had ordered other men to come after him; they, too, had run across a deserted pier through shimmering pools of floodlights and the mist. If he could find that man! If he found him he would peel the suntanned flesh from the face until he was told what he had to know.

He got to his feet and began limping rapidly toward the guard who was running at him, weapon extended.

"*Fermati! Alza le mani!*"

"*Un errore!*" Havelock shouted back, his voice both aggressive and apologetic; he had to get by the man, not be detained. He took several bills from his pocket, holding them in front of him so they could be seen in the spill of the floodlights. "What can I tell you?" he continued in Italian. "I made a mistake—which benefits *you*, doesn't it? You and I, we spoke before, remember?" He pressed the money into the guard's hand while slapping him on the back. "Come on, put that thing away. I'm your friend, remember? What harm is there? Except I'm a little poorer and you're a little richer. Also, I've had too much wine."

"I thought it was you!" said the guard grudgingly, taking the bills and ramming them into his pocket, his eyes darting about. "You're crazy in the head! You could have been shot. For *what?*"

"You told me the *Teresa* wasn't sailing for hours."

"It's what *I* was told! They're bastards, *all* bastards! They're crazy too! They don't know what they're doing."

"They know exactly what they're doing," said Michael quietly. "I've got to get along now. Thanks for your help." Before the angry guard could answer, Havelock started forward rapidly, wincing in pain as he tried to control his throbbing legs and aching chest. *For God's sake, hurry!*

He reached the stretch of fence that enclosed the *Cristóvão*'s pier, his hand now in his pocket, grateful for the weapon. The unconscious guard was still on the ground in the lower shadows of the glass booth. He had neither moved nor been moved in the five minutes, perhaps six, that he had lain there. Was the man in the overcoat still on the pier? The odds favored it; logic dictated that he would have looked for the guard because he did not see him in the booth and, when he found him, would have questioned the fallen man. In doing so, some part of the unconscious body would have been moved; it had not been.

But why would the *capo regime* remain on the pier for so long? The answer came from the sea through the fog and the wind. Shouts, questions, followed by commands and further questions. The man in the overcoat was still on the pier, his gorillas screaming from the waters below.

Michael clenched his teeth, forcing the pain from his mind. He slid along the side wall of the warehouse, past the door from which the blond decoy had emerged, to the corner of the building. The morning light was growing brighter, the mists rising, the absence of the freighter permitting the early rays of the sun to spread over the dock. In the distance, on the water, another ship was steaming slowly toward the harbor of Civitavecchia; it might well be heading for the berth recently vacated by the *Cristóvão*. If so, there was very little time remaining before the shape-up crews arrived. He had to move swiftly, act effectively, and he was not at all sure he was capable of doing either.

A stretch of unpatrolled coastline. Did the man only yards away from him now know which? He must find out. He had to be capable.

He rounded the corner, holding the weapon against the cloth of his jacket. He could not use it, he understood that; it would serve no purpose because it would only eliminate his source and draw attention to the pier. But the threat had to be conveyed as genuine; his anger had to seem desperate. He was capable of that.

He stared through the rising mist. The man in the overcoat was at the edge of the dock, excitedly barking instructions in a low voice; he, too, was obviously afraid of drawing attention from stray crewmen who might be loitering on the adjacent pier. The effect was comic. From what Michael could gather, one of the men below was hanging on to a piling strut, reluctant to let go because he apparently couldn't swim. The negotiator was ordering the second man to support his companion and the man was apparently refusing, concerned that he might be pulled under by his incompetent associate.

"Don't talk anymore!" Havelock said sharply in Italian, the words clear if not precise, his voice commanding though not loud.

The startled man spun around, his right hand reaching under his overcoat.

"If I see a gun," continued Michael, moving closer, "you'll be dead and in the water before you can raise it. Move away from there. Walk toward me. Now to your left. Over to the wall. Move! Don't stop!"

The man lurched forward. "I could have had you killed, signore. I did not. Surely, that is worth something to you."

"It is—obviously. I thank you."

"Nor was anything on your person taken, I assume you are aware of that. My orders were clear."

"I'm aware. Now tell me why. On both counts."

"I am neither a killer nor a thief, signore."

"Not good enough. Raise your hands! Lean against the wall and spread your legs!" The Italian complied; it was not the first time such orders had been given him. Havelock came up behind him, kicking the man's right calf as he whipped his hand around the *capo regime*'s waist, pulling the gun from the Italian's belt. He glanced at it, impressed. The weapon was a Spanish automatic, a Llama .38 caliber, with grip and manual safeties. A quality gun, undoubtedly less expensive on the waterfront. He shoved it into his own belt. "Tell me about the girl. Quickly!"

"I was paid. What more can I tell you?"

"A great deal." Michael reached up and grabbed the man's left hand; it was soft. The negotiator was not a violent man, the term *capo regime*, which the guard had used, was misapplied. This Italian was no part of the Mafia; a mafioso at his age would have come up through violent ranks and would not have soft hands.

A sudden cacophony of ship's whistles erupted from the harbor. They were joined by panicked shouts from the lone man in the slapping waters below the pier. Taking advantage of the sounds, Michael rammed the pistol into the negotiator's kidney. The man screamed. Then Havelock crashed the handle into the side of the Italian's neck and there was another scream, which was followed by a series of whimpering pleas. "Signore . . . signore! You are American; we speak American! Do not do this to me! I saved your life—my word on it!"

"We'll get to that. The *girl!* Tell me about the girl! Quickly!"

"I do favors around the docks. Everyone knows that! She needed a favor. She paid!"

"To get out of Italy?"

"What else?"

"She paid for a lot more than that! How many did *you* pay? For the setup."

"Che cosa vuol dire? Set . . . up?"

"That show you put on! The pig who walked out of that door over there!" Havelock gripped the Italian by the shoulder and spun him around, slamming him back into the wall. "Right around that corner," he added, gesturing. "What was that all about? Tell me! She paid for that, too. *Why?"*

"As you say, signore. She paid. *Spiegazioni* . . . explanations . . . were not required."

Michael jammed the barrel of the pistol deep into the man's stomach. "Not good enough. *Tell* me!"

"She said she had to *know,"* the negotiator spat out, doubling over.

"Know what?" Havelock slapped the man's hat off and, grabbing him by the hair, crashed his head into the wall. "Know *what?"*

"What you would do!"

"How did she know I'd follow her here?"

"She did not!"

"Then why?"

"She said you *might* do so! You were . . . *ingegnoso* . . . a resourceful man. You've hunted other men; you have means at your disposal. Contacts, sources."

"That's too loose! *How?"* Michael bunched the Italian's hair in his fist, pulling it half out of its roots.

"Signore . . . she said she spoke to three drivers on the *piattaforma* before she found a taxi to take her to Civitavecchia! She was afraid!"

It made sense. It had not occurred to him to look for a taxi ramp at the Ostia; taxis were not in oversupply in Rome. In truth, he had simply not been thinking; he had been bent only on moving.

"Per favore! Aiuto! Mio Dio!" The screams came from the water below.

The ships in the harbor were beginning to fill the air with whistles and vapor. There was so little time left; soon the crews would come, men and machinery crawling all over the pier. He had to learn exactly what the negotiator had sold; he gripped the man's throat with his left hand.

"She's on the *Teresa,* isn't she?"

"*Sì!*"

Havelock recalled the words of Il Tritone's owner: the *Teresa* sailed to Marseilles. "How is she to be taken off the ship?"

The Italian did not answer; Michael plunged his fingers deeper into the man's throat, choking him. He went on: "Understand me, and understand me well. If you don't tell me, I'll kill you now. And if you lie, and she gets past me in Marseilles, I'll come back for you. She was right, I'm resourceful and I've hunted a great many men. I'll find you."

The negotiator went into a spasm, his mouth gaping as he tried to speak. Havelock reduced the pressure on the man's neck. The Italian coughed violently, grabbing his throat, and said, "What's it to me, anyway, so I'll tell you. I don't want *afflizione* with the likes of you, signore! I should have known better. I should have listened better!"

"Go on."

"Not Marseilles. San Remo. The *Teresa* stops at San Remo. How or where she is to be brought ashore, I do not know—my word on it! She buys her way to Paris. She's to be taken across the border at Col des Moulinets. When, I do not know—my word! From there to Paris. I swear on the blood of Christ!"

The negotiator did not have to swear he was telling the truth; his terrified eyes proved it. He was being honest out of fear, extraordinary fear. What had Jenna told him? Why hadn't the man ordered him killed? Also, why had nothing been stolen? Michael released his grip on the Italian's neck.

He spoke quietly. "You said you could have had me killed, but you didn't. Now tell me why."

"No, signore, I will not say it," whispered the man. "In the name of God, you'll never see me again! I say nothing, know nothing!"

Havelock raised the pistol slowly, resting the point of the barrel on the man's left eye. "Say it," he said.

"Signore, I have a small, profitable business here, but I have never once —*never*—involved myself with political activities! Or anything remotely connected to such things. I swear on the tears of the Madonna! I thought she was lying, appealing to me with lies! I never once believed her!"

"But I wasn't killed, nothing on my person taken, I think you said." Michael paused, then shouted as he jammed the barrel into the Italian's eye. "*Why?*"

The man screamed, spitting out the words. "She said you were an

American working with the *comunisti!* With the Soviets. I did not believe her! I know nothing of such things! But caution would naturally call for —caution. In Civitavecchia we are outside of such wars. They are too . . . *internazionali* for people like us who make our few unimportant lire on the docks. These things mean nothing to us—my word on it! We wish no trouble from you, any of you! . . . Signore, you can understand. You attacked a woman—a *puttana,* to be certain, but a woman—on the pier. Men stopped you, pulled you away, but when I saw, I stopped *them!* I told them we should be cautious. We had to think . . ."

The frightened man continued to babble, but Havelock was not listening. What he had heard stunned him beyond anything he imagined he might hear. *An American working with the Soviets.* Jenna had said this? It was insane!

Had she tried to appeal to the man with a lie, only to instill a very real fear in the small-time operator after the fact, *after* the trap? The Italian had not equivocated; he had repeated her story out of fear. He had not lied.

Did she believe it? Was that what he had seen in her eyes on the platform at the Ostia station? Did she really believe it—just as he had believed beyond any doubt in his mind that she was a deep-cover officer for the Voennaya?

Oh, *Christ!* Each turned against the other with the same maneuver! Had the evidence against him been as airtight as the evidence against her? It had to have been; that was also in her eyes. Fear, hurt . . . pain. There was no one she could trust, not now, not for a while, perhaps not ever. She could only run—as he had kept running. *God!* What had they *done? Why?*

She was on her way to Paris. He would find her in Paris. Or fly to San Remo or Col des Moulinets and intercept her at one or the other. He had the advantage of fast transport; she was on an old freighter plodding across the water and he would be flying. He had time.

He would use that time. There was an intelligence officer at the embassy in Rome who was about to know the depth of his anger. Lieutenant Colonel Lawrence Baylor Brown was going to supply answers or all the exposés of Washington's clandestine activities would be seen as mere footnotes compared with what he would reveal: the incompetences, the illegalities, the miscalculations and errors costing the lives of thousands the world over every year.

He would start with a black diplomat in Rome who funneled secret orders to American agents throughout Italy and the western Mediterranean.

"Capisce? You *do* understand, signore?" The Italian was pleading, buying time, his eyes glancing furtively to the right. Across on the second pier three men were walking through the early light toward the far pilings; two blasts of a ship's whistle told why. The freighter steaming into port was to be tied up at the *Elba's* berth. In moments additional crews would arrive. "We are cautious . . . *naturalmente,* but we know nothing of such things! We are men of the docks, nothing more."

"I understand," said Michael, touching the man's shoulder and turning him around. "Walk to the edge," he ordered quietly.

"Signore, please! I beg you!"

"Just do as I say. *Now."*

"I swear on the patron saint of mercy Himself! On the blood of Christ, on the tears of the Holy Mother!" The Italian was weeping, his voice rising. "I am an insignificant merchant, signore! I know nothing! Say nothing!"

As they reached the edge of the pier, Havelock said, "Jump," and pushed the negotiator over the side.

"Mio Dio! Aiuto!" screamed the henchman below as his employer joined him in the water.

Michael turned and hobbled back to the corner of the warehouse wall. The dock was still deserted, but the guard was beginning to move, shaking his head, trying to pull himself up in the shadows of the booth. Havelock slapped open the cylinder of the pistol and shook the bullets out of their tracks; they clattered onto the dock. He hurried toward the gate, and when he reached the door of the glass booth, he threw the weapon inside. He ran as fast as he was capable of running through the gate, toward the rented car.

Rome. There would be answers in Rome.

7

The four men around the table in the white-walled room on the third floor of the State Department building were youngish by upper-echelon Washington standards. Their ages ranged from the mid-thirties to the late forties, but their lined faces and hollow look made them old beyond their years. The work they did led to sleepless nights and prolonged periods of anxiety, made worse by their insular life: none of them could discuss the crises they faced in that room with anyone outside it. These were the strategists of covert operations, the air traffic controllers of clandestine activities; roving condors could be shot down on their slightest miscalculation. Others above them might request the broad objectives; others below might design the specific assignments. But only these men were aware of every conceivable variation, every likely consequence of a given operation; they were the clearinghouse. Each was a specialist, each an authority. Only they could give the final nod for the condors to fly.

Yet they had no radar grids or circling antennae to aid them; they had only the projections of human behavior to guide them. They had to examine actions and reactions, not simply those of the enemy but those of their own people in the field as well. Evaluation was a never-ending struggle, which was rarely resolved to everyone's satisfaction. The "what if" probabilities were geometrically compounded with each new twist of events, each human reaction to abruptly altered circumstances. They were psychoanalysts in an endless labyrinth of abnormality, their patients the products of that disorder. They were specialists in a macabre way of life where the truth was usually a lie and lies too often were the only means of survival. Stress was the factor that frightened them most, for under maximum or prolonged stress both one's enemies and one's own people saw things and did things they might not do otherwise. The totally unpredictable added to the abnormal became dangerous territory.

This was the conclusion the four men had reached regarding the crisis late that night. Lieutenant Colonel Lawrence Baylor Brown in Rome had sent his cable on priority cipher; its contents required the opening of a dead file so that each strategist could study the facts.

They were beyond dispute. The events at that isolated beach on the Costa Brava had been verified by two on-site confirmations, one of them Foreign Service Officer Havelock himself, the other a man unknown to Havelock named Steven MacKenzie, one of the most experienced under-cover operatives working in Europe for the Central Intelligence Agency. He had risked his life to bring back proof: torn garments stained with blood. Everything had been microscopically examined, the results positive: Jenna Karas. The reasons for a backup confirmation had not been made explicit, nor was that necessary. The relationship between Havelock and the Karas woman was known to those who had to know; a man under maximum stress might fall apart, be incapable of carrying out what had to be done. Washington had to know. Agent MacKenzie had been positioned two hundred feet north of Havelock; his view was clear, his confirmation absolute, his proof incontrovertible. The Karas woman had been killed that night. The fact that Steven MacKenzie had died of a heart seizure three weeks after he returned from Barcelona, while sailing in Chesapeake Bay, in no way diminished his contribution. The doctor who had been summoned by the Coast Guard patrol was a well-established physician on the Eastern Shore, a surgeon named Randolph with impeccable credentials. A thorough postmortem was conclusive: MacKenzie's death was from natural causes.

Beyond Costa Brava itself, the evidence against Jenna Karas had been subjected to the most exhaustive scrutiny. Secretary of State Anthony Matthias had demanded it, and the strategists knew why. There was another relationship to take into consideration: one that had existed between Matthias and Michael Havelock for nearly twenty years since student had met teacher in the graduate program at Princeton University. Fellow Czechs by birth, one had established himself as perhaps the most brilliant geopolitical mind in the academic world, while the other, a young, haunted expatriate, was desperately searching for his own identity. The differences were considerable, but the friendship was strong.

Anton Matthias had come to America over forty years ago, the son of a prominent doctor from Prague who had hurried his family out of Czechoslovakia under the shadow of the Nazis and was welcomed by the medical community. Havelock's immigration, on the other hand, was managed covertly as a joint exercise of American and British intelligence; his origins were obscured, initially for the child's own safety. And where Matthias's meteoric rise in government was sparked by a succession of influential political figures who openly sought his counsel and publicly extolled his brilliance, the much younger man from Prague proceeded to establish his own worth through clandestine accomplishments that would never see the light of day. Yet in spite of the dissimilarities of age and reputation, intellect and temperament, there existed a bond between them, held firm by the elder, never taken advantage of by the younger.

Those who confirmed the evidence against the Karas woman understood that there was no room for error, just as the strategists understood now that the cable from Rome had to be studied carefully, handled delicately. Above all, for the time being, it had to be kept from Anthony Matthias. For though the media had announced that the Secretary of State was off on a well-deserved holiday, the truth was something else. Matthias was ill—some, in whispers, said gravely ill—and although he was in constant touch with State through his subordinates, he had not been in Washington for nearly five weeks. Even those perceptive men and women of the press corps who suspected another explanation beneath the vacation ploy said nothing and printed nothing. No one really wanted to think about it; the world could not afford it.

And Rome could not become an additional burden for Anthony Matthias.

"He's hallucinating, of course," said the balding man named Miller, putting his copy of the cable down on the table in front of him. Paul Miller, M.D., was a psychiatrist, an authority on diagnosing erratic behavior.

"Is there anything in his record that might have warned us?" asked a red-haired, stocky man in a rumpled suit and an open collar, his tie unknotted. His name was Ogilvie; he was a former field agent.

"Nothing you would have read," replied Daniel Stern, the strategist on Miller's left. His title was Director of Consular Operations, which was a euphemism for section chief of State's clandestine activities.

"Why not?" asked the fourth strategist, a conservatively dressed man who might have stepped out of an advertisement in the *Wall Street Journal* for IBM. He was seated next to Ogilvie. His name was Dawson; he was an attorney and a specialist in international law. He pressed his point. "Are you saying there were—are—omissions in his service file?"

"Yes. A security holdover from years ago. No one ever bothered to reassess, so the file remained incomplete. But the answer to Ogilvie's question might be found there. The warning we missed."

"How so?" asked Miller, peering over his glasses, his fingers spread across his balding hairline.

"He could be finally burned out. Over the edge."

"What do you mean?" Ogilvie leaned forward, his expression none too pleasant. "Evaluation depends on available data, goddamn it."

"I don't think anyone thought it was necessary. His record's superior. Except for an outburst or two, he's been extremely productive, reasonable under very adverse conditions."

"Only, now he's seeing dead people in railroad stations," interrupted Dawson. "Why?"

"Do you know Havelock?" asked Stern.

"Only from a field personnel interview," answered the attorney. "Eight or nine months ago; he flew back for it. He seemed efficient."

"He was," agreed the director of Cons Op. "Efficient, productive, reasonable—very tough, very cold, very bright. But then he was trained at an early age under rather extraordinary circumstances. Maybe that's what we should have looked at." Stern paused, picked up a large manila envelope, and removed a red-bordered file folder, sliding it out carefully. "Here's the complete background dossier on Havelock. What we had before was basic and acceptable. A graduate student from Princeton with a Ph.D. in European history and a minor in Slavic languages. Home: Greenwich, Connecticut. A war orphan brought over from England and adopted by a couple named Webster, both cleared. What we all looked at, of course, was the recommendation from Matthias, someone even then to be reckoned with. And what the recruiters here at State saw sixteen years ago was fairly obvious. A highly intelligent Ph.D. from Princeton willing to work for bureaucratic spit, even willing to perfect his linguistic dialects and go into deep-cover work. But that wasn't necessary—the language part. Czech was his native tongue; he knew it better than we thought he did. That's what's here; it's the rest of his story and could be the reason for the breakdown we're witnessing now."

"That's a hell of a leap backward," said Ogilvie. "Can you sketch it for us? I don't like surprises; retired paranoids we don't need."

"Apparently, we've got one," interjected Miller, picking up the cable. "If Baylor's judgment means anything—"

"It does," Stern broke in. "He's one of the best we've got in Europe."

"Still, he's Pentagon," added Dawson. "Judgment's not a strong point."

"It is with him," corrected the Cons Op director. "He's black and had to be good."

"As I was about to say," continued Miller, "Baylor includes a strong recommendation that we take Havelock seriously. He saw what he saw."

"Which is impossible," said Ogilvie. "Which means we've got a whacko. What's in there, Dan?"

"An ugly early life," replied Stern, lifting the cover of the file and turning several pages. "We knew he was Czech, but that's all we knew. There were several thousand Czechoslovakian refugees in England during the war, and that was the explanation given for his being there. But it wasn't true. There were two stories: one real, the other a cover. He wasn't in England during the war, nor were his parents. He spent those years in and around Prague. It was a long nightmare and very real for him. It started when he was old enough to know it, see it. Unfortunately, we can't get inside his head, and that could be vital now." The director turned to Miller. "You'll have to advise us here, Paul. He could be extremely dangerous."

"Then you'd better clarify," said the doctor. "How far back do we go? And why?"

"Let's take the 'why' first," said Stern, removing a number of pages from the dossier. "He's lived with the specter of betrayal since he was a child. There was a period during adolescence and early adulthood—the high school and college years—when the pressures were absent, but the memories must have been pretty horrible for him. Then for the next sixteen years—these past sixteen years—he's been back in that same kind of world. Perhaps he's seen too many ghosts."

"Be specific, Daniel," pressed the psychiatrist.

"To do that," said the director, his eyes scanning the top page in his hand, "we have to go back to June of 1942, the war in Czechoslovakia.

You see, his name isn't Havelock, it's Havlíček. Mikhail Havlíček. He was born in Prague sometime in the middle thirties, the exact date unknown. All the records were destroyed by the Gestapo."

"Gestapo?" The attorney, Dawson, leaned back in his chair. "June, 1942 . . . came up in the Nuremberg trials."

"It was a sizable item on the Nuremberg agenda," agreed Stern. "On May twenty-seventh Reinhard Heydrich, known as *der Henker*—the hangman—of Prague, was killed by Czech partisans. They were led by a professor who'd been dismissed from Karlova University and who worked with British intelligence. His name was Havlíček and he lived with his wife and son in a village roughly eight miles outside of Prague where he organized the partisan cells. The village was Lidice."

"Oh, Christ," said Miller, slowly dropping the cable from Rome on the table.

"He wasn't noticeably in evidence," commented Stern dryly as he shifted the pages in his hand. "Afraid that he might have been seen at the site of Heydrich's assassination, Havlíček stayed away from his house for nearly two weeks, living in the cellars at the university. *He* hadn't been spotted, but someone else from Lidice had been; the price was set for Heydrich's death: execution for all adult males; for the women, conscription—slave labor for the factories, the more presentable sent to the officers' barracks to be *Feldhuren*. The children . . . they would simply 'disappear.' *Jugendmöglichkeiten*. The adaptable would be adopted, the rest gassed in mobile vans."

"Efficient bastards, weren't they?" said Ogilvie.

"The orders from Berlin were kept quiet until the morning of June tenth, the day of the mass executions," continued Stern, reading. "It was also the day Havlíček was heading home. When the word went out—the proclamations were nailed to telephone poles and broadcast over the radio—the partisans stopped him from going back. They locked him up, sedated him with drugs; they knew there was nothing he could do, and he was too valuable. Finally, he was told the worst. His wife had been sent to the whore camps—it was later learned that she killed herself the first night, taking a Wehrmacht officer with her—and his son was nowhere to be found."

"But he hadn't, obviously, been taken with the other children," said Dawson.

"No. He'd been chasing rabbits, and he came back in time to see the roundups, the executions, the corpses thrown in ditches. He went into shock, fled into the woods and, for weeks, lived like an animal. The stories began spreading through the countryside: a child was seen running in the forest, footprints found near barns, leading back into the woods. The father heard them and knew; he had told his son that if the Germans ever came for him, he was to escape into the forests. It took over a month, but Havlíček tracked the boy. He had been hiding in caves and trees, terrified to show himself, eating whatever he could steal and scratch from the ground, the nightmare of the massacre never leaving him."

"A lovely childhood," said the psychiatrist, making a note on a pad.

"It was only the beginning." The director of Cons Op reached for another page in the dossier. "Havlíček and his son remained in the Prague-Boleslav sector and the underground war accelerated, with the father as the partisan leader. A few months later the boy became one of the youngest recruits in the Dĕtská Brigáda, the Children's Brigade. They were used as couriers, as often as not, carrying nitroglycerin and plastic explosives as messages. One misstep, one search, one soldier hungry for a small boy, and it was over."

"His father *let* him?" asked Miller incredulously.

"He couldn't stop him. The boy found out what they'd done to his mother. For three years he lived that lovely childhood. It was uncanny, macabre. During those nights when his father was around, he was taught his lessons like any other school kid. Then during the days, in the woods and the fields, others taught him how to run and hide, how to lie. How to kill."

"That was the training you mentioned, wasn't it?" said Ogilvie quietly.

"Yes. He knew what it was like to take lives, see friends' lives taken, before he was ten years old. Grisly."

"Indelible," added the psychiatrist. "Explosives planted almost forty years ago."

"Could the Costa Brava have triggered them forty years later?" asked the lawyer, looking at the doctor.

"It could. There're a couple of dozen blood-red images floating around, some pretty grim symbols. I'd have to know a hell of a lot more." Miller turned to Stern, pencil poised above his pad. "What happened to him then?"

"To all of them," said Stern. "Peace finally came—I should say the formal war was over—but there was no peace in Prague. The Soviets had their own plans, and another kind of madness took over. The elder Havlíček was visibly political, jealous of the freedom he and the partisans had fought for. He found himself in another war, as covert as before and just as brutal. With the Russians." The director turned to another page. "For him it ended on March tenth, 1948, with the assassination of Jan Masaryk and the collapse of the Social Democrats."

"In what sense?"

"He disappeared. Shipped to a gulag in Siberia or to a nearer grave. His political friends were quick; the Czechs share a proverb with the Russians: 'The playful cub is tomorrow's wolf.' They hid young Havlíček and reached British M.I.6. Someone's conscience was stirred; the boy was smuggled out of the country, and taken to England."

"That proverb about the cub turning into tomorrow's wolf," interjected Ogilvie. "Proved out, didn't it?"

"In ways the Soviets could never envision."

"How did the Websters fit in?" asked Miller. "They were his sponsors over here, obviously, but the boy was in England."

"It was chance, actually. Webster had been a reserve colonel in the war, attached to Supreme Command Central. In '48 he was in London on business, his wife with him, and one night at dinner with wartime friends they heard about the young Czech brought out of Prague, living at an orphanage in Kent. One thing led to another—the Websters had no children, and God knows the boy's story was intriguing, if not incredible —so the two of them drove down to Kent and interviewed him. That's the word here. 'Interviewed.' Cold, isn't it?"

"They obviously weren't."

"No, they weren't. Webster went to work. Papers were mocked up, laws bent, and a very disturbed child flown over here with a new identity. Havlíček was fortunate; he went from an English orphanage to a comfortable home in a well-to-do American suburb, including one of the better prep schools and Princeton University."

"And a new name," said Dawson.

Daniel Stern smiled. "As long as a cover was deemed necessary, our reserve colonel and his lady apparently felt Anglicization was called for in Greenwich. We all have our foibles."

"Why not their name?"

"The boy wouldn't go that far. As I said before, the memories had to be there. Indelibly, as Paul put it."

"Are the Websters still alive?"

"No. They'd be almost a hundred if they were. They both died in the early sixties when Havelock was at Princeton."

"Where he met Matthias?" asked Ogilvie.

"Yes," answered the director of Cons Op. "That softened the blow. Matthias took an interest in him, not only because of Havelock's work but, perhaps more important, because his family had known the Havlíčeks in Prague. They were all part of the intellectual community until the Germans blew it apart and the Russians—for all intents and purposes—buried the survivors."

"Did Matthias know the full story?"

"All of it," replied Stern.

"That letter in the Costa Brava file makes more sense now," said the lawyer. "The note Matthias sent to Havelock."

"He wanted it included," explained Stern, "so there'd be no misunderstanding on our part. If Havelock opted for immediate withdrawal, we were to permit it."

"I know," continued Dawson, "but I assumed when Matthias made a reference to how much Havelock had suffered in . . . 'the early days,' I think he wrote, he meant simply losing both parents in the war. Nothing like *this.*"

"Now you know. We know." Stern again turned to the psychiatrist. "Any guidance, Paul?"

"The obvious," said Miller. "Bring him in. Promise him *anything,* but bring him in. And we can't afford any accidents. Get him here alive."

"I agree that's the optimum," interrupted the red-haired Ogilvie, "but I can't see it ruling out every option."

"You'd better," said the doctor. "You even said it yourself. Paranoid. Whacko. Costa Brava was intensely personal to Havelock. It could very well have set off those explosives planted thirty years ago. A part of him is back there protecting himself, building a web of defenses against persecution, against attack. He's running through the woods after having witnessed the executions in Lidice; he's with the Children's Brigade, nitroglycerin strapped to his body."

"It's what Baylor mentions in his cable." Dawson picked it up. "Here it is. 'Sealed depositions,' 'tales out of school.' He could do it all."

"He could do anything," continued the psychiatrist. "There are no behavioral rules. Once he's hallucinated, he can slip back and forth between fantasy and reality, each phase serving the dual objectives of convincing himself of the persecution and at the same time ridding himself of it."

"What about Rostov in Athens?" asked Stern.

"We don't know that there *was* any Rostov in Athens," Miller said. "It could be part of the fantasy, retroactively recalling a man in the street who looked like him. We *do* know the Karas woman was KGB. Why would a man like Rostov suddenly appear and deny it?"

Ogilvie leaned forward. "Baylor says Havelock called it a blind probe. Rostov could have taken him, gotten him out of Greece."

"Then why *didn't* he?" asked Miller. "Come on, Red, you were in the field for ten years. Blind probe or no blind probe, if you were Rostov and knowing what you knew was back at the Lubyanka, wouldn't you have taken Havelock under the circumstances described in that cable?"

Ogilvie paused, staring at the psychiatrist. "Yes," he said finally. "Because I could always let him go—if I wanted to—before anyone knew I'd taken him."

"Exactly. It's inconsistent. Was it Rostov in Athens, or anywhere else? Or was our patient fantasizing, building his own case for persecution and subsequent defenses?"

"From what this Colonel Baylor says, he was damned convincing," interjected the lawyer, Dawson.

"A hallucinating schizophrenic—if that's what he is—can be extraordinarily convincing because he believes totally what he's saying."

"But you can't be sure, Paul," insisted Daniel Stern.

"No, I can't be. But *we're* sure of one thing—two things, actually. The Karas woman *was* KGB and she was killed on that beach on the Costa Brava. The evidence was irrefutable for the first, and we have two on-site confirmations for the second, including one from Havelock himself." The psychiatrist looked at the faces of the three men. "That's all I can base a diagnosis on; that and this new information on one Mikhail Havlíček. I'm in no position to do anything else. You asked for guidance, not absolutes."

" 'Promise him anything . . .' " repeated Ogilvie. "Like that goddamned commercial."

"But bring him in," completed Miller. "And just as fast as you can. Get him into a clinic, under therapy, but find out what he's done and where he's left those defense mechanisms of his. The 'sealed depositions' and 'tales out of school.' "

"I don't have to remind anyone here," interrupted Dawson quietly. "Havelock knows a great deal that could be extremely damaging if revealed. The damage would be as extensive to our own credibility—here and abroad—as from anything the Soviets might learn. Frankly, more so.

Ciphers, informers, sources—all these can be changed, the networks warned. We can't go back and rewrite certain incidents where intelligence treaties were violated, the laws of a host country broken by our people."

"To say nothing of the domestic restrictions placed on us over here," added Stern. "I know you included that, I just want to emphasize it. Havelock knows about them; he's negotiated a number of exchanges as a result of them."

"Whatever we've done was justified," said Ogilvie curtly. "If anyone wants proof, there's a couple of hundred files that show what we've accomplished."

"And a few thousand that don't," objected the attorney. "Besides, there's also the Constitution. I'm speaking adversarily, of course."

"Horseshit!" Ogilvie shot back. "By the time we get court orders and warrants, some poor son of a bitch over here has a wife or a father shipped to one of those gulags over there, when someone like Havelock could have made a deal. *If* we could have placed a tap on time, assigned surveillance, and found out what was going on."

"It's a gray area, Red," explained Dawson, not unsympathetically. "When is homicide justified, *really* justified? On balance, there are those who would say our accomplishments don't justify our failures."

"One man crossing a checkpoint to our side justifies them." Ogilvie's eyes were cold. "One family taken out of a camp in Magya-Orszag or Krakow or Dannenwalde or Liberec justifies them. Because that's where they are, Counselor, and they shouldn't *be* there. Who the hell gets hurt, *really* hurt? A few screaming freaks with political hatchets and outsized egos. They're not worth it."

"The law says they are. The Constitution says they are."

"Then fuck the law, and let's put a couple of holes in the Constitution. I'm sick to death of its being used by loudmouthed, bushy-haired smart-asses who mount any cause they can think of just to tie our hands and draw attention to themselves. I've seen those *rehabilitation* camps, Mr. Lawyer. I've *been* there."

"Which is why you're valuable here," interposed Stern quickly, putting out the fire. "Each of us has a value, even when he renders judgments he'd rather not. I think the point Dawson's making is that this is no time for a Senate inquiry, or the hanging judges of a congressional oversight committee. They could tie our hands far more effectively than any mob from the aging radical-chic or the wheat-germ-and-granola crowd."

"Or," said Dawson, glancing at Ogilvie, his look conveying a mutuality of understanding, "representatives of a half a dozen governments showing up at our embassies and telling us to shut down certain operations. You've been there, too, Red. I don't think you want that."

"Our patient can make it happen," interjected Miller. "And very probably will unless we reach him in time. The longer his hallucinations are allowed to continue without medical attention, the farther he'll slip into fantasy, the rate of acceleration growing faster. The persecutions will multiply until they become unbearable to him and he thinks he has to strike out—strike back. With his own attacks. They're his defense mechanisms."

"What form might they take, Paul?" asked the director of Cons Op.

"Any of several," replied the psychiatrist. "The extreme would be his making contact with men he's known—or known of—in foreign intelligence circles, and offering to deliver classified information. That could be the root fantasy of the Rostov 'encounter.' Or he could write letters—with copies to us—or send cables—easily intercepted by us—that hint at past activities we can't afford to have scrutinized. Whatever he does, he'll be extremely cautious, secretive, the reality of his own expertise protecting his manipulative fantasies. You said it, Daniel; he could be dangerous. He *is* dangerous."

" '*Offering* to deliver,' " said the attorney, repeating Miller's phrase. "Hinting . . . not delivering, not giving outright?"

"Not at first. He'll try to force us—blackmail us—into telling him what he wants to hear. That the Karas woman is alive, that there was a conspiracy to retire him."

"Neither of which we can do convincingly because there's not a damn thing we can offer him as proof," said Ogilvie. "Nothing he'll accept. He's a field man. Whatever we send him he'll filter, chew it around for accuracy, and spit it back in the horseshit pile. So what do we tell him?"

"Don't *tell* him anything," answered Miller. "You *promise* to tell him. Put it any way you like. The information's too classified to send by courier, too dangerous to be permitted outside these rooms. Play his game, suck him in. Remember, he desperately wants—needs, if you like—his primary hallucination confirmed. He *saw* a dead woman; he has to believe that. And the confirmation's over here; it could be irresistible to him."

"Sorry, Headman." The red-haired former field agent raised his hands, palms up. "He won't buy it, not that way. His—what did you call it? his 'reality' part?—would reject it. That's buying a code in a box of Cracker

Jacks. It just doesn't happen. He'll want something stronger, much stronger."

"Matthias?" asked Dawson quietly.

"Optimum," agreed the psychiatrist.

"Not yet," said Stern. "Not until we have no other choice. The quiet word is that he's aware of his failing condition; he's conserving his strength for SALT Three. We can't lay this on him now."

"We may *have* to," insisted Dawson.

"We may, then again we may not." The director turned to Ogilvie. "Why does Havelock have to buy anything concrete, Red?"

"So we can get close enough to grab him."

"Couldn't a sequence be designed—say, one piece of information leading to another, each more vital than the last—so as to draw him in, suck him in, as Paul says? He can't get the last unless he shows up?"

"A treasure hunt?" asked Ogilvie, laughing.

"That's what he's on," said Miller quietly.

"The answer's no." The red-haired man leaned forward, his elbows on the table. "A sequence operation depends on credibility; the better the field man, the firmer the credibility. It's also a very delicate exercise. The subject, if he's someone like Havelock, will use decoys, blind intermediaries. He'll reverse the process by programming his decoys with information of their own, give his intermediaries questions they want answered on the spot; he'll suck *you* in. He won't expect perfect answers; he'd be suspicious as hell if he got them, but he'll want what we use to call a 'stomach consensus.' It's not something you can write down on paper and analyze; it's a gut feeling for believability. There aren't that many good men who could fool Havelock in sequence. One substantial misstep and he closes the book and walks away."

"And sets off the explosions," said Miller.

"I see," said Stern.

And it was clear that the men around that table *did* see. It was one of those moments when the unkempt, irascible Ogilvie confirmed his value, as he did so frequently. He had been out in that labyrinth called the "field," and his summations had a peculiar eloquence and sagacity.

"There is a way, however," continued the former agent. "I'm not sure there's any other."

"What is it?" asked the director of Cons Op.

"Me."

"Out of the question."

"Think about it," said Ogilvie quickly. *"I'm* the credibility. Havelock knows me—more important, he knows I sit at this table. To him I'm one of *them,* a half-assed strategist who may not know what he's asking for, but sure as hell knows why. And with me there's a difference; a few of them out there might even count on it. I've been where they've been. None of the rest of you have. Outside of Matthias, if there's anyone he'll listen to, anyone he'll meet with, it's me."

"I'm sorry, Red. Even if I agreed with you, and I think I do, I can't permit it. You know the rules. Once you step inside this room, you never go out in the field again."

"That rule was *made* in this room. It's not Holy Writ."

"It was made for a very good reason," said the attorney. "The same reason our houses are watched around the clock, our cars followed, our regular telephones tapped with our consent. If any of us was taken by interested parties, from Moscow to Peking to the Persian Gulf, the consequences would be beyond recall."

"No disrespect, Counselor, but those safeguards were designed for people like you and the Headman here. Even Daniel. I'm a little different. They wouldn't try to take me because they know they'd wind up with nothing."

"No one doubts your capabilities," countered Dawson. "But I submit—"

"It hasn't anything to do with capabilities," interrupted Ogilvie, raising his hand to the lapel of his worn tweed jacket; he turned up the flap toward the lawyer next to him. "Look closely, Counselor. There's a slight bulge an inch from the tip here."

Dawson's eyes dropped to the fabric, his expression noncommittal. "Cyanide?"

"That's right."

"Sometimes, Red, I find you hard to believe."

"Don't mistake me," said Ogilvie simply. "I don't ever want to use this —or the others I've got conveniently placed. I'm no macho freak trying to shock you. I don't hold my arm over a fire to show how brave I am any more than I want to kill someone or have him try to kill me. I've got these pills because I'm a coward, Mr. Lawyer. You say we're being watched, guarded twenty-four hours a day. That's terrific, but I think you're overreacting to something that doesn't exist. I don't think there *is* a file on you in Dzerzhinsky Square; at least not on you or the doctor here. I'm sure there's one on Stern, but grabbing him is like codes in Cracker Jacks, or us going in and grabbing someone like Rostov. It doesn't happen. But there's a file on me—you can bet your legal ass on that—and I'm not retired. What I know is still very operative, more so ever since I stepped inside this room. That's why I've got these little bastards. I know how I'd go in and how I'd come out, and they know I know. Strangely enough, these pills are my protection. They know I've got them and they know I'd use them. Because I'm a coward."

"And you've just spelled out the reasons why you can't go into the field," said the director of Consular Operations.

"Have I? Then either you didn't listen or you should be fired for incompetence. For not taking into account what I *didn't* spell out. What do you want, Teacher? A note from my doctor? Excusing me from all activity?"

The strategists glanced briefly at each other, looking uncomfortable. "Come on, Red, cut it out," said Stern. "That's not called for."

"Yes, it is, Dan. It's the sort of thing you consider when making a decision. We all know about it; we just don't talk about it, and I suppose that's another kind of consideration. How long have I got? Three months, maybe four? It's why I'm here, and *that* was an intelligent decision."

"It was hardly the sole reason," offered Dawson softly.

"If it didn't weigh heavily in my favor, it should have, Counselor. You should always pick someone from the field whose longevity—or lack of it—can be counted on." Ogilvie turned to the balding Miller. "Our doctor knows, don't you, Paul?"

"I'm not your doctor, Red," said the psychiatrist quietly.

"You don't have to be; you've read the reports. In five weeks or so the pain will start getting worse . . . then worse after that. I won't feel it, of course, because by then I'll be moved to a hospital room where injections will keep it under control, and all those phony cheerful voices will tell me I'm actually getting better. Until I can't focus, or hear them, and then they don't have to say anything." The former field man leaned back in his chair, looking now at Stern. "We've got here what our learned attorney might call a confluence of beneficial prerogatives. Chances are that the Soviets won't touch me, but if they tried, nothing's lost for me, you can be goddamned sure of that. And I'm the only one around who can pull Havelock out in the open, far enough so we can take him."

Stern's gaze was steady on the red-haired man who was dying. "You're persuasive," he said.

"I'm not only persuasive, I'm right." Suddenly Ogilvie pushed his chair back and stood up. "I'm so right I'm going home to pack and grab a cab to Andrews. Get me on a military transport to Italy; there's no point in advertising the trip on a commercial flight. Those KGB turkeys know every passport, every cover I've ever used, and there's no time to be inventive. Route me through Brussels into the base at Palombara. Then cable Baylor to expect me. . . . Call me Apache."

"Apache?" asked Dawson.

"Damn good trackers."

"Assuming Havelock will meet with you," said the psychiatrist, "what'll you say to him?"

"Not a hell of a lot. Once he's an arm's length away he's mine."

"He's experienced, Red," said Stern, studying Ogilvie's face. "He may not be all there, but he's tough."

"I'll have equipment," replied the dying man, heading for the door. "And I'm experienced, too, which is why I'm a coward. I don't go near anything I can't walk away from. Mostly." Ogilvie opened the door and left without another word. The exit was clean, swift, the sound of the closing door final.

"We won't see him again," said Miller.

"I know," said Stern. "So does he."

"Do you think he'll reach Havelock?" asked Dawson.

"I'm sure of it," replied the director of Cons Op. "He'll take him, turn him over to Baylor and a couple of resident physicians we've got in Rome, then he'll disappear. He told us. He's not going into that hospital room and all those lying voices. He'll go his own way."

"He's entitled to that," said the psychiatrist.

"I suppose so," agreed the lawyer without conviction, turning to Stern. "As Red might say, 'No disrespect,' but I wish to God we could be certain about Havelock. He's *got* to be immobilized. We could be hauled in by authorities all over Europe, fuel for the fanatics of every persuasion. Embassies could be burned to the ground, networks scattered, time lost, hostages taken, and—don't fool yourself—a great many people killed. All because one man fell off balance. We've seen it happen with far less provocation than Havelock could provide."

"That's why I'm so sure Ogilvie will bring him in," said Stern. "I'm not in Paul's line of work, but I think I know what's going through Red's mind. He's offended, deeply offended. He's watched friends die in the field—from Africa to Istanbul—unable to do anything because of his cover. He saw a wife and three children leave him because of his job; he hasn't seen his kids in five years. Now he's got to live with what he's got —die from what he's got. All things considered, if *he* stays on track, what gives Havelock the right, the privilege, to go over the edge? Our Apache's on his last hunt, setting his last trap. He'll see it through because he's angry."

"That and one other thing," said the psychiatrist. "There's nothing else left for him. It's his final justification."

"For what?" asked the lawyer.

"The pain," answered Miller. "His *and* Havelock's. You see, he respected him once. He can't forget that."

8

The unmarked jet swept down from the skies forty miles due north of the airport at Palombara Sabina. It had flown from Brussels, avoiding all military and commercial air routes, and soaring over the Alps east of the Lepontine sector; its altitude was so great and its descent so rapid that the probability of observation was practically nonexistent. Its blip on defense radar screens was prearranged: it would appear and disappear without comment, without investigation. And when it landed at Palombara, it would bring in a man who had been taken on board secretly at three o'clock in the morning, Brussels time. A man without a conventional name, referred to only as the Apache. This man, as with many like him, could not risk the formalities of identification at immigration desks or border checkpoints. Appearances might be altered and names changed, but other men watched such places, knowing what to look for, their minds trained to react like memory banks; too often they were successful. For the Apache—as for many like him—the current means of travel was more the norm than otherwise.

The engines were cut back as the pilot—trained in carrier landings—guided his aircraft over the forests in the stretched-out, low approach to the field. It was a mile-long black strip cut out of the woods, with maintenance hangars and traffic towers set back and camouflaged, odd yet barely visible intrusions on the countryside. The plane touched down, and the young pilot turned in his seat as the reverse thrust of the jets echoed throughout the small cabin. He raised his voice to be heard, addressing the red-haired middle-aged man behind him.

"Here we are, Indian. You can take out your bow and arrows."

"Funny boy," said Ogilvie, releasing the clamp that held the strap across his chest. He looked at his watch. "What's the time here? I'm still on a Washington clock."

"Oh-five-fifty-seven; you've lost six hours. You're working on midnight, but here it's morning. If you're expected at the office, I hope you got some sleep."

"Enough. Is transport arranged?"

"Right to the big chief's wigwam on the Via Vittorio."

"Very cute. The embassy?"

"That's right. You're a special package. Delivery guaranteed straight from Brussels."

"That's wrong. The embassy's out."

"We've got our orders."

"I'm issuing new ones."

Ogilvie walked into the small office reserved for men like himself in the maintenance building of the unmapped airfield. It was a room devoid of windows, with only basic furniture; there were two telephones, both routed perpetually through electronic scrambler systems. The outside corridor that led to the office was guarded by three men dressed innocuously in overalls. Under the bulging fabric, however, each carried a weapon, and should any unidentified persons interfere with the incoming passenger or the presence of a camera even be suspected, the weapons would be bared, used instantly if necessary. These accommodations were the result of extraordinary conferences between unknown men of both governments whose concerns transcended the stated limits of covert cooperation; quite simply, they were necessary.

Governments everywhere were being threatened from without and within, from fanatics of the left and the right committed solely to the destruction of the status quo. Fanaticism fed upon itself, upon sensationalism, upon the spectacular interruption of normal activity; clandestine access had to be given those who fought the extremists in any form. It was presumed that those who passed through Palombara were such fighters, and the current passenger knew beyond any doubt that he was one. Unless he brought in a rogue agent, a dangerous paranoid whose mind held the secret histories of a thousand untold intelligence operations going back sixteen years, that man could destroy alliances and networks throughout Europe. Sources would disappear, potential sources evaporate. Michael Havelock had to be found and taken; no terrorist could inflict greater damage.

Ogilvie walked to the desk, sat down, and picked up the telephone on his left; it was black, signifying domestic use. He dialed the number he had committed to memory, and twelve seconds later the sleepy voice of Lieutenant Colonel Lawrence Baylor Brown was on the line.

"Brown. What is it?"

"Baylor Brown?"

"Apache?"

"Yes. I'm at Palombara. Have you heard anything?"

"Not a word. I've got tracers out all over Rome; there's not a line on him."

"You've got *what?*"

"Tracers. Every source we can pay or who owes us a favor—"

"Goddamn it, call them off! What the hell do you think you're doing?"

"Hey, easy, buddy. I don't think we're going to get along."

"And I don't give a duck's fuck whether we do or not! You're not dealing with a G-two crossword puzzle; he's a snake, *buddy.* You let him find out you're going after him, he figures you've broken the rules. And he *will* find out; that's when he bites. Jesus, you think he's never been traced before?"

"You think I don't know my tracers?" countered Baylor angrily, defensively.

"I think we'd better talk."

"Come on in, then," said the colonel.

"That's another thing," replied Ogilvie. "The embassy's out."

"Why?"

"Among other things, he could be in a window across the street."

"So?"

"He knows I'd never show up in-territory. KGB cameras operate around the clock, aimed at every entrance."

"He doesn't even know you're coming," protested Baylor. "Or who you are."

"He will when you tell him."

"A *name*, please?" said the army officer testily.

"Apache'll do for now."

"That'll mean something to him?"

"It will."

"It doesn't to me."

"It's not supposed to."

"We're definitely not going to get along."

"Sorry about that."

"Since you won't come in, where do we meet?"

"The Borghese. In the gardens. I'll find you."

"That'll be easier than my finding *you.*"

"You're wrong, Baylor."

"About *that?*"

"No. I think we will get along." Ogilvie paused briefly. "Make it two hours from now. Our target may try to reach you by then."

"Two hours."

"And, Baylor?"

"What?"

"Call off those duck-fucking tracers, *buddy.*"

The month of March was not kind to the Borghese. The chill of the Roman winter, mild as the winter was, still lingered, inhibiting the budding of flowers and the full explosion of the gardens that in spring and summer formed rows and circles of dazzling colors. The myriad paths that led through the tall pines toward the great museum seemed just a little dirty, the green of the pine trees tired, dormant. Even the benches that lined the narrow foot roads were layered with dust. A transparent film had descended over the park that was the Villa Borghese; it would disappear with the April rains, but for now the lifelessness of March remained.

Ogilvie stood by the thick trunk of an oak tree on the border of the gardens behind the museum. It was too early for any but a few students and fewer tourists; a scattering of these strolled along the paths waiting for the guards to open the doors that led to the Casino Borghese's treasures. The former field man, now in the field again, looked at his watch, wrinkles of annoyance spreading across his deeply lined face. It was nearly twenty minutes to nine; the army intelligence officer was over a half hour late. Ogilvie's irritation was directed as much at himself as toward Baylor. In his haste to veto his going to the embassy as well as making it clear that he was the control and no one else, he had chosen a poor rendezvous and he knew it. So would the colonel, if he thought about it; perhaps he had, perhaps that was why he was late. The Borghese at this hour was too quiet, too remote, with far too many shadowed recesses from which those who might follow either of them could observe their every move, every word, visually and electronically. Ogilvie silently swore at himself; it was no way to initiate his authority. The attaché-conduit had probably taken a circuitous, change-of-vehicle route, employing frequency scanners in hopes of exposing and thus losing presumed surveillance. KGB cameras *were* trained on the embassy; the colonel had been put in a difficult situation thanks to an abrasive source from Washington enigmatically called Apache. A cover from the back of a cereal box.

The enigma was there, but not the foolishness, not the cereal box. Seven years ago in Istanbul two undercover field men, code names Apache and Navajo, nearly lost their lives trying to prevent a KGB assassination on the Mesrutiyet. They had failed, and in the process Navajo had been cornered on the deserted Ataturk at four o'clock in the morning, KGB killer teams at both entrances. It was a total-loss situation until Apache sped across the bridge in a stolen car, screeching to a stop by the pedestrian alley, shouting at his associate to climb in or get his head blown off. Ogilvie had then raced through a fusillade of gunfire, receiving a graze wound at his temple and two bullets in his right hand while breaking through the thunderous early-morning barricade. The man called Navajo seven years ago would not readily forget Apache. Without him Michael Havelock would have died in Istanbul. Ogilvie counted on that memory.

Snap. Behind him. He turned; a black hand was held up in front of him, the black face beyond the hand immobile, eyes wide and steady staring at him. Baylor shook his head sharply twice, bringing his index finger to his lips. Then slowly, moving closer and pulling both of them behind the tree trunk and the foliage, the army officer gestured toward the south garden, at the rear entrance of the stone museum. About forty yards away a man in a dark suit was glancing about, his expression indecisive, as he moved first in one direction, then in another, unable to choose a path. In the distance there were three rapid blasts of a high-pitched automobile horn, followed by the gunning of an engine. Startled, the man stopped, then broke into a run toward the direction of the intruding sounds and disappeared beyond the east wall of the Borghese.

"This is one dumb location," said the colonel, checking his watch.

"That horn was yours?" asked Ogilvie.

"It's parked by the Veneto gates. It was near enough to be heard; that was all that mattered."

"Sorry," said the former field man quietly. "It's been a long time. I don't usually make mistakes like this. The Borghese was always crowded."

"No sweat. And I'm not sure it was a mistake."

"Let the needle out. Don't stick me with kindness."

"You're not reading me. Your feelings aren't any concern of mine. I've never been put under KGB surveillance before—not that I know of. Why now?"

Ogilvie smiled; he was the control, after all. "You put out the tracers. I think I mentioned that."

The black officer was silent, his dark eyes aware. "Then I'm finished in Rome," he said finally.

"Maybe."

"No maybe. I'm finished, anyway. It's why I'm late."

"He reached you." The red-haired agent made the statement softly.

"With full artillery and I'm the first who'll be exposed. He picked up the Karas woman's trail and followed her to the port of Civitavecchia, where she got out. He won't say how or on what ship. It was a trap; he waded through and reversed it, targeting the man responsible—a small-time operator on the docks. Havelock broke him, and what he learned— what he *thinks* he learned—has turned him into a stockpile of nitro."

"What is it?"

"Double programming. Same tactic supposedly employed with him. She was sandbagged against him by us."

"How?"

"By someone convincing her he'd gone over to the Soviets, that he was going to kill her."

"That's a crock of shit."

"I'm only repeating what he said—what he was told. All things considered, it's not without logic. It would explain a lot. The KGB's got some pretty fair actors; they could have put on a performance for her. It's sound strategy. He's out and she's running. A productive team neutralized."

"I mean the whole *thing's* a crock of shit," countered Ogilvie. "There is no Jenna Karas; she died on a beach called Montebello on the Costa Brava. And she *was* KGB—a deep-cover VKR field officer. No mistakes were made, but even that doesn't matter now. The main point is she's dead."

"He doesn't believe it; when you talk to him you may not, either. I'm not sure I do."

"Havelock believes what he wants to believe, what he has to believe. I've heard the medical terms, and reduced to our language, he's gone over the edge. He crosses back and forth between what is and what isn't, but fundamentally he's gone."

"He's damned convincing."

"Because he's not lying. That's part of it. He saw what he saw."

"That's what he says."

"But he couldn't have; that's also part of it. His vision's distorted. When he goes over, he doesn't see with his eyes, only his head, and that's damaged."

"You're convincing too."

"Because I'm not lying and my head's not damaged." Ogilvie reached into his pocket for a pack of cigarettes. He extracted one and lit it with an old, tarnished Zippo purchased a quarter of a century ago. "Those are the facts, Colonel. You can fill in the blank spaces, but the bottom line's firm. Havelock's got to be taken."

"That won't be so easy. He may be running around in his own foggy tunnels, but he's not an amateur. He may not know where he's going, but he's survived in the field for sixteen years. He's smart, defensive."

"We're aware of that. It's the reality part. You told him I was here, didn't you?"

"I told him a man named Apache was here." The army officer paused. "Well?"

"He didn't like it. Why you?"

"Why not me?"

"I don't know. Maybe he doesn't like you."

"He owes me."

"Maybe that's your answer."

"What are you, a psychologist? Or a lawyer?"

"A little of both," said the colonel. "Constantly. Aren't you?"

"Right now I'm just annoyed. What the hell are you driving at?"

"Havelock's reaction to you was very quick, very vocal. 'So they sent the Gunslinger,' he said. Is that your other name?"

"Kid stuff. A bad joke."

"He didn't sound amused. He's going to call at noon with instructions for you."

"At the embassy?"

"No. I'm to take a room at the Excelsior. You're to be there with me; you're to get on the phone."

"Son of a bitch!" Ogilvie sucked breath through his teeth.

"That's a problem?"

"He knows where I am but I don't know where he is. He can watch me but I can't watch him."

"What difference does it make? He's obviously willing to meet you. In order to take him, you've got to meet with him."

"You're the new boy on the block, Colonel, no offense intended. He's forcing my hand at the top."

"How so?"

"I'll need two men—Italians, preferably, as inconspicuous as possible —to follow me when I leave the hotel."

"Why?"

"Because he could take *me,*" said the former field man reflectively. "From behind. On any crowded sidewalk. There isn't a jump he doesn't know. . . . A man collapses in the street, a friend helps him to a nearby car. Both Americans, nothing out of the ordinary."

"That presumes I won't be with you. Still, I'm the conduit. I could make a case for my being there."

"Definitely the new boy; he'd head for Cairo. And if you tried to keep me in sight, I have an idea he'd spot you. No—"

"Offense intended. . . . There *are* drawbacks. . . . I'll get you your cover." The officer paused again, then continued, "But not two men. I think a couple would be better."

"That's good. You've got possibilities, Colonel."

"I've also got a recommendation to make that I'll deny if it's ever ascribed to me. And considering that sobriquet Gunslinger, I don't think I'd have any difficulty saying I heard it from you."

"I can't wait to hear it myself."

"I'm responsible for a large territory in this area of operations. The work I do for the Pentagon and State gets compounded; it's unavoidable. I need a favor, or someone needs one from us, so the circle quietly grows bigger, even if we've never met each other."

"I hate to repeat myself," interrupted Ogilvie, "but what the hell are you driving at now?"

"I have a lot of friends out there. Men and women who trust me, trust my office. If I have to go, I'd like the office to remain intact, of course, but there's something more basic. I don't want those friends—known and unknown—to get hurt, and Havelock could hurt them. He's worked Italy, the Adriatic, the Ligurian—from Trieste across the borders, along the northern coast all the way to Gibraltar. He could provoke reprisals. I don't think one messed-up retired field man is worth it."

"Neither do I."

"Then take him out. Don't just take him, take him *out.*"

"You could have heard that from me."

"Do I hear it now?"

The man from Washington was silent for a moment; then he replied, "No."

"Why not?"

"Because the act could bring about the consequences you don't want."

"Impossible. He hasn't had time."

"You don't know that. If this thing's been growing since Costa Brava, there's no way to tell what deposits he's made or where he's made them. He could have left documents in half a dozen countries with specific instructions to release them if scheduled contacts are missed. During the last six weeks he's been in London, Amsterdam, Paris, Athens and Rome. Why? Why those places? With the whole world to choose from, and with money in his pocket, he returns to the cities where he operated extensively under cover. It could be a pattern."

"Or coincidence. He knew them. He was out; he felt safe."

"Maybe, maybe not."

"I don't follow the logic. If you simply take him, he still won't make those contacts."

"There are ways."

"The clinics, I assume. Laboratories where doctors inject serums that loosen tongues and minds?"

"That's right."

"And I think you're wrong. I don't know whether he saw the Karas woman or not, but whatever he saw—whatever happened—happened during the past twenty-four hours. He hasn't had time to do a *goddamned thing.* He may tell you he has, but he hasn't."

"Is that an opinion, or are you clairvoyant?"

"Neither. It's fact. I listened to a man in shock. A man who'd just gone through a mind-blowing experience—his phrase, incidentally. It wasn't the result of a festering mental aberration; it had just *happened.* When you talk about what he could have done, the deposits he could have made, you're using the words I gave you because they're the words he said to me. He was speculating on what he *might* do, not what he did. There's a hell of difference, Mr. Strategist."

"And because of it you want him dead?"

"I want a lot of other people to live."

"So do we. That's why I'm here."

"So you can bring him back alive," said Baylor sardonically. "Just like Frank Buck."

"That'll do."

"No, it won't. Suppose you miss? Suppose he gets away?"

"It won't happen."

"Opinion or clairvoyance?"

"Fact."

"No way. It's conjecture, a probability factor I don't want to count on."

"You don't have a choice, *soldier.* The chain of command has spoken."

"Then let me spell it out for you, *civilian.* Don't talk to me about chains of command. I've worked my black ass off in this white man's army—white at the top, black at the bottom—until they had to make me a vital cog in the big white wheel. Now you come along with your secret-agent act, and a code name right out of—"

"The back of a cereal box?" interjected Ogilvie.

"You got it. A cereal box. No name I can point to, no identification I can bargain with to get me off the hook, just a balloon from a comic strip. And if you do miss, and Havelock does get away, I'm on the firing line—as the target. Coffee-Face blew it; his network's compromised. Take him out of the big white wheel."

"You hypocritical bastard," said the man from Washington in disgust. "The only thing you're interested in saving is your own skin."

"For a lot of reasons too benign for you to understand. There're going to be more like me, not less. . . . Wherever you go in this town, I'm not far behind. You take him your way, that's fine with me. I'll get you back to Palombara and strap the two of you into a jet myself with a letter of recommendation written in classical Latin. But if you can't hack it, and he breaks, he goes down my way."

"That doesn't sound like the man who believed his story, who pleaded his case."

"I didn't plead his case, I reported it. And it doesn't make any difference whether I believe him or not. He's an active, dangerous threat to me and my function here in Rome and a large part of the network I've cultivated on the orders of my government and at the expense of the

American taxpayer." The colonel stopped; he smiled. "That's all I have to know to pull a trigger."

"You could go far."

"I intend to, I've got points to make."

Ogilvie stepped away from the tree; he looked past the bordering foliage at the dormant gardens beyond. He spoke quietly, his voice flat, noncommittal. "I could lose you, you know. Kill you, if I had to."

"Right on," agreed the officer. "So I'll forget about the Excelsior. You take a room in my name and when the call comes from Havelock, you pretend to be me. He expects me to be there, confirm your presence; he knows I've got a stake in this. And by the way, when you talk to him as me, don't make it too nigger. I'm a Rhodes Scholar. Oxford, '71."

The agent turned. "You're also something else. I can bring you up on charges, a court-martial guaranteed. Direct disobedience of a superior in the field."

"For a conversation that never took place? Or perhaps it did, and I exercised on-spot military judgment. The subject found the contact unacceptable; I wanted another man in Rome. How does that grab you, *Gunslinger?*"

Ogilvie did not answer for the better part of a minute. He threw his cigarette on the ground, crushing it underfoot, grinding his shoe into the dirt. "You're talented, Colonel," he said finally. "I need you."

"You really want him, don't you?"

"Yes."

"I thought so. It was in your voice on the phone. I wanted that confirmation, Mr. Strategist. Just consider me an insurance policy you don't want to carry, but your accountant says you must. If I have to pay off, nothing's lost. I can justify the act better than anyone around a D.C. conference table. I'm the only one who's spoken to him. I know what he's done and what he hasn't done."

"A very short time could prove you wrong."

"I'll chance it. That's how sure I am."

"You won't have to. There'll be no payoff from you because I won't miss, and he won't get away."

"Glad to hear it. Outside of the couple who'll pick you up when you leave the hotel, what else do you need?"

"Nothing. I brought my equipment with me."

"What are you going to tell him?"

"Whatever he wants to hear."

"What are you going to use?"

"Experience. Have you made arrangements for the room?"

"Forty-five minutes ago," said Baylor. "Only, it's not a room, it's a suite. That way there're two phones. Just in case you're tempted to give me a wrong rendezvous, I'll be listening to everything he says."

"You're boxing me in, boy."

"I'll let that pass. Look at it this way. When today's over, you'll be heading back to Washington either with him or without him, but with no hooks in you. If you've got him, fine. If not, I'll take the heat. My judgment's respected at the Pentagon; under the circumstances the solution will be 'last extremity,' and acceptable."

"You know that book, don't you?"

"Right down to a hundred-odd contradictions. Go back to the good life, Mr. Strategist. Be well and happy in the Georgetown circuit. Make your pronouncements from a distance and leave the field to us. You'll live better that way."

Ogilvie controlled the wince that was about to crease his face. He could feel the sharp pain shooting up through his rib cage, clawing at the base of his throat. It was spreading; every day it went a little further, hurt a little more. Signals of the irreversible. "Thanks for the advice," he said.

9

The Palatine, one of the seven hills of Rome, rises beyond the Arch of Constantine, its sloping fields dotted with the alabaster ruins of antiquity. It was the rendezvous.

A quarter of a mile northwest of the Gregorio gate was an ancient arbor, with a bust of the emperor Domitian resting upon a fluted pedestal at the end of a stone path bordered on both sides by the marble remnants of a jagged wall. Branches of wild olive cascaded over the chiseled rock while vines of brown and green crept underneath, filling crevices and spreading a spidery latticework across the cracked yet ageless marble. At the end of the path, behind the blotched, stern face of Domitian, were the remains of a fountain built into the hill. The arbor abruptly stopped; there was no exit.

The peaceful setting gave rise to images: stately men in togas strolling in the sunlight filtering through the overhanging branches, meditating on the great affairs of Rome, and on the ever-expanding boundaries of the empire, uneasy over the increasing abuses that came with unchallenged might and undiluted power—wondering, perhaps, when the beginning of the end would commence.

This sylvan fragment of another time was the contact ground. Time span: thirty minutes—between three o'clock and half past the hour, when the sun was at midpoint in the western sky. Here two men would meet, each with different objectives, both aware that the differences might cause the death of one or the other, neither wanting that finality. Wariness was the order of the afternoon.

It was twenty minutes before three, the start of the span. Havelock had positioned himself behind a cluster of bushes on the next hill overlooking the arbor, several hundred feet above the bust of Domitian. He was concerned, angry, as his eyes roamed over the stone path and the untamed fields beyond the walls below. A half hour ago, from a sidewalk café across the Via Veneto from the Excelsior, he had seen what he was afraid he might see. Within seconds after the red-haired Ogilvie had walked through the glass doors onto the pavement he had been picked up by a man and a woman who had emerged casually—too casually, a bit too swiftly—from a jewelry shop next door. The store had a wide-angled display-case entrance, affording observers inside a decent range of vision. The man from Washington had veered briefly to his right and stopped before entering the stream of pedestrians heading left. It was a sighting backup, the unobtrusive movement of a hand or a fleeting glance at the pavement, gestures that marked him in the crowds. There would be no taking the Apache unawares before he reached the Palatine. Ogilvie had anticipated that the attempt might be made; he had no intention of losing control, and so he had protected himself. On the phone, the former field man, now a vaunted strategist, had offered only accommodation. He had reasonable—if highly classified—data to deliver; in them would be found the answers Michael sought.

Not to worry, Navajo. We'll talk.

But if the Apache had reasonable explanations to offer, he did not require protection. And why had Ogilvie agreed so readily to the out-of-the-way rendezvous? Why hadn't he simply suggested meeting on the street, or at a café? A man confident of the news he bore did not set up defenses, yet the strategist had done just that.

Instead of an explanation, had Washington sent another message?

Dispatch? Call me dead?

I didn't say we'd kill you. We don't live in that kind of country. . . . On the other hand, why not? Lieutenant Colonel Lawrence Baylor Brown, intelligence conduit, U.S. embassy, Rome.

If Washington had reached that conclusion, the planners had sent a qualified assassin. Havelock respected Ogilvie's talents, but he did not admire the man. The former operative was one of those men who justify their violence too glibly with self-serving scraps of philosophy that imply personal revulsion for committing even necessary acts of violence. Associates in the field knew better. Ogilvie was a killer, driven by some inner compulsion to avenge himself against his own personal furies, which he concealed from all but those who worked closely with him under maximum stress; and those who knew him tried their level best never to work with him again.

After Istanbul, Michael had done something he had never thought he would do. He had reached Anthony Matthias and advised him to take Red Ogilvie out of the field. The man was dangerous. Michael had volunteered to appear before a closed hearing with the strategists, but, as always, Matthias had the better, less divisive method. Ogilvie was an expert; few men had his background in covert activities. The Secretary of State had ordered him up the ladder, making Ogilvie a strategist himself.

Matthias was out of Washington these days. It was not a comforting thought. Decisions were often arrived at without accountability for the simple reason that those who should be apprised in depth were not accessible. The urgency of a given crisis was frequently a green light for movement.

That was it, thought Havelock, as his eyes settled on a figure in the distance, in the sloping field beyond the right wall. It was the man who had accompanied the woman out of the jewelry store next to the Excelsior, the one who had picked up Ogilvie. Michael looked to his left; there was the woman. She was standing by the steps of an ancient bath, a sketch pad in her left hand. But there was no sketching pencil in her right, which she held under the lapel of her gabardine coat. Havelock returned to the man in the field on the right. He was sitting on the ground now, legs stretched, a book open on his lap—a Roman finding an hour's peace, reading. And by no coincidence his hand, too, was held in place at the upper regions of his coarse tweed jacket. The two were in communication and Michael knew the language. Italian.

Italians. No subordinates from the embassy, no CIA stringers, no Baylor—no Americans in sight. When Ogilvie arrived, he'd be the only one. It fit; remove all U.S. personnel, all avenues of record. Use only local backups, men or women themselves beyond salvage. Dispatch.

Why? Why was he a crisis? What had he done or what did he know that made men in Washington want him dead? First they wanted him out by way of Jenna Karas. Now dead. Christ in heaven, what was it?

Besides the couple, were there others? He strained his eyes against the sun, studying every patch of ground, separating the terrain into blocks—an awkward puzzle. The arbor of Domitian was not a prominent site on the Palatine; it was a minor scrap of antiquity left to decay. The dismal month of March had further reduced the number of trespassers. In the distance, on a hill to the east, a group of children played under the watchful glances of two adults. Teachers, perhaps. Below, to the south, there was an uncut green lawn with marble columns of the early empire standing like upright, bloodless corpses of widely differing heights. Several tourists laden with camera equipment—straps over straps, and bulging cases—were taking photographs, posing one another in front of the fluted remains. But other than the couple covering both sides of the arbor's entrance, there was no one in the immediate vicinity of Domitian's retreat. If they were competent marksmen, no additional backups were necessary. There was only one entrance, and a man climbing a wall was an easy target; it was a gauntlet with a single exit. That, too, fit the policy of dispatch. Use as few locals as possible, remembering always that they can snap back with extortion.

The irony had come about unconsciously. Michael had roamed the Palatine that morning, selecting the site for the very advantages that now could be used against him. He looked at his watch: fourteen minutes to three. He had to move quickly, but not until he saw Ogilvie. The Apache was smart; he knew the odds favored his remaining out of sight as long as possible, riveting his adversary's concentration on his anticipated appearance. Michael understood, so he concentrated on his options: on the woman with a sketch pad in her hand, and the man reclining on the grass.

Suddenly, he was there. At one minute to three the red-haired agent came into view, his head and shoulders seen first as he walked up the path from the Gregorio gate, passing the man in the field without acknowledgment. Something was odd, thought Havelock, something about Ogilvie himself. Perhaps it was his clothes, as usual rumpled, ill-fitting . . . but too large for his stocky frame. Whatever, he seemed different; not the face —he was too far away for his face to be seen clearly. It was in his walk, the way he held his shoulders, as if the gentle slope of the hill were far steeper than it was. The Apache had changed since Istanbul; the seven years had not been kind.

Ogilvie reached the remnants of the marble arch that was the arbor's entrance; he would remain inside. It was three o'clock; the time span had begun.

Michael crept away from his recess behind the cluster of wild bush and crawled rapidly through the descending field of high grass, keeping his body close to the ground and making a wide arc north until he came to the base of the hill. He glanced at his watch; it had taken him nearly two minutes.

The woman was now above him, roughly a hundred yards away in the center of the field below and to the right of Domitian's arbor. He could not see her, but he knew she had not moved. She had chosen her sight lines carefully, a backup killer's habit. He started up the slope on his hands and knees, separating the blades of grass in front of him, listening for the sounds of unexpected voices. There were none.

He reached the crest. The woman was directly ahead, no more than sixty feet away, still standing on the first rung of curving white steps that led down to the ancient marble bath. She held the sketch pad in front of her, but her eyes were not on it. They were staring at the entrance of the arbor, her concentration absolute, her body primed to move instantly. Then Havelock saw what he had hoped he would see: the heavyset woman's right hand was no longer on her lapel. It was now concealed under her gabardine coat, without question gripping an automatic she could remove quickly and aim accurately, unencumbered by the awkwardness of a pocket. Michael feared that weapon, but he feared the radio more. In moments it might be an ally; now it was his enemy, as deadly as any gun.

He looked at his watch again, annoyed at the sight of the seconds ticking off; he had to move swiftly. He did so, staying below the crest of the field, working his way around toward the broken stone trench that led to the well of the Roman bath. Huge weeds sprang up from the sides and from the cracks in the trench, covering it and giving it the appearance of an ugly giant centipede. Havelock parted the moist, filthy overgrowth, slid forward on his stomach, and crawled along the jagged marble ditch. Thirty seconds later he emerged from the weeds into the ancient remains of the circular pool that centuries ago had held the oiled, pampered bodies of emperors and courtesans. Seven feet above him—eight decayed steps away—was the woman whose function was to kill him should her current employer be incapable of doing so. Her back was to him, her thick legs planted like those of a sergeant major commanding a machine-gun squad.

He studied the remains of the marble staircase; it was fragile, and was protected by a twelve-inch iron fence on the second rung to prevent onlookers from venturing farther down. The weight of a body on any single step could cause the stone to crack, and the sound would be his undoing. But what if the sound was accompanied by the impact of a severe physical blow? He knew he had to decide quickly, move quickly. Every minute that went by was adding to the growing alarm of the assassin in Domitian's arbor.

Silently he moved his hands about under the tangled weeds; his fingers struck a hard, rough-edged object. It was a fragment of marble, a chiseled part of an artisan's design two thousand years ago. He gripped it in his right hand and, with the other, removed from his belt the Llama automatic he had taken from the would-be mafioso in Civitavecchia. Long ago he had trained himself to fire with his left hand as well as with his right, a basic precaution. The skill would serve him now; it was his own particular backup. If his tactic failed, he would kill the woman hired to make certain he died on the Palatine. But it was a backup, merely an option to make sure he stayed alive. He wanted to keep his rendezvous in Domitian's arbor.

He brought his legs slowly into a crouch and, extending a knee, prepared to spring. The woman was less than four feet away, directly above him. He raised his right arm, the heavy, jagged fragment in his hand, and lunged as he hurled the heavy piece of marble at the wide expanse of gabardine between her shoulders, whipping his arm with all the force he could muster, sending the rock at enormous speed over the short distance.

Sound triggered instinct. The woman started to turn, but the impact came. The jagged fragment crashed into her neck at the base of her skull, blood matting her dark hair instantly. Havelock surged up the steps and, grabbing her coat at the waist, pulled her down over the small iron fence while jamming his forearm against her mouth and choking off the scream. The two of them plunged down into the marble well, Michael twisting the woman's body as they fell. They hit the hard surface; he rammed his knee into her chest between her breasts and thrust the barrel of the Llama deep against her throat.

"You listen to me!" he whispered harshly, knowing that neither the embassy nor Ogilvie would employ a backup who was not fluent in English and might misinterpret orders. "Get on your radio and tell your friend to come over here as fast as he can! Say it's an emergency. Tell him to use the woods below the archway. You don't want the American to see him."

"Cosa dici?"

"You heard me and you understand me! Do as I say! Tell him you think you've both been betrayed. *Prudente! Io parlo italiano! Capisci?"* added

Havelock, applying further pressure both with his knee and the barrel of the gun. *"Presto!"*

The woman grimaced, sucking her breath between her clenched teeth, her broad, masculine face stretched like that of a striking cobra caught in a snake fork. Haltingly, as Michael removed his knee, she raised her right hand to her lapel and folded it back, revealing a transistorized microphone in the shape of a thick button attached to the cloth. In the center was a small, flat transmission switch; she pressed it. There was a brief hum, the signal traveling three hundred feet due west on the Palatine; she spoke.

"Trifoglio, trifoglio," she said rapidly for identification. *"Ascolta! C'è un' emergenza . . . !"* She carried out Michael's orders, the whispered urgency of her voice conveying the panic she felt as the Llama was shoved deeper into her throat. The response came in the sound of startled, metallic Italian.

"Che avete?"

"Sbrigatevi!"

"Arrivo!"

Havelock spun off the woman and pulled her to her knees, ripping her coat apart as he did so. Held in place above her waist by a wide strap was an elongated holster; protruding from it was the handle of a powerful magnum automatic. The outsized leather case accommodated an added appendage attached to the barrel: a perforated cylinder—a silencer, permanently secured and zeroed for accuracy. The woman was, indeed, a professional. Michael quickly removed the weapon and shoved it under his belt. He yanked the woman to her feet and pushing her violently into the curving stairs, forcing her up to the second step so both of them could see—between the spikes of the small iron fence—over the top of the ancient bath. He was behind her, his body pressed into hers locking her in place, the Llama at her right temple, his left arm around her neck. In seconds he saw her companion, crouching as he raced through the foliage below the arbor; it was all he had to see. Without warning, he snapped his left arm back, choking the breath out of the woman's throat and forcing her head forward into the crushing vise. Her body went limp; she would remain unconscious until it was dark on the Palatine. He did not want to kill her; he wanted her to tell her story to the patriots who had hired her. He moved to the side, and she slid down the cracked marble to the weed-infested well below. He waited.

The man emerged cautiously on the sloping field, his hand beneath his tweed jacket. Too many minutes; time was passing too swiftly, the span half over. Much longer, and the assassin sent by Washington would become alarmed. If he walked outside the arbor he would know that his guards were not in place, that his control was lost; he would run. It must not happen! The answers Havelock sought were fifty yards away inside a remnant of antiquity. Once the control was shifted— *only* if it was shifted —could those answers be learned. *Make your move, employee,* thought Havelock, as the Italian approached.

"Trifoglio, trifoglio!" said Michael in a sharp whisper as he grabbed debris from the steps and threw it over the top of the marble casement to his right, at the opposite end of the circular enclosure.

The man broke into a run toward the sound of the voice repeating the code and the sight of flying dirt. Havelock moved to his left and crouched on the third step, his hand on a spoke of the fence, his feet constantly testing the stone beneath; it *had* to hold him.

It did. Michael lurched over the top as the Italian reached the marble rim, so startling the man that he gasped in shock, his panic immobilizing him. Havelock lunged, swinging the Llama into the Italian's face, shattering bone and teeth; blood burst from his mouth and splattered his shirt and jacket. The man started to collapse; Havelock rushed forward to grab him, then turned and propelled him over the side of the marble bath. The Italian plummeted, arms and legs flailing; at the bottom he lay motionless, sprawled over the body of the woman, his bloody head on her stomach. He, too, would have a story to tell, thought Michael. It was important that the strategists in Washington hear it, for if the answers were not forthcoming during the next few minutes, the Palatine was only the beginning.

Havelock forced the Llama into the inside pocket of his jacket and felt the uncomfortable pressure of the outsized magnum automatic beneath his belt. He would keep both weapons; the Llama was a short piece and easily concealed, while the magnum with its permanently attached silencer could be advantageous in circumstances demanding the absence of sound. Suddenly a cold wind of depression swept through him. Twenty-four hours ago he had thought that he would never again hold a gun in his hand for the rest of his life—his new life. In truth, he loathed weapons, feared and hated them, and for this reason he had learned to master them so that he could go on living and use them to still other weapons—the guns of his childhood. The early days, the terrible days; in a way they were what his whole life had been about, the life he had thought he had put finally to rest. Root out the abusers, permit life to the living—destroy the killers of Lidice in any form. He had left that life, but the killers were still there, in another form. And now he was back again. He buttoned his jacket and started toward the entrance of the arbor, and the man who had come to kill him.

As he approached the decrepit marble archway his eyes instinctively scanned the ground, his feet avoiding stray branches that could snap underfoot, announcing his presence. He reached the jagged wall of the arch and silently sidestepped his way to the opening. Gently he pushed away the cascading vines and looked inside. Ogilvie was at the far end of the stone path by the pedestaled bust of Domitian. He was smoking a cigarette, studying the hill above the arbor to his right, the same hill—the same area with the cluster of wild bushes—where Michael had concealed himself nineteen minutes before. The Apache had made his own assessment, the accuracy of his analysis apparent.

There was a slight chill in the air, and Havelock noted that Ogilvie's wrinkled, ill-fitting jacket was buttoned. But he also saw that this did not prevent swift access to a gun. Then Michael focused on the strategist's face; the change was startling. It was paler than Havelock could remember ever having seen it. The lines that had been there before were chiseled deeper now and drawn longer, like the ridges of decay in the faded marble of the ancient arbor. One did not have to be a doctor to know that Ogilvie was a sick man and that his illness was severe. If there was a great deal of strength left in him, it was as concealed as the weapons he carried.

Michael stepped inside, watching intently for any sudden movement on the part of the former field man. "Hello, Red," he said.

Ogilvie's head turned only slightly, conveying the fact that he had seen Havelock out of the corner of his eye before the greeting. "Good to see you, Navajo," answered the strategist.

"Drop the 'Navajo.' This isn't Istanbul."

"No, it isn't, but I saved your ass there, didn't I?"

"You saved it after you damn near got me killed. I told you the bridge was a trap, but you, my so-called superior—a label you overworked, incidentally—insisted otherwise. You came back for me because I told you it was a trap in front of our control in the Mesrutiyet. He would have racked you in his briefing report."

"Still, I came *back*," pressed Ogilvie quickly, angrily, color spreading across his pallid face. Then he checked himself, smiled wanly and shrugged. "What the hell, it doesn't matter."

"No, it doesn't. I think you'd risk blowing yourself and all your kids apart to justify yourself, but as you say, you did come back. Thanks for that. It was quicker, if not necessarily safer, than jumping into the Bosporus."

"You never would have made it."

"Maybe, maybe not."

Ogilvie threw his cigarette on the ground, crushed it underfoot, and stepped forward. "Not the kids, Havelock. Me, yes. Not the kids."

"All right, not the kids." At the reference to children—his unthinking reference—Michael felt momentary embarrassment. He recalled that Ogilvie's children had been taken away from him. This suddenly old man was alone in his shadow world with his personal furies.

"Let's talk," said the man from Washington, walking toward a marble bench on the border of the stone path. "Sit down . . . Michael. Or is it Mike? I don't remember."

"Whatever you like. I'll stand."

"I'll sit. I don't mind telling you, I'm beat. It's a long way from D.C., a lot of flying time. I don't sleep well on planes."

"You look tired."

At the remark, Ogilvie stopped and glanced at Havelock. "Cute," he said, and then sat down. "Tell me something, Michael. Are *you* tired?"

"Yes," said Havelock. "Of the whole goddamned lie. Of everything that's happened. To her. To me. To all of you in your sterile white offices, with your filthy minds—God help me, I was part of you. What did you think you were doing? Why did you *do* it?"

"That's a large indictment, Navajo."

"I told you. Drop that fucking name."

"Like from a cereal box, huh?"

"Worse. For your enlightenment, the Navajos were related to the Apaches, but unlike the Apaches, the tribe was essentially peaceful, defensive. The name didn't fit in Istanbul, and it doesn't fit now."

"That's interesting; I didn't know that. But then, I suppose it's the sort of thing someone not born in a country—brought over after a pretty harrowing childhood somewhere else—would find out about. I mean, studying that kind of history is a way of saying 'Thanks,' isn't it?"

"I don't know what you're talking about."

"Sure, you do. A kid lives through wholesale slaughter, sees friends and neighbors machine-gunned down in a field and thrown into ditches, his own mother sent away to God knows what, knowing he'll never see her again. This kid is something. He hides in the woods with nothing to eat except what he can trap or steal, afraid to come out. Then he's found and spends the next few years running through the streets with explosives strapped to his back, the enemy everywhere, any one of them his potential executioner. All this before he's ten years old, and by the time he's twelve, his father's killed by the Soviets. . . . Christ, a kid like that, when he finally gets to a safe harbor, he's going to learn everything he can about the place. He's really saying 'Thanks for letting me come here.' Wouldn't you agree . . . *Havlíček?*"

So the inviolate was not impenetrable by the strategists. Of course they knew, he should have realized that; his own actions had brought it about. The sole guarantee he had been given was that his true file would be provided only on a need-to-know basis to the highest levels of personnel screening. Those below would be shown the British M.I.6 addendum. A Slovak orphan, parents killed in a Brighton bombing raid, cleared for adoption and immigration. It was all they had to know, all they should know. Before. Not now.

"It's not pertinent."

"Well, maybe it is," said the former field man, shifting his position on the bench, his hand casually moving toward his jacket pocket.

"Don't do that."

"What?"

"Your hand. Keep it out of there."

"Oh, sorry . . . As I was saying, all that early stuff *could* be pertinent. A man can take just so much over the years; it accumulates, you know what I mean? Then one day something snaps, and without his realizing it, his head plays tricks on him. He goes back—way back—to when things happened to him—terrible things—and the years and the motives of people he knew *then* get mixed up with the years and the people he knows *now.* He begins to blame the present for all the lousy things that happened in the past. It happens a lot to men who live the way you and I have lived. It's not even unusual."

"Are you *finished?*" asked Havelock harshly. "Because if you *are*—"

"Come on back with me, Michael," interrupted the man from Washington. "You need help. We can help you."

"You traveled five thousand miles to tell me *that?*" shouted Havelock. "That's the *data,* your *explanation?*"

"Take it easy. Cool it."

"No, *you* take it easy! *You* cool it, because you're going to need every cold nerve you've got! All of you! I'll start here in Rome and work my way

up and over, through Switzerland, Germany . . . Prague, Krakow, Warsaw
. . . right up into Moscow, if I have to! And the more I talk, the more
of a mess you'll be in, every one of you. Who the hell are you to explain
what or where my head is? I saw that woman. She's *alive!* I followed her
to Civitavecchia, where she faded, but I found out what you said to her,
what you *did* to her! I'm going after her, but every day it takes will cost
you! I'll start the minute I get out of here and you won't be able to stop
me. Listen to the news tonight and read the morning papers. There's a
conduit here in Rome, a respected first-level attaché, a member of a
minority—one hell of a screen. Only, he's going to lose his value *and* his
network before the sun goes down! You *bastards!* Who do you think you
are?"

"All right, all *right!"* pleaded Ogilvie, both hands in the air, pressing
the space in front of him. "You've got it all, but you can't blame me for
trying. Those were the orders. 'Get him back so we can tell him over here,'
that's what they said. 'Try anything, but don't *say* anything, not while he's
out of the country.' I told them it wouldn't work, not with you. I made
them give me the disclosure option; they didn't want to, but I hammered
it out of them."

"Then *talk!"*

"Okay, okay, you've got it." The man from Washington expelled his
breath, shaking his head slowly back and forth. "Jesus, things get screwed
up."

"Unscrew them!"

Ogilvie looked up at Michael, raising his hand to the upper left area
of his rumpled jacket. "A smoke, do you mind?"

"Pull it back."

The strategist peeled back his lapel, revealing a pack of cigarettes in his
shirt pocket. Havelock nodded; Ogilvie took out the cigarettes and a book
of matches behind the pack. He shook a cigarette into his right hand and
flipped open the matchbook cover; the book was empty. "Shit," he muttered. "Have you got a light?"

Michael reached into his pocket, took out matches and brought them
over. "What you've got to say had better make a great deal of sense—"

Oh, my God! Whether it was the slight movement of the head of red
hair below him, or the odd position of Ogilvie's right hand, or the flash
of sunlight reflecting off the cigarette pack's cellophane, he would never
know, but in that confluence of unexpected factors, he knew the trap had
been sprung. He lashed his left foot out, catching the strategist's right arm

and reeling it back; the force of the blow threw Ogilvie off the bench.
Suddenly the air was filled with a billowing cloud of mist. He dived to his
right, beyond the path, holding his nostrils, closing his eyes, rolling on the
ground until he slammed into the remains of the jagged wall, out of range
of the gaseous cloud.

The collapsible vial had been concealed in the pack of cigarettes, and
the acrid odor that permeated the arbor told him what the vial had
contained. It was a nerve gas that inhibited all muscular control if a target
was caught in the nucleus; its effect lasted no less than an hour, no more
than three. It was used almost exclusively for abduction, rarely if ever as
a prelude to dispatch.

Havelock opened his eyes and got to his knees, supporting himself on
the wall. Beyond the marble bench the man from Washington was thrashing around on the overgrown grass, coughing, struggling to rise, his body
in convulsions. He had been caught in the milder periphery of the burst,
just enough to make him momentarily lose control.

Michael got to his feet, watching the bluish-gray cloud evaporate in
the air above the Palatine, its center holding until diffused by the breezes.
He opened his jacket, feeling the pain of the scrapes and bruises made
by the magnum under his belt as a result of his violent movements. He
took out the weapon with the ugly perforated cylinder on the barrel, and
walked unsteadily across the grass to Ogilvie. The red-haired man was
breathing with difficulty, but his eyes were clear; he stopped struggling
and stared up at Havelock and then at the weapon in Michael's hand. "Go
ahead, Navajo," he said, his voice barely above a whisper. "Save me the
trouble."

"I thought so." Havelock looked at the former field man's gaunt, lined
face that had the chalk-white pallor of death about it.

"Don't think. Shoot."

"Why should I? Make it easier, I mean. Or harder, for that matter. You
didn't come to kill me, you came to take me. And you don't have any
answers at all."

"I gave them to you."

"When?"

"A couple of minutes ago . . . *Havlíček*. The war. Czechoslovakia,
Prague. Your father and mother. Lidice. All those things that aren't
pertinent."

"What the *hell* are you talking about?"

"Your head's damaged, Navajo. I'm not lying about that."

"*What?*"

"You didn't see the Karas woman. She's dead."

"She's *alive!*" shouted Michael, crouching beside the man from Washington, grabbing him by the lapel of his rumpled coat. "Goddamn you, she saw me! She ran from me!"

"No way," said Ogilvie, shaking his head. "You weren't the only one at Costa Brava, there was someone else. We have his sighting; he brought back proof—fragments of clothing, matching blood, the works. She died on that beach at the Costa Brava."

"That's a *lie!* I was there all night! I went down to the road, down to the beach. There weren't any pieces of clothing; she was running, she wasn't touched until after she was dead, after the bullets hit her. Whoever she was, her body was carried away intact, nothing torn, nothing left on the beach! How *could* there be? *Why* would there be? That sighting's a lie!"

The strategist lay motionless, his eyes boring up into Havelock's, his breathing steadier now. It was obvious that his mind was racing, filtering truth where he could find the truth. "It was dark," he said in a monotone. "You couldn't tell."

"When I walked down to the beach, the sun was up."

Ogilvie winced, forcing his head into his left shoulder, his mouth stretched, a searing pain apparently shooting up through his chest and down his arm. "The man who made that sighting had a coronary three weeks later," said the strategist, his voice a strained whisper. "He died on a goddamned sailboat in the Chesapeake   If you're right, there's a problem back in D.C. neither you nor I know about. Help me. We've got to get out to Palombara."

"*You* get out to Palombara. I don't come in without answers. I told you that."

"You've got to! Because you're not getting out of here without me, and that's Holy Writ."

"You've lost your touch, Apache. I took this magnum from that pretty face you hired. Incidentally, her *gumbà* is with her now, both resting at the bottom of a marble bath."

"Not them! *Him!*" The man from Washington was suddenly alarmed. He pushed himself up on his elbows, his neck craning, his eyes squinting into the sun, scanning the hill above the arbor. "He's waiting, watching us," he whispered. "Put the gun down! Get off the advantage. Hurry up!"

"Who? Why? What for?"

"For Christ's sake, do as I say! Quickly!"

Michael shook his head and got to his feet. "You're full of little tricks,

Red, but you've been away too long. You've got the same stench about you that I can smell all the way from the Potomac—"

"Don't! *No!*" screamed the former field man, his eyes wide, straining, focused on the high point of the hill. Then drawing from an unreasonable reservoir of strength, he lurched off the ground, clutching Havelock and pulling him away from the stone path.

Havelock raised the barrel with heavy cylinder attached and was about to crash it into Ogilvie's skull when the snaps came, two muted reports from above. Ogilvie gasped, then exhaled audibly, making a terrible sound like rushing water, and went limp, falling backwards on the grass. His throat was ripped open; he was dead, having stopped the bullet meant for Michael.

Havelock lunged to the wall; three more shots came, exploding marble and dirt all around him. He raced to the end of the jagged wall, the magnum by his face, and peered through a V-shaped break in the stone.

Silence.

A forearm. A shoulder. Beyond a cluster of wild bush. *Now!* He aimed carefully and fired four shots in rapid succession. A bloody hand whipped up in the air, followed by a pivoting shoulder. Then the wounded man lurched out of the foliage and limped rapidly over the crest of the hill. The hair on the hatless figure was close-cropped and black, the skin deep brown. Mahogany. The would-be assassin on the Palatine was Rome's conduit for covert activities in the northern sector of the Mediterranean. Had he squeezed the trigger in anger, or fear, or a combination of both, afraid and furious that his cover and his network would be exposed? Or had he coldly followed orders? Another question, one more shapeless fragment in the mosaic.

Havelock turned and leaned against the wall, exhausted, frightened, feeling as vulnerable as in the early days, the terrible days. He looked down at Red Ogilvie—John Philip Ogilvie, if he remembered correctly. Minutes ago he was a dying man; now he was a dead man. Killed saving the life of another he did not want to see die. The Apache had not come to dispatch the Navajo; he had come to save him. But safety was not found among the strategists in Washington; they had been programmed by liars. Liars were in control.

Why? For what purpose?

No time. He had to get out of Rome, out of Italy. To the border at Col des Moulinets, and if that failed, to Paris.

To Jenna. Always Jenna, now more than ever!

10

The two phone calls took forty-seven minutes to complete from two separate booths in the crowded Leonardo da Vinci Airport. The first was to the office of the *direttore* of Rome's Amministrazione di Sicurezza, Italy's watchdog over covert foreign activities. With succinct references to authentic clandestine operations going back several years, Havelock was put through without identification to the director's administrative assistant. He held the man on the line for less than a minute, hanging up after saying what he had to say. The second call, from a booth at the opposite end of the terminal, was placed to the *redattore* of *Il Progresso,* Rome's highly political, highly opinionated, largely anti-American newspaper. Considering the implied subject matter, the editor was a far less difficult man to reach. And when the journalist interrupted Michael for identification and clarification, Havelock countered with two suggestions: the first, to check with the administrative assistant to the *direttore* of the Amministrazione di Sicurezza; the second, to watch the United States embassy during the next seventy-two hours, with particular attention paid to the individual in question.

"Mezzani!" fumed the editor.

"Addio," said Michael, replacing the phone.

Lieutenant Colonel Lawrence Baylor Brown, diplomatic attaché and a prime example of America's recognition of minorities, was out of a job. The conduit was finished, his network rendered useless; it would take months, possibly a year, to rebuild. And regardless of how seriously he was wounded, Brown would be flown out of Rome within hours to explain the death of the red-haired man on the Palatine.

The first floodgate had been opened. Others would follow. *Every day it takes will cost you.*

He meant it.

"I'm glad you got here," said Daniel Stern, closing the door of the white, windowless room on the third floor of the State Department building. The two men he addressed were sitting at the conference table: the balding psychiatrist, Dr. Paul Miller, going through his notes; the attorney named Dawson gazing absently at the wall, his hand resting on a yellow legal pad in front of him. "I've just come from Walter Reed—the Baylor briefing. It's all confirmed. I heard it myself, questioned him myself. He's one torn-apart soldier, physically and emotionally. But he's reining tight; he's a good man."

"No deviations from the original report?" asked the lawyer.

"Nothing substantive; he was thorough the first time. The capsule was secreted in Ogilvie's cigarettes, a mild diphenylamine compound released through a C-O-Two cartridge triggered by pressure."

"That's what Red meant when he told us he could take Havelock if he got him within arm's reach," interrupted Miller quietly.

"He nearly did," said Stern, walking into the room. There was a red telephone on a small table beside his chair; he flipped a switch on the sloping front of the instrument and sat down. "Hearing Baylor tell it is a lot more vivid than reading a dry report," said the director of Consular Operations, and fell silent; the two strategists waited. Stern continued softly. "He's quiet, almost passive, but you look at his face and you know how deeply he feels. How responsible."

Dawson leaned forward. "Did you ask him what tipped Havelock off? It wasn't in the report."

"It wasn't there because he doesn't know. Until the last second, Havelock didn't appear to suspect anything. Just as the report says, the two of them were talking; Ogilvie took the cigarettes out of his pocket and apparently asked for a light. Havelock reached into his pocket for matches, brought them over to Red, and then it happened. He suddenly kicked out, sending Ogilvie reeling off the bench, and the capsule exploded. When the smoke cleared, Red was on the ground and Havelock was standing over him with a gun in his hand."

"Why didn't Baylor shoot *then?* At that moment?" The lawyer was disturbed; it was in his voice.

"Because of us," replied Stern. "Our orders were firm. Havelock was to be brought in alive. Only a 'last extremity' judgment could intervene."

"He could have been," said Dawson quickly, almost questioningly. "I've read Brown's—Baylor's—service report. He's a qualified expert in weapons, special emphasis on side arms. There's very little he's not a 'qualified expert' in; he's a walking advertisement for the NAACP *and* the officer corps. Rhodes scholar, Special Forces, tactical guerrilla warfare. You name it, he's got it in his file."

"He's black; he's had to be good. I told you that before. What's your point?"

"He could have wounded Havelock. Legs, shoulders, the pelvic area. Between them, he and Ogilvie *could* have taken him."

"That's asking for a lot of accuracy from seventy-five to a hundred feet."

"Twenty-five to thirty yards. Almost the equivalent of a handgun firing range, and Havelock was standing still. He wasn't a moving target. Did you question Baylor about that?"

"Frankly, I didn't see any reason to. He's got enough on his mind, including a shot-up hand that may spell him out of the army. In my opinion, he acted correctly in a hairy situation. He waited until he saw Havelock point his gun at Ogilvie, until he was convinced Red didn't have a chance. He only fired then, at the precise moment Ogilvie lunged up at Havelock, taking the bullet. Everything corresponds with the autopsy in Rome."

"The delay cost Red his life," said Dawson, not satisfied.

"Shortened it," corrected the doctor. "And not by much."

"That's also in the autopsy report," added Stern.

"This may sound pretty cold under the circumstances," said the attorney, "and perhaps it's related. We overestimated him."

"No," disagreed the director of Cons Op. "We underestimated Havelock. What more do you need? It's been three days since the Palatine, and in those three days he's destroyed a conduit, frightened off the locals in Rome—no one wants to work for us now—and collapsed a network. Added to this he routed a cable through Switzerland to the chairman of Congressional Oversight, alluding to CIA incompetence and corruption in Amsterdam. And this morning we get a call from the chief of White House security, who doesn't know whether to be panicked or outraged. He, too, received a cable, this one in sixteen-hundred cipher, implying that there was a Soviet mole close to the President."

"That comes from Havelock's so-called confrontation with Rostov in Athens," said Dawson, glancing at the yellow legal pad. "Baylor reported it."

"And Paul here doubts that it ever took place," said Stern, looking at Miller.

"Fantasy and reality," interjected the psychiatrist. "If all the information we've gathered is accurate, he slips back and forth, unable to distinguish which. *If* our data is accurate. In all likelihood, there's a degree of incompetence, perhaps minor corruption, in Amsterdam. However, I'd think it's just as unlikely that a Soviet mole could break into the presidential circle."

"We can and do make mistakes *here*," offered Stern, "as well as at the Pentagon, and, God knows, in Langley. But over there the chances of that type of error are minuscule. I don't say it can't happen or hasn't happened, but anyone close to the Oval Office has had every year, every month, every week of his life put under the microscope, even the President's closest friends. The bright recruits are researched as if they might be Stalin's heirs; it's been standard procedure since '47." The director paused again, again not finished. His eyes strayed to the sheaf of loose notes in front of the doctor. He continued slowly, pensively. "Havelock knows which buttons to press, which people to reach, the right ciphers to use; even old ciphers have impact. He can create panic because he gives his information authenticity. . . . How far will he go, Paul?"

"No absolutes, Daniel," said the psychiatrist, shaking his head. "Whatever I say is barely above guesswork."

"Trained guesswork," interrupted the lawyer.

"How would you like to try a case without the benefit of pretrial examination?" asked Miller.

"You've got depositions, statistics, a current on-site briefing, and a detailed dossier. It's fair background."

"Bad analogy. Sorry I brought it up."

"If we can't find him, how far will he go?" pressed the director of Cons Op. "How long have we got before he starts costing lives?"

"He already has," broke in Dawson.

"Not in a controlled sense," contradicted Miller. "It was a direct reaction to a violent attack on his own life. There's a difference."

"Spell out the difference, Paul."

"As *I* see it," said the psychiatrist, picking up his notes and adjusting his glasses. "And to use a favorite phrase of Ogilvie's, I don't claim it's Holy Writ. But there are a couple of things that shed a little light, and I'll be honest with you, they disturb me. The key, of course, is in whatever was said between Havelock and Ogilvie, but since we can't know what it was, we can only go by Baylor's detailed description of the scene, the physical movements, the general tone. I've read it over and over again, and until the final moments—the eruption of violence—I was struck by a note I didn't expect to find. The absence of sustained hostility."

"Sustained hostility?" asked Stern. "I don't know what that implies in behavioral terms, but I hope it doesn't mean they didn't argue, because they did. Baylor makes that clear."

"Of course they argued; it was a confrontation. There was a prolonged outburst on Havelock's part, restating the threats he's made before, but then the shouting stopped; it had to. Some kind of accommodation was reached. It couldn't have been otherwise in light of what followed."

"In light of what followed?" questioned Stern, bewildered. "What followed was Ogilvie's trap, the diphenylamine gas, the explosion."

"I'm sorry, you're wrong, Daniel. There was a retreat before then. Remember, from the moment Havelock showed himself until that instant at the bench when he kicked out, aborting the trap, there was no show of physical violence, no display of weapons. There was talk, *conversation.* Then the cigarettes, the matches. It's too damned reasonable."

"What do you mean?"

"Put yourself in Havelock's place. Your grievance is enormous, your anger at fever pitch, and a man you consider your enemy asks you for a light. What do you do?"

"It's only a match."

"That's right, only a match. But you're consumed, your head throbbing with anxiety, your state of mind actually vicious. The man in front of you represents betrayal at its worst, at its most personal, most deeply felt. These are the things a paranoid schizophrenic feels at a time like this, with a man like this. And that man, that enemy—even if he's promised to tell you everything you want to hear—asks you for a light. How do you react?"

"I'd give it to him."

"How?"

"Well, I'd—" The section chief stopped, his eyes locked with Miller's. Then he completed the answer, speaking quietly. "I'd throw it to him."

"Or tell him to forget about it, or shove it, or just to keep on talking. But I don't think you'd take a pack of matches from your pocket and walk over, handing them to that man as though it were a momentary pause in an argument rather than an interruption of a highly charged moment of extreme personal anxiety. No, I don't think you'd do that. I don't think any of us would."

"We don't know what Ogilvie said to him," objected Stern. "He could have—"

"It almost doesn't matter, don't you see?" interrupted the psychiatrist. "It's the pattern, the goddamned *pattern.*"

"Discerned from a pack of *matches?*"

"Yes, because it's symptomatic. Throughout the entire confrontation, with the exception of a single outburst, there was a remarkable absence of aggressiveness on Havelock's part. If Baylor is as accurate as you say —and I suspect he is, because under the circumstances he'd be prone to exaggerate any threatening movements or gestures—Havelock exercised extraordinary control . . . rational behavior."

"What does that tell you?" asked Dawson, breaking his silence, watching Miller closely.

"I'm not sure," said the doctor, returning the lawyer's stare. "But I know it doesn't fit the portrait of the man we've convinced ourselves we're dealing with. To twist a phrase, there's too much reason afoot, not enough madness."

"Even with his slipping in and out of reality?" continued Dawson.

"It's not relevant here. His reality is the product of his whole experience, his everyday living. Not his convictions; they're based largely on his emotions. Under the conditions of the rendezvous, they should have surfaced more, distorting his reality, forcing him into listening less, into a more aggressive posture. . . . He listened too much."

"You know what you're saying, don't you, Paul?" said the attorney.

"I know what I'm *implying,* based on the data we've all accepted as being totally accurate . . . from the beginning."

"That the man on the Palatine three days ago doesn't fit the portrait?" suggested Dawson.

"Might not fit it. No absolutes, only 'trained' guesswork. We don't know what was said, but there was too much rationality in what was described to suit me. Or the portrait."

"Which was predicated on information we've considered infallible," concluded the lawyer. "In your words, 'from the beginning.' From Costa Brava."

"Exactly. But suppose it wasn't? Suppose it *isn't?*"

"Impossible!" said the director of Consular Operations. "That information was filtered through a dozen sieves, then filtered again through twenty more. There was *no* margin for error. The Karas woman *was* KGB; she *died* at Costa Brava."

"That's what we've accepted," agreed the psychiatrist. "And I hope to God it's accurate, and that my guesswork observations are worthless reactions to an *in*accurately described scene. But if it's not and they're not, if there's the remotest possibility that we're not dealing with a psychopath but with a man who's telling the truth because it *is* the truth, then we're faced with something I don't even want to think about."

The three men fell silent, each grappling with the enormity of the implication. Finally Dawson spoke. "We have to think about it."

"It's appalling even to consider it," said Stern. "There was MacKenzie's confirmation, and it *was* a confirmation. The torn clothing, parts of a blouse, a skirt, they *belonged* to her, it was established. And the blood type, A-negative. *Hers.*"

"And Steven MacKenzie died of a coronary three weeks later," interrupted Miller. "We looked into it, but it just faded away."

"Come on, Paul," objected Stern. "That doctor in Maryland is one of the most respected on the Eastern Shore. What's his name? . . . Randolph. Matthew Randolph. Johns Hopkins, Mayo Clinic, on the boards of Massachusetts General, New York's Mount Sinai, and with his own medical center. He was thoroughly interviewed."

"I'd like to talk to him again," the doctor said.

"And I remind you," pressed the director of Cons Op. "MacKenzie had just about the finest record that ever came out of the Central Intelligence Agency. What you're suggesting is inconceivable."

"So was the horse in Troy," said the lawyer. "When it was conceived." He turned to Miller, who had removed his glasses. "Trained guesswork, Paul. Let's take it all the way; we can always scratch it, but say there's substance. What do you think he'll do now?"

"I'll tell you what he won't do—if there's substance. He won't come in, and we can't trick him with ploys because he understands—rationally —that whatever's happened we're either a part of it, or ignorant of it, or it's beyond our control. The attack's been made on him; he'll mount every defense he's learned in the sixteen years he's been in the field. And from here on in he'll be ruthless, because he *has* been betrayed. By men he can't see in places where they shouldn't be." The psychiatrist looked at Stern. "There's your answer, Daniel, if there's substance. Oddly enough, he's really back in his early days now—the machine guns, Lidice, betrayal. He's running through the streets wondering who in the crowds might be his executioner."

A sharp, abrasive hum erupted from the red telephone on the small, low table next to Stern. The director reached down and picked it up, his eyes still on Miller. "Yes?"

Thirty seconds of silence followed, interrupted only by quiet acknowledgments on Stern's part as he listened, staring across at the psychiatrist's notes, absorbing the information being given him. "Stay on the line," he said finally, snapping the switch and looking up at both strategists. "This is Rome. They've found a man in Civitavecchia, the name of a ship. It may *be* the girl. Or a Soviet hoax; that's entirely possible. It was Baylor's theory and he still holds to it. . . . The original order stands. Take Havelock, but not in dispatch; he's not to be considered 'beyond salvage.' . . . Now, I've got to ask you a question—primarily you, Paul, and I know I can't hold you to absolutes."

"That's the only absolute."

"We've acted on the assumption that we're dealing with an unbalanced man, with someone whose paranoia may compel him to place documents or statements exposing past operations with third parties, to be released on instructions. Is that right?"

"Basically, yes. It's the sort of manipulation a schizophrenic mentality would indulge in, the satisfaction derived as much from revenge as from the threat. Remember, the third parties in question would undoubtedly come from undesirable elements; respectable people would shun such a person, and underneath he knows that. It's a compulsive, involuntary game. He really can't win, only seek vengeance, and there's the danger."

"Would a sane man play that game?"

The psychiatrist paused, fingering his glasses. "Not the same way."

"How do you mean?"

"Would you?"

"*Please,* Paul."

"No, I'm serious. You'd be more concerned with the threat than with the revenge. You want something; revenge may be down the road, but it's not what's primarily on your mind now. You want answers. Threats might get them for you, but risking exposure of classified information by delivering it to highly suspect brokers defeats the purpose."

"What would a sane man do?"

"Probably get word to those he's threatening as to the kind of information he intends to reveal. Then he'd proceed to reach qualified third parties—publishers, perhaps, or men and women who head organizations that legitimately, openly, resist the kind of work we do here—and make arrangements with them. That's a sane man's approach, his attack, his ultimate threat."

"There's no evidence that Havelock's done any of these things."

"It's only been three days since the Palatine; he hasn't had time. These things take time."

"Lending credence to the matches. To his sanity."

"I think so, and I'm biting the bullet. I gave him the label—based on what we had—and now I'm wondering if it should be removed."

"And if we remove it, we accept the possibility of a sane man's attack. As you said, he'll be ruthless, far more dangerous than a schizophrenic."

"Yes," agreed the psychiatrist. "An unbalanced man can be repudiated, blackmailers dealt with . . . and it's important to realize that since Costa Brava no such extortionists have tried to reach us. But legitimate interests, no matter how misguided, could inflict extraordinary damage."

"Costing networks, informants, sources, years of work . . ." The director's hand reached down to the telephone, to the switch. "And lives."

"Yet *if* he's sane," interrupted Dawson sharply, once again breaking a silence, "if it *is* the girl, that presupposes a much deeper problem, doesn't it? Her guilt, her death, everything's in question. All that *infallible* information that was filtered through all those high-level sieves suddenly looks like a massive deception where deception shouldn't *be*. Those are the answers Havelock wants."

"We know the questions," replied Stern quietly, his hand still on the telephone switch, "and we can't *give* him the answers. We can only stop him from inflicting extraordinary damage." The director of Cons Op fell silent for a moment, his eyes on the telephone. "When each of us entered this room, we understood. The only morality here is pragmatic morality, no philosophy but our own brand of utilitarianism: the greatest advantage for the many—over the few, over the individual."

"If you put him 'beyond salvage,' Daniel," continued the attorney softly but emphatically, "I can't support you. And not from an ethical point of view, but from a very practical one."

Stern looked up. "What is it?"

"We need him for tracing the second, deeper problem. If he's sane, there's an approach we haven't tried, an approach he may listen to. As you said, we've acted on the assumption that he was unbalanced; it was the only reasonable assumption we could make. But if he isn't, he may listen to the truth."

"What truth?"

"That we don't *know*. Let's grant him that he *did* see the Karas woman, that she *is* alive. Then tell him we want the answers as badly as he does. Perhaps more so."

"Assuming we can get that word to him, suppose he doesn't listen, suppose he demands only the answers we can't give, and considers everything else a trick to take him. Or take him out. What then? We've got the Costa Brava files; they contain the names of everyone involved. What help can he really be? On the other hand, we know the damage he can do, the panic he can create, the lives he can cost."

"The victim becomes the villain," said Miller wearily. "Jesus Christ."

"We take our problems in order of appearance and priority," said Stern, "and in my judgment these are two separate crises. Related but separate now. We go after the first. What else can we do?"

"We can admit we don't know!" answered Dawson urgently.

"Every effort will be made to comply with the original order, to take him alive. But they have to be given the option."

"By giving it you're telling them he's a traitor. They'll use it on the slightest provocation. They'll kill him. I repeat, I can't support you."

The director slowly looked up at the lawyer; there were deep creases around his tired eyes, which were filled with doubt. "If we're this far apart, then it's time," he said quietly, reluctantly.

"For what?" asked Miller.

"To give this to Matthias's office. They can reach the old man, or not, knowing that time's running out. I'll go up myself and summarize." Stern flipped the switch on the telephone. "Rome? Sorry to keep you hanging, and I'm afraid it's going to get worse. Keep the ship under air surveillance, and send your people to Col des Moulinets, their radio frequency on scrambler for instructions. If they don't get their orders by the time they land, they're to reach you every fifteen minutes. You stay by this line and close it down—for your use only. We'll get back to you as soon as we can, either myself or someone upstairs. If it's not me, the code will be . . . Ambiguity. Have you got that? Ambiguity. That's all for now, Rome." The director of Cons Op replaced the phone, snapped the switch, and got up from his chair. "I hate like hell doing this . . . at a time like this," he said. "We're supposed to be the shield with a thousand eyes, all-seeing, all-knowing. Others can plan, others execute, but we're the ones who give the word. The lousy decisions are supposed to be made here, that's our *function,* goddamn it."

"We've needed help before," said the psychiatrist.

"Only on tactical questions that Ogilvie couldn't answer, never on matters of evaluation. Never for anything like this."

"Dan, we're not playing corporate chairs in the boardroom," added Dawson. "We inherited Costa Brava, we didn't initiate it."

"I know that," said Stern, going to the door. "I suppose it's a consolation."

"Do you want us to go with you?" asked Miller.

"No, I'll present it fairly."

"Never doubted it," interjected the attorney.

"We're running against a clock in Rome," continued the director. "The fewer of us, the fewer questions. It's reduced to one anyway. Sane or insane. 'Beyond salvage' or not." Stern opened the door and left as the two strategists watched, an uneasy sense of relief apparent on both their faces.

"Do you realize," said Miller, turning in his chair, "that for the first time in three years the phrase 'I can't support you' was used? Not 'I don't think so' or 'I disagree,' but 'I can't support you.' "

"I couldn't," said Dawson. "Daniel's a statistician. He sees numbers—fractions, equations, totals—and they spell out the odds for him. God knows he's brilliant at it; he's saved the lives of hundreds with those statistics. But I'm a lawyer; I see complications, ramifications. Parties of the first part turning on parties of the second part. Prosecutors stymied because a point of law prohibits them from connecting one piece of evidence to another when it should be permitted. Criminals outraged over minor discrepancies of testimony when the only things outrageous were their crimes. I've seen it all, Paul, and there are times when the odds aren't found in numbers. They're found in things you can't perceive at the moment."

"Strange, isn't it? The differences between us, I mean. Daniel sees

numbers, you see complications, and I see—full-blown possibilities based
on particles."

"A book of matches?"

"I guess so." The psychiatrist leveled his eyes at the attorney. "I believe
in those matches. I believe in what they stand for."

"So do I. At least in the possibility they represent. That's the complication, Headman—as Ogilvie would have said. If there's a possibility that
Havelock's sane, then everything he says is true. The girl—false guilt
generated in our deepest laboratories—alive, running. Rostov in Athens
—bait not taken to the Lubyanka for reasons unknown, a Soviet mole at
1600 . . . Complications, Doctor. We need Michael Havelock to help us
unravel a melted ball of wax. *If* it's happened—whatever it is—it's frightening." Dawson abruptly pushed his chair back and stood up. "I've got
to get back to the office. I'll leave a message for Stern; he may want to
come over and talk. How about you?"

"What? Oh, no, thanks," answered Miller, preoccupied. "I've got a
five-thirty session at Bethesda, a marine from Teheran." He looked up.
"It *is* frightening, isn't it?"

"Yes, Paul. Very."

"We did the right thing. No one in Matthias's section will put Mikhail
Havlíček 'beyond salvage.' "

"I know. I counted on it."

The director of Consular Operations came out of the office on the fifth
floor, L Section, of State, closing the door quietly behind him—closing,
too, a part of the problem from his mind. It was shared now, the responsibility spread. The man he had shared it with—the man who would reach
Rome under the code name Ambiguity and render the judgment—was
chosen carefully. He was one of Anthony Matthias's inner circle, someone
the Secretary of State trusted implicitly. He would consider all the options
before making the decision—undoubtedly not alone.

The issue was as clear as it could be. If Havelock was sane and telling
the truth, he was capable of doing extraordinary damage because he had
been betrayed. And if that was the case, there was treason here in Washington in inconceivable places. Related but separate crises. Should he then
be placed immediately "beyond salvage," so that his death would prevent
the great harm he could inflict on intelligence operations throughout all
Europe? Or should the order for his execution be delayed, in the hope that

something might happen that would reconcile a man who was an innocent victim to those who would *not* betray him?

In Col des Moulinets the only way was to find the woman and, if it *was* Jenna Karas, to bring her to Havelock, let them join forces and together run down the second, potentially greater crisis here in Washington. But if it was *not* Jenna Karas, if it was a Soviet ploy, if she did not exist except as a deadly puppet hoax to drive a man mad and into treason, what then? Or if she was alive and they could not find her, would Havelock listen? Would Mikhail Havlíček, victim, survivor of Lidice and Soviet Prague, listen? Or would he see betrayal where there was none, and in turn betray his own? Could the delay then be justified? God knew it could not be justified to dismantled networks or to undercover agents who found themselves in the Lubyanka. And if that was the answer, there was the possibility—the probability—that a man had to die because he was right.

The only morality here is pragmatic reality, no philosophy but our own brand of utilitarianism: the greatest advantage for the many—over the few, over the individual.

That was the real answer, the statistics proved it. But this was the inner territory of Anthony Matthias's domain. Would they see it here? In all likelihood they would not, Stern realized. Fear would compel the man he had talked with to reach Matthias, and the revered Secretary of State would delay.

And a part of Daniel Stern—not the professional but the person inside—did not object. A man should not die because he is right, because he is sane. Yet Stern had done his professional best to make the options clear, to justify that death if it came down to it. And he had been fortunate in one respect, he thought as he approached the door to the outer reception room. He could not have brought the problem to a fairer, more level-headed man. Arthur Pierce's title—like that of so many other young middle-aged men in the department—was Undersecretary of State, but he was head and shoulders above the many others. There had been around twenty senior personnel still in L Section when Stern reached the fifth floor, but Pierce's name had stood out. To begin with, Pierce was not in Washington every day; he was assigned to the United Nations in New York as chief liaison between the ambassador and the State Department, a position decreed by Anthony Matthias, who knew what he was doing. Given a respectable amount of time, Arthur Pierce would be made the U.N. ambassador, and a good man, a decent man, would be rewarded not only for his high intelligence but for his decency.

And God knew decency was needed now. . . . Or was it? wondered Stern, startling himself, his hand reaching for the knob of the reception-room door. *The only morality here is pragmatic morality* . . . There was decency in that for hundreds of potential victims in the field.

No matter, it was out of his hands, Stern thought as he opened the door. The decision to be made and transmitted under the code name Ambiguity was on Pierce's conscience now. Quiet, bright, understanding Arthur Pierce—outside of Mikhail Havlíček, closest to Matthias—would ponder all sides of the question, then bring in others. The decision would be made by committee, if it was to be made. *They* were Ambiguity now.

"Mr. Stern?" the receptionist called out as he passed her, heading for the elevator.

"Yes?"

"Message for you, sir."

It said: "Daniel, I'll be at my office for a while. If you're of a mind, come over for a drink. I'll drive you home, chicken."

Dawson had not signed his name, nor was it necessary. The often aloof, circumspect attorney always seemed to know when quiet talk was called for; it was his warmer side. The two cold, analytical men every now and then needed the solace of each other's rarely seen lighter traits. The humorous offer to drive him home was a reference to Stern's distaste for Washington traffic. He took taxis everywhere, to the annoyance of his personal surveillance. Well, whatever team was on now, it could take a break and pick him up later at home in Virginia; Dawson's guards could serve them both until then.

Ogilvie had been right, the whole business was foolish, a hangover from the Angleton days in Langley. Stern looked at his watch; it was twenty minutes past seven, but he knew the lawyer would still be at his office, still waiting for the quiet talk.

They talked for over an hour before going down to Dawson's car, analyzing and reanalyzing the events at Costa Brava, realizing there was no explanation, no answer within their grasp. Each had called his wife; both women were inured to the interminable hours demanded at State, and claimed to understand. Each lied and both husbands understood; the clandestine regions of government placed too much strain on the marriage vows. This nether life would all come to an end one day. There was a far healthier world beyond the Potomac than either man had known for too many years.

"Pierce will go to Matthias, and Matthias won't consider it, you know that, don't you?" said Dawson, turning off the crowded highway onto the backcountry road in Virginia, passing luminous signs that read CONSTRUCTION AHEAD. "He'll demand a review."

"My conference with Pierce was one-on-one," said Stern, absently glancing at the rearview mirror outside the window, knowing that a pair of headlights would be there in moments. The watchdogs stayed on their leashes. "I was balanced but firm; either decision has merit, both have drawbacks. When he talks to his committee they may decide to go around Matthias because of the time factor. I emphasized it. In less than three hours our people will be in Col des Moulinets; so will Havelock. They have to know how to proceed."

"Whatever comes down, they'll first try to take him alive."

"That's the priority; no one here wants it otherwise." Stern looked through the flashing shadows at the attorney. "But I don't kid myself, you were right before. If it comes down 'beyond salvage,' he's dead. It's a license to kill someone who'll kill you if he can."

"Not necessarily. I may have overreacted. If the order's clear—dispatch the last resort—I could be wrong."

"You're wrong now, I'm afraid. Do you think Havelock will give them a choice? He survived the Palatine; he'll use every trick in his very thick book. No one'll get close enough to take him. But getting him in a rifle sight is another matter. That can be done and no doubt will be."

"I'm not sure I agree."

"That's better than not supporting me."

"It's easier," said Dawson, smiling briefly. "But Havelock doesn't know we found the man in Civitavecchia; he doesn't know we're on him in Col des Moulinets."

"He'll assume it. He told Baylor about the Karas woman getting out, how he's convinced she got out. He'll expect us to follow up. We'll concentrate on her, of course. If it *is* Jenna Karas, she's the answer to everything; we'd be home free without a shot. Then *with* Havelock we can go after the mess here. That's the optimum, and I hope to Christ it happens. But it may not."

"And then we're left with a man in the cross hairs of a rifle scope," said Dawson with an edge to his voice, as he accelerated down the flat stretch of backcountry road. "If it *is* the Karas woman, we've got to find her. We *have* to."

"No matter who it is, we'll do our damnedest," said Stern, his eyes again straying to the mirror outside the window. There were no headlights. "That's odd. The watchdogs strayed, or your foot's outracing them."

"There was a lot of traffic on the highway. If they got in a slow lane, they could crack their butts breaking out. It's Friday in Virginia, swizzle time for the hunt-country diplomats. On nights like this, I begin to understand why you don't drive."

"What team's on tonight, by the way?"

The question was never answered. Instead, an ear-shattering scream exploded from the attorney's throat as the deafening impact came, smashing the windshield into a thousand blades of flying glass, piercing flesh and eyes, severing veins and arteries. Metal shrieked against metal, twisting, breaking, curling, crushing against itself as the left side of the car rose off the ground, throwing the bodies into the well of deep-red rivulets below.

The steel behemoth of yellow and black, its colors glistening in the reflection of its single front floodlight, vibrated thunderously; the giant treads of its spiked cables rolled through the huge wheel casings, relentlessly pressing the monster forward. This enormous machine that moved earth from mountains and forests now crawled ahead, crushing the demolished vehicle as it sent it over and beyond the road. The attorney's car plunged down the steep incline of a shallow ravine; the fuel tank exploded, and fire spread everywhere, consuming the bodies within the car.

Then the brightly colored machine, its curved implement of destruction hydraulically raised in triumph, jerked back and forth, its massive gears remeshing, the pitch of the sound higher—an animal proclaiming its kill. And with sporadic but deliberate movements it retreated across the road into its lair at the edge of the woods.

High in the darkness of the cab the unseen driver turned off the engine and raised a hand-held radio to his lips.

"Ambiguity terminated," he said.

"Get out of there," was the reply.

The long gray sedan roared out of the highway exit into the backcountry road. As the license plates indicated, the vehicle was registered in the State of North Carolina, but a persistent investigator could learn that the individual in Raleigh listed as the owner was in reality one of twenty-four men stationed in Washington, D.C. They were a unit, each having had extensive experience in military police and counterintelligence; they were assigned to the Department of State. The car now racing down the dark country road in Virginia was one of a fleet of twelve; they, too, were assigned to State, Division of Consular Operations.

"File a report with the insurance company in Raleigh," said the man sitting next to the driver, speaking into a microphone attached to a large radio console beneath the dashboard. "Some clown sideswiped us, and we plowed into a guy from Jersey. There was no damage to us, of course, but he doesn't have much of a trunk left. We wanted to get out of there, so we told him—"

"*Graham!*"

"What?"

"Up ahead! The fire!"

"*Jesus Christ! Move!*"

The gray sedan leaped forward, the sound of its powerful engine echoing through the dark Virginia countryside. Nine seconds later it reached the steep incline that fronted the shallow ravine, and tires screeched as the brakes were applied. Both men leaped out and raced to the edge, the heat of the flames directly below causing both to step back, with their hands shielding their eyes from the fire.

"Oh, my *God!*" cried the driver. "It's Dawson's car! Maybe we can—"

"*No!*" shouted the man named Graham, stopping his associate from crawling down the flank of the ravine. His eyes were drawn to the yellow-and-black bulldozer standing motionless in its recess on the side of the road. Then . . . "Miller!" he screamed. "Where's *Miller?*"

"The chart said Bethesda, I think."

"Find him!" ordered Graham, running across the road, crouching, reaching behind for the weapon in his hip holster. "Get Bethesda! *Raise him!*"

The head nurse at the reception counter on the sixth floor of the Bethesda Naval Hospital was adamant. Neither did she appreciate the aggressive tone of voice used by the man on the telephone; it was a poor connection to begin with, and his shouting only made it worse.

"I repeat, Dr. Miller is in psychiatric session and can't be disturbed."

"You get him on the line and you get him on *now!* This is a Four Zero emergency, Department of State, Consular Operations. This is a direct order routed and coded through State's switchboard. Confirm, please."

"Confirmed," said a third voice flatly. "This is operator one-seven, State, for your recheck."

"Very well, operator one-seven, and you may be sure we *will* check."

The nurse jammed her forefinger on the hold button, cutting off further conversation, as she got out of her chair and walked around the counter. It was hysterical men like the so-called special agent from Consular Operations that kept the psychiatric wards in full operation, she thought as she proceeded down the white corridor toward the row of therapy rooms. They screamed emergency for the flimsiest reason, more often than not trying to impress everyone with their so-called authority. It would serve special agent Consular-whatever right if the doctor refused to come to the phone. But he would not refuse; the head nurse knew that. Dr. Miller's brilliance in no way thwarted his genuine kindness; if he had a fault, it was his excessive generosity. He had checked into T.R. 20; she approached it, noting that the red light at the side of the door was on, signifying occupancy. She pressed the intercom button.

"Dr. Miller, I hate to interrupt, but there's a man from the State Department on the telephone. He says it's an emergency."

There was no reply; perhaps the intercom was not working. The head nurse pressed the button again, applying more pressure, speaking louder. "Dr. Miller? I realize this is highly irregular, but there's a man on the phone from State. He's most insistent and the operator *did* confirm the status of the call."

Nothing. Silence. No sound of the knob being turned, no acknowledgment whatsoever. The doctor obviously could not hear her; the intercom was not working. She rapped on the door.

"Dr. Miller? Dr. *Miller?*"

Really, the man was not deaf. What was he *doing?* His patient was a marine, one of the hostages from Teheran. Not violent; overly passive, actually. Had there been a regression? The nurse turned the knob and opened the door of Therapy Room 20.

She screamed—again and again.

Crouched in the corner, trembling, was the young marine in his government-issue bathrobe. He was staring through the light of the desk lamp, his gaze riveted on the figure sprawled back on the chair. Miller's eyes were open wide, glasslike—dead. In the center of his forehead was a single bullet hole from which blood poured out, rolling down his face and into the collar of his white shirt.

The man in Rome looked at his watch. It was a quarter past four in the morning, his men in position in Col des Moulinets, and still no word from Washington. The only other person in the code room was the radio operator; bored with the inactivity, he was absently scanning his dials, picking up insignificant traffic signals from ships mainly. Every now and then he would lean back and flip through the pages of an Italian magazine, mouthing the phrases that had become his third language—the radio was his second.

The light on the telephone preceded the hum. The man picked it up. "Rome," he said.

"This is Ambiguity, Rome." The voice was clear, deliberate. "That name gives me complete authority regarding all orders issued to your unit at Col des Moulinets. I assume Director Stern made that clear to you."

"Very clear, sir."

"Are we on total scrambler?"

"Total."

"We're not to be taped or logged. Is that understood?"

"Understood. No tape, no log. What's the word?"

" 'Beyond salvage.' Complete."

"That's it, then."

"Not yet. There's more."

"What?"

"Clarification. There's been no contact with the freighter, has there?"

"Of course not. Small-plane surveillance until it's too dark, then we shift to parallel coast sightings."

"Good. She'll be put ashore somewhere before San Remo, I'd guess."

"We're ready."

"Is the Corsican in charge up there?" asked the voice from Washington.

"The one who came on board three days ago?"

"Yes."

"He is. He put the unit together, and I can tell you we owe him. Our drones over here have dwindled."

"Good."

"Speaking of clarification, I assume the colonel's order still holds. We bring the woman in."

"Inoperative. Whoever she is, she's *not* the Karas woman; she was killed at Costa Brava, we know that."

"Then what do we do?"

"Let Moscow have her back. This one's Soviet poison, a lure to drive the target out of his head. It worked; he's already talked. He's—"

" 'Beyond salvage.' "

"Just get her out of there. We don't want any trail that could lead back to us, no reopened speculations on Costa Brava. The Corsican will know what to do."

"I've got to say it, I'm not sure I understand."

"You don't have to. We just want proof of dispatch. *His* dispatch."

"You'll have it. Our man with the eyes is up there."

"Have a good day, Rome. A good day with no mistakes."

"No mistakes, no tape, no log."

"Out," said the voice known only as Ambiguity.

The man behind the desk was outlined in silhouette. He was in front of a window overlooking the grounds below the Department of State, the soft glow of faraway streetlamps the only light intruding on the dark office. The man had been facing the window, the telephone held close to his lips. He swiveled in his chair, his features in shadow, as he replaced the phone and leaned forward, resting his forehead on the extended fingers of both hands; the curious streak of white that shot through his dark hair gleamed even in the dim light.

Undersecretary of State Arthur Pierce, born Nikolai Petrovich Malyekov in the village of Ramenskoye, southeast of Moscow, and raised in the State of Iowa, breathed deeply, steadily, imposing a calm over himself as he had learned to do throughout the years whenever a crisis called for swift, dangerous decisions; he knew full well the consequences of failure. That, of course, was the strength of men like him: they were not afraid to fail. They understood that the great accomplishments in history demanded the greatest risks; that, indeed, history itself was shaped by the boldness not only of collective action but of individual initiative. Those who panicked at the thought of failure, who did not act with clarity and determination when the moments of crisis were upon them, deserved the limitations to which their fears committed them.

There had been another decision to make, a decision every bit as dangerous as the one he had transmitted to Rome, but there was no avoiding it. The strategists of Consular Operations had reopened the events of that night on the Costa Brava; they had been peeling away the layers of deceit, about which they knew *nothing*. It all had to be buried —*they* had to be buried. At all costs, at all risk. Costa Brava had to be submerged again and become an obscure deception in a convoluted world of lies. In a few hours word would be sent from Col des Moulinets: "The order for 'beyond salvage' has been carried out. Authorization: Code

Ambiguity—established and cleared by D. S. Stern, director of Consular Operations."

But only the strategists knew whom Stern had come to with his ambiguous dilemma. In fact, Stern himself had not known whom he would approach until he had emerged on the fifth floor and studied the roster of senior personnel on the premises; he had made that clear. No matter, thought Arthur Pierce in the dark office as he glanced at the inscribed photograph of Anthony Matthias on the wall. All things considered, it would have been unthinkable for him not to have been consulted regarding the crisis. It was simply more convenient for him to have been in his office when Stern and the other strategists had made the decision to bring the insoluble problem upstairs. Had he not been on the floor, he would have been reached, his counsel sought. The result would have been the same: 'Beyond salvage.' Only the method would have been different: an unacknowledged consensus by a faceless committee. Everything worked out for the best; the past two hours had been orchestrated properly. Failure had been considered, but not contemplated. Failure had been out of the question. The strategists were dead, all links to code name Ambiguity severed.

They needed time. Days, a week, a month. They had to find the man who had accomplished the incredible—with *their help.* They would find him, for he was leaving a trail of fear—no, not fear, terror—and trails could be tracked. And when they found him, it would not be the meek who inherited the earth. It would be the Voennaya.

There were so few of them left on this side of the world. So few, but so strong, so right. They had seen it all, lived it all. The lies, the corruption, the essential rot at the cores of power; they had been part of it for a greater cause. They had not forgotten who they were, or what they were. Or *why* they were. They were the travelers, and there was no higher calling; its concept was based in reality, not in romantic illusions. They were the men and women of the new world, and the old one needed them desperately. They were not many in numbers—less than a hundred, committed beyond life—but they were finely tuned units, prepared to react instantly to any opportunity or emergency. They had the positions, the right papers, the proper vehicles. The Voennaya was generous; they, in turn, were loyal to the elite corps of the KGB.

The death of the strategists had been crucial. The resulting vacuum would paralyze the original architects of Costa Brava, stunning them into silence. They would say nothing; cover-up would be paramount. For the man in shadows behind the desk had not lied to Rome: there could be no reopened speculations on Costa Brava. For either side.

Darkness obscuring his movements, Arthur Pierce, the most powerful *paminyatchik* in the Department of State, rose from the desk and walked silently to the armchair against the wall. He sat down and stretched his legs; he would remain there until morning, until the crowds of senior and subordinate personnel began to fill up the fifth floor. Then he would mingle with the others, signing a forgotten roster sheet; his morning presence would be temporary, for he was needed back in New York. He was, after all, Washington's senior aide to the ambassador of the American delegation at the United Nations. In essence, he was the State Department's major voice on the East River; soon he would be the ambassador. That had been Anthony Matthias's design; everyone knew it. It would be yet another significant step in his extraordinary career.

Suddenly Malyekov-Pierce bolted up in the chair. There was a last phone call to be placed to Rome, a last voice to be stilled: a man in a radio room who answered a sterile telephone and took an untaped, unlogged message.

11

"She's not on board, I *swear* it!" protested the harassed captain of the freighter *Santa Teresa*, seated at his desk in the small cabin aft of the wheelhouse. "Search, if you wish, signore. No one will interfere. We put her ashore three . . . three and a half hours ago. *Madre di Dio!* Such madness!"

"How? *Where?*" demanded Havelock.

"Same as you. A motor launch came out to meet us twelve kilometers south of Arma di Taggia. I swear to you, I knew *nothing!* I'll *kill* that pig in Civitavecchia! Just a political refugee from the Balkans, he said—a woman with a little money and friends in France. There are so many these days. Where is the sin in helping one more?"

Michael leaned over and picked up the outdated diplomatic identification card that gave his status as consular attaché, U.S. Department of State, and said calmly, "No sin at all, if that's what you believed."

"It's true, signore! For nearly thirty years I've pushed my old cows through these waters. Soon I leave the sea with a little land, a little money. I grow grapes. Never *narcotici!* Never *contrabbandi!* But people—yes. Now and then *people,* and I am not ashamed. Those who flee places and men you and I know nothing about. I ask you again, where is the sin?"

"In making mistakes."

"I cannot believe this woman is a criminal."

"I didn't say that. I said we had to find her."

The captain nodded his head in resignation. "Badly enough to report me. I leave the sea for prison. *Grazie, gran Signor Americano.*"

"I didn't say that, either," said Michael quietly.

The captain's eyes widened as he looked up, his head motionless. *"Che cosa?"*

"I didn't expect you to be what you seem to be."

"Che dice?"

"Never mind. There are times when embarrassment should be avoided. If you cooperate, nothing may have to be said. *If* you cooperate."

"In any way you wish! It's a gift I did not expect."

"Tell me everything she said to you. And do it quickly."

"There was much that was meaningless—"

"That's not what I want to hear."

"I understand. She was calm, obviously highly intelligent, but, beneath, a very frightened woman. She stayed in this cabin."

"Oh?"

"Not with me, I can assure you. I have daughters her age, signore. We had three meals together; there was no other place for her, and my crew is not what I would have my daughters eat with. Also, she carried a great deal of lire on her person. She had to; the transportation she purchased did not come cheap. . . . She looked forward to much trouble. Tonight."

"What do you mean?"

"She asked me if I had ever been to the village of Col des Moulinets in the Ligurian mountains."

"She told you about Col des Moulinets?"

"I think she assumed I knew, that I was merely one part of her journey, aware of the other parts. As it happened, I *have* been to Moulinets several times. The ships they give me are often in need of repairs, here in San Remo, or Savona, or Marseilles, which, incidentally, is my farthest port of call. I am not what is known as a *capitano superiore*—"

"Please. Go on."

"We have been dry-docked here in San Remo a few times and I have gone up to the mountains, to Col des Moulinets. It's across the French border west of Monesi, a lovely town filled with mountain streams and— How do you say it? *Ruote a pale?"*

"Paddle wheels. *Moulinets* can also mean paddle wheels in French."

"*Sì*. It's a minor pass in the lower Alps, not used very much. It's difficult to reach, the facilities poor, the transportation poorer. And the border guards are the most lax in the Ligurians and the Maritimes; they barely have time to take the Gauloises out of their mouths to glance at papers. I tried to assure my frightened refugee that she would have no trouble."

"You think she'll try to go through a checkpoint?"

"There's only one, a short bridge across a mountain river. Why not? I doubt it would be necessary even to bribe a guard; if she was one woman among a group of well-dressed people at night, no doubt evidencing fine *vino*. What concern is it of theirs?"

"Men like me."

The captain paused; he leaned back in his chair appraising the American official, as if in a somewhat different light. "Then you would have to answer that yourself, signore. Who else knows?" Both men looked at each other, neither speaking. The captain nodded and continued. "But I tell you this, if she doesn't use the bridge, she will have to make her way through very dense forest with much steep rock, and don't forget the river."

"Thanks. That's the kind of information I need. Did she say why she was getting out this way?"

"The usual. The airports were watched; the train stations also, as well as the major roads that cross into France."

"Watched by whom?"

"Men like you, signore?"

"Is that what she said?"

"She did not have to say anything more than she did, and I did not inquire. That is the truth."

"I believe you."

"Will you answer the question, then? Do others know?"

"I'm not sure," said Michael. "The truth."

"Because if they do, I am arrested. I leave the sea for prison."

"Would that mean it's public information?"

"Most certainly. Charges would be brought before *la commissione*."

"Then I don't think they'll touch you. I have an idea that this incident is the last thing on earth the men I'm involved with want known. If they haven't reached you by now—by radio, or a fast boat, or by helicopter— they either don't know about you, or they don't want to touch you."

Again the captain paused, looking carefully at Havelock. "Men you are involved with, signore?" he said, the words suspended.

"I don't understand."

"Involved with, but not *of*, is that correct?"

"It's not important."

"You wish to help this woman, do you not? You are not after her to . . . penalize her."

"The answer to the first is yes. The second, no."

"Then I will tell you. She asked me if I knew the airfield near Col des Moulinets. I did not. I never heard of it."

"An airfield?" Michael understood. It was added information he would not have been given ten seconds ago. "A bridge over a mountain river, and an airfield. Tonight."

"That is all I can tell you."

The mountain road leading out of Monesi toward the French border was wide enough, but the profusion of rock and boulder and bordering overgrowth made it appear narrow, more suited to heavy-wheeled trucks and rugged jeeps than to any normal automobile. It was the excuse that Michael used to travel the last half-mile on foot, to the relief of the taxi driver from Monesi.

He had learned there was a country inn just before the bridge, a watering spot for the Italian and French patrols, where both languages were sufficiently understood by the small garrisons on either side, as well as by the few nationals and fewer tourists who occasionally passed back and forth. From what little Havelock had seen and had been told, the captain of the *Santa Teresa* was right. The border checkpoint of Col des Moulinets was at a minor pass in the lower Alps, not easily accessible and poorly staffed, manned no doubt because it was there—had been for decades—and no bureaucratic legislation had bothered to remove it. The general flow of traffic between the two countries used either the wide coast roads of the Mediterranean fifteen miles south or the larger, more accommodating passes in the north, such as Col de Larche or Col de la Madeleine, west of Turin.

The late-afternoon sun was now a fan-shaped arc of deep orange and yellows, spraying up from behind the higher mountains, filling the sky above the Maritimes with receding echoes of light. The shadows on the primitive road were growing longer, sharper; in minutes their outlines would fade and they would become obscure shapes, indistinguishable in the gray darkness of early evening. Michael walked along the edge of the woods, prepared to spring into the underbrush at the first sounds not part of the forest. He knew that every move he made had to be prejudged on the assumption that Rome had learned about Col des Moulinets. He had not lied to the captain of the *Santa Teresa;* there could be any number of reasons why those working for the embassy would stay away from a ship in international waters. The slow freighter could be tracked and watched —very likely had been—but it was another matter to board her in a legitimate official capacity. It was a high-risk tactic; inquiries too easily could be raised with a *commissione.*

Had Rome found the man in Civitavecchia? He could only presume that others could do what he had done; no one was that exceptional or that lucky. He had in his anger—no, his outrage—shouted the name of the port city into the phone and Baylor had repeated it. If the wounded intelligence officer was capable of functioning after the Palatine, he would order his people to prowl the Civitavecchia waterfront and find a broker of illegal passage.

Yet there were always gaps, spaces that could not be filled. Would the man in Civitavecchia name the specific ship, knowing that if he did so, he'd never again be trusted on the waterfront? Trusted, hell; he could be killed in any one of a dozen mist-filled back streets. Or might he plead ignorance to that phase of the escape—sold by others unknown to him —but reveal Col des Moulinets so as to curry favor with powerful Americans in Rome, who everyone knew were inordinately generous with those they favored. . . . "One more refugee from the Balkans, where was the sin, signori?"

So many gaps, so little that was concrete . . . so little time to think, so many inconsistencies. Who would have thought there'd be a tired, aging captain opposed to trafficking in the profitable world of narcotics and contraband but perfectly willing to smuggle refugees out of Italy—no less a risk, no less a cause for imprisonment?

Or blunt Red Ogilvie, a violent man who never stopped trying to justify violence. There was ambivalence in that strange justification. What had driven John Philip Ogilvie? Why does a man strain all his life to break out of self-imposed chains? Who really was the Apache? The Gunslinger? Whoever and whatever, he had died violently at the very moment he had understood a violent truth. The liars were in control in Washington.

Above all, Jenna. His love who had not betrayed that love but, instead, had been betrayed. How could she have believed the liars? What could they have said to her, what irrefutable proof could they have presented that she would accept? Most important of all, *who* were the liars? What were their names and where had they come from?

He was so close now that he could sense it, feel it with every step he took on the darkening mountain road. Before the disappearing sun came up on the other side of the world, he would have the answers, have his love back. If his enemies had come from Rome, they were not a match for him; he knew that. His belief in himself swelled within him; it was unjustified all too often, but it was necessary. One did not come out of the early days, the terrible days, and survive without it. Each step and he was nearer.

And when he had the answers, and his love, the call would be made to a cabin in another range of mountains thousands of miles away. To the Blue Ridge and the Shenandoah, U.S.A. His mentor, his *přítel,* Anton Matthias, would be presented with a conspiracy that reached into the bowels of clandestine operations, its existence incontrovertible, its purpose unknown.

Suddenly he saw a small circle of light up ahead, shining through the foliage on the left-hand side of the road. He crouched and studied it, trying to define it. It did not move; it was merely there, where no light had been before. He crept forward, mesmerized, frightened; what *was* it?

Then he stood up, relieved, breathing again. There was a bend in the road, and in its cradle were the outlines of a building; it was the country inn. Someone had just turned on an outside post lamp; other lights would follow shortly. The darkness had come abruptly, as if the sun had dropped into a chasm; the tall pines and the massive boulders blocked the shafts of orange and yellow that could still be seen in the sky. Light now appeared in windows, three on the nearest side, more in front—how many he could not tell, but at least six, judging from the spill that washed over the grass and graveled entrance of the building.

Michael stepped into the woods to check the underbrush and foliage. Both were manageable, so he made his way toward the three lighted windows. There was no point in staying on the road any longer; if there were surprises in store, he did not care to be on the receiving end.

He reached the border of the woods, where the thick trunk of a pine tree stood between him and a deeply rutted driveway of hard mud. The drive extended along the side of the inn and curved behind it into some kind of parking area next to what appeared to be a delivery entrance. The distance to the window directly across was about twenty-five feet; he stepped out from behind the tree.

Instantly he was blinded by headlights. The truck thundered out of the primitive road thirty yards to his right, careening into the narrow driveway of ridged mud. Havelock spun back into the foliage, behind the trunk of the pine tree, and reached for the Spanish automatic strapped to his chest. The truck bounced past, pitching and rolling over the hardened ruts of the drive like a small barge in choppy water. From inside the van could be heard the angry shouts of men objecting to the discomfort of their ride.

Havelock could not tell whether he had been seen or not; again he crouched for protective cover and watched. The truck lurched to a stop at the entrance of the wide, flat parking area; the driver opened his door and jumped to the ground. Prepared to race into the woods, Michael crept back several feet. It was not necessary; the driver stretched while swearing in Italian, his figure suddenly caught in the spill of a floodlight someone had switched on from inside the building. What the light revealed was bewildering: the driver was in the uniform of the Italian army, the insignia that of a border guard. He walked to the back of the truck and opened the large double doors.

"Get out, you bastards!" he shouted in Italian. "You've got about an hour to fill your kidneys before you go on duty. I'll walk up to the bridge and tell the others we're here."

"The way you drive, Sergeant," said a soldier, grimacing as he stepped out, "they heard you halfway back to Monesi."

"Up yours!"

Three other men got out, stamping their feet and stretching; all were guards.

The sergeant continued, "Paolo, you take the new man. Teach him the rules." As the noncommissioned officer lumbered up the driveway past Havelock, he scratched his groin and pulled down the underwear beneath his trousers—signs of a long, uncomfortable trip.

"You, Ricci!" shouted a soldier at the rear of the truck, looking up into the van. "Your name's Ricci, right?"

"Yes," said the voice from inside, and a fifth figure emerged from the shadows.

"You've got the best duty you'll find in the army, *paesano!* The quarters are up at the bridge, but we have an arrangement: we damn near live *here*. We don't go up there until we go on. Once you walk in, you sign in, understand?"

"I understand," said the soldier named Ricci.

But his name was not Ricci, thought Michael, staring at the blond man slapping his barracks hat against his left hand. Havelock's mind raced back over a dozen photographs; his mind's eye selected one. The man was not a soldier in the Italian army—certainly no border guard. He was a Corsi-

can, a very proficient drone with a rifle or a handgun, a string of wire or
a knife. His real name was irrelevant; he used too many to count. He was
a "specialist" used only in "extreme prejudice" situations, a reliable executioner who knew his way around the western Mediterranean better than
most such men, as much at home in the Balearic Islands as he was in the
forests of Sicily. His photograph and a file of his known accomplishments
had been provided Michael several years ago by a CIA agent in a sealed-off
room at Palombara. Havelock had tracked a Brigate Rosse unit and was
moving in for a nonattributable kill; he had rejected the blond man now
standing thirty feet away from him in the floodlit driveway. He had not
cared to trust him then, but Rome did now.

Rome *did* know. The embassy had found a man in Civitavecchia, and
Rome had sent an executioner—for a nonattributable kill. Something or
someone had convinced the liars in Washington that a former field officer
was now a threat only if he lived, so they had put out the word that he
was "beyond salvage," his immediate dispatch the highest priority. Nonattributable, of course.

The liars could not let him reach Jenna Karas, for she was part of their
lie, her mock death on the Spanish coast intrinsic to it. Yet Jenna was
running too; somehow, some way after Costa Brava she had escaped. Was
she now included in the execution order? It was inevitable; the bait could
not be permitted to live, and therefore the blond assassin was not the only
killer on the bridge at Col des Moulinets. On, or near it.

The four soldiers and the new recruit started toward the rear entrance
of the country inn. The door beneath the floodlight was opened, and a
heavyset man spoke in a loud voice. "If you pigs spent all your money in
Monesi, stay the hell out of here!"

"Ah, Gianni, then we'd have to close you up for selling French girls
higher than ours!"

"*You* pay!"

"Ricci," one of the soldiers said, "this is Gianni the thief. He owns this
dung heap. Be careful what you eat."

"I have to use the bathroom," said the new recruit. He had just looked
at his watch; it was an odd thing to do.

"Who doesn't?" shouted another soldier as all five went inside.

The instant the door closed, Havelock ran across the drive to the first
window. It looked in on a dining room. The tables were covered with
red-checked cloths, with cheap silver and glassware in place, but there
were no diners; either it was too early for the kitchen or there were no

takers that afternoon. Beyond, separated only by a wide archway that extended the length of the wall, was the larger central barroom. From what he could see, there were a number of people seated at small round tables—between ten and fifteen would be his estimate, nearly all men. The two women in his sight lines were in their sixties, one fat, one gaunt, sitting at adjacent tables with mustachioed men; they were both talking and drinking beer. Teatime in the Ligurian Alps. He wondered if there were any other women in that room; he wondered—his chest aching—if Jenna was huddled at a corner table he could not see. If that was the case, he had to be able to watch a door from the rear quarters —from the kitchen, perhaps—from which the five soldiers had to emerge into the barroom. He *had* to be able to see. The next few minutes could tell him what he needed to know: who among the clientele in that barroom would the blond killer recognize, if only with a glance, a twitch of his lips, or an almost imperceptible nod?

Michael crouched and ran to the second window along the drive; the angle of vision was still too restricting. He raced to the third, appraised the view and rejected it, then rounded the corner of the building to the first window in front. He could see the door now—CUCINA, the lettering said; the five soldiers would walk out of that door any second, but he could not see all the tables. There were two windows remaining that faced the stone path leading to the entrance. The second window was too close to the door for reasonable cover, but he held his breath and crawled swiftly to it, then stood up in the shadow of a spreading pine. He inched his face to the glass, and what he saw allowed him to let out the breath he had held. Jenna Karas was not an ambushed target sitting in a corner. The window was beyond the inside archway; he could see not only the kitchen entrance but every table, every person in the room. Jenna was not there. And then his eyes strayed to the far-right wall; there was another door, a narrow door with two separate lines of letters. *Uomini* and *Hommes*, the men's room.

The door labeled CUCINA swung open and the five soldiers straggled in; Gianni the thief had his hand on the shoulder of the blond man whose name was not Ricci. Havelock stared at the killer, stared at the eyes with all his concentration. The owner of the inn gestured to his left—Michael's right—and the assassin started across the room toward the men's room. The eyes. Watch the eyes!

It came! Barely a flicker of the lids, but it was there, the glance was there. Recognition. Havelock followed the blond man's line of sight.

Confirmed. Two men were at a table in the center of the room; one had lowered his eyes to his drink while talking, the other—bad form—had actually shifted his legs so as to turn his head away from the path of the killer's movement. Two more members of the unit—but only one of them was active. The other was an observer. The man who had shifted his legs was the agent of record who would confirm the dispatch but in no way participate. He was an American; his mistakes bore it out. His jacket was an expensive Swiss windbreaker, wrong for the scene and out of season; his shoes were soft black leather, and he wore a shiny digital chronometer on his wrist—all so impressive, so irresistible to a swollen paycheck overseas, so in contrast to the shabby mountain garments of his companion. So American. The agent of record—but it was a file no more than six men alive would ever see.

Something else was inconsistent; it was in the numbers. A unit of three with only two active weapons was understaffed, considering the priority of the kill and the background of the foreign service officer who was the primary target. Michael began studying every face in the room, isolating each, watching eyes, seeing if any strayed to the oddly matched pair at the center table. After the faces came the clothes, especially those belonging to the few faces angled away from him. Shoes, trousers and belts where they could be seen; shirts, jackets, hats and whatever jewelry was visible. He kept trying to spot another chronometer or an Alpine windbreaker or soft leather shoes. Inconsistencies. If they were there, he could not find them. With the exception of the two men at the center table, the drinkers at the inn were a ramshackle collection of mountain people. Farmers, guides, storekeepers—apparently French from across the bridge—and, of course, the border guards.

"Ehi! Che avete?" The words were hurled at him, a soldier's challenge. The sergeant from the truck stood, with his hand on his holster, in the semidarkness of the path that led to the entrance of the inn.

"Mia sposa," said Havelock quickly, his voice low, urgent, properly respectful. *"Noi siamo molto disturbati, Signor Maggiore. Io vado ad aiutare una ragazza francese. Là mia sposa mi seguirà!"*

The soldier grinned and removed his hand from the gun case. He admonished Havelock in barracks Italian: "So the men of Monesi still go across the border for French ass, eh? If your wife's not in there, she's probably back in your own bedroom being pumped by a Frenchman! Did you ever think of that?"

"The way of the world, Major," replied Michael obsequiously, shrugging, and wishing to Christ the loudmouthed dolt would go inside and leave him alone. He had to get back to the window!

"You're not from Monesi," said the sergeant, suddenly alarmed. "You don't talk like a man from Monesi."

"The *Swiss* border, Major. I come from Lugano. I moved here two years ago."

The soldier was silent for a moment, his eyes squinting. Havelock slowly moved his hand in the shadows toward his waist, where, secured uncomfortably under his belt, was the heavy magnum with the silencer attached. There could be no sounds of gunfire, if it came to that.

Finally the sergeant threw up his hands, shaking his head in disgust. "Swiss! *Italian*-Swiss, but more *Swiss* than Italian! All of you! Sneaky bastards. I won't serve in a battalion north of Milan, I swear it. I'll get out of the army first. Go back to your sneaking, *Swiss!*" He turned and stalked into the inn.

Inside, another door—the narrow door to the men's room—was opened. A man walked out, and Michael not only knew he had found a third weapon in the unit from Rome, but realized there had to be a fourth. The man was part of a team—two demolition experts who worked together—veteran mercenaries who had spent several years in Africa blowing up everything from dams and airports to grand villas suddenly occupied by inept despots in Graustarkian regalia. The CIA had found them in Angola, on the wrong side, but the American dollar was healthier then, and persuasive. The two experts had been placed in a single black-bordered file deep in the cabinets of clandestine operations.

And their being at the bridge of Col des Moulinets gave Havelock a vital piece of information: a vehicle or vehicles were anticipated. Either one of these two demolition specialists could pause for ten seconds by an automobile, and ten minutes later it would explode, killing everyone in the immediate vicinity. Jenna Karas was expected to cross the border by car; minutes later she would be dead, a successful, nonattributable kill.

The airfield. Rome had learned about the airfield from the man in Civitavecchia. Somewhere on the road out of Col des Moulinets, whatever conveyance she was in would be blown into the night sky.

Michael dropped to the ground behind the pine tree. Through the window he could see the explosives expert walking directly to the front door of the inn; the man glanced at his watch, as the blond killer had done minutes ago. A schedule was in progress, but *what* schedule?

The man emerged; his swarthy face looked even darker in the dim light of the post lamp at the end of the path. He began walking faster, but the acceleration was barely perceptible; this was a professional who knew the value of control. Havelock rose cautiously, prepared to follow; he glanced at the window, then looked again, alarmed. Inside, by the bar, the sergeant was talking to the blond recruit he called Ricci, obviously delivering an unwanted order. The killer seemed to be protesting, raising his beer as if it were much needed medicine and thus an excuse for not obeying. Then he grimaced, drank his drink in several swallows, and started for the door.

The schedule was being adhered to. Through prearrangement, someone at the bridge had been instructed to call for the new recruit in advance of the duty hour; he was to be rostered *before* the shift was over. Procedural methods would be the cover, and no one would argue, but it was not procedure, it was the schedule.

They knew. The unit from Rome knew that Jenna Karas was on her way to the bridge. A motor launch had been picked up in Arma di Taggia, and the party had been followed; the vehicle in which she traveled into the Ligurian mountains was now spotted within minutes of its arrival at the checkpoint of Col des Moulinets. It was logical: what better time to cross a border than at the end of a shift, when the soldiers were tired, weary of the dull monotony, waiting for relief, more careless than usual?

The door opened, and Michael crouched again, peering to his right through the branches of the pine tree at the road beyond the post lamp. The mercenary had crossed diagonally to the shoulder on the other side, bearing left toward the bridge—an ordinary stroller, a Frenchman perhaps, returning to Col des Moulinets. But in moments he would fade into the woods, taking up a predetermined position east of the bridge's entrance, from which he could crawl to an automobile briefly held up by the guards. The blond killer was now halfway to the post lamp; he paused, lighting a cigarette, an action that gave another reason for his delay. He heard the sound of the door being opened, and was satisfied. The "soldier" continued on his way as the two men from the center table—the American agent of record and his roughly dressed companion, the second weapon in the unit from Rome—came out.

Havelock understood now. The trap had been engineered with precision; in a matter of minutes it would be in place. Two expert marksmen would take out the intruder who tried to interfere with the car carrying Jenna Karas—take him out instantly, the second he came in sight, with a fusillade of bullets; and two demolition specialists would guarantee that the automobile waved through would explode somewhere in the streets of Col des Moulinets, or on a road to an unmarked airfield.

Another assumption could be made beyond the fact that there was a schedule in progress that included a car on its way to the bridge. The unit from Rome knew he was there, knew he would be close enough to the border patrols to observe all those in any vehicle offering passports to the guards. They would examine closely every male figure that came into view, their hands on their weapons as they did so. Their advantage was in their numbers, but he, too, had an advantage and it was considerable: he knew who they were.

The well-dressed American and his employee, the second gun, separated at the road, the agent of record turning right in order to remove himself from the execution ground, the killer going left and to the bridge. Two small trucks clattered up the road from Monesi, one with only a single headlight, the other with both headlights but no windshield. Neither the American nor his hired weapon paid any attention; they knew the vehicle they were waiting for, and it was neither of these.

If you know a strategy, you can counter a strategy—his father's words so many years ago. He could recall the tall, erudite man patiently explaining to a cell of partisans, calming their fears, channeling their angers. Lidice was their cause, the death of Germans their objective. He remembered it all now as he crept back to the driveway and raced across into the woods.

He got his first glimpse of the bridge from three hundred yards away on the edge of the bend in the road that led to the country inn—the curve he had avoided by heading into the woods. From what he could see, it was narrow and not long, which was a blessing for drivers because two cars crossing at the same time would no doubt graze fenders. A dual string of naked bulbs was now lit; it arced over the central steel span, sagging between the struts; several of the bulbs had burned out, to be replaced when others joined them. The checkpoint itself consisted of two opposing structures that served as gatehouses, the windows high and wide, each with a ceiling light fixture; between the two small, square buildings a hand-winched barrier painted with intense, light-reflecting orange fell across the road. To the right of the winch was a shoulder-high gate that opened onto the pedestrian walk.

Two soldiers in their brown uniforms with the red and green stripes were on either side of the second truck, talking wearily but animatedly with the driver. A third guard was at the rear, his attention not on the truck but on the woods beyond the bridge. He was studying the areas on both sides as a hunter might when stalking a wounded mountain cat; he stood motionless, his eyes roving, his head barely turning. He was the blond assassin. Who would suspect that a lowly soldier at a border check-point was a killer with a range of accomplishments that spanned the Mediterranean?

A fourth man had just been passed through the pedestrian gate. He was trudging slowly up the slight incline toward the midpoint of the bridge. But this man had no intention of crossing to the other side, no intention of greeting the French patrols in Ligurian patois, claiming as so many did that the air was different in *la belle France* and thank God for slender women. No, thought Michael, this crudely dressed peasant of the moun-tains with the drooping trousers and the large, heavy jacket would remain in the center shadows and, if the light was dim enough, would check his weapon, no doubt a braced, repeating, rapid-fire machine gun, its stock a steel bar clamped to the shoulders, easily concealed beneath garments. He would release the safety and be prepared to race down to the check-point at the moment of execution, ready to kill the Italian guards if they interfered, intent on firing into the body of a man coming out of the darkness to reach a woman crossing the border. This man, last seen at a center table in the country inn, was the backup support for the blond-haired killer.

It was a gauntlet, at once simple and well manned, using natural and procedural roadblocks; once the target entered, he was trapped both within and without. Two men waited with explosives and weapons at the mouth of the trap, one at its core, and a fourth at its outer rim. Well conceived, very professional.

12

The tiny glow of a cupped cigarette could be seen in the bushes diagonally across the dark road. Bad form. The agent of record was an indulgent man denying himself neither chronometers nor cigarettes during the early stages of a kill. He should be replaced; he would be replaced.

Havelock judged the angle of the cigarette, its distance to the ground; the man was crouched or sitting, not standing. Because of the density of the foliage it was impossible for the man to see the road clearly, which meant that he did not expect the car with Jenna Karas for some time yet; he was being too casual for an imminent sighting. The sergeant had said in the driveway that the soldiers had an hour to fill their kidneys; twenty minutes had passed, leaving forty. Yet not really forty. The final ten minutes of the shift would be avoided because the changing of the guard would require an exchange of information, no matter how inconsequential or pro forma. Michael had very little time to do what had to be done, to mount his own counterstrategy. First, he had to learn all he could of Rome's.

He sidestepped his way back along the edge of the foliage until the distant spill of light from the bridge was virtually blocked by the trees. He ran across the road and into the underbrush, turning left, testing every step to ensure the silence that was essential. For a brief, terrible moment he was back in the forests outside Prague, the echoes of the guns of Lidice in his ears, the sight of screaming, writhing bodies before his eyes. Then he snapped back to the immediate present, remembering who and where he was. He was the mountain cat; the most meaningful lair of his life had been soiled, corrupted by liars who were no better than those who commanded the guns at Lidice—or others who ordered "suicides" and gulags when the guns were stilled. He was in his element, in the forest, which had befriended him when he had no one to depend on, and no one understood it better.

The agent of record was sitting on a rock and, true to his indulgence, was playing with his watch, apparently pushing buttons, controlling time, master of the half-second. Havelock reached into his pocket and took out one of the items he had purchased in Monesi, a four-inch fish-scaling knife encased in a leather scabbard. He parted the branches in front of him, crouched low, then lunged.

"*You! Jesus Christl! . . . Don't!* What are you doing? Oh, my *God!*"

"You talk above a whisper, you won't have a face!" Michael's knee was rammed into the agent's throat, the razor-sharp, jagged blade pressed against the man's cheek below his left eye. "This knife cleans fish, you son of a bitch. I'll peel your skin off unless you tell me what I want to know. Right *now.*"

"You're a maniac!"

"And you're the loser, if you believe that. How long have you been here?"

"Twenty-six hours."

"Who gave the order?"

"How do I know."

"Because even an asshole like you would cover yourself! It's the first thing we learn in dispatch, isn't it? The *order!* Who gave it?"

"*Ambiguity!* The code was Ambiguity," cried the agent of record, as the scaling edge of the blade dug into his face. "I swear to Christ, that's all I know! Whoever used it was cleared by Cons Op–D.C. It can be traced back *there! Jesus,* I only know our orders came from the code! It was our clearance!"

"I'll accept it. Now, give me the step schedule. *All* of it. You picked her up in Arma di Taggia, and she's been followed ever since. How?"

"Change of vehicles up from the coast."

"Where is she now? What's the car? When's it expected?"

"A Lancia. The ETA, as of a half hour ago, barring—"

"Cut it out! *When?*"

"Seven-forty arrival. A bug was planted in the car; they'll be here at twenty of eight."

"I know you don't have a radio, a radio'd be evidence in your case. How were you contacted?"

"The phone at the inn. *Jesus!* Get that thing away from me!"

"Not yet, sane man. The schedule, the steps? Who's on the car now?"

"Two men in a beat-up truck, a quarter of a mile behind. In case you intercept, they'll hear it and be on you."

"If I don't, then what?"

"We've made arrangements. Starting at seven-thirty, everyone crossing the border gets out of his car or truck or whatever. Vehicles are searched —we spread lire—so one way or the other she'll have to show herself."

"That's when you figured I'd come out?"

"If we . . . *they* . . . don't find you first. They think they'll spot you before she gets here."

"And if they don't?"

"I don't know! It's *their* plan."

"It's *your* plan!" Havelock broke the skin on the agent's face; blood streaked down his cheek.

"Christ! Don't, *please!*"

"Tell me!"

"It's made to look like you attacked. They know you've got a weapon whether you show it or not. They nail you and pull it out if it's not in your hand. It doesn't matter; it's only for confusion. They'll run; the truck's got a good engine."

"And the car? What about the *car?*"

"It's shoved through. We just want it out of there. She's not Karas, she's a Soviet lure. We're to let Moscow have her back. The French won't argue, a guard was paid."

"Liar! Goddamned *liar!*" Michael slid the blade of the fishing knife across the agent's face to the other cheek. "Liars should be marked! You're going to be *marked, liar!*" He broke the skin with the point. "Those two nitro clowns, the ones who worked Africa—Tanzania, Mozambique, Angola—they're not here for the mountain air, *liar!*"

"Oh, *Jesus!* You're killing me!"

"Not yet, but it's entirely possible. What's their act?"

"They're just backups! Ricci brought them!"

"The Corsican?"

"I don't know . . . Corsican."

"The blond."

"*Yes!* Don't cut me! *Please*, don't *cut* me!"

"Backups? Like your friend at the table?"

"The *table?* Christ, what *are* you?"

"An observer, and you're stupid. For you, they're only guns?"

"Jesus, *yes!* That's what they *are!*"

So the liars in Washington lied even to their own in Rome. Jenna Karas did not exist. The woman in the car was to be dispatched beyond Rome's cognizance. Liars! Killers!

Why?

"Where are they?"

"I'm bleeding! I've got blood in my mouth!"

"You'll drown in it if you don't tell me. *Where?*"

"One on both sides! Twenty, thirty feet before the gate. *Christ,* I'm *dying!*"

"No, you're not dying, agent of record. You're just marked; you're finished. You're not worth surgery." Havelock switched the knife to his left hand and raised his right, his fingers straight out, taut, the muscles of the palm's underside rigid. He crashed his hand into the man's throat; he would be immobilized for no less than an hour. It would be long enough; it *had* to be.

He crawled through the underbrush, sure of his footing, at home in the friendly forest.

He found him. The man was on his knees hunched over a canvas bag —a knapsack or a small duffel; the light from the bridge was just bright enough to outline the figure and too dim to make it clearly visible if one did not know what to look for. Suddenly there was the growing sound of an engine accompanied by the clatter of a loose tailpipe or a bumper making contact with the rock-filled road. Michael spun around, holding his breath, his hand reaching toward his belt. A broken-down van came into view. A sickening feeling spreading through him, he wondered, Had the agent lied? He looked back at the explosives specialist; the man crouched lower, making no other move at all, and Havelock slowly let out his breath.

The van rattled by and stopped at the bridge. The blond killer was standing by a guard; he had obviously been instructed to observe procedure, but instead, his eyes were roaming the woods and the road below. Loud voices filled the gate area: a couple in the van was objecting to the unexpected demand to get out; apparently, they made the trip daily across the border.

Michael knew the noise was his cover; he crept forward. He was within seven feet of the man when the rear door of the van was opened and the shouted obscenities rose to a crescendo. The door was slammed shut. Havelock lunged out of the underbrush, arms extended with fingers curved for the attack.

"*Che mai . . . ?*"

The specialist had no chance to experience further shock. His head was slammed into soft earth and rock, his neck vised by Michael's right hand; he coughed spastically and went limp. Havelock turned the unconscious body over, and whipping the man's belt out of the trousers, he slipped it under the arms beneath the shoulder blades, and yanked it taut, then looped it over and knotted it. He removed the Llama automatic from his chest holster and brought the short barrel down on the man's head above the right temple, extending the time during which the expert would remain unconscious.

Michael tore into the canvas bag. It was a specialist's mobile laboratory, filled with compact blocks of dynamite and soft rolls of plastic explosive. The devices with wires extending from miniaturized clocks with radium dials were detonators, with positive and negative poles plugged into one another across the lethal powder, set to emit charges at a given minute by a twist of the fingers. There was also another type of detonating device: small, flat, circular modules, no larger than the face of a man's watch; these were without wires, having only a bar with a luminous numerical readout, and a tiny button on the right with which to set the desired time. These were designed specifically for the plastic charges, buried inside, and were accurate within five seconds over a time span of twenty-four hours. Havelock felt the casing of a single *plastique*. On the top surface was a self-sealing lip through which a module was inserted, and the bottom was marked by a flap that was to be peeled away several minutes before placement. The peeling process released an epoxy stronger than a weld; it would adhere to a second surface through earthquake and hurricane. He removed three charges and modules, and put them in his pockets. Then he crawled away, pulling the canvas bag behind him; ten feet farther into the forest he shoved it under a fallen pine branch. He looked at his watch. Twelve minutes to go.

The yelling had stopped at the bridge. The angry couple was back in the van, the guards apologizing for the crazy temporary regulations. *Burocrati!* The engine was started, a series of metallic groans preceding the full roar of an accelerator pressed to the floor. The headlights were turned back on and the orange barrier raised as the gears ground abrasively and the decrepit vehicle crept onto the bridge. The clatter was louder now, actually deafening as the van rumbled across the surface of the bridge ridged with narrow, open metal struts. The noise echoed below and above, filling the air with an unrelenting staccato that made one of the guards wince and put both hands to his ears. The clatter, the headlights: the first was diversion; the second, distraction. If he could get into a decent line of sight, he might—just possibly—eliminate his backup executioner; he would not make the attempt unless the odds were his.

The burly man in the heavy jacket would hug the rail, leaning over, perhaps, to be as inconspicuous as possible in the glare of the headlights, a weary pedestrian with too much wine in him. No single shot could be counted on; no man was that accurate at eighty-plus feet. But the magnum was a powerful weapon, the permanently attached silencer designed for zero sighting as much as any handgun could be. Therefore a marksman firing five or six rounds at a given target would have the probabilities on his side, but only if the bullets were fired in what amounted to a single burst; each instant of separation was a margin for error. It would require a steady arm supported by a solid object, a view undistorted by light and shadow. It would not hurt to get closer, either.

With his concentration split equally between the overgrowth in front of him and the blond assassin, whom he could see through the trees on his left, he made his way as swiftly, as silently, as he could to the edge of the river gorge.

A flashlight beam shot out behind him. He scrambled behind a huge boulder, sliding partially down the smooth surface and catching his foot on a protruding ridge. His sanctuary was the top of a jagged wall of rock and bush that led to the roiling waters several hundred feet below. His vision at the far side was clear; he stared at the end of the beam of light. Some part of the foliage he had raced through had snapped, and the blond killer was standing motionless with the flashlight in his hand. Gradually his attention waned: an animal or a night bird, he judged; there was no human being to be seen.

Above, the clattering truck neared the midpoint of the bridge. There he was! Less than seventy feet away, he leaned over the rail, his head huddled deep in the collar of his heavy jacket. The clanging was thunderous now, the echoes full, as the backup executioner was caught in the glare of the headlights. Havelock spun around on the boulder, steadying his feet on the flanking rocks. There would be no more than a second to make the decision, no more than two or three to fire the magnum during the short space of time when the rear of the van would block the view from the booths at the entrance. Full of uncertainty, Michael pulled the heavy weapon from his belt and braced his arm against the boulder, his feet anchored by pressure, his left hand gripping his right wrist to steady the barrel that was aimed diagonally above. He had to be *sure*; he could not risk the night and everything the night stood for. But if the odds were his . . .

They *were*. As the hood of the van passed the man he stood up, now silhouetted in the back light, a large immobile target. Havelock fired four rounds in rapid succession in concert with the deafening clatter on the bridge. The support killer arched backward, then sank down into the shadows of the solid steel barricade of the pedestrian walk.

The clanging receded as the van reached the far side of the bridge. There was no orange barrier across the entrance on the French side: francs had been paid; the two guards leaning against a gatehouse wall smoked their cigarettes. However, another sound intruded; it came from behind, quite far behind, down the road from Monesi. Michael curved his spine into the surface of the rock and slid back into the edge of the woods, crouching instantly, shoving the warm magnum under his belt. He glanced through the trees at the checkpoint; the two authentic soldiers in the nearest gatehouse on the right could be seen beyond the large glass windows, nodding at each other as if counting something in their hands —lire had reached the second level. The blond impostor was outside, an outsider as far as the current transaction was concerned; he was staring down the road, squinting in the dim light.

He raised his hand to the midpoint of his chest and shook his wrist twice—an innocuous gesture, a man restoring circulation to a forearm strained by carrying too much weight too recently. It was a signal.

The killer brought his hand down to his right hip, and it took no imagination to realize he was releasing the snap on his holster while keeping his concentration on the road below. Havelock crept rapidly through the woods until he reached the unconscious figure of the explosives specialist. The sound of a motor grew louder, joined now by a faint, bass-toned hum in the farther distance—a second vehicle steadily increasing its speed. Michael parted the thick branches of an overhanging pine and looked to his left. Several hundred yards down the road the glistening grille of a large automobile could be seen, reflecting the light from the bridge. It swung into the curve; the car was a Lancia. It was Jenna! Havelock imposed a control over his mind and body he had not thought was possible. The next few minutes would bring into play everything he had learned—that no one should ever have to learn—since he was a child in Prague, every skill he had absorbed from the shadow world in which he had lived so long.

The Lancia sedan drew nearer, and sharp bolts of pain shot through Michael's chest as he stared at the windshield. Jenna was not there. Instead, two men could be seen in the wash of the dashboard, the driver smoking, his companion apparently talking garrulously, waving his hands for emphasis. Then the driver turned his head sideways, addressing a remark to someone in the back seat. The Lancia began to slow down; it was within two hundred feet of the checkpoint.

The blond impostor at the orange barrier turned and walked quickly to the gatehouse booth; he knocked on the window, then pointed to the approaching vehicle and then to himself. He was the eager recruit telling his veteran superiors that he could handle the immediate assignment. The two soldiers looked up, annoyed at the intrusion, perhaps wondering if the intruder had seen money changing hands; they nodded, waving him away.

Instead of leaving immediately, the assassin employed by Rome reached into his pocket and took out an object while moving unobtrusively toward the closed door of the booth. He reached down and inserted the object into the frame below the window, the movements of his shoulders indicating that he used considerable force. Havelock tried to imagine what it was, what the killer was doing. And then it was clear; the door of the booth was a sliding door, but it would not slide now. The man called Ricci had wedged a thin steel plate with small angled spikes into the space between frame and panel; the door was jammed. The more force that was used to open it, the deeper the tiny spikes would embed themselves, until all movement would be impossible. The two soldiers were trapped inside, and as with checkpoints everywhere—no matter how minor—the booth was sturdily constructed with thick glass in the windows. Yet there was a fallacy: a simple call to the barracks somewhere on the other side would bring assistance. Michael peered through the dim light above the gatehouse, and saw there was no fallacy. Dangling from the limb of a tree was a heavy-gauge telephone wire; it had been severed. The killers from Rome controlled the checkpoint.

The blond man strode to the metal plank that separated the road from the entrance to the bridge, assumed a military stance—the feet apart, the left hand at his waist, the right held up in the "Halt" position—and faced the oncoming sedan.

The Lancia came to a stop. The front windows were rolled down and passports were offered by the two men in the front seat. The killer walked to the driver's window and spoke quietly—too quietly for Havelock to hear the words—while looking past the driver into the rear seat.

The driver was explaining something and turned to his companion for confirmation. The second man leaned across the seat, nodding his head, then shaking it, as if in sorrow. The false guard stood back and spoke louder, with a soldier's authority.

"Regrets, signori and signora," he said in Italian. "Tonight's regulations require that all passengers step out of their automobiles while they are examined."

"But we were assured that we could proceed across into Col des Moulinets as rapidly as possible, *Caporale,*" protested the driver, raising his voice. "The dear woman buried her husband less than two hours ago. She is distraught. . . . Here are her papers, her passport. Ours also. Everything is in order, I can assure you. We are expected for an eight o'clock mass. She is from a fine family, a Franco-Italian marriage tragically ended by a dreadful accident. The mayors of both Monesi and Moulinets were at the funeral—"

"Regrets, signore," repeated the killer. "Please, step out. There is a truck behind you and it is not right for you to hold up the line."

Havelock turned his head, looking at the run-down truck with the powerful engine. There was no one inside. Instead, the two men were on opposite shoulders of the road, dressed in mountain clothes, their eyes scanning the country road and the woods, their hands in their pockets. Backups for backups, support for support. The border belonged to the unit from Rome, secure in its knowledge that no one could pass through without being seen, and if the target was seen, the target would die.

And if he was not seen? Would the secondary order hold? Would the secondary target—the bait—be eliminated in Col des Moulinets because she was no longer feasible bait? The answer was as painful for Michael to admit to himself as it was self-evident. She had to be. She did not exist, her existence was too dangerous for the liars who gave orders to strategists and embassies alike. The unit would return to Rome without its primary kill, the only loser an agent of record who had not been apprised of the secondary target.

The tall, slender figure in black climbed out of the car—a woman in mourning, an opaque veil of black lace falling from her wide-brimmed hat and covering her face. Havelock stared; the pain in his chest was almost unbearable. She was no more than twenty feet away, yet the gulf was filled with death, her death to follow shortly whether his came or not.

"My regrets again, signora," said the killer in uniform. "It will be necessary for you to remove your hat."

"Good Lord, *why?*" asked Jenna Karas, her voice low, controlled, but with a trace of a throb, which could be a sign of grief as well as of fear.

"Merely to match your face with the photograph on the passport, signora. Surely you know it's customary."

Jenna slowly lifted the veil from her face, and then the hat from her head. The skin that was so often bronzed by the sun was chalk-white in the dim, eerie light of the bridge; her delicate features were taut, the high cheekbones masklike, and her long blond hair was pulled back and knotted severely. Michael watched, breathing slowly, silently, a part of him wanting to cry out while another desperately, foolishly, placed them back in another time . . . lying together on the grass overlooking the Moldau, walking down the Ringstrasse, holding hands as children might, laughing at the irony of two deep-cover agents behaving like human beings. . . . In bed, holding each other, telling themselves they would somehow break out of their movable prison.

"The signora has lovely hair," said the blond killer, with a smile that denied his rank. "My mother would approve. We, too, are from the north."

"Thank you. May I replace my veil, *Caporale?* I am in mourning."

"In one moment, please," replied Ricci, holding up the passport but not looking at it. Instead, he was glancing everywhere at once without moving his head, his anger obviously mounting. Jenna's escorts stood motionless by the car, avoiding the soldier's eyes.

Behind the Lancia, on either side of the run-down truck, the support assassins were tense, peering into the shadows, then repeatedly looking in the vicinity of the country inn, anticipation on their faces. It was as though they all expected him to materialize out of the darkness, to appear suddenly, walking either casually or resolutely up the path from the inn, or from behind the thick trunk of a pine tree on the edge of the road, calling out to the woman by the automobile. It was what they expected; these were the moments they had calculated as the crisis span—the target would be found now if he had not been found before. And from their viewpoint, it had to happen. Everything was clean, nothing wrinkled. The target had not crossed over the bridge within the past twenty-six hours —and if he had crossed over prior to minus-twenty-six, it would have been stupid. There was no way he could know which vehicle carried Jenna Karas or which road it would take through Col des Moulinets. Beyond these deductions, there was no reason for the man marked for dispatch to know there was a unit from Rome at the checkpoint. It would happen now, or it would not happen.

The tension at the scene was stretched to the breaking point. It was compounded by the two soldiers inside the gatehouse booth who were trying to open the door and shouting through the windows, their voices muted by the thick glass. Nothing was lost on Jenna Karas or her paid escorts; the driver had edged toward the door, his companion toward the border of the road and the woods. A trap was in the making, but for reasons they could not understand, it was clearly not a trap for them; if it were, they would have been summarily taken.

Havelock knew that everything now was timing: the eternal wait until the moment came, and then that instant when instinct told him to move. He could not rearrange the odds to favor him, but he could reduce them against him. Against Jenna.

"Finirà in niente," said the uniformed killer, just loud enough to be heard; he brought his hand to his waist and shook his wrist twice as he had done before, giving a signal as he had given it before.

Michael reached into his pocket and took out a packet of plastic explosive and a module. The luminous readout was at 0000; he pressed the timer button delicately until he had the figures he wanted, then inserted the module into the self-sealing lip. He had checked and rechecked his position in the darkness; he knew the least obstructed path and used it now. He snaked his way eight feet into the forest, observed the outlines of the branches against the night sky, and threw the packet into the air. The moment it was out of his hand, he scrambled back toward the road, arcing to his left, now parallel to the run-down truck, ten feet from the backup killer dressed in mountain clothes. He had two shells left in the magnum; it was possible he would have to use both before he cared to, but the muted sounds were preferable to explosions from the Llama automatic. Seconds now.

"Regrets again for the delay, signora and signori," said the assassin sent by Rome, walking away from the Lancia toward the winch that operated the orange barrier. "Procedures must be followed. You may return to your automobile now, all is in order." The blond man passed the windows of the booth, ignoring the angry shouts of the soldiers inside; he had no time to waste on minor players. A plan had failed, a finely tuned strategy had been an exercise in futility; anger and frustration were second only to his professional instincts to get out of the area. There was only one chore left to finish, which an agent of record was to know nothing about. He raised the orange barrier and immediately stepped back out into the center of the entrance, blocking passage. He removed a notebook and a pencil from his pocket—the border guard attending to his last procedure, taking down the numbers of a vehicle's license. It, too, was a signal.

Only seconds.

Jenna and her two escorts climbed back in the car, the faces of the two men betraying bewilderment and cautious relief. The doors slammed shut, and at the sound a short, stocky man came slowly out of the foliage across the road near the trunk of the Lancia. He walked directly to the rear of the automobile, but his attention was not on the car but on the woods beyond the road. He raised his right hand to his waist, and shook his wrist twice, perplexed at the lack of response to his signal. He stood for a moment, his frown conveying minor alarm but not panic. Men in his business understood the problems of equipment malfunction; they were sudden and deadly, which was why the two specialists traveled as a team. He turned his head quickly toward the checkpoint; the blond assassin was impatient. The man knelt down, took an object out of his left hand and transferred it to his right. He reached under the car, the area directly beneath the fuel tank.

There were no seconds left. The target could not wait.

Havelock had the man in the sights of his magnum. He fired; the specialist screamed as his body crashed up into the metal of the fender, the packet flying out of his hand as his arm whipped back; the bullet had lodged in his spine and his body arched in searing pain. Though in agony, the killer turned toward the source of the explosive spit, pulled an automatic from his pocket and leveled it instantly. Frantically Michael rolled out of the area until the dense underbrush stopped his movement. The gunshots echoed everywhere, bullets spraying the ground, as Havelock raised the magnum and fired its last round. The muffled report was followed by a loud gasp from the man by the truck as his neck was blown away.

"Dov'è? Dov'è?" shouted the blond assassin at the checkpoint, racing around the Lancia.

The explosion filled the air, the blinding light of the detonated *plas-*

tique bathing the darkness of the woods, echoing throughout the mountains. The assassin lunged to the ground and, aiming at nothing, began shooting at everything. The Lancia's engine roared, its wheels spun, and the sedan surged onto the bridge. Jenna was *free*.

Seconds more. He had to do it.

Michael got to his feet and raced out of the forest, the empty magnum in his belt, the Llama in his hand. The assassin saw him in the light of the spreading flames in the woods; the blond man got up on his knees and, supporting his right arm with his left, aimed at Havelock. He fired rapidly, repeatedly; the bullets shrieked in ricochets and snapped the air above and to the right of Michael as he lurched for the cover of the truck. But it was no cover; he heard the scraping, then the footsteps behind him, and whirled around, his back against the door. At the rear of the truck the killer-driver came, crouching—the movements of a professional cornering a quarry at close range—as he raised his weapon and fired. Havelock dropped to the ground at first sighting and returned two shots; feeling the ice-like pain in his shoulder, he knew he had been hit, but not how seriously. The driver rolled spastically off the edge of the road; if he was not gone, he would be soon.

Suddenly, the dirt exploded in front of Michael; the blond assassin was free to resume firing now that his associate was finished. Havelock dived to his right, then plunged under the truck, crawling in panic to the other side. *Seconds. Only seconds left.* He sprang to his feet and sidestepped to the door. The crowd of frightened people down at the inn were shouting at one another, running in all directions. There was so little time; men would race out of barracks, perhaps were racing even now. He reached for the handle and yanked the door open; he saw what he wanted to see: the keys were in the ignition as he had dared to think they would be. The unit from Rome had been in control, and control meant being able to get away from the execution ground instantly.

He leaped up into the seat, his head low, his fingers working furiously. He turned the key; the engine caught, and at the first sound, gunfire came from the road ahead and bullets embedded themselves in metal. There was a pause, and Michael understood; the assassin was reloading his gun. *These were the crucial seconds.* He switched on the headlights; like the motor, they were powerful—blinding. Up ahead, the blond man was crouched off the shoulder of the road, slamming a clip into the base of his automatic. Havelock jammed the clutch, pulled the gearshift, and pressed the accelerator to the floor.

The heavy truck jolted forward, its tires screeching over rock and dirt.

Michael spun the wheel to his right as the engine roared with the gathering speed. Rapid gunshots; the windshield was punctured and a web of cracks spread throughout the glass as bullets screamed into the cab. Havelock raised his head just high enough to see what he had to see; the killer was centered in the glare of the headlights. Michael kept his course until he felt and heard the impact, accompanied by a scream of fury, which was abruptly cut short as the assassin lurched and twisted, but was held in place, his legs crushed under the heavy cleated tires of the truck. Havelock spun the wheel again, now to his left, back into the road proper; he sped past the two gatehouses onto the bridge, noting as he raced by that the two guards were prone on the floor of the booth.

There was chaos on the French side, but no barrier to block his way. Soldiers were running to and from the checkpoint, shouting orders at no one and everyone; inside a lighted booth four guards were huddled together, one screaming into a telephone. The road into Col des Moulinets bore to the left off the bridge, then curved right, heading straight into a silhouetted patchwork of small wood-framed houses, set close together, with sloping roofs, typical of a thousand villages in this part of the Alps. He entered a narrow cobblestone street; several pedestrians jumped onto the narrow pavement, startled as much by the sound as by the sight of the heavy Italian truck.

He saw the red lights . . . the wide, rear lights of the Lancia. It was far in the distance; it turned into a street— God only knew what street, there were so many. Col des Moulinets was one of those villages where every long-ago path and pasture bypass had been paved with stone; some had been converted into streets, others merely into quaint alleyways, barely wide enough for produce carts. But he would know it when he came to it; he *had* to.

The intersecting streets grew wider, the houses and shops set farther back; narrow pavements became sidewalks, and more and more villagers were seen strolling past the lighted storefronts. The Lancia was nowhere; it had disappeared.

"Pardon! Ou est l'aéroport?" he yelled out the window to an elderly couple about to step off the curb into the cobblestone street.

"Airport?" said the old man in French, the word itself pronounced in an accent that was more Italian than Gallic. "There is no airport in Col des Moulinets, monsieur. You can take the southern roadway down to Cap Martin."

"There *is* an airport near the village, I'm sure of it," cried Havelock, trying to control his anxiety. "A friend, a very *good* friend, told me he was flying into Col des Moulinets. I'm to meet him. I'm late."

"Your friend meant Cap Martin, monsieur."

"Perhaps not," called out a younger man who was leaning against the doorframe of a shop closed for the evening. "There is no real airport, monsieur, but there is an airfield fifteen, twenty kilometers north on the road to Tenda. It's used by the rich who have estates in Roquebillière and Breil."

"That's it! What's the fastest way?"

"Take your next right, then right again back three streets to Rue Maritimes. Turn left; it will lead you into the mountain auto route. Fifteen, eighteen kilometers north."

"Thank you."

Time was a racing montage of light and shadow, filled with peopled streets and leaping figures, small interfering cars and glaring headlights, gradually replaced by fewer buildings, fewer people, fewer streetlamps; he had reached the outskirts of the village. If the police had been alerted by the panicked border guards, he had eluded them by the odds of a small force versus a large area. Minutes later—how many he would never know —he was tearing though the darkness of the Maritimes countryside, the rolling hills everywhere that were introductions to the mountains beyond, barricades to be negotiated with all the speed the powerful truck could manage. And as the grinding gears strained and the tires under him screamed to a crescendo, he saw the silhouettes of paddle wheels; like the hills, they were everywhere, alongside houses by mountain streams and rivulets, slowly turning, a certain majesty in their never-ending move-ments—proof again that time and nature were constant. In a strange way, Michael needed the reaffirmation; he was losing his mind!

There were no lights on the auto route, no red specks in the darkness. The Lancia was nowhere to be seen. Was he even going in the right direction? Or had anxiety warped his senses? So close and yet so terribly far away, one gulf traversed, one more to leap. Traversed? We said it better in Prague. *Přejezd* said it better.

Miluji vás, má drahá. We understand these words, Jenna. We do not need the language of liars. We never should have learned it. *Don't listen to the liars! They neutralized us; now they want to kill us. They have to because I know they're there. I know, and so will you.*

A searchlight! Its beam was sweeping the night sky. Beyond the nearest hills, diagonally up ahead on the left. Somewhere the road would turn; somewhere minutes away was an airfield and a plane—and Jenna.

The second hill was steep, the other side of it steeper, with curves; he held the wheel with all his strength, careening into each turn. *Lights.* Wide white beams in front, two red dots behind. It was the Lancia! A mile, two miles ahead and below; it was impossible to tell, but the field was there. Parallel lines of yellow ground lights crossed each other at forty-plus degree points; the valley winds had been studied for maximum lift. The airfield was in a valley, sufficiently wide and long for small jets as well as prop aircraft—*used by the rich who have estates in Roquebillière and Breil.*

Havelock kept the accelerator on the floor, his left foot grazing the brake for those instants when balance was in jeopardy. The road leveled out and became a flat track that circled the fenced-off airfield. Within the enormous compound were the vivid reflections of glistening wings and fuselages; perhaps a dozen stationary planes were moored to the ground in varying positions off the runways—the yachts of yesterday had been replaced by silver tubes that sailed through the skies. The ten-foot-high hurricane fence was strung with barbed wire across the top and angled an additional four feet inside. The rich of Roquebillière and Breil cared for their airborne possessions. Such a fence—a double mile in length—carried a price of several hundred thousand dollars; and that being the case, would there be a security gate and guards somewhat more attentive than the French and Italian military?

There were. He screeched into the entrance roadway. The heavy ten-foot gate was closing three hundred feet in front of him. Inside, the Lancia was racing across the field. Suddenly its lights were extinguished; somewhere within the expanse of grass and asphalt its driver had spotted a plane. Lights would reveal markings, and markings were traces; if he could see the Lancia's headlights several miles away in the darkness of the valley, his, too, could be seen. There were only seconds and half-seconds now, each minuscule movement of a clock narrowing the final gulf or widening it.

While gripping the wheel, he jammed the palms of both hands on the rim of the truck's horn, hammering out the only alarm code that came to him: *Mayday, Mayday, Mayday!* He repeated it over and over again as he sped down the entrance drive toward the closing gate.

Two uniformed guards were inside the fence, one pushing the thick metal crossbar of the gate, the other standing by the latch, prepared to receive the sliding bar and insert the clamp. As the gate reached the three-quarter mark, both guards stared through the wire mesh at the powerful truck bearing down on them; the blaring series of notes was not lost on them. Their terrified faces showed they had no intention of staying in the path of the wild vehicle about to crash into their post. The guard at the crossbar released it and ran to his left; the gate swung back partially —only partially—when he withdrew his grip. The man by the latch scrambled to his right, diving into the grass and the protection of the extended fence.

The impact came, the truck ripping the gate away, twisting it up off its hinges and smashing it into the small booth, shattering glass and severing an electrical wire that erupted in sparks and static. Michael raced the truck onto the field, his wounded shoulder pitched in pain; the truck careened sharply, narrowly missing two adjacent planes parked in the shadows of a single wide hangar. He spun the wheel to his left, sending the truck in the direction the Lancia had been heading less than a minute ago.

Nothing. Absolutely *nothing!* Where was it? Where *was* it?

A flicker of light. Movement—at the far end of the field, beyond the glowing yellow lines of the north runway, slightly above the farthest ground row. The cabin of a plane had been opened, an interior light snapped briefly on, then instantly turned off. He whipped the wheel to the right—blood from his wrenched wounded shoulder spreading through his shirt—and raced diagonally across the enormous compound; heavy, weatherproof bulbs exploded under the tires as he sped toward the now darkened area where seconds ago there had been the dim flash of light.

There it was! Not a jet, but a twin-engine, single-wing, its propellers suddenly revving furiously, flames belching from its exhausts. It was not on the runway but beyond the glow of the parallel lines of yellow lights; the pilot was about to taxi into the takeoff position. But he was not moving now; he was holding!

The Lancia. It was behind and to the right of the plane. Again, a light! Not from the aircraft now, but from the Lancia itself. Doors opened; figures leaped out, dashing for the plane. The cabin door, another light! For an instant Michael considered ramming the fuselage or crashing into the nearest wing, but it could be a tragic error. If he struck a fuel tank, the aircraft would blow up in seconds. He swerved the heavy truck to the right, then to the left, and screeching to a stop yards in front of the plane, he leaped out.

"Jenna! *Jenna! Poslouchám já! Stůj! Listen to me!*"

She was climbing on board, pushed up the steps by the driver of the Lancia, who followed her inside and closed the door. He ran, oblivious to everything but her; he had to *stop* her! The plane spun in place like a grotesque, dark cormorant. Its path was free of the Lancia!

The blow came out of the shadows, muffled and at the same time magnified by the furious winds of the propeller's wash. His head snapped back as his legs buckled, blood matting the hair above his right temple. He was on his knees, supporting himself with his hands, staring up at the plane, at the window of the moving plane, and he could *not move!* The cabin lights remained on for several seconds and he saw her face in the glass, her eyes staring back at him. It was a sight he would remember for as long as he lived . . . if he lived. A second blow with a blunt instrument was delivered to the back of his neck.

He could not think about the terrible sight now, about *her* now! He could hear the sirens screaming across the field, see the glare of search-lights shooting over the runway, catching the glistening metal of the plane as it sped down between the yellow lights. The man who had struck him twice was running toward the Lancia; he had to *move!* He had to move *now,* or he would not be permitted to live, permitted ever to see her again. He struggled to his feet as he pulled the Llama automatic from under his jacket.

He fired twice above the roof of the sedan; the man leaping into the seat could have killed him moments ago; he would not kill that man now. His hands were too unsteady, the flashing, sweeping lights too bewilder-ing to ensure inflicting only a wound. But he *had* to have the car. He fired again, the bullet ricocheting off the metal as he approached the window.

"Get out or you're dead!" he shouted, gripping the door handle. "You heard what I said! Get *out!*" Havelock yanked the man by the cloth of his coat and pulled him, propelling him onto the grass. There was no time for a dozen questions he wanted to ask. He had to escape! He slid behind the wheel and slammed the door shut; the motor was running.

For the next forty-five seconds he crisscrossed the airfield at enormous speeds, evading the airfield's security police by weaving in and out of searchlight beams. A dozen times he nearly crashed into stationary aircraft before reaching the demolished gate. He raced through, not seeing the road, functioning only on nerves and instinct.

He could not shut out the terrible sight of Jenna's face in the window of the moving plane. In Rome her face had shown raw fear and confusion. Moments ago there had been something else; it was in her eyes.

Cold, immaculate hatred.

13

He drove southwest to Provence, then due south toward the coast, to the small city of Cagnes-sur-Mer. He had worked the northern Mediterranean for years and knew a doctor between Cagnes and Antibes; he needed help. He had ripped the sleeve of his shirt and tied a knot around the wound in his shoulder, but it did not prevent the loss of blood. His entire chest was soaked, the cloth sticking to his skin, and there was the sweet-acrid odor that he knew only too well. His neck was merely bruised—a paramedical opinion that in no way diminished the pain—but the blow to his head required stitches; the slightest graze would reopen the laceration that was sealed with barely coagulated blood.

He needed other help, too, and Dr. Henri Salanne would provide it. He had to reach Matthias; to delay any longer was asinine. Specific identities could be traced from orders, from a code name, Ambiguity; there was enough information. Surface evidence of the massive conspiracy was clear from Jenna's having survived Costa Brava—when she had been officially recorded as dead—and his own condemnation as "beyond salvage." The first Matthias would accept from his *přítele*, the second could be confirmed from sealed black-bordered directives in the files of Consular Operations. Granted the whys were beyond Havelock's reach, but not the facts—they existed, and Matthias could act on them. And while the Secretary of State acted, Michael had to get to Paris as quickly as possible. It would not be simple; every airport, highway and train station in Provence and the Maritimes would be watched, and Matthias could do nothing about it. Time and communications were on the side of the liars. Issuing covert orders was far easier then rescinding them; they spread like a darkening web of ink on soft paper, as the recipients disappeared, each wanting credit for the kill.

Within an hour—if it had not happened by now—Rome would be apprised of the events at Col des Moulinets. Telephones and little-used radio frequencies would be employed to send out the word: *The man "beyond salvage" is loose; he can cost us too much that's valuable, including time and our lives. All network personnel are on alert; use every source, every weapon available. Zero area: Col des Moulinets. Radius: Maximum two hours' travel, reported to be wounded. Last known vehicles: A nondescript farm truck with a powerful engine, and a Lancia sedan. Find him. Kill him.*

No doubt the liars on the Potomac had already reached Salanne but as with so many in the shadow world, there were hidden confidences—things in and of his past—that those who cleared payrolls in Washington or Rome or Paris knew nothing about. And for drones such as Dr. Henri Salanne, only certain men in the field who had been on a given scene at a given time knew them, and stored away their names for future personal use should the necessity ever arise. There was even a vague morality about this practice, for more often than not the incriminating information or the events themselves were the result of a temporary crisis or a weakness that did not require that the man or the woman be destroyed—or killed.

With Salanne, Havelock had been there when it happened—to be precise, eleven hours after the act took place, time enough to alter the consequences. The doctor had sold out an American agent in Cannes who coordinated a small fleet of oceangoing pleasure craft for the purpose of monitoring Soviet naval positions in the sector. Salanne had sold him for money to a KGB informant, and Michael had not understood; neither money nor betrayal was a motive that made sense where the doctor was concerned. It took only one low-key confrontation to learn the truth, and it was a truth—or a juxtaposition of truths—as old as the grotesque world in which they all lived. The gentle if somewhat cynical middle-aged doctor was a compulsive gambler; it was the primary reason why years ago a brilliant young surgeon from L'Hôpital de Paris had sought out a practice in the Monte Carlo triangle. His credentials and references were honored in Monaco, which was a good thing, but his losses at the casino were not.

Enter the American, whose cover was that of a yacht-owning jet-setter, and who spent the taxpayers' money cautiously but obnoxiously at the tables. His obnoxiousness, however, did not end at chemin de fer; he was a womanizer with a preference for young girls, an image, he rationalized, that did nothing to harm his cover. One of the girls he brought to his busy bed was Salanne's daughter, Claudie, an impressionable child who suffered a severe depression when nothing further came of the relationship.

The Soviets were in the market; the doctor's losses could be covered, and a preying *coureur* removed from the scene. *Pourquoi pas?* The act had taken place.

Enter Havelock, who had traced the betrayal, got the American out before the boats were identified, and confronted Henri Salanne. He never reported his findings; there was no point, and the doctor understood the conditions of his "pardon." Never again . . . and an obligation was assumed.

Michael found a telephone booth at a deserted corner in the downtown district of Cagnes-sur-Mer. He braced himself with difficulty, and got out of the car, clutching his jacket around him as he stood up; he was cold, bleeding still. Inside the booth, he pulled out the Llama from his holster, smashed the overhead light, and studied the dial in the shadows. After what seemed like an interminable wait, he was given Salanne's number by Antibes information.

"*Votre fille, Claudie, comment va-t-elle?*" he asked quietly.

There was dead silence. Finally the doctor spoke, his use of English deliberate. "I wondered if I'd hear from you. If it *is* you, they say you may be hurt."

"I am."

"How badly?"

"I need cleaning up and a few sutures. That's all, I think."

"Nothing internal?"

"Not that I can tell."

"I hope you're right. A hospital would be in questionable taste right now. I suspect all emergency rooms in the area are being watched."

Michael was suddenly alarmed. "What about you?"

"There's only so much manpower. They won't waste it on someone they assume would rather see ten patients die on an operating table than be cut off from their generosity."

"Would you?"

"Let's halve it," said Salanne, laughing softly. "In spite of my habits, my conscience couldn't take more than five." The doctor paused but not long enough for Havelock to speak. "However, there could be a problem. They say you're driving a medium-sized truck—"

"I'm not."

"Or possibly a dark gray Lancia sedan," continued Salanne.

"I am."

"Get rid of it, or get away from it."

Michael looked at the large automobile outside the booth. The engine had overheated; steam was escaping from the radiator, vapor rising and diffusing under the light of the streetlamp. All this was calling attention to the car. "I'm not sure how far I can walk," he said to the doctor.

"Loss of blood?"

"Enough so I can feel it."

"*Merde!* Where are you?"

Havelock told him. "I've been here before, but I can't remember much."

"Disorientation or absence of impressions?"

"What difference does it make?"

"Blood."

"I feel dizzy, if that's what you mean."

"It is. I think I know the corner. Is there a *bijouterie* on the other side? Called something and Son?"

Michael squinted through glass beyond the Lancia. "Ariale et Fils?" he said, reading the raised white letters of a sign above a dark storefront across the street. "'Fine Jewelry, Watches, Diamonds.' Is that it?"

"Ariale, of course. I've had good nights, too, you know. They're much more reasonable than the thieves in the Spélugues. Now then, several shops north of Ariale is an alley that leads to a small parking lot behind the stores. I'll get there as fast as I can, twenty minutes at the outside. I don't care to race through the streets under the circumstances."

"Please don't."

"Nor should you. Walk slowly, and if there are automobiles parked there, crawl under one and lie flat on your back. When you see me arrive, strike a match. As little movement as possible, is that understood?"

"Understood."

Havelock left the booth, but before crossing the street, he opened his jacket, pulled the blood-soaked shirt out of his belt and squeezed it until drops of dark red appeared on the pavement. Leaning over, he took a dozen rapid steps straight ahead past the corner building into the shadows, scuffing the blood with the soles of his shoes, streaking it backwards; anyone studying the Lancia and the immediate area would assume he had run down the intersecting street. He then stopped, awkwardly removed both shoes, and sidestepped carefully to the curb, pulling his jacket around him. He reversed direction and hobbled across the intersection to the side of the street that housed Ariale et Fils.

He lay on his back, matches in his hand, staring up at the black grease-laden underside of a Peugeot facing the parking-lot wall, keeping his mind alert with an exercise in the improbable. Proposition: The owner returned with a companion, and both got into the car. What should Michael do and how would he do it without being seen? The answer to the first was to roll out—obviously—but on which side?

Twin headlight beams pierced the entrance of the parking lot, cutting short his ruminations. The headlights were turned off ten feet inside the unmanned gate; the car stopped, the motor still running. It was Salanne, telling him he had arrived. Havelock crawled to the edge of the Peugeot's chassis and struck a match. Seconds later the doctor was above him, and within minutes they were driving south on the road toward Antibes, Michael in the back seat, angled in the corner, legs stretched, out of sight.

"If you recall," said Salanne, "there is a side entrance to my house, reached by the driveway. It leads directly to my office and the examining room."

"I remember. I've used it."

"I'll go inside first, just to make certain."

"What are you going to do if there are cars in front?"

"I'd rather not think about it."

"Maybe you should."

"Actually, I have. There's a colleague of mine in Villefranche, an elderly man, above reproach. I'd prefer not to involve him, of course."

"I appreciate what you're doing," said Havelock, looking at the back of the doctor's head in the coruscating light, noting that the hair touched with gray only a year or so ago was practically white now.

"I appreciate what you did for me," replied Salanne softly. "I assumed a debt. I never thought otherwise."

"I know. That's pretty cold, isn't it?"

"Not at all. You asked how Claudie was, so let me tell you. She is happy and with child and married to a young intern at the hospital in Nice. Two years ago she nearly took her own life. How much is that worth to me, my friend?"

"I'm glad to hear it."

"Besides, what they say about you is preposterous."

"What do they say?"

"That you are insane, a dangerous psychopath who threatens us all with exposure—certain death from roving jackals of the KGB—if you are allowed to live."

"And that's preposterous to you?"

"As of an hour ago, *mon ami méchant.* You remember the man in Cannes who was involved with my indiscretion?"

"The KGB informant?"

"Yes. Would you say he's knowledgeable?"

"As any in the sector," replied Havelock. "To the point where we left him alone and tried to feed him disinformation. What about him?"

"When the word came through about you, I rang him up—from a public booth, of course. I wanted confirmation of this new, incredible judgment, so I asked him how soft the market was, how flexible in terms of price for the American consular attaché whose origins were in Prague. What he told me was both startling and specific."

"Which was?" asked Michael, leaning forward in pain.

"There is no market for you, no price—high, low or otherwise. You are a leper and Moscow wants no part of your disease. You are not to be touched, even acknowledged. So whom could you expose in this manner?" The doctor shook his head. "Rome lied, which means that someone in Washington lied to Rome. 'Beyond salvage'? Beyond *belief.*"

"Would you repeat those words to someone?"

"And by doing so, call for my own execution? There are limits to my gratitude."

"You won't be identified, my word on it."

"Who would believe you without naming a source he could check?"

"Anthony Matthias."

"*Matthias?*" cried Salanne, whipping his head to the side, gripping the wheel, his eyes straining to stay on the road. "Why would *he* . . . ?"

"Because you're with me. Again, my word on it."

"A man like Matthias is beyond one's well-intentioned word, my friend. He asks and you must tell him."

"Only if you cleared it."

"Why would he believe you? Believe *me?*"

"You just said it. The attaché whose origins were in Prague. So were his."

"I see," said the doctor pensively, his head turned front again. "I never made the connection, never even thought about it."

"It's complicated, and I don't talk about it. We go back a long time, our families go back."

"I must think. To deal with such a man puts everything in another perspective, doesn't it? We are ordinary men doing our foolish things; he is not ordinary. He lives on another plane. The Americans have a phrase for what you ask."

"A different ballgame?"

"That's the one."

"It's not. It's the same game, and it's rigged against him. Against all of us."

There were no strange automobiles within a four-block radius of Salanne's house, no need to travel to Villefranche and an elderly physician above reproach. Inside the examining room, Havelock's clothes were removed, his body sponged, and the wounds sutured, the doctor's petite, somewhat uncommunicative wife assisting Salanne.

"You should rest for several days," said the Frenchman, after his wife had left, taking Michael's garments to wash out what she could and burn the irrecoverable. "If there are no ruptures, the dressing will hold for five, perhaps six days, then it should be changed. But you should rest."

"I can't," answered Havelock, grimacing, raising himself into a sitting position on the table, his legs over the edge.

"It hurts to move even those few inches, doesn't it?"

"Only the shoulder, that's all."

"You've lost blood, you know that."

"I've lost more, I know that, too." Michael paused, studying Salanne. "Do you have a dictating machine in your office?"

"Of course. Letters and reports—medical reports—must be dealt with long after nurses and receptionists have gone home."

"I want you to show me how to use it, and I want you to listen. It won't take long, and you won't be identified on the tape. Then I want to place an overseas call to the United States."

"Matthias?"

"Yes. But the circumstances will determine how much I can tell him.

Who's with him, how sterile the phone is; he'll know what to do. The point is, after you hear what I've got to say, the tape in your machine, you can decide whether to speak to him or not—if it comes up."

"You place a burden on me."

"I'm sorry—there won't be many more. In the morning, I'll need clothes. Everything I had is back in Monesi."

"No problem. Mine would not fit, but my wife buys for me. Tomorrow, she will buy for you."

"Speaking of buying, I've got a fair amount of money, but I'll need more. I have accounts in Paris; you'll get it back."

"Now you embarrass me."

"I don't mean to, but, you see, there's a catch. In order for you to get it back, I have to get to Paris."

"Surely Matthias can effect swift, safe transportation."

"I doubt it. You'll understand when you hear what I say in your office. Those who lied to Rome are very high in Washington. I don't know who or where they are, but I know they'll transmit only what they want to. His orders will be sidetracked, because *their* orders have gone out and they don't want them voided. And if I say where I am, where I can be reached, they'll send in men after me. In any case, they might succeed, which is why I need the tape. May we do it now, please?"

Thirty-four minutes later, Havelock depressed the switch on the cassette microphone and placed it on the Frenchman's desk. He had told it all, from the screams at Costa Brava to the explosions at Col des Moulinets. He could not refrain from adding a last judgment. The civilized world might well survive the compromising of any sprawling, monolithic intelligence service—regardless of race, creed or national origin—but not when one of the victims was a man that the same civilized world depended on: Anthony Matthias, a statesman respected by geopolitical friends and adversaries everywhere. He had been systematically lied to regarding a matter to which he had addressed himself in depth. How many more lies had been fed him?

Salanne sat across the office, deep in a soft leather armchair, his body motionless, his face rigid, his eyes staring at Havelock. He was stunned, speechless. After several moments he shook his head and broke his silence.

"Why?" he asked in a barely audible voice. "It's all so preposterous, as preposterous as what they say about you. *Why?*"

"I've asked myself that over and over again, and I keep going back to what I said to Baylor in Rome. They think I know something I shouldn't know, something that frightens them."

"Do you?"

"He asked me that."

"Who?"

"Baylor. And I was honest with him—perhaps too honest—but the shock of seeing her had blown my mind. I couldn't think straight. Especially after what Rostov had said in Athens."

"What did you say?"

"The truth. That if I *did* know something, I'd forgotten it, or it had never made much of an impression on me."

"That's not like you. They say you are a walking data bank, someone who recalls a name, a face, a minor event that took place years ago."

"Like most such opinions, it's a myth. I was a graduate student for a long time, so I developed certain disciplines, but I'm no computer."

"I'm aware of that," said the Frenchman quietly. "No computer would have done what you did for me." Salanne paused, leaning forward in the chair. "Have you gone over the months preceding Costa Brava?"

"Months, weeks, days—everything, every place we were . . . I was. Belgrade, Prague, Krakow, Vienna, Washington, Paris. There was nothing remotely startling, but I suppose that's a comparative term. With the exception of an exercise in Prague where we got some documents out of the Státní Bezpečnost—the secret police headquarters—everything was pretty routine. Gathering information, which damn near any tourist could have done, that's all."

"Washington?"

"Less than nothing. I flew back for five days. It's an annual event for field men, an evaluation interview, which is mostly a waste of time, but I suppose they catch a whacko now and then."

"Whacko?"

"Someone who's crossed over the mental line, thinks he's someone he's not, who's fantasized a basically routine job. Cloak-and-dagger flakes, I suppose you could call them. It comes with the stress, with too often pretending you *are* someone you're not."

"Interesting," said the doctor, nodding his head in some abstract recognition. "Did anything else happen while you were there?"

"Zero. I went to New York for a night to see a couple I knew when

I was young. He owns a marina on Long Island, and if he ever had a political thought in his head, I've never heard it. Then I spent two days with Matthias, a duty visit, really."

"You *were* close . . . *are* close."

"I told you, we go back a long time. He was there when I needed him; he understood."

"What about those two days?"

"Less than zero. I only saw him during the evenings when we had dinner together—two dinners, actually. Even then, although we were alone, he was constantly interrupted by phone calls and by harried people from State—supplicants, he called them—who insisted on bringing him reports." Havelock stopped, seeing a sudden tight expression on Salanne's face, but continued quickly, "No one saw me, if that's what you're thinking. He'd confer with them in his study, and the dining room's on the other side of the house. Again, he understood; we agreed not to display our friendship. For my benefit, really. No one likes a great man's protégé."

"It's difficult for me to think of you that way."

"It'd be impossible if you'd had dinner with us," said Michael, laughing quietly. "All we did was rehash papers I'd written for him nearly twenty years ago; he could still punch holes in them. Talk about total recall, he has it." Havelock smiled, then the smile faded as he said, "It's time," and reached for the telephone.

The lodge in the Shenandoah was reached by a sequence of telephone numbers, the first activating a remote mechanism at Matthias's residence in Georgetown, which in turn was electronically patched into a line a hundred and forty miles away, in the Blue Ridge Mountains, ringing the private telephone of the Secretary of State. If he was not on the premises, that phone was never answered; if he was, only he picked it up. The original number was known to perhaps a dozen people in the nation, among them the President and Vice-President, the Speaker of the House, the chairman of the Joint Chiefs, the Secretary of Defense, the president of the Security Council of the United Nations, two senior aides at State, and Mikhail Havlíček. The last was a privilege that Matthias had insisted upon for his *krajana*, his *spolopracovníka* from the university, whose father in Prague had been a colleague in intellect and spirit, if not in good fortune. Michael had used it twice during the past six years. The first time, when he was briefly in Washington for new instructions, Matthias had left word at his hotel that he should do so, and the call was merely social.

The second was not pleasant for Havelock to recall. It had concerned a man named Ogilvie who Michael felt strongly should be removed from the field.

The Antibes operator offered to ring him back when the call to Washington, D.C., was put through, but experience had taught Havelock to stay on the line. Nothing so tested the concentration of an operator as an open circuit; calls were more swiftly completed by remaining connected. And while he listened to the series of high-pitched sounds that signified international transmission, Salanne spoke.

"Why haven't you reached him before now?"

"Because nothing made sense, and I wanted it to. I wanted to give him something concrete. A name or names, a position, a title, some kind of identity."

"But from what I've heard, you still can't do that."

"Yes, I can. The authorization for dispatch had a source. Code name Ambiguity. It could only come from one of three or four offices, the word itself cleared by someone very high at State who was in touch with Rome. Matthias reaches Rome, has the incoming logs checked, talks to the receiver, and learns who gave Ambiguity its status. There's another name, too, but I don't know how much good it'll do. There was a second, so-called confirmation at Costa Brava, including torn pieces of blood-stained clothing. It's all a lie; there were no clothes left behind."

"Then find that man."

"He's dead. They say he died of a heart attack on a sailboat three weeks later. But there are things to look for, if they haven't been obscured. Where he came from, who assigned him to Costa Brava."

"And if I may add," said the Frenchman, "the doctor who made out the death certificate."

"You're right." The singsong tones disappeared from the line, replaced by two short, steady hums, then a break of silence, followed by a normal ring. The electronic remote had done its work; the telephone in the Shenandoah lodge was ringing. Michael felt the pounding in his throat and the shortness of breath that came with anxiety. He had so much to say to this *přítele;* he hoped to Christ he could say it and so begin the ending of the nightmare. The ringing stopped; the phone had been picked up. *Thank God!*

"Yes?" asked the voice over four thousand miles away in the Blue Ridge Mountains, a male voice, but not the voice of Anton Matthias. Or was the sound distorted, the single word too short to identify the man?

"Jak se vám daří?"

"What? Who's this?"

It was *not* Matthias. Had the rules been changed? If they had, it did not make sense. This was the emergency line, Matthias's personal phone, which was swept for intercepts daily; only he answered it. After five rings the caller was to hang up, dial the regular telephone number and leave his name and whatever message he cared to, aware that confidentiality was far less secure. Perhaps there was a simple explanation, an offhand request by Matthias for a friend nearer to the ringing phone to pick it up.

"Secretary of State Matthias, please?" said Havelock.

"Who's calling?"

"The fact that I used this number relieves me of the need to answer that. The Secretary, if you please. This is an emergency *and* confidential."

"Mr. Matthias is in conference at the moment and has asked that all calls be held. If you'd give me your name—"

"Goddamn it, you're not listening! This is an emergency!"

"He has one, too, sir."

"You break into that conference and say the following words to him. *Krajan* . . . and *bouře.* Have you got that? Just two words! *Krajan* and *bouře.* Do it now! Because if you don't, he'll have your head and your job when I talk to him! *Do* it!"

"Krajan," said the male voice hesitantly. *"Bouře."*

The line went silent, the silence interrupted once by the low undercurrent of men talking in the distance. The waiting was agony, and Michael could hear the echoes of his own breathing. Finally the voice came back.

"I'm afraid you'll have to be clearer, sir."

"What?"

"If you'd give me the details of the emergency and a telephone number where you can be reached—"

"Did you give him the message? The *words!* Did you say them?"

"The Secretary is extremely busy and requests that you clarify the nature of your call."

"Goddamn it, did you *say* them?"

"I'm repeating what the Secretary said, sir. He can't be disturbed now, but if you'll outline the details and leave a number, someone will be in contact with you."

"Someone? What the hell *is* this? Who *are* you? What's your name?"

There was a pause. "Smith," said the voice.

"Your name! I want your *name!"*

"I just gave it to you."

"You get Matthias on this phone—!"

There was a click; the line went dead.

Havelock stared at the instrument in his hand, then closed his eyes. His mentor, his *krajan*, his *přítel*, had cut him off. What had happened?

He had to find out; it made no sense, no sense at all! There was another number in the Blue Ridge Mountains, the home of a man Matthias saw frequently when he was in the Shenandoah, an older man whose love of chess and fine old wine took Anton's mind off his monumental pressures. Michael had met Leon Zelienski a number of times, and was always struck by the camaraderie between the two academics; he was happy for Matthias that such a person existed whose roots, though not in Prague, were not so far away, in Warsaw.

Zelienski had been a highly regarded professor of European history brought over to America years ago from the University of Warsaw to teach and lecture at Berkeley. Anton had met Leon during one of his early forays into the campus lecture circuit; additional funds were always welcome to Matthias. A friendship had developed—mostly by way of the mails and over chess—and upon retirement and the death of Zelienski's wife, Anton had persuaded the elderly scholar to come to the Shenandoah.

The Antibes operator took far longer with the second call, but finally Havelock heard the old man's voice.

"Good evening?"

"Leon? Is that you, Leon?"

"Who is this?"

"It's Michael Havelock. Do you remember me, Leon?"

"Mikhail! Do I *remember!* No, of course not, and I never touch kielbasa, either, you young *baranie!* How are you? Are you visiting our valley? You sound so far away."

"I'm very far away, Leon. I'm also very concerned . . ." Havelock explained his concern; he was unable to reach their beloved mutual friend, and was old Zelienski planning to see Anton while Matthias was in the Shenandoah?

"If he's here, Mikhail, I do not know it. Anton, of course, is a busy man. Sometimes I think the busiest man in this world . . . but he doesn't find time for me these days. I leave messages at the lodge, but I'm afraid he ignores them. Naturally, I understand. He moves with great figures . . . he *is* a great figure, and I am hardly one of them."

"I'm sorry to hear that . . . that he hasn't been in touch."

"Oh, men call me to express his regrets, saying that he rarely comes out to our valley these days, but I tell you, our chess games suffer. Incidentally, I must settle for another mutual friend of ours, Mikhail. He was out here frequently several months ago. That fine journalist Raymond Alexander. Alexander the Great, I call him, but as a player he's a far better writer."

"Raymond Alexander?" said Havelock, barely listening. "Give him my best. And thank you, Leon." Havelock replaced the phone and looked over at Salanne. "He hasn't time for us anymore," he said, bewildered.

14

He had reached Paris by eight o'clock in the morning, made contact with Gravet by nine and, by a quarter past eleven, was walking south amid the crowds in the Boulevard St. Germain. The fastidious art critic and broker of secrets would approach him somewhere between the Rue de Pontoise and the Quai St. Bernard. Gravet needed the two hours to seek out as many sources as possible relative to the information Havelock needed. Michael, on the other hand, used the time to move slowly, to rest— leaning upright against walls, never sitting—and to improve his immediate wardrobe.

There had been no time for Salanne's wife to buy him clothes in the morning, no thought but to get to Paris as quickly as he could, for every moment lost widened the distance between Jenna and himself. She had never been to Paris except with him, and there were only so many options open to her; he had to be there when she narrowed them down.

The doctor had driven for three and a half hours at very high speed to Avignon, where there had been a one o'clock produce train bound for Paris. Michael had caught it, dressed in what could be salvaged from his own clothes, in addition to a sweater and an ill-fitting gabardine topcoat furnished by Salanne. Now he looked at his reflection in a storefront window; the jacket, trousers, open shirt and hat he had purchased off the rack in the Raspail forty-five minutes ago suited his purpose. They were loose and nondescript. A man wearing such clothes would not be singled out, and the brim of the soft hat fell just low enough over his forehead to cast a shadow across his face.

Beyond the window was a narrow pillar of clear glass, part of the merchandise display, a mirror. He was drawn to it, to the face in the shadow of the hat brim. *His* face. It was haggard, with black circles under the eyes and the stubble of a dark beard. He had not thought of shaving even when he had been shopping in the Raspail. There had been mirrors in the store, but he had looked only at the clothes while concentrating his thoughts on the Paris he and Jenna Karas had known together: one or two embassy contacts; several colleagues-in-cover, as they were; a few French friends—government mainly, whose *ministères* brought them into his orbit; and three or four acquaintances they had made at late-night cafés having nothing whatsoever to do with the world in which he made his living.

Now in the St. Germain the ashen face he saw reminded him of how tired and racked with pain he was, how much he just wanted to lie down and let his strength come back to him. As Salanne had said, he needed rest badly. He had tried to sleep on the train from Avignon, but the frequent stops at rural depots that were farmers' points of delivery had jolted him awake whenever he dozed. And when awake, his head had throbbed, his mind filled with a profound sense of loss, confusion, and anger. The one man on earth to whom he had given his trust and love, the giant who had replaced his father and had shaped his life, had cut him loose and he had no idea why. Throughout the years, during the most harrowing and isolated times, he was somehow never alone because the presence of Anton Matthias was always with him. Anton was the spur that drove him to be better than he was, his protection against the memories of the early terrible days, because his *přítel* had given them meaning, perspective. Certainly no justification, but a reason for doing what he was doing, for spending his life in an abnormal world until something inside him told him he could join the normal one. He had fought against the guns of Lidice and the arbiters of gulag termination in whatever form he had found them.

Those guns will always be with you, my přiteli. *I wish to Almighty God you could walk away from them, but I don't think you can. So do what lessens the pain, what gives you purpose, what removes the guilt of having survived. Absolution is not here among the books and argumentative theoreticians; you have no patience with their conceptualism. You have to see practical results. . . . One day you will be free, your anger spent, and you will return. I hope I am alive to witness it. I intend to be.*

He had come so close to being free, his angers reduced to an abstract sense of futility, his return to a normal world within his grasp and understanding. It had happened twice. Once with the woman he loved, who had given another breadth of meaning to his life . . . and then without her, loving neither her nor the memory of her, believing the lies of liars, betraying his innermost feelings—and her. Oh, *God!*

And now the one man who could fulfill the prophecy he had made years ago to his *krajanu,* his student, his son, had thrown him out of his life. The giant was a mortal, after all. And now his enemy.

"Mon Dieu, you look like a graduate of Auschwitz!" whispered the tall Frenchman in the velvet-collared overcoat and gleaming black shoes standing several feet to the right of Havelock in front of the window. "What *happened* to you? . . . No, don't tell me! Not here."

"Where?"

"On the Quai Bernard, past the university, is a small park, a playground for children mostly," continued Gravet, admiring his own figure in the glass. "If the benches are occupied, find a place by the fence and I'll join you. On your way, purchase a bag of sweets and try to look like a father, not a sexual deviant."

"Thanks for the confidence. Did you bring me anything?"

"Let's say you are heavily in my debt. Far more than your impecunious appearance would suggest you could pay."

"About *her?"*

"I'm still working on that. On her."

"Then *what?"*

"The Quai Bernard," said Gravet, adjusting his scarlet tie and tilting his gray homburg as he regarded his reflection in the window. He turned with the grace of a ballet master and walked away.

The small park was chilled by the winds off the Seine, but they did not deter the nurses, nannies and young mothers from bringing their boisterous charges to the playground. Children were everywhere—on the swings, jungle gyms, seesaws—it was bedlam. Fortunately for Michael's waning strength, there was a vacant bench against the far back wall, away from the more chaotic center of the riverside park. He sat down, absently picking tiny colored mints out of a white paper bag while looking at a particularly obnoxious child kicking a tricycle; he hoped that whoever might be observing him would think the youngster was his, reasoning that the small boy's real guardian would stay as far away as possible. The child stopped punishing the three wheels long enough to return his stare with an astonishing malevolence.

The elegant Gravet walked through the red-striped entrance and levitated his way around the rim of the playground, nodding pleasantly, benignly to the screaming children in his path, an elder full of kindness toward the young. It was quite a performance, thought Havelock, knowing that the epicene critic loathed the surroundings. Finally he reached the bench and sat down, snapping a newspaper out in front of him.

"Should you see a doctor?" asked the critic, his eyes on the paper.

"I left one only hours ago," replied Michael, his lips by the edge of the white paper bag. "I'm all right, just tired."

"I'm relieved, but I suggest you clean yourself up, including a shave. The two of us in this particular park could bring on the *gendarmes*. The opposite poles of an obscene spectrum, would be the conclusion."

"I don't feel like being funny, Gravet. What have you got?"

The critic folded the paper, snapping it again, as he spoke. "A contradiction, if my sources are accurate, and I have every reason to believe they are. A somewhat incredible contradiction, in fact."

"What is it?"

"The KGB has no interest in you whatsoever. I could deliver you, a willing, garrulous defector snapped from the jaws of imperialists, to their Paris headquarters—an importing firm on the Beaumarchais, but I suspect you know that—and I wouldn't get a sou."

"Why is that a contradiction? I said the same thing to you several weeks ago on the Pont Royal."

"*That* isn't the contradiction."

"What is?"

"Someone else is looking for you. He flew in last night because he thinks you're either in Paris now or on your way here. The word is he'll pay a fortune for your corpse. He's not KGB in the usual sense, but make no mistake about it, he's Soviet."

"Not . . . in the usual sense?" asked Havelock, bewildered, yet sensing the approach of an ominous memory, a recent memory.

"I traced him through a source in the Militaire Etranger. He's from a special branch of Soviet intelligence, an elite corps of—"

"*Voennaya Kontra Razvedka,*" Michael broke in harshly.

"If the shortened form is VKR, that's it."

"It is."

"He wants you. He'll pay dearly."

"Maniacs."

"Mikhail, I should tell you. He flew in from Barcelona."

"Costa Brava!"

"Don't look at me! Move to the edge of the bench!"

"Do you know what you just *told* me?"

"You're upset. I must leave."

"No! . . . All right, all *right!*" Havelock lifted the white paper bag to his face; both his hands were trembling and he could hardly breathe as the pain in his chest surged up to his temples. "You know what you've got to deliver now, don't you? You've got it, so give it to me."

"You're in no condition."

"I'll be the judge of that. *Tell* me!"

"I wonder if I should. Quite apart from the payment I may never see, there's a moral dilemma. You see, I like you, Mikhail. You're a civilized man, perhaps even a good man, in a very unsavory business. You took yourself out; have I the right to put you back in?"

"I *am* back in!"

"The Costa Brava?"

"Yes!"

"Go to your embassy."

"I *can't!* Don't you understand that?"

Gravet broke his own sacrosanct rule: he lowered the newspaper and looked at Havelock. "My God, they couldn't," he said quietly.

"Just tell me."

"You leave me no choice."

"Tell me! Where is he?"

The critic rose from the bench, folding the paper, as he spoke. "There's a run-down hotel on the Rue Etienne. La Couronne Nouvelle. He's on the second floor, Room Twenty-three. It's in the front; he observes every-one who enters."

The bent-over figure of the tramp was like that of a derelict in any large city. His clothes were ragged but thick enough to ward off the cold in deserted alleyways at night, his shoes cast-off heavy-soled boots, the laces broken and tied in large, awkward knots. On his head was a wool knit cap set low on his brow; his eyes focused downward, avoiding the world in which he could not compete, and which in turn found his presence unnerving. But over the tramp's shoulder was his soiled canvas satchel, the oily straps held in a firm grip, as if he were proclaiming the dignity of possession: This is my all, what is left of me, and it is mine. The man approaching La Couronne Nouvelle had no age; he measured time only by what he had lost. He stopped at a wire trash basket and dug through the contents with methodical patience—a sidewalk archaeologist.

Havelock separated a torn lamp shade from a soggy bag of half-eaten lunch, and angled the small tinted mirror between them, his hands concealed by the filthy fabric of the shade. He could see the Russian directly above in the second-floor window; the man was leaning against the sill, watching the street, studying the pedestrians, waiting. He would stay by that window for a simple reason: his strike force was deployed; had a counterstrike been mounted? Michael knew him—not by name or reputation, or even from a photograph in a file, but he knew him, knew the set of the face, the look in the eyes. Havelock had been where this man had been—where he was now. The process had been set in motion, the word cautiously put out; word was awaited back at the command post of one. The lethal compromisers had been reached, none having allegiance to anything or anybody except the dollar, the franc, the pound and the deutsche mark. A sliding scale of incentive payments had been circulated, bonuses matching the value of various contributions, the highest, of course, the kill with proof of the kill. Word and method of the target's arrival, sightings at specific locations, alone or with known or unknown associates, a hotel, a café, a *pension*, a rooming house—all had value in terms of immediate payment. A competition had been created among the qualified practitioners of violence, each professional enough to know that one did not lie to the command post. Today's loss was another day's kill.

Sooner or later the man in the window would start getting his responses. A few would be mere speculation based on secondhand information; others would be honest error, which would not be penalized but analyzed for what it was. Then a single call would come, its authenticity established by a descriptive phrase or a certain reaction—unmistakably the target's —and the command post would have its first breakthough. A street, a café, a bench perhaps in a children's park on the Seine—the practitioners would have spread out everywhere. The hunt was on, the prize many times a year's income. And when the hunt came to an end, the man in the window would come out of his movable prison. Yes, thought Michael, he had been there. The waiting was the worst part.

He looked at his watch, his hand buried in the refuse. There was a second wire trash basket down the block, on the other side of the hotel's entrance; he wondered if it would be necessary to go to it and continue foraging. He had gone past the hotel twice in a taxi—projecting his movements on foot, calculating his timing—before he had sought out the used-clothing shops in the Séverine—those and an obscure shop on the Sommerard where he had purchased ammunition for the Llama automatic and the magnum. He had phoned Gravet seven minutes ago and told him the clock was on; the Frenchman would place his call from a booth in the Place Vendôme; the crowds would guarantee his untraceable anonymity. What was holding him up? There were so many possibilities. Occupied booths, out-of-order phones, a talkative acquaintance who insisted on prolonging a street-corner conversation, all were reasonable assumptions, but whatever, Havelock knew he could not stay where he was any longer. Awkwardly, like an old man in pain—and indeed he was a not so young man in pain—he began to push himself up. He would force a deliberately unfocused eye to see what it should not see.

The man in the window whipped his head around. An intrusion had interrupted his concentration on the street; he walked back into the shadows of the room. Gravet had made his call. *Now.*

Michael lifted the satchel off the ground, dropped it in the wire receptacle and rapidly walked diagonally across the pavement toward the short flight of steps that led to the hotel's entrance. With each stride he lessened his stooped posture to return gradually to normal height. As he climbed the concrete steps he placed his hand on the side of his face, his fingers gripping the edge of the wool knit cap. No more than eight feet above was the window in which the Soviet VKR officer had been standing only seconds ago, and in seconds he would return. Gravet's call would be brief, professional; in no way could it be construed as a device. There was a possible sighting in the Montparnasse. Was the target injured? Did he walk with a pronounced limp? Whatever answers the Russian gave, the call would be terminated, probably in mid-sentence. If it *was* the target, he was heading for the Métro; the hunter would call back.

Inside the dark, musty lobby with the cracked tile floor and the cobwebs spanning the four corners of the ceiling, Havelock took off his cap, flattened the lapels of his disheveled jacket and ripped the already torn cloth that hung from the bottom of his coat. It was not much of an improvement, but in the dim light and with erect bearing, it was not inappropriate for a hotel that catered to drifters and whores. It was not an establishment that scrutinized its clientele—only the legitimacy of their currency.

It had been Michael's intention to project the image of a man painfully coming out of a long drunk, seeking a bed in which to shake through the final ordeal. It was not necessary; an obese *concierge* behind the cracked marble counter was dozing in a chair, his soft, fat hands folded on his protruding stomach. There was one other person in the lobby: a gaunt old man seated on a bench, a cigarette dangling from his lips below an unkempt gray moustache, his head bent forward as he squinted at a newspaper in his hands. He did not look up.

Havelock dropped the cap on the floor, side-kicked it toward the wall, and walked to his left, where there was a narrow staircase, the steps worn smooth from decades of use and neglect, the banister broken in several places. He started up the creaking steps and was relieved that the staircase was short. There were no turns, no midpoint landings; the steps led straight from one level to the next. He reached the second floor and stood motionless, listening. There was no sound other than the distant hum of traffic, punctuated by sporadic shrieks of impatient horns. He looked at the door ten feet away, at the faded painted number, *23*. He could discern no vocal undercurrent of a one-sided telephone conversation; the call from Gravet was over and the Soviet VKR officer was back at his window, the elapsed time no more than forty-five seconds. Michael unbuttoned his ragged jacket, reached underneath, and gripped the handle of the magnum. As he pulled the gun out from under his belt, the perforated cylinder caught briefly on the leather; with his thumb he released the safety and started down the dark, narrow hallway toward the door.

A creak on the floorboards—not his, not under him, *behind* him! He spun as the first door on the left beyond the staircase was pulled slowly open. Since it had been left ajar, there had been no sound of a turning knob; the open crack was a line of sight for someone inside. A short, heavyset man emerged, shoulders and spine against the frame, a weapon in his hand at his side. He raised the gun. Havelock had no time for assessment or appraisal, he could only react. Under different circumstances he might have held up his hand and whispered sharply a word, a signal, a note of warning to avert a terrible error; instead he fired. The man was blown off his feet, buckling back into the doorframe. Michael looked at the gun still gripped in the man's hand. He had been right to shoot; the weapon was a Graz-Burya, the most powerful, accurate auto-matic produced in Russia. The VKR officer was not alone. And if there was one . . .

A knob was being turned; it was the door directly across from Room 23. Havelock lurched to the wall to the right of the frame; the door opened and Michael spun around, the magnum raised chest-high, pre-pared to fire or deliver a blow—or drop his arm if it should turn out to be an innocent hotel guest. The man was in a crouch, and held a gun. Havelock crashed the barrel of the magnum on the man's head. The Russian fell back inside the room; Michael followed and gripped the door to prevent it from slamming shut. He held the crack open less than an inch, stood still and waited. There was silence in the hall except for the faraway sounds of traffic. He backed away from the door, the magnum leveled at it, his eyes scanning the floor for the man's gun. It was several feet behind the prone, unconscious figure; he kicked it forward beside the body, kneeled down and picked it up. It, too, was a Graz-Burya; the detail sent to Paris was equipped with the best. He shoved it into his jacket pocket, reached over and pulled the Russian toward him; the man was limp and would not be conscious for hours.

He got to his feet, went to the door and let himself out. The violent movements had drained him; he leaned against the wall breathing slowly, deeply, trying to put out of his mind the weakness and pain in his body. He couldn't stop now. There was the first man in the door beyond the staircase; the door was open. Someone walking past would look inside and go into hysterics—after no doubt furtively checking the dead man's pock-ets for money. Michael pushed himself away from the wall, and silently, on the balls of his thick-soled feet, made his way down the narrow corridor past the staircase. He pulled the door shut and started back toward Room 23.

He stood facing the barely legible numbers and knew he had to find the strength. There was nothing for it but to depend on the shock of the totally unexpected. He tensed his chest and stepped back from the door, then rushed forward leading with his unwounded shoulder, and crashed the full weight of his body against the wood. The door splintered and broke open; the VKR officer pivoted away from the window, his hand reaching for the exposed holster strapped to his belt. He stopped, swiftly thrusting both hands out in front of him, his eyes staring at the huge barrel of the magnum pointed at his head.

"I believe you were looking for me," said Havelock.

"It appears I trusted the wrong people," answered the Russian quietly in well-accented English.

"But not your own people," interrupted Michael.

"You're special."

"You lost."

"I never ordered your death. They might have."

"Now you're lying, but it doesn't matter. As I said, you lost."

"You're to be commended," mumbled the VKR officer, his eyes straying above Havelock's shoulder to the broken door.

"You didn't hear me. You lost. There's a man in the room across the hall; he won't be attending you."

"I see."

"And another down the way, beyond the staircase. He's dead."

"Nyet! Molniya!" The Soviet agent blanched; his fingers were stretched, taut, six inches from his belt.

"I speak Russian, if you prefer."

"It's immaterial," said the startled man. "I'm a graduate of the Massachusetts Institute of Technology."

"Or of the American compound in Novgorod, KGB degree."

"Cambridge, not Novgorod," objected the Russian, disdain in his voice.

"I forgot. The VKR is an elite corps. A degree from the parent organization might be considered an insult. The untutored and unskilled conferring honors upon its in-house superiors."

"There are no such divisions in the Soviet government."

"My ass."

"This is pointless."

"Yes, it is. What happened at Costa Brava?"

"I have no idea what you mean."

"You're VKR, Barcelona! The Costa Brava is in your sector! What happened that night on January fourth?"

"Nothing that concerned us."

"Move!"

"What?"

"Against the wall!"

It was an outside wall, built of mortar and heavy brick, solid for decades, weight pressing against weight, impenetrable. The Russian moved slowly, haltingly in front of it. Havelock continued.

"I'm so special your sector chief in Moscow doesn't know the truth. But you do. It's why you're here in Paris, why you put out the premium on me."

"You've been misinformed. It is a crime tantamount to treason to withhold information from our superiors. As to my coming from Barcelona, surely you understand that. It was your last assignment and I was your last counterpart. I had the most up-to-date information on you. Who better to send in after you?"

"You're very good. You glide well."

"I've told you nothing you don't know, nothing you could not learn."

"You missed something. Why am I special? Your colleagues at the KGB haven't the slightest interest in me. On the contrary, they won't touch me; they consider me a bad text. Yet you say I'm special. The Voennaya wants me."

"I won't deny there's a degree of interservice rivalry, even departmental. Perhaps we learned it from you. You have an abundance of it."

"You haven't answered my question."

"We know certain things our comrades are not aware of."

"Such as?"

"You were placed 'beyond salvage' by your own government."

"Do you know why?"

"The reasons at this juncture are secondary. We offer refuge."

"The reasons are never secondary," corrected Michael.

"Very well," agreed the Soviet officer reluctantly. "A judgment was made that you are unbalanced."

"On what basis?"

"Pronounced hostility, accompanied by threats, cables. Delusions, hallucinations."

"Because of Costa Brava?"

"Yes."

"Just like that? One day walking around sane, filing reports, honorably retired; the next a cuckoo bird whistling at the moon? Now you're not very good. You're not gliding well at all."

"I'm telling you what I know," insisted the Russian. "I do not make these determinations, I follow instructions. The premium, as you call it, was to be paid for a meeting between us. Why should it be otherwise? If killing you were the objective, it would be far simpler to pay for your whereabouts and telephone your embassy in the Gabriel, asking for a specific extension; I can assure you we know it. The information would reach the proper personnel and we would not be involved, no possibility of errors leading to future repercussions."

"But by offering me refuge and bringing me in, you take back a trophy your less talented comrades avoided because they thought I was a trap, programmed or otherwise."

"Basically, yes. May we talk?"

"We're talking." Havelock studied the man; he was convincing, quite possibly telling his version of the truth. Refuge or a bullet, which was it? Only the exposure of lies would tell. One had to look for the lies, not a subordinate's interpretation of the truth. In his peripheral vision Michael caught the reflection of a dull mirror above a shabby bureau against the wall; he spoke again. "You'd expect me to deliver information you know I've got."

"We'd be saving your life. The order for 'beyond salvage' termination will not be rescinded, you know that."

"You're suggesting I defect."

"What choice do you have? How long do you think you can keep running? How many days or weeks will it be before their networks and their computers find you?"

"I'm experienced. I have resources. Maybe I'm willing to take my chances. Men have been known to disappear—not into gulags, but to other places—and live happily ever after. What else can you offer?"

"What are you looking for? Comfort, money, a good life? We offer these. You deserve them."

"Not in your country. I won't live in the Soviet Union."

"Oh?"

"Suppose I told you I've picked out a place. It's thousands of miles away in the Pacific, in the British Solomons. I've been there; it's civilized but remote, no one would ever find me. Given enough money, I could live well there."

"Arrangements can be made. I am empowered to guarantee that."

Lie number one. No defector ever left the Soviet Union and the VKR officer knew it.

"You flew into Paris last night. How did you know I was here?"

"Informants in Rome, how else?"

"How did they learn?"

"One doesn't question informants too closely."

"The hell one doesn't."

"*If* they are trusted."

"You ask for a source. You don't leave a station and fly to a city hundreds of miles away without being pretty damn sure the source can be confirmed."

"Very well," said the VKR officer, gliding confidently with the cross-currents again. "There was an investigation; a man was found in Civitavecchia. He said you were on your way to Paris."

"When did you get the word?"

"Yesterday, of course," replied the Russian impatiently.

"When yesterday?"

"Late afternoon. Five-thirty, I believe. Five-thirty-five, to be precise."

Lie number two, the falsehood found in the precision. The decision to head for Paris was forced on him after Col des Moulinets. Eight o'clock at night.

"You're convinced that what I can divulge about our European intelligence operations is of such value to you that you are willing to accept the retaliations that come with defection at my level?"

"Naturally."

"That opinion isn't shared by the directors' committee of the KGB."

"They're fools. Frightened, tired rabbits among the wolves. We'll replace them."

"You're not troubled that I may be programmed? That whatever I tell you could be poison, useless?"

"Not for a moment. It's why you're 'beyond salvage.' "

"Or that I'm paranoid?"

"Never. You're neither paranoid nor hallucinatory. You are what you have always been, a highly intelligent specialist in your field."

Lie number three. Word of his supposed psychotic condition had been spread. Washington believed it; the dead Ogilvie had confirmed it on the Palatine.

"I see," said Havelock, grimacing, feigning pain that needed very little pretense. "I'm so goddamned tired," he said, lowering the magnum slightly, turning slightly to his left, his eyes millimeters from making contact with the mirror on the wall. "I took a bullet. I haven't had any sleep. As you said, I just keep running, trying to figure it out . . ."

"What more is there to figure?" asked the Russian, his voice now gliding into compassion. "It's basically an economic, time-saving decision, you know that. Rather than altering codes, networks and sources, they've decided to eliminate the man who knows too much. Sixteen years of service in the field and this is your retirement bonus. 'Beyond salvage.' "

Michael lowered the gun further, his head bent down but his eyes now on the mirror. "I have to think," he whispered. "It's all so crazy, so impossible."

Lie number four—the most telling lie! The Russian went for his gun!

Havelock spun around and fired; the bullet snapped into the wall. The VKR officer grabbed his elbow as blood erupted through his shirt and dripped onto the floor. *"Ubliudok!"* he cried.

"We've only just begun!" whispered Michael with controlled fury. He approached the Russian and pushed him against the wall, then removed the exposed weapon from the holster and threw it across the room. "You're too sure of yourself, comrade, too sure of your facts! Never state them so confidently; leave room for error because there may *be* one. You had several."

The Russian answered him with silence, his eyes full of both loathing and resignation. Havelock knew those eyes, knew the combination of hatred and the recognition of mortality; they were intrinsic to the nature of certain men, trained for years to hate and die. By any name they were recognizable: *Gestapo, Nippon Kai, Palestinian Liberationists, Voennaya.* . . . And there were lesser leagues, amateurs who knew nothing beyond arrogance and hate—their own deaths being no part of their childish bargains—screeching fanatics who marched to the drums of sanctimonious loathing.

Michael returned silence for silence, look for look. And then he spoke.

"Don't waste the adrenaline," he said quietly. "I'm not going to kill you. You're prepared for that; you've been ready for it for years. Damned if I'm going to accommodate you. Instead, I'm going to blow off both your kneecaps—and then your hands. You're not trained to live with the results. No one is, really, especially not your kind. So many routine things'll be beyond you. Simple things. Walking to a door or a locked file cabinet, opening either one. Dialing a phone or going to the toilet. Reaching for a gun and pulling a trigger."

The Russian's face went pale and his lower lip began to tremble. *"Nyet,"* he whispered hoarsely.

"Da," said Havelock. "There's only one way you can stop me. Tell me what happened at Costa Brava."

"I *told* you! *Nothing!*"

Michael lowered the magnum and fired into the Soviet's thigh; blood splattered against the wall. The Russian started to scream, collapsing on the floor; Havelock gripped his mouth with his left hand.

"I missed the kneecap. I won't miss now. Either one." He stood up, leveling the weapon downward.

"No! Stop!" The VKR officer rolled over, clutching his leg. He was broken; he could accept death, but not what Michael had promised him. "I'll tell you what I know."

"I'll know if you're lying. My finger's on the trigger, the gun pointed at your right hand. If you lie, you won't have it anymore."

"What I told you *is* true. We were not at Costa Brava that night."

"Your code was broken. Washington broke it. I saw it, I *sent* it!"

"Washington broke nothing. That code was abandoned seven days prior to the night of January fourth. Even if you sent it and we accepted it, we could not have responded. It would have been physically impossible."

"Why?"

"We were nowhere near the area, any of us. We were sent out of the sector." The Russian coughed in pain, his face twisted. "For the period of time in question, all activities were canceled. We were prohibited from going within twenty miles of the Montebello beach on the Costa Brava."

"Liar!"

"No," said the VKR officer, his bleeding leg pulled up under him, his body taut, his eyes staring at Michael. "No, I am not lying. Those were the orders from Moscow."

BOOK
TWO

15

It was raining that night in Washington. Angry, diagonal sheets were driven by erratic winds, making drivers and pedestrians alike mistrust their vision; headlights refracted, diffused, blinded in suddenly shifting angles. The chauffeur at the wheel of the limousine heading down 14th Street toward the East Gate of the White House was not immune to the problem. He slammed on his brakes and swerved to avoid an onrushing compact, whose high beams gave the illusion of a huge attacking insect. The small car was well to his left on its side of the line, so the maneuver had been unnecessary. The chauffeur wondered if his very important passengers had noticed the error.

"Sorry, sirs," he said, his voice directed at the intercom, his eyes on the rearview mirror and the glass partition that separated him from them.

Neither man responded. It was as if neither had heard him, yet he knew both had; the blue intercom light was on, which meant that his voice was transmitted. The red light, of course, was dark; he could not hear anything being said in the rear seat. The red light was always off, except when instructions were being given, and twice every day the system was checked in the garage before he or any other driver left the premises. It was said that tiny circuit breakers had been installed that tripped at the slightest tampering with the intercom mechanism.

The men who rode in these limousines had been assigned them by the President of the United States, and the chauffeurs who drove them were continuously subjected to the most stringent security checks. Each of them was unmarried and without children, and each was a combat veteran —proven under fire—with extensive experience in guerrilla warfare and diversionary tactics. The vehicles they drove were designed for maximum protection. The windows could withstand the impact of .45-caliber bullets; homing devices were implanted throughout the undersides, and small jets that released two separate types of gas with a flick of a switch were positioned at all points of the frame—one gas merely numbed and was used for riots and unruly protesters, while the other was a lethal dioxide compound, which was designed for terrorists. The chauffeurs were told: "Guard your passengers with your lives." These men held the secrets of the nation; they were the President's closest advisers in times of crisis.

The driver glanced at the dashboard clock. It was nine-twenty, nearly four hours since he had driven the same vehicle back into the garage after completing a previous assignment, waited for the electronics check, and left for the night. Thirty-five minutes later he had been having a drink at a restaurant on K Street and was about to order dinner when the jarring one-note signal of his beeper erupted from its case on his belt. He had telephoned the unlisted number for Security Dispatch and was ordered to the garage immediately: *Aquarius One emergency, Scorpio descending.* Out of context and out of orbit, but the message was clear. The Oval Office had pushed a button; the senior drivers were now on duty, all prior schedules aborted.

Back in the garage he had been mildly surprised to see that only two vehicles had been prepared for transport. He had expected to find six or seven black-stretch Abrahams wheeled out of their docks and ready to roll; instead, there were just two—one ordered to an address in Berwyn Heights, Maryland, and the second—his—to Andrews Field to await the arrival of two men being flown in on army jets from separate islands in the Caribbean. Times had been coordinated; the ETA's were within fifteen minutes of each other.

The younger of the two old men had arrived first, and the driver recognized him instantly; not everyone would have done so. His name was Halyard, like the line on a sailboat, but his reputation had been made on land. Lieutenant General Malcolm Halyard: WW II, Korea, Vietnam. The bald soldier had started off commanding platoons and companies in France and across the Rhine, then battalions in Kaesong and Inchon, and, finally, armies in Southeast Asia, where the driver had seen him more than once in Danang. He was something of an oddball in the upper ranks of the military; he was never known to have held a press conference, and he had been known to bar photographers—military and civilian alike—from wherever he happened to be. "Tightrope" Halyard was considered a brilliant tactician, one of the first to state for the *Congressional Record* that Vietnam was no-win idiocy. He avoided publicity with the same tenacity that he showed on the battlefield, and his low profile, it was said, appealed to the President.

The general had been escorted to the limousine and, after greeting the driver, had waited in the back seat without another word.

The second man had arrived twelve minutes later. He was as far removed from "Tightrope" Halyard as the eagle is from the lion, but both were superb examples of their species. Addison Brooks had been a lawyer, an international banker, a consultant to statesmen, an ambassador, and finally an elder statesman himself and adviser to presidents. He was the embodiment of the Eastern Establishment aristocracy, the last of the old-school-tie crowd, the ultimate WASP, who tempered the image with a swift wit that could be as gentle and compassionate as it could be devastating. He had survived the political wars by exercising the same agility displayed by Halyard on the battlefield. In essence, both men would compromise with reality, but not with principle. This was not, of course, the driver's own judgment; he had read about it in the *Washington Post*, his interest having been drawn to a political column that had analyzed the two advisers because he knew the ambassador and had seen the general in Danang. He had driven the ambassador on a number of occasions, flattered that old Brooks remembered his name and always had a little personal something to say to him: "I have a grandson who swears he saw you play your one two-minute game for the Steelers, Jack." Or: "Damn it, Jack, don't you ever put on weight? My wife makes me drink my gin with some God-awful diet fruit juice." The last had to be an exaggeration; the ambassador was a tall, slender man, his silver hair, aquiline features and perfectly groomed gray moustache making him look more English than American.

Tonight, however, there had been no personal greeting at Andrews Field, and no jokes. Instead, Brooks had nodded absently when the driver opened the rear door for him; then he had paused as his eyes made contact with the general inside. At that moment only one word was spoken. "Parsifal," the ambassador said, his voice low, somber; it was the sole greeting.

After Brooks had climbed in beside Halyard, they talked briefly, their faces set, glancing frequently at each other, as if asking questions neither could answer. Then they fell silent, or so it appeared, at least, whenever the driver's eyes strayed to the rearview mirror. The few times he had looked at them, as he was looking at them now, both the diplomat and the soldier had been staring straight ahead, neither speaking. Whatever the crisis that had brought them to the White House, each from an island in the Caribbean, it was obviously beyond discussion.

The driver's memories were stirred as he turned into the short drive that led to the East Gate guardhouse. Like many collegiate athletes whose ability was somewhat greater on the playing field than in the classroom or laboratory, he had taken a course in music appreciation that had been suggested by his coaches. They had been wrong; it was a bitch. Still, he remembered. *Parsifal* was an opera by Wagner.

The driver of Abraham Seven turned off the Kenilworth Road into the residential section of Berwyn Heights, Maryland. He had been to the house twice before, which was why he had been selected for the route tonight despite his previous request not to be given Undersecretary of State Emory Bradford as an assignment again. When Security Dispatch had asked why, he could only answer that he did not like him.

"That doesn't really concern us, Yahoo," had been the reply. "Your likes and dislikes have yet to become policy around here. Just do your job."

Of course that was the point—the job. If part of the job was to protect Bradford's life at a risk to his own, he was not sure he could comply. Twenty years ago the cold, analytical Emory Bradford had been one of the best and the brightest, the new breed of young pragmatists who skewered adversaries right and left in the pursuit of power. And the tragedy at Dallas had done nothing to slow this pursuit; the mourning had been quickly replaced by adjustment to a changed situation. The nation was in peril and those endowed with the capacity to understand the aggressive nature of factionalized Communism had to stand firm and rally the forces of strength. The tight-lipped, unemotional Bradford became an impassioned hawk. A game called dominoes was suddenly a theory on which the survival of freedom was based.

And in Idaho a strapping farm boy was caught up in the fever. He answered the call; it was his personal statement against the long-haired freaks who burned flags and draft cards and spat on things that were decent and—*American*. Eight months later the farm boy was in the jungles watching friends getting their heads blown away, and faces and arms and legs. He saw ARVN troops running from firefights and their commanders selling rifles and jeeps and whole consignments of battalion rations. He came to understand what was so obvious to everyone but Washington and Command Saigon. The so-called victims of the so-called atheistic hordes didn't give a doodilly shit about anything except their hides and their profits. They were the ones who were spitting and burning everything that could not be traded or sold, and laughing. *Jesus*, were they laughing! At their so-called saviors, the pink-faced, round-eyed suckers who took the fire and the land mines, and lost heads and faces and arms and legs.

And then it had happened. The frenzied hawk that was Emory Bradford in Washington saw the light, a different light. In an extraordinary public display of mea culpa he appeared before a Senate committee and announced to the nation that something had gone wrong, the brilliant planners—himself included—had erred grievously. He advocated immediate withdrawal; the impassioned hawk became a passionate dove.

He was accorded a standing ovation. While heads and faces and arms and legs were scattered over the jungles, and a farm boy from Idaho was doing his damnedest not to want to die as a prisoner of war. A *standing ovation*, goddamn it!

No, Mr. Emory Bradford, I will not risk my life for you. I will not die for you—again.

The large three-story Colonial house was set back beyond a manicured lawn that promised a pool and a tennis court hidden somewhere. The best and the brightest also frolicked; it was part of their life-style, intrinsic to their worth and their image. The farm boy from Idaho wondered how Undersecretary of State Emory Bradford would behave in a river cage infested with water rats in the Mekong Delta. Probably very well, goddamn it.

The driver reached under the dashboard and pulled out the retractable microphone. He pressed the button and spoke.

"Abraham Seven to Dispatch."

"Go ahead, Abraham Seven."

"Have reached location. Please raise cargo by phone."

"Will do, Seven. Good timing. You and Abraham Four should reach Aquarius at about the same time."

"Glad you approve. We try to please."

The three descended in the elevator together, the two older men astonished that the conference was to take place in one of the underground strategy rooms and not in the Oval Office. The undersecretary of State, briefcase in hand, seemed to understand why. The advantages, of course, were found in the equipment. There were computers and projectors that threw images and information onto a huge wall screen, communications devices that linked the White House to just about anybody anywhere in the world, and data-processing machines that isolated facts from volumes of useless scholarship. Yet all the sophisticated equipment in Washington was in itself useless without a breakthrough. Had it happened? wondered the older advisers as each looked questioningly at the other. Had the breakthrough come? If it had, the summons from the President had given no indication of it. Instead, the opposite had been conveyed. "Scorpio descending" was akin to catastrophe, and each felt the tightening of his stomach muscles as the lower level was reached and the elevator door opened onto the pristine white-walled corridor. They emerged and walked in unison down the hallway toward the assigned room and the President of the United States.

President Charles Berquist greeted each man curtly, and each understood. It was not in the nature of the stocky Minnesotan to be cold—tough, yes, very tough, but not cold; he was frightened. He gestured impatiently at the raised U-shaped conference table at the end of the room; it faced the wall screen thirty feet away where images would be projected. The three men walked up the two steps with the President and took their places at the table; at each place was a small Tensor lamp angled down on a note pad. Addison Brooks sat on Berquist's right, General Halyard on his left, and the younger Emory Bradford beyond the statesman, one chair removed so he could address the three. It was a pecking order rooted in logic; most of the questions would be directed at Bradford, and he in turn would ask most of the questions directed at anyone brought in for interrogation. Below the U-shaped table and facing it midway to the screen was another table, smaller, rectangular, with two swivel chairs that enabled whoever sat in them to turn and watch the images projected on the wall.

"You look tired, Mr. President," said Brooks, once all were seated and the lamps adjusted.

"I *am* tired," agreed Berquist. "I'm also sorry to bring you and Mal back to this rotten weather."

"Insofar as you saw fit to call us back," commented Halyard sincerely, "I'd say the weather is the least of our problems."

"You're right." The President pressed a button embedded in the table on his left. "The first slide, if you please." The overhead lights were extinguished and only the Tensors remained on; the photographs of four men appeared on a split screen at the end of the room. "Do you know any of these men?" asked Berquist, then added hastily, "The question's not for Emory. He does."

The ambassador and the general glanced at Bradford, then turned to the photographs. Addison Brooks spoke. "The fellow on the upper right is named Stern. David or Daniel Stern, I believe. He's over at State, isn't he? One of the European specialists, bright, analytical, a good man."

"Yes," confirmed Berquist quietly. "What about you, Mal? Recognize anybody up there?"

"I'm not sure," said the retired general, squinting at the screen. "The one below this Stern, lower right. I think I've seen him before."

"You have," said Bradford. "He spent time at the Pentagon."

"I can't picture the uniform, the rank."

"He didn't wear one, have one. He's a doctor; he testified before a number of panels on P.O.W. trauma. You were seated on two or three, I believe."

"Yes, of course, I remember now. He's a psychiatrist."

"One of the leading authorities on stress behavior," said Bradford, watching the two old men.

"What was that?" the ambassador asked urgently. "Stress behavior?"

The words startled the advisers. The old soldier leaned forward. "Is there a connection?" he demanded of the undersecretary.

"To Parsifal?"

"Who the hell else would I mean? *Is* there?"

"There is, but that's not it."

"What isn't?" asked Brooks apprehensively.

"Miller's specialization. That's his name. Dr. Paul Miller. We don't think his link to Parsifal has anything to do with his studies of stress."

"Thank *God,*" muttered the general.

"Then what *is?*" the elder diplomat pressed impatiently.

"May I, Mr. President?" asked Bradford, his eyes on the Commander in Chief. Berquist nodded silently; the undersecretary turned to the screen and the photographs. "The two men on the left, top and bottom, respectively, are John Philip Ogilvie and Victor Alan Dawson."

"Dawson's an attorney," interrupted Addison Brooks. "I've never met him but I've read a number of his briefs. He's brilliant in the area of international treaty negotiations. He has a gut feeling for foreign legal systems and their nuances."

"Brilliant," agreed the President softly.

"The last man," continued Bradford rapidly, "was no less an expert in his line of work. He was an undercover agent for nearly twenty years, one of the most knowledgeable tacticians in the field of covert operations."

The undersecretary's use of the past tense was not lost on the two advisers. They looked at each other, and then at President Berquist. The Minnesotan nodded.

"They're dead," said the President, bringing his right hand to his forehead, his fingers nervously massaging his brows. "All of them. Ogilvie died four days ago in Rome, a misplaced bullet, the circumstances acceptable. The others were not accidents; they were killed here. Dawson and Stern simultaneously, Miller twenty miles away at the same time."

The ambassador leaned forward, his eyes on the screen. "Four men," he said anxiously. "One an expert in European affairs and policies, another an attorney whose work was almost exclusively in international law, the third a veteran undercover agent with broad tactical experience, and the fourth a psychiatrist acknowledged to be a leading specialist in stress behavior."

"An odd collection of targets," concluded the old soldier.

"They're connected, Mal," said Brooks. "To each other before Parsifal. Am I correct, Mr. President?"

"Let Emory explain," replied Berquist. "He has to take the heat, so let him explain."

Bradford's glance conveyed the fact that the explanation might be his to give but responsibility should be shared. Nevertheless, his slow intake of breath and the quiet delivery of his voice also indicated that he expected the worst.

"These men were the strategists of Consular Operations."

"Costa Brava!" The name exploded in a whisper from the ambassador's lips.

"They peeled it away and found us," said Halyard, his eyes filled with a soldier's angry acceptance. "And they paid for it."

"Yes," agreed Bradford. "but we don't know how it happened."

"How they were *killed*," said the general incredulously.

"We know that," replied the undersecretary. "Very professionally, the decision made quickly."

"Then what don't you understand?" Brooks was annoyed.

"The connection to Parsifal."

"But you said there *was* a connection," insisted the elder statesman. "Is there or isn't there?"

"There has to be. We just can't follow it."

"I can't follow you," said the soldier.

"Start from the beginning, Emory," interrupted the President. "As you understand the beginning. From Rome."

Bradford nodded. "Five days ago the strategists received a priority cable from our conduit in Rome, a Lieutenant Colonel Baylor—cover name Brown. He oversees the clandestine-activities network."

"Larry Baylor?"

"Yes, General."

"One hell of a fine officer. Give me twenty Negroes like him, and you can throw out the War College."

"Colonel Baylor's black, Mr. Ambassador."

"Apparently, Mr. Undersecretary."

"For Christ's sake, Emory," said Berquist.

"Yes, Mr. President. To continue, Colonel Baylor's cable referred to a meeting he had with—" Bradford paused. He delivered the name reluctantly: "Michael Havelock."

"Costa Brava," muttered the soldier quietly.

"Parsifal," added Brooks, halting briefly, then continuing, his words a protest. "But Havelock was ruled out. After the clinic and his separation, he was watched, tested, his every move placed under what I believe is called a microscope. We were assured there was nothing, absolutely *nothing.*"

"Less than nothing," agreed the man from State. "Under controlled circumstances he accepted a teaching position—an assistant professorship —at Concord University in New Hampshire. For all intents and purposes, he was completely out and we were back with the original scenario."

"What changed it?" asked the soldier. "What changed Havelock's status?"

Again Bradford paused, once more his delivery reluctant. "The Karas woman," he said quietly. "She surfaced; he saw her. In Rome."

The silence around the table conveyed the shock. The faces of the two old men hardened, both pairs of eyes boring into the undersecretary, who accepted the looks with granite resignation. Finally the ambassador spoke. "When did this happen?"

"Ten days ago."

"Why weren't we informed, Mr. President?" continued Brooks, his eyes still on Bradford.

"Quite simply," replied the undersecretary before the President could speak, his eyes locked with the statesman's, "because *I* wasn't informed."

"I find that unacceptable."

"Intolerable," added the old soldier sharply. "What the hell are you running over there?"

"An extremely efficient organization that responds to input. In this case, perhaps too efficient, too responsive."

"Explain that," ordered Halyard.

"These four men," said Bradford, gesturing at the projected photographs of the dead strategists, "were convinced beyond doubt that the Karas woman was killed at Costa Brava. How could they think otherwise? We played everything out— *carried* everything out—down to the smallest detail. Nothing was left to speculation; her death was witnessed by Havelock, later confirmed by bloodstained clothing. We wanted it accepted and no one questioned it, least of all Havelock himself."

"But she surfaced," insisted Halyard. "You say he *saw* her. I presume that information was in Colonel Baylor's cable."

"Yes."

"Then why wasn't it reported immediately?" demanded Brooks.

"Because they didn't believe it," answered Bradford. "They thought Havelock was crazy—hallucinating-crazy, the real thing. They sent Ogilvie to Rome, which in itself was extraordinary, indicating how serious they considered the situation to be. Baylor confirmed it. He said Ogilvie told him Havelock had gone over the edge, seeing things that weren't there, the hallucinations brought on by deep, latent hostilities and years of pressure. He simply exploded; at least that's what Ogilvie implied."

"That'd be Miller's judgment," interrupted the President. "It's the only one he could have arrived at when you think of it."

"Havelock's behavior deteriorated rapidly," continued the undersecretary. "He threatened to expose past and present covert operations, which would have compromised us all over Europe, if he wasn't given answers, explanations. He even sent disrupting cables to show what he could do. The strategists took him very seriously. Ogilvie was in Rome either to bring Havelock back—or to kill him."

"Instead, he was killed himself," said the soldier. A statement.

"Tragically. Colonel Baylor was covering Ogilvie's meeting with Havelock on the Palatine Hill; it was an isolated area. There was an argument, a premature eruption of nerve gas triggered by Ogilvie, and when the device failed, Havelock went after him with a gun. As Baylor tells it, he waited until he couldn't wait any longer. He fired at the precise moment he believed Havelock was about to kill Ogilvie, and apparently he was right. Ogilvie must have felt the same thing; at that same moment he lunged up and caught the bullet. It's all in Baylor's report, available to you both, of course."

"Those were the acceptable circumstances, Mr. President?" asked Brooks.

"Only in terms of explanation, Addison."

"Naturally," said Halyard, nodding, looking at Bradford. "If those are Larry Baylor's words, I don't need the report. How's he taking it? That buck doesn't like to lose or goof up."

"He was severely wounded in his right hand. It was shattered and may not come back. Naturally, it'll curtail his activities."

"Don't wash him out; it'd be a mistake. Put him behind a field desk."

"I'll recommend that to the Pentagon, General."

"Let's get back to the Cons Op strategists," said the statesman. "It's still not clear to me why they didn't report Colonel Baylor's information, especially the reasons behind Havelock's actions—those 'disrupting cables,' I believe you called them. Incidentally, how disrupting were they?"

" 'Alarming' is a better word; 'false alarming' better still. One message came here—in a recent sixteen-hundred priority cipher—stating that there was a deep-cover Soviet agent in the White House. Another was sent to Congressional Oversight; it claimed there was CIA corruption in Amsterdam. In both instances the use of the cipher and naming names in Amsterdam obviously lent authority to the data."

"Any substance?" asked the soldier.

"None whatsoever. But the reactions were volatile. The strategists knew they could get worse."

"All the more reason why they should have reported Havelock's motives," insisted Brooks.

"They may have," answered Bradford softly. "To someone. We'll get to that."

"Why they were killed? What's their connection to Parsifal?" The general lowered his voice. "To Costa Brava."

"There was no 'Costa Brava' until we invented it, Mal," said the President. "But that, too, has to be told in sequence. It's the only way we can make sense out of it . . . if there is any sense."

"It never should have happened," interjected the silver-haired statesman. "We had no right."

"We had no *choice*, Mr. Ambassador," said Bradford, leaning forward.
"Secretary of State Matthias built the case against the Karas woman, we
know that. His objective, as near as we can determine, was to remove
Havelock from service, but we could never be certain. Their friendship
was strong, going back years, their family ties stronger, reaching back to
Prague. Was Havelock part of Matthias's plans or not? Was he a willing
player following orders, pretending to do what others would call perfectly
understandable, or was he the unknowing victim of a terrible manipulation? We had to find out."

"We *did* find out," protested Addison Brooks quietly, indignantly. "At
the clinic in Virginia. He was probed with everything doctors and
laboratories can probe with; he knew absolutely nothing. As you said, we
were back to the original scenario, completely in the dark ourselves. Why
did Matthias want him out? It's the unanswered, perhaps now unanswer-
able, question. When we understood that, we should have told Havelock
the truth."

"We couldn't." The undersecretary leaned back in the chair. "Jenna
Karas had disappeared; we had no idea whether she was alive or dead.
Under the circumstances Havelock would have raised questions that can-
not be raised outside the Oval Office—or a room like this."

"Questions," added the President of the United States, "which, if
exposed, would plunge the world into a global nuclear war in a matter of
hours. If the Soviets or the People's Republic of China knew this government is out of control, ICBM's would be launched from both hemi-
spheres, a thousand submarines poised in both oceans for secondary tactical strikes—obliteration. And we *are* out of control."

Silence.

"There's someone I'd like you to meet," said Bradford finally. "I had
him flown in from an Alpine pass called Col des Moulinets. He's out of
Rome."

"Nuclear war," whispered the President, as he pressed the button on
the huge, curved desk, and the screen went dark.

16

Havelock drew two lines through the seventeenth and eighteenth names on the list, hung up the telephone on the wall and left the shabby café in Montmartre. Two calls per phone were all he permitted himself. Sophisticated electronic scanners could pick up a location in a matter of minutes, and should any of those he reached be patched into equipment at the American embassy, it would be no different from his calling the Paris conduit of Cons Op and setting the time for his own execution. Two calls per phone, each phone a minimum of six blocks from the previous one, no conversation lasting more than ninety seconds. He had gone through half the list, but now the rest of the names would have to wait. It was nearly nine o'clock; the gaudy lights of Montmartre battered the streets with frenzied eruptions of color that matched the frantic caco- phony of the district's nighttime revels. And he was to meet Gravet in an alley off the Rue Norvins. The art critic had spent the afternoon tracking down anyone and everyone in his peculiar world who might have knowledge of Jenna Karas.

In a way, so had Michael, but his initial work had been cerebral. He had retrieved his clothes from a Métro locker, purchased basic toiletries, a note pad and a ball-point pen, and taken a room at a cheap hotel around the corner from La Couronne Nouvelle. He reasoned that if the wounded VKR officer raised help, he would not think to send his killers down the street for the target. Havelock had shaved and bathed, and now lay on the decrepit bed, his body resting but not his mind. He had gone back in time, disciplining his memory, recalling every moment he and Jenna had shared in Paris. He had approached the exercise academically, as a graduate student might doggedly follow a single development chronologically through a chaotic period in history. He and Jenna, Jenna and he; where they had gone, what they had seen, whom they had spoken with, all in order of sequence. Each place and scene had a location and a reason for their being there; finally, each face that had any meaning had a name, or if not a specific name, the identity of someone who knew him or her.

After two hours and forty minutes of probing, he had sat up, reached for the note pad and pen he had placed on a bedside chair, and had begun his list. A half hour later it was complete—as complete as his memory permitted—and he had relaxed, back on the bed, knowing that the much needed sleep would come. He knew also that the clock in his mind would awaken him when daylight ended. It did. And minutes later he was out in the streets, going from one telephone booth to another, one café with a TÉLÉPHONE sign in the window to the next, each instrument six blocks away from the last.

He began the conversations quickly but casually, and kept his ears primed to pick up any telltale signs of alarm in the responses. In each case his approach was the same; he was to have met Jenna that noon at the Meurice bar, each having flown into Paris from a different city, but his plane had been hours late. And since Jenna had mentioned the person's name frequently—fondness implied—Michael wondered if she had called him or her, perhaps looking for an afternoon companion in a city she barely knew.

Most were mildly surprised to hear from Havelock, especially so casually, and even more surprised that Jenna Karas would have remembered their names, much less having recalled them with affection; they were by and large only brief acquaintances. However, in no instance was there the slightest hesitation other than the normal caution required when confronted with the unexpected. Eighteen names. Nothing. Where had she gone? What was she doing? She could not go underground in Paris, not without his finding her; she had to know that. *Christ, where are you?*

He reached the Rue Ravignan and began the steep ascent up the Montmartre hill, passing the dark old houses that were once the homes of legends, and emerging on the small square that was the Place Clément, he started down the Rue Norvins. The street was crowded, the revels of would-be Bohemians fueled by the genuine residents who dressed their roles and later went home to count their profits. The alley Gravet had described was just before the narrow Rue des Saules; he could see the break in the row of ancient buildings up ahead and walked faster.

The old brick alleyway was dark and empty. The ersatz Bohemians knew there were limits to their pretense that they belonged in Montmartre; a mugging on the sacred hill of martyrs was little different from a taped iron pipe in Soho or the East Village. Havelock went inside, his right hand instinctively edging toward the break in his jacket and belt where the magnum was awkwardly in place. Gravet was late, a discourtesy the critic himself found abhorrent. What had happened?

Michael found a shadowed doorway in the dimly lit thoroughfare; he leaned against the brick frame, took out a cigarette and struck a match. As he cupped the flame his mind leaped back to the Palatine, to a book of matches and a man who had tried to save his life, not take it. A dying man who had died only moments later, knowing there was betrayal at the highest levels of his government.

There was a sudden commotion out on the Rue Norvins, a brief flare-up of tempers as two men collided. Then a tall, slender man stood momentarily erect, and let forth a stream of invective in French. His much younger, stockier adversary made a sullen comment about the man's ancestry and moved along. The injured party smoothed his lapels, turned to his left and entered the alley. Gravet had arrived, not without his customary *élan*.

"*Merde!*" the critic spat out, seeing Havelock walk out of the shadows into the dim light. "It's those filthy, ragged field jackets they wear! You just know they dribble when they eat and their teeth are yellow. God knows when they last bathed or spoke civilly. Sorry to be late."

"It's only a few minutes. I just got here."

"I'm late. I intended to be in the Rue Norvins a half hour ago to make sure you weren't followed."

"I wasn't."

"Yes, you'd know that, wouldn't you?"

"I'd know. What kept you?"

"A young man I've cultivated who works in the catacombs of the Quai d'Orsay."

"You're honest."

"And you misinterpret." Gravet moved to the wall, turning his head back and forth, looking at both entrances of the alley; he was satisfied. "Since you called after your business at the Couronne Nouvelle—a call, incidentally, I wasn't sure you'd ever make—I've been in touch with every conceivable contact who might know something about a lone woman in Paris looking for sanctuary, or papers, or secret transportation, and no one could help. It was really quite illogical; after all, there are only so many sources of illegal machinations, and precious few I'm not aware of. I even checked the Italian districts, thinking her escorts from Col des Moulinets might have provided her with a name or two. Nothing. . . . Then it occurred to me. *Illegal* efforts? Perhaps I was searching in the wrong areas. Perhaps, instead, such a woman might seek more legitimate assistance, without necessarily detailing her illegitimate reasons. After all, she was an experienced field operative. She had to know—or know of—certain personnel in allied governments if only through you."

"The Quai d'Orsay."

"*Naturellement.* But the undersides, the catacombs, where distinctly unpublicized conveniences had to exist for you."

"If they did, I'm not aware of them. I crossed paths with a number of people in the ministries but I never heard of the catacombs."

"London's Foreign Office calls them Clearing Centres. Your own State Department refers to them less subtly. Division of Diplomatic Transfers."

"Immunity," said Havelock. "Did you find something?"

"My young friend spent the last several hours tracing it down. I told him the timing was advantageously narrow. If anything happened, it could only have happened today. So he returned to his little cave after the dinner hour on some pretext or other and riffled through the day's security duplicates. He thinks he may have found it, but he can't be certain and neither can I. However, you might be able to make the connection."

"What is it?"

"At ten-forty-five this morning there was a memorandum from the Ministère des Affaires Etrangères ordering up an open identity. Subject: white female, early thirties, languages: Slavic, Russian, Serbo-Croatian, cover name and statistics requested immediately. Now, I realize there are dozens—"

"What section at the ministry?" interrupted Havelock.

"Four. Section Four."

"Régine Broussac," said Havelock. "Madame Régine Broussac. First Assistant Deputy, Section Four."

"That's the connection. It's the name and signature on the request."

"She's twenty-ninth on my list, twenty-ninth out of thirty-one. We saw her—*I* saw her—for less than a minute on the street almost a year ago. I barely introduced Jenna. It doesn't make sense; she hardly knows her, *doesn't* know her."

"Were the circumstances of your seeing her a year ago notable?"

"I suppose so. One of their people was a double agent at the French embassy in Bonn; he made periodic flights to the East by way of Luckenwalde. We found him on the wrong side of Berlin. At a meeting of the *Geheimdienst.*"

"The Moscow puppet's offspring of the S.S. I'd say quite notable." Gravet paused, unfolding his hands. "This Broussac. She's an older woman, isn't she? Years ago a heroine of the Résistance?"

"She and her husband, yes. He was taken by the Gestapo; what they found of him wasn't pleasant."

"But she carried on."

"Yes."

"Did you, perhaps, tell any of this to your friend?"

Havelock thought back as he drew on the cigarette, then dropped it, crushing it underfoot. "Probably. Régine's not always easy to take; she can be abrupt, caustic, some call her a bitch, but she's not. She *had* to be tough."

"Then let me ask you another question, the answer to which I'm vaguely familiar with, but it's based merely on rumor; nothing I've read that pretended to be official." The critic folded his hands again. "What prompted your friend to do what she did, to live the sort of life she led with you, and obviously before you?"

"1968," replied Havelock flatly.

"The Warsaw-bloc invasion?"

"The *černý den* of August. The black days. Her parents had died, and she was living in Ostrava with her two older brothers, one married. Both were Dubček activists, the younger a student, the older an engineer who was forbidden any meaningful work by the Novotný regime. When the tanks rolled in, the younger brother was killed in the streets, the older one rounded up by advance Soviet troops for 'interrogation.' He was crippled for life—arms and legs—totally helpless. He blew his brains out and his wife disappeared. Jenna traveled to Prague, where no one knew her, and went underground. She knew whom to reach, what she wanted to do."

Gravet nodded; his face looked drawn even in the dim light. "The people who do what you do, quietly, so efficiently, you all have different stories, yet common themes run through them. Violence, pain . . . loss. And genuine revenge."

"What did you expect? Only ideologues can afford to shout; we've generally got other things on our minds. It's why we're sent in first. It doesn't take much to make us efficient."

"Or to recognize one another, I imagine."

"Under certain circumstances, yes. We don't make too much of it. What's your point?"

"The Broussac woman. Your friend from the Costa Brava would remember her. A husband, brothers, pain, loss . . . a woman alone. Such a woman would remember another woman who carried on."

"She obviously did, I just wouldn't have thought so." Havelock nodded silently. "You're right," he said quietly. "Thanks for giving it perspective. Of course she would."

"Be careful, Michael."

"Of what?"

"Genuine revenge. There has to be a *sympathie* between them. She could turn you over to your own, trap you."

"I'll be careful; so will she. What else can you tell me about the memorandum? Was a destination mentioned?"

"No, she could be going anywhere. That will be set at Affaires Etrangères and kept quiet."

"What about her cover? A name?"

"That was processed and beyond my young friend's eyes, at least this evening. Perhaps tomorrow he can pry into files that are locked tonight."

"Too late. You said the memorandum asked for an immediate response. That passport's been mocked up and issued. She's on her way out of France. I have to move quickly."

"What's one day? Twelve hours from now perhaps we can find a name. You call the airlines on an emergency basis and they check their manifests. You'll know where she's gone."

"But not how."

"Je ne comprends pas."

"Broussac. If she's done this much for Jenna, she'll do more. She wouldn't leave her on her own at an airport somewhere. Arrangements were made. I have to know what they are."

"And you think she'll tell you?"

"She has to." Havelock buttoned his loose-fitting jacket and pulled the lapels up around his neck. The alley was a tunnel for the damp breezes from below, and there was a chill. "One way or the other, she has to tell me. Thanks, Gravet, I owe you."

"Yes, you do."

"I'll see Broussac tonight and leave in the morning . . . one way or the other. But before I go, there's a bank here in Paris where I've got a safety deposit box; I'll clean it out and leave an envelope for you at the vault cage. Call it part payment. It's the Banque Germaine on the Avenue George Cinq."

"You're most considerate, but is it wise? In all modesty, I'm something of a public figure and must be careful in my associations. Someone there might know you."

"Not by any name you've ever heard of."

"Then what name shall I use?"

"None. Just say the 'gentleman from Texas'; he's left an envelope for you. If it makes you feel any better, say you've never met me. I'm negotiating a painting for an anonymous buyer in Houston."

"And if there are complications?"

"There won't be. You know where I'm going tonight, and, by extension, tomorrow."

"At the last, we're professionals, aren't we, Michael?"

"I wouldn't have it any other way. It's cleaner." Havelock extended his hand. "Thanks again. You know the help you've been. I won't belabor it."

"You can forget about the envelope, if you like," said Gravet, shaking hands, studying Michael's face in the shadows. "You may need the money, and my expenses were minimal. I can always collect on your next trip to Paris."

"Don't change the rules, we've lived too long by them. But I appreciate the vote of confidence."

"You were always civilized, and I don't understand any of this business. Why her? Why you?"

"I wish to God I knew."

"That's the key, isn't it? Something you *do* know."

"If it is, I haven't the vaguest idea what it could be. Good-bye, Gravet."

"*Non, au revoir.* I really don't want the envelope, *Mikhail.* Come back to Paris. You owe me." The distinguished critic turned and disappeared up the alley.

There was no point in being evasive with Régine Broussac; she would sense the evasion instantly, the coincidence of timing being too unbeliev-

able. On the other hand, to give her the advantage of naming the rendezvous was equally foolish; she would stake out the area with personnel the
Quai d'Orsay had no idea were on its payroll. Broussac was tough, knowing
when and when not to involve her government, and depending upon what
Jenna had told her, she might consider any dealings with an unbalanced
retired American field officer more suited to treatment by unofficial methods. There were no checks and balances in those methods; they were
dangerous because there was no line of responsibility, only diverted monies that no one cared to acknowledge. Drones by any other names or
payments were first cousins to the practitioners of violence—whether
employed by Rome in Col des Moulinets or by a VKR officer in a cheap
hotel on the Rue Etienne. All were essentially lethal, it was merely a
question of degree, and all should be avoided unless one was the employer.
Havelock understood; he had to get Broussac alone, and to do that, he
had to convince her that he was not dangerous—to her—and might have
information that could be extraordinarily valuable.

An odd thought struck him as he descended the endless steps of Montmartre. He was talking to himself about the truth. He would tell her part
of it, but not all of it. Liars twisted the truth and she might listen to their
version of the truth, not his.

She was in the Paris telephone book. Rue Losserand.

". . . I've never given you wrong information and I'm not going to start
tonight. But it's out of sanction. Way out. So that you can judge just how
far, use someone else's name at the Quai d'Orsay and call the embassy.
Ask about my status, directing the inquiry to the senior attaché of Consular Operations. Say I called you from somewhere in the South and wanted
to set up a meeting. As an official of a friendly government, request
instructions. I'll call you back in ten minutes, not on this phone, of
course."

"Of course. Ten minutes."

"Régine?"

"Yes?"

"Remember Bonn."

"Ten minutes."

Havelock walked south to Berlioz Square, checking his watch frequently, knowing he would add an additional five to seven minutes beyond
the stated ten. Stretching a call-back under tension often exposed more
than the recipient intended to reveal. There was a *cabine* on the corner,

a young woman inside screaming into the phone, gesturing frantically. In a fit of temper she slammed down the receiver and stalked out of the booth.

"*Vache!*" exclaimed the angry girl as she passed Havelock, furiously adjusting the shoulder strap of her large purse.

He opened the door and walked in; the extended stretch time had reached nine minutes. He made the call and listened.

"Yes?" Broussac's voice broke off the first ring. She was anxious; she had reached the embassy.

"Did you speak to the attaché?"

"You're late. You said ten minutes."

"Did you speak to him?"

"Yes. I'll meet with you. Come to my flat as soon as you can."

"Sorry. I'll call you back in a little while."

"*Havelock!*"

He hung up and walked out of the booth, his eyes scanning the street for a vacant taxi.

Twenty-five minutes later he was in another booth, the numbers indistinguishable in the shadows. He struck a match and dialed.

"*Yes!*"

"Take the Métro to the Bercy station, and walk up into the street. Several blocks down on the right is a row of warehouses. I'll be in the area. Come alone, because I'll know if you don't. And if you don't, I won't show."

"This is *ridiculous!* A lone woman at night in Bercy!"

"If there's anyone around at this hour, I'll warn him about you."

"Preposterous! What are you *thinking* of?"

"A year ago in another street," said Michael. "Of Bonn." He lowered the phone into the cradle.

The area was deserted, the row of warehouses dark, the streetlights dim, the wattage low by municipal decree. It was a favorable hour and location for a drop that entailed more than a pickup or an exchange of merchandise. A conversation could be held without the din of crowded streets or the jostling of impatient pedestrians, and unlike a café or a city park, there were few places where an unknown observer could conceal himself. The few residents who emerged from the lighted cavern of the Métro up the street could be watched—hesitation or sudden disappearance could be noted; a stray automobile could be seen blocks away. The complete advantage was found, of course, in being there at the rendezvous before it was established. He was; he left the booth and started across the Boulevard de Bercy.

Two trucks were parked, one behind the other, at the curb in front of a loading platform. Their open-planked carriages were empty, stationary symbols of an early-morning call for the drivers. He would wait between the two vehicles, the sight lines in either direction clear. Régine Broussac would come; the agitated huntress, prodded and provoked, would be unable to resist the unexplained.

Eleven separate times he heard the muted rumble of the underground trains and felt the vibrations in the concrete and earth beneath him. Starting with the sixth, he concentrated on the Métro's entrance; she could not have arrived before it did. However, radio dispatch was commonplace and rapid; only minutes after the second call he had begun to study the street, the infrequent automobiles, the less frequent bicycles. He saw nothing that alarmed him, and the most insignificant intrusion would have done so.

The twelfth rumble stopped, the faint vibrations still echoing underfoot, and by the time the below-ground thunder commenced again he could see her climbing up the steps; her short, broad figure emerging from the brighter light into the dimly lit street. A couple preceded her; Michael watched them carefully. They were elderly, older than Broussac, their pace slow and deliberate; they would be of no value to her. They turned left, around the squared iron latticework of the entrance, and away from the trucks and the warehouses; they were no part of a night unit. Régine continued forward with the hesitant stride of an apprehensive older woman aware of her vulnerability, her head turning slowly, reluctantly at each odd noise, real and imagined. She passed under a streetlight and Havelock remembered; her skin was as gray as her short-cropped hair, testimony to years of unacknowledged torments, yet her face was softened by wide blue eyes as often expressive as they were clouded. As she passed through the light into the shadows, Gravet's words came back to Havelock: "Violence, pain, loss." Régine Broussac had lived through it all and survived—quiet, wary, silently tough, and in no way beaten. She reveled in the secret, unseen powers her government had given her; it helped her get even. Michael understood; after all, she was one of them. A survivor.

She came alongside him on the pavement. He called out softly from between the trucks, "Régine."

She stopped, standing motionless, her eyes straight ahead, not looking at him. She said, "Is it necessary to hold a weapon on me?"

"I have no gun aimed at you. I have a gun, but it's not in my hand."

"Bien!" Broussac spun around, her purse raised. An explosion blew a hole through the fabric, and the concrete and stone shattered beneath Havelock's feet, fragments of rock and cement piercing his trousers, scraping his flesh. "For what you did to Jenna Karas!" shouted the woman, her face contorted. "Do not move! One step, one gesture, and I will put a hole in your throat!"

"What are you *doing?*"

"What have you *done?* Whom do you work for *now?*"

"Myself, goddamn you! Myself and *Jenna!*" Havelock raised his hand, an instinctive move but no less a plea. It was not accepted.

A second explosion came from the shattered purse, the bullet grazing his outer palm, ricocheting off the truck's metal, whining out into the night.

"Arrêtez! I'd as soon deliver a corpse as a breathing body. Perhaps more so in your case, *cochon.*"

"Deliver to whom?"

"You said you would call me 'in a little while'—were they not your words? Well, in a little while several colleagues of mine will be here, a time span I was willing to risk. In less than thirty minutes you would have felt secure; you would have shown yourself. When they arrive we'll drive to a house out in the countryside where we shall have a session with you. Then we'll give you to the Gabriel. They want you very badly. They called you dangerous, that's all I had to know . . . with what I already knew."

"Not to *you!* I'm dangerous to *them,* not you!"

"What do you take me for? Take *us* for?"

"You saw Jenna. You helped her—"

"I saw her. I listened to her. I heard the truth."

"As she believes it, not as it *is!* Hear *me!* Listen to *me!*"

"You'll talk under the proper conditions. You know what they are as well as I do."

"I don't need chemicals, you bitch! You won't hear anything different!"

"We'll follow procedures," said Broussac, removing her hand and the gun from the ruptured purse. "Move out of there," she continued, gesturing with the weapon. "You're standing in the shadows. I don't like it."

Of course she didn't like it, thought Havelock, watching the old woman
blink her eyes. As with many aging people, it was clear that night was no
friend to her vision. It accounted for her constantly moving head as she
walked away from the lighted entrance of the Métro; she had been as
concerned with the unexpected shadows as with sounds. He had to keep
her talking, divert some part of her concentration.

"You think the American embassy will tolerate what you're doing?"
said Michael, stepping out of the patterned shadow created by the slats
of the open truck and the spill of the streetlamps.

"There'll be no international incident; we had no alternative but to
sedate you. In their words, you're dangerous."

"They won't accept that and you know it."

"They'll have little choice. The Gabriel has been alerted that a situation
of extreme abnormality exists in which a former American intelligence
officer—a specialist in clandestine activities—may be attempting to compromise an official of the Quai d'Orsay. The anticipated confrontation will
take place twenty miles from Paris, near Argenteuil, and the Americans
are requested to have a vehicle with armed personnel in the vicinity. A
radio frequency has been established. We will turn over an American
problem to the Americans once we learn the nature of the extortion. We
protect the interests of our government. Perfectly acceptable, even generous."

"Christ, you're thorough."

"Very. I've known men like you. And women; we used to shave their
heads. I despise you."

"Because of what she told you?"

"Like you, I know when I've heard the truth. She did not lie."

"I agree. Because she believes it all—just as I did. And I was wrong—
God, was I wrong—just as she's wrong now. We were used, both of us
used."

"By your own people? For what purpose?"

"I don't *know!*"

She was listening, her concentration beginning to split. She could not
help herself, the unexplored was too compelling.

"Why do you think I reached you?" he asked. "For Christ's sake, if I
had the leverage to find you, I could have bypassed you! I don't need you,
Régine. I could have learned what I wanted to learn without you. I called
you because I trusted you!"

Broussac blinked, the gray flesh around her eyes wrinkling in thought. "You'll have your chance to talk—under the proper conditions."

"Don't do this!" cried Michael, taking a short step forward. She did not fire; she did not move her gun. "You've set it in motion; you'll have to turn me over! They know it's me and you'll be forced to. Your friends'll insist. They're not going to go down with you, no matter what you hear from me—under proper conditions!"

"Why should we go down?"

"Because the embassy is being lied to. By people way the hell up!"

The old woman's eyes now blinked rapidly as she flinched. She had not fired when he moved only seconds ago.

Now!

Havelock lunged forward, his right arm extended, rigid, as straight as an iron bar, his left hand under his wrist. He made contact with the gun, sweeping it aside as a third explosion broke the silence of the deserted street. With his left hand he grabbed the barrel and ripped it out of her grip, then slammed her against the wall of the warehouse.

"Cochon! Traître!" screamed Broussac, her face twisted. *"Kill* me! You'll learn nothing from me!"

He held his forearm across her throat—in agony from the wound in his shoulder—as he pressed her head back into the brick, the weapon in his hand. "What I want can't be forced from you, Régine," he said while gasping for breath. "Don't you understand? It has to be given."

"Nothing! Which *terroristes* bought you? Meinhof cowards? Arab pigs? Isracli fanatics? Brigate Rosse? Who wants what you can sell? . . . She knew. She found out! And you must kill her! Kill me first, *betrayer!"*

Slowly Havelock released the pressure of his arm and, slower still, he moved his body away from hers. He knew the risk; he did not take it lightly. On the other hand, he knew Régine Broussac. After all, she was one of them; she had survived. He removed his arm and stood in front of her, his eyes steady, looking into hers.

"I've betrayed no one except myself," he began. "And through myself a person I love very much. I meant what I said. I can't force you to tell me what I have to know. Among other things, you could lie to me too easily, too successfully, and I'd be back where I was ten days ago. I won't do that. If I can't find her, if I can't have her back, perhaps it doesn't matter. I know what I did and it's killing me. I love her . . . I need her. I think we both need each other more than anything else in the world just now. We're all each other has left. But I've learned something about futility over the years." He raised the gun in his left hand, taking the barrel with his right. He held it out to her. "You've fired three times; there are four shells left."

Broussac stood still, staring at him, studying his face, his eyes. She took the weapon and leveled it at his head, her own eyes questioning, roaming his. Finally her grimacing features softened, astonishment replacing hostility. Slowly she lowered the gun.

"*C'est incroyable,*" she whispered. "This is the truth, then."

"The truth."

Régine looked at her watch. "*Vite!* We must leave. They'll be here in minutes; they'll search everywhere."

"Where to? There are no taxis—"

"The Métro. We'll take it to the Rochereau. There's a small park where we can talk."

"What about your team? What'll you tell them?"

"That I was testing their alertness," she said, taking his arm as they started up the pavement toward the lighted entrance of the underground train. "That I wanted to see how they would react in a given situation. It's consistent: it's late, they're off duty, and I'm a bitch."

"You've still got the embassy."

"I know, I was thorough. I'll have to think about that."

"Maybe I never showed up," said Havelock, rubbing his shoulder, grateful that the pain was receding.

"*Merci.*"

The vest-pocket park in Denfert Rochereau was a plot of grass dotted with stone benches, sculptured trees and a graveled path circling a small pool with a fountain in its center. The only source of light was a streetlamp thirty feet away, its spill filtered by the branches of the trees. They sat beside each other on the cold bench. Michael told Broussac what he had seen—and what he had not seen—at the Costa Brava. He then had to ask the question. "Did she tell you what happened?"

"She was warned, told to follow instructions."

"By whom?"

"A high government official from Washington."

"How could she accept him?"

"He was brought to her by a man identified as the senior attaché from Madrid's Consular Operations."

"Consular . . . *Madrid?* Where was *I?*"

"Madrid."

"Jesus, right down to the hour!"

"What was?"

"The whole goddamned thing. What instructions was she given?"

"To meet a man that night and leave Barcelona with him."

"Did she?"

"No."

"Why not?"

"She panicked. In her words, everything had collapsed for her. She didn't feel she could trust *anyone.* She ran."

"Thank God. I don't know who was killed on that beach, but it was meant to be Jenna. In a way, it makes the whole thing even more obscene. Who was she? Someone who didn't know a damn thing? A woman brought there and told to chase a Frisbee in the moonlight, suddenly shot at, knowing she was going to die? *Christ,* what kind of people *are* they?"

"Find out through Madrid. The attaché from Consular Operations."

"I can't. She was fed another lie. There's no Cons Op unit in Madrid; the climate's too rotten. It operates an hour away out of Lisbon."

Régine was silent, her eyes on him. "What's happening, Michael?"

Havelock watched the fountain in the dark pool. Its cascading spray was diminishing, folding, dying; somewhere a hand was turning a dial, shutting it off for the remainder of the night. "Liars are operating at very high places in my government. They've penetrated areas I used to think were impenetrable. They're controlling, killing—lying. And someone in Moscow is working with them."

"Moscow? Are you sure?"

"I'm sure. On the word of a man who wasn't afraid to die, but was afraid of living the way I promised him he'd be forced to live. Someone in Moscow, someone the controllers of the KGB know nothing about, is in contact with the liars."

"For what purpose. *You?* To destroy your credibility, then kill you? To void some recent accomplishment by maligning the record of a dead man?"

"It's not me; I'm only a part of it. I wasn't important before, but I am now." Havelock turned his head and looked at old Broussac, her face now soft and compassionate, yet still ashen in the dim light. "Because I saw Jenna; because I found out she was alive. Now they have to kill me. They have to kill her, too."

"Why? You were the best!"

"I don't know. I only know that Costa Brava is where I have to look for answers. It's where it started for Jenna and me . . . where it was supposed to end. One of us dead, the other dying inside, finished. Out."

"It is she who is dying inside now. It astonishes me that she can function as she does, move as she does. She's remarkable." Régine paused. The fountain's spray had collapsed, and only trickles of water dripped over its saucerlike basin into the pool. "She loved you, you know."

"Past tense?"

"Oh, yes. We all learn to accept new realities, don't we? We're better at it than most people because sudden change is an old acquaintance as well as our enemy. We constantly seek out betrayal in others; we preach it. And all the while we're being tested ourselves, our adversaries intent on seducing our minds and our appetites. Sometimes we succeed, sometimes they do. That's the reality."

"The futility," said Havelock.

"You are too much the *philosophe* for this business."

"It's why I got out." Michael looked away. "I saw her face in the window of the plane in Col des Moulinets. Her eyes. Christ, it was awful."

"I'm certain it was. It happens. Hatred replaces love, doesn't it? It's the only defense in these cases. . . . She'll kill you if she can."

"Oh, God . . ." Havelock leaned forward on the bench, his elbows on his knees, hands cupped under his chin, staring at the fountain. "I love her so. I loved her when I killed her that night, knowing a part of me would always be at that beach for the rest of my life, my eyes seeing her running, falling in the sand, my ears hearing her screams . . . wanting to race down and hold her, tell her the whole world was a *lie* and nothing mattered but us! Just *us* . . . Something inside me was trying to tell me that terrible things were being done to us, and I wouldn't listen. . . . I was too hurt to listen to myself. I, I, *I! Me!* I couldn't get *me* out of the way and hear the truth she was screaming!"

"You were a professional in a professional crisis," said Régine softly, touching his arm. "According to everything you'd learned, everything you'd lived with for years, you were doing what you had to do. A professional."

Michael turned his head and looked at her. "Why wasn't I myself?" he asked simply. "Why didn't I listen to the other screams, the ones I couldn't get out of my throat?"

"We can't always trust what we call instinct, Michael. You know that."

"I know that I love her . . . loved her when I thought I hated her, when that professional in me expected to see her die because I'd closed the trap on an enemy. I didn't hate her, I loved her. Do you know why I know that?"

"Why, *mon cher?*"

"Because there was no satisfaction in winning, not the slightest. Only revulsion, only sadness . . . only wanting things to be the way they couldn't be."

"That's when you got out, isn't it? It's what we'd heard, what I found so difficult to believe. I understand now. You loved her very much. I *am* sorry, Michel."

Havelock shook his head, closing his eyes, the darkness comforting for a moment. "In Barcelona," he said, opening his eyes again, looking at the quiet pool in front of them, "what happened to her? Tell me what she told you."

"She can't understand what happened. Did the Soviets actually buy you or did Washington order her execution? It's an enigma to her—a violent enigma. She got out of Spain and went to Italy, going from city to city, seeking out those few people she thought she could trust to help her, hide her. But always there were the questions: Where were *you?* Why was she alone and not with *you?* At first, she was afraid to say, and when she did, no one believed her. Whenever she told the story and it was rejected, she felt she had to run again, convinced the few would reach you, and you would come after her. She lives with the nightmare that you're always there, following—hunting her down. And when she settled briefly into a safe cover, a Russian appeared, someone you both knew in Prague, a KGB butcher. Coincidence? Who was to tell? She ran again, this time stealing a large sum of money from her employer."

"I wondered about that. How she could buy her way out of Italy, get across the border, and up into Paris. Compared with some other routes, she traveled first-class."

Broussac smiled, her blue eyes lively in the shadows, telling him that a brief moment of amusement was to follow. "She laughed about it—quietly, to be sure—but the laughter was good; that she could laugh was good, Michael. Do you see what I mean? For a minute or two she was like a little girl remembering a prank."

"I hear her laughter in my sleep . . . when I don't hear her screams. Her laugh was always quiet, never loud, but somehow full . . . an echo from deep inside her. She loved to laugh; it was a release for her, something not usually permitted and therefore enjoyed so much more when it happened." He paused, his eyes again on the still fountain. "How did she steal the money? Where?"

"Milan."

"The Soviets are crawling all over Milan. Whomever she saw was a migratory coincidence. . . . Sorry, what happened?"

"She was working in that enormous store in the Piazza del Duomo, the one that sells books and magazines and newspapers from all over the world. Do you know it?"

"I've seen it."

"Her languages got her the job, and she dyed her hair, wore glasses, all the usual things. But her figure also got her the undivided attention of the owner, a pig with a large wife he was terrified of and eight children. He was forever asking her into his office and mauling her and promising her the Galleria Vittorio for her favors. One day at noon the Russian came in; she recognized him and knew she had to run; she was afraid that he was connected to you, that you were scouring Europe for her. . . . At the lunch hour, she literally assaulted the manager in his office, claiming that she could no longer wait for *his* favors, and that only a small loan stood between them and absolute ecstasy. By this time she had her blouse off and the poor man's billfold under a chair. In a state of near apoplexy, the idiot opened the safe, where several days' receipts were stored—it was a Friday, if you recall."

"Why should I?" interrupted Havelock.

"We'll get to that," said Régine, a partial smile on her lips. "Regardless, when the aging, perspiring Lothario had the safe open and our Jenna was removing her brassiere, he counted out a few thousand lire in his quivering hands and she struck him in the head with a desk clock. She then proceeded to empty the safe, positively stunned by the amounts of money filling the bank-deposit pouches. That money was her passport and she knew it."

"It was also an invitation for a police hunt."

"A hunt that could be delayed, the delay permitting her to get out of Milan."

"How?"

"Fear, confusion, and embarrassment," replied Broussac. "Jenna closed the safe, stripped the owner naked, and marked him everywhere with streaks of lipstick. She then called his home and, speaking with a maid, said an urgent matter required the man's wife to come to the store in an hour, not before and not later."

"Fear, confusion, and embarrassment," agreed Michael, nodding. "She tapped him again, making sure he'd stay where he was, figuring he'd hardly rush to the safe in front of his wife, compounding the mess he was already in. . . . And obviously, she took his clothes with her," added Havelock, smiling, remembering the woman who was Jenna Karas.

"Obviously. She used the next several hours to gather her things together, and realizing that a police warrant would be issued sooner or later, removed the dye from her hair. She then joined the crowds at the Milan railroad station."

"The railroad . . . ?" Michael sat back on the bench and looked at Régine. "The train. She took the train to Rome! That's where I saw her!"

"It's a moment she'll never forget. There you were, standing there, staring at her. The man who had forced her into hiding, into running, who'd caused her to alter her appearance and change the sequence of her languages. The one person on earth she was terrified might find her, kill her—and there *she* was, all her disguise gone, recognized by the one she most feared."

"If the shock hadn't been so paralyzing, if only I'd been quicker . . . so much would have been so different." Michael arched his neck back and brought his hands to his face, covering his eyes. "Oh, *Christ*, we were so *close!* I yelled to her, I screamed and kept screaming, but she disappeared. I lost her in the crowds; she didn't hear me—she didn't *want* to hear me—and I lost her." Havelock lowered his hands and gripped the edge of the stone bench. "Civitavecchia came next. Did she tell you about that?"

"Yes. It was where she saw a crazed animal try to kill her on a pier—"

"It *wasn't* her! How could she think I thought it was? Jesus, a fucking whore from the docks!" Michael checked himself; it served no purpose to lose control.

"She saw what she saw," said old Broussac quietly. "She couldn't know what you were thinking."

"How did she know I'd go to Civitavecchia? A man there told me she thought I'd question the taxi drivers. I didn't. There's a strike, although a few are running, I suppose."

"There are, and you are the best of hunters. You yourself taught her that the surest way to get out of a country unseen is to go to a busy waterfront in the early hours of the morning. There is always someone willing to broker space, if only in a cargo hold. She asked people on the train, pretending to be a Polish merchant seaman's wife, her husband on a freighter. People are not stupid; they understood; one more couple leaving the arms of the Bear. 'Civitavecchia,' they said. 'Try Civita-vecchia!' She assumed you might reach the same conclusion—based on what you'd taught her—and so she made her preparations. She was right; you arrived."

"By a different route," said Havelock. "Because of a conductor on the third car of the train who remembered a *bella ragazza.*"

"Regardless, she assumed the possibility and acted on it, placing herself in a position to observe. As I said, she's remarkable. The strain, the pressures. To do what she did without panic, to mount the strategy alone . . . remarkable. I think you were a splendid teacher, Michael."

"She had ten years of training before I met her. There was a lot she could teach me, and did. You gave her a cover and diplomatic clearance. Where did she go? What arrangements did you make?"

"How did you learn this?"

"Don't make me pay the price, I owe him. Instead, let me send him to you. Don't turn him in; use him yourself. You won't regret it, but I need the guarantee."

"Fair enough. Talent should be shared, and I respect the sender. I remember Bonn."

"Where did she go?"

"Outside of a few remote islands in the Pacific, the safest place in the world for her now. The United States."

Havelock stared in astonishment at the old woman. "How did you figure *that?*"

"I went back over the restricted cables from your State Department looking for any mention of Jenna Karas. Indeed, it was there. A single insertion dated January tenth, detailing briefly the events at the Costa Brava. She was described as an infiltrator caught in a reverse trap where she had lost her life, her death confirmed by two separate sightings and forensic examination of bloodstained clothing. The file was closed to the satisfaction of Consular Operations."

"The rotes have it," said Michael. "Aye, aye, sir. Next case, please."

"The implausibility was glaring, of course. Sightings can be erroneous, but a forensic laboratory has to work with materials. Yet they couldn't have, not with any legitimacy. Not only was Jenna Karas very much alive and sitting in my office, but she had never gone to that beach on the Costa Brava. The forensic confirmation was a lie, and someone had to know it, someone who wanted the lie accepted as the truth." Broussac paused. "I assumed it was you. Termination carried out, execution as scheduled. If you had been bought by the Soviets, what better proof could they have than from the Department of State? If you had been carrying out Washington's instructions, you could not allow them to think you had failed."

"In light of what she told you, I can understand."

"But I wasn't satisfied; the acceptance was too simple, so I looked further. I went to the data-processing computers and placed her name in the security scanner relevant to the past three months. . . . It was extraordinary. She appeared no less than twelve times, but never on State Department communiqués. They were all on cables from the Central Intelligence Agency, and couched in very odd language. It was always the same, cable after cable: the U.S. government had an alert out for a woman matching her description who *might* be using the name of Karas—but it was third or fourth on a list of a half-dozen *false* names. It was a highly classified search, but obviously an intense one, the widest cooperation sought. It was strange, almost amateurish. As though one branch of your intelligence community did not want the other to know what it was doing."

"That didn't exonerate me?"

"On the contrary. You had been found out, the lie had been exposed."

"Then why wasn't there an alert out for *me?*"

"There was, is. As of five days ago."

Five days, thought Havelock. The Palatine. "But you weren't aware of it."

"Those in the Quai d'Orsay who've listed you as an American liaison knew of it, and in time it would have crossed my desk as a matter of routine. However, neither you nor I have ever listed each other in our reports. That was the understanding between us."

"It served the purpose. Is the alert specific? Am I given a label?"

"No. Only that it is imperative that you be located—as a matter of internal security. Again, I presumed: you had been exposed, either as a defector or as one who had lied to his superiors and disappeared. It really didn't matter which. Because of Jenna Karas, you were the enemy in either case. It was confirmed for me when I called the embassy."

"I forgot. I'm dangerous."

"You are. To someone. I checked with London, Brussels, Amsterdam and Bonn. Both alerts have been circulated, both highest priority, but not connected."

"You still haven't answered the question. Why did you send her to the States?"

"I just did answer you; you weren't listening. The search for her—and now you—is centered in Europe. Rome, the Mediterranean, Paris, London . . . Bonn. The curve is arcing north, the destination presumed to be the Eastern bloc. This is the line of progress they're concentrating on, where their agents have fanned out, pulling in sources and contacts. They won't think to look in their own barnyard."

"Backyard," said Michael absently.

"Qu'est-ce que c'est?"

"C'est americain. Peu importe. When did she leave?"

"Three-thirty this afternoon . . . yesterday afternoon now. Air France to New York, diplomatic status, cover name drawn from a dead file—unblemished, of course."

"And unknown."

"Yes, it's not relevant. It will be changed."

"What are the arrangements?"

"She's to see a man; no doubt she's already seen him. *He* will make the arrangements, and it is our policy never to inquire what they are. You have the same sort of men over here—in Paris, London, Amsterdam, wherever. They do not speak with us directly."

"The landlords of the halfway houses," said Havelock, "guiding the people we send them into safe territories, providing identities, papers, families to live with, the towns and cities chosen carefully. We make our payments through blind conduits, and after contact we're not involved. We've never heard of them; ignorance is the order of the day. But there's another side, too, isn't there? We don't really know what happens to those people, do we?"

"With safe transfer, our obligations are fulfilled. They ask no more and we offer no more, that's always been the understanding between us. I, for one, have never been curious."

"I'm not *curious*, Régine, I'm going out of my mind! She's in sight now, I can find her! I *can find her!* For Christ's sake, help me! Whom did you send her to?"

"You ask a great deal, Michael. You're asking me to violate a confidence I've sworn never to break. I could lose a valuable man."

"I could lose *her!* Look at me! Tell me I wouldn't do the same for you! If it was your husband and I was there and the Gestapo came for him, look at me and tell me I wouldn't *help* you!"

Broussac closed her eyes briefly, as if struck. "The reference is unkind but not without truth. You are much like him. . . . Yes, you would have helped."

"Get me out of Paris. Right away. *Please!*"

Régine was silent for a moment, her eyes again roaming his face. "It would be better if you did so yourself. I know you can."

"It could take me days! I'd have to route myself through a back door in Mexico or Montreal. I can't lose the time. With every hour she's farther away. You know what can happen. She could get swallowed up, moving from one circle into the next, no one telling anyone anything. She could disappear and I'd never find her!"

"Very well. Tomorrow, the noon flight on the Concorde. You'll be French, a member of the United Nations delegation. Flush the papers down a toilet the minute you're in the Kennedy terminal."

"Thanks. Now the halfway man. Who is he?"

"I'll get word to him, but he may choose to tell you nothing."

"Get word to him. Who is he?"

"A man named Handelman. Jacob Handelman. Columbia University."

17

The man with a single strip of tape on each cheek sat at the small table below the curved dais in the underground strategy room of the White House. The flesh on his square face was taut, held in place by the sutures beneath the brown adhesive; the effect was robotlike, macabre. His replies in a subdued monotone to the questions put to him heightened the image of a man not totally whole, yet overcontrolled. In truth, he was afraid; the agent of record from Col des Moulinets would have been more afraid thirty-five minutes before, when the panel of men facing him was complete. There had been four men then; now there were only three. The President had removed himself. He was observing the proceedings from an unseen cubicle behind the platform, through a pane of coated glass that was part of the inner wall and indistinguishable from it. Words were being said in the room that could not be said in his presence; he could not bear witness to orders of dispatch at an Alpine pass, and prior communications that included the phrase "beyond salvage."

The interrogation was at midpoint, Undersecretary of State Emory Bradford probing the salient points while Ambassador Brooks and General Halyard made notes on their pads under the harsh glare of the Tensor lamps.

"Let me get this clear," said Bradford. "You were the field officer of record and the only one in contact with Rome. Is that correct?"

"Yes, sir."

"And you're absolutely certain no other member of the unit was in touch with the embassy?"

"Yes, sir. No, sir. I was the only channel. It's standard, not only for the security blackout, but to make sure there's no foul-up in the orders. One man transmits them, one man receives them."

"Yet you say Havelock referred to two of the unit's personnel as explosives specialists, a fact you were not aware of."

"I wasn't."

"But as the field officer of record—"

"Agent of record, sir."

"Sorry. As the *agent* of record, shouldn't you have known?"

"Normally, I would have."

"But you weren't and the only explanation you can give us is that this new recruit, a Corsican named Ricci, hired the two men in question."

"It's the only reason I can think of. If Havelock was right; if he wasn't lying."

"The reports from Col des Moulinets stated that there were numerous explosions in the vicinity of the bridge's entrance at the time." Bradford scanned a typewritten page in front of him. "Including a massive detonation in the road that occurred approximately twelve minutes after the confrontation, killing three Italian soldiers and four civilians. Obviously, Havelock knew what he was talking about; he wasn't lying to you."

"I wouldn't know, sir. I was unconscious . . . bleeding. The son of— Havelock cut me up."

"You're getting proper medical attention?" interrupted Ambassador Brooks, looking up from the yellow pad under the Tensor lamp.

"I guess so," replied the agent, his right hand slipping over his left wrist, his fingers massaging the glistening stainless-steel case of his chronometer. "Except the doctors aren't sure the wounds'll require plastic surgery. I think I should have it."

"That's their province, of course," said the statesman.

"I'm . . . valuable, sir. Without that surgery I'm *marked*—sir."

"I'm sure Undersecretary Bradford will convey your feelings to Walter Reed," said the general, reading his notes.

"You say you never saw this man Ricci," continued Bradford, "prior to the briefing in Rome, just before the unit flew to Col des Moulinets. Is that correct?"

"Yes, sir. No, sir. I never saw him. He was new."

"And you didn't see him when you regained consciousness after the events at the bridge?"

"No, I didn't."

"You don't know where he went?"

"No, sir."

"Neither does Rome," added the undersecretary quietly, pointedly.

"I learned that an Italian soldier was hit by a truck and was pretty badly mangled, screaming his head off. Someone said he had blond hair, so I figured it was Ricci."

"And?"

"A man came out of the woods—someone with a gash in his head— put the soldier in a car, and drove him away."

"How did you learn this?"

"I asked questions, a lot of questions . . . after I got first aid. That was my job, sir. It was a madhouse up there, Italians and French yelling all over the place. But I didn't leave until I found out everything I could— without permitting anyone to ask *me* questions."

"You're to be commended," said the ambassador.

"Thank you, sir."

"Let's assume you're right." Bradford leaned forward. "The blond man *was* Ricci, and someone with a head wound got him out of there. Have you any idea who that someone might be?"

"I think so. One of the men he brought with him. The other was killed."

"So Ricci and this other man got away. But Rome hasn't heard from Ricci. Would you say that's normal?"

"No way, sir. It's not normal at all. Whenever any of those people are damaged, they bleed us for everything they can get, and they don't waste time about it. Our policy in black operations is clear. If we can't evacuate the wounded—"

"I think we understand," interrupted Halyard, an old soldier's antennae picking up a signal couched in a soldier's vocabulary.

"Then it's your opinion that if Ricci and this demolitions expert got away intact, they'd have reached our embassy in Rome as quickly as they could."

"Yes, sir. With their hands out and shouting all the way. They would have expected attention pronto and threatened us with the kind we don't want if they didn't get it."

"What do you think happened?"

"I'd say it's pretty obvious. They didn't make it."

"What was that?" asked Brooks.

"There isn't any other explanation. I know those people, sir. They're garbage; they'd kill their mothers if the price was right. They would have been in touch with Rome, believe me."

" 'Didn't make it'?" repeated Halyard, staring at the man from Col des Moulinets. "What do you mean?"

"The roads, sir. They wind up and down those mountains like corkscrews, sometimes without lights for miles at a time. A wounded man driving, the other one banged up and screaming; that vehicle's a candidate for a long fall up there."

"Head wounds can be deceptive," Halyard commented. "A bloody nose looks a hell of a lot worse than it is."

"It strikes me," said Brooks, "that same man acted with considerable presence of mind amid the chaos. He functioned—"

"Forgive me, Mr. Ambassador," interrupted Bradford, his voice rising slightly but deferentially. The intrusion was not a breach of manners but a signal. "I think the field officer's point is well taken. A thorough search of those roads will undoubtedly reveal a car somewhere at the bottom of a precipice."

Brooks exchanged looks with the man from State; the signal was acknowledged. "Yes, of course. Realistically, there is no other explanation."

"Just one or two more points and we're finished," said Bradford, rearranging his papers. "As you know, whatever is said here is confidential. There are no hidden microphones, no recording devices; the words spoken here are stored only in our memories. This is for the protection of all of us—not just you—so feel perfectly free to speak candidly. Don't try to soften the truth; we're in the same boat."

"I understand, sir."

"Your orders with regard to Havelock were unequivocal. He was officially classified 'beyond salvage' and the word from Rome was to terminate with 'extreme prejudice.' Is that correct?"

"Yes, sir."

"In other words, he was to be executed. Killed at Col des Moulinets."

"That's what it meant."

"And you received those instructions from the senior attaché, Consular Operations, Rome. A man named Warren. Harry Warren."

"Yes, sir. I was in constant touch with him, waiting for the determination . . . waiting for Washington to give it to him."

"How could you be certain the man you spoke with was Harry Warren?"

The agent seemed perplexed, as if the question were foolish, though the man who asked it was not foolish at all. "Among other things, I worked with Harry for over two years. I knew his voice."

"Just his voice?"

"And the number in Rome. It was a direct line to the embassy's radio room, unlisted and very classified. I knew that, too."

"Did it occur to you that when he gave you your final instructions he might have been doing so under duress? Against his will?"

"No, sir, not at all."

"It never crossed your mind?"

"If that had been the case, he would have told me."

"With a gun at his head?" said Halyard. "How?"

"The code had been established and he used it. He wouldn't have if there'd been anything wrong."

"Explain that, please," said Brooks. "What code?"

"A word or a couple of words that originate in Washington. They're referred to when decisions are transmitted; that way you know the authorization's there without naming names. If anything had been wrong, Harry wouldn't have used the code, and *I* would have known something wasn't right. I'd have asked for it and he would have given me a different one. He didn't and I didn't. He used the correct one up front."

"What was the code for Col des Moulinets?" asked Emory Bradford.

"Ambiguity, sir. It came direct from Cons Op, Washington, and will be listed in the embassy telephone logs, classified files."

"Which is proof of authorization," said Bradford, making a statement.

"Yes, sir. Dates, times and origins of clearance are in those logs."

Bradford held up an eight-by-ten-inch photograph of a man's face, adjusting the Tensor lamp so it could be seen clearly. "Is this Harry Warren?"

"Yes, sir. That's Harry."

"Thank you." The undersecretary put down the photograph and made a check mark on the border of his notes. "Let me go back a bit; there's something I'm not sure is clear. Regarding the woman, she was to be sent across the border unharmed, if possible. Is that correct?"

"The operative words were 'if possible.' Nobody was going to risk anything for her. She was just a needle."

"A needle?"

"To stick into the Soviets. Let Moscow know we didn't buy the plant."

"Meaning she was a Russian device. A woman similar in appearance —perhaps someone who had undergone cosmetic surgery—whom the Soviets surfaced repeatedly at selected locations for Havelock's benefit, letting him get close, but never close enough to take her. Is that what you mean?"

"Yes, sir."

"The purpose being to shock Havelock into a state of mental instability, to the point of defection?"

"To drive him nuts, yes, sir. I guess it worked; the 'beyond salvage' came from Washington."

"From Ambiguity."

"Ambiguity, sir."

"Whose identity can be traced in the embassy's telephone logs."

"Yes, sir. The logs."

"So it was established beyond doubt that the woman at the bridge was *not* Jenna Karas."

"Beyond doubt. She was killed at Costa Brava, everyone knew that. Havelock himself was the agent of record at that beach. He went crazy."

Ambassador Brooks slapped down his pencil and leaned forward, studying the man from Col des Moulinets. The sharp, echoing crack of the pencil, and the movement itself, were more than an interruption; they combined to indicate an objection. "This entire operation, didn't it strike you as . . . well, *bizarre*, to say the least? To be quite candid, was execution the only solution? Knowing what you all knew—presumed you knew— couldn't you have tried to take the man, spare his life, get him back here for treatment?"

"With respect, sir, that's a lot easier said than done. Jack Ogilvie tried in Rome and never left the Palatine. Havelock killed three men on that bridge that we know of; another two may be dead by now and probably are. He dug a knife into my face— He's a psycho." The agent paused, not finished. "Yes, sir. All things considered, we kill him. That's 'beyond salvage,' and has nothing to do with me. I follow orders."

"An all too familiar phrase, sir," said Brooks.

"But justified under the circumstances," Bradford broke in quickly, writing out the word *Ambiguity* on the page in front of him and continuing before anyone else could speak, or object. "What happened to Havelock? Did you learn?"

"They said an *assassino pazzo*—crazy man, killer—drove the truck hellbent across the bridge and out of sight. It had to be Havelock. There are alerts out all through the provinces—the towns and cities and up and down the Mediterranean coast. He worked the coast; he'll get in touch with someone and they'll find him. They said he was wounded; he won't get far. My guess is a couple of days at the outside, and I wish I was there to take him myself."

"Again quite justified," said Bradford. "And we want to thank you for your cooperation this evening. You've been very concise and helpful. You may leave now, and good luck to you."

The man got out of the chair, nodded awkwardly and walked to the door. He stopped, touching his left cheek and the tape as he turned to face the powerful men on the dais. "I'm worth the surgery," he said.

"I'm sure you are," replied the undersecretary.

The agent of record from Col des Moulinets opened the door and stepped out into the white-walled corridor. The instant the door was shut, Halyard turned to Bradford and shouted, "Get hold of Rome! Get those logs and find this *Ambiguity!* It's what you were trying to tell us, isn't it? This is the link to Parsifal!"

"Yes, General," answered Bradford. "The Ambiguity code was established by the director of Consular Operations, Daniel Stern, whose name appears in the embassy logs, entered by the Cons Op senior attaché, Harry Warren. Warren was clear in his entry; the transcript was read to me. He wrote the following"—the undersecretary picked up a note on top of his papers—" 'Code: Ambiguity. Subject: M. Havelock. Decision pending.' "

" 'Pending'?" asked Brooks. "When was it *made?*"

"According to the embassy logs, it wasn't. There were no further entries that night making any reference whatsoever to Ambiguity, Havelock, or the unit at Col des Moulinets."

"Impossible," protested the general. "You heard that man. The go-ahead was given, the authorization code was delivered. He didn't mince words. That call *had* to have come through."

"It did."

"Are you saying that the entry was deleted?" asked Brooks.

"It was never made," said Bradford. "Warren never made it."

"Then get him," said Halyard. "Nail him. He knows who he talked to. Goddamn it, Emory, get on that phone. This is Parsifal!" He turned in his chair, addressing the wall. "Mr. *President?*"

There was no reply.

The undersecretary separated the papers in front of him and removed a thin manila envelope from the rest. He opened it, took out a second photograph and handed it to the former ambassador. Brooks studied it, a sharp intake of breath accompanying his first glance. Silently he passed it to Halyard.

"*Jesus* . . ." Halyard placed the photograph under the beam of the Tensor. The surface was grainy, the infinitesimal lines the result of a transmitting machine, but the image was clear. It was a photograph of a corpse stretched out on a white table, the clothes torn and bloody, the face bruised terribly but wiped clean for identification. The face of the dead man was the same as that in the first photograph Bradford had shown the agent from Col des Moulinets only minutes before. It belonged to Harry Warren, senior attaché, Cons Op, Rome.

"That was telexed to us at one o'clock this afternoon. It's Warren. He was run down on the Via Frascatti in the early hours of the morning two days ago. There were witnesses, but they couldn't help much, except to tell our people the car was a large sedan with a powerful engine; it roared down the street, apparently gathering speed just before impact. Whoever drove it wasn't taking any chances of missing; he caught Warren stepping onto the curb and hammered him into the pole of a streetlight, doing considerable damage to the automobile. The police are searching for it, but there's not much hope. It's probably at the bottom of a river in the hills."

"So the link is gone." Halyard pushed the photograph toward Brooks.

"I mourn the man," said the undersecretary, "but I'm not sure how much of a link he was."

"Someone thought so," said the soldier.

"Or was covering a flank."

"What do you mean?" asked Brooks.

"Whoever made that final call authorizing 'beyond salvage' couldn't know what Stern told Warren. All *we* know is that the decision hadn't been made."

"Please be clearer," the statesman insisted.

"Suppose the strategists of Consular Operations decided they couldn't *reach* a decision. On the surface, it wouldn't appear that difficult—a psychopath, a rogue agent capable of causing extraordinary damage, a potential defector, a killer—the decision wasn't one that stretched their consciences. But suppose they learned something, or suspected something, that called everything into question."

"The Karas woman," said Halyard.

"Perhaps. Or maybe a communication, or a signal from Havelock that contradicted the assumption that he was a maniac. That he was as sane as they were; a sane man caught in a terrible dilemma not of his own making."

"Which is, of course, the truth," interrupted Brooks quietly.

"The truth," agreed Bradford. "What would they do?"

"Get help," said Halyard. "Advice."

"Guidance," added the statesman.

"Or practically speaking," said the undersecretary, "especially if the facts weren't clear, they'd spread the responsibility for the decision. Hours later it was made, and they were dead . . . and we don't know who made it, who placed that final call. We only know it was someone sufficiently cleared, sufficiently trusted to be given the code Ambiguity. That man made the decision; he made the call to Rome."

"But Warren didn't log it," said Brooks. "Why didn't he? How could it happen?"

"The way it's happened before, Mr. Ambassador. A routed line traceable only to a single telephone complex somewhere in Arlington is used, the authorization verified by code, and a request made on the basis of *internal* security: There is to be no log, no tape, no reference to the transmission; it's an order, actually. The recipient is flattered; he's been chosen, deemed by men who make important decisions to be more reliable than those around him. And what difference does it make? The authorization can always be traced through the code—in this case through the director of Cons Op, Daniel Stern. Only, he's dead."

"It's appalling," said Brooks, looking down at his notes. "A man is to be executed because he's right, and when the attempt fails, he's held responsible for the death of those who try to kill him and labeled a killer himself. And we don't know who officially gave the order. We can't *find* him. What kind of people are we?"

"Men who keep secrets." The voice came from behind the dais. The President of the United States emerged from the white-paneled door set into the white wall. "Forgive me, I was watching you, listening. It's often helpful."

"Secrets, Mr. President?"

"Yes, Mal," said Berquist, going to his chair. "The words are all there, aren't they? Top Secret, Eyes Only, Highly Classified, Maximum Clearance Required, Duplication Forbidden, Authorization to Be Accompanied by Access Code . . . so many words. We sweep rooms and telephone lines with instruments that tell us whether bugs and intercepts have been placed, and then develop hardware that misdirects those same scanners when we implant our own devices. We jam radio broadcasts— including satellite transmissions—and override the jamming with laser beams that carry the words we want to send. We put a national security lid on information we don't want made public so we can leak selected sections at will, keeping the rest inviolate. We tell a certain agency or department one thing and another something else entirely, so as to conceal a third set of facts—the damaging truth. In history's most advanced age of communications, we're doing our damnedest to louse it up, to misuse it, really." The President sat down, looked at the photograph of the dead man in Rome, and turned it over. "Keeping secrets and diverting the flow of accurate information have become prime objectives in our ever-expanding technology—of communications. Ironic, isn't it?"

"Unfortunately, often vital, sir," said Bradford.

"Perhaps. If only we could be certain when we applied them. I often wonder—late at night, watching the lights on the ceiling as I'm trying to sleep—if we hadn't tried to keep a secret three months ago, whether we would be faced with what we're faced with now."

"Our options were extremely limited, Mr. President," the undersecretary said firmly. "We might have faced worse."

"Worse, Emory?"

"Earlier, then. Time is the only thing on our side."

"And we have to use every goddamn minute," agreed Berquist, glancing first at the general and then at Brooks. "Now you're both aware of what's happened during the past seventy-two hours and why I had to call you back to Washington."

"Except the most relevant factor," said the statesman. "Parsifal's reaction."

"None," replied the President.

"Then he doesn't know," said Halyard rapidly, emphatically.

"If you'd get that written in stone, I could sleep at night," said Berquist.

"When did he last communicate with you?" asked Brooks.

"Sixteen days ago. There was no point in reaching you; it was another demand, as outrageous as the others and now as pointless."

"There's been no movement on the previous demands?" continued the statesman.

"Nothing. As of fifteen days ago we've funneled eight hundred million dollars into banks throughout the Bahamas, the Caymans and Central

America. We've set up every—" The President paused as he touched the photograph in front of him, folding a corner until part of a bloodied trouser leg could be seen. "—every code and countercode he's asked for, so he could verify the deposits whenever he wished, have the monies sent to blind accounts in Zurich and Bern where they would be accessible to him. He hasn't moved a cent, and except for three verifications he's made no contact at all with the other banks. He has no interest in the money; it's only a means of confirming our vulnerability. He knows we'll do anything he asks." Berquist paused again; when he spoke, his voice was barely audible. "God help us, we can't afford not to."

There was silence on the dais, an acknowledgment of the unthinkable. It was broken by the general's businesslike comment. "There are a couple of holes here," he said, reading his notes, then looking at the undersecretary. "Can you fill them in?"

"I can speculate," replied Bradford. "But to do even that, we've got to go back to the very beginning. Before Rome."

"Costa Brava?" asked Brooks disdainfully.

"Before then, Mr. Ambassador. To when we all agreed there had to *be* a Costa Brava."

"I stand rebuked," said the statesman icily. "Please go on."

"We go back to when we learned that it was Matthias himself who initiated the investigation of Jenna Karas. It was the great man himself, not his aides, who relayed information from unnamed informants, sources so deep in Soviet intelligence that even to speculate on their identities was tantamount to exposing our own operations."

"Don't be modest, Emory," interrupted the President. "*We* didn't learn that it was Matthias. *You* did. You had the perspicacity to go around the 'great man,' as you call him."

"Only with a sense of sadness, sir. It was you, Mr. President, who demanded the truth from one of his aides in the Oval Office and he gave it to you. He said they *didn't* know where the information had come from, only that Matthias himself had brought it in. He never would have told me that."

"The room did it, I didn't," said Berquist. "You don't lie to the man sitting in that room . . . unless you're Anthony Matthias."

"In fairness, Mr. President," said Brooks softly, "his intention was not to deceive you. He believed he was right."

"He believed he should have been sitting in my chair, my office! Good Christ, he still *believes* it. Even now! There's no end to his goddamned megalomania! Go on, Emory."

"Yes, sir." Bradford looked up. "We concluded that Matthias's objective was to force Havelock to retire, to get his old student and one of the best men we had out of Consular Operations. We've covered that before; we didn't know why then and we don't know why now."

"But we went along," said Berquist, "because we didn't know what we had. A broken foreign service officer who didn't want to go on, or a fraud — *worse* than a fraud. Matthias's lackey, willing to see a woman killed so he could work for the *great* man on the outside. Oh, and the work he could have done! The international emissary for Saint Matthias. Or was it Emperor Matthias, ruler of all the states and territories of the republic?"

"Come on, Charley." Halyard touched the President's arm; no one else in that room would have risked such an intimate gesture. "It's over. It's not why we're here."

"If it wasn't for that son of a bitch Matthias we wouldn't *be* here! I find *that* hard to forget. And so could the world one day . . . if there's anyone left with a memory."

"Then may we return to that infinitely more ominous crisis, Mr. President?" said Brooks gently.

Berquist leaned back; he looked at the aristocratic statesman, then at the old general. "When Bradford came to me and convinced me that there was a pattern of deception at the highest levels of State involving the great Anthony Matthias, I asked for you two—and only you two. At least, for now. I'd better be able to take your criticism, because you'll give it to me."

"Which I think is why you asked for us," said Halyard. "Sir."

"You're a ball-breaker, Mal." The President nodded toward the man from State. "Sorry. All right, we didn't know then, and we don't know now, why Matthias wanted Havelock out. But Emory brought us the scenario."

"An incredible scenario," agreed Bradford, his hands on top of the papers, no longer needing his notes. "The case that Matthias concocted against the Karas woman was a study in meticulous invention. A reformed terrorist from Baader-Meinhof suddenly appears looking for absolution; he'll trade information for relocation and the cancellation of his death sentence. Bonn agrees—reluctantly—and we buy his story. The woman working with a Cons Op field officer then in Barcelona is actually a member of the KGB. A method of transferring orders is described, which entails the passing of a key, and a small overnight suitcase is located at an airport, *her* suitcase, filled with all the evidence needed to convict her —detailed analyses of the activities she and Havelock had been involved with during the past five weeks, summaries of in-depth, classified information Havelock had sent back to the State Department, and copies of the current codes and radio frequencies we used in the field. Also in that overnight bag were instructions from Moscow, including the KGB code that she was to employ should contact with KGB Northwest Sector be required. We tested the code and got a response; it was authentic."

Brooks raised his left hand no more than a few inches above the surface of the dais, the gesture of a man used to commanding attention. "General Halyard and I are familiar with much of this, albeit not the specifics. I assume there's a reason for your restating it in such detail."

"There is, Mr. Ambassador," agreed Bradford. "It concerns Daniel Stern. Please bear with me."

"Then while you're at it," said the general, "how did you verify that KGB code?"

"By using the three basic maritime frequencies for that area of the Mediterranean. It's standard procedure for the Soviets."

"That's pretty damn simple of them, isn't it?"

"I'm no expert, General, but I'd say it's pretty damn smart. I've studied the way we do it—I've had to—and I'm not sure ours is more effective. The frequencies we select are usually the weaker ones, not always clear, and easily jammed if discovered. You don't tamper with maritime channels, and no matter how much traffic, the codes get through within a reasonable period of time."

"You're very impressive," said Brooks.

"I've had a series of crash courses during the past three months. Thanks to an executive order from the President, I've also had the benefit of the best brains in the intelligence community."

"The reason for that executive order was not explained," interrupted Berquist, glancing at the older men, then turning back to Bradford. "All right, you verified the KGB code to be authentic."

"It was the most incriminating document in that suitcase; it couldn't have been faked. So her name was put through the wheels at Central Intelligence—very deep wheels." Bradford paused. "As you may or may not know, General—Mr. Ambassador—it was at this point that I came on the scene. I didn't seek to be included; I was sought out by men I'd worked with during the Johnson administration . . . and in Southeast Asia."

"Remnants of the benevolent AID in Vientiane who stayed with the Agency?" asked Halyard sardonically.

"Yes," replied the undersecretary; there was no apology in his answer. "Two men whose wide experience in undercover operations—favorable and unfavorable—led them to become what's called source controls for informants deep within the Soviet apparatus. They phoned me at home one night, said they were at a local bar in Berwyn and why didn't I join them for a drink—old times' sake. When I said it was late, the one I was talking to pointed out that it was also late for them, and Berwyn Heights was a long drive from McLean and Langley. I understood and joined them."

"I've never heard this," interrupted the former ambassador. "Am I to infer that these men did not report back through normal channels but, instead, went directly to you?"

"Yes, sir. They were disturbed."

"Thank God for the communion of past sinners," said the President. "When they returned to those normal channels, they did it our way. It was beyond their scope, they reported. They pulled out and left it in Bradford's lap."

"The information requested about the Karas woman was a basic intelligence query," said Halyard. "Why were they disturbed?"

"Because it was a highly negative inquiry that presupposed the subject was too deep, too concealed for CIA detection. She was going to be found guilty no matter what the Agency came back with."

"Then it was the arrogance that angered them?" suggested Brooks.

"No, they're used to that from State. What *disturbed* them was that the supposition couldn't possibly be true. They reached five separate sources in Moscow, none aware of the others—moles who had access to every black file in the KGB. Each probe came back negative. She was clean, but someone at State wanted her dirty. When one of the men routinely called an aide of Matthias to get further background from Cons Op, he was told simply to send back a nonproductive report—State had everything it needed. In other words, she was hanged no matter what the Agency returned, and the source control had the distinct impression that whatever was sent back to State would be buried. But Jenna Karas was no part of the KGB and never had been."

"How did your friends explain the KGB code?" asked the soldier.

"Someone in Moscow provided it," said Bradford. "Someone working with or for Matthias."

Again the silence on the dais suggested the unthinkable, and once again it was broken by the general. "We ruled that *out!*" he cried.

"I'd like to revive it," said Bradford quietly.

"We've explored the possibility to the point of exhaustion," said Brooks, staring at Bradford. "Practically and conceptually, there's no merit in the theory. Matthias is inexorably bound to Parsifal; one does not exist without the other. If the Soviet Union had any knowledge of Parsifal, ten thousand multiple warheads would be in position to destroy half our cities and all our military installations. The Russians would have no choice but to launch, posing their final questions after the first strike. We have intelligence penetration to alert us to any such missile deployment; there's been no such alert. In your words, Mr. Bradford, time is the only thing on our side."

"I'll stay with that judgment, Mr. Ambassador. Still, the KGB code found its way into the manufactured evidence against the Karas woman even though she was clean. I can't believe it was for sale."

"Why not?" asked the general. "What isn't for sale?"

"Not a code like that. You don't *buy* a code that changes periodically, erratically, with no set schedule of change."

"What's your point?" Halyard interrupted.

"Someone in Moscow *had* to provide that code," said Bradford, raising his voice. "We may be closer to Parsifal than we think."

"What's your thesis, Mr. Undersecretary?" Brooks leaned forward, his elbow on the dais.

"There's someone trying to find Parsifal as frantically as we are—for the same reasons we are. Whoever he is, he's here in Washington—he may be someone we see every day, but we don't know who he is. I only know he's working for Moscow, and the difference between him and us right now is that he's been looking longer than we have. He knew about Parsifal *before* we did. And that means someone in Moscow knows." Bradford paused. "That's the reason for the most God-awful crisis this country has ever faced—the world has ever faced. There's a mole here in Washington who could tip the balance of power—of basic global recognition of our physical and moral superiority, which *is* power—if he reaches Parsifal first. And he may, because he knows who he is and we don't."

18

The man in the dark overcoat and low-brimmed hat that shadowed his face climbed out of the two-toned coupe; with difficulty he avoided stepping into a wide puddle by the driver's door. The sounds of the night rain were everywhere, pinging off the hood and splattering against the glass of the windshield, thumping the vinyl roof and erupting in the myriad pools that had formed throughout the deserted parking area on the banks of the Potomac River. The man reached into his pocket, took out a gold-plated butane lighter and ignited it. No sooner had the flame erupted than he extinguished it; replacing the lighter in his pocket, he kept his gloved hand there. He walked to the railing and looked down at the wet foliage and the border of thick mud that disappeared into the black flowing water. He raised his head and scanned the opposite shoreline; the lights of Washington flickered in the downpour. Hearing the footsteps behind him, leather scraping over the soaked gravel, he turned.

A man approached, coming into view through blocks of darkness. He wore a canvas poncho printed with the erratic shapes of green and black that denoted military issue. On his head was a heavy wide-brimmed leather hat, a cross between a Safari and a Digger. The face beneath the hat was thirtyish, hard, with a stubble of a beard and dull eyes set far apart, which could barely be seen between the squinting flesh. He had been drinking; the grin that followed recognition was as grotesque as the rest of him.

"Hey, how about it, *huh!*" cried the man in the poncho, his speech guttural, slurred. "*Wham!* Splat! Boom . . . *kaboom!* Like a fuckin' gook rickyshaw hit by a tank! *Wham!* You never seen nothin' like it!"

"Very fine work," said the man in the overcoat.

"You betch-er ass! I caught 'em at the pass, and *kaboom!* Hey, I can't hardly see you. It *is* you, ain't it?"

"Yes, but you disappoint me."

"Why? I did good!"

"You've been drinking. I thought we agreed you wouldn't."

"A couple of balls, that's all. In my room, not at no gin mill . . . no sir!"

"Did you talk with anyone?"

"Christ, *no!*"

"How did you get out here?"

"Like you said. On a bus . . . three buses . . . and I walked the last couple of miles."

"In the road?"

"*Off* it. Way off, like it was an S and D in Danang."

"Good. You've earned your R and R."

"Hey, Major . . . ? Sorry, I mean . . . sir."

"What is it?"

"How come there was nothin' in the papers? I mean it was one big blow! Musta' burned for hours, seen for a couple of miles. How come?"

"They weren't important, Sergeant. They were only what I told you they were. Bad men who betrayed people like you and me, who stayed over here and let us get killed."

"Yeah, well, I evened a few scores. I guess I should go back now, huh? To the hospital."

"You don't have to." The civilian who had been addressed as "Major" calmly took his gloved hand out of his pocket. In it was a .22-caliber automatic, concealed by the darkness and the rain. He raised it at his side and fired once.

The man fell, his bleeding head sinking into the wet poncho. The civilian stepped forward, wiping the weapon against the cloth of his overcoat. He knelt down and spread the fingers of the dead man's right hand.

The two-tone coupe rounded the curve in the backcountry road, the headlights sweeping over a rock-strewn Maryland field, the high grass bending under the force of the wind and the night rain. The driver in the dark overcoat and low-brimmed hat saw what he expected to see and slowed down, switching off the lights before coming to a stop. On the shoulder of the road, standing motionless by a barbed-wire fence, was a glistening white ambulance, the license plates those of the federal government, the black lettering on the door proclaiming co-ownership with the taxpayer as well as the identification: BETHESDA NAVAL HOSPITAL, EMERGENCY UNIT 14.

The driver drove the coupe alongside the long white vehicle. He took out his lighter, flicked the top and held the flame briefly toward the opposite window. The door of the ambulance opened, and a man in his late twenties jumped out into the rain, his government-issue raincoat parting to reveal the white uniform of a hospital attendant.

The driver lowered the right window by pressing a button above his armrest. "Get in!" he yelled through the sound of the downpour. "You'll get soaked out there!"

The man climbed in, slamming the door shut and wiping his face with his right hand. He was Hispanic, his large eyes two stones of shining hard coal, his hair jet-black, matted to the dark skin of his forehead.

"You owe me, mama," said the Latin. "Oh, big mama owes me one big *montón de dinero.*"

"You'll be paid, although I suppose I could say that you simply canceled an old debt you owed me."

"*Olvídalo,* mama Major!"

"You would have been executed in the field or still be pushing rocks around Leavenworth if it weren't for me. Don't you forget it, Corporal."

"I wasted that shrinker for you! You *pay!*"

"You wasted—as you put it—two MP's in Pleiku who caught you stealing narcotics from a Med-Evac truck. Weren't you lucky I was around? Two more MIA's in a river."

"Sure, mama, *real* lucky! Who was the *puerco* who *told* me about the truck? *You,* Major!"

"I knew you were enterprising. These past years I've kept my eye on you. You never saw me, but I saw you. I always knew where to find you, because debts should be paid."

"Yeah, well, you're wrong, Major. I saw you the other night on the TV news. You were getting out of a big limousine in New York. At the United Nations place, wasn't it? It *was* you, wasn't it?"

"I doubt it."

"Sure, it was! I know big mama when I see her. You must be something! You pay, mama. You're going to pay a lot."

"My God, you're irritating."

"Just pay me."

"The gun first," said the man in the overcoat. "I gave it to you and I want it back. I protected you; no one could trace it ballistically."

The hospital attendant reached into his raincoat pocket and took out a small gun, identical in size and caliber with the weapon the driver of the coupe had used an hour ago in a parking area overlooking the Potomac.

"You won't find no bullets in it," said the Hispanic, holding out the automatic in the darkness. "Here, take it."

"Give it to me."

"*Take* it! For Christ's sake, I can't see nothin' in here! *Ouch! Shit!* What the *hell* . . . ?"

The driver's hand had slipped beyond the short barrel of the weapon, pushing the attendant's wide sleeve partially up his forearm. "Sorry," said the man in the overcoat. "My class ring is twisted. Did I scrape you?"

"Forget it, mama. The money. Give me the fuckin' *dinero!*"

"Certainly." The man took the gun and slipped it into his pocket. He picked up his lighter from his lap and ignited it; on the seat between them was a stack of money held together with an elastic band. "There it is. Fifty one-hundred-dollar bills—laundered, of course. Do you want to count it?"

"What for? I know where I can find you now," said the attendant, opening the door. "And you're going to see a lot of me, big mama."

"I look forward to it," replied the driver.

The wind again whipped the attendant's raincoat away from his white uniform as he slammed the door and started toward the ambulance. The man in the coupe leaned over in the shadows, watching through the opposite window with his fingers on the door latch beside him, prepared to leap out of the car the instant he saw what he expected to see.

The attendant began to stagger, rushing forward off balance, his arms stretched out, his hands clutching the side of the ambulance. He raised his head and screamed, the rain pounding his face; three seconds later he collapsed on the wet grass.

The man in the overcoat jumped out of the coupe and walked around the trunk while removing a tubular glass object from his left pocket. He reached the attendant, knelt down and pushed the wide sleeve up the immobile arm. He then adjusted the glass vial in his left hand and, with his right, extracted a hypodermic needle. He plunged it into the soft flesh, depressed the shaft until the vial of white liquid was emptied into the arm, and let the long needle remain where it was, firmly embedded in the skin. Reaching across the attendant's body, he pulled the lifeless hand toward the vial, pressed the fingers around the glass tube, with the thumb firmly down on the plunger, and then let the hand fall away.

The man stood up, seeing in the night light the scattered bills, many held in place by the weight of the attendant's body. He turned and opened the door of the ambulance; the inside was neat, the equipment in place, as befitted a trusted employee of the Bethesda Naval Hospital. He took out the small automatic from his pocket and threw it onto the seat. He then reached inside his overcoat for the contents of another pocket. Four additional glass vials, two filled, two empty. He checked the labels; each read the same:

Bethesda Naval Hospital
Security-Control-Supply
Contents: $C_{17} H_{19} NO_3 H_2O$
M O R P H I N E

He held them out and dropped them on the floor of the ambulance.

Suddenly a gust of wind came swirling off the field, forcing the rain to fall in diagonal sheets. The man reached for his hat but it was too late. Caught in an updraft, the hat was lifted off his head and hurled against the side of the coupe. He walked across the grass to retrieve it. Even in the darkness the shock of white could be seen streaking from his forehead through his wavy black hair.

In truth, Nikolai Petrovich Malyekov was annoyed, and his dripping hair was only part of his irritation. Time was running short. In his identity as Undersecretary of State Arthur Pierce, he would have to change his clothes and make himself presentable. A man in his position in the United States government did not run around in the mud and the pouring rain;

he would phone for his limousine the minute he reached home. He had agreed to have late-night drinks with the British ambassador, as there was another OPEC problem, matters of state to be attended to.

It was not what his people in Moscow wanted, but knowledge of another Anglo-American oil strategy was not to be dismissed. All such information brought the Voennaya closer to the power they had been seeking since Yagoda set them on their path over a half century ago. Yet only the man who could not be found, the man who knew the secret of Anthony Matthias, could lead the Voennaya to its destiny—for the good of the world.

Arthur Pierce, raised as an Iowa farm boy but born in the Russian village of Ramenskoye, turned toward his car in the rain. There was no time to be tired, for the charade never stopped. Not for him.

Ambassador Addison Brooks stared at Bradford across the dais. "You say this mole *knows* who Parsifal is, *knew* about him before *we* did!" he exclaimed. "On what basis do you make that extraordinary statement?"

"Costa Brava," said the undersecretary. "And the past seventy-two hours."

"Take them in sequence," ordered the President.

"In the final hours of Costa Brava, Havelock was provided with a radio transmitter whose frequency calibrations had been altered by CIA technicians in Madrid. They were working under blind orders; they had no idea what the transmitter was for or who was going to use it. As you know, the entire Costa Brava assignment was controlled by a man named Steven MacKenzie, the most experienced black-operations officer in Central Intelligence; the security was guaranteed."

"Completely," interrupted Berquist. "MacKenzie died of a coronary three weeks after we pulled him out of Barcelona. There was nothing suspicious. The doctor's a respected, well-known physician and was thoroughly questioned. MacKenzie's death was from natural causes."

"Only *he* knew all the details," continued Bradford. "He'd hired a boat, two men, and a blond woman who spoke Czech and was to scream in the distance—in the dark—during the grisly scene they were performing on that beach. The three of them were the dregs—small-time narcotics dealers and a prostitute—picking up a sizable fee. They didn't ask questions. Havelock sent out his transmission in KGB code to what he thought was a Baader-Meinhof unit in the boat offshore. MacKenzie caught it on his scanner and signaled the boat to come in. A few minutes later Havelock saw what we wanted him to see—or he *thought* he saw it. The Costa Brava operation was over."

"Again," interrupted the ambassador impatiently, "General Halyard and I are aware of the essentials—"

"It was over, and except for the President and the three of us, no one else knew about it," said the undersecretary, rushing ahead. "MacKenzie had structured it in fragments, no one group knowing what the other was doing. The only story we issued was the trapped-double-agent version, no buried reports, no file within a file that contradicted it. And with MacKenzie's death, the last man on the outside who knew the truth was gone."

"The last man, perhaps," said Halyard. "Not the last woman. Jenna Karas knew. She got away from you, but she knew."

"She knew only what she was told, and I was the one who spoke with her at the hotel in Barcelona. The story she was given had a dual purpose. One, to frighten her into doing exactly what we asked of her so we could ostensibly save her life; and two, to put her into a disturbed frame of mind that would startle Havelock, help convince him she *was* a KGB officer if he had any last doubts or emotional hurdles. If she'd followed my instructions she'd be safe. Or if we'd been able to find her, she wouldn't be running from the men who have to kill her now—and kill Havelock—so as to keep the truth about Costa Brava secret. Because they *know* the truth."

Ambassador Brooks whistled softly; it was a low, swelling whistle, the sound made by a man genuinely astonished. "We've reached the last seventy-two hours," he said, "beginning with an untraceable call to Rome preceded by an authorization code established by Daniel Stern."

"Yes, sir. Col des Moulinets. I saw the outlines of the connection when I read the agent of record's report, but nothing was clear. Just shapes, shadows. Then it became clearer when he told us here tonight the things he did."

"A man named Ricci he'd never seen before," said Brooks, "two demolitions experts he knew nothing about."

"And a massive explosion that detonated some twelve minutes *after* the gunfire at the bridge," added Bradford. "Then his description of the woman as a 'needle' for the Soviets, a Russian plant that Moscow could have back and be taught a lesson."

"Which was a lie," objected Halyard. "That bomb was meant for the car she was in. It killed how many? Seven people on the road to the bridge? Christ, it was powerful enough to blow that vehicle out of sight and everyone in it beyond recognition. And our own people weren't to know a goddamned thing about it."

"By way of a man named Ricci," said Bradford, "a Corsican no one knew and two so-called small-arms backup personnel who were in reality explosives experts. They were sent by Rome, but the two who escaped never tried to get in touch with the embassy afterward. In our agent's words, that's not normal. They didn't dare return to Rome."

"They were sent by our people," said Berquist. "But they didn't *come* from our people. They had a separate arrangement with the same person who made the last untraceable call from Washington to Rome. Ambiguity."

"That same person, Mr. President, who was able to reach into Moscow and pull out an authentic KGB code—anything less would never have been accepted by Havelock. Someone who knew the truth about Costa Brava, and was as anxious, perhaps as desperate, as we are to keep a blackout on it."

"Why?" asked the general.

"Because if we went back and examined every aspect of the operation we might find he was there."

The President and the general reacted as though each had been told of an unexpected death; only Brooks remained impassive, watching Bradford carefully, a first-rate mind acknowledging the presence of another.

"That's a hell of a jump, son," said Halyard.

"I can't think of any other explanation," said Bradford. "Havelock's execution had been sanctioned, the sanction was understood even by those who respected his record. He'd turned; he was a 'psycho,' a killer, dangerous to every man in the field. But why was the woman at Col des Moulinets to be sent across the border? Why was the point made that she was a 'needle,' a plant? Why was her escape supposed to be a lesson to the Soviets, when all the while a bomb timed to explode minutes later would have blown her away beyond recognition?"

"To maintain the illusion that she had died at Costa Brava," said Brooks. "If she remained alive, she'd ask for asylum and tell her story; she'd have nothing to lose."

"Forcing the events of that night on the beach to be reexamined," the President said, completing the thought. "She had to be killed away from that bridge while still preserving the lie that she had died at Costa Brava."

"And the person who made the call authorizing Havelock's execution," said Halyard, frowning, with uncertainty in his voice, "who used the

Ambiguity code and put this Ricci and the two nitro men in Col des Moulinets by way of Rome . . . you say he was on the beach that night?"

"Everything points to it, yes, General."

"For Christ's sake, *why?*"

"Because he knows Jenna Karas is alive," replied Brooks, still watching Bradford. "At least, he knows she wasn't killed at Costa Brava. No one else does."

"That's speculation. It may have been kept quiet, but we've been looking for her for nearly four months."

"Without ever acknowledging it *was* her," explained the undersecretary, "without ever admitting she *was* alive. The alert was for a person, not a name. A woman whose expertise as a deep-cover agent could lead her to people she'd worked with previously under multiple identities. The emphasis was on physical appearance and languages."

"What I can't accept is your jump." Halyard shook his head, the gesture of a military strategist who sees a practical gap in a plan for a field maneuver. "MacKenzie put Costa Brava together in pieces, reporting only to you. The CIA in Langley didn't know about Madrid, and Barcelona was kept away from both. Under those conditions, how could someone penetrate what wasn't there? Unless you figure MacKenzie sold you out or loused it up."

"I don't think either." The undersecretary paused. "I think the man who took over the Ambiguity code was already involved with Parsifal months ago. He knew what to concentrate on and became alarmed when Havelock was ordered to Madrid under a Four Zero security."

"Someone with maximum clearance right here in the State Department," the ambassador broke in. "Someone with access to confidential memoranda."

"Yes. He kept tabs on Havelock's activities and saw that something was happening. He flew to Spain, picked him up in Madrid, and followed him back to Barcelona. *I* was there; so was MacKenzie. He almost certainly would have recognized me, and as I met with MacKenzie twice, it's reasonable to assume we were seen together."

"And presuming you were, it's also reasonable to assume that Moscow had a file on MacKenzie thick enough to alarm Soviet intelligence." Brooks leaned forward, once again locking his eyes with Bradford's. "A photograph wired to the KGB, and the man we're looking for, who saw you together in Barcelona, knew a black operation was in progress."

"It could have happened that way, yes."

"With a lot of conjecture on your part," said Halyard.

"I don't think the undersecretary of State is finished, Mal." The ambassador nodded his head at the papers Bradford had just separated and was scanning. "I don't believe he'd permit his imagination to wander into such exotic regions unless something triggered it. Am I right?"

"Substantially, yes."

"How about just plain yes," said the President.

"Yes," said the man from State. "I suppose I could be prosecuted for what I did this afternoon, but I considered it essential. I had to get away from the phones and the interruptions; I had to reread some of this material and provoke whatever imagination I have. I went to the classified files of Cons Op, removed Havelock's summary of Costa Brava under 'Chemical Therapy' and took it home. I've been studying it since three o'clock—and remembering MacKenzie's verbal report after he came back from Barcelona. There are discrepancies."

"In what way?" asked Brooks.

"In what MacKenzie planned and in what Havelock saw."

"He saw what we wanted him to see," said the President. "You made a point of it a few minutes ago."

"He may have seen more than we think, more than MacKenzie engineered."

"MacKenzie was *there*," protested Halyard. "What the hell are you talking about?"

"He was approximately seventy yards away from Havelock, with only a peripheral view of the beach. He was more concerned with watching Havelock's reactions than with what was taking place below. He'd rehearsed it a number of times with the two men and the blond woman. According to those practice sessions, everything was to take place near the water, the shots fired into the surf, the woman falling into the wet sand, her body rolling with the waves, the boat close by, within reach. The distance, the darkness—everything was for effect."

"Visually convincing," interrupted Brooks.

"Very," agreed Bradford. "But it wasn't what Havelock described. What he saw was infinitely *more* convincing. Under chemicals at the clinic in Virginia he literally relived the entire experience, including the emotional trauma that was part of it. He described bullets erupting in the sand, the woman running up to the road, not down by the water, and two men carrying the body away. *Two* men."

"Two men were hired," said Halyard, perplexed. "What's the problem?"

"*One* had to be in the boat; it was twenty feet offshore, the engine running. The *second* man was to have fired the shots and pulled the woman into the water, throwing her 'dead body' *into* the boat. The distance, the darkness, the beam of a flashlight—these were part of MacKenzie's scene, what he'd rehearsed with the people he'd hired. But the flashlight was the only constant between what MacKenzie planned and what Havelock saw. He didn't witness a performance; he saw a woman actually killed."

"*Jesus.*" The general sat back in his chair.

"MacKenzie never mentioned any of this?" said Brooks.

"I don't think he saw it. All he said to me was 'My employees must have put on a hell of a show.' He stayed where he was on that hill above the road for several hours watching Havelock. He left when it began to get light; he couldn't risk Havelock's spotting him."

Addison Brooks brought his right hand to his chin. "So the man we're looking for, the man who pulled the trigger at Costa Brava, who was given the Ambiguity code by Stern and put Havelock 'beyond salvage,' is a Soviet agent in the State Department."

"Yes," said the undersecretary.

"And he wants to find Parsifal as desperately as we do," concluded the President.

"Yes, sir."

"Yet, if I follow you," said Brooks quickly, "there's an enormous inconsistency. He hasn't passed on his astonishing information to his normal KGB controls. We'd know it if he had. Good *God,* we'd know it!"

"Not only has he held it back, Mr. Ambassador, he's purposely misled one of the ranking directors of the KGB." Bradford picked up the top page of his notes and slid it respectfully to the silver-haired statesman on his right. "I've saved this for last. Not, incidentally, to startle you or shock you, but only because it didn't make any sense unless we looked at everything else in relationship to it. Frankly, I'm still not sure I understand. It's a cable from Pyotr Rostov in Moscow. He's director of External Strategies, KGB."

"A cable from *Soviet intelligence?*" said Brooks, astonished, picking up the paper.

"Contrary to what most people believe," added the undersecretary, "strategists from opposing intelligence services often make contact with one another. They're practical men in a deadly practical business. They can't afford wrong signals. . . . According to Rostov, the KGB had nothing to do with the Costa Brava and he wanted us to know it. Incidentally, Colonel Baylor in his report said that Rostov trapped Havelock in Athens, and although he could have gotten him out of Greece and into Russia by way of the Dardanelles, he chose not to."

"When did you get this?" asked the statesman.

"Twenty-four hours ago," answered the President. "We've been studying it, trying to figure it out. Obviously, no response is called for."

"Read it, Addison," said Halyard.

"It was sent to D. S. Stern, Director of Consular Operations, United States Department of—" Brooks looked up at Bradford. "Stern was killed *three days* ago. Wouldn't Rostov have *known* that?"

"He wouldn't have sent it if he had. He wouldn't have permitted the slightest speculation that the KGB was involved in Stern's death. He sent that cable because he *didn't* know Stern was dead—or the others."

"Only Miller's death was released," said Berquist. "We couldn't keep it quiet; it was all over Bethesda. We put a blackout on Stern and Dawson, at least for the time being, until we could learn what was happening. We moved their families to the Cheyenne security compound in Colorado Springs."

"Read it," said the general.

Brooks held the paper under the glare of the Tensor lamp. He spoke slowly, reading in a monotone. " 'The betrayal at Costa Brava was not ours. Nor was the bait taken in Athens. The infamous Consular Operations continues its provocative actions and the Soviet Union continues to protest its disregard for human life as well as the crimes and terrorist acts it inflicts upon the innocent—peoples and nations alike. And should this notorious branch of the American Department of State believe it has collaborators within the walls of Dzerzhinsky, be assured such traitors will be rooted out and face the punishments demanded. I repeat, Costa Brava was not ours.' " The statesman finished; the cable was over. He let his hand drop to the dais, the page still held between his thumb and forefinger. "Good *Lord*," he whispered.

"I understand the words," said Halyard, "but not what he's trying to tell us."

" 'Better a Satan you know than one you don't,' " replied Brooks. "There are no walls in Dzerzhinsky Square."

"That's *it,*" said Bradford, turning to the President. "That's what we didn't connect with. The walls are in the *Kremlin.*"

"Outside and inside," continued the former ambassador. "He's telling you that he knows Costa Brava could not have taken place without a collaborator or collaborators in Moscow—"

"We understood that," interrupted Berquist. "What about the walls? The Kremlin? How do you read that?"

"He's warning us. He's saying he doesn't know who they are, and since he doesn't, they're not controllable."

"Because they're outside the normal channels of communication?" asked the President.

"Even abnormal channels," said Brooks.

"A power struggle." Berquist turned to the undersecretary. "Has there been anything of a serious nature about this from any of our intelligence departments?"

"Only the usual frictions. The old guard dying, the younger commissars anxious, ambitious."

"Where do the generals stand?" inquired the general.

"Half wanting to blow up Omaha, half wanting SALT Three."

"And Parsifal could unite them," said the statesman. "*All* their hands would be on the nuclear switches."

"But Rostov doesn't *know* about Parsifal," protested Bradford. "He has no *conception*—"

"He senses it," the ambassador broke in. "He knows Costa Brava was a Department of State operation somehow in conjunction with elements in Moscow. He's tried to trace them down and can't; that alarms him immensely. There's an imbalance, a shift from the norm at the highest levels."

"Why do you say that?" The President took the cable from Brooks, scrutinizing it as if trying to see what he had not seen before.

"It's not in there, sir," said Bradford, nodding at Brooks as he spoke. "Except for the word 'bait,' which refers to Havelock. Remember, he didn't take Havelock in Athens. Rostov's aware of the very unusual relationship between Michael Havelock and Anthony Matthias. Czech and Czech, teacher and student, survivors really—in many ways father and son; where does one end and the other begin? Is one or are both of them dealing with someone in Moscow? And for what purpose? Reasonable objectives can be ruled out; avoiding normal channels would indicate that. Not too many months ago we wondered the same thing: What had

Matthias done, and where did Havelock stand? We created Costa Brava because of it."

"And then Parsifal reached us and it didn't make any difference," interrupted Berquist. "We were at the wall. We're still at the wall—only, now it's grown larger, broken away from itself until there are two walls, our backs to each no matter which way we turn. The search for Parsifal is joined with another search for another man. Someone right here who's watching every move we make. A Soviet mole capable of pulling a buried code out of Moscow, and deep enough to change the face of Costa Brava. . . . My *God*, we've got to blow him out of the ground! If he finds Parsifal before we do, he and the madmen he answers to in the Kremlin can dictate whatever terms they like to this country."

"You know where he is," said the general. "Go after him! He's at State. High up; with access to embassy cables, and obviously goddamned close to Matthias. Because if *I* follow you now, he nailed the Karas woman. He supplied that code; he had it placed in her suitcase. He *nailed* her!"

"I think he supplied everything." Bradford shook his head slowly, arching his brows, as if recalling the impossible. "Including the suitcase, the Baader-Meinhof informer, our own codes and the instructions from Moscow. Everything just appeared in Barcelona—out of nowhere. And no one really knows how."

"I imagine it's pointless to press Matthias further?" said Brooks, asking the question nevertheless.

"Pointless," replied Bradford. "He repeats what he's maintained from the beginning. 'The evidence was there. It was true. It was channeled to me.' "

"The bells are heard by Saint Anthony!" exploded the President.

"The mole at *State*," Halyard persisted. "Good *Christ*, he can't be that hard to find. How many people would Stern talk to? What kind of time frame was involved? A few minutes? A few hours? Go back and trace every move he made."

"The Cons Op strategists operated in total secrecy," said Bradford. "There were no appointment calendars, no conference schedules. A call would come to a specific person upstairs, or over at the Agency, or the NSC, and the decks would be cleared for whichever strategist it was, but no record of the meeting was ever written down. Internal security again; a great deal could be pieced together by informers with access to such records or memoranda."

"Misdirect the flow of accurate information at all costs," said the President softly.

"By our estimates, Stern could have spoken to any of sixty to seventy-five people," continued Bradford. "And we could be *underestimating* that figure. There are authorities within teams of specialists, specialists among those considered authorities. The lists are endless, and all those people have maximum clearance."

"But we're talking about the *State Department,*" said Brooks emphatically. "Sometime between Stern's last conversation with Rome and four hours later when the authorization was given to Col des Moulinets. That narrows down the possibilities considerably."

"And whoever it is knows that," said the undersecretary. "It further obscures his movements. Even the check-ins and check-outs won't show him to be where he was."

"Didn't anyone *see* Stern?" persisted Brooks. "Surely, you've asked."

"As quietly as we could. Not one of those we questioned admitted seeing him within twenty-four hours of the period in question, but then we didn't expect the one who did to say so."

"*Nobody* saw him?" asked the general, frowning in disbelief.

"Well, yes, someone did," said Bradford, nodding. "The outside receptionist on the fifth floor, L Section. Dawson had left a message for Stern; he picked it up on his way to the elevator. He could have been in any of seventy-five offices beyond the reception-room door."

"Who was inside at the time?" The ambassador shook his head the instant he asked the question, as if to say, Sorry, never mind.

"Exactly," said Bradford, accepting the statesman's unspoken afterthought. "It wasn't any help. Twenty-three people were listed as not having checked out. There were conferences, secretaries taking notes, and briefings by division personnel. Everything was substantiated. No one left a meeting long enough to place that call."

"But, damn it, you've got a floor!" cried the soldier. "Seventy-five offices, seventy-five people. That's not a hundred and fifty, or a thousand; it's seventy-five and one of them's your mole! Start with those closest to Matthias and pull them in. Put every goddamn one of them into a clinic if you have to!"

"There'd be panic; the entire State Department would be demoralized," said Brooks. "*Unless*—Is there a clique, a particular group, closest to Matthias?"

"You don't understand him." Bradford brought his folded hands to his chin, searching for words. "He's first, last and always *Dr.* Matthias, teacher, enlightener, provoker of thought. He's a hustling Socrates on the Potomac, gathering his worshipers wherever he can find them, extolling those who see the light, striking down the disbelievers with the cruelest humor I've ever heard. Cruel but always couched in brilliantly humble phrases. And like most self-appointed arbiters of an elite, his arrogance makes him fickle as hell. A section will catch his eye and they're his fair-haired boys and girls for a while, until another group comes along and flatters him at the right moment, and there's suddenly a new court of supplicants he can lecture. Naturally, during the past year it's gotten worse —but it was always there." Bradford permitted himself the start of a strained smile. "Then, of course, I could be biased. I was never allowed in one of those charmed circles."

"Why do you think you were excluded?" asked the ambassador.

"I'm not sure. I had a certain reputation of my own once; perhaps he was uncomfortable with it. But I think it was because I used to watch him very closely, very hard. I was fascinated, and I know he was uncomfortable with that. . . . You see, the 'best and the brightest' were led down a lot of strange paths by men like him. Some of us grew up, and I don't think Matthias approved of that growth. Skepticism comes with it. The Thomistic leap isn't good enough anymore; blind faith can ruin the eyesight —and the perspective." Bradford leaned forward, his eyes on Halyard. "I'm sorry, General. My answer to both you and Ambassador Brooks is that there is no one group I'd zero in on, no guarantee that our mole would be caught before he panicked and ran. And we can't let that happen. I know I'm right. If we can find him, he can lead us to the man we call Parsifal. He may have lost him temporarily, but he knows who Parsifal is."

The older men were silent; they looked at each other, then turned back to Bradford. The general frowned, a questioning look in his clear eyes. The President nodded his head slowly, bringing his right hand to his cheek and staring at the man from State.

The ambassador spoke, his slender figure rigid in his chair. "I commend you, Mr. Undersecretary. May I try to reconstruct the new scenario? . . . For reasons unknown, Matthias needed an incontrovertible case against the Karas woman, which would lead to Havelock's retirement. By now, because of what he's done, Matthias is Parsifal's puppet—his prisoner, really—but Parsifal knows it's in his interest to carry out Matthias's obsession. He goes to a well-entrenched Soviet agent in the upper regions of the State Department and the incriminating evidence against the Karas woman is provided, studied and accepted. Except that two source controls from the CIA come to you and tell you it can't be true—any of it—and you, Emory Bradford, enter the picture. In fact, the President, alarmed by what appears to be a conspiracy at State brings us *all* into the picture —and we in turn recruit a black-operations officer to mount the Costa Brava exercise. That exercise—that scene—is turned into murder, and at this juncture, it's your thesis that the mole lost sight of Parsifal."

"Yes. Parsifal, whoever he is, got what he wanted from the mole, then dropped him. The mole is stunned, possibly frantic. He's undoubtedly made promises to Moscow—based on assurances from Parsifal—that projected a major setback for American foreign policy, conceivably its collapse."

"Either," interjected the President in a quiet monotone, "would be a benevolent alternative."

"And whoever has the information contained in Parsifal's documents will assume control of the Kremlin." Brooks remained rigid, his aristocratic face pale, drawn. "We're at war," he added softly.

"I repeat," said Halyard. "Go after those seventy-five offices at State. Mount a sweep, call it a medical quarantine; it's simple but effective, even acceptable. Do it in the early evening after they've left work. Round them up in their homes, restaurants; pull them in and get them down to your laboratories. Find your mole!" The general's forceful rendering of the tactic impressed the civilians, who remained silent. Halyard lowered his voice. "I know it smells, but I don't think you've got a choice."

"We'd need two hundred men posing as medical technicians and drivers," said Bradford. "Between thirty and forty government vehicles. No one knowing anything."

"We'd also be dealing with families and neighbors and 'technicians' knocking on doors at night," countered Berquist. "*Christ,* that son of a bitch! That *man* for all *seasons!*" The President stopped; he took a deep breath, then continued, "We'd never get away with it; the rumors would spread like a Mesabi brush fire in a dry July. The press would break it open and call us everything in the book, everything we deserve. Mass arrests without explanation—there's none we could give—interrogations without due process, storm troopers . . . chemicals. We'd be crucified on every editorial page in the country, hanged in effigy on every campus, denounced from every pulpit and soapbox, to say nothing of the acid from our legislative brethren. I'd be impeached."

"More important, Mr. President," said the ambassador, "and I'm sorry to say I mean that, the action itself would undoubtedly throw Parsifal into panic. He'd see what we were doing, know whom we were trying to unearth in order to find him. He could carry out his threats, carry out the inconceivable."

"Yes, I know. We're damned if we move, helpless if we don't."

"It could *work,*" persisted the general.

"Handled correctly, it might, Mr. President," added Bradford.

"For God's sake, how?"

"Anyone who objected strenuously, to the point of refusal or evasion, would probably be our man," replied Bradford.

"Or someone with something else to hide," said Brooks gently. "We're in the age of anxiety, Mr. Undersecretary, and this is a city with a low threshold for privacy. You might very well corner a person who has nothing more to conceal than an unopened closet, or the loathing of a superior, an unpopular viewpoint, or an office affair. Parsifal will see only what his insanity compels him to see."

Bradford listened, reluctantly accepting the statesman's judgment. "There's another approach we haven't had time to implement. An itinerary check. Tracing the whereabouts of every person on that floor during the week of Costa Brava. If we're right—if I'm not wrong—he wasn't here. He was in Madrid, in Barcelona."

"He'd cover himself," objected Halyard.

"Regardless, General, he'd have to account for being away from Washington. How many such absences can there be?"

"When can you start?" asked Berquist.

"First thing in the morning—"

"Why not tonight?" the general interrupted.

"If those records were accessible, I could. They're not, and to call someone in to open them at this hour would cause talk. We can't afford that."

"Even in the morning," said the ambassador, "how can you suppress curiosity, keep it quiet?"

Bradford paused before speaking, his eyes cast downward, seeking an answer. "Time study," he replied, looking up, the phrase bordering on a question. "I'll tell whoever controls those records that it's a routine time study. Someone's always doing something like that."

"Acceptable," agreed Brooks. "Banal and acceptable."

"Nothing's acceptable," said the President of the United States quietly, staring at the white wall, where an hour ago the faces of four dead men had been projected. " 'A man for all seasons,' they call him. The original was a scholar, a statesman, the creator of Utopia . . . *and* a burner of heretics—they conveniently forget that, don't they? 'Condemn the non-believers; they don't see what I see, and I'm—inviolate.' . . . Goddamn it, if I had my way, I'd do what fat Henry did with Thomas More. I'd cut off Matthias's head, and instead of London Bridge, I'd jam it on top of the Washington Monument as a reminder. Heretics, too, are citizens of the republic and so, *holy* man, there can be no heresy! *Goddamn* him!"

"You know what would happen, don't you, Mr. President?"

"Yes, Mr. Ambassador, I do. The people would look up at that bleeding neck, at that ever-benign face—no doubt with those tortoiseshell glasses still intact—and in their infinite wisdom they'd say he was right, had been right all along. Citizens—heretics included—would canonize him, and that's the lousy irony."

"He could still do it, I think," Brooks mused. "He could walk out and the cries would start again. They'd offer him the crown and he'd refuse and they'd persist—until it became inevitable. Another irony. Hail not Caesar but Anthony—a coronation. A constitutional amendment would be rammed through the House and the Senate and President Matthias would sit in the Oval Office. As incredible as it might seem, he could probably still do it. Even now."

"Maybe we should let him," said Berquist softly, bitterly. "Maybe the people—in their *infinite* wisdom—are right, after all. Maybe *he's* been right all along. Sometimes I don't know anymore. Perhaps he really does see things others don't see. Even now."

The aristocratic statesman and the plainspoken general left the underground room. The four would meet again at noon the next day, each arriving separately at the South Portico entrance, away from the inquisitive eyes of the White House press corps. If, in the morning, there were any startling developments in Bradford's research at State, the time would be moved up, the President's calendar erased. The mole took all precedence. He could lead them to a madman the President and his advisers called Parsifal.

"I commend you, Mr. Undersecretary," said Berquist, lowering his voice in an amateur's imitation of the ambassador's fluid and graceful speech. It was an imitation with only a trace of rancor; respect was also there. "He's the last of the originals, isn't he?"

"Yes, sir. There aren't many left, and none that I know of who care that much. Taxes and the great democratization have removed them—or alienated them. They feel uncomfortable, and I think it's the country's loss."

"Don't be sepulchral, Emory, it doesn't suit you. We need him; the power brokers on the Hill are still in awe of him. If there ever was an answer to Matthias, it's Addison Brooks. The *Mayflower* and Plymouth Rock, New York's Four Hundred and fortunes built on the backs of immigrants—leading to the guilt feelings of the inheritors. Benevolent liberals who weep at the sight of swollen black bellies in the Mississippi Delta. But for Christ's sake, don't take away the Château d'Yquem."

"Yes, Mr. President."

"You mean 'No, Mr. President.' It's in your eyes, Emory; it's always in the eyes. Don't mistake me, I admire old elegant-ass, respect what's in that head of his. Just as I think Tightrope Halyard's one of the few military relics who've actually read the Constitution and understand what civilian authority really means. It's not that war's too important to leave to the generals; that's horseshit. We'd both be rotten pincering up the Rhine. It's the *ending* of wars, the aftermath. The generals are reluctant to accept the first and have no concept of the second. Halyard's different, and the Pentagon knows it. The Joint Chiefs listen to him because he's better than they are. We need him, too."

"I agree."

"That's what this office is all about. Need. Not likes or dislikes, only need. If I ever get back to Mountain Iron, Minnesota, alive and in one piece, I can think about whether I like someone or not. But I can't do that now. It's only what I need. And what I need right now is to stop Parsifal, stop what he's done, what he did to Anthony Matthias." The President paused, then continued, "I meant what I said—*he* said. I *do* commend you. It was a hell of a job."

"Thank you, sir."

"Especially what you didn't say. Havelock. Where is he?"

"Almost certainly in Paris; it's where Jenna Karas was heading. Between pages this afternoon I placed a number of calls to people I know in the Assembly, the Senate, several ministries, the Quai d'Orsay, and our own embassy. I applied pressure, hinting that my orders came from the White House, but without mentioning you by name."

"You could have."

"Not yet, Mr. President. Perhaps never, but certainly not now."

"Then we understand each other," said Berquist.

"Yes, sir. Necessity."

"Halyard might have understood; he's a practical soldier. Brooks wouldn't; underneath that diplomatic exterior he's a thorough moralist."

"That was my assessment, why I didn't clarify Havelock's status."

"It remains what it was at Col des Moulinets. If he exposed Costa Brava, it would panic Parsifal more quickly than anything we might do in the State Department. Havelock was at the center—from the beginning."

"I understand, sir."

Berquist's eyes strayed to the blank white screen at the far end of the room. "In World War Two, Churchill had to make a decision that tore him apart. The German code machine Enigma had been broken by Allied intelligence, a feat that meant that military strategies issued from Berlin could be intercepted and hundreds of thousands—ultimately perhaps millions—of lives could be saved. Word came that a massive air strike had been called against Coventry. It was a single transmission, coded through Enigma. But acknowledging it, evacuating the city or even mounting sudden, abnormal defenses, would have revealed that the riddle of Enigma had been solved. . . . Coventry had to be bombed half out of existence so the secret could be kept. The secret of Costa Brava cannot be exposed for the same reason—millions of lives are in the balance. . . . Find Havelock, Mr. Undersecretary Find him and have him killed. Reinstate the order for his execution."

19

Havelock knew he had been spotted: a newspaper was abruptly lowered as he walked between the roped stanchions of Air France's disembarkation lounge at Kennedy into the corridor that led to immigration. He had been pre-cleared on diplomatic status, the papers Broussac had provided guaranteeing a rapid exit through U.S. customs, and because of this accommodation he understood that he had to destroy those papers as quickly as possible. He carried his small suitcase—officially lock-taped and stamped *Diplomatique* in Paris—and once through the corridor he would be admitted through the heavy metal doors that led into the terminal by simply showing his United Nations credentials and declaring that he had no other luggage. A dead-file name would be checked against a dead-file name on the manifest, and he would be free to search or be killed in the United States of America. It was all so simple.

However, for Régine Broussac's protection—and ultimately his own—he had to get rid of the false papers that made all this possible. Too, he had to find out who had lowered the newspaper. The gray-faced man had risen slowly from his seat, folding the newspaper under his arm, and started for the outer, crowded hallway that paralleled the inner corridor that led to questionable freedom. Who was that man?

If he could not find out, it was entirely possible that he would be killed before he could search, before he reached a halfway broker named Jacob Handelman. And that was not acceptable.

The uniformed immigration officer was astute, polite. He asked the proper questions while looking Havelock directly in the eyes.

"You have no luggage, sir?"

"*Non, monsieur.* Only the one piece here."

"Then you don't expect to be on First Avenue very long?"

"A day, forty-eight hours," replied Michael with a Gallic shrug. "*Une conférence.*"

"I'm sure your government has made arrangements for transportation into the city. Wouldn't you care to wait for the rest of your party?"

The official was *very* good, thought Havelock. "Forgive me, monsieur, you force me to be candid." Michael smiled awkwardly, as though his dignity had been somewhat compromised. "There is a lady waiting for me; we see each other so seldom. Perhaps it is noted on your information, I was posted at—First Avenue for several months last year. Haste, *mon ami,* haste is on my mind."

Slowly the official returned the smile as he checked off the name and reached for a button. "Have a good day, sir," he said.

"Many thanks," said Havelock, walking rapidly through the parting steel checkpoint. *Vivent les amours des gentilhommes français,* he thought.

The gray-faced man was standing by a short row of telephones, each occupied; he was second in line behind the third. The newspaper, which had been folded under the arm, was instantly removed and snapped open. He had not been able to make his call, and under the circumstances that was the best sight Michael could hope to see.

He started walking in the man's direction, passing him quickly and looking straight ahead. He took his first left into an intersecting wide corridor crowded with streams of departing passengers heading for their gates. He swung right into a narrower hallway, this one with far fewer people and the majority of these in the uniforms of the various airlines.

Left again, the corridor longer, still narrow, even fewer people, mostly men in white overalls and in shirt sleeves; he had entered some kind of freight complex, the office section. There were no passengers, no business suits, no briefcases or carry-on bags.

There were no public telephones. The walls were stark, broken up by widely spaced glass doors. The nearest phones were far behind, around the corner in the first, main hallway. Out of sight.

He found the men's room; it said, AIRPORT EMPLOYEES ONLY. Michael pushed the door open and walked inside. It was a large tiled room, two air vents whirring on the far wall, no windows. A row of toilet stalls was on the left, sinks and urinals on the right. A man in overalls with the words *Excelsior Airline Caterers* was positioned in front of the fourth urinal; a flush came from one of the stalls. Havelock went to a sink, placing his suitcase under it.

The man at the urinal stepped back and zipped up his overalls; he glanced at Michael, his eyes taking in an expensive dark suit purchased that morning in Paris. Then, as if to say, All right, Mr. Executive, I'll wash my hands, he ambled to the nearest sink and turned on the water.

A second man emerged from a stall; he pulled his belt taut and started for the door, swearing under his breath, the plastic I.D. tag pinned to his shirt indicating he was a harried supervisor.

The man in overalls ripped a paper towel out of a stainless-steel machine, cursorily wiped his hands and threw the brown paper into a receptacle. He opened the door and stepped out. As the door swung back Havelock ran to catch it, holding it open no more than an inch, and peered outside.

The unknown surveillance was fifty-odd feet up the corridor, casually leaning against the wall next to an office door, reading the folded newspaper. He looked at his watch, then glanced at the frosted glass panel; he was the image of a visitor waiting for a friend to come out and join him for a late lunch or drinks, or a drive to a motel near the airport. There was nothing menacing about him, but in that control Michael knew there was menace, professionalism.

Still, two could have control, two could wait, be professional. The advantage belonged to the one behind a door; he knew what was inside. The one outside did not, and could not afford to move away—to a telephone, perhaps—because once he was out of sight the quarry could escape.

Wait. Keep the control. And get rid of the false papers that could lead the pursuers to Régine Broussac and a halfway man named Jacob Handelman. A dead-file name on an aircraft's manifest was meaningless, inserted by mindless computers that could not say who punched the keys, but the papers could be traced to their origin. Havelock tore the documents into shreds, which he flushed down a toilet. With a penknife he sliced the ribbed *Diplomatique* tape, which guaranteed the absence of official inspection, and opened his suitcase in a stall at the end of the row. He removed the short-barreled Llama automatic from beneath his folded clothes, and a passport case containing his own very authentic papers. Presented properly, the papers were essentially harmless. The objective, however, was not to have to present them at all, and they were rarely required in the streets of his adopted country, one of the benefits for which he was profoundly thankful.

Between the time he destroyed the mocked-up papers and inserted his passport case and weapon in their proper places, the employees' men's room had two more visitors. They came in together—an Air France pilot and his first officer, to judge from their conversation; Michael remained in the stall. They argued, urinated, swore at preflight red tape, and wondered how much their Havana Monte Cristos would bring at the bar of L'Auberge au Coin, a restaurant apparently in midtown Manhattan. They continued talking about their profits on the way out.

Havelock took off the jacket of his suit, rolled it up, and waited in the stall. He held the door open no more than a quarter of an inch and looked at his watch. He had been inside the lavatory nearly fifteen minutes. It would happen soon, he thought.

It did. The white metal door swung slowly back and Havelock saw part of a shoulder first, then the edge of a folded newspaper. The unknown surveillance *was* professional: no folded jacket or coat concealed a gun— no draped cloth that could be grabbed and twisted, to be used against the holder—just a loose newspaper that could be easily discarded and the weapon fired cleanly.

The man whipped around the door, his back against the metal panel, his eyes scanning the walls, the vents, the row of stalls. Satisfied, he bent his knees, lowering himself, but apparently not for the purpose of checking the open spaces under the doors of the first several stalls. His eyes darted back and forth. His body was turned away from Michael. What was he doing?

And then he did it, and the image of another professional on the bridge at Col des Moulinets came to Michael, a blond professional in the uniform of an Italian guard. But the killer "Ricci" had come prepared, knowing what his landscape was, knowing there was a gatehouse door to be jammed. This gray-faced professional had improvised, the test of on-site ingenuity. He had broken off a piece of wood, a small strip of cheap industrial molding—found in a dozen places in any airport corridor—and was now wedging it under the door. He stood up, placed his foot against the strip, and pulled on the metal knob. The door was jammed; they were alone. The man turned.

Peering from inside the stall, Havelock studied him. The menace was not at first glance in the man's physical equipment. He was perhaps in his mid-fifties, with thinning hair above a flat gray face with thick eyebrows and high cheekbones. He was no more than five feet, eight inches, and his shoulders were narrow, compact. But then, Michael saw the left hand—the right was concealed beneath the newspaper; it was huge, a peasant's powerful hand, formed by years of working with heavy objects and equipment.

The man started down the row of stalls, the sides of each about two inches above the tiled floor, which made it necessary for him to be within three feet of a front panel to ascertain whether it was occupied. Wearing shoes with thick rubber soles, he moved in total silence. Suddenly he spun his right hand in a circle, flipping off the newspaper. Havelock stared at the gun as the intruder approached the final three stalls. He was angry but bewildered—the weapon was a Graz-Burya. The Russian bent over . . .

Now. Michael threw his rolled-up suit jacket over the side of the stall on his right. The sound made the Russian leap up, spinning to his left, his gun raised.

In simultaneous movements Havelock grabbed the handle of his suitcase and yanked the door open, then swung the heavy luggage in a lateral arc toward the gray-faced man. He reached for the Graz-Burya with his left hand and tore it out of the man's hand. The Russian spun away, his powerful arms blocking Havelock; Michael used them—he locked the man's left arm under his right, wrenched it forward until the Russian's face was stretched in pain, then he pried the weapon loose and crashed the barrel into the man's head. As the Russian started to fall, Havelock crouched and jammed his shoulder into the man's kidney, propelling him back into the row of urinals.

The gray-faced man fell to his knees, supporting himself on his right hand and holding his left arm across his chest in pain. He gasped for breath, shaking his head. *"Nyet, nyet,"* he choked. "Talk only! Only *talk.*"

"With the door as good as locked and a gun in your hand?"

"Would you have agreed to a conversation if I had come up and introduced myself? In Russian, perhaps?"

"You should have tried me."

"You did not stay still long enough. . . . May I?" The Russian leaned back on his knees, holding his arm and raising one leg as he requested permission to stand.

"Go ahead," said Havelock, the Graz-Burya steady in his hand. "You were trying to make a phone call."

"Certainly. To relay word that you had been found. What would you have done? Or I don't know, perhaps I should not ask."

"What *do* you know? How did you find me?" Michael raised the gun, aiming it at the man's head. "I'd advise you to tell me the truth. I haven't got a thing to lose with your corpse in here."

The Russian stared at the barrel and then at Havelock's eyes. "No, you have nothing to lose; you would not hesitate. A younger man should have been sent out here."

"How did you know I'd be on that plane?"

"I didn't. No one knows anywhere. . . . A VKR officer was shot in Paris; he had nowhere to turn but to us."

"An importing firm on the Beaumarchais?" interrupted Michael. "KGB headquarters, Paris?"

The Russian overlooked the interruption. "We knew you had connections throughout the French government. Military intelligence, the Quai d'Orsay, the Deputies. If it was your intention to leave France, there was only one way you could do it. Diplomatic cover. All Air France flights listing diplomatic personnel are being watched. Everywhere. London, Rome, Bonn, Athens, the Netherlands, all of South America—everywhere. It's my misfortune that you chose to come back here; it was not expected. You are 'beyond salvage.' "

"That seems to be a well-publicized piece of information."

"It has been circulated in certain quarters."

"Is that what you wanted to talk about? Because if it is, Moscow's wasting a lot of man-hours in all those airports."

"I bring you a message from Pyotr Rostov. He believes that after Rome, you might listen."

"Rome?" What about Rome?"

"The Palatine. It would seem it was conclusive for you. You were meant to die on the Palatine."

"I was?" Havelock watched the man's eyes, the set of his lips. So Rostov knew about the Palatine; it was to be expected. Bodies had been found there: the corpse of a former American agent known for jugular operations and his two wounded Italian drones who had nothing to lose and something to bargain with by telling the truth. Certainly Moscow knew. But Rostov did not know about Jenna Karas or Col des Moulinets, or he would have included them in his opening lure. Under different circumstances it might have been necessary for the words to have been shouted quickly: *Jenna Karas is alive! Col des Moulinets!* Both were far more persuasive. "What's the message?"

"He says to tell you the bait's been reconsidered. He'll take it now and thinks you should agree. He says he's not your enemy any longer, but others are who may be his as well."

"What does that mean?"

"I can't answer you," said the man, his thick eyebrows motionless above his deep-set peasant eyes. "I'm merely the messenger. The substance is for you to know, not me."

"You knew about the Palatine."

"The death of a maniac travels fast, especially if he's your adversary—most especially if he's killed a number of your friends. . . . What was the name his own people gave him? The Gunslinger, I believe. A romantic figure from your Western films, which, incidentally, I enjoy immensely. But in history such a fellow was invariably a filthy, unprincipled pig, devoid of morals or ideology, motivated solely by profit or pathological brutality. In these times he might be the president of an enormous corporation, no?"

"Spare me. Save it for the state schools."

"Rostov would like a reply, but you don't have to give it at once. I can reach you. A day, two days—a few hours from now. You may name the drop. We can get you out. To safety."

Again Michael studied the Russian's face. Like Rostov in Athens before him, the man was relaying the truth—as he knew the truth, and as he knew the word of his superior in Moscow. "What does Rostov offer?"

"I told you. Safety. You know what's ahead of you here. The Palatine."

"Safety in exchange for what?"

"That's between you and Rostov. Why should I invent conditions? You would not believe them."

"Tell Rostov he's wrong."

"About Rome? The Palatine?"

"The Palatine," said Havelock, wondering briefly if a KGB director ten thousand miles away would perceive the essential truth within the larger lie. "I don't need the safety of the Lubyanka."

"You refuse his offer, then?"

"I refuse the bait."

There was a sudden thud against the men's-room door, followed by a muffled voice swearing, then repeated banging against the metal panel.

The strip of wood wedged under the door scraped the tile; it gave less than an inch, which was enough to make the intruder shout while continuing to pound, "Hey, what the hell *is* this! Open up!"

The Russian glanced at the door; Havelock did not. The man spoke rapidly: "Should you change your mind, there is a row of trash cans in Bryant Park, behind your Public Library. Place a red mark on the front of one of them—I suggest a felt marker or, better yet, a spot of woman's nail polish. Then, starting at ten o'clock that same night, walk north and south on Broadway, between Forty-second and Fifty-third streets, staying on the east-side pavement. Someone will reach you, giving you the address of the contact. It will be outside, naturally. No traps."

"What's going *on* in there? Fa' *Christ's sake,* open this goddamned *door!*"

"I thought you said I could pick the drop."

"You may. Simply tell the man who reaches you where you want to meet. Just give us three hours."

"To sweep it?"

"Son of a bitch! *Open up!*" The metal door was smashed back several inches, the strip of wood scratching against the tiles.

A second, authoritative voice joined that of the angry intruder. "All right, what's this all about?"

"The door's jammed! I can't get in, but I hear 'em talkin'! They jammed the fuckin' door!" Another crash, another screech, another inch.

"We take precautions, just as you do," said the Russian. "What's between you and Rostov . . . is between you and Moscow. We are not in Moscow, *I* am not in Moscow. I do not call for the police when I'm in trouble in New York City."

"All *right* in there!" shouted the second voice in lower-register officiousness. "Fair warning, you punks! Obstruction of normal operating procedures at an international airport constitutes a felony, and that includes the toilets! I'm calling Airport Security!" The stern-toned one addressed the angry intruder. "If I were you, I'd find another men's room. These kids use needles; they can get hopped up and pretty violent."

"I've gotta take one pisser of a leak, man! And they don't *sound* like no kids— There's a cop! Hey, *Fuzz!*"

"He can't hear you. He's walking past. I'll get to a phone."

"*Shit!*"

"Let's go," said Havelock, reaching down for his jacket and slipping it on.

"My life, then?" asked the Russian. "No corpse in a men's room?"

"I want my reply delivered. Forget the nail polish on those trash cans."

"Then, if I may, my weapon, please?"

"I'm not that charitable. You see, you *are* my enemy. You have been for a long time."

"It's difficult to explain a missing weapon. *You* understand."

"Tell them you sold it on the open market; it's the first step in capitalism. Buy cheap—or get it for nothing—and sell high. The Burya's a good gun; it'd bring a large profit."

"Please!"

"You don't understand, *comrade.* You'd be surprised how many hustlers in Moscow would respect you. Come *on!"* Havelock grabbed the man by the shoulder, propelling him toward the door. "Kick out the wood," he ordered, shoving the weapon into his belt and picking up his suitcase.

The Russian did as he was told. He pressed the side of his shoe on the protruding wedge, moving it back and forth, as he pushed the door shut. The wedge came loose; he swept it away with his foot and pulled the door open.

"Jesus *Christ!"* exclaimed an obese man in sky-blue overalls. "A couple of fuckin' fairies!"

"They're *coming!"* yelled a shirt-sleeved man, running out of an office door across the corridor.

"I think you're too late, Mr. Supervisor," said the wide-eyed freight employee, staring at Havelock and the Russian. "Here're your fuckin' punks. Two old queens who figured the parking lot was too cold."

"Let's *go!"* whispered Havelock, grabbing the Russian's elbow.

"Disgusting! Revolting!" shouted the supervisor. "At your age! Have you no *shame?* Perverts *everywhere!"*

"You won't change your mind about the weapon?" asked the Russian, walking breathlessly up the corridor, wincing as Michael gripped his damaged left arm. "I'll be severely disciplined. I haven't used it in years; it's really a form of dress, you know."

"Perverts! You should all be in jail, not in public toilets! You're a menace!"

"I'm telling you, you'll get a promotion if the right people think you made a bundle."

"Faggots!"

"Let go of my arm. That idiot's marking us."

"Why? You're adorable."

They reached the second hallway, turning left toward the center of the terminal. There were, as before, men in overalls and shirt sleeves milling about, watching an occasional secretary emerge from an office door. Up ahead was the main corridor, crowds surging in both directions, toward departing gates and luggage areas.

In seconds they were swept into the flow of arrivals. Seconds later a trio of uniformed police could be seen breaking through the stream of departing passengers, pushing aside shoulders and small suitcases and plastic garment bags. Havelock switched sides with the Russian, yanking him to the left, and as the police came parallel in the opposite aisle Michael crashed his shoulder into his companion, pummeling him into a blue uniform.

"Nyet! Kishki!" yelled the Russian.

"Goddamn it!" shouted the police officer as he plunged off balance to his right, tripping one of his associates, who in turn fell on top of an elderly blue-haired woman, who screamed.

Havelock accelerated his pace, threading his way past startled passengers who were rushing toward an escalator on the right that led to the baggage area, where they could retrieve their belongings. On the left was someone's idea of a celestial arch, which led into the central terminal; he headed toward it, walking faster still as the path became less congested. In the terminal the bright afternoon sunlight streamed through the huge floor-to-ceiling windows. He looked around as he went toward the exit door marked *Taxis.* There were rows of counters beneath panoplies of white-lettered schedules, isolated slots constantly in motion; circular booths selling knickknacks and gewgaws were dotted about in the middle of the domelike building. Along the walls were banks of telephones and indented racks of telephone books. He veered toward the nearest one.

Thirty seconds later he found it: Handelman, J. The address was in upper Manhattan, on 116th Street, Morningside Heights.

Jacob Handelman, halfway man, broker of sanctuary for the pursued and the dispossessed. The man who would conceal Jenna Karas.

"Stop over there," said Havelock, leaning forward in the seat and pointing to a blue canopy emblazoned with a small gold crown and the name THE KING'S ARMS HOTEL across the scalloped valance. He hoped he would not have to spend the night—each hour put greater distance between Jenna and himself—but on the other hand, he could not walk around Columbia

University, carrying even a small suitcase while tracking down Jacob Handelman. He had told the cab driver to take the Triborough Bridge, heading west toward the Hudson and south into Morningside Heights; he wanted to pass the address on 116th, then find a secure place to leave his luggage. It was midafternoon and the halfway man could be anywhere within the sprawling urban campus.

Michael had been to Columbia twice while a graduate student at Princeton, once for a lecture on Europe after Napoleon delivered by a visiting bore from Oxford, and the second time for an inter-graduate-school seminar on university placement for budding Carl Schorskes. Neither occasion was memorable, both were brief, and as a result he really knew nothing about the place. That was probably irrelevant, but the fact that he knew absolutely nothing about Jacob Handelman was not.

The King's Arms was around the corner from Handelman's apartment. It was one of those small hotels that somehow manage to survive tastefully within the environs of a city university, upper Manhattan's answer to the old Taft in New Haven or, stretching a point, the Inn at Princeton—in essence, a campus fixture, temporary quarters for visiting lecturers rather than an undergraduate drinking spot. It had the appearance of dark-leather English comfort and the smell of Academe. It was only an outside possibility, but since the hotel was so close to Handelman's residence, there was a chance someone might know him.

"Certainly, Mr. Hereford," said the clerk, reading the registration card. "Dr. Handelman stops in now and then—a little wine or dinner with friends. A delightful gentleman, a most charming sense of humor. We here, like most everyone else, all call him the Rabbi."

"I didn't know that. His being a rabbi, I mean."

"I'm not sure he is formally, although I doubt anyone would question his credentials. He's Jarmaine Professor of Philosophy, and I understand he lectures frequently at the Jewish Theological Seminary. You'll enjoy your interview."

"I'm sure I will. Thank you."

"Front," said the clerk, tapping a bell.

Handelman's apartment building was between Broadway and Riverside Drive, the street sloping toward Riverside Park and the Hudson. It was a solid structure of heavy white stone—once a monument to New York's exploding upward mobility—which had been permitted to age gently, and to pass through periods of brief renaissance, only to recede into that graveyard of tall, awkwardly ornate edifices too cumbersome for efficient economics. Once there had been a doorman standing in front of the glass-and-ironwork façade; now there were double locks on the inner door and a functioning communications system between visitor and resident.

Havelock pressed the bell, intending merely to make sure Handelman was home; there was no reply from the speaker. He rang again. Nothing.

He went back outside, crossing the street to a doorway, and considered his options. He had telephoned the university's information center and was given the location and number of Handelman's office. A second call —placed anonymously as an administration clerk requesting a Thursday stat sheet—revealed the fact that Handelman had doctoral appointments scheduled through 4:00 P.M. It was now nearly five o'clock, and Michael's frustration was growing. Where *was* Handelman? There was, of course, no guarantee that he would come directly home from his office, but a broker of sanctuary who had just placed— or was placing—a woman fugitive from Paris had certain obligations. Havelock had considered going to Handelman's office or intercepting him on the street; he considered both options again. Perhaps an appointment had run late, or he had accepted an invitation for dinner; someone could still be there who might know, who might help him.

Coping with the tension of waiting—a practice he was normally superb at—was causing him pain, actual physical pain in his stomach. He breathed deeply; he could not confront the halfway man in an office or on the street or in any public place and he knew it. The meeting had to take place where there were names and numbers, maps and codes; these were the tools of a halfway man. They would only be kept where he could store them safely, reach them quickly. Under a floorboard, or deep in a wall, or microscopically reduced and in the toe of a shoe or implanted in shirt buttons.

He had not seen a photograph of Handelman, but he knew what he looked like. The florid-faced bartender at the King's Arms Hotel— himself apparently a fixture, with the flair and verbosity of a fifth-rate poet from Dublin—had described "the Rabbi." Jacob Handelman was a medium-tall man with long white hair and a short gray beard, given slightly to overweight and more than slightly to a paunch. His walk was "slow and stately," the bartender said, "as if he was the Judaic blood-royal, sir, forever partin' the waters, or mountin' the ark to discourse with the animals. Ah, but he has a gleam in his eye and a lovely heart, sir."

Havelock had listened to the man and ordered a double Scotch.

Three minutes past five. *Breathe deep. Really breathe and think of Jenna, think what you're going to say to her. It could be an hour or two, or longer, perhaps half the night. Half the night for the halfway man. Don't dwell on it.*

Dusk lingered, the orange sun inflaming the New Jersey skyline beyond the Hudson River. The West Side Highway was jammed, and Riverside Drive, parallel to it, was barely less so. The temperature was dropping and gray clouds joined the darkening sky; snow was in the air.

And across the street a medium-tall man, wide at the girth, in a full black overcoat, walked slowly down the pavement. His bearing was indeed stately, matching the distinguished image created by his pure-white hair, which fell several inches below the brim of his black hat. In the light of a streetlamp, Michael could see the gray beard; it was the halfway man.

Jacob Handelman approached the outer glass doors of his apartment building and was now in the stronger light of the large entrance lamps. Havelock stared, at once mesmerized and disturbed; did he know the halfway man? Had "the Rabbi" been part of an operation eight . . . ten years ago? Perhaps in the Middle East, Tel Aviv, Lebanon? Michael had the distinct feeling that he *did* know him. Was it the walk? The deliberate pace that seemed almost anachronistic, as if the figure should be strolling in medieval robes? Or was it the thin steel-rimmed glasses, set so firmly in the center of the large face?

The moment passed; it was, of course, possible that a halfway man might have crossed his path in any number of situations. They could have been in the same sector at one time or another, a respected professor supposedly on holiday but, in reality, meeting with someone like Régine Broussac. Entirely possible.

Handelman went inside the enclosed entranceway, climbed the inner steps and stopped at the row of mailboxes. It was all Michael could do to restrain himself; the desire to race across the street and confront the halfway man was nearly overpowering.

He may choose to tell you nothing. Broussac.

An old man who did not care to negotiate could scream on a staircase and yell for help. And the one who *needed* help did not know what was behind a door across the street, what devices a group of intelligent city dwellers had mounted to defend themselves from hallway thugs. Security alarms had flooded the market; he had to wait until Jacob Handelman was safely in his flat. And then a knock on the door and the words "Quai d'Orsay" would be enough; there was respect for a man who could elude alarms, an inherent threat in someone outside a door who knew that the one inside was a halfway man. Handelman would see him; he could not afford to refuse.

The old man disappeared through the inner door, the heavy panel of ironwork and glass swinging slowly shut behind him. Havelock waited three minutes; the lights went on in several front windows on the fourth floor. It was logical that Handelman's apartment number was 4A. A halfway man had certain things in common with deep-cover field personnel and the Soviet VKR; he had to be able to watch the streets.

He was not watching now; there was no figure behind the window shades. Michael stepped out of the doorway and crossed the street. Inside the ornate entranceway he struck a match and held it waist-high as he looked down the row of names above the buttons.

R. Charles, Superintendent 1D.

He pressed the button and put his lips close to the webbed speaker.

"Yes, what is it?" asked the male voice in clear, well-spoken English.

"Mr. Charles?" said Havelock, not knowing why the man's voice struck him as odd.

"Yes, it's Charles. Who's this?"

"United States government, Department of State—"

"*What?*"

"Nothing to be alarmed about, Mr. Charles. If you'll come to the door, you can check my identification through the glass, and either admit me or I can give you a number to call."

R. Charles paused, then answered slowly, "Fair enough."

Thirty seconds later a huge, muscular young man appeared in the hallway beyond the door. He was wearing track shorts and a sweatshirt marked with a large number 20. It was either a proclamation of age or the gridiron identity of one of Columbia's larger linebackers. This, then, was the protection the apartment dwellers on Morningside Heights had chosen. Again, logical: take care of your own to take care of you. Free lodgings for an imposing presence. Michael held up his old ID card in its black plastic case; the dates, of course, were blurred.

R. Charles squinted through the glass, shrugged, and opened the door.

"What the hell is this?" he asked, more curiosity than hostility in his voice. A man his size did not have to be aggressive; his thick legs and neck and muscular arms were sufficiently intimidating. Also his youth.

"There's a man here I'd like to see on official State Department business, but he's not in. I rang, of course; he's a friend."

"Who is it?"

"Dr. Jacob Handelman. He's a consultant for us but he doesn't advertise it."

"Nice old guy, Handelman."

"The best, Mr. Charles. However, I think he'd be alarmed if he thought I might be recognized." Havelock grinned. "Also, it's damned cold out there."

"I can't let you in his apartment. I *won't* let you in."

"And I wouldn't allow you to. I'll just wait here, if it's all right."

R. Charles hesitated, his eyes dropping to the open ID case still in Michael's hand. "Yeah, well, okay. I'd ask you into my place but my roommate and I are busting our humps for a midterm tomorrow."

"Please, I wouldn't think of it . . ."

Havelock was interrupted by the appearance of an even larger young man in a doorway at the end of the hall. He was in a full sweatsuit, a book gripped in one hand, a pair of glasses in the other. "Hey, man, what is it?"

"Nothing. Someone looking for the Rabbi."

"Another one? Come on, we're wasting time. You're the brain, I just want to get through tomorrow."

"Your roommate on the team?" asked Michael, trying to appear contemporary.

"No. He wrestles. That is, he does when they don't throw him out for dirty holds. Okay, Mastiff, coming." The roommate went inside.

"Thanks again."

"Sure. You even sound official. The Rabbi ought to show up any minute."

"Pretty punctual, huh?"

"Like a Swiss clock." Number 20 turned, then looked back at Havelock. "You know, I figured something like this. Like you, I mean."

"How so?"

"I don't know . . . the people who come to see him, I guess. Late at night sometimes; not exactly campus types."

There was nothing to lose in asking, thought Michael. The young man himself had provided the opening. "We're most concerned about the woman, I don't mind telling you that. For the Rabbi's sake we hope she got here. Did you by any chance see her? A blond woman, about five feet five, probably in a raincoat, maybe a hat. Yesterday? Today?"

"Last night," said the young man. "I didn't, but Mastiff did. Foxy lady, he told me. But nervous; she rang the wrong bell and got old Weinberg —he's in Four-B and even more nervous."

"We're relieved she's here. What time last night?"

"About now, I guess. I was on the phone when Weinberg buzzed us on the intercom."

"Thank you." *Twenty-four hours. A halfway man upstairs. She was within reach—he could feel it, sense it!* "Incidentally, by sheer coincidence, you've been given privileged information. Please respect it."

"Man, you *are* official. I never saw you, Mr. Havalatch. But if they institute that draft, I may look you up."

"Do that. Thanks again."

"Take care." The huge student walked down the hallway to the open door.

The instant it was closed, Havelock moved quickly to the wide stone staircase in the center of the foyer, the steps worn smooth, indented from decades of use. He could not use the elevator beyond; its sound might well alarm a trusting muscular student who could suddenly reject the concept of privileged information in favor of less esoteric responsibilities.

In Paris when Michael had purchased the expensive black shoes to match his suit, he had had the presence of mind to have them resoled with hard rubber. They served him well on the staircase; he went up swiftly, silently, taking the steps two and three at a time, rounding the landings without a sound. In less than half a minute he reached the fourth floor; apartment 4A was at the end of the tiled, dimly lit hallway. He stood for several moments catching his breath, then approached the door and pressed the small button embedded in the molding. From beyond he heard the bell chime softly and seconds later the sound of footsteps.

"Yes?" said the curiously high-pitched voice, in a guttural European accent.

"Dr. Jacob Handelman?"

"Who is this, please?" The speech was Jewish-rooted German.

"I have news from the Quai d'Orsay. May we talk?"

"Vos?" The silence was brief, the words that followed rushed. "You are

mistaken. I have no idea what you are talking about. I know no one in
. . . what you say, the Quai d'Orsay?"

"In that case, I'll have to get in touch with Paris, and tell my contact
she's made a dreadful error. Naturally, Jacob Handelman will be removed
from the catacomb's computer terminal."

"Just one minute, please. I must jog this old man's memory."

Havelock could hear the moving footsteps again, faster now, receding,
then returning long before the stated minute was up. The metallic sounds
of several locks were heard behind the thick wood; the door opened and
the halfway man stared at him, then gestured with his head for Michael
to come inside.

What was it? Why was he so certain he knew this man, this old man
with the gray beard and the long white hair? The large face was soft, but
the eyes, in the creased flesh behind the heavy-lensed glasses with the thin
steel rims, were— He was not sure, he could not tell.

"You are in my house, sir," said Handelman, closing the door and
manipulating the locks. "I've traveled widely, of course, not always by my
own wishes, like so many thousands in my situation. Perhaps we have a
mutual friend I cannot at the moment recall. At the Quai d'Orsay.
Naturally, I know a number of professors at the Sorbonne."

Was it the high-pitched, singsong voice? Or the questioning tilt of the
head? Or the way the old man stood, feet planted firmly, the posture soft,
yet somehow rigid? No, it was not any single thing; it was all of them
. . . somehow.

" 'A mutual friend' isn't quite accurate. You know a name. Broussac.
Ministry of Foreign Affairs, Section Four. She was to have reached you
today; she's a person of her word. I think she did."

"Ah, but my office is filled with scores of messages only my secretary
is aware of, Mr. . . . Mr. . . . ?"

"Havelock."

"Yes, Mr. Havellacht. Come in, come in. I knew a Habernicht in Berlin
in the old days. Friedrich Habernicht. Quite similar, no?"

"Close, I guess." *Was it the walk?* The same deliberate stride that he
had seen outside. The stately . . . arrogant steps that should be cloaked
in medieval robes, or a high priest's cassock. He had to ask. "We've met
before, haven't we?"

"*We?*" The halfway man's eyebrows arched; he adjusted his steel-
rimmed glasses and peered at Michael. "I cannot imagine where. Unless
you were a student in a large class of mine, but that would have to be a

number of years ago, I would think. In such a case, you would remember me, but I would not necessarily remember you. Age and the sheer mass of numbers, you understand."

"Never mind." *A number of years ago. How many years?* "Are you telling me you haven't heard from Broussac?"

"I'm telling you nothing. . . . Sit down, do sit down. . . . I am merely saying that I do not know. You say this person Broussac sent me a message today, and *I* am saying I receive dozens of messages *every* day that I frequently do not get to for *many* days. Again, age and the sheer mass of numbers."

"I heard you before," interrupted Havelock; he remained standing, his eyes scanning the room. There were bookshelves everywhere, old furniture —overstuffed chairs, fringed lamps, hassocks—nothing Spartan. Once more the smell of Academe. "Jenna Karas!" said Michael suddenly, rapidly, raising his voice.

"Another message?" asked Handelman ingenuously, an old man bemused by a younger antagonist. "So many messages— I must have a talk with my secretary. She overprotects me."

"Jenna Karas came to see you last night, I know that!"

"Three . . . no, *four* people came to see me last night, each a student of mine. I even have their names over here, and the outlines of two graduate papers." Handelman walked to a cluttered desk against the wall.

"Cut it out!" shouted Havelock. "You packaged her and I've got to *find* her! That was Broussac's message."

"So many messages," intoned the halfway man, as if chanting a Talmudic passage. "Ahh, here are the names, the graduate outlines," continued Handelman, bending over the disorganized pile of papers. "So many visitors . . . so many messages. Who can keep track?"

"Listen to me! Broussac wouldn't have given me your name or told me where to find you if I weren't telling you the truth. I have to *reach* her! A terrible thing was done to her—to *us*—and she doesn't understand!"

" 'The Filioque Denials in the Councils of Arius,' " chanted Handelman, standing erect and holding a sheaf of papers under the light of a floor lamp. "Those would be the Nicene rejections of the Eastern Church around the fifth century. Very little understood—speaking of understanding."

He may choose to tell you nothing. "Goddamn you, where did you *send* her? Stop *playing* with me! Because—if I have to—I'll—"

"Yes?" Jacob Handelman turned his head in the spill of the floor lamp and peered once again through the steel-rimmed glasses. He took several steps to his left and replaced the papers on the desk.

It was there, at that moment. It was all there. The eyes behind the thin rims of steel, the rigid posture of the soft body . . . the walk. Not the measured gait of a high prelate of the church or of a medieval baron entering a great hall . . . but the strutting of a man in uniform. A black uniform!

Sheets of lightning filled Havelock's eyes. His mind exploded . . . *then and now, now and then!* Not eight or ten years ago but the early years, the terrible years! He was one of *them!* The images of his memory confirmed it; he saw the man in front of him now as he was then. The large face—without a beard, the hair straight and long, not white but *Aryan yellow.* Walking . . . *strutting* . . . down to rows of ditches. *Machine-gun fire. Screams.*

Lidice!

As if in a trance, Michael started toward the halfway man, his hands taut and hard, his fingers curving into claws, tensed for combat with another animal—a lower form of animal.

"Vos?" Handelman drew out the sibilant *s* in his high-pitched whine. "What is the matter with you? Are you crazy, perhaps? Look at you . . . are you sick? Stay away from me!"

"The *Rabbi . . . ?* Oh, Christ, you son of a bitch! You *incredible son of a bitch!* What were you—*Standartenführer? Sturmbannführer? . . .* No, it was *Obergruppenführer!* It was *you! Lidice!*"

The old man's eyes widened; magnified by the thick lenses, they looked monstrous. "You are mad, completely, utterly *mad!* Leave my house! You are not welcome here. With the pain I've suffered, I will not listen to the ravings of a madman!"

The intense singsong chant of the words covered the halfway man's movement. His right hand slipped down to the desk, to the clutter of papers. Havelock lunged as a gun emerged in Handelman's hand, placed there minutes ago by an *Obergruppenführer* who could never afford to forget his origins. The halfway man was a killer of Czechs and Poles and Jews, a man who had taken the identity of a ragged inmate he had sent into a shower of gas or a cave of fire.

Havelock grabbed the hand with the gun, jamming his third finger behind the trigger, slamming it repeatedly against the edge of the desk. It would not come loose! The halfway man was arched beneath him, pinning his right arm, the face grotesque, the mouth stretched like a rabid dog's, the soft body suddenly hard, writhing in spasms. Handelman's left hand surged up and clapped Michael's face, the fingers digging into his eyes.

Havelock twisted violently back and forth, and the halfway man slipped out from under him. They were at the edge of the desk, immobilized by each other's arms bent to the breaking point. Suddenly Michael freed his right hand; he clenched it into a fist and brought it crashing down like a hammer into where he could see the blur of Handelman's face.

The steel-rimmed glasses shattered. The German screamed, and the gun clattered to the floor as he brought both his hands to his face.

Havelock leaped backward, yanking the German to his feet, and clamped his hand across the ugly mouth. Havelock's eyes burned, and tears and specks of blood clouded his vision. But he could see; the Nazi could not.

"You raise your voice, old man, I'll kill you the instant you do. Now, sit down!"

He pulled the German away from the desk and pushed him into the nearest chair with such force that the halfway man's neck snapped back. The shattered glasses, however, remained secure on Handelman's face; they were a part of that face, part of the ugliness.

"You have blinded me!" whined the soldier from Lidice. "A madman comes into my house—"

"Forget it!" said Michael. "I was *there!*"

"Madness!" Gasping, Handelman raised his hands to remove his glasses.

"Leave them alone!" ordered Havelock. "Let them stay right where they are."

"Young man, you are—"

"Don't talk! Listen. I can put out a trace on a man named Jacob Handelman, going back fifty years. Everything about him— old pictures, Germans still alive who knew him, if he ever existed. Then circulate a photograph of you, minus the beard, of course, in certain sections of Prague. You were there; I saw you later and wanted to kill you. A boy of nine or ten wanted to put a knife in your back in the street. And someone still living in Prague or Rudna or Kladno would want to do the same even now. That's the bottom line, you *bastard!* So don't talk to me about people who weren't here last night, tell me about the one who was. Where *is* she?"

"I am a very valuable man—"

"I'll bet you are. Who'd know more about finding safe territories than someone who did it so well. And who could protect himself better than someone who could expose the whereabouts of so many. You've covered yourself, *Mörder*. But not with me, do you understand that? Because I don't care. Now, where is *Jenna Karas?*"

"While not addressing myself to the preposterous accusations you make," whined the German, "there are considerations of exchange."

"You have your life," said Havelock. "I'm not interested in it. It's enough that you know I'm out there and can end it anytime I like. That's your exchange. Where is she?"

"The top drawer of the desk." The halfway man gestured with his trembling hand, his eyes unseeing behind the shattered glasses. "Lift up the pencil rack. There's a folded green paper."

Michael went to the desk, opened the drawer, and pulled out the concave receptacle for pens and pencils. There was the light green paper; he picked it up and unfolded it. It was a page of memorandum stationery from the Columbia University Graduate Faculty of Philosophy. In precise, handwritten block letters was the information Havelock would have killed for; it was everything.

> BROUSSAC. APPLICANT FOR DOCTORAL CANDIDATE
> NAME: ARVIDAS CORESCU. C/O KOHOUTEK
> RFD 3, MASON FALLS, PENNA.

"Is Corescu the name she's using?" asked Havelock sharply.

"Temporarily. The papers are only temporary; they had to be manufactured in a few hours. Others will follow . . . if they are to follow."

"Which means?"

"They must be paid for. Nothing is for nothing."

"Naturally; the hook's sunk in and the line keeps reeling out. You must have some very impressive fish out there."

"You could say I have powerful—friends. In many places."

"Who's this Kohoutek?"

"A Slav," said the halfway man, shrugging derisively. "He has farm land."

"When did she leave?"

"She was picked up this morning."

"What's her cover?"

"Another destitute refugee—a niece, perhaps—gotten out of the Balkans, or wherever. Away from the Bear, as they say. Kohoutek will get her work; he has friends in the textile unions."

"From which she pays him *and* you, or the papers don't follow."

"One needs papers," whined Handelman, "to drive a car, or use a bank—"

"Or to be left alone by immigration," interrupted Michael. "That threat's always there, isn't it?"

"We are a nation of laws, sir."

"You make me *sick,*" said Havelock approaching the chair, looking down at the animal from Lidice. "I could kill you now, feeling nothing but joy," he added quietly. "Can you understand that, philosopher? But I won't, because I want you to know what it's like to realize it can happen any moment, any day, any night. With a knock on your door. You live with that, *du altes Luder. Heil Hitler.*"

He turned and started for the door.

There was a sharp sound, as of something cracking, behind him. He spun around to see the long blade of a knife streaking toward him directly at his chest. The halfway man had torn the shattered glasses off his face and seized the weapon concealed in the overstuffed chair; the musty smell of Academe was suddenly the putrid odor of a no-man's-land in a faraway battlefield. Havelock jumped back, but not before the blade had ripped through the jacket of the suit, the razor-sharp edge slitting his flesh and marking his white shirt with a line of blood.

His right hand whipped under his coat for the Llama automatic. He kicked wildly in front of him, hoping to make contact with any part of the German's body. As the blade came arcing back he spun away from its trajectory and raised his gun, aiming at the face.

He fired twice; the halfway man fell to the floor, his head soaked in blood, one eye blown away.

A gun had stilled another gun from Lidice. But there was no joy; it had ceased to matter.

There was only Jenna. He had found her! She could not stop him from reaching her now. She might kill him, but first she would have to look into his eyes. That *did* matter.

He shoved the Llama into his belt, the page of green paper into his pocket, and raced out of the apartment.

20

"The name's Broussac, Mr. President," said Emory Bradford into the phone at his desk in the State Department. "Madame Régine Broussac. The Quai d'Orsay, Foreign Ministry, Section Four. She contacted the embassy the night before last, instructing a radio-car unit to be in the vicinity of Argenteuil for the purpose of picking up a former American intelligence officer who was to meet her there. Under highly unorthodox circumstances, she said."

"Havelock?"

"She's admitted that much, yes."

"And?"

"The car drove up and down the streets of Argenteuil all night. It was never contacted."

"What did this Broussac say? I assume she's been questioned."

"Angrily. She claims he never showed up."

"Well?"

"Our people think she's lying."

"Why?"

"One of our men went around to her flat and asked some questions. He learned that she returned home by one o'clock in the morning. If that was the case—and apparently it was; two neighbors confirmed it—why didn't she phone the embassy and call off the car?"

"Has she been asked about this?"

"No, sir. Our people are waiting for instructions. It's not customary for embassy personnel to go around asking questions surreptitiously about officials of the Quai d'Orsay."

Charles Berquist paused, then spoke firmly. "Have Ambassador Richardson call Madame Broussac and respectfully request that she accept an invitation to come to the embassy as soon as it's convenient, preferably within the hour. A limousine will be sent for her, of course. The President of the United States wishes to speak with her on a confidential basis."

"Mr. *President*—"

"Just do as I say, Mr. Undersecretary."

"Yes, sir."

"And, Emory?"

"Sir?"

"How's the other task coming? The seventy-odd diplomats who may have been out of town during the Spanish problem?"

Bradford paused before answering. When he spoke, it was apparent he was trying to control his voice. "As of this moment, five are missing."

"*What?*"

"I didn't want to say anything until noon, until I have all the information, but the last report indicates that nineteen personnel were off the premises. Fourteen are accounted for, five aren't."

"Get it! Get *all* your information!"

"I'm trying."

"By noon! Get it!"

The cold rain of the night before had lingered with diminishing strength, and the sky outside the Oval Office was dark. A drop of only a degree or two in temperature and there would be thin, erratic patches of snow on the White House lawn. Berquist stood by the window, briefly wondering how deep the drifts were in Mountain Iron, Minnesota. And how he wished to Christ he were back there now. There was a buzzing from his telephone console. He glanced at his watch as he walked to the desk; it was eleven-fifteen.

"Yes?"

"Your call from Paris, sir."

"Thank you." Berquist pushed the appropriate red button. "Madame Broussac?"

"*Oui, Monsieur le Président.* It is an honor, sir. I am flattered to have been summoned to speak with you." The old woman's voice was strong, but not without astonishment. And a measure of fear.

"And I'm most grateful, madame. As I instructed, are we alone?"

"Yes, *Monsieur le Président.* Ambassador Richardson most courteously permitted me the use of his office. Quite honestly, I am, as you might say, bewildered."

"You have the word of the President of the United States that we *are* alone, Madame Broussac. There is no interference on this telephone, no third parties or mechanical devices to record our conversation. Will you accept that word?"

"Assuredly. Why would such an august figure deceive a mere functionary of the Quai d'Orsay?"

"For a lot of reasons. But I'm not."

"*Mais oui.* Then I am convinced."

"Good. I need your cooperation in a matter of the utmost importance and delicacy. It in no way affects the government of France, but any help you might give us could only be in its ultimate interests. Again, you have my word on it, the word of this office."

"It is sufficient, *Monsieur le Président.*"

"It's imperative we reach a retired foreign service officer recently separated from the Department of State. His name is Michael Havelock."

"*S'il vous plaît, Monsieur le—*"

"No, please," interrupted Berquist. "Let me finish. This office has too many staggering concerns to be involved with the work you do, or with the activities Mr. Havelock was engaged in. I only ask you to help us locate him. A destination, a routing, a name he might be using. Whatever you tell me will be held in the strictest confidence; no detail will be compromised, or ever used against you or your operations. I promise you that."

"*Monsieur—*"

"Lastly," continued the President, overriding her voice, "no matter what he may have told you, his government has never meant him harm. We have too much respect for his service record, too much gratitude for his contributions. The tragedy he thinks is his alone is all of ours, and that is all I can tell you, but I hope you consider the source—the office from which it comes. Will you help us, help *me*, Madame Broussac?"

Berquist could hear the breathing over the line from Paris, as well as the pounding tattoo in his own chest. He looked out the window; fine flecks of white were intermingling with the mottled drizzle. The virgin drifts in the fields of Mountain Iron were the most beautiful at sundown; one caressed them with the eyes, touched the colors from a distance, never wanting them to change.

"As you are trying to find him," began Broussac, "he is looking for someone else."

"We know that. We've been looking for her too. To save her life. To save his." The President closed his eyes; it was a lie he would remember back in the hills of the Mesabi country. But then, he would remember, too, Churchill and Coventry. Enigma . . . Costa Brava.

"There is a man in New York."

"New *York?*" Berquist sat forward, startled. "He's *here?* She's—?"

"It surprises you, *Monsieur le Président?*"

"Very much."

"It was intended to. It was I who sent her. Sent him."

"This man in New York?"

"He must be approached with a great deal of—as you mentioned—delicacy. He cannot be compromised. You have the same such people in Europe; we all need them, *Monsieur le Président.* Even when we know of those who belong to other—companies, we leave them alone."

"I understand perfectly." Berquist did; the warning was clear. "This man can tell us where he is?"

"He can tell you where *she* is. That's what you need to know. But he must be convinced he is not compromised."

"I'll send only one man and only he will know. My word."

"*Je le respecte.* I must tell you, I do not know him, except through his dossier. He is a great man with much compassion, a survivor, monsieur. In April of 1945, he was taken out of the Bergen-Belsen camp in Germany."

"He will be accorded all the respect this office can summon, as well as the confidentiality I promised you. His name, please."

"Jacob Handelman. Columbia University."

The three men listened intently as Emory Bradford slowly, methodically delivered his findings in the strategy room in the underground complex of the White House. Speaking in a deliberate monotone, he described the confirmed whereabouts of all nineteen State Department personnel from the fifth floor, L Section, who were not in Washington during the week of Costa Brava. When he finished, each man's expression conveyed both pain and frustration, none more so than the President's. He leaned forward on the dais, his heavy Scandinavian face worn and lined, his intelligent eyes angry.

"You were so *sure* this morning," he said. "You told me five were missing, five not accounted for. What happened?"

"I was wrong, Mr. President."

"Goddamn it, I didn't want to hear that."

"Neither did King Richard when news reached him that Richmond had landed," said Addison Brooks quietly. "He struck down the messenger."

Berquist turned to his ambassador, studying him before replying, "Richard the Third had already received two messages he considered lies. He could have been testing the latest."

Brooks shook his head, admiration in his eyes. "You constantly amaze me, Mr. President."

"I shouldn't. You worked for Truman. He knew more about history than all the Commagers and Schlesingers put together. I've done some reading myself, and this is a waste of time." Berquist turned back to the undersecretary of State. "Who were the five?"

"The woman who was having surgery. It was an abortion. Her husband's a lawyer and has been in protracted litigation at The Hague for several months. They've been apart. The picture was pretty clear."

"How could you even consider a woman?" demanded Halyard. "No double standard implied, but a woman would leave her mark somewhere."

"Not if she—through Moscow—controlled men. Actually, I was quite excited when her name surfaced. I thought, Good God, it's perfect. It wasn't."

"Keep it surgery, and tell that to whomever you spoke with. Who were the others?"

"The two attachés at our embassy in Mexico. They'd been recalled for change-of-policy briefings, then didn't return to Mexico City until January fifth."

"Explanation?" asked the President.

"Furlough time. They went their separate ways and their families joined them. One to a ski lodge in Vermont, the other to the Caribbean. Credit-card charges confirmed everything."

"Who else?" pressed Berquist.

"Arthur Pierce."

"Pierce?" interrupted the general, startled. "The fellow at the U.N. now?"

"Yes, General."

"I could have straightened you out there. So could have Addison here."

"So would Matthias," agreed Bradford. "If there was anyone at State who maintained clear access to Matthias for a longer period of time, I don't know who it is. He appointed Pierce to the U.N. with the obvious intention of submitting him for the ambassadorship."

"If you'll permit me the correction," said Berquist, "*I* appointed him after Matthias gave him to us and then took him away. He worked over here with the NSC for a couple of months last year before the great man said he was needed in New York."

"And he was one fellow *I* told the Pentagon to bribe the hell out of," exclaimed the general. "I wanted to keep him in the army; he was too good to lose. He didn't like that mess in Southeast Asia any more than I did, but his record was as good as mine. . . . Let's face it; it was a damn sight better."

The ambassador leaned back in his chair. "I know Pierce. He was brought to my attention by an old-line career foreign officer. I suppose I was as responsible as anyone for bringing him into the State Department. Knowing what I do, Iowa farm boy, rather humble beginnings, I believe, and then a brilliant academic record, everything on scholarship. He was one of the few in this day and age who really went from rags to riches. Well, influential if not literally rich, but he could have been. A dozen or so of the country's largest corporations were after him, not to mention Rand and the Brookings Institution. I was persuasive and quite practical. Patriotism aside, I pointed out that a tour of duty with the Department of State could only enhance his value in the marketplace. Of course, he's still a relatively young man; with his accomplishments, if he leaves government, he'll be able to name his own price anywhere. He's cornstalk American success story—how could you possibly conceive of a Moscow connection?"

"I didn't *preconceive* anything, especially not in this case," said Bradford. "Arthur Pierce is a friend—and I don't have many. I consider him one of the best men we have at State. But in spite of our friendship, I went by the reports given me. Only me, incidentally. Not to my secretary or any assistant. Only to me."

"What did you get that made you think Pierce could possibly have anything to do with Soviet intelligence? Christ, he's mother, God, apple pie and the flag."

"An error in the U.N. message logs. The initial report showed that during the last days of December and the first three days of January— the week of Costa Brava—Pierce hadn't responded to four separate queries from the Middle East Section. Then, of course, they showed up—four replies that could be entered in a diplomatic analyst's handbook. They were as penetrating as anything I've read on that area and dovetailed with the specific proceedings in the Security Council. As a matter of fact, they were used to block a particularly aggressive Soviet proposal."

"The error in the logs was the explanation?" said Brooks.

"That's the maddening thing. There's always an explanation, then a confirmation of an explanation. Message traffic's so heavy, twenty percent of it gets misplaced. Pierce's responses had been there all along."

"Who's the last man?" Berquist was not going to let up. From his eyes it was apparent he could not readily accept the altered findings.

"One I was so convinced might be the mole that I nearly had a White House Secret Service detail pick him up. Thank God I didn't; he's volatile, a screamer."

"Who?"

"Nikolai Sitmarin. Born and raised in Leningrad, parents dissident immigrants over a dozen years ago. He's the State Department's most accomplished analyst of Soviet internal affairs, proven accurate about seventy percent. He's a prize, and in his case I thought, What better way for Moscow to put a mole into the ground? An eighteen-year-old son of immigrants, dissidents permitted a family visa when they were damned hard to come by."

"Is Sitmarin Jewish?" asked the general.

"No, but I expect most people think he is; in my view it added to his cover. Soviet dissidence isn't the exclusive province of Russian Jews, although that seems to be the general impression. Also, he's received a fair amount of media exposure—the thirty-year-old *Wunderkind* carrying out a personal vendetta. It all seemed so logically convoluted, so right."

"What were the circumstances?" The President's words were clipped.

"Again, an unexplained absence. He was gone from his office from mid–Christmas week until January eighth. He just wasn't in Washington and no assignment was listed for his not being here. I had a time-stat man call the section head; the explanation was given."

"Which was?" pressed Berquist.

"A personal leave was granted. Sitmarin's mother was gravely ill in Chicago."

"Pretty damned convenient illness, wasn't it?"

"So much so she nearly died. The Cook County General Hospital confirmed it."

"But she didn't die," interrupted Brooks.

"I spoke personally to the physician of record and he had a very clear idea of the gravity of my inquiry. He quoted from his files."

"Have them sent to you," ordered the President. "There are too damned many explanations; one of them's a lie."

"I agree, but which one?" added Bradford. "Not just these five, but the entire nineteen. Someone who thinks he's—or she's—doing a superior a harmless favor is concealing Ambiguity from us, hiding the mole. What's going down as a few extra days' skiing or going to the Caribbean or shacking up—excuse me."

"Oh, for Christ's sake. Go back and tear into every explanation given you. Find one that won't hold up."

"One that has a discrepancy in it," added the ambassador. "Meetings that didn't take place, a conference that was postponed, credit-card charges where the signatures are questionable—a gravely ill woman who just may have been given an assumed name."

"It'll take time," said the undersecretary.

"You've accomplished a great deal in something over twelve hours," continued Brooks sympathetically. "Again, I commend you."

"And you have the authority of this office to get you what you need, anything you need. Use it! Find the mole!" Berquist shook his head in exasperation. "He and we are in a race after a madman we call Parsifal. If the Soviets reach him first, this country has no viable foreign policy. And if Parsifal panics, it won't make a damn bit of difference." The President put his hands on the dais. "Is there anything else? I'm keeping two curious senators waiting and it's no time to do it. They're on the Foreign Relations Committee and I've a gut feeling they've got wind of Matthias." Berquist stopped; he got up and looked at Bradford. "Reassure me again—that *every man* at Poole's Island is secure."

"Yes, sir. Each was screened down to his fingernails, and no one leaves that island for the duration."

"That, too, will run its course," said Brooks. "What *is* the duration? It's an unnatural condition."

"These are unnatural circumstances," broke in General Halyard. "The patrols are armed, the place a fortress."

"Armed?" The President spoke softly, in his own personal anguish. "Of course, they're armed. Insane!"

"What about Havelock?" asked the statesman. "Has there been anything?"

"No," replied the commander in chief, leaving the dais and heading for the door. "Call me later, Mr. Undersecretary," he said without explanation. "Call me at three o'clock."

The snow, though not heavy, was a whipping snow. It careened off the windshield, tiny white flakes targeting into the glass and bouncing silently away like thousands of miniature asteroids passing through galactic space. Havelock, in his rented car, had driven past the sign several minutes before, the letters reflected in the headlights: MASON FALLS 3 MILES.

He had checked out of the King's Arms Hotel, relieved to see a different clerk on duty, and had taken a cab to LaGuardia Airport. A hastily purchased map pinpointed Mason Falls, Pennsylvania; his only choice was a domestic flight to Pittsburgh. He was not at the time concerned with further Soviet surveillance. The Russian he had trapped had undoubtedly reported his arrival, but even if he had not, LaGuardia was not an international terminal. No diplomatic personnel came through its gates on overseas flights.

He had been issued a last-moment seat on US Air's 7:56 P.M. plane, reached Pittsburgh by nine-fifteen, and rented a car, the signed credit slip permitting him to drop it off at any Hertz location. By nine-forty-five he was driving south through the long stretches of dark countryside on Route 51.

MASON FALLS

ESTABLISHED 1858

Through the swirling pockets of snow—thicker now, fuller—Michael could see the glow of a red neon sign up ahead on the right. He approached, slowing down, and read the letters; a touch of the absurd had intruded: HARRY'S BAR. Either someone along the banks of the Monongahela had a sense of humor, or there was a man named Harry who did not know how far away he was from Venice or Paris. Or perhaps he did.

He obviously did. Inside, there were enlarged World War II photographs on the walls depicting Parisian scenes, several showing a soldier standing outside the door of Paris's Harry's Bar on the Right Bank. The place was rustic—thick wood dulled by use and totally untouched by furniture polish—heavy glasses and high-backed barstools. A jukebox in the corner was bleating out country music to the bored half-dozen or so patrons at the bar. They were in keeping with their surroundings: everyone male, a profusion of red-checkered flannel shirts, wide-ribbed corduroy trousers and ankle-length boots worn in the fields and in barns. These were farmers and farmhands; he might have assumed as much from the pickup trucks outside, but the biting wind had distracted him—that and the fact that he was in Mason Falls, Pennsylvania.

He looked around for a wall telephone; it was inappropriately placed six feet from the jukebox. That did not concern him, but the absence of a telephone book did; he needed an address. There had been no time at LaGuardia to find the correct book for Mason Falls, and as Pittsburgh was an international airport, he wanted to get out of the terminal as fast as possible. He walked to the bar, stood between two empty stools, and waited for an aging, morose-looking Harry to serve him.

"Yeah, what'll it be?"

"Scotch on the rocks, and a telephone book, if you've got one, please."

The owner studied Havelock briefly. "I don't get much call for Scotch. It ain't the best."

"I probably wouldn't know the best."

"It's your throat." Harry reached under the bar to his right, but instead of coming up with a glass and ice, he put a thin telephone book in front of Michael. He then walked to his left, to a row of bottles on a lighted shelf.

Havelock leafed through the pages rapidly, his index finger descending the row of *K*'s.

Kohoutek, Janos RFD 3 Box 12

Goddamn it!

Rural Free Delivery, routing number 3, could be anywhere in Mason Falls, which, although small in population, was large in square mileage. Acres and acres of farmland, winding roads that threaded through the countryside. And to call the number was to give an alarm; if there were special words, he did not know them, and all things considered, there undoubtedly *were* special words. To mention Jacob Handelman over the phone was asking for a confirmation call to be made to New York. There would be no answer on the dead halfway man's phone until he was found, possibly in the morning, possibly not for several days.

"Here y'are," said Harry, placing the drink on the bar.

"Would you know a man named Kohoutek?" asked Havelock softly. "Janos Kohoutek?"

The owner squinted in minor thought. "Know the name, not him, though. He's one of them foreigners with some land over in the west end."

"Would you know where in the west end?"

"No. Doesn't it tell you there?" Harry gestured at the telephone book.

"It only gives an RFD and a box number."

"Call him, for Christ's sake."

"I'd rather not. As you say, he's a foreigner; he might not understand over the phone."

"Hey!" yelled Harry over the sounds of the country music. "Any you assholes know a guy named Kohoutek?"

"Foreigner," said one red-checkered flannel shirt.

"He's got more'n forty acres over west," added a hunting cap farther down. "Fuckin' refugees with their government handouts can afford it. We can't."

"Would you know where?" asked Havelock.

"It's either on Chamberlain or Youngfield, maybe Fourforks, I don't know which. Don't it say in the book?"

"No, just RFD-three, that's all. And a box number."

"Route three," said another patron, this one with a growth of beard and bleary eyes. "That's Davey Hooker's route. He's a carrier, and that son of a bitch soaks 'em. Got the job through his uncle, the fuckin' grafter."

"Would you know where the route is?"

"Sure. Fourforks Pike. Heads due west from the depot a mile down Fifty-one."

"Thanks very much." Michael raised the glass to his lips and drank. It was not very good; it was not even Scotch. He reached into his pocket, pulled out his money, and left two dollars on the bar. "Thanks again," he said to the owner.

"It's sixty cents," said Harry.

"For old times' sake," replied Havelock. "For the other place in Paris."

"Hey, you *been* there?"

"Once or twice."

"You shoulda told me! You woulda gotten decent whisky! Let me tell you, in '45 me and—"

"I'm really sorry, I don't have time."

Michael pressed himself away from the bar and started for the door. He did not see a man at the far end of the room get off his stool and walk to the telephone.

Fourforks Pike became a slowly curving, interminable backcountry road less than a mile west of the old railroad depot. The first post-office box was marked 5; prominently anchored in the ground on his right, it was clearly visible through the snow in the glare of the headlights. The next, however, Havelock would have missed had he not suddenly become aware of a break in the foliage; it was a narrow dirt road on his left, and the box could not be seen from the pike. It was number 7, negating the rule that said odd and even numbers meant different sides in a delivery route. He would have to drive more slowly and keep his eyes more alert.

The next three boxes were all within a half mile, each in sequence, the last number 10. Two hundred yards beyond, the road split—the first of presumably four forks on the pike. He took the straighter line, the fork on the right. Number 11 did not appear until he had driven nearly a mile and a half; when he saw it he briefly closed his eyes in relief. For several agonizing moments he had been convinced he had taken the wrong road. He pressed his foot on the accelerator, his mouth dry, the muscles of his face rigid, his eyes straining.

If the road was interminable—made worse by the spiraling snow against the windshield—the wait for the final sighting was torturously so. He entered a long, seemingly endless stretch of flat, straight ground, which, as near as he could determine, was bordered by fields or pastures; but there were no houses, no lights anywhere. Had he passed it? Was his vision so distorted by the silent pounding of the snow that the post-office box had gone by without his spotting it? Was there an unseen road on his right or his left, a metal receptacle off the shoulder, covered perhaps? It was not logical; the snow was heavier, but not yet heavy, and the wind was too strong for the snow to settle.

It was *there!* On the right. A large black mailbox, shaped like a miniature Quonset hut, the covered opening wide enough to receive small packages. The number 12 was stenciled in white—thick white enamel that threw back the light as though challenged in the darkness. Havelock slowed down and peered through the window; again there were no lights beyond, no signs of life whatsoever. There was only what appeared to be a long road that disappeared into a wall of trees and further darkness.

He drove on, eyes straining, looking for something else, something he could not miss if and when he came across it. He only hoped it would be soon, and several hundred yards beyond box number 12, he found a reasonable facsimile. Not ideal but, with the snow, acceptable. It was a bank of wild foliage that had crept toward the edge of the road, the end of a property line, or a demarcation signifying no responsibility. Whatever it was, it would do.

He drove the car off the shoulder and into the cluster of bushes and high grass. He extinguished the headlights and opened his suitcase in the front seat. He removed all identification and shoved it into the elasticized rear pocket, then took out a heavy leaded plastic bag impervious to X-rays, the kind often used for transporting exposed film. He peeled it open and removed the Llama automatic; the magazine was full. Last, he reached into the suitcase for the scaling knife he had used at Col des Moulinets; it was sheathed in a thin leather scabbard with a clip. Awkwardly he pulled up the sides of his topcoat and shoved it behind his trousers into the small of his back, clipping it to his belt at the base of his spine. He hoped neither weapon would be called for; words were infinitely preferable, frequently more effective.

He got out of the car, locked it, pushed the snow-swept foliage up around the sides, obliterated the tracks, and started down the Fourforks Pike toward P.O. Box 12, RFD 3, Mason Falls, Pennsylvania.

He had walked no more than thirty feet off the highway into the long, narrow road that seemed to disappear into a wall of darkness beyond when he stopped. Whether it was the years he had spent instinctively studying alien ground—aware that an unknown path at night might hold lethal surprises—or the wind off the fields that caused him to angle his head downward against it, he could not tell. He was merely grateful that he saw it: a tiny greenish dot of light on his right about two feet above the snow-patched earth. It appeared to be suspended, but he knew it wasn't. Instead, it was wired to the end of a thin black metal tube that was sunk at least another two feet into the ground for stability. It was a photoelectric cell, its counterpart across the road, an invisible beam of light crossing the darkness, connecting both terminals. Anything breaking that beam for more than a second or with a weight density of more than fifty pounds would trigger an alarm somewhere. Small animals could not do it; automobiles and human beings could not fail to do it.

Michael sidestepped cautiously to his right through the cold, wet overgrowth to pass beyond the device. He stopped again at the edge of the tangled bushes, aware of a line of flickering white parallel with his shoulders, knowing suddenly that there was another obstacle. It was a barbed-wire fence bordering an adjacent field, flakes of snow clinging briefly to the barbs before being whipped away. He had not seen it entering the side road marked by post-office box number 12; he looked back and understood. The fence did not begin until the foliage was high enough to conceal it. And that meant he understood something else; again, weight density. Sufficient pressure against the thinly spaced wires would set off further alarms. Janos Kohoutek was very security-conscious. Considering his location, he had paid for the best he could get.

This, then, was the path, thought Havelock. Between the green trip light and the shoulder-high barbed-wire fence. For if there was one photoelectric alarm, there were others along the way because the expectation of malfunction was an innate part of protection technology. He wondered how long "the way" was; he could see virtually nothing but foliage and darkness and swirling snow in front of him. He started to literally push ahead, bending the tangled brush and webbed branches with his hands and arms, as he kept his eyes riveted on the ground for dots of eerie green light.

He passed three, then four, each spaced roughly two hundred and fifty to three hundred feet apart. He reached the wall of tall trees, the fence growing higher as if commanded by nature. He was soaked now, his face cold, his brows iced, but movement was easier through the thick-trunked trees that seemingly had been planted at random but nevertheless formed a visual wall. Suddenly he realized he was heading downward, descending. He looked over at the road; the decline there was sharper, the mottled surface of dirt and snow no longer in sight. There was a break in the trees; the narrow, sloping path he had to take was still overgrown, the high grass and untamed bushes bending in the wind and glazed with white.

And then spread below him was a sight that both hypnotized and disturbed him, in the same way he had reacted to the first sight of Jacob Handelman. He plunged down through the thickets of brush, falling twice into the cold, prickly bushes, his eyes on the bewildering view below.

At first glance it was like any farm buried in the deeper countryside, protected in the front by sloping fields, endless woods beyond. There was a group of buildings, solid, simple, constructed of heavy wood for severe winters, the lights in various windows flickering in the snowfall: a main house and several barns, a silo, tool sheds and shelters for tractors and plows and harvesting equipment. They were indeed what they seemed to be, Havelock was sure, but he knew they were more. Much more.

It began with the gate at the end of the sloping road. It was framed unpretentiously with iron piping; the mesh was ordinary mesh, but it was higher than it had to be, higher than it should be for the entrance to a farm. Not higher to a conspicuous degree, but simply higher than seemed necessary, as if the builder had made a slight error in the height specification and had decided to live with the mistake. Then there was the fence that spanned out from both sides of the unprepossessing gate; it, too, was strange, somehow askew, also higher than it had to be for the purpose of containing animals in the ascending grazing fields before it. Was it just the height? It was no more than seven feet, Michael judged as he drew closer; it had appeared much shorter from above—again nothing strange . . . but somehow wrong. And then he realized what it was, why the word "askew" had come to mind. The top of the barbed-wire fence was angled *inward.* That fence was not meant to keep animals from breaking in, it was designed to keep people from breaking out!

Suddenly the blinding beam of a searchlight shot out from the upper regions of the silo; it was arcing around—toward *him.*

This was the 1980s, but he was standing in front of a symbol of human carnage that went back forty years. It was a concentration camp!

"We wondered how long it would take you," said a voice behind him.

He spun around, reaching for his weapon. It was too late.

Powerful arms gripped him around the neck, arching him backwards, as a pair of hands plunged a soft, wet, acrid-smelling cloth into his face.

The beam of the searchlight zeroed in on him. He could see it, feel it, as his nostrils began to burn. Then the darkness came, and he could neither see nor feel.

21

He felt the warmth first; he found it not particularly pleasant but merely different from the cold. When he opened his eyes, his vision blurred, coming into focus slowly, he simultaneously became aware of the nausea in his throat and the stinging sensation on his face. The pungent odor lingered in his nostrils; he had been anesthetized with pure ethyl ether.

He saw flames, logs burning behind a black-bordered screen, in a large brick fireplace. He was on the floor in front of the slate hearth; his topcoat had been removed, and his wet clothes were heating up uncomfortably. But part of the discomfort was in the small of his back; the scaling knife was still in place, the leather scabbard irritating his skin. He was grateful for the pain.

He rolled over slowly, inch by inch, his eyes half closed, observing what he could by the light of the fire and several table lamps. He heard the sound of muffled voices; two men were talking quietly beyond a plain brown sofa at the other end of the room; they stood together in a hallway. They had not noticed his movement, but they were his guards. The room itself was in concert with the rustic structures outside—solid, functional furniture, thick plaited rag rugs scattered about over a wide-beamed floor, windows bordered by red-checkered curtains that might have come from a Sears Roebuck catalogue.

It was a simple living room in a country farmhouse, nothing more or less, and nothing suggesting it might be something else—or someplace else—to disturb a visitor's eye. If anything, the room was Spartan, without a woman's touch, entirely male.

Michael slid his watch slowly into view. It was one o'clock in the morning; he had been unconscious for nearly forty-five minutes.

"Hey, he's awake!" cried one of the men.

"Get Mr. Kohoutek," said the other, walking across the room toward Havelock. He rounded the sofa and reached under his leather jacket to pull out a gun. He smiled; the weapon was the Spanish Llama automatic that had traveled from a mist-laden pier in Civitavecchia, through the Palatine and Col des Moulinets, to Mason Falls, Pennsylvania. "This is good hardware, Mr. No-Name. I haven't seen one like it in years. Thanks a lot."

Michael was about to answer, but was interrupted by the rapid, heavy-footed entrance of a man who walked out of the hallway carrying a glass of steaming liquid in his hand.

"You are very free with odds and ends," thundered Janos Kohoutek. "Be careful or you'll walk barefoot in the snow."

Nie shodz sniegu bez butow.

Kohoutek's accent was that of the dialect of the Carpathian Mountains south of Otrokovice. The words alluding to bare feet in the snow were part of the Czech-Moravian admonition to wastrels who did not earn their keep or their clothes. *To understand the cold, walk barefoot in the snow.*

Kohoutek came around the guard and was now fully in view. He was a bull of a man, his open shirt emphasizing the thickness of his neck and chest, the stretched cloth marking the breadth of his heavy shoulders; age had not touched his physique. He was not tall, but he was large, and the only indication of his years was in his face—more jowl than face—deeply lined, eyes deeply set, the flesh worn by well over sixty years of driven living. The hot, dark brown liquid in the glass was tea—black Carpathian tea. The man holding it was Czech by birth, Moravian by conviction.

"So here is our invader!" he roared, staring down at Havelock. "A man with a gun, but with no identification—not even a driver's license or credit card, or a billfold to carry such things in—attacks my farm like a commando! Who is this stalker in the night? What is his business? His name?"

"Havlíček," said Michael in a low, sullen voice, pronouncing the name in an accent close to Moravian. "Mikhail Havlíček."

"*Český?*"

"*Ano.*"

"*Obchodní?*" shouted Kohoutek, asking Havelock his business.

"*Má žena,*" replied Michael, answering "The woman."

"*Co, žena?*" demanded the aging bull.

"The one who was brought here this morning," said Havelock, continuing in Czech.

"Two were brought in this morning! Which?"

"Blond hair . . . when we last saw her."

Kohoutek grinned, but not with amusement. "*Chlípný,*" he said, leering.

"Her body doesn't interest me, the information she has does." Michael raised himself. "May I get up?"

"*Vžádním případě!*" The mountain bull roared again as he rushed forward, lashing his right foot out, the boot catching Havelock in the throat, making reel him back on the slate hearth.

"*Proklatě!*" shouted Havelock, grabbing his neck. It was the moment to react in anger, the beginning of the words that mattered. "I *paid!*" he yelled in Czech. "What do you think you're doing!"

"You paid what? To ask about me on the highway? To sneak up on my house in the middle of the night? To carry a gun into my farm? I'll pay *you!*"

"I did what I was told!"

"By whom?"

"Jacob Handelman."

"Handelman?" Kohoutek's full, battered face was stretched into an expression of bewilderment. "You paid Handelman? *He* sent you?"

"He told me he would phone you, get in touch with you," said Michael quickly, using a truth from Paris that the halfway man had denied in New York, denied for profit. "I wasn't to call you under any circumstances. I was to leave my car on the highway past your mailbox and walk down the road to your farm."

"The highway? You asked questions about me in a café on the highway!"

"I didn't know where the Fourforks Pike was. How could I? Did you have a man there? Did he call you?"

The Czech-Moravian shook his head. "It doesn't matter. An Italian with a truck. He drives produce for me sometimes." Kohoutek stopped; the menace returned to his eyes. "But you did not walk down my road. You came in like a thief, an armed thief!"

"I'm no fool, *přiteli.* I know what you have here and I looked for trip alarms. I was with the Podzemí. I found them and so I was cautious; I wanted no dogs on me or men shooting at me. Why do you think it took me so long to get here from that café on the highway?"

"You *paid* Handelman?"

"Very handsomely. May I get up?"

"Get up! Sit, *sit!*" ordered the mountain bull, pointing to a short deacon's bench to the left of the fireplace, his expression more bewildered than seconds before. "You gave him money?"

"A great deal. He said I'd reach a point in the road when I could see the farm below. Someone would be waiting for me by the gate, wave me down with a flashlight. There was nobody I could see, no one at the gate. But then the weather's rotten, so I came down."

Gripping his steaming glass of tea, Kohoutek turned and walked across the room to a table against the wall. There was a telephone on it; he put down the glass, picked up the phone, and dialed.

"If you're calling Handelman—"

"I do not call Handelman," the Czech-Moravian broke in. "I never call Handelman. I call a man who calls another; he phones the German."

"You mean the Rabbi?"

Kohoutek raised his head and looked at Havelock. "Yes, the Rabbi," he said without comment.

"Well, whoever . . . there won't be any answer at his apartment. That's all I wanted to tell you."

"Why not?"

"He told me he was on his way to Boston. He's lecturing at someplace called Brandese or Brandeis."

"Jew school," said the bull, then talked into the phone: "This is Janos. Call New York. The name you will give is Havlíček, have you got that? *Havlíček.* I want an explanation." He hung up, grabbed his tea, and started back toward the fireplace. "Put that away!" he commanded the guard in the leather jacket who was rubbing the Llama against his sleeve. "Stand in the hall." The man walked away as Kohoutek approached the fire, sitting down opposite Michael in a rustic-looking rocking chair. "Now we wait, Mikhail Havlíček. It won't be long, a few minutes, ten—fifteen perhaps."

"I can't be responsible if he's not home," said Havelock, shrugging. "I wouldn't be here if we didn't have an agreement. I wouldn't know your name or where to find you if he hadn't told me. How could I?"

"We'll see."

"Where's the woman?"

"Here. We have several buildings," answered the man from the Carpathians as he sipped his tea and rocked slowly back and forth. "She's upset, of course. It is not quite what she expected, but she will understand; they all do. We are their only hope."

"How upset?"

Kohoutek squinted. "You are interested?"

"Only professionally. I've got to take her out and I don't want trouble."

"We shall see."

"Is she all right?" asked Michael, controlling his anxiety.

"Like some others—the educated ones—she lost her reason for a while." Kohoutek grinned, then coughed an ugly laugh as he drank his tea. "We explained the regulations, and she told us they were not acceptable. Can you imagine? Not *acceptable!*" The bull roared, then his voice dropped. "She will be watched carefully, and before she is sent outside she will understand. As they all understand."

"You don't have to worry. I'm taking her."

"You say that."

"I paid."

Kohoutek leaned forward, stopping the motion of the chair. "How much?"

It was the question the Czech-Moravian had wanted to ask several minutes ago, but Carpathian progress was serpentine. Michael knew he was on a tightrope; there would be no answer in New York. He was about to negotiate, and both men knew it.

"Wouldn't you rather hear it from Handelman? If he's home."

"Perhaps I would rather hear it from you, *příteli.*"

"How do you know you can trust me?"

"How do I know I can trust the Rabbi? How do you know *you* can trust him?"

"Why shouldn't I? I found you, found this place. Not in the way I would have preferred, but I'm here."

"You must represent influential interests," said Kohoutek, veering quickly, as was the custom of mountain men in negotiations.

"So influential I don't carry identification. But then you know that."

The aging lion began rocking again. "Such influence, however, always carries money."

"Enough."

"How much did you pay Handelman?" All movement stopped as the question was asked.

"Twenty thousand dollars American."

"*Twenty* . . . ?" Kohoutek's weathered face lost some of its color and his deep-set eyes squinted through the slits of flesh. "A considerable sum, *přiteli.*"

"He said it was reasonable." Havelock crossed his legs, his damp trousers warmed by the fire. "We were prepared for it."

"Are you prepared to learn why he did not reach me?"

"With the complicated arrangements you have for contacting one another, I'm not surprised. He was on his way to Boston, and if someone was not by a phone—"

"Someone is always by a phone; he is a cripple. And you were on your way to a trap that would have cost you your life."

Michael uncrossed his legs, his eyes riveted on Kohoutek. "The trip lights?"

"You spoke of dogs; we have dogs. They only attack on command, but an intruder does not know that. They circle him, barking viciously. What would you have done?"

"Used my gun, of course."

"And for that you would have been shot."

Both men were silent. Finally, Havelock spoke. "And the Rabbi has twenty thousand dollars you don't know about and I can't tell you because I'm dead."

"Now you see."

"He'd *do* that to you—for twenty thousand dollars?"

The mountain bull again started to rock his chair. "There could be other considerations. I've had minor troubles here—nothing we cannot control—but this is a depressed area. Certain jealousies arise when you have a successful farm. Handelman might care to replace me, have a reason to replace me."

"I don't understand."

"I would have a corpse on my hands, a corpse who might have made a telephone call while he was alive. He could have told someone where he was going."

"You shot an intruder, a man with a gun, who probably used his gun. You were defending your property, no one would blame you."

"No one," agreed Kohoutek, still rocking. "But it would be enough. The Moravian is a troublemaker, we cannot afford him. Cut him off."

"From what?"

The mountain man sipped his tea. "You spent twenty thousand dollars. Are you prepared to pay more?"

"I might be persuaded. We want the woman; she's worked with our enemies."

"Who is 'we'?"

"That I won't tell you. It wouldn't mean anything to you if I did. . . . Cut you off from what?"

Kohoutek shrugged his heavy shoulders. "This is only the first step for these people—like the Corescu woman."

"That's not her name."

"I'm certain it's not, but that's no concern of mine. Like the others, she'll be pacified, work out of here for a month or two, then be sent elsewhere. The South, Southwest—the northern Midwest, wherever we place her." The bull grinned. "The papers are always about to arrive— just another month, one more congressman to pay, a senator to reach. After a while, they're like goats."

"Even goats can rebel."

"To what end? Their own? To be sent back to the place where they came from? To a firing squad, or a gulag, or garrote in an alleyway? You must understand, these are panicked people. It's a *fantastic* business!"

"Do the papers ever arrive?"

"Oh, yes, frequently. Especially for the talented, the productive. The payments go on for years."

"I'd think there'd be risks. Someone who refuses, someone who threatens you with exposure."

"Then we provide another paper, *přiteli.* A death certificate."

"My turn to ask. Who is 'we'?"

"My turn to answer. I will not tell you."

"But the Rabbi wants to cut you out of this fantastic business."

"It's possible." The telephone rang, its bell abrasive. Kohoutek got out of the rocking chair and walked rapidly across the room. "Perhaps we shall learn now," he said, placing his tea on the table, and picking up the phone in the middle of the second bell. "Yes?"

Havelock involuntarily held his breath; there were so many probabilities. A curious university athlete whose responsibility was the well-being of his tenants, who might have walked out into the hallway. A graduate student with an appointment. So many accidents . . .

"Keep trying," said the Carpathian.

Michael breathed again.

Kohoutek came back to the chair, leaving his tea on the table. "There is no answer on Handelman's phone."

"He's in Boston."

"How much could you be persuaded to pay?"

"I don't carry large sums with me," replied Havelock, estimating the amount of cash in his suitcase. It was close to six thousand dollars—money he had taken out of Paris.

"You had twenty large sums for the Rabbi."

"It was prearranged. I could give you a down payment. Five thousand."

"Down payment on what?"

"I'll be frank," said Michael, leaning forward on the deacon's bench. "The woman's worth thirty-five thousand to us; that was the sum allocated. I've spent twenty."

"With five, that leaves ten," said the bull.

"It's in New York. You can have it tomorrow, but I've got to see the woman tonight. I've got to take her tonight."

"And be on a plane with my ten thousand dollars?"

"Why should I do that? It's a budget item and I don't concern myself with finances. Also, I suspect you can collect a fair amount from Handelman. A thief caught stealing from a thief. You've got him now; you could cut *him* out."

Kohoutek laughed his bull of a laugh. "You are from the mountains, Čechu! But what guarantees do I have?"

"Send your best man with us. I have no gun; tell him to keep his at my head."

"Through an airport? I am not a goat!"

"We'll drive."

"Why tonight?"

"They expect her in the early morning. I'm to bring her to a man at the corner of Sixty-second Street and York Avenue, at the entrance of the East River Drive. He has the remaining money. He's to take her to Kennedy Airport, where arrangements have been made on an Aeroflot flight. Your man can make sure; she docsn't get into the car until the money is paid. What more do you want?"

Kohoutek rocked, his squint returning. "The Rabbi is a thief. Is the Čech as well?"

"Where's the hole? Can't you trust your best man?"

"I am the best. Suppose it was me?"

"Why not?"

"*Done!* We shall travel together, the woman in the back seat with me. One gun at her head, the other at yours. Two guns, *přiteli!* Where is the five thousand dollars?"

"In my car up on the road. Send someone with me, but I get it myself; he stays outside. That's the condition or we have no negotiation."

"You Communists are all so suspicious."

"We learned it in the mountains."

"*Čechu!*"

"Where's the woman?"

"In a back building. She refused to eat before, threw the tray at our Cuban. But then, she's educated; it is not always a favorable thing, although it brings a higher price later. First, she must be broken; perhaps the Cuban has already begun. He's a hot-tempered *macho* with balls that clank on the floor. Her type of woman is his favorite."

Michael smiled, it was the most difficult smile he had rendered in his life "Are the rooms wired?"

"What for? Where are they going? What plans can they hatch alone? Besides, to install and service such items could raise gossip. The alarms on the road are enough trouble; a man comes from Cleveland to look after them."

"I want to see her. Then I want to get out of here."

"Why not? When I see five thousand dollars." Kohoutek stopped rocking and turned to his left, shouting in English. "*You!* Take our guest up in the truck to his automobile. Have him drive and keep your gun on his head!"

Sixteen minutes later, Havelock counted out the money into the Moravian's hands.

"Go to the woman, *přiteli,*" said Kohoutek.

He walked across the fenced-in compound to the left of the silo, the man with the Spanish Llama behind him.

"Over there, to your right," said the guard.

There was a barn at the edge of the woods, but it was more than a barn.

There were lights in several windows above the ground level; it was a second floor. And silhouetted in those lights were straight black lines; they were bars. Whoever was behind those windows could not get out. It was a barracks. *Ein Konzentrationslager.*

Michael could feel the welcome pressure of the leather scabbard at the base of his spine; the scaling knife was still in place. He knew he could take the guard *and* the Llama—a slip in the snow, a skid over iced grass and the man in the leather jacket was a dead man—but not yet. It would come later, when Jenna understood, when—and if—he could convince her. And if he could not, both of them would die. One losing his life, the other in a hell that would kill her.

Listen to me! Listen to me, for we are all that's left of sanity! What happened to us? What did they do to us?

"Knock on the door," said the man behind.

Havelock rapped on the wood. A voice with a Latin accent answered. "Yes? What is it?"

"Open up, Mr. K's orders. This is Ryan. Hurry!"

The door was opened two or three inches by a stocky man in a bolero and dungarees. He stared first at Michael, then saw the guard and opened the door completely.

"Nobody called," he said.

"We thought you might be busy," said the man behind Havelock, a snide laugh in his voice.

"With what? Two pigs and a crazy woman?"

"She's the one we want to see. *He* wants to see."

"He better have a *pene* made like rock, I tell you no lie! I looked in ten minutes ago; she's asleep. I don't think she slept for a couple of days maybe."

"Then he can jump her," said the guard, pushing Michael through the door.

They climbed the stairs and entered a narrow corridor with doors on both sides. Steel doors with slits in the center, sliding panels for peering inside.

We are in our movable prison. Where was it? Prague? Trieste? . . . Barcelona?

"She's in this room," said the Latin, stopping at the third door. "You want to look?"

"Just open the door," said Havelock. "And wait downstairs."

"*Ojalá—*"

"Mr. K's orders," broke in the leather-jacketed guard. "Do what the man says."

The Cuban took a key from his belt, unlocked the cell door, and stood aside.

"Get out of here," said Michael.

The two men walked up the corridor.

Havelock opened the door.

The small room was dark, and the dark light of night grudgingly spilled through the window, the white flakes bouncing off the glass and the bars. He could see her on the bed, more cot than bed. Fully dressed, she was lying face down, her blond hair cascading over her shoulders, one arm hanging down limp, the hand touching the floor. She lay on top of the covers, her clothes disheveled, the position of her body and the sound of her deep breathing proof of exhaustion. Watching her, he ached, pain pressing his chest for the pain she had endured, so much of it because of him. Trust had fled, instincts rejected, love repulsed; he had been no less an animal than the animals who had done this to her . . . he was ashamed. And filled with love.

He could see the outline of a floor lamp next to the bed; lighted, it would shine down on her. A cold fear went through him and his throat tightened. He had faced risks before, but never a danger like this, never a moment that meant so much to him. If he lost it—lost her, the bond between them shattered irremediably—nothing would matter except the death of liars. He was profoundly aware that he would willingly give up years of life for the moment to be frozen, not to have to turn on the light —simply to call out her name softly, as he had called it a hundred times a hundred, and have her hand fall into his, her face come against his. But the waiting, too, was self-inflicted torture; what were the words? *Between the acting of a dreadful thing and the first motion, all the interim is like a phantasma or a hideous dream.* It would end or it would begin when he turned on the lamp. He walked silently to the bed.

An arm shot up in the darkness. Pale skin flashing in the dim light, a hand plunged into his abdomen. He felt the impact of a sharp pointed object—not a knife, something else. He leaped back and grabbed the hand, twisting yet not twisting—to cause her further pain was not in him. He could not hurt her.

She'll kill you if she can. Broussac.

Jenna rolled off the bed, her left leg bent, her knee crashing into his kidney, her sharp fingernails clawing his neck, digging into his skin. He could not strike her, he could not do it. She grabbed his hair, pulling his face down, and her right knee smashed into the bridge of his nose. The darkness was splintered into fragments of white light.

"*Čuně!*" she cried in a muted voice, made guttural by her fury.

He understood; he had taught her well. *Use an enemy. Kill him only if you must. But use him first.* Escape was her intent; it accounted for the disheveled clothes, the skirt pulled up to expose her thigh. He had attributed it all to exhaustion, but he had been wrong; it was a sight for a *prase* peering through a slot in the cell door.

"*Stůj!*" he whispered harshly as he held her, twisting nothing, damaging nothing. "*Těsí mě!*" He freed his left hand and pulled her writhing body across the small room to the lamp. He reached over and found the switch; he snapped it on, her face in front of his.

She stared at him, her wide brown eyes bursting from their sockets with that strange admixture of fear and loathing he had seen in the window of the small plane in Col des Moulinets. The cry that was wrenched from her throat came also from the center of her life; the scream that grew from it was prolonged and horrible—a child in a cellar of terror, a woman who faced the return of infinite pain. She kicked wildly, and spun away, breaking his grip, and threw herself across the bed and against the wall. She whipped her hand back and forth, slashing madly, a crazed animal cornered, with nothing left but to end its life screaming, clawing, thrashing as the trap snapped shut. In her hand she grasped the instrument that had been her only hope for freedom; it was a fork, its tines tinted with his blood.

"*Listen* to me!" he whispered sharply again. "It was done to both of us! It's what I've come to tell you, what I tried to tell you at Col des Moulinets!"

"It was done to *me!* You tried to *kill* me . . . how many times? If I'm to die, then you—"

He lunged, and pinning her hand against the wall, her right arm under his, he forced her to stop writhing.

"Broussac *believed* you . . . but then she believed *me!* Try to understand. She knew I told her the truth!"

"You don't know the truth! Liar, *liar!*" She spat in his face; she was kicking, twisting, digging the nails of her trapped hand into his back.

"They wanted me out and you were the way! I don't know why, but I know men have been killed . . . a woman, too, who was meant to be you! They want to kill us both now, they *have* to!"

"*Liar!*"

"There are liars, yes, but I'm not one of them!"

"You are, you *are!* You sold yourself to the *zvířata! Kurva!*"

"No!" He twisted her hand, the bloodied fork protruding from her clenched fist. She winced in pain as he pulled her wrist down. Then she slowly reduced her counterpressure, her wide eyes frightened still, hating still, but piercing, too, with confusion. He placed the fork against his throat and whispered. "You know what to do," he said carefully, clearly. "The windpipe. Once punctured there's no way out for me here. . . . But there is for you. Pretend to go along with them; be passive, but watch the guard—as you know, he's a goat. The sooner you're cooperative, the sooner they'll find you work on the outside. Remember, all you want are your papers; they're everything to you. But when they let you out, somehow get to a phone and reach Broussac in Paris—you can do it. She'll help you because she knows the truth." He stopped and took his hand away, leaving hers free. "Now, do it. Either kill me or believe me."

Her stare was to him a scream echoing in the dark regions of his mind and hurling him into the horror of a thousand memories. Her lips trembled, and slowly it happened. Fear and bewilderment remained in her eyes, but the hatred was receding. Then the tears came, welling up slowly; they were the balm that meant the healing could begin.

Jenna dropped her hand and he took it, holding it in his own. The fork fell from her unclenched hand, and her body went limp, as the deep, terrible sobs came.

He held her. It was all he could do, all he wanted to do.

The sobs subsided and the minutes went by in silence. All they could hear was their own breathing, all they felt was each other as they clung together. Finally he whispered, "We're getting out, but it won't be clean. Did you meet Kohoutek?"

"Yes, a horrible man."

"He's going with us, supposedly to pick up a final payment for you."

"But there isn't any," said Jenna, pulling her face back, studying his, her eyes absorbing him, enveloping him. "Let me look at you, just look at you."

"There isn't time—"

"Shhh." She placed her fingers on his lips. "There must be time, because there's nothing else."

"I thought the same when I was walking over here, and when I was looking down at you." He smiled as he stroked her hair and gently caressed her lovely face. "You played well, *překrásně.*"

"I've hurt you."

"A minor cut and a few major scratches. Don't be insulted."

"You're bleeding . . . your neck."

"And my back, and a fork scrape—I guess you'd call it—on my stomach," said Michael. "You can nurse me later and I'll be grateful, but right now it fits the picture they have. I'm bringing you back on Aeroflot."

"Do I continue fighting?"

"No, just be hostile. You're resigned; you know you can't win. It'll go harder for you if you struggle."

"And Kohoutek?"

"He says you're to stay in the back seat with him. He'll have us both under a gun."

"Then I shall smoke a great deal. His hand will drop."

"Something like that. It's a long trip, a lot can happen. A gas station, a breakdown, no lights. He may be a mountain bull but he's close to seventy." Havelock held her shoulders. "He may decide to drug you. If he does, I'll try to stop him."

"He won't give me anything dangerous; he wants his money. I'm not concerned. I'll know you're there and I know what you can do."

"Come on."

"*Mikhail.*" She gripped his hands. "What *happened?* To me . . . to *you?* They said such dreadful things, such *terrible* things! I couldn't believe them, yet I had to believe. It was *there!*"

"It was all there. Down to my watching you die."

"Oh, *God* . . ."

"I've been running away ever since, until that night in Rome. Then I started running in a different direction. After you, after them—after the liars who did this to us."

"How did they do it?"

"There's no time now. I'll tell you everything I can later, and then I want to hear *you.* Everything. You have the names, you know the people. Later."

They stood up and embraced, holding each other briefly, feeling the warmth and the hope each gave the other. Michael pulled a handkerchief from his breast pocket and held it against his neck. Jenna took his hand away and blotted the deep scratches herself; she touched the bridge of his nose, where she had struck him with her knee, then smoothed his hair at the temples.

"Remember, my darling," she whispered. "Treat me sternly. Push me and shove me and grab my arm firmly as you do it. A man who's been scratched by a woman, whether she's his enemy or not, is an angry man. Especially among other men; his masculinity suffers more than the wounds."

"Thank you, Sigmund Freud. Let's go."

The guard in the black leather jacket smiled at the sight of Havelock's bleeding neck while the Cuban nodded his head, his expression confirming a previous judgment. As instructed, Michael held Jenna's arm in a viselike grip, propelling her forward at his side, his mouth set, his eyes controlled but furious.

"I want to go back to Kohoutek and get out of here!" he said angrily. "And I don't care for any discussion, is that understood?"

"Did the great big man get hurt by the little bitty girl?" said the guard, grinning.

"Shut up, you goddamned idiot!"

"Come to think of it, she's not that little."

Janos Kohoutek was dressed in a heavy mackinaw coat, a fur-lined cap on his head. He, too, smiled at the handkerchief held in place on Havelock's neck. "Perhaps this one's a witch from the Carpathians," he said, speaking English, his stained teeth showing. "The old wives' tales say they have the strength of mountain cats and the cunning of demons."

"Spell it with their *b, přiteli.* She's a *bitch.*" Michael pressed Jenna toward the door. "I want to get started; the snow will make for a longer trip."

"It's not so bad, more wind than anything," said the bull, taking a roll of thick cord out of his pocket and walking toward Jenna. "They keep the turnpike clear."

"What's that?" asked Havelock, gesturing at the cord.

"Hold out her hands," ordered Kohoutek, addressing the guard. "You may care to put up with this cat, but *I* do not."

"I smoke," protested Jenna. "Let me smoke, I'm very nervous. What can I *do?*"

"Perhaps you would prefer a needle? Then there will be no thought of smoking."

"My people won't accept drugs," interrupted Michael firmly. "The airports are watched, especially our departure gates. No narcotics."

"Then she'll be tied. Come, take her hand." The guard in the leather jacket approached Jenna; haltingly she put out her hands, so as not to be touched more than necessary. Kohoutek stopped. "Has she been to the toilet?" he asked harshly of no one, and no one answered. "Tell me, woman, have you been to the toilet?"

"I'm all right," said Jenna.

"For a number of hours? There'll be no stops, you understand? Even to sit on the side of the road with a gun at your head, there'll be no stops. *Rozumíš?*"

"I said I'm all right."

"Tie her, and let's go." Havelock took several impatient steps toward the door, passing the Moravian and glancing at Jenna. Her eyes were cool glass; she was magnificent. "I assume this refugee from a *žalář* will take us up in the truck."

The guard looked angry as Kohoutek grinned. "You are not far wrong, Havlíček. He's been put away for aggravated assault several times. Yes, he'll take us." The bull pulled the cord tight around Jenna's hands, then turned and shouted, *"Axel!"*

"He has my weapon," said Michael, gesturing at the man in the leather jacket. "I'd like it back."

"You shall have it. At a street corner in New York."

The second guard entered the room from the hallway, the same man who had first seen Havelock awake on the floor.

"Yes, Mr. Kohoutek?"

"You're handling the schedules tomorrow, no?"

"Yes, sir."

"Stay in radio contact with the north trucks and have one pick me up in Monongahela after my plane arrives tomorrow. I will phone from the airport and give you the time of the flight."

"Right."

"We go," said the mountain bull, heading for the door.

Michael took Jenna's arm, the guard in the leather jacket following. Outside, the wind was stronger than before, the snow angrier, whipping in circles and stinging the face. With Kohoutek leading, they ran down the farmhouse path to the truck in the road. A third guard, wearing a white parka, stood by the gate fifty yards away; he saw them and walked to the center latch.

The truck was enclosed; there were facing wooden benches in the van for transporting a cargo of five to six on each side, and coiled ropes hung on the walls. At the sight of the covered, windowless quarters Jenna was visibly shaken, and Havelock understood. Her country—his native country—had seen too many such vehicles over the years, heard too many stories told in whispers of convoys carrying away men and women and children who were never seen again. This was Mason Falls, Pennsylvania, U.S.A., but the owners and drivers of these trucks were no different from their brothers in Prague and Warsaw, late of Moscow—before then, Berlin.

"Get in, get *in!*" shouted Kohoutek, now waving a large .45 automatic as the guard held the handle of the rear door.

"I'm not your prisoner!" yelled Havelock. "We negotiated! We have an agreement!"

"And part of that agreement, *přiteli,* is that you are my guest as well as my hostage until we reach New York. After delivery—both deliveries —I shall be happy to put away the gun and buy you dinner."

The mountain bull roared with laughter as Jenna and Michael climbed into the van. They sat next to each other, but this was not to Kohoutek's liking. He said, "The woman sits with me. You move across. *Quickly.*"

"You're paranoid," said Havelock, moving to the other side, seeking out the shadows.

The door was closed, the latch and lock manipulated by the guard. A dim light came through the windshield. In seconds, thought Michael, the headlights would be turned on, the reflected spill partially illuminating the van. In the darkness he pulled up his coat and reached behind him with his right hand, inching toward the knife clipped to his belt in the small of his back. If he did not remove it now, it would be infinitely more difficult later when he was behind the wheel of his car.

"What's *that?*" shouted the bull, raising his gun in the shadows, pointing it at Havelock's head. "What are you doing?"

"The bitch cat clawed my back; the blood's sticking to my shirt," said Michael in a normal voice. Then he yelled, "Do you want to see it, *feel* it?"

Kohoutek grinned, glancing at Jenna. "A Carpathian *čarodějka.* The moon's probably full but we can't see it." He laughed his crude mountain laugh once more. "I trust the Lubyanka is as tight as it ever was. She'll eat your guards up!"

At the mention of the word "Lubyanka," Jenna gasped, shuddering. "Oh, God! Oh, my *God!*"

Kohoutek looked at her again, and again Havelock understood—she was covering for him. He quickly pulled the knife out of the scabbard and palmed it in his right hand. It had all taken less than twelve seconds.

The driver's door opened; the guard climbed in and switched on the lights. He looked behind; the old bull nodded and he turned the ignition key. The vehicle had a powerful engine, and a minute later they had passed through the gate and were climbing the steep hill, the heavy-treaded tires crunching the snow and the soft earth beneath them, lurching, vibrating, rolling with the uneven pitch of the ground. They reached the wall of trees where the road flattened out; there was perhaps three-eighths of a winding mile to go before the Fourforks Pike. The guard-driver gathered speed, then suddenly stepped on the brake, stopping the truck instantly. A red light was flashing on the dashboard. He reached over for a switch, then another, and snapped both. There was a prolonged burst of static over the radio as an excited voice shouted through the eruptions: "Mr. Kohoutek! Mr. Kohoutek!"

"What is it?" asked the guard, grabbing a microphone from the dash-board and depressing a button. "You're on the emergency channel."

"The sparrow in New York—he's on the phone! Handelman's dead! He heard it on the radio! He was shot in his apartment, and the police are looking for a man . . ."

Havelock lunged, twisting the handle of the knife into his clenched fist, the blade protruding downward, his left hand reaching for the barrel of the .45 automatic. Jenna sprang away; he gripped the long, flat steel as Kohoutek rose, then slamming the gun back down on the wooden bench, he plunged the knife through the mountain bull's hand, the point embedding—through flesh and bone—in the wood, the bloody hand impaled.

Kohoutek screamed; the guard in the front seat spun around as Jenna threw herself at him, crashing her roped hands down on his neck, and pulled the microphone out of his grip, cutting off the transmission. Have-lock swung the gun up into the old bull's head; Kohoutek lurched back into the wall and fell forward on the floor of the van, his arm stretched out, his hand still nailed to the wooden bench.

"*Mikhail!*"

The guard had recovered from Jenna's blows and was pulling the Llama out of his leather jacket. Michael sprang forward and jammed the heavy barrel of the .45 into the man's temple; reaching over his shoulder, he pressed down, holding the Llama in place.

"Mr. Kohoutek? Have you *got* it?" yelled the voice through the radio static. "What should the sparrow do? He wants to know!"

"Tell him you've got it," ordered Havelock, breathing hard, thumbing back the hammer of the gun. "Say the sparrow should do nothing. You'll be in touch."

"We've got it." The guard's voice was a whisper. "Tell the sparrow not to do anything. We'll be in touch."

Michael yanked the microphone away and pointed to the Llama. "Now, just hand it to me slowly," he said. "Use your fingers, just *two* fingers," he continued. "After all, it's mine, isn't it?"

"I was going to give it back," said the frightened guard, his lips trembling.

"How many years can you give back to the people you drove in this thing?"

"That hasn't anything to do with me, I swear it! I just work for a living. I do what I'm told."

"You all do." Havelock took the Llama and moved the automatic around the man's head, pressing it into the base of his skull. "Now, drive us out of here," he said.

22

The slender, middle-aged man with the straight dark hair opened the door of the telephone booth at the corner of 116th Street and Riverside Drive. The wet city snow was clinging to the glass, blurring the rotating red lights of the police cars up the block. He inserted the coin, dialed *o*, then five additional digits; he heard the second tone and dialed again. In moments a private phone was ringing in the living quarters of the White House.

"Yes?"

"Mr. President?"

"Emory? How did it go?"

"It didn't. He's dead. He was shot."

The silence from Washington was interrupted only by the sound of Berquist's breathing. "Tell me what happened," said the President.

"It was Havelock, but the name wasn't reported correctly. We can deny the existence of any such person at State."

"Havelock? At . . . ? Oh my God!"

"I don't know all the details, but enough. The shuttle was delayed by the snow and we circled LaGuardia for nearly an hour. By the time I got here there were crowds, police cars, a few press and an ambulance."

"The *press?"*

"Yes, sir. Handelman's prominent here. Not only because he was a Jew who survived Bergen-Belsen, but because of his standing at the university. He was respected, even revered."

"Oh, Christ . . . What did you learn? *How* did you learn it? Your name won't surface, will it?"

"No, sir. I used my rank at State and reached the precinct up here; the detective was cooperative. Apparently Handelman had an appointment with a female graduate student, who came back to the building twice before ringing the superintendent. They went up to Handelman's apartment, saw the door was unlocked, went inside, and found him. The superintendent called the police, and when they got here, he admitted having let in a man who had State Department credentials. He said his name was Havilitch; he didn't recall the first name, but insisted the ID was in order. The police are still in Handelman's apartment getting fingerprints, cloth and blood scrapings."

"Have the details been made public?"

"In this town they can't wait. It was all released twenty minutes ago. There was no way I could stop it, if I wanted to. But State doesn't have to clarify; we *can* deny."

The President was silent, then he spoke. "When the time is right, the Department of State will cooperate fully with the authorities. Until then I want a file built—and circulated on a restricted basis—around Havelock's activities since his separation from the government. It must reflect the government's alarm over his mental state, his apparent homicidal tendencies—his loyalty. However, in the interests of national security, that file will remain under restricted classification. It will not be made public."

"I'm not sure I understand."

"The facts will be revealed when Havelock is no longer a threat to this country's interests."

"Sir?"

"One man is insignificant," said the President softly. "Coventry, Mr. Undersecretary. The Enigma . . . Parsifal."

"I accept the reasoning, sir, not the assumption. How can we be sure we'll find him?"

"He'll find us; he'll find *you*. If everything we've learned about Havelock is as accurate as we believe, he wouldn't have killed Jacob Handelman unless he had an extraordinary reason. And he would never have killed him if he hadn't learned where Handelman sent the Karas woman. When he reaches her, he'll know about you."

Bradford paused, his breath visible, the vapor briefly interrupted. "Yes, of course, Mr. President."

"Get back here as fast as you can. We have to be ready . . . *you* have to be ready. I'll have two men flown up from Poole's Island. They'll meet you at National; stay in airport security until they arrive."

"Yes, sir."

"Now, listen to me, Emory. My instructions will be direct, the explanation clear. By presidential order you are to be given round-the-clock protection; your life is in their hands. You are being hunted by a killer who's sold his government's secrets to the enemy. Those will be the words *I* use; *yours* will be different. You will use the language of Consular Operations: Havelock is 'beyond salvage.' Every additional hour he lives is a danger to our men in the field."

"I understand."

"Emory?"

"Sir?"

"Before all this happened I never really knew you, not personally," said Berquist softly. "What's your situation at home?"

"Home?"

"It's where he'll come for you. Are there children at home?"

"Children? No, no, there are no children. My older son's in college, my younger boy away at boarding school."

"I thought I heard somewhere that you had daughters."

"Two. They're with their mother. In Wisconsin."

"I see. I didn't know. Is there another wife?"

"There were. Again, two. They didn't last."

"Then there are no women living in your house?"

"There are frequently, but not at the minute. Very few during the past four months."

"I see."

"I live alone. The circumstances are optimum, Mr. President."

"Yes, I guess they are."

Using the coiled ropes on the wall of the van, they tied the guard to the steering wheel, Kohoutek to the bench.

"Find whatever you can and bind his hand," said Michael. "I want him alive. I want someone to ask him questions."

Jenna found a farmer's kerchief in the glove compartment. She removed the scaling knife from the old mountain bull's huge hand, ripped the cloth in two, and expertly bound the wound, stemming the blood at both the gash and the wrist.

"It will hold for three, perhaps four hours," she said. "After that, I don't know. If he wakes and tears it, he could bleed to death. . . . Knowing what I know, I have no use for prayers."

"Someone'll find him. Them. This truck. It'll be light in an hour or so, and the Fourforks Pike's a county route. Sit down for a minute." Havelock started the engine and, reaching over the guard's leg, depressed the clutch and shoved the truck in gear. Wrenching the man back and forth over the steering wheel, he maneuvered the vehicle so that it was broadside across the road. "Okay, let's get out."

"You can't leave me here!" whined the guard. *"Jesus!"*

"Have you been to the toilet?"

"What?"

"I hope so, for your sake."

"Mikhail?"

"Yes?"

"The radio. Someone might come along and free him. He'd use it. We need every minute."

Havelock picked up the .45 from the seat and smashed the thick, blunt handle repeatedly into the dials and switches until there was nothing but shattered glass and plastic. Finally, he ripped the microphone out of its receptacle, severing the wires; he opened the door and turned to Jenna. "We'll leave the lights on so no one smashes into it," he said, stepping out and pulling the seat forward for her. "One more thing to do. Come on."

Because of the wind, the Fourforks Pike had less than an inch of snow on the surface except for the intermittent drifts that had been pummeled into the bordering grass. Michael handed the .45 to Jenna, and switched the Llama to his right hand. "That makes too much noise," he continued. "The wind might carry it down to the farmhouse. Stay here."

He ran to the back of the van and fired twice, blowing out both rear tires. He raced up the other side and fired into the front tires. The truck rocked back and forth as the tires deflated and settled into the road. To clear the highway, it could be driven into the grass, but it would go no farther than that. He put the Llama into his pocket.

"Let me have the forty-five," he said to Jenna, pulling his shirt out of his trousers.

She gave it to him. "What are you going to do?"

"Wipe it clean. Not that it'll do much good, our prints are all over inside the van. But they may not brush there; they will this."

"So?"

"I'm gambling that our driver in his own self-interest will yell like hell that it's not his, that it belongs to his employer, your host, Kohoutek."

"Ballistics," said Jenna, nodding. "Killings on file."

"Maybe something else. That farm will be torn apart, and when it is, they may start digging around those acres. There could be killings not on file." He held the automatic with his shirttail, opened the door of the truck and arced the weapon over the front seat into the covered van.

"Hey, come *on*, for Christ's sake!" shouted the driver, twisting and turning against the ropes. "Let me out of here, will ya? I didn't do nothing to you! They'll send me back for ten years!"

"They're a lot easier on people who turn state's evidence. Think about it." Havelock slammed the door and walked rapidly back to Jenna. "The car's about a quarter of a mile down on the other side of Kohoutek's road. Are you all right?"

She looked at him; particles of snow stuck to her blond hair swirling in the wind and her face was drenched, but her eyes were alive. "Yes, my darling, I'm all right. . . . Wherever we are at this moment, I'm home."

He took her hand and they started down the road. "Walk in the center so our footsteps will be covered."

She sat close to him, touching him, her arm through his, her head intermittently resting on his shoulder as he drove.

The words between them were few, the silences comforting; they were too tired and too afraid to talk sensibly, at least for a while. They had been there before; they knew a little peace would come with the quiet—and being with each other.

Remembering Kohoutek's words, Havelock headed north to the Pennsylvania Turnpike, then east toward Harrisburg. The old Moravian had been right; the low-flying winds virtually swept the wide expanse of highway, and the subfreezing temperature kept the snow dry and buoyant. Although the visibility was poor, the traveling was fast.

"Is this the main auto route?" asked Jenna.

"It's the state turnpike, yes."

"Is it wise to be on it? If Kohoutek's found before daybreak, might not men be watching this 'turnpike' as they do the *Bahnen* and the *dráha?*"

"We're the last people on earth he wants the police to find. We know what that farm is. He'll stall, use the intruder story, say *he* was the hostage, the victim. And the guard won't say anything until he hasn't got a choice, or until they find his record, and then he'll bargain. We're all right."

"That's the police, darling," said Jenna, her hand gently touching his forearm. "Suppose it is not the police? You want it to be the police, so you convince yourself. But suppose it is someone else? A farmer or a driver of a milk truck. I think Kohoutek would pay a great deal of money to get safely back to his home."

Michael looked at her in the dim light of the dashboard. Her eyes were tired, with dark circles under them; fear was still in the center of her stare. Yet in spite of the exhaustion and the dread, she was thinking—better than he. But then she had been hunted far more often than he, more recently than he. Above all, she would not panic; she knew the value of control even when the pain and the fear were overwhelming. He leaned over and brushed his lips on her face.

"You're magnificent," he said.

"I'm frightened," she replied.

"And you're also right. There's a childish song that says 'wishing will make it so.' It's a lie, and only for children, but I was counting on it, hoping for it. The odds of the police finding Kohoutek, or a citizen reporting what he found to the police, are no better than seventy-thirty. Against. We'll get off at the next exit and head south."

"To where? Where are we going?"

"First, where we can be alone, and not moving. Not running."

She sat in a chair by the motel window, the early light spreading up and over the Allegheny Mountains outside in the distance. The yellow rays heightened the gold in the long blond hair that fell across her shoulders. Alternately she would look at him, then turn her face away and close her eyes; his words were too painful to hear in the light.

When he finished, he was still caught in the anguish that came with the admission: he had been her executioner. He had killed his love and there had been no love left in him.

Jenna rose from the chair and stood silently by the window. "What did they *do* to us?" she whispered.

Havelock stood across the room watching her; he could not look away. And then he was drifting back through indeterminate time, through the rolling mists of a haunting, obsessive dream that never left him. The images were there, the moments remembered, but they had been pushed out of his life only to rise up and attack him, inflaming him whenever the memories refused to stay buried. *What's left when your memory's gone, Mr. Smith?* Nothing, of course, yet how often had he wished for oblivion, with no images or remembered moments—trading nothingness for the absence of pain. But now he had passed through the nightmare of interrupted sleep and had come to life, just as the tears had come to Jenna's eyes and washed away the hatred. But the reality was fragile; its fragments had to be pieced together.

"We have to find out why," said Michael. "Broussac told me what happened to you, but there were gaps I couldn't understand."

"I didn't tell her everything," said Jenna, gazing at the snow outside. "I didn't lie to her, but I didn't tell her everything. I was afraid she wouldn't help me."

"What did you leave out?"

"The name of the man who came to see me. He's been with your government for a number of years. He was once quite controversial, but still respected, I think. At least, I'd heard of him."

"Who was it?"

"A man named Bradford. Emory Bradford."

"Good *God* . . ." Havelock was stunned. Bradford was a name from the past, a disquieting past. He had been one of the political comets born under Kennedy and winning dubious spurs with Johnson. When the comets had faded from the Washington firmament, heading for the international banks and the foundations, the prestigious law offices and the corporate boardrooms, Bradford had remained—less celebrated, to be sure, and less influential, certainly—where the political wars had been fought. It was never understood why. A degree of personal wealth aside, he could have done a thousand other things, but he had chosen not to. *Bradford,* thought Havelock, the name echoing in his head. All these years, had Emory Bradford merely been marking time, waiting for another version of Camelot to carry him into another time of self-aggrandizing glory? It had to be. If he had reached Jenna in Barcelona, he was at the core of the deception at Costa Brava, a deception that went far beyond himself and Jenna, two lovers turned against each other. It linked unseen men in Moscow with powerful men in the United States government.

"Do you know him?" asked Jenna, still staring out the window.

"Not personally. I've never met him. But you're right, he *was* controversial, and most everyone knows him. The last I heard he was an undersecretary of State with a low profile but a pretty high reputation—buried but valuable, you could say. He told you he was with Cons Op out of Madrid?"

"He said he was on special assignment with Consular Operations, an emergency involving internal security."

"Me?"

"Yes. He showed me copies of documents found in a bank vault on the Ramblas." Jenna turned from the window. "Do you recall telling me you had to go to the Ramblas on several occasions?"

"It was a drop for Lisbon, I also told you that. Never mind, it was orchestrated."

"But you can understand. The Ramblas stayed in my mind."

"They made sure of it. What were the documents?"

"Instructions from Moscow that could only have been meant for you. There were dates, itineraries; everything corresponded to where we'd been, where we were going. And there were codes; if they weren't authentic, then I'd never seen a Russian cipher."

"The same materials *I* was given," said Havelock, his anger surfacing.

"Yes, I knew it when you told me what they gave you in Madrid. Not all, of course, but many of the same documents and much of the same information they showed you they showed me. Even down to the radio in the hotel room."

"The maritime frequency? I thought you'd been careless; we never listened to the radio."

"When I saw it, a great part of me died," said Jenna.

"When I found the key in your purse and it matched the one the evidence in Madrid said you would have—a key to an airport locker—I couldn't stay in the same room with you."

"That was it, wasn't it? The final confirmation for both of us. I had changed, I couldn't help it. And when you came back from Madrid, *you* were different. It was as if you were being pulled violently in several directions, but with only one true commitment, and it was not to me, not to us. You had sold yourself to the Soviets for reasons I couldn't understand. . . . I even tried to rationalize; perhaps after thirty years there was news of your father—stranger things have happened. Or you were going into deep cover without me; a defector in the process of becoming a double agent. I simply knew that the transition—whatever it was—did not include me." Jenna turned back to the window. She continued, her voice barely audible, "Then Bradford reached me again; this time he was panicked, nearly out of control. He said the word had just been intercepted—Moscow had ordered my execution. You were to lead me into a trap, and you were going to do it that night."

"At the Costa Brava?"

"No, he never mentioned the Costa Brava. He said a man would call around six o'clock while you were out, using a phrase or description I'd recognize as coming only from you. He would say that you could not get to a telephone, but I was to take the car and drive down the coast to Villanueva, that you would meet me by the fountains in the plaza. But you wouldn't, because I'd never get there. I'd be taken on the road."

"I *told* you I was going to Villanueva," said Michael. "It was part of the Cons Op strategy. With me supposedly twenty miles south on business, you had time to get up to the Montebello beach on the Costa Brava. It was the final proof against you. I was to witness it—I demanded that, hoping to Christ you'd never show up."

"It all fit, it was *made* to fit!" cried Jenna. "Bradford said if that call came, I was to run. Another American would be in the lobby with him, watching for the KGB. They'd take me to the consulate."

"But you didn't leave with them. The woman I saw die wasn't you."

"I couldn't. I suddenly couldn't trust anyone. . . . Do you remember the incident that night at the café in the Paseo Isabel just before you went to Madrid?"

"The drunk," said Havelock, remembering all too well. "He bumped into you—fell into you, actually—then insisted on shaking your hand and kissing it. He was all over you."

"We laughed about it. You more than I."

"I didn't a couple of days later. I was convinced that was when you were given the key to the airport locker."

"Which I never knew about."

"And which I found in your purse because Bradford put it there while he was in the hotel room and I was in Madrid. I assume you excused yourself for a moment or two."

"I was in shock; I was ill. I'm sure I did."

"It explains the radio, the maritime frequency. . . . What about the drunk?"

"He was the other American in the lobby of the hotel. Why was he there? Who *was* he? I went back up as fast as I could."

"He didn't see you?"

"No, I used the staircase. His face frightened me, I can't tell you why. Perhaps because he had pretended to be someone else before, someone so different, I don't know. I *do* know his eyes disturbed me; they we angry, but they did not look around. He *wasn't* watching the lobby for the KGB; he only kept glancing at his watch. By then I was in a panic myself—confused, and hurt more than I'd ever been hurt in my life. *You were going to let me die, and suddenly I couldn't trust them."*

"You went back to the room?"

"God, no, I'd have been cornered. I went up to the floor, stayed in the stairwell, and tried to think things through. I thought perhaps I was being hysterical, too frightened to act reasonably. Why *didn't* I trust the Americans? I'd about made up my mind to go back down when I heard noises from the corridor inside. I opened the door a bit . . . and knew that I was right to do what I did."

"They came after you?"

"The elevator. Bradford knocked on the door several times, and while he was knocking, the other man—the drunk from the café—took out a gun. When there was no answer, they waited until they were sure there was no one in the hallway. Then, with one kick, the man with the gun broke down the door and rushed inside. It was not the action of men who'd come to save someone. I ran."

Havelock, watching her, tried to think. There were so many ambiguities . . . *ambiguity.* Where were the outlines of the man who had used the code Ambiguity?

"How did they get your suitcase?" he asked.

"As you described it, it was an old one of mine. The last I recall I simply left it in the basement of the flat I leased in Prague. You may have carried it down, in fact."

"The KGB would find it."

"The *KGB?"*

"Someone in the KGB."

"Yes, you said that, didn't you? . . . There has to be someone."

"What was the phrase or description the man gave you over the phone? The words you were to think came from me."

"Again Prague. He said there was 'a cobblestone courtyard in the center of the city.' "

"*Veřejná mistnost,"* said Michael, nodding. "Prague's Soviet police. They'd know about that. In a report I sent to Washington I described how you got out of that place, how great you were. And how I damn near died watching you from a window three stories above."

"Thank you for the commendation."

:ting all our points together, remember? We were going
our movable prison."
:re going to teach."

:re going to have children—"
"And send them off to school—"
"And love them and scold them."
"And go to hockey-ball games."
"You said there were no such things—"
"I love you . . ."
"Mikhail?"

The first steps were tentative, but the pavane was suddenly finished.
They ran to each other, and held each other, pushing time away, and hurt,
and a thousand moments of anguish. Her tears came, washing away the
final barricades mounted by liars and men who served the liars. Their arms
grew stronger around each other, the straining of their bodies an exertion
each understood; their lips met, swollen, probing, searching for the release
they held for each other. They were trapped as never before in their
movable prison—they understood that, too—but for the moment they
were also free.

The dream had come fully to life, the reality no longer fragile. She was
beside him, her face touching his shoulder, her lips parted, the breath of
her deep, steady breathing warming his skin. As so often in the past,
strands of her hair fell across his chest, somehow a reminder that even in
sleep she was a part of him. He turned carefully, so as not to waken her,
and looked down at her. The dark shadows under her eyes were still there,
but they were fading as a hint of color returned to her pale flesh. It would
take days, perhaps weeks, for the fear in her eyes to disappear. Yet in spite
of it, her strength was there; it had carried her through unbearable tensions.

She moved, stretching, and her face was bathed in the sunlight that
streamed through the windows. As he watched her he thought of what
she had been through, what resources she must have had to summon in
order to survive. Where had she been? Who were the people who had
helped her, hurt her? There were so many questions, so many things he
wanted to know. A part of him was a callow adolescent, jealous of the
images he did not wish to imagine, while another part of him was a
survivor who knew only too well the prices one had to pay to remain alive
in their disorderly, so frequently violent world. The answers would come

with time, revealed slowly or in eruptions of memory or resentment, but they would not be provoked by him. The healing process could not be forced; it would be too easy for Jenna to sink back and relive the terrors and, by reliving them, prolong them.

She moved again, her face returning to him, her breath warm. And then the absurdity of his thoughts struck him. Where did he think he was . . . *they* were? What did he think would be permitted them? How could he dare to think in terms of any time at all?

Jacob Handelman was dead, his killer as good as identified—certainly known by now to the liars in Washington. The manhunt would be given respectability; he could see the story in the newspapers: a beloved scholar brutally slaughtered by a deranged former foreign service officer wanted by his government for all manner of crimes. Who would possibly believe the truth? That a kindly old Jew who had suffered the horrors of the camps was in reality a strutting man-monster who had ordered up the guns of Lidice? *Insane!*

Broussac would turn; anyone he might have counted on would not touch him now, touch *them* now. There was no time for healing, they needed every hour; the swiftness of their strikes—*his* strikes—was essential. He looked at his watch; it was two-forty-five, the day three-quarters gone. There were strategies to consider—liars to reach at night.

Yet there had to be *something.* For them, only themselves; to ease the ache, erase the vestiges of fragility. If there was not, there was nothing.

He did what he had dreamt of, waking up in sweat whenever the dream had recurred, knowing it could never be. It could be now. He whispered her name, calling out to her across the chasms of sleep.

And as if the moments away from each other had never been, her hand reached for his. She awoke, and her eyes roamed his face; then without speaking, she raised the covers and came to him. She pressed her naked body against his, her arms enveloping him, her lips against his.

They were silent as their excitement grew; only the throated cries of need and anxiety were heard in the room. The need was each for the other, and the anxiety was not to be feared.

They made love twice more, but the third time was more successful in the attempt than in the completion. The rays of the sun no longer streaked through the window; instead there was an orange glow that was the reflection of a country sundown. They sat up in bed, Michael lighting her cigarette, both laughing softly at their misguided energies, their temporary exhaustion.

"You're going to throw me out for a hot-blooded stag from Ankara."

"You have nothing at all to apologize for, my darling . . . my Mikhail. Besides, I really don't like their coffee."

"I'm relieved."

"You're a love," she said, touching the bandage on his shoulder.

"I'm *in* love. There's so much to make up for."

"Both of us, not you alone. You must not think that way. I accepted the lies, just as you did. Incredible lies, incredibly presented. And we don't know why."

"But we know the purpose, which gives us part of the why. To get me out but keep me under control, under a microscope."

"With *my* defection, *my* death? There are other ways of terminating a man you no longer want."

"Killing him?" said Havelock, nodding; then he paused and shook his head. "It's one way, yes. But then there's no way to control whatever damaging evidence he may have left behind. The possibility that such a man has left that information often keeps him alive."

"But they want to kill you *now*. You're 'beyond salvage.' "

"Someone changed his mind."

"This person called Ambiguity," said Jenna.

"Yes. Whatever I know—or they think I know—has been supplanted by a larger threat much more dangerous to them. Again, me. What I found, what I learned."

"I don't understand."

"You," said Havelock. "The Costa Brava. It has to be buried."

"The Soviet connection?"

"I don't know. Who was the woman on the beach? What did she think she was doing there? Why wasn't it you—thank Christ, it wasn't—but *why* wasn't it? Where were they taking you?"

"To my grave, I think."

"If that was the case, why weren't you sent to that beach? Why weren't you killed there?"

"Perhaps they felt I wouldn't go. I didn't leave the hotel with them."

"They couldn't have known that then. They thought they had you—frightened, in shock, wanting protection. The point is, they never mentioned the Costa Brava; they didn't even try to *prime* you."

"I would have driven there that night—all you had to do was call me. I would have come. They could have had their execution; you would have seen what they wanted you to see."

"It doesn't make sense." Michael struck a match and lit a cigarette for himself. "And that's the basic inconsistency, because whoever put Costa Brava together was a hell of a technician, an expert in black operations. It was brilliantly structured, down to split-second timing. . . . It doesn't make sense!"

Jenna broke the long silence. "Mikhail," she said quietly, sitting forward, her eyes clouded, focused inward. *"Two* operations," she whispered.

"What?"

"Suppose there were two operations, not one?" She turned to him, her eyes alive now. "The first set in motion in Madrid—the evidence against *me*—then carried forward to Barcelona—the evidence against *you.* "

"Still one blanket," said Havelock.

"But then it was *torn,* " insisted Jenna. "It became *two.* "

"How?"

"The original operation is intercepted," she said. "By someone not part of it."

"Then altered," he said, beginning to understand. "The cloth is the same but the stitches are twisted, ending up being something else. A *different* blanket."

"Still, for what purpose?" she asked.

"Control," he answered. "Then you got away and the control was lost. Broussac told me there's been a coded alert out for you ever since Costa Brava."

"Very coded," agreed Jenna, crushing out her cigarette. "Which could mean whoever intercepted the operation and altered it might not have known that I *had* gotten out of Barcelona alive."

"Until I saw you and let *everyone* know—everyone who counted. At which point we both had to die; one by the black-operations book—that was me. The other out of strategy—no one in sanction aware—a bomb blowing up a car outside of Col des Moulinets. You. Everything buried."

"Again Ambiguity?"

"No one else could have done it. No one else but a man with the clearance code could have infiltrated the strategy at that bridge."

Jenna looked at him, then across at the windows; the orange glow was fading. "There are still too many omissions. Too many gaps."

"We'll fill some of them in, maybe all."

"Emory Bradford, of course."

"And someone else," said Havelock. "Matthias. Four days ago I tried to reach him from Cagnes-sur-Mer on his private line—very few people have the number. I couldn't understand it, but he wouldn't talk to me.

You can't know how crazy it was—in a way, unbelievable. But he wouldn't and I thought the worst: the man closest to me had cut me off. Then you tell me about Bradford, and I'm beginning to think I was wrong."

"How do you mean?"

"Suppose Anton wasn't there? Suppose others had taken over that private place, that very private line?"

"Bradford?"

"And whatever's left of his tribe. The return of the political comets, looking for a way to get their fires back. According to *Time* magazine, Matthias is off on an extended holiday, but what if he's not? What if the most celebrated Secretary of State in history is being held incommunicado. In a clinic somewhere, unable to get word out."

"But that's incredible, Mikhail. A man like that would have to stay in touch with his office. There are daily briefings, decisions—"

"It could be done through second and third parties, aides known to State personnel."

"It's too preposterous."

"Maybe it's not. When they told me Anton wouldn't talk to me, I couldn't accept it. I made another call—to an old man, a neighbor of Matthias's whom he saw whenever he went to his lodge in the Shenandoah. His name's Zelienski and he's good for Anton—a retired professor brought over from Warsaw a number of years ago. They'd sit around playing chess, talking about the old days. He was a tonic for Matthias and both of them knew it, especially Anton, but when I spoke to Zelienski he said Anton didn't have time for him these days. Didn't have time."

"It's entirely possible, Mikhail."

"But not consistent. Matthias would *make* the time; he wouldn't cut off an old friend without at least some kind of explanation, any more than he would me. It is not like him."

"How do you mean?"

"I remember Zelienski's words. He said he'd leave messages for Anton and men would call him back expressing Matthias's regrets, saying he rarely drove out to the valley anymore. But he did; he was there in the valley when I called. Or he was *supposed* to be. My point is, he may not have been."

"Now *you're* not consistent," broke in Jenna. "If what you say is true, why didn't they simply say he wasn't there?"

"They couldn't. I used the private line and it's to be answered only if he's on the premises, and only by him. Someone picked up the phone by mistake and tried to cover it."

"Someone working for Bradford?"

"Someone who's part of a conspiracy against Matthias, at any rate, and I wouldn't exclude Bradford. Men in Washington are dealing secretly with men in Moscow. Together they built Costa Brava, convincing Matthias you're a Soviet agent—his note to me made that clear. We don't know whether everything went off the track or not, but we do know Matthias had nothing to do with it and Bradford did. Anton didn't trust Emory Bradford and his crowd; he considered them the worst sort of opportunists. He kept them away from extremely sensitive negotiations because he believed they'd use them for their own ends. He had a point; they did it before, letting the country know only what they wanted people to hear, using the classification stamp so that it became their signature." Michael paused, inhaling on his cigarette as Jenna looked at him. "He may be doing it again, God knows for what purpose. It'll be dark soon and we can drive. We'll head across into Maryland, then down to Washington."

"To Bradford?"

Havelock nodded. Jenna touched his arm and said, "They'll connect you with Handelman and assume you reached me. They'll know the first name I'd give you is Bradford's. They'll guard him."

"I know that," said Michael. "Let's get dressed. We've got to eat and find a newspaper, one that carries the wire services. We'll talk in the car." He began walking toward his suitcase, then stopped. "My God, your clothes. I didn't think; you don't have your clothes."

"Kohoutek's people took them, took everything. They said foreign labels, European luggage, mementos—anything like that—had to be confiscated for our own good. There could be no traces of where we came from. They would supply me with something suitable later."

"Suitable for what?"

"I was too frightened to think."

"Take all your possessions, and leave you alone in a cell." *So much to make up for.* "Let's go," he said.

"We should stop somewhere and pick up a Red Cross kit," added Jenna. "That dressing on your shoulder should be changed. I can do it."

So much to make up for!

23

At a diner on the outskirts of Hagerstown, they saw a dispenser for newspapers reflected in the light of the entrance. There were two papers left, both afternoon editions of the Baltimore *Sun*. They took both, to see whether any photographs had been released that might alert someone inside the roadside restaurant. Shaving the negative odds was instinct.

They sat across from each other in a corner booth. They turned the pages rapidly, and when they had gone through them all, they breathed easier. There were no photographs. They would go back and study the article in a moment; it was on page three.

"You must be starved," said Havelock.

"To tell you the truth, I'd like a drink, if they serve one here."

"They do. I'll order." He glanced at the counter and held up his hand.

"I haven't even thought about eating."

"That's strange. Kohoutek said you wouldn't eat last night, that you threw the tray at his Cuban."

"A tray full of scraps. I ate; you always told me never to leave food when you're in a bad situation. That you never know when you'll get another meal."

"Listen to Mother."

"I listened to a child running for his life through the woods."

"History. Why did you throw the tray? To keep him away from you?"

"To get the fork. There was no knife."

"You're something, lady."

"I was desperate. Stop complimenting me."

A plump, overly-made-up waitress approached the table, her eyes appraising Jenna with a mixture of sadness and envy. Michael understood, neither with satisfaction nor in condescension; he merely understood. Jenna Karas was that often-forgotten person, whether she was forced to kill in order to survive, or be seduced so she might live. She was a lady. Havelock ordered their drinks. The waitress smiled as she nodded and left quickly; she would return quickly.

"Let's get to the bad news," said Michael, opening the newspaper.

"It's on the third page."

"I know. Did you read it?"

"Only the bottom line where it said 'continued on page eleven.' I thought they might have included a photograph there."

"So did I." Havelock began reading as Jenna watched him. The waitress returned, placing their drinks on the table. "We'll order food in a minute," said Michael, his eyes riveted on the paper. The waitress left as Havelock quickly flipped the pages, snapping the paper in place. As he read on he experienced relief, then concern and, finally, alarm. He finished and leaned back in the booth, staring at Jenna.

"What is it? What does it say?"

"'They're covering it up," he said softly.

"*What?*"

"They're protecting me . . . actually protecting me."

"You couldn't have read it properly."

"I'm afraid I did." He leaned forward, his fingers scanning the lines in the column of the paper. "Listen to this. 'According to the State Department, no such individual matching the name, the description, or the fingerprints is currently or has ever been in the employ of the Department of State. Further, a spokesman for State said that to speculate on the similarity of the reported name of the killer with that of any present or past employee would be grossly unfair and inaccurate. A thorough computer check was made upon receipt of the Manhattan police report, and the results were negative. However, the State Department's report revealed that the slain Professor Handelman had acted as a consultant to the Department in the area of European refugee displacement, with emphasis on those persons who had survived the Nazi period. According to a spokesman, the Manhattan police theorize that the killer may be a member of a terrorist organization violently hostile to the Jewish community. The State Department pointed out that it is not uncommon for terrorists in all countries to assume the identities of government personnel.' " Havelock stopped and looked up at Jenna. "That's it," he said. "They've thrown everybody off."

"Could they believe it?"

"Not possible. To begin with, there are a hundred people in and out of State who know I was with Consular Operations. They'd put the names together and come up with mine. Second, my fingerprints had to be all over Handelman's apartment; they're on file. Last, Handelman had nothing whatsoever to do with any part of the government; that was his strength. He was a halfway man for the Quai d'Orsay, and they never would have used him if they thought he'd ever be under government scrutiny. It isn't done; we're all off-limits."

"What do you make of it?"

Michael sank back in the booth, reached for his whisky, and drank. "It's too blatant," he mused, holding the glass in front of his lips.

"A trap, then," said Jenna. "They want you to come in—presumably after Bradford—and take you."

"To a point 'beyond salvage,' to coin a phrase. And once I'm dead, I can't talk, but they can explain they trapped a killer. Reaching Bradford would be easy, coming out with him impossible. . . . Unless I could draw *him* out, make him come to *me."*

"They'll never permit it. He'll be flanked by guards and they'll be watching for you. They'll kill you on sight."

Havelock drank again, a thought stirring at the bottom of his mind but as yet unclear. "Watching for me," he repeated, putting the glass down. *"Looking* for me . . . But no one's *looking* for me except the men who did this to us."

"The liars, as you call them," said Jenna.

"Yes. We need help, but I assumed we couldn't get it, that anyone I might want to reach wouldn't touch us. That's not the case now; they called *off* the hunt."

"Don't be foolish, Mikhail," interrupted Jenna. "It's part of the trap. There's an alert out for you as well as for me, and yours isn't coded; there's nothing ambiguous about it. You're you, and every agency that might be of value has you on its list. Whom in your government do you think you could trust?"

"No one," agreed Havelock. "And no one who could survive a 'beyond salvage' association, if I did trust him."

"Then what are you saying?"

"Cagnes-sur-Mer," said Michael, squinting. "At Salanne's house, when I couldn't reach Anton I called old Zelienski—I told you, remember? He mentioned him. 'Alexander the Great,' he called him. Raymond Alexander. Not just a mutual friend, but a pretty damned good friend—of mine as well as Matthias. He could do it."

"How?"

"Because he's *outside* the government. Outside but in a way very much a part of it; Washington needs him and he needs Washington. He's a writer for *The Potomac Review,* and knows as much about the government as anyone I've ever met. But he relies on his contacts; he'd never let me get near him if I'd been identified in the newspapers, but I wasn't."

"How could he help us?"

"I'm not sure. Maybe draw out Bradford for me. He does in-depth interviews, and to be interviewed by him is a plus for anyone in the government. He's above suspicion. They might drive Bradford out in a tank, but they'd let him go inside the house by himself. I could hint at something unexpected, a substantive change in the State Department with Bradford at the center. Then suggest an interview—with me in the house to listen, to verify."

"The house?"

"He works at home; it's part of his mystique. Like James Reston at the *Times.* If a politician or a bureaucrat says he was at Fiery Run, everyone knows what he means; there'll be a story by Scotty Reston. If he says he was out at Fox Hollow, the same people know he was interviewed by Raymond Alexander. Fox Hollow's in Virginia just west of Washington. We could be there in an hour and a half, two hours at the most."

"Would he do it?"

"He might. I won't tell him why, but he might. We're friends."

"The university?"

"No, but there's a connection. I met him through Matthias. When I first started at State, Matthias would come down to Washington on one thing or another, building his contacts, charming the asses off influential asses, and I'd frequently get a hurry-up call from Anton, asking me to join them both for dinner. I never refused, not only because of the company, but the restaurants were the kind way beyond my income."

"That was gracious of your *přítele.*"

"And not very bright for a brilliant man, considering the nature of my training. He was the *učitel* extolling his not too gifted student from Praha, when the last thing I needed was any sort of notice. I explained this quietly to Alexander. We both laughed and, as a result, had dinner now and then when Anton was safely back in his tower at Princeton, tending his academic gardens and not trying to grow arbors in Washington. Make no mistake, the great Matthias was not above fertilizing the seeds he'd sown."

"You'd have dinner at Alexander's home?"

"Always. He understood that he also wasn't someone I wanted to be seen with in public."

"Then you *are* good friends."

"Reasonably so."

"And he's influential?"

"Of course."

Jenna reached over and touched his arm. "Mikhail, why not tell him *everything?*"

Havelock frowned and put his hand over hers. "I don't think he'd want to hear it. It's the sort of thing he runs from."

"He's a writer. In *Washington.* How can you say that?"

"He's an analyst, a commentator. Not an investigative reporter, not a muckraker. He doesn't like stepping on toes, only on opinions."

"But what you have to tell him is extraordinary."

"He'd tell me to go straight to the State Department security bureau on the basis that I'd get a fair hearing. I wouldn't. I'd get a bullet in my head. Alexander's a sixty-five-year-old curmudgeon who's heard it all— from Dallas to Watergate—and he thinks a hundred and ten percent of it is a conspiracy of horseshit. And if he found out what I'd done— Handelman excluded—he'd call security himself."

"He's not much of a friend."

"By his lights he is; just don't transgress." Michael paused, turning her hand over. "But beyond the possibility that he'd bring Bradford out to Fox Hollow, there's something he might clear up. My *přítel.* I'll ask him to find out where Matthias is, say that I don't want to call myself because I may not have time to see him and Anton would be upset. He'd do it; with his connections he *could* do it."

"Suppose he can't?"

"Then that'll tell us something, won't it? In which case, I'll force him to get Bradford out there, if I have to put a gun to his head. But if he does reach Matthias at a lodge in the Shenandoah . . . we'll know something else, and it frightens the hell out of me. It will mean that the Secretary of State has a Moscow connection in the KGB."

The village of Fox Hollow was small. The streets were lit by gas lamps and the architecture was Colonial by township decree; the stores were called shops and their clientele was among the wealthiest in the Washington–New York orbit. The village's charm was not only apparent, it was proclaimed, but it was not for the benefit of outsiders—tourists were discouraged, if not harassed. The minimum police force had maximum arms and a communications system that proportionately rivaled that of the Pentagon, where it was probably designed. Fox Hollow was an island in a landlocked area of Virginia as surely as if its square mileage were surrounded by an impassable sea.

The air had been warmed by the Potomac River, and the snow had receded on the outskirts of Harpers Ferry. It had turned into a cold drizzle at Leesburg, by which time Havelock had prepared his scenario for Raymond Alexander. Its bureaucratic plausibility lent it conviction, plausibility based on genuine anxiety where present or past covert operations were concerned. There had been a killing in New York—if Alexander had not heard of it, he would by morning; he was a voracious reader of newspapers —and the killer had mocked up an impersonation, including an ID and an appearance uncomfortably close to Michael's own. The State Department had flown him back from London on military transport; any assistance the retired foreign service officer could give Consular Operations would be appreciated; also, he had been in London, hadn't he?

The Bradford ploy would be refined as their conversation progressed, but the basic thrust would be that the once controversial undersecretary of State was about to be rehabilitated and put back in the limelight. In London, Havelock would say, he had been given a detailed report of Bradford's extensive but secret negotiations in the touchy matter of NATO missile deployment; it was a major shift in policy. It was also sufficiently explosive to get Alexander's juices running. It was the sort of advance leak he thrived on, giving him time to put together an exhaustive analysis of the pros and cons. But if the old warhorse wished to interview Emory Bradford—with on-site but unseen verification, possibly confrontation—he had to persuade the undersecretary to come out to Fox Hollow in the morning. Havelock had a reservation on the afternoon flight back to London—and, of course, time and schedules permitting, he wanted to drop in on his old mentor Anthony Matthias, if only for a few minutes. If Alexander knew where he could find him.

As for Bradford, he had no choice. If summoned by the redoubtable journalist, he would comply. Other things—such as Costa Brava—might be paramount, but he still had to maintain his low profile at all costs, and one way to lose it was to refuse to be interviewed by Raymond Alexander. And when he came into the house in Fox Hollow, with his guards remaining outside in a limousine, Michael would take him. His disappearance would baffle the liars and the guards hired by the liars. The journalist's large, rambling house was surrounded by miles of dense woods, overgrown fields and steep ravines. No one knew forests the way Mikhail Havlíček knew them; he would take Bradford through them until they came to a backcountry road somewhere, and a car, and the woman that Bradford had used in Barcelona. After his meeting with Alexander, they would have all night to study the map and travel the roads, watching for the Fox Hollow police, explanations at the ready if they were stopped. They could do it. They *had* to do it.

"It's lovely!" cried Jenna, charmed by the gas-lit streets and the small alabaster columns of the storefronts.

"It's wired," said Michael, spotting a blue-and-white patrol car at the curb in the middle of the block.

"Get down!" he ordered. "Stay out of sight."

"What?"

"Please."

Jenna did as she was told, curling up on the floor.

He slowed down, pulling alongside the police car; he saw the officer in the window, then eased to his right, and parked directly in front.

"What are you doing?" whispered Jenna, bewildered.

"Showing my credentials before anyone asks for them."

"That's very good, Mikhail."

Havelock got out of the coupe and walked back to the patrol car. The police officer rolled down the window, first studying the license plate on Michael's rented car. It was precisely what Michael wanted him to see; it could be of value later that night if a "suspicious vehicle" was reported.

"Officer, could you tell me where there's a pay phone around here? I thought there was one on the corner, but then I haven't been back here in a couple of years."

"You've been here before?" asked the policeman, his voice friendly, his eyes not.

"Oh, sure. Used to spend weekends out here a lot."

"You have business in Fox Hollow, sir?"

"Well . . ." Havelock paused, as if the question bordered on impertinence. Then he shrugged, as if to say, After all the police have a job to do. He spoke in a slightly lower tone. "All right, I understand. My business is with an old friend, Raymond Alexander. I want to call and tell him I'm here. . . . Just in case someone's dropped in on him he'd prefer I not meet. It's standard procedure with Mr. Alexander, Officer, but you probably know that. I could drive around for a while. I'll probably have to later on anyway."

The policeman's posture had visibly improved at the mention of Alexander's name. Limousines and military staff cars were common sights on the road to the venerated political commentator's retreat. There was no such vehicle in front of him now, but the operative phrases were printed in the officer's eyes: "An old friend"; "Used to spend weekends . . ."

"Yes, sir. Of course, sir. There's a restaurant five blocks up with a phone in the lobby."

"The Lamplighter?" said Havelock, remembering.

"That's it."

"I don't think so, Officer. It could be a busy night. Isn't there a booth on the street?"

"There's one over on Acacia."

"If you'll tell me how to get there, both R.A. and I would appreciate it."

"You can follow me, sir."

"Thanks very much." Michael started for his car, then stopped and returned to the window. "I know this sounds silly, but I was usually driven out here. I think I know the way to his home. I take a left on Webster to Underhill Road, then straight out for two or three miles, isn't that it?"

"It's nearer six miles, sir."

"Oh? Thanks."

"After you make your call, I could lead you out, sir. It's quiet in town tonight."

"That's *very* kind of you. But really, I couldn't ask you."

"No problem. That's what we're here for."

"Well, thanks, again. I appreciate it."

The call to Raymond Alexander brought forth the response Havelock expected. Nothing would do but that he drop in and see the journalist if only for a drink. Michael said he was glad Raymond was free, not only to renew an old friendship but because he had learned something in London that Alexander might want to know about. It might even make up partially for a great many expensive dinners Havelock had enjoyed at Raymond's expense.

On the way back to his car from the booth, Michael stopped at the police officer's window. "Mr. Alexander wanted me to get your name. He's very grateful to you."

"It's nothing, sir. My name's Lewis. Officer Lewis; there's only one."

Lewis, he thought. Harry Lewis, professor of political science, Concord University. He could not think about Harry now, but he would have to think about him soon. Lewis must be convinced he had dropped out of civilization. He had, and to reenter it, liars would have to be found and exposed.

"Is something the matter, sir?"

"No, nothing at all. I know a man named Lewis. I remembered I was to call him. Thanks once again. I'll follow you."

Havelock climbed behind the wheel of the rented car and looked at Jenna. "How are you doing?"

"Uncomfortable and frightened out of my mind! Suppose that man had come over?"

"I would have stopped him, called to him from the booth, but I didn't think it was likely. The police in Fox Hollow stay close to their radios. I just don't want you seen, if we can help it. Not around here, not with me."

The drive out to Alexander's house took less than twelve minutes. The white post-and-rail fence marking the journalist's property shone in the glare of the headlights of both cars. The home itself was set far back from the road. It was a tasteful combination of stone and wood, with floodlights shining down on the circular drive in front of wide slate steps that led to the heavy oak entrance door. The grounds were cleared in the front and on the sides of the house; thick, tall trees shot up at random about the close-cropped lawn. But where the lawn ended, on either side the dense woods abruptly began. From memory, Michael pictured the rear of the house; the woods were no farther away from the large back patio than they were from the sides of the building. He would use those woods and Bradford would enter them with him.

"When you hear the police car leave," he said to Jenna, "get up and stretch, but don't get out. I don't know what kind of alarms Alexander has around here."

"It's been a strange introduction to this free country of yours, Mikhail."

"Also, don't smoke."

"Děkuji."

"You're welcome."

Havelock purposely touched the rim of the horn as he got out of the car; the sound was abrupt and short, easily explained. There were no dogs. He walked toward the patrol car in front, hoping the horn would serve its function before he reached the window. It did; the front door opened and a uniformed maid stood in the frame, looking out.

"Hello, Margaret!" yelled Michael over the hood of the police car. "Be right there." He looked down at the police officer, who had glanced at the door, the scene not lost on him. "Thanks again, Officer Lewis," he said, taking a bill from his pocket. "I'd like to—"

"Oh, no, sir, thanks just the same. Have a good evening, sir." The officer nodded with a smile, pulled the gear in place, and drove off.

Havelock waved; no police, no dogs, only unseen alarms. As long as Jenna stayed in the car, she was safe. He walked up the slate steps to the door and the maid.

"Good evening, sir," said the woman in a distinct Irish brogue. "My name is Enid, not Margaret."

"I'm terribly sorry."

"Mr. Alexander is expecting you. I never heard of a Margaret; the girl before me was Gretchen. She lasted four years, may the Lord rest her soul."

Raymond Alexander got up from the soft easy chair in his book-lined, wood-paneled library and walked toward Michael, his hand outstretched. His gait was more lively than one might have expected from his portly figure; his cherubic face with the clear green eyes was topped by a mass of disheveled hair that managed to stay darker than the years normally permitted. In keeping with his anachronistic life-style, he wore a deep red velvet smoking jacket, something Havelock had not seen since his adolescent days in Greenwich, Connecticut.

"Michael, how *are* you? My God, it's been four, five years now!" cried the journalist in his clipped, high-pitched voice.

"They've served you well, Raymond. You look great."

"*You* don't! Forgive me, young man, but you look like something one of my cats would have left outside. I don't think retirement agrees with you." Alexander released Havelock's hand and quickly raised both of his own. "Yes, I know all about it. I keep track when friends answer questions. Pour yourself a drink; you know the rules here and you look like you need one."

"I will, thanks," said Michael, heading for the familiar copper dry-bar against the wall.

"I suppose you'd look better with some sleep. . . ."

It was the opportune opening. Havelock sat down opposite the journalist and told him the story of the killing in New York and State's flying him back from London at 4:00 A.M., U.K. time.

"I read about that this morning," said Alexander, shaking his head. "Naturally, I thought of you—the name, of course—but knew right away it was ridiculous. You, of all people, with *your* background? Did someone steal an old identification of yours?"

"No, it was mocked, that's what we think. At any rate, it's been a long two days. For a while I thought I was a prisoner."

"Well, they never would have brought you over this way if Anton had been apprised, I can tell you that."

Only Matthias's closest friends called him by his Czech first name, and because Michael knew it, the statement alarmed him. By necessity, it reversed the sequence that Havelock had intended, but it would have been unnatural not to inquire. The Bradford ploy would come last; Matthias now.

"I wondered about that," said Havelock, revolving the glass in his hand, his voice casual. "I simply figured he was too damned busy. As a matter of fact, I was going to ask you if he was in Washington. I'd like to drop in and see him, but my time's limited. I have to get back to London, and if I call him myself . . . well, you know Anton. He'd insist I spend a couple of days."

Alexander leaned forward in the heavily cushioned chair, his intelligent face expressing concern. "You don't know, then?"

"Know what?"

"Damn it, that's when government paranoia goes too far! He's the closest thing you have to a father and you're the closest thing he has to a son! You who've kept the secrets of a thousand operations and they haven't told you."

"Told me what?"

"Anton's ill. I'm sorry you have to hear it from me, Michael."

"How ill?"

"The rumors range from serious to fatal. Apparently he's aware of whichever it is, and, true to form, thinks of himself last. When State learned that I'd found out, he sent me a personal note swearing me to secrecy."

"How did you learn of it?"

"One of those odd things you don't really think about . . . until you think about it. I was inveigled into going to a party in Arlington several weeks ago—you know how I detest those exhausting exercises in verbal endurance, but the hostess was a close friend of my late wife."

"I'm sorry," interrupted Havelock, only vaguely remembering the journalist's wife, a willowy thing who had opted for gardens and flower arrangements. "I didn't know."

"It's all right. It's been over two years now."

"The party in Arlington?"

"Yes, well to my embarrassment a youngish woman who was quite drunk virtually assaulted me. Now, if she'd been a predatory female intent on a sexual liaison, I could have understood her being drawn to the most desirable man on the premises, but I'm afraid it wasn't the case. Apparently, she had marital difficulties of a most unusual nature. Her husband was an army officer absent from the household—read 'connubial bed'— for nearly three months, and no one at the Pentagon would tell her where he was. She feigned illness, which I doubt took a great deal of self-persuasion, and he was brought back on emergency leave. When she got him in her net, she demanded to know where he'd been, what he was doing—read 'other woman.' He refused to tell her, so when soldier-boy was asleep she went through his clothes and found a security pass for a post she'd never heard of; I hadn't either, as a matter of fact. I gather she battered him awake and confronted him, and this time in self-defense he blurted out that it was the highest-priority classification. It was where a very important man was being treated, and he couldn't say any more."

"Anton?" broke in Michael.

"I didn't piece it together until the next morning. The last thing she said to me—before some charitable or oversexed guest drove her home— was that the country should be told about such things, that the government was behaving like Mother Russia. That morning she phoned me, quite sober and in serious panic. She apologized for what she described as her 'ghastly behavior' and pleaded with me to forget everything she'd told me. I was entirely sympathetic, but added that perhaps her instincts were right, although I wasn't the person she should appeal to; there were others who would serve her better. She replied something to the effect that her husband could be ruined, a brilliant military career destroyed. So that was that."

"That was *what?* How did you find out it was Matthias?"

"Because that same morning I read in the *Washington Post* that Anton was prolonging a brief vacation and would not appear before the Senate Foreign Relations Committee. I kept thinking about the woman and what she'd said . . . and the fact that Anton rarely gave up a chance to perform for the Senate newsreels. And then I thought, Why not? Like you, I know where he spends every free moment he has—"

"The Shenandoah lodge," interrupted Havelock, feeling a sense of déjà vu.

"Exactly. I reasoned that if the story was true and he was taking an extra few days, we might get together for some valley fishing or his beloved chess. Like you, again, I have the telephone number, so I called him."

"He wasn't there," said Michael.

"They didn't say that," corrected the journalist. "They said he couldn't come to the phone."

"*That* phone?"

"Yes . . . *that* phone. It was the private line."

"The one that goes unanswered unless he's there."

"Yes." Alexander raised his brandy glass and drank.

Havelock was close to screaming. He wanted to rush over to the portly writer and shake him: *Go on! Go on, tell me!* Instead, he said quietly, "That must have been a shock."

"Wouldn't it have been to you?"

"Certainly." *It was. Can't you see it in my eyes?* "What did you do?"

"The first thing was to call Zelienski. You remember old Leon, don't you? Whenever Matthias drove or flew out to the lodge it was standard procedure for Zelienski to be summoned for dinner—has been standard for years now."

"Did you reach him?"

"Yes, and he told me a very odd thing. He said he hadn't seen Anton in months, that Matthias never answered his calls anymore—not personally—and that he didn't think our great man had time for the valley these days."

The déjà vu was complete for Michael. Then he remembered. "You're a friend of Zelienski's, aren't you?"

"Through Anton, mainly. Very much the way we met. He comes up now and then for lunch and chess. Never for dinner, though; he won't drive at night. But my point is that the one place where Matthias should have been for a holiday he wasn't. I really can't imagine his not seeing old Leon, can you? After all, Zelienski lets him win."

"I can't imagine your letting the issue drop, either."

"You're quite right, I didn't. I called Anton's office and asked to speak with his first assistant. I emphasized that I expected someone who represented the Secretary of State in his absence, as I considered my inquiry to be that substantive. Of *all* people, guess who was put on to me."

"Who?"

"Emory Bradford. Do you remember him? Bradford the 'boomerang,' scourge of the warlords where once he'd been their spokesman. I was fascinated because actually I admire him for having had the courage to reverse himself, but I always thought Matthias detested the whole flock. If anything, he was more sympathetic to those who went down in flames because they *didn't* change their minds."

"What did Bradford tell you?" Michael gripped the glass in his hand, suddenly terrified that he might break it.

"You mean, what did he tell me after I told him what I thought had happened? Naturally, I never mentioned the woman and, God knows, it wasn't necessary. Bradford was in shock. He begged me not to say anything or write anything, that Matthias himself would be in touch with me. I agreed, and by midafternoon, I received Anton's note by messenger. I've abided by his request—until now. I can't for a minute believe he'd want you excluded."

"I don't know what to say." Havelock lessened the pressure on the glass, breathing deeply, the moment to be interpreted in any way the journalist wished. But for Michael it was the prelude to the most important question he might ever have asked in his life. "Do you remember the name of the post where the woman's husband was stationed? The one you'd never heard of before?"

"Yes," said Alexander, studying Havelock. "But no one knows I know. Or my source."

"Will you tell me? No one will ever know *my* source, you have my word on it."

"For what purpose, Michael?"

Havelock paused, then smiled. "Send a basket of fruit probably. A letter, of course."

The journalist nodded his head, smiled and answered, "It's a place called Poole's Island, somewhere off the coast of Georgia."

"Thank you."

Alexander noted his empty glass. "Come now, we're both out. Freshen yours and do mine while you're at it. That's also part of the rules, remember?"

Michael got out of the chair, shaking his head, smiling still, despite the tension he felt. "Be happy to pour yours, but I really have to get going." He picked up the journalist's glass. "I was expected in McLean an hour ago."

"You're *leaving?*" exclaimed the old warhorse, his eyebrows arched, turning in the chair. "What about this piece of information from London you claimed would make up for some of the best meals you ever had, young man?"

Havelock stood at the copper dry-bar, pouring brandy. "I was thinking about that as I drove out here," he said pensively. "I may have been impetuous."

"Spoilsport," said Alexander, chuckling.

"Well, it's up to you. It concerns a very complicated, deep-cover intelligence operation, which in my judgment will take us nowhere. Do you want to hear it?"

"Stop there, dear boy! You've got the wrong scribbler, I wouldn't touch it. I subscribe to Anton's maxim. Eighty percent of all intelligence is a chess game played by idiots for the benefit of paranoid morons!"

Michael climbed into the car; there was the faint odor of cigarettes. "You've been smoking," he said.

"Feeling like a little boy in a graveyard," replied Jenna, curled up on the floor. "What about Bradford? Will your friend bring him out here?"

Havelock started the engine, engaged the gear, and swung rapidly around the circular drive toward the entrance. "You can get up now."

"What about *Bradford?*"

"We're going to let him sweat for a while, stretch him out."

Jenna crawled up on the seat, staring at him. "What are you saying, Mikhail?"

"We're going to drive all night, rest for a while in the morning, then keep going. I want to get there late tomorrow."

"My God, *where?*"

"A place called Poole's Island, wherever it is."

24

The island was off the coast, east of Savannah; five years ago it had been a sparsely populated island of less than two square miles before it was taken over by the government for oceanic research. Several times a week, said the fishermen, helicopters from Hunter Air Force Base could be seen skimming above the water toward an unseen pad somewhere beyond the tall pines that bordered the rocky shoreline.

They had reached Savannah by three-thirty in the afternoon and, by four, had found a nondescript motel on the ocean highway. At four-twenty they walked onto the pier of a commercial marina across the way in time to watch a dozen or so fishing boats come in with the day's catch. By a quarter past five they had talked to various fishermen, and at five-thirty Havelock had a quiet conversation with the manager of the marina. By ten to six $200 had exchanged hands, and a fifteen-foot skiff with a twelve-horsepower outboard had been made available to him, with the hours at his discretion and the night watchman of the marina informed of the rental.

They drove back along the highway to a shopping center in Fort Pulaski where Michael found a sporting-goods store and purchased the items he needed. These included a wool knit hat, tight sweater, chinos and thick, rubber-soled ankle boots—all black. In addition to the clothes, he bought the following: a waterproof flashlight and an oilcloth packet, a hunting knife, and five packages of 72-inch rawhide shoelaces.

"A sweater, a hat, a torch, a knife," Jenna said rapidly, angrily. "You buy one of each. Buy two. I'm going with you."

"No, you're not."

"Do you forget Prague and Warsaw? Trieste or the Balkans?"

"No, but you do. In each place—everywhere we went—there was always a secondary we could fall back on, if only to buy time. Someone at an embassy or a consulate who was given the words that constituted a counterthreat."

"We never used such people."

"We were never caught."

She looked at him, her eyes reluctantly accepting his logic. "What words do *I* have?"

"I'll write them out for you. There's a stationery store across the mall. I want to get a yellow legal pad and carbon paper. Let's go."

Jenna sat in an armchair next to the motel desk where Havelock wrote. Taking the carbon copies from him as he tore them off the yellow pad, she checked the blue impressions for legibility. He had filled up nine pages, each line in precise block letters, each item numbered, every detail specific, every name accurate. It was a compendium of selected top-secret intelligence operations and penetrations perpetrated by the United States government throughout Europe during the past eighteen months. It included sources, informants, deep-cover and double agents, as well as a list of diplomats and attachés in three embassies who, in reality, were controls for the Central Intelligence Agency. On the tenth page he gave an account of Costa Brava naming Emory Bradford and the men he had spoken with who had confirmed evidence that could only have been obtained with the cooperation of the KGB, and of a VKR officer in Paris who admitted Soviet knowledge of the deception. On the eleventh page he wrote of the fatal meeting on the Palatine, and of an American intelligence officer who had died saving his life and, moments before his death, had exclaimed that there were lies being told by powerful men in Washington. On the twelfth he briefly described the events at Col des Moulinets and the order for his execution issued under the code name Ambiguity. On the thirteenth and last page he told the truth about a killer from Lidice who had called himself Jacob Handelman and the purpose of a farm in Mason Falls, Pennsylvania, which sold the services of slaves as efficiently as any camp that had provided labor for Albert Speer. The final line was concise: *Secretary of State Anthony Matthias is being held against his will at a government installation called Poole's Island in Georgia.*

"There are your words," he said, handing Jenna the last page and getting up to stretch. His body ached; he had written furiously for nearly two hours. While Jenna read he lit a cigarette and walked to the window overlooking the highway and the ocean beyond. It was dark, the moon intermittently shining through a night sky streaked with clouds. The weather was fair, the seas normal; he hoped both would stay that way.

"They're strong words, Mikhail," said Jenna, placing the last carbon on the desk.

"It's the truth."

"Forgive me for not approving. You could cost the lives of many people, many friends, with this."

"Not the last four pages. There're no friends there . . . except the Apache, and he's gone."

"Then use only the last four pages," said Jenna.

Havelock turned from the window. "No, I have to go all the way or not at all. There's no middle ground now; they've got to believe I'll do it. More important, they've got to believe *you'll* do it. If there's the slightest doubt, I'm dead and you might as well be. The threat's got to be real, not hollow."

"You're assuming you'll be caught."

"If I find what I think I'm going to find, I intend to be."

"That's insane!" cried Jenna, quickly getting to her feet.

"No, it isn't. You're not usually wrong, but you are now. That island's the shortcut we've been looking for." He walked toward the chair where he had dropped the purchases from the sporting-goods store. "I'll get dressed and we'll work out a telephone relay."

"You mean this, don't you?"

"I mean it."

"Booths, then," she said reluctantly. "No call over twelve seconds."

"But only one number." Michael changed direction and went to the desk. He picked up a pencil, wrote on the pad, tore off the page and gave it to Jenna. "Here it is; it's the Cons Op emergency reception. Dial direct —I'll show you how—and have a pocketbook full of change."

"I have no pocketbook."

"And no money, and no clothes," added Havelock, taking her by the shoulders, pulling her to him. "Remedy that, will you? It'll take your mind off things for a while. Go shopping."

"You're mad."

"No, I mean it. You won't have much time, but most of the stores in that shopping center stay open until ten-thirty. Then there's a bowling alley, a couple of restaurants, and an all-night supermarket."

"I don't *believe* you," she exclaimed, pulling her face back and looking at him.

"Believe," he said. "It's safer than telephone booths on the highway." He glanced at his watch. "It's ten of nine now, and Poole's Island is only a mile and a half offshore. It shouldn't take me more than twenty minutes to reach it—say, by ten. At eleven I want you to start calling that number and say the words 'billiards or pool.' Got it?"

"Certainly. 'Billiards or pool.' "

"Good. If you don't get an immediate response, hang up and get to another phone. Call every fifteen minutes."

"You say a response. What will it be?"

Havelock frowned. " 'We prefer pool.' "

" 'We prefer pool.' Then what?"

"A last call, again fifteen minutes later. Someone else other than the operator will be patched into the emergency line. He won't use a name but he'll give the response. The second he does, read him the first two lines on the first page. I'll take the carbons with me so the words match. Do it fast and hang up."

"And then the waiting begins," said Jenna, holding him, her cheek against his. "Now, our immovable prison."

"Very immovable—stationary, in fact. Pick up food at the supermarket and stay here. Don't go out. I'll reach you."

"How long will it be, do you think?"

Havelock gently pulled his cheek away from hers and looked at her. "It could be as long as a day, two days. I hope not, but it may be."

"And if . . ." Jenna could not finish the sentence, and tears came to her eyes, her face drawn.

"After three days call Alexander in Fox Hollow and tell him I've been killed or taken, that Anton Matthias is being held prisoner. Say you've got the proof in my own handwriting, plus my voice on the tape I made at Salanne's house in Cagnes-sur-Mer. Under the circumstances, he can't walk away from you. He won't. His beloved republic is being poisoned."

Michael paused. "Just the last four pages," he said quietly. "Burn the first nine. You're right, they don't deserve to die."

Jenna closed her eyes. "I cannot promise you that," she said. "I love you so. If I lose you, none of them matters. None."

The water was choppy, as it often was when coastal currents were interrupted by sudden offshore land masses. He was about a quarter of a mile from the island's rocky coastline, approaching from the leeward side, the wind carrying the minimal sound of the engine out to sea. He would cut it off soon and use the oars, rowing forward toward the darkest section of the surrounding pines, guided by the soft glow of light beyond the treetops.

He had made his own separate arrangements with the marina's night watchman, tenuous arrangements any experienced field man would attempt to make if he hired a boat with the possibility that he might have to abandon it. One never gave up means of escape unless it was absolutely necessary, but one obscured those means as best one could, if only to buy time; five minutes of confusion was often the difference between capture and escape. So far, however, the trip had been clean. He would propel the skiff into the blackest inlet and beach it.

Now was the moment. He pushed in the throttle; the engine coughed quietly and died. He jumped to the mid-seat, body forward, and lifted the oars into their locks. The outgoing current was stronger than he had expected, he pressed against the seaward tide, hoping it would alter before his arms and shoulders weakened. The wound from Col des Moulinets was beginning to hurt; he had to be careful and use the weight of his body. . . .

Sound. Not his, not the abrasive creaking of oarlocks or the lapping of waves against the bow. A muffled sound . . . an engine.

A light, a searchlight, sweeping the water about half a mile to his right. It was a patrol boat rounding the far point of the island, veering starboard, directly at him. Did the island's security system include sonar? Sonic beams shooting over the water, rising and falling with the tides, capable of picking up small craft approaching the shore? Or was the boat on a routine patrol? It was not the moment to speculate. Keeping his body low, Havelock swiftly lifted the oars out of their locks, shoving both under the slatted seats so they rested on the floor of the hull. He reached forward for the mooring line, throwing it over the bow, and then slipped over the side into the ocean, breathing deeply and tensing his muscles to ward off the cold. He slid back and held on to the propeller shaft, splashing water over the outboard motor, cooling the top surface. He had traveled at very low throttle; in minutes only a sensitive hand would be able to determine whether the engine had been running—if anyone thought to check.

The searchlight suddenly blinded him; the skiff had been spotted. The faraway engine roared through the wind, joined by the wobbling wail of a siren. The patrol boat accelerated, bearing down on him. He dived under the water, swimming out, away from the island, the current propelling him. The skiff was still nearly a quarter-mile from the shoreline, too far for a swimmer to attempt comfortably in these waters; it was a fact that might weigh in his favor when the boat was found.

By the time the large patrol boat had side-slipped into the skiff and cut its motors, Michael was twenty yards behind its stern, breaking the surface, pulling the wet wool knit hat down over his head. The searchlight was crisscrossing the water everywhere; he went under twice, his eyes open, reemerging when the beam had passed. It continued scanning the area, but no longer behind, only in the front and the sides. Two men with grappling hooks had the skiff in tow; the one at the bow shouted.

"Leo's Marina, Lieutenant! Out of Savannah! Marker number GA zero-eight-two!"

"Tell base to raise Leo's Marina in Savannah and cut us in!" yelled the officer to an unseen radio operator in the open cabin. "The number's GA zero-eight-two! Get a reading!"

"Yes, sir!" came the reply.

"And inform base of our location. Have a security check run on sector four."

"This thing couldn't have gotten in there, Lieutenant," said the man with the stern hook. "It'd be tripped by the flat nets. Everywhere there ain't no rocks we got flat nets."

"Then what the hell's it doing here? Are there any clothes, any equipment? Anything?"

"Nothin', sir!" yelled the first man, climbing down into the skiff. "Stinks of fish, that's all."

Havelock watched while treading and bobbing in the water. He was struck by an odd thing: the men on the patrol boat were in khaki fatigues, the officer in a field jacket. They were army, not navy. Yet the boat had a naval registration.

"Lieutenant!" The voice came from within the cabin as a face with a headset framing it appeared in the open archway. "The watchman at Leo's said a couple of drunks had that skiff out and brought it in late. He figured they didn't tie it up proper and it went out with the tide. He'd appreciate it if we towed it in; it'd be his ass. The boat's shit, but the outboard's worth money."

"I don't like it," said the officer.

"Hey, come on, sir. Who's gonna swim a half-mile in these waters? The fishermen've seen sharks around here."

"Suppose it's *been* in?"

"With the flat nets?" asked the man with the stern hook. "No place else to park, Lieutenant."

"Fuck it! Throw up the line and let's circle around nearer the nets and rocks. This Leo owes us."

And Havelock knew he owed a night watchman far more than the hundred dollars he had given him. The patrol boat's engines roared as the first man climbed aboard and another tied the skiff's mooring line to a stern cleat. In seconds the surface prowler was heading toward the shoreline, crisscrossing the waters as its powerful searchlight roamed the darkness.

Flat nets. Fields of lightweight fabric, stretched and held afloat just below the surface by buoyant cork or Styrofoam, woven together with strands of piano wire. Fish could not break the wires, but propellers could, and if they did, the alarms went off *Rocks.* Stretches of the island's coastline that were prohibitive to vessels of any size. He had to keep the patrol boat in sight; it was approaching the rocks.

Sharks. He did not care to think about them; there simply was no point.

What he had to concentrate on was reaching land. The current was almost intolerable, but by breaststroking between the waves and the undertow beneath he made slow progress, and when he could see the beams of a dozen flashlights shining through the pines, he knew he was getting closer. Time was irrelevant, its passage reflected only in the straining pain in his arms and legs, but his concentration was complete. He had to reach a net or a rock, or some other obstruction beneath him that told him he could stand.

A net came first. He worked himself to the right, hand over hand, slipping on the thick nylon cord, until he felt a huge floating Styrofoam barrel shaped like an ocean buoy. He rounded it and pulled himself in on the border of cord until his knees struck two sharp objects that told him he had reached the rocks. He held on to the net, his body battered by the incoming surf, and waited, gasping for air. The flashlight beams were receding into the pines; the security check in sector four had proven fruitless. When the last beam disappeared between the trunks, he inched his way toward the shore, holding on to the wired net with all his strength as the waves crashed over him. He had to stay away from the rocks! They loomed above him—white, jagged points of stone made razor-sharp by millennia of rushing waters. One enormous wave and he would be impaled.

He lurched to his left, spreading himself over the net, when suddenly it was gone. It was gone! He could feel the sand under him. He had crossed the man-made barrier reef and was on land.

He crawled out of the water, barely able to lift his arms; his legs were drained, weightless appendages that kept collapsing into the wet softness beneath him. The moon made one of its sporadic appearances, illuminating a dune of wild grass twenty yards ahead; he crept forward, each foot bringing him nearer a resting place. He reached the dune and climbed up onto its dry sand; he rolled over on his back and stared at the dark sky.

He remained motionless for the better part of a half hour, until he could feel the blood filling his arms again, the weight returning to his legs. Ten years ago, even five, he reflected, the gauntlet he had struggled through would have taken him fifteen minutes, at most, from which to recover. Now, he would appreciate several hours', if not a night's, sleep and a hot bath.

He lifted his hand and looked at the dial of his watch. It was ten-forty-three. In seventeen minutes Jenna would place her first call to Cons Op emergency reception. He had wanted an hour on the island—to explore, to make decisions—before that first call, but it was not to be. He was forty-three minutes behind schedule. On the other hand, there would have been no schedule at all to adhere to if he had failed to cross the island's barrier reef.

He got to his feet, tested his legs, shook his arms and twisted his torso back and forth, barely noticing the discomfort of his soaked clothing and the abrasive scraping of sand over his entire body. It was enough that he could function, that signals from brain to muscle still filtered through the proper motor controls. He could move—swiftly if he had to—and his mind was clear; he needed nothing else.

He checked his gear. The waterproof flashlight was hooked into a strap around his waist next to the oilcloth packet on his left; the hunting knife in its scabbard was on the right. He removed the packet, unzipped the waterproof flap and felt the contents. The thirteen folded pages were dry. So was the small Spanish automatic. He took out the weapon, shoved it under his belt, and replaced the packet on the strap. He then checked his trouser pockets; the rawhide shoelaces were soaked but intact—each lace separate, rolled into a ball—five in his right-hand pocket, five in the left. If more than ten were needed, then none would be needed. They would all be worthless. He was ready.

Footsteps . . . Were there footsteps? If so, the sound was incongruous with the sand and the soft earth that had to be beneath the ocean pines. It was a slow tattoo of sharp cracks—leather heels beating a hard surface. Havelock crouched and raced toward the cover of the tall trees and peered diagonally to his right in the direction of the sound.

A second tattoo, now on his left, farther away, but coming closer. It was similar to the first—slow, deliberate. He crawled deeper into the pines until he came within several feet of the edge, where he dived prone on the ground; he immediately raised his head to see what the sudden new light would reveal. What he saw explained the sound of the footsteps, but nothing else. Directly ahead was a wide, smoothly surfaced concrete road, and just beyond it was a stockade fence at least twelve feet high extending as far as the eye could see in both directions. The light came from behind it; a roof of light hung everywhere. It was the glow he had seen from the water, now much brighter, but still oddly soft, lacking intensity.

The first soldier appeared on the right, walking slowly. Like the crew on the patrol boat, he wore army fatigues, but strapped to his waist was a government-issue Colt .45 automatic. He was a young foot soldier on guard duty, his bored face reflecting the waste of time and motion. His counterpart emerged from the shadows on the left, perhaps fifty yards away; his walk, if anything, was slower than that of his comrade. They approached each other like two robots on a treadmill, meeting no more than thirty feet from Havelock.

"Did anyone fill you in?" asked the soldier on the right.

"Yeah, some rowboat with a motor drifted out from Savannah with the tide, that's all. No one in it."

"Anybody check the engine?"

"What do you mean?"

"The oil. The oil stays warm if it's been running. Like any motor."

"Hey, come on. Who the hell could get in here, anyway?"

"I didn't say they could. I just said it was one way to tell."

"Forget it. They're still doing a three-sixty search—in case somebody's got wings, I guess. The whips around here are all swacked in the head."

"Wouldn't you be?"

The guard on the left looked at his watch. "You've got a point. See you inside."

"If Jackson shows up, you will. Last night he was a half hour late. Can you believe it? He said he had to see the end of a lousy TV movie."

"He pulls that a lot. Willis told him the other night that someday someone's going to just walk off and say he took over. Let him hang."

"He'd talk his way out of it."

Each man turned and began trudging back on his familiar, useless course. Michael pieced together the essentials of their conversation. A search party was combing the island and the guards' watch was about over —a watch that was apparently loose, if a midnight relief could be a half hour late. It was an inconsistency; the island was a security fortress, yet guard duty was treated as though it were a futile if necessary performance. Why?

The answer, he surmised, might be found in an old observation. Barracks personnel and low-level superiors were the first to perceive unnecessary duty. Which could only mean that the shoreline alarms were matched by interior sensors. Michael studied the high stockade fence. It was new, the wood a pale tan, and it took little imagination to picture the trips wired behind it—dual beams set off by mass, weight and body heat, impossible to tunnel under or vault over or cut through. And then he saw what he had not concentrated on: the fence curved—as the concrete road curved—on both sides. Gates had to be beyond the sight lines, entrances manned by personnel at the only points of penetration. Not casual at all.

A three-sixty search.

Soldiers with flashlights treading through the pines and over the beaches, looking for the shadow of a possibility. They had begun directly behind him, on a stretch of the coastline called sector four, moving quickly—perhaps a dozen men, maybe a thirteen-man squad. Wherever they had come from, they would undoubtedly return to the same place once they had completed the circle . . . and the night was dark, the moonlight increasingly infrequent. Using the search party as part of his strategy was an outside possibility—the only one he could think of—but for the tactic to work, he had to move. *Now.*

The soldier on the right not only was closest but was the most logical to deal with first. He was nearly out of sight, rounding the bend in the road, disappearing beyond the angle of the fence. Havelock got up and ran across the road, then started racing down the sandy shoulder, furious at the sound of his waterlogged boots. He reached the bend; there were gate lights up ahead, perhaps six hundred feet away. He ran faster, closing the gap between himself and the slow-moving guard, hoping the wind rustling through the trees muffled the spongelike crunching beneath him.

He was within twelve feet when the man stopped, alarmed, his head whipping to the side. Havelock sprang, covering the final six feet in midair; his right hand clamped on the soldier's mouth and his left grabbed the base of the man's skull, controlling both their falls to the ground. He held the soldier firmly, his knee under the young man's back, arching the body over it.

"Don't try to shout!" he whispered. "This is only a security exercise—like war games, you understand? Half the garrison here knows about it, half doesn't. Now, I'm going to take you across the road and tie you up and gag you, but nothing'll be too tight. You're simply out of maneuvers. Okay?"

The young guard was too much in shock to respond other than to blink repeatedly with his large, frightened eyes. Michael could not trust him—more accurately, he could not trust him not to panic. He reached for the fallen barracks cap and rose with the soldier, pulling the young man up, his hand still clamped on the mouth; they both dashed across the road, turning right, and headed for the pines. Once in the darkness under the branches, Havelock stopped and tripped the soldier to the ground; they were far enough into sector four.

"Now, I'm going to take my hand away," said Michael, kneeling, "but if you make a sound, I'll have to chop you out, you got that? If I didn't, I'd lose points. Okay?"

The young man nodded and Havelock slowly removed his hand, prepared to clamp it back at the first loud utterance. The guard rubbed his cheeks and said quietly, "You scared the shit out of me. What the hell's going on?"

"Just what I told you," said Michael, unstrapping the soldier's weapons belt and yanking off his field jacket. "It's a security exercise," he added, reaching into his own pocket for a rawhide lace and pulling the guard's arms behind him. "We're going to get inside." He tied the guard's wrists and forearms together, weaving the rawhide up to the elbows.

"Into the compound?"

"That's right."

"No way, man. You lose!"

"The alarm system?"

"It's seven ways to Memphis and back. A pelican got burned on the fence the other night; it sizzled for a goddamn half an hour. Son of a bitch if we didn't have chicken the next day."

"What about inside?"

"What about it?"

"Are there alarms inside?"

"Only in Georgetown."

"What? What's Georgetown?"

"Hey, I know the rules. All I've got to give you is my name, rank, and serial number!"

"The gate," said Havelock menacingly. "Who's on the gate?"

"The gate detail, who else? What goes out comes in."

"Now, you *tell* me—"

A faint glow of light caught Michael's eye; it was far away, through the trees, a distant beam of a flashlight. The search party was rounding the island. There was no more time for conversation. He tore off part of the soldier's shirt, rolled it up and stuffed it into the protesting mouth, then strung another rawhide lace around the young man's face and tied it at the back of his neck, holding the gag in place. A third lace bound his ankles.

Havelock put on the field jacket, strapped the weapons belt around his waist, removed his wool knit hat and shoved it into a pocket. He put the barracks cap on his head, pulling it down as far as he could, then reached under his soaked sweater and unhooked the waterproof flashlight. He judged the angles of passage through the trees, the distance of the emerging beams of light, and started running diagonally to his right through the pines—toward an edge of a rock or beach, he had no idea which.

He clung to the rock, the crashing sea beneath him, the wind strong, and waited until the last soldier passed above. The instant he did, Michael pulled himself up and raced toward the receding figure; with the experience born of a hundred such encounters, he grabbed the man around the neck, choking off all sound as he yanked him to the ground. Thirty seconds later the unconscious soldier was bound—arms, legs and mouth. Havelock ran to catch up with the others.

"All right, you guys!" shouted an authoritative voice. "Screw-off time is over! Back to your kennels!"

"Shit, Captain," yelled a soldier. "We thought you were bringing in a boatload of broads and this was a treasure hunt!"

"Call it a trial run, *gumbà*. Next time you may score."

"He can't even score on the pinball!" shouted another. "What's he gonna do with a broad?"

Havelock followed the beams of light through the pines. The road appeared—the light-colored smooth concrete reflecting the harsh glare of the gate lights. The squad crossed the road in a formless group, Michael jostling himself ahead so there would be soldiers behind him. They passed through the steel structure, a guard shouting off the numbers as each man went past.

"*One, two, three, four . . .*"

He was number eight; he put his head down, rubbing his eyes.

"*Seven, eight, nine . . .*"

He was inside. He took his hands away from his eyes as he moved with the squad across an oddly smooth surface, and looked up.

His breathing stopped, his legs froze. He was barely able to move forward, for he was in another time, another place. What he saw in front of him and around him was surreal. Abstract images, isolated fragments of an unearthly scene.

He was not inside a compound on a small land mass off the Georgia coast called Poole's Island. He was in Washington, D.C.

25

It was something out of a macabre dream, reality twisted, abstracted, deformed to fulfill a demonic fantasy. Scaled-down models of familiar sights were alongside six-foot-high photographic blowups of places he knew only too well. There were small, narrow, tree-lined streets, abruptly starting, suddenly ending, falling off into dirt, and street signs and street-lamps—all in miniature. The soft glow of light that came from the lamps washed over massive, life-size doorways and on buildings—which were not buildings but only the façades of buildings.

There were the glass doors of the Department of State. And over there, the stone entrance of the new FBI Building, and across the way, beyond a tiny park dotted with small white benches, the brown steps leading to the main doors of the Pentagon. Far to his left he could see a tall black wrought-iron fence with an opening in the center to accommodate a drive flanked by two tiny glass-enclosed guardhouses. It was the South Portico entrance to the White House.

Incredible!

And automobiles of normal sizes glistening. A taxi, two army staff cars, two outsized limousines, all parked separately, stationary symbols of another place. And there were the unmistakable symbols seen in the distance to his right beyond the miniature park: small alabaster models—no more than four feet in size—of the Jefferson Memorial, the Washington Monument, and small compact duplicates of the Reflecting Pool on the Mall . . . all bathed in light . . . from far away perfect renditions, unmistakable landmarks.

It was all there, all *insane!* It was a spread-out movie set, filled with outlandish grainy photographs, miniaturized models, partial structures. The whole scene could have been the product of a mad imagination, a film maker intent on exploring a white-light nightmare that was his warped, personal statement about Washington, D.C.

Uncanny.

A bizarre, false world had been created to present a distorted version of the real one hundreds of miles away!

It was more than Havelock could absorb. He had to break away and find a few moments of sanity, to try to piece together the meaning of the macabre spectacle. To find Anton Matthias.

The squad began to separate, several to the left, others to the right. Beyond the false façade of State was a receding lawn, and low-hanging willows, then darkness. Suddenly a prolonged burst of cursing came from behind, from the entrance gate, and Michael tensed.

"Goddamned son-of-a-bitch-fuck-off, where *is* he!"

"Who, Sergeant?"

"Jackson, Lieutenant! He's late again!"

"He goes on report, Sergeant. This duty's become far too lax. I want it tightened up."

There were amused rumblings from the search-party squad, a number looking behind, laughing quietly. Havelock took advantage of the moment to slip down the street and around the corner into the shadows of the lawn.

He leaned against a cinder-block wall; it was solid. It enclosed something within and was not part of the false front. He crouched in the darkness trying to think, trying to understand. And that was the problem: it was beyond his understanding. He knew, of course, about the Soviet training center in Novgorod called the American Compound, a vast complex where everything was "Americanized," where there were stores and supermarkets and motels and gas stations, where everyone used U.S. currency and spoke American English, slang and different dialects. And he had heard about further Soviet experiments in the Urals, where entire U.S. army camps had been built, American military customs and regulations followed with extraordinary accuracy, and where, again, only American English was spoken, barracks language encouraged, everything authentic down to the most minute detail. Then, of course, there were the *paminyatchiki*—the so-called travelers—a deep-cover operation scorned as a paranoid fantasy by Rostov in Athens, but still alive, still functioning. These were men and women who had been brought over as infants and placed in homes as sons and daughters, growing up entirely within the American experience, but whose mission as adults was to serve the Soviet Union. It was said—and confirmed by Rostov—that the *paminyatchik* apparatus had been absorbed by the Voennaya, that maniacally secretive cult of fanatics that even the KGB found difficult to control. It was further rumored that some of these fanatics had reached positions of power and influence. Where did rumor stop and reality begin? What was the reality here?

Was it possible? Was it even conceivable that Poole's Island was peopled by graduates of Novgorod and the Urals, whose lower ranks were filled out by *paminyatchiki* coming of age, and whose highest ranks were run by still other *paminyatchiki* who had risen to positions of power at State, who were capable of abducting Anton Matthias? Emory Bradford . . . was *he* . . . ?

Perhaps it was all rumor and nothing else. Men in Washington were working with men in Moscow; there was madness enough in that acknowledged connection.

He was not going to learn anything crouched in the shadows of a cinder-block wall; he had to move, explore—above all, not be caught. He edged his way to the corner of the building and peered around it at the softly lit tree-lined streets and the tiny structures that surrounded it. Beyond the guard detail at the gate a trio of officers strolled through the miniature park in the direction of the alabaster monuments in the distance, and four enlisted men hurried toward a large Quonset hut set back on a lawn between two unfamiliar brick structures that looked like the first floors of some tasteful apartment complex. Then, to Havelock's surprise, a civilian emerged from the doorway of the brick building on the left, followed by another, in a white laboratory coat, who seemed to be speaking quietly but emphatically. Michael wondered briefly if the language was Russian. The two men walked down the path and turned right to a set-piece "intersection," whose simulated traffic lights, however, were not operating. They turned right again, continuing their conversation, the first civilian now upbraiding his white-coated companion, but not obstreperously. Nothing was loud; the scene was still, with only the penetrating cacophony of the crickets breaking the stillness. Whatever secrets Poole's Island held, they were buried beneath a peaceful exterior—itself a lie created by liars.

As the two civilians walked down the allée and out of sight, Havelock noticed the metal sign affixed to a post on the other side of the street. Had he seen it before? Of course he had! Every time he had driven or taken a cab out to Matthias's house in Georgetown. There was a blue arrow preceded by the words CHESAPEAKE AND OHIO CANAL. It was the picturesque waterway that separated the stridency of Washington from the tranquillity of the residential enclaves in Georgetown, whose quiet streets housed the wealthiest and most powerful men in the nation's capital.

Georgetown.

Are there alarms inside?

Only in Georgetown.

Anton Matthias was somewhere down that street, somewhere over a bridge, with or without water, in a house that was a lie. My *God!* Had they simulated his house so as to rehearse his abduction? It was entirely possible; Anton's residence was protected by presidential order, guards were on duty around the clock to protect the nation's most valuable living asset. It was not only possible, it was the only way it could have been done. Matthias *had* to have been taken at home, the alarms circumvented, the guards pulled away and replaced by State Department orders—orders issued by liars. A mission had been rehearsed and executed.

He moved out into the street, walking casually—an enlisted man getting some air or getting away from his fellow soldiers. He reached the brick building on the left and crossed over the lawn to the sidewalk; the receding street was dark, no lamps shone above the line of short trees. He walked faster, feeling more comfortable in the shadows, and noted the paths that turned to the right, leading to a row of three Quonsets—there were lights in several windows and the glow of a few television sets. He assumed these were the living quarters of whatever officers there were and their civilian counterparts. Graduates of Novgorod and the Urals?

Suddenly, civilization stopped. The street and the sidewalk ended and there was nothing ahead but a dirt road bordered by high foliage and darkness. But it was a road; it led somewhere. Havelock began a slow lope; jogging would be his excuse if he was stopped—before he took out his interrogator. He thought of Jenna, going from telephone booth to telephone booth five miles away on the mainland, reaching a bewildered Cons

Op emergency operator and saying words that brought no response: there might never be a response. Michael understood that, and, strangely, it served only to infuriate him. One accepted the risks in his profession and treated them with respect, for they induced fear and caution—a valuable protection—but one could not accept betrayal by one's own. It was the final circle of futility, proof of the ultimate sham—of a wasted life.

A glow of light. Far down the road, to the left. He broke into a run, and as he came nearer he knew what it was: the outlines of a house, part of a house, a house that stopped at the second floor—but the first two stories were unmistakable. It was the façade of Anton's home in Georgetown, the area of the street accurate in every detail. He approached the end of the dirt road and halted where the tarred surface began on the left. He stared in disbelief.

The brick steps were the same brick steps that led up to the porticoed entrance with the white door and the carriage lamps and the brass hardware. Everything was identical with its original hundreds of miles away, even to the lace curtains in the windows; he could picture the rooms inside and knew that they, too, were the same. The lessons of Novgorod had been learned well, their fruits transplanted to a small island minutes away from the coast of the United States, *seconds* by air. *My God, what's happened?*

"Stay right where you are, soldier!" The command came from behind. "What the *hell* do you think you're doing out here!"

Havelock turned, covering the .45 as best he could. A guard stepped out of the foliage with a gun in his hand, but he was not military; he was dressed in civilian clothes. Havelock said, "What's wrong with you? A guy can't take a walk?"

"You weren't walking, you were running."

"Jogging, pal. Ever heard of it?"

"Every morning, *pal*, when I don't pull this late-night crap. But on the island road with everybody else, not down here. You know the rules. No one goes past sector six; you don't go off the macadam."

"Hey, come on, man," said Havelock. "Don't be a hard-nose—"

A sudden swelling of music burst from the house, filling the night and drowning out the crickets. Michael knew it well; it was one of Matthias's favorites. Handel's *Water Music*. His *přitel* was there!

"Every night, a goddamn concert," said the civilian.

"How come?"

"How the hell do I know? He goes into the garden and plays that stuff for an hour or more."

Music is for thought, Mikhail. The better the music, the better the thinking. There's a causal relationship, you know.

"Nice of you people to let him have it."

"Why not? What else has he got, and where's he going to go? But *you're* going to get your GI ass in a sling if you don't get out of here." The guard holstered his gun inside his jacket. "You're lucky I don't— Hey, wait a minute! You've got a weapon!"

Havelock lunged, gripped the man's throat and hurled him to the ground over his left leg. He fell on the guard and rammed his knee into the man's chest as he ripped the field jacket open and pulled out the hunting knife. "You're not lucky at all!" he whispered. "Where are you from, *skotina?* Novgorod? The Urals? A *paminyatchik?*" Michael held the point of the knife's blade between the guard's nostrils and lips. "I'm going to cut your face off unless you tell me what I want to know. First, how many men are up there? *Easy!*" He released the pressure on the man's throat; the guard coughed.

"You'll . . . never get off here," he choked.

Havelock drew blood, the trickle covering the man's lips. "Don't push me, butcher! I have a lot of memories, *ponimayu.* How many *men?*"

"One."

"*Liar!*"

"No, *one!* The two of us are on till four. One outside, one inside!"

"Alarms. Where are they? *What* are they?"

"Crossbeams, shoulder to knee. In the door."

"That's *all?*"

"It's all that's on. To keep him in."

"The garden?"

"Wall. Too high. For Christ's sake, where's he going to *go?* Where are *you* going to go?"

"We'll see." Michael pulled the guard's head up by his hair, then dropped the knife and struck him, a sharp, hard blow behind the right ear; the man collapsed. Havelock took out a rawhide lace, cut it in two with the knife, and bound the guard's hands and feet. Finally, he gagged the man with his own handkerchief, tying the cloth in place with one of the three remaining laces. He dragged the unconscious body into the foliage and started for the "house."

The *Water Music* soared into its thematic march, horns and strings intermingling, reverberating above and behind the half-house. Havelock climbed the short hill that bordered the brick steps until he was within ten feet of the first lace-curtained window. He crouched and crept to it, his head below the sill, then stepped to the side and stood up. He inched his face to the glass. The room was exactly as he remembered it from another time and place. The worn, fine Oriental rugs, the heavy, comfortable armchairs, the brass lamps; it was Matthias's sitting room—his parlor, as he called it—a place to greet visitors. Michael had spent many pleasant hours in that room, yet this was not that room.

He crouched and made his way to the edge of the strange structure, rounded the corner, and started toward the rear, toward a wall he could picture in his mind, a wall that enclosed a garden—hundreds of miles away. There were three windows to pass, to duck under, to check, and the second window told him what he had to know. Inside, a heavyset man sat on a couch, smoking a cigarette, his feet on a coffee table, watching television. The volume was high, apparently to counteract the stereophonic sound of the music.

Havelock ran to the wall and jumped; he clung to the top with both hands, and then, his chest aching and the wound close to tearing apart, he pulled himself up. He lay prone, catching his breath, letting the pain subside.

Below, the eerily lit garden was as he remembered it. Soft light coming from the house, a single lamp on the all-important chess table between two brown wicker chairs, other white wicker furniture, and a slate path roaming in circles around the beds of flowers.

There he was, his beloved *přítel,* sitting in a chair at the end of the garden, his eyes closed, seeing images the music evoked in his mind. The tortoiseshell glasses were still in place; the silver hair waved back over his strong head.

Silently Havelock swung his legs over the side, rolled on his stomach and dropped to the ground. He stayed in the shadows for several moments; the music had dropped to pianissimo, and the sound of the television could be heard distinctly. The guard would remain inside—that was to say, he would remain inside until Michael wanted him. And when he had taken the hired gun of liars, he would use him or kill him. Somehow.

Havelock came away slowly from the wall and walked down the circular path toward Matthias.

For no apparent reason the statesman suddenly opened his eyes. Michael rushed forward holding up both hands, the gesture a command for silence—but it was ignored. Matthias spoke, his deep voice rising with the music. *"To je dobré srovnání,* Mikhail. So good of you to come around. I was thinking about you the other day, about that paper you wrote several weeks ago. What was it? The 'Effects of Hegelian Revisionism' or some such immodest and inappropriate title. After all, my *darebák akademik*, Hegel is his own best revisionist, no? The *revisionist maximus!* How do you like that?"

"Anton . . . ?"

Again suddenly, without warning, Matthias rose from his chair, eyes wide in a face that was contorted. He began backing away unsteadily, his arms crossed in front of his chest, his voice now a horrible whisper: *"No! You cannot . . . you must not . . .* come near me! You don't understand, you can never understand! *Get away from me!"*

Havelock stared; the shock was as unbearable as the truth.

Anthony Matthias was insane.

BOOK THREE

26

"Raise your hands! Walk to the wall and spread your legs! *Move!* . . . *Now!* Lean into the brick, palms *straight out!*"

As if in a trance, his eyes still on Matthias, who was crouching like a child on one knee by a rosebush, Havelock did as the guard ordered. He was in shock, his impressions a blur, his thoughts suspended. His *přítel,* his mentor . . . his father . . . was mad. The shell of the man who had astonished the world with his brilliance, with his perceptions, was cowering by the flowers, his head trembling, the frightened eyes behind the glasses filled with a terror no one knew but himself.

Havelock had heard the guard's footsteps on the slate and known the blow was coming. Somehow it had not mattered. Nothing mattered.

A spreading web of pain shuddered through his head, and the darkness came.

He was on a parlor rug, circles of bright white light spinning in front of his eyes, his temples throbbing, his drenched, sand-filled trousers pressing against his skin. He could hear men rushing up the steps outside, barking orders in panic. As they came through the door he felt his jacket, his waist; his gun had been taken, but he had not been searched. Presumably, that process and the interrogation would be left to the guard's superiors.

Two men approached: one in uniform, a major; the other, a civilian. He knew the latter; he was from State, an agent from Cons Op he had worked with in London or Beirut, or Paris or . . . he could not recall.

"That's him," said the civilian. "Bradford told me it might be—he didn't know how—but it is. He gave me the details; you're not involved."

"Just get him out of here," replied the soldier. "What you do is your business."

"Hello, Havelock." The man from State looked down with contempt. "You've been busy. It must have been fun killing that old guy in New York. What were you doing? Setting him up for contingency funds, with a little more of the same down here? Get on your feet, you bastard!"

Body and head racked, Michael slowly rolled onto his knees and pushed himself up. "What happened to him? What *happened?*"

"I don't answer questions."

"Somebody has to . . . for Christ's sake, *somebody* has to!"

"And give you a free ticket? No way, you son of a bitch." The civilian addressed the guard, who was standing across the room. "Did you search him?"

"No, sir. I just removed his weapon and punched the alarm. There's a flashlight on his belt and some kind of pouch."

"Let me help you, Charley," said Havelock, spreading the field jacket and reaching for the oilcloth packet. "It *is* Charley, isn't it? Charley Loring . . . was it Beirut?"

"It was, and keep your goddamned hands still!"

"What you want's in there. Go on, take it. It won't detonate."

The man from State nodded at the major; the soldier stepped forward and grabbed Michael's hands as Charles Loring ripped the packet off the webbed belt.

"Open it," continued Havelock. "It's from me to you. All of you."

The Cons Op agent unzipped the packet and took out the folded yellow pages. The major released his grip as the civilian walked to a floor lamp and began reading. He stopped, looked over at Michael, then spoke to the soldier. "Wait outside, Major. And you," he added, glancing at the guard. "In the other room, please."

"Are you sure?" asked the officer.

"Very," said Charley. "He's not going anywhere, and I'll shout if I need you." The two men left, the soldier out the front door, the guard into the next room. "You're the lowest piece of garbage I've ever known," said the man from State.

"It's a carbon, Charley."

"I can see that."

"Call Cons Op emergency. Every fifteen minutes since eleven o'clock they've gotten a message. It's in the form of a question: 'Billiards or pool?' The response is, 'We prefer pool.' Tell them to give it."

"Then what?"

"Patch yourself into the next call, give the response, and listen."

"So some other piece of garbage can read this to me."

"Oh, no, just twelve seconds' worth. No way to trace. And don't bother to think about giving me a needle. I've been in therapy before, so I took precautions. I have no idea where the calls are coming from, take my word."

"I wouldn't take your word for a goddamn thing, *garbage!*"

"You'd better right now, because if you don't, copies of those pages will be sent to appropriate addresses all over Europe. From Moscow to Athens, from London to Prague—from Paris to Berlin. Get on the phone."

Twenty-one minutes later the man from State stared at the wall as he gave the response to Jenna Karas. Eleven seconds after that he hung up and looked over at Havelock. "You're everything they said you were. You're filth."

"And 'beyond salvage'?"

"That's right."

"Then so are you, because you're programmed, Charley. You're useless. You forgot how to ask questions."

"*What?*"

"You just accepted the verdict on me. You knew me—knew my record —but it didn't make any difference. The word came down and the good little sheep said, 'Why not?' "

"I could *kill* you."

"And live with the consequences? Don't do that. Call the White House."

He could hear the deafening roar of the giant helicopter's rotating blades and knew that the President of the United States had arrived at Poole's Island. It was midmorning, and the Georgia sun was burning the pavements outside the open window. He was in a room, but there was no question that it was a cell even though there were no bars in the single window. He was two stories off the ground; there were four soldiers beneath, and the eerie façades and photographs of familiar buildings could be seen beyond. A world of lies, of artifice, of transplanted, warped reality.

Havelock walked back to the bed—more cot than bed—and sat down. He thought of Jenna, what she must be going through—again; what resources she had to summon to survive the unbearable tension. And of Matthias—good God, what had *happened?* Michael relived the horrible scene in the garden, trying to find a thread of sense.

You must not come near me. You don't understand. You can never understand!

Understand *what?*

He had no idea how long he sat there thinking; he only knew that his thoughts were interrupted by the crack of the glass panel in the center of the door. A face appeared; it was under the gold braid of a visored cap. The door opened, and a broad-shouldered, middle-aged colonel walked in, gripping a pair of handcuffs.

"Turn around," he ordered. "Extend your arms."

Havelock did as he was told, and the cuffs were clamped around his wrists. "What about my feet?" asked Michael curtly. "Aren't they considered weapons?"

"I'll have a much more effective one in my hand," said the officer, "and I'll be watching you every second. You pull one thing I could even misinterpret, I'm inside, and you're dead."

"A one-on-one conference. I'm flattered."

The colonel spun Havelock around. "I don't know who you are, or what you're doing, or what you've done, but you remember this, cowboy. That man is my responsibility, and there's no way I wouldn't blow you out of this room and ask questions later."

"Who's the cowboy?"

As if to punctuate his threat, the officer shoved Michael back into the wall. "Stay there," he commanded, and left the room.

Thirty seconds later the door was opened again, and President Charles Berquist walked in. In his hand were the thirteen carbons of Havelock's indictment. The President stopped, and looked at Michael. He raised the yellow pages.

"This is an extraordinary document, Mr. Havelock."

"It's the truth."

"I believe you. I find a great part of it beneath contempt, of course, but then, I tell myself that a man with your record would not cavalierly cause the exposure and death of so many. That, basically, this is a threat —an irresistible threat—to make yourself heard."

"Then you'd be telling yourself another lie," said Michael, motionless against the wall. "I was placed 'beyond salvage.' Why should I concern myself with anyone?"

"Because you're an intelligent man who knows there have to be explanations."

"Lies, you mean?"

"Some are lies and they will remain lies for the good of this country."

Havelock paused, studying the hard Scandinavian face of the President, the steady eyes that were somehow a hunter's eyes. "Matthias?"

"Yes."

"How long do you think you can bury him here?"

"For as long as we possibly can."

"He needs help."

"So do we. He had to be stopped."

"What have you done to him?"

"I was only part of it, Mr. Havelock. So were you. We all were. We made him an emperor when there were no personal empires to be allocated by divine right, much less ours. We made him a god when we didn't own the heavens. There's only so much the mind can absorb and act upon when elevated to such heights in these very complicated times. He was forced to exist in the perpetual illusion of being unique, above all other men. We asked too much. He went mad. His mind—that extraordinary instrument—snapped, and when it could no longer control itself, it sought control elsewhere. To compensate, perhaps, to convince himself that he was what we said he was, although a part of him told him he wasn't. Not any longer."

"What do you mean 'sought control elsewhere'? How could he do that?"

"By committing this nation to a series of obligations that were, to say the least, unacceptable. Try to understand, he had feet of quicksilver, not of clay, like you and me. Yes, even me, the President of the United States, some say the most powerful man in the world. It's not true. I'm bound by the body politic, subject to the goddamn polls, guided by the so-called principles of a political ideology, with my head on a congressional chopping block. Checks and balances, Mr. Havelock. But not him. We made him a superstar; he was bound to nothing, accountable to no one. His word was law, all other judgments were subordinate to his brilliance. And then there was his charm, I might add."

"Generalities," said Michael. "Abstractions."

"Lies?" asked Berquist.

"I don't know. What are the specifics?"

"I'm going to show you. And if after what you've seen, you still feel compelled to carry out your threat, let it be on your head, not mine."

"I don't have a head. I'm 'beyond salvage.' "

"I told you, I've read these pages. All of them. The order's been rescinded. You have the word of the President of the United States."

"Why should I accept it?"

"If I were you, I probably wouldn't. I'm simply telling you. There are many lies and there will continue to be lies, but that's not one of them. . . . I'll have the handcuffs removed."

The scene in the large, dark, windowless room was an unearthly depiction of a science-fiction nightmare. There were a dozen television screens mounted in a row on the wall, monitors that recorded and taped the activities seen by the various cameras. Below the screens was an enormous console manned by four technicians; several white-jacketed doctors entered, watching a scene or scanning tapes, writing notes, leaving quickly or conferring with colleagues. And the object of the whole sophisticated operation was to record and analyze every movement made and every word spoken by Anthony Matthias.

His face and body were projected on seven screens at once, and under each monitor was a green digital readout showing the exact hour and minute of the filming; the screen on the far left was marked *Current.* The day was an illusion for Matthias, starting with morning coffee in the garden identical with his own in Georgetown.

"Before he wakes, he's given two injections," said the President, sitting next to Havelock at a second, smaller console at the rear wall. "One's a muscle relaxant that reduces physical and mental tensions; the other, a stimulant that accelerates the heart, pumping blood, without interfering with the first narcotic. Don't ask me the medical terms, I don't know them; I just know it works. He's free to associate with a degree of simulated confidence—in a way, a replica of his former self."

"Then his day begins? His . . . simulated day?"

"Exactly. Read the monitors from right to left. His day starts with breakfast in the garden. He's brought intelligence reports and newspapers corresponding to the dates of whatever issue is being probed. Then in the next screen you see him walking out of his 'home' and down his steps with an aide who's talking to him, refining the options of the problem, building up the case, whatever it is. Everything, by the way, is taken from his logs; that remains constant throughout 'the day.' " Berquist paused, and gestured at the third monitor from the right. "There you see him in his limousine, the aide still talking, bringing his focus back. He's driven around for a while, then gradually brought in sight of places that are familiar to him, the Jefferson Memorial, the monument, certain streets, past the South Portico—the sequence is irrelevant."

"But they're not *whole,*" insisted Michael. "They're fragments!"

"He doesn't see that; he sees only the impressions. But even if he did see that they are fragments, as you call them, or miniatures of the existing places, the doctors tell me his mind would reject that and accept the reality of the impressions. Just as he refused to accept his own deterioration, and kept pressing for wider and wider responsibilities, until he simply reached out and took them. . . . Watch the fourth screen. He's getting out at the State Department, going inside, and telling his aide something; it will be studied. In the fifth, you can see him walking into his office— the same in every respect as his own on the eighth floor—and immediately scanning the cables and reading the day's appointments, again identical with those that were there at the time. The sixth shows him taking a series of phone calls, the same calls he had taken before. Often his responses are meaningless, a part of him rejecting a voice, or a lack of authentic repartee, but other times what we learn is mind-blowing. . . . He's been here nearly six weeks, and there are times when we think we've only scratched the surface. We're only beginning to learn the extent of his massive excesses."

"You mean the things he's done?" asked Havelock, recoiling from the frightening turn of events.

Berquist looked at Michael in the glow of the console and the flickering light emanating from the screens across the room. "Yes, Mr. Havelock, the—'things'—he's done. If ever a man in the history of representative government exceeded the authority of his office, Anthony Matthias is that man. There were no limits to what he promised—what he *guaranteed*— in the name of the United States government. Take today. A policy was set and in the process of being implemented, but it did not suit the Secretary of State at this particular moment of irrationality, so he altered

it. . . . Watch the seventh screen, the one marked *Current.* Listen. He's
at his desk, and in his mind he's back about five months, when a bipartisan
decision had been made to close an embassy in a new African country
slaughtering its citizens with mass hangings and death squads, revolting
the civilized world. The aide is explaining."

Mr. Secretary, the President and the Joint Chiefs, as well as the Senate,
have gone on record as opposing any further contact at this time . . .

Then we won't tell them, will we? Antediluvian reactions cannot be a
keystone of a coherent foreign policy. I shall make contact myself and
present a cohesive and judicious plan. Arms and well-sweetened butter are
international lubricants, and we shall provide them.

Michael was stunned. "He said that? He *did* that?"

"He's reliving it now," replied Berquist. "In a few minutes he'll place
a call to the mission in Geneva, and another unbelievable commitment
will be made. . . . This, however, is only a minor example, one they're
working on this morning. Actually, as outrageous as it is, it's insignificant
compared with so many others. So many—so dangerous—so incredible."

"Dangerous?"

"One voice overriding all others, entering unthinkable negotiations,
processing agreements contrary to everything this nation supposedly
stands for—agreements that would make an outraged Congress impeach
me for even considering. But even that fact—and it *is* a fact—is insignificant. We can't let the world know what he's done. We'd be humiliated,
a giant on its knees, begging forgiveness, and if it was not forthcoming
there would be guns and bombs. You see, he's put it all in writing."

"Could he *do* that?"

"Not constitutionally, no. But he was the superstar. The uncrowned
king of the republic had spoken, a god had given his word. Who questions
kings or gods? The mere existence of such documents is the most fertile
grounds on earth for international extortion. If we can't quietly invalidate
those negotiations—diplomatically void them by anticipated congressional rejection—they *will* be exposed. If they are, every treaty, every
agreement we've concluded during the past decade—all the sensitive
alliances we're currently negotiating everywhere in the world—will be
called into question. This country's foreign policy will collapse; we'd never
be trusted again. And when a nation such as ours has no foreign policy,
Mr. Havelock, it has war."

Michael leaned over the console, staring at the *Current* screen, and brought his hand to his forehead; he felt the beads of perspiration. "He's gone this far?"

"Beyond. Remember, he's been Secretary of State for nearly six years, and before he took office his influence was significant, perhaps too much so, in the two previous administrations. He was nothing short of an ambassador-plenipotentiary for both, roaming the globe, cementing his power bases."

"But they were for *good,* not this!"

"They were, and no one knew it better than I did. I'm the one who convinced him that he should chuck the consulting business and take over. I said the world needed his imprimatur, the time was right. You see, I appealed to his ego; all great men have outrageous egos. De Gaulle was right: the man of destiny knows it before anybody else. What he doesn't know is the limit of his capabilities. God knows Matthias didn't."

"You said it a few minutes ago, Mr. President. We made him a god. We asked too much of him." Havelock shook his head slowly, overwhelmed.

"Just hold it there," answered Berquist, his voice cold, his eyes penetrating in the incandescent reflections of light. "I said it by way of an oversimplified explanation. No one makes a man a god unless that man wants to *be* one. And, Christ-on-a-raft, Matthias has been looking for that divine appointment all his life! He's been tasting the holy water for years —in his mind, *bathing* in it. . . . You know what someone called him the other day? A hustling Socrates on the Potomac, and that's exactly what he was. A hustler, Mr. Havelock. A grade-A, high-IQ, brilliant *opportunist.* A man with extraordinarily persuasive words, capable of first-rate global diplomacy—the best we could field—as long as *he* was the eye of the worldwide hurricane. He could be magnificent and, as I also said, no one knew it better than I did and I used him. But for all of that, he was a hustler. He never stopped pushing the *omniscient* Anthony Matthias."

"And knowing this," said Michael, refusing to permit Berquist's stare to cower him, "you still used him. *You* pushed him as much as he pushed himself. You appealed to a 'man of destiny,' wasn't that it?"

The President lowered his eyes to the dials on the console. "Yes," he said softly. "Until he blew.apart. Because I was watching a performance, not the man, and I was blinded. I didn't see what was really happening."

"Jesus!" exclaimed Havelock, his whisper a cry. "It's all so hard to believe!"

"On that assumption," interrupted Berquist, regaining his composure, "I've had several tapes prepared for you. They're reenactments of actual conversations that took place during his final months in office. The psychiatrists tell me they're valid, and the papers we've unearthed bear them out. Put on the earphones and I'll press the appropriate buttons. . . . The images will appear on the last monitor on the right."

What took place on that screen during the next twelve minutes was a portrait of a man Havelock did not know. The tapes showed Matthias at emotional extremes as he was psychologically stimulated by the combined effects of the chemicals and the visual trappings, and prodded by aides using his own words. He was screaming one moment, weeping the next, cajoling a diplomat over the phone with charm and flattery—and brilliant humility—then condemning the man as a fool and a moron once the conversation was finished. Above all were the lies, where once there had been essential truth. The telephone was his instrument; his resonant voice with its European cadence, the organ.

"This first," said Berquist, angrily stabbing a button, "is his response to me when I had just told him I wanted a reassessment of foreign aid in San Miguel."

Your policy is firm, Mr. President, a clear call for decency and human rights. I applaud you, sir. Good-bye. . . . Idiot! Imbecile! One does not have to endorse a brother, one must merely accept geopolitical realities! Get me General Sandoza on the line. Set up a very private appointment with his ambassador. The colonels will understand we back them!

"This little number followed a joint House and Senate resolution, which I thoroughly endorsed, to withhold diplomatic recognition . . ."

You understand, Mr. Prime Minister, that our existing accords in your part of the world prohibit what you suggest, but you should know that I am in agreement with you. I'm meeting with the President . . . no, no, I assure you he will have an open mind . . . and I have already convinced the chairman of the Senate Foreign Relations Committee. A treaty between our two countries is desirable progress, and should it be in contradistinction to prior agreements . . . well, enlightened self-interest was the essence of Bismarck's reign.

"I can't believe this," said Havelock, mesmerized.

"Neither did I, but it's true." The President pushed a third button. "We're now in the Persian Gulf . . ."

You are, of course, speaking unofficially, not as your country's Minister of Finance but as a friend, and what you are seeking are additional guaran-

tees of eight hundred and fifty million for your current fiscal year, and one billion two hundred million for the next. . . . Contrary to what you may believe, my good friend, they are entirely plausible figures. I say this confidentially, but our territorial strategies are not what they appear. I shall prepare, again on a confidential basis, a memorandum of intent.

"Now we're in the Balkans, a Soviet satellite, loyal to Moscow, and at our throats. . . . Insanity!"

Mr. Premier, the restrictions on arms sales to your nation, if they cannot be lifted outright, will be overlooked. I find specific and considerable advantages in our cooperating with you. "Equipment" can and will be funneled through certain North African regimes considered to be in our adversary's camp but with whom I've met—shall we say ex- et non-officio —recently and frequently. Confidentially, a new geopolitical axis is being formed . . .

"Being formed!" exploded Berquist. "Suicide! Here's a coup in the Yemens. Instability on course, wholesale bloodshed guaranteed!"

The emerging of a great new independent nation, Sirach Bal Shazar, though slow to gain the recognition you deserve, will have the quiet support of this administration. We recognize the necessity of dealing firmly and realistically with internal subversion. You may be assured that the funds you ask for will be allocated. Three hundred million once transferred will indicate to the legislative branch of our government the faith we place in you.

"Finally," said the President, touching a last button, his whisper strained, his lined face looking exhausted, "the new madman of Africa."

To speak frankly and in the utmost confidence, Major General Halafi, we approve of your proposed incursion north into the Straits. Our so-called allies there have been weak and ineffectual, but, naturally, our disassociation must, because of the current treaties, be gradual. The educating process is always difficult, the reeducating of the entrenched unfortunately a maddening chess game, fortunately played by those of us who understand. You shall have your weapons. Salaam, my warrior friend.

What Michael had watched and listened to was paralyzing. Alliances not in the interests of the United States had been tacitly formed or half formed, and treaties proposed or negotiated that were in violation of existing treaties; guarantees of billions had been made that Congress would never tolerate and the American taxpayer would never accept; military obligations had been assumed that were immoral in concept, crossing the bounds of national honor, and irrationally provocative. It was a portrait of a brilliant mind that had fragmented itself in a profusion of global commitments, each a lethal missile.

Michael slowly recovered from his state of shock. Suddenly the gap came into focus; it had to be filled, explained. Havelock took off the earphones and turned to the President. "Costa Brava," he whispered harshly. "*Why?* Why 'beyond salvage'?"

"I was part of the first, but I did not call for the second. As near as we can determine, it was not officially sanctioned."

"Ambiguity?"

"Yes. We don't know who he is. However, I should tell you, I personally confirmed the salvage order later."

"*Why?*"

"Because I accepted one aspect of the oath you signed when you entered the service of your government."

"Which was?"

"To lay down your life for your country, should your country need it desperately enough to ask for it. Any of us would, you know that as well as I do. Nor do I have to remind you that untold thousands have done so even when the needs were questionable."

"Meaning the need for my life—my death—was not questionable?"

"When I gave the order, no, it was not."

Michael held his breath. "And the Czechoslovakian woman? Jenna Karas?"

"Her death was never sought."

"It *was!*"

"Not by us."

"Ambiguity?"

"Apparently."

"And you don't know . . . Oh, my *God*. But my execution was sanctioned. By *you.*"

The President nodded, his Nordic face less hard than before, his eyes still level, still steady, but no longer a hunter's eyes.

"May the condemned man ask why?"

"Come with me," said Berquist, rising from the console in the dim, flickering light. "It's time for the last phase of your education, Mr. Havelock. I hope to God you're ready for it."

They left the monitor room and entered what appeared to be a short, white corridor, guarded by a huge master sergeant whose face and display of ribbons conveyed many tours and many battles. He cracked to

attention the instant he saw the President; his commander in chief nodded and proceeded toward a wide black door at the end of the enclosure. However, it was not a door, Michael realized as he drew nearer
behind Berquist. It was a vault, its wheel in the center, a small hand-
sensor plate to the right of the frame. The President pressed his right
palm against it; a tiny row of colored lights raced back and forth above
the plate, settling on green and white. He then reached over with his
left hand and gripped the wheel; the lights were tripped again, a combination of three greens this time.

"I'm sure you know more about these devices than I do," said Berquist,
"so I'll only add that it can be released solely by myself . . . and one other
person in the event of my death."

The significance was obvious and required no comment. The President
swung the heavy vault back, reached up and pressed an unseen plate on
the inner frame; somewhere crossbeam trips were deactivated. Once again
he nodded at the soldier, gesturing for Havelock to enter. They stepped
inside as the master sergeant approached the steel panel and closed it,
then spun the wheel into its locked position.

It was a room, but not an ordinary room, for there were no windows,
no prints on the walls, no extraneous furniture, no amenities, only the
quiet whir of ventilating machines. There was an oblong conference table
in the center with five chairs around it, note pads, pencils, and ashtrays
in place, a paper shredder in the far left corner; it was a table in a room
preset for immediate consultation and instant destruction of whatever
came from a given meeting. Whereas the room they had just left had
twelve television monitors across the wall, this had a single large reflector
screen, an odd-shaped projector bracketed into the opposite wall next to
a panel of circular switches.

Without speaking, Charles Berquist went directly to the panel,
dimmed the overhead lights and snapped on the projector. The screen
across the dark room was instantly filled with a double image, a straight
black line dividing the two photographs. Each was a single page of two
separate documents, both obviously related, the forms nearly identical.
Havelock stared at them in growing terror.

"This is the essence of what we call Parsifal," said the President quietly.
"Do you recall Wagner's last opera?"

"Not well," replied Havelock, barely able to speak.

"No matter. Just bear in mind that whenever Parsifal took up the spear
used at Christ's crucifixion and held it against wounds, he had the power

to heal. Conversely, whoever holds these has the power to rip them open. All over the world."

"I . . . don't . . . *believe* this," whispered Havelock.

"I wish to God I didn't have to," said Berquist, raising his hand and pointing to the projected document on the left. "This first agreement calls for a nuclear strike against the People's Republic of China, executed by the combined forces of the United States of America and the Soviet Union. Objective: the destruction of all military installations, government centers, hydroelectric plants, communications systems and seven major cities ranging from the Manchurian border to the China Sea." The President paused and gestured at the document on the right. "This second agreement calls for a nearly identical strike against the Union of Soviet Socialist Republics carried out by the combined forces of the United States and the People's Republic of China. The differences are minor, vital only to a few million people who will be burned to death in the nuclear fires. There are an additional five cities, inclusive of Moscow, Leningrad and Kiev. Total destruction: twelve cities obliterated from the face of the earth. . . . This nation has entered into two separate agreements, one with the Soviet Union, the other with the People's Republic of China. In each instance, we have committed the full range of our nuclear weapons to a combined strike with a partner to destroy the mutual enemy. Two diametrically opposed commitments, and the United States is the whore serving two studs gone berserk. Mass annihilation. The world has its nuclear war, Mr. Havelock, engineered with brilliant precision by Anthony Matthias, superstar."

27

"These are . . . *insane!*" whispered Havelock, his eyes riveted on the screen. "And we're a partner to *each?* Each commits us to a nuclear strike —a *first* strike?"

"A second also, and a third, if necessary, from submarines ringing the coasts first of China, then of Russia. Two insane agreements, Mr. Havelock, and we are, indeed, a party to each. There it is in writing."

"My *God* . . ." Michael scanned the lines of both documents, as if studying the deformed appendages of an obscene, horrible thing. "If these are ever exposed, there's nothing left."

"Now you understand," said Berquist, his gaze, too, fixed on the agreements that filled both sides of the screen, his face drawn, his eyes hollow. "That's the unendurable threat we're living with. Unless we follow to the letter the instructions delivered to my office, we face global catastrophe in the truest sense. The threat is simple: the nuclear pact with Russia will be shown to the leaders of the People's Republic of China, and our agreement with the PRC will be given to Moscow. Both will know they've been betrayed—by the richest whore in history. That's what they'll believe, and the world will go up in a thousand nuclear explosions. The last words heard will be: 'This is not an exercise, this is *it!*' And that is the truth, Mr. Havelock."

Michael felt the trembling in his hands, the throbbing at his temples. Something Berquist had just said triggered a sudden uneasiness, but he could not concentrate to identify its source. He could only stare at the two documents projected on the screen. "There's nothing here about dates," he said, almost pointlessly.

"It's on a separate page—these are memoranda of intent. Conferences are to be held during the months of April and May, at which the precise dates of the strikes will be determined. April is scheduled for the Soviets, May is for China. Next month and the month after. The strikes are to occur within forty-five days of each conference."

"It's . . . beyond belief." Overwhelmed, Havelock suddenly felt the paralysis again. He stared at Berquist. "You connected *me* with *this? These?*"

"You *were* connected. God knows not through your own doing, but dangerously connected. We know how; we don't know why. But the 'how' was enough to place you 'beyond salvage.' "

"For Christ's sake, *how?*"

"To begin with, Matthias built the case against your friend Jenna Karas."

"Matthias?"

"It was he who wanted you out. But we couldn't be sure. Were you out, or were you simply changing jobs? From the government of the United States to the holy empire of Matthias the Great."

"Which is why I was watched. London, Amsterdam, Paris . . . God knows where else."

"Everywhere you went. But you gave us nothing."

"And that was grounds for 'beyond salvage'?"

"I told you, I had nothing to do with the original order."

"All right, it was this Ambiguity. But later it was *you.* You reconfirmed it."

"Later, much later; when we learned what *he* had learned. Both orders were given, one in sanction, one not, for the same reason. You were penetrating the manipulation—the structure—behind these documents, the link between men in Washington and their unknown counterparts in the KGB. We're in a race. One miscalculation on your part, one exposure of the flaw in that structure and we have every reason to believe that these agreements, these invitations to Armageddon, would be shown to the leaders in Moscow and Peking."

"Wait a minute!" cried Havelock, bewildered, angry. "That's what you

said before! Goddamn it, these were *negotiated* with Moscow and Peking!"

The President of the United States did not reply. Instead, he walked to the nearest chair at the table and sat down, the back of his large head and his thinning blond hair reflected in the shaft of light. And then he spoke. "No, they were not, Mr. Havelock," he said, looking at the screen. "These are the detailed fantasies of a brilliant but mad mind, the words of a superb negotiator."

"Good *God*, then *deny* them! They aren't real!"

Berquist shook his head. "Read the language!" he said sharply. "It's literally *beyond* deniability. There are detailed references to the most secret weapons in our arsenals. Locations, activating codes, specifications, logistics—information that men would be labeled traitors for revealing, their lives ended in prison, none sentenced to less than thirty years for their acts. In Moscow or Peking, those even remotely associated with the armaments data in these documents would be shot without a hearing on the mere possibility they had divulged, knowingly or unknowingly, even a part of it." The President paused, turning his head slightly to the left, his eyes still on the screen. "What you must understand is that should the leaders in either Moscow or Peking be shown the adversary document, they would be convinced beyond doubt of its authenticity. Every strategic position, each missile capability, every area of destructive responsibility, has been hammered out down to the last detail, nothing left to debate —even to the hours of vehicular robot-controlled occupation of territories."

"Hammered out?" asked Michael, the phrase a glaring intrusion.

Berquist turned around, his eyes once again the hunter's, but wary, afraid. "Yes, Mr. Havelock, hammered out. Now you've reached the core of Parsifal. These agreements were negotiated by two extraordinary—and extraordinarily informed—minds. *Two* men *hammering out* every detail, each step, each point, as though his stature in history depended on the task. A nuclear chess game, the universe to the winner—what's left of it."

"How do you know that?"

"Language again. It's the product of two minds. It doesn't take a psychiatrist, or a pathologist, to spot the different inputs. More to the point, Matthias couldn't have created these by himself, he didn't have the in-depth information that readily available. But with another—a Russian, as knowledgeable about Chinese capabilities as we are—together they could do it. *Did* it. Two men."

His gaze fixed on the President, Havelock spoke in a monotone. "Parsifal is that other man, isn't he?" he asked quietly. "The one who could rip open wounds—all over the world."

"Yes. He has the original set of these agreements, the only other set that exists, he claims. We have to believe him. He's got a nuclear gun to our heads—my head."

"Then he's been in touch with you," said Michael, his eyes shifting to the screen. "You got these from *him*, not Anton."

"Yes. His demands at first were financial, growing with each contact, until they were beyond being outrageous; they were astronomical. Millions upon millions—and millions after that. We assumed his motive had to be political. He had the resources to buy lesser governments, to finance revolutions throughout the Third World, to promote terrorism. We kept dozens of unstable countries under the closest intelligence scrutiny, penetrating their most entrenched elements with our best people, telling them only to look for the slightest substantive change. We thought we might trace him, trap him. And then we learned that Parsifal had not gone near the money; it was merely the means that told him we would do as he ordered. He's not interested in money; he never was. He wants control, power. He wants to dictate to the strongest nation on earth."

"He *has* dictated. That's where you made your first mistake."

"We were buying time. We're still buying it."

"At the risk of annihilation?"

"In the all-consuming hope of preventing it. You still don't understand, Mr. Havelock. We can and probably will parade Anthony Matthias before the world as a madman, destroying the credibility of ten years' worth of treaties and negotiations, but it will not answer the fundamental question. How in the name of *God* did the information in these agreements get there? Was it given to a man certifiably insane? If it was, whom else has he divulged it to? And do we willingly deliver to potential enemies the innermost secrets of our offensive and defensive capabilities? Or let them know how deeply we've penetrated their own weapons systems? . . . We have no monopoly on nuclear maniacs. There are men in Moscow and Peking who, at the first perusal of these, would reach for the buttons and launch. Do you know why?"

"I'm not sure. . . . I'm not sure of anything."

"Welcome to a very elite club. Let me tell you why. Because it's taken all of us forty years and uncountable billions to get where we are today. Atomic knives at each other's throats. There's no time and not enough money left to begin again. In short, Mr. Havelock, in the desperate attempt to avert a global nuclear holocaust, we might start one."

Michael swallowed, conscious of doing so, the blood draining from his face. "Simplistic assumptions are out," he said.

"They're not even fashionable," replied Berquist.

"Who is Parsifal?"

"We don't know. Any more than we know who Ambiguity is."

"You don't *know?*"

"Except that they're connected. We can assume that."

"*Wait* a minute!"

"You keep saying that."

"You've got *Matthias!* You're running him through a computerized charade here. Tear into his head! You've got a hundred therapies! Use them. Find out!"

"You think we haven't tried? There's nothing in the annals of therapy that hasn't been used—isn't *being* used. He's erased reality from his mind; he's convinced himself he negotiated with the militarists in Peking and Moscow. He can't allow it to be otherwise; his fantasies have to be real to him. They protect him."

"But Parsifal's *alive,* he's *not* a fantasy! He has a face, eyes, features! Anton's got to be able to give you *something!*"

"Nothing. Instead, he describes—accurately, to be sure—known extremists in the Soviet Presidium and China's Central Committee. Those are the people he sees when these agreements are mentioned—with or without chemicals. That mind of his, that incredible instrument, is as creative in protecting him now as it was when instructing the world of lesser mortals before."

"*Abstractions!*" cried Havelock.

"You've said that, too."

"This Parsifal's *real!* He exists! He's got you under a gun!"

"My words, I believe."

Michael ran to the table and pounded it with his clenched fist. "I can't *believe* this!"

"Believe," said the President, "but don't do that again. There's some kind of sonic thing that registers solid decibels, not conversations. If I don't speak immediately, the vault is opened and you could lose your life."

"Oh, my *God!*"

"I don't need your vote. There's no third term any longer—if there is an 'any longer'—and I wouldn't seek it, anyway."

"Are you trying to be funny, Mr. President?"

"Possibly. In times like these, and if circumstances permit you to grow older, you may find a certain comfort in the rare attempt. But I'm not sure . . . I'm not sure of anything any longer. Millions to build this place, secrecy unparalleled, the finest psychiatrists in the country. Am I being sold a bill of goods? I don't know. I just know I have nowhere else to go."

Havelock sank into the chair at the end of the table, feeling vaguely uncomfortable at sitting down in Berquist's presence without having been instructed to do so. "Oh," he said meaninglessly, his voice trailing off, looking abjectly at Berquist.

"Forget it," said the President. "I ordered up your own personal firing squad, remember?"

"I still don't understand why. You say I penetrated something, a flaw in some structure or other. That if I kept going, these"—Michael looked up at the screen, wincing—"would be given to Moscow and Peking."

"Not would, *might.* We couldn't take the slightest chance that Parsifal might panic. If he did, he'd undoubtedly head for Moscow. I think you know why."

"He has a Soviet connection. The evidence against Jenna, everything that happened in Barcelona; none of it could have taken place without Russian intelligence."

"The KGB denies it; that is, a man denies it on an official basis. According to the Cons Op records and a Lieutenant Colonel Lawrence Baylor, that man met with you in Athens."

"Rostov?"

"Yes. He didn't know what he was denying, of course, but he as much as told us that if there was a connection, it wasn't sanctioned. We think he's a worried man; he has no idea how justified he is."

"He may," said Havelock. "He's telling you it could be the VKR."

"What the hell is that? I'm no expert in your field."

"Voennaya Kontra Rozvedka. A branch of the KGB, an elite corps that frightens anyone possessing a scrap of sanity. Is that what I penetrated?" Michael stopped and shook his head. "No, it couldn't be. I broke it in Paris, after Col des Moulinets. A VKR officer from Barcelona who came after me. I was placed 'beyond salvage' in Rome, not Paris."

"That was Ambiguity's decision," said Berquist. "Not mine."

"But for the same reason. Your words—sir."

"Yes." The President leaned forward. "It was the Costa Brava. That night on the Costa Brava."

The frustration and the anger returned; it was all Michael could do to control himself. "The Costa Brava was a sham! A fraud! I was *used,* and for that you pinned the label on me! You knew about it. You said you were a *part* of it!"

"You saw a woman killed on that beach."

Havelock got up swiftly and gripped the back of the chair. "Is this another attempt to be funny—Mr. *President?*"

"I don't remotely feel like being amusing. No one was to be killed that night on the Costa Brava."

"No one . . . *Christ!* You *did* it! You and Bradford and those bastards in Langley I spoke with from Madrid! Don't tell me about Costa Brava, I was *there!* And you were responsible, all of you!"

"We initiated it, we set it in motion, but we didn't finish it. And that, Mr. Havelock, is the truth."

Michael wanted to rush to the screen and smash his hands against the terrible images. Instead, the words, Jenna's words, came back to him. *Not one operation, but two.* Then his own. *Intercepted. Altered.*

"Wait a minute," he said.

"Find another expression."

"No, please. You started it, and without your knowing it the scenario was read, then taken over, the threads altered, going into another weave."

"Those phrases aren't in my lexicon."

"They're very clear. You're making a rug and the birds in the pattern are swans; suddenly they turn into condors."

"I stand corrected. That's what happened."

"*Shit!* Excuse me."

"I'm from Minnesota. I've shoveled more than you've ever seen, most of it in Washington." Berquist leaned back in his chair. "Do you understand now?"

"I think so. It's the flaw that could trap him. Parsifal was at Costa Brava."

"*Or* his Soviet connection," amended the President. "When you saw the Karas woman three months later, you began probing that night. If you exposed it, you might have alarmed Parsifal. We don't *know* that you would have, but as long as the possibility existed, we couldn't risk the consequences."

"Why didn't anyone tell me? Why didn't anyone reach me and spell it out?"

"You wouldn't come in. The strategists at Consular Operations went to extreme lengths to bring you in. You eluded them."

"Not because of"—Havelock gestured helplessly, angrily at the screen —"*these*. You could have *told* me, not tried to kill me!"

"There was no time, nor could we send couriers with any part of this information or with the slightest intimations as to Matthias's mental condition. We didn't know what you'd do at any given moment, what you might say about that night, or whom you might say it to. In our judgment —in my judgment—if the man we call Parsifal *was* at Costa Brava, or was part of the altered strategy, and he thought he was being identified with that night, he could well have been provoked into doing the unthinkable. We could not permit even the possibility of that."

"So many questions . . ." Michael blinked in the harsh glare of light. "So much I can't fit together."

"You may when and if the decision is made on both our parts to bring you all the way in."

"The Apache," said Havelock, avoiding Berquist's comment, "the Palatine . . . Red Ogilvie. Was it an accident? Was that shot meant for me, or was it really meant for him because he knew about something back here. He mentioned a man who died of a heart attack on the Chesapeake."

"Ogilvie's death was exactly what it appeared to be. A mistake. The bullet was meant for you. The others, however, were not accidents."

"What others?"

"The remaining three strategists at Consular Operations were murdered in Washington."

Havelock stood motionless, absorbing the information in silence.

"Because of me?" he asked finally.

"Indirectly. But then, you're at the core of everything because of the single, imponderable question: Why did Matthias do what he did to you?"

"Tell me about the strategists, please."

"They knew who Parsifal's Soviet connection was," said the President. "Or they would have known the next night if you had been killed at Col des Moulinets."

"Code name Ambiguity. He's here?"

"Yes. Stern gave him the clearance code. We know where he is, not who he is."

"Where?"

"You may or may not be given that information."

"For *God's sake!* With all due respect, Mr. President, hasn't it occurred to you even now to *use* me? Not kill me, but *use* me!"

"Why should I? Could you help me? Help us?"

"I've spent sixteen years in the field, hunting and being hunted. I speak five languages fluently, three marginally, and more dialects than I can count. I know one side of Anthony Matthias better than anyone else alive; I know his *feelings.* More to the immediate point, I've uncovered as many double entries—agents—as any other man in Europe. Yes, I think I can help."

"Then you must give me your answer. Do you intend to carry out your threat? These thirteen pages that could—"

"Burn them," interrupted Havelock; he was watching the President's eyes, believing him.

"They're carbons," said Berquist.

"I'll reach her. She's a couple of miles away in Savannah."

"Very well. Code name Ambiguity is on the fifth floor of the State Department. One of sixty-five, maybe seventy men and women. The word, I believe, is 'mole.' "

"You've narrowed it down that *far?*" asked Michael, sitting down.

"Emory Bradford did. He's a better man than you think. He never wanted to harm the Karas woman."

"Then he was incompetent."

"He'd be the first to agree with that. Still, if she'd followed his instructions, she'd eventually have been told the truth; the two of you would have been brought in."

"Instead, I was put 'beyond salvage.' "

"Tell me something, Mr. Havelock," said the President, once again leaning forward in the chair. "If you were I, knowing what you know now, what would you have done?"

Michael looked at the screen, the astonishing words burning into his mind. "The same thing you did. I was expendable."

"Thank you." The President rose. "Incidentally, no one here on Poole's Island knows anything about these. Neither the doctors, nor the technicians, nor the military. Only five other men are aware of them. Or of Parsifal. One of them is a psychiatrist from Bethesda, a specialist in hallucinatory disorders, who flies down once a week to work with Matthias only in this room."

"I understand."

"Now, let's get out of here while we're still sane," said Berquist as he walked to the projector; he snapped it off, then turned on the overhead lights. "Arrangements will be made to fly the two of you to Andrews Air Force Base this afternoon. We'll find you a place somewhere in the country, not in Washington. We can't risk your being seen."

"If I'm going to be effective, I'll have to have access to records, logs, files. They can't be moved to the country, Mr. President."

"If they can't be, we'll bring you in under very controlled circumstances. . . . There'll be two more chairs placed at the table. You'll be given clearance for everything under another name. And Bradford will brief you as soon as possible."

"Before I leave here, I want to talk to the doctors. I'd also like to see Anton, but I understand; it'll be brief, only a few minutes."

"I'm not sure they'll permit it."

"Then overrule them. I want to talk to him in Czech, his own language. I've got to dig around something he said to me. He said, 'You don't understand. You can never understand.' It's deep inside of him, something between himself and me. Maybe I'm the only one who can get it out. It could be everything, why he did what he did, not only to me but to himself. Somewhere in my head there's a bomb, I've known it from the beginning."

"The doctors are overruled. But I remind you, you spent twelve days at a clinic, a total of eighty-five hours in chemical therapy, and you couldn't help us."

"You didn't know where to look. God help me, neither do I."

The three doctors were not able to tell him anything he could not have guessed from Berquist's descriptions, and in fact, the psychiatric terminology tended to obscure the picture for him. The President's characterization of a delicate, remarkable instrument exploding under the inhuman pressures of responsibilities was far more graphic than the dry explanation of the limits of stress tolerance. Then one of the analysts interrupted—the youngest, as it happened: "There is no reality for him in the accepted sense of the word. He filters his impressions, permitting only those that support what he wants to see and hear. These are his reality—more real to him, perhaps, than anything was before—because they're his fantasies and they've got to protect him now. He has nothing else, only fragmented memories."

Not only was President Charles Berquist adept at description, thought Michael, but he also listened.

"The deterioration can't be reversed?" asked Havelock.

"No," said another psychiatrist. "The cellular structure has degenerated. It's irreversible."

"He's too old," said the younger man.

"I want to see him. I'll be brief."

"We've registered our objections," said the third doctor, "but the President feels differently. Please understand, we're working here under virtually impossible conditions, with a patient who's failing—how rapidly it's difficult to tell. He has to be both artificially repressed and stimulated in order for us to achieve any results at all. It's extremely delicate, and a prolonged trauma could set us back days. We haven't the time, Mr. Havelock."

"I'll be quick. Ten minutes."

"Make it five. *Please.*"

"All right. Five minutes."

"I'll take you over," said the younger psychiatrist. "He's where you saw him last night. In his garden."

Outside on the street, the white-jacketed doctor directed Michael to an army jeep behind the red-brick building. "You were getting pissed off in there," he said. "You shouldn't have. They're two of the best men in the country and nobody was exaggerating. Sometimes this place seems like Futilityville."

"Futility what?"

"The results don't come fast enough. We'll never catch up."

"With what?"

"With what he's done."

"I see. You can't be too much of a slouch yourself," said Havelock, as they drove down the tree-lined street toward the dirt road that approached Matthias's mocked-up house.

"I've written a couple of papers, and I'm good with stats, but I'm happy to be a go-fer for these guys."

"Where'd they find you?"

"I worked with Dr. Schramm at Menninger's—he's the one who insisted on the five minutes, and the finest neuropsychiatrist in the business. I operated machines for him—brain scanners, electrospectographs, that sort of thing. I still do."

"There's a lot of machinery around here, isn't there?"

"No expense spared."

"I can't get over it," exclaimed Michael, glancing around at the reced-

ing scenery, at the macabre façades and the alabaster models, the miniature streets and streetlamps and odd-shaped blowups placed on manicured
lawns. "It's incredible. It's something out of a movie—a weird movie.
Who the hell built it, and how were they convinced not to say anything?
The rumors must be flying all over south Georgia."

"Not because of them—the people who built it, I mean."

"How could you stop them?"

"They're nowhere near here. They're hundreds of miles away working
on a half-dozen other projects."

"*What?*"

"You just said it," explained the young doctor, grinning. "A movie.
This whole complex was built by a Canadian film company that thinks
it was hired by a cost-conscious producer on the West Coast. They started
the scenic construction twenty-four hours after the Corps of Engineers
threw up the stockade and converted the existing buildings for our use."

"What about the helicopters that fly in from Savannah?"

"They're routed on a path and into a threshold beyond the stockade;
they can't see anything. And anyway, except for the President and one
or two others, they're all from Quartermaster, bringing in supplies.
They've been told it's an oceanic research center and have no reason to
think otherwise."

"What about the personnel?"

"We doctors, the technicians who can handle just about everything, a
few aides, the guards, and a platoon of enlisted men and five officers. The
last is all army, even the ones who man the patrol boat."

"What have they been told?"

"As little as possible. Outside of us, the technicians and the aides know
more than anyone else, but they were screened as if they were being sent
to Moscow. Also the guards, but I guess you know that. I gather you're
acquainted."

"With one, anyway." The jeep entered the rutted dirt road, the island
dust billowing behind them. "I can't figure the army. How do they keep
it quiet?"

"To begin with, they don't go anywhere. None of us do, that's the
official word. And even if they did, they wouldn't worry about the officers.
They're all from the Pentagon Rolodex and each one sees himself as a
future chairman of the Joint Chiefs. They wouldn't say anything; it's their
guarantee of quick rank."

"And the enlisted men? They've got to be a boiling pot."

"That's stereotypical thinking, isn't it? Young guys like that took a lot of beaches once, fought in a lot of jungles."

"I only meant there's got to be gossip, wild tales all over the place. How are they contained?"

"For starters, they don't see that much, not of anything that counts. They're told Poole's Island is a simulated exercise in survival, everything top secret, ten years in a stockade if the secrecy's broken. They're also screened, all regular army; they've got a home here. Why louse it up?"

"It still sounds loose."

"Well, there's always the bottom line. I mean, before too long it's not going to make a hell of a lot of difference, is it?"

Havelock whipped his head around and stared at the psychiatrist. *Incidentally, no one here on Poole's Island knows anything about these. Neither the doctors, the technicians* . . . Berquist's words. Had that vault, that very odd room, been entered? "What do you mean?"

"One of these days Matthias will quietly slip away. When he's gone, the rumors won't make any difference. All great men and women have postmortem stories told about them; it's part of the ballgame."

If there is a ballgame, Doctor.

Dobré odpoledne, přіteli," said Michael softly, as he walked out of the house into the sun-drenched garden. Matthias was sitting in the same chair at the end of the winding slate path where he had been seated the night before, protected from the sun by the shade of a traveler's palm that fanned out in front of the wall. Havelock continued speaking, quickly and gently, in Czech. "I know you're upset with me, my dear friend, and I wish only to put to rest the difficulty between us. After all, you are my beloved teacher, the only father I have left, and it isn't right for fathers and sons to be estranged."

At first Matthias recoiled in the chair, pulling himself farther into the shadows of the palm, the intermittent streaks of light crossing his frightened, contorted face. But a mist began to cover the wide eyes behind the tortoiseshell glasses, a film of uncertainty; perhaps he was remembering words from long ago—a father's words in Prague, or a child's plea. It did not matter. The language, the soft, deliberate cadence—they were having their effect. It was crucial now to touch. The touch was vital, a symbol of so much that was of another language, of another country—of remembered trust. Michael approached, the words flowing softly, the cadence rhythmic, evoking another time, another land.

"There are the hills above the Moldau, our great Vltava with its beautiful bridges, and the Wencelas when the snow falls . . . the Stříbrné Lake in summer. And the valleys of the Váh and the Nitra, sailing with the currents toward the mountains."

They touched, the student's hand on the teacher's arm. Matthias trembled, breathing deeply, his own hand rising haltingly from his lap and covering Havelock's.

"You told me I didn't understand, that I could never understand. It's not so, my teacher . . . my father . . . I *can* understand. Above all, I *must* understand. There should be nothing between us . . . ever. I owe everything to you."

The mist in Matthias's eyes began to clear, the focus returning, and in that focus there was something suddenly wild—something mad.

"No, *please*, Anton," said Michael quickly. "Tell me what it is. Help me, help me to understand."

The hollow whisper began as it had in the darkness of the garden before. Only now there was blinding sunlight and the language was different, the words different.

"The most dreadful agreements on earth are the ultimate *solution.* That is what you could never understand. . . . But you saw them all . . . all coming and going, the negotiators of the world! Coming to me! Pleading with me! The world knew I could do it and it came to *me!*" Matthias stopped, and then as suddenly as the night before, the deep whisper was replaced by a scream that seemed to block out the sunlight, a nightmare in the middle of the afternoon. *"Get away from me!* You will betray me! You will betray us *all."*

"How can I?"

"Because you *know!*"

"I *don't* know!"

"Betrayer! Betrayer of your countrymen! Your father! Betrayer of the world!"

"Then why not *kill me!*" roared Michael, knowing there was nothing left, nowhere else to go with Anton Matthias. "Why didn't you have me *killed?*"

"Havelock, cut it out!" shouted the young doctor from the doorway.

"Not now!" yelled Michael in English.

"Yes, goddamn it!"

"Já slyším!" screamed Havelock into Matthias's face, returning to Czech. "You could have killed me but you didn't! Why not? I'm nothing

compared to the world, to *your solutions* for the world! What stopped you?"

"That's it, mister!"

"Let me alone! He's got to tell me!"

"Tell you *what?*"

"*Ted', starý pane?*" Michael gripped the arms of Matthias's chair, locking him into it. "What *stopped* you?"

The hollow whisper returned, the wild eyes now clear of uncertainty. "You left the conference and we did not see you, we could not find you. We had to know what you had done, whom you had told."

Madness.

"You're finished here, Havelock!" said the psychiatrist, gripping Michael's arm and pulling him away from the chair. "What were you two talking about? I know it's Czech, but that's *all* I know. What did he tell you? I want it verbatim!"

Havelock tried to shake the numbness from his mind, the utter sense of futility. He looked at the doctor, remembering his use of the word; he would not corrupt it as the young man had. "It wouldn't do you any good. He was back in his childhood; it was meaningless rambling . . . an angry, frightened child. I thought he was going to tell me something. He didn't."

The doctor nodded, his eyes those of a learned, older man. "He does that a lot," said the psychiatrist, voice and face relaxing. "It's a degenerative syndrome in old people born in another country, with a different language. It doesn't make much difference whether they're sane or insane; they go back. And why not? They're entitled to the comfort. . . . Sorry. Nice try. Come on, I have to get you out of here. There's a chopper waiting for you at the pad."

"Thanks." Michael backed away on the slate path, and looked, he knew, for the last time at Anton Matthias . . . *přítel*, mentor, father. The once great man was cowering again, seeking sanctuary in the shadows of the palm tree.

Madness. Or was it?

Was it *possible?* Did he—Mikhail Havlíček—know the answer? *Did he know Parsifal?*

28

It was called Sterile House Five—Sterile Five for short—and was ten miles south of Alexandria in the Fairfax countryside. Once the estate of a horse breeder, it had been purchased by an elderly, apparently wealthy, retired couple who were in fact buyers of record for the United States government. They were appropriate "owners" because they had spent their adult lives in the foreign service; they had been attached to various embassies and given various titles, but in reality they were two of the most proficient cryptanalysts in U.S. intelligence. Their cover was simple; he had been an investment banker living in Europe for several decades. It was eminently acceptable to the distant, affluent neighbors and accounted for the frequent sight of limousines turning off the country road into the half-mile drive that led to the house. Once a visitor arrived, the "owners" were rarely visible—unless visibility was prearranged—for their quarters were in the north wing, a separate section of the house, with a separate entrance and independent facilities.

Sterile Five was another form of halfway house, serving clients who had far more to offer the United States government than the castaway inmates of Mason Falls, Pennsylvania. Over the years it had seen a procession of high-level defectors pass through its doors for periods of interrogation and debriefing. Scientists, diplomats, espionage agents, military men—all had been residents at one time or another. Sterile Five was reserved for those people Washington felt were vital to the immediate interests of the country at given moments of crisis. Havelock and Jenna Karas arrived in an unmarked government vehicle at twenty minutes past four. Undersecretary of State Emory Bradford was waiting for them.

The recriminations were brief; there was no point in going over past errors. Bradford had spoken with the President and understood that there would be "two new chairs at the table." At Sterile Five, however, they sat in the "owner's study," a small room outfitted for a country squire: a couch and thick armchairs; leather, brass and expensive wood in harmony; mementos signifying little of substance on the walls. There was a heavy pine table behind the single couch, and on it was a silver tray with glasses, ice and bottles. Havelock made himself and Jenna drinks; Bradford declined.

"What have you told Miss Karas?" asked the undersecretary.

"Everything I learned at Poole's Island."

"It's difficult to know what to say—what to think," said Jenna. "I suppose I'm awestruck and terrified at the same time."

"It's a good combination," agreed Bradford.

"What I want from you," Havelock said to Bradford as he went around the couch with the drinks and sat down beside Jenna, "is everything you have, the names of everyone involved—no matter how remotely—from the beginning. I don't care how long it takes; we can be here all night. As you go along I'll ask questions, make notes, and when you're finished I'll give you a list of what I need."

It took less than four minutes for Michael's first question: "MacKenzie? CIA? Black operations. One of the best out of Langley."

"I was told *the* best," Bradford said.

"He set up Costa Brava, then?"

"Yes."

"He was the second sighting, the one who brought back the blood-stained clothing for forensic?"

"I was about to—"

"Tell me," interrupted Havelock. "Did he die of a stroke—a coronary—on the Chesapeake?"

"In his boat, yes."

"Was there an inquest? An autopsy?"

"Not formally, but, again, the answer is yes."

"What does that mean?"

"With a man like that, you don't promote speculation. The doctor was cooperative and thoroughly questioned; he's a very respected physician. X-rays were examined by him and our own people, the conclusion was unanimous. A massive aortal hemorrhage." Bradford lowered his voice. "It was the first thought we had when we heard the news. We didn't overlook a thing."

"Thanks," said Havelock, writing a note to himself. "Go on."

Jenna placed her drink on the coffee table. "Was he the man with you in the lobby of the hotel in Barcelona?"

"Yes, it was his operation."

"He was an angry man. His eyes were angry, not concerned, just angry."

"He was in an angry occupation."

"He crashed my door in; he had a gun in his hand."

"He was worried, we both were. Miss Karas, if you'd come downstairs or even stayed in your room—"

"Please, go on," Michael broke in.

The undersecretary continued as Havelock and Jenna listened intently, interrupting whenever either had a question or felt details should be clarified. Within the hour it was apparent to Bradford that Jenna Karas had a mind to contend with and the experience to match. She asked nearly as many questions as Michael, frequently pursuing specifics until possibilities not previously considered were suddenly brought to light.

Bradford reached the night when the three strategists were killed, when the unknown Ambiguity routed the call to Rome placing Havelock "beyond salvage." The undersecretary of State was thorough, detailing the checks he had made on the personnel in the L Section of the fifth floor during the hours in question. None, he was certain, could be Ambiguity.

"Because the conferences and briefings they held were . . . how do you say it?" Jenna looked at Michael. *"Potvrdit?"*

"Confirmed," said Havelock, watching her. "Logged in the official records."

"Yes, official." She turned back to Bradford. "Is this the reason you rule out these people?"

"None left their meetings long enough to have reached Rome on a code circuit."

"Forgive me," continued Jenna, "but do you exclude the possibility that this Ambiguity might have associates? Persons who would lie for him?"

"I don't even want to think about it," said the undersecretary. "But considering the diversity of those who were there, I *do* think it's mathematically impossible. I know too many of those people, have known them for years, some for nearly two decades."

"Still . . ."

"*Paminyatchiki?*" asked Havelock, his eyes on Jenna.

"*Proč ne? To je možné.*"

"*Nemluv o tom.*"

"*Vy nemáte pravdu.*"

"What are you talking about?" asked Bradford.

"We're being rude," said Jenna. "Sorry. I thought—"

"She thought it was something to think about," interrupted Michael. "I explained that the numbers didn't add up. Go on, please."

Jenna looked at Havelock and reached for her drink.

The undersecretary of State spoke for nearly four hours, half the time answering questions and refining countless details until the elegant den came to seem like a quietly charged courtroom. Bradford was the reluctant hostile witness facing two agile and relentless prosecuting attorneys.

"How are you dealing with Jacob Handelman?"

"Unsolved. The President read me what you wrote over the phone. It's incredible . . . about Handelman, I mean. Are you sure you weren't mistaken?"

"It was his gun, his knife. There was no mistake."

"Berquist said you had to have had an extraordinary reason to kill him."

"Oddly enough, I didn't. I wanted him to sweat—for years, if I could. He came after me. Are you going to tell the truth about him?"

"The President says no. What purpose would it serve? He says the Jews have been through enough; let it be."

"Another necessary lie?"

"Not necessary, but compassionate, I think."

"Kohoutek? That farm in Mason Falls?"

"He's being taken now."

"His clients?"

"Each case will be studied individually and determinations made, again compassionately."

Havelock leafed through the pages of his notebook, then put it down on the coffee table and reached for his empty glass. He glanced at Jenna; she shook her head. He got up and walked around the couch to pour himself a drink. "Let me try to put this together," he began quietly.

"Ambiguity's somewhere on the fifth floor of the State Department and he's probably been there for years, feeding Moscow everything he gets his hands on." Michael paused and walked aimlessly to the thick-paned window; outside, the floodlights illuminated the landscaped grounds. "Matthias meets this Parsifal and together they create these incredible— no, not incredible—*unthinkable* agreements." Havelock stopped, turning suddenly from the window and looking hard at Bradford. "How could it have happened? For Christ's sake, where *were* all of you? You saw him every day, talked to him, watched him! Couldn't you see what was happening to him?"

"We never knew what role he was playing," said the undersecretary of State, returning the stare, slow anger finally surfacing. "Charisma has many facets, like a diamond seen in different lights, different turns. Was he Dean Matthias sitting in academic judgment, or Dr. Matthias at a lectern, holding forth for an enraptured convocation? Or was he the European Mr. Chips, over sherry, with Handel in the background, enlightening his favorite idolators of the moment? He did that very well. Then there was the *bon vivant,* the darling of Georgetown, Chevy Chase and the Eastern Shore. My God, what a coup for a hostess! And how magnificently he performed . . . what charm! What wit! The sheer force of his personality, a paunchy little man who suddenly emanated power! If he'd been capable, he could have had any woman he wanted. Then, of course, there was the office tyrant. Demanding, petulant, self-seeking, jealous—so conscious of his image he scoured the papers for the most minor mention, swelling up with the headlines, furious at the slightest criticism. And speaking of criticism, what did he do last year when a lowly senator questioned his motives at the Geneva conference? He went on television, voice choking, close to tears, and said he would remove himself from public life. *Jesus,* what an uproar! That senator's a *pariah* today!" Bradford paused, shaking his head, embarrassed at his outburst. He continued, lowering his voice. "Then there was Anthony Matthias, the most brilliant Secretary of State in this nation's history. . . . No, Mr. Havelock, we saw him but we didn't see him. We didn't know him because he was too many people."

"You're nit-picking a man's vanity," said Michael, walking toward the couch. "They're called shortcomings; you may not have any, the rest of us do. He *was* many people; he had to be. Your problem is that you hated him."

"No, you're wrong." Again Bradford shook his head. "You don't hate a man like Matthias," he continued, glancing at Jenna. "You may be awestruck, or frightened, or mesmerized—but you don't hate."

"Let's get back to Parsifal," said Havelock, sitting on the arm of the couch. "Where do you think he came from?"

"He came from nowhere and he disappeared into nowhere."

"The second he may have done, the first he couldn't have. He came from somewhere. He met with Matthias time after time, certainly for weeks, possibly months."

"We've checked Matthias's calendars over and over again. Also his logs, his telephone records, his classified appointments, his every travel itinerary—where he went, whom he met, from diplomats to doormen. There were no consistent repeats. Nothing."

"I'll want them all. Can you arrange it?"

"It's arranged."

"Anything on a time span?"

"Yes, spectroanalysis of the copy-page type indicates recent impressions. Within six months."

"Very good."

"We could have assumed it."

"Do me a favor," said Michael as he sat down and reached for his notebook.

"What's that?" asked the undersecretary.

"Never assume." Havelock wrote on the pad, and added, "Which is exactly what I'm going to do right now. Parsifal's a Russian. Most likely an untouched, unlisted defector."

"We've . . . assumed that. Someone with extraordinary knowledge of the Soviet Union's strategic-arms capabilities."

"Why do you say that?" asked Jenna Karas.

"The agreements. They contain offensive and defensive nuclear-strike data that match our deepest and most accurate penetrations of their systems."

Michael wrote another note for himself. "Just as important," he said, looking at Jenna, "Parsifal knew where to find Ambiguity. The connection is made, the mole reaches Moscow and the evidence against you is provided—for my benefit. Then Ambiguity moves into Costa Brava, rewriting the scenario on the beach." Michael turned back to the undersecretary of State. "It's here you think the break came, isn't it?"

"I do, and I agree with you. I think it was Ambiguity on that beach, not Parsifal. I believe further that Ambiguity returned to Washington and found he'd lost Parsifal. He'd been used, then discarded, a situation that must have panicked him."

"Because in order to get the KGB to cooperate he obviously had to promise something extraordinary?" asked Havelock.

"Yes, but then, there's Rostov's cable and it's a snag. He as much as told us that if there was a connection, it wasn't sanctioned, or even controllable."

"He was right. I explained it to Berquist, and it fits . . . from the beginning. It's the answer to Athens. Rostov was referring to a *branch* of the KGB, a descendant of the old OGPU slaughterhouse maniacs, a pack of wolves."

"Voennaya Kontra Razvedka," said Jenna, adding quietly, "VKR."

"Ambiguity isn't just a major or a colonel in the KGB, he's a member of the wolf pack. Those are the men he's dealing with, and that, Mr. Bradford, is about the worst news you could hear. The KGB with all its paranoia is a stable intelligence-gathering organization compared with the fanatics of the Voennaya."

"Fanatics and anything nuclear are a combination this world can't afford."

"If the Voennaya reaches Parsifal first, that's precisely the combination the world is stuck with." Michael drank, swallowing more than he intended to, fear enveloping him. He picked up the notebook. "So we have a mole called Ambiguity who cooperated with a fellow Russian we've labeled Parsifal, Matthias's partner in creating these insane agreements that could blow up the globe. Matthias virtually collapses, is taken into custody—and therapy—at Poole's Island, and Parsifal goes on alone. But now really alone because he's dropped the mole."

"You agree with me, then," said Bradford.

Havelock looked up from the pad. "If you were wrong, we'd know it. Or maybe we wouldn't; maybe we'd be a pile of ashes. . . . Or from a less melodramatic, though hardly less tragic, point of view in my judgment, the Soviet Union would be running this country with the blessings of the rest of the world. 'The giant ran amok; for God's sake, chain him.' Moscow might even get a vote of confidence from our own citizens. 'Better dead than Red' is not a euphemism I care to test. When push comes to shove, people opt for living."

"But you and I know what that living is, Mikhail," broke in Jenna. "Would you opt for it?"

"Of course," said the undersecretary of State, mildly surprising the other two. "You can't change anything by dying—unless you're a martyr —or by taking yourself out. Especially when you've seen the worst."

Havelock looked again at Bradford, now studying him. "I think the jury just came back in for you, Mr. Undersecretary. That's why you stayed in this city, isn't it? You saw the worst."

"I'm not the issue."

"You were for us for a while. It's nice to know the terrain's firmer. Call me Havelock, or Michael, or whatever you like, but why not drop the 'Mr.'?"

"Thanks. I'm Emory—or whatever you like."

"I'm Jenna, and I'm starved."

"There's a fully stocked kitchen with a cook in residence. He's also one of the guards. When we're finished, I'll introduce you."

"Just a few more minutes." Havelock tore off a page from his notebook. "You said you were checking the whereabouts of everyone on the fifth floor at the time of Costa Brava."

"Rechecking," interrupted Bradford. "The first check was negative all the way. Everyone was accounted for."

"But we know someone wasn't," said Michael. "He was at Costa Brava. One of those checks of yours ran into a smoke screen, the man inside leaving and returning while supposedly he had stayed in place."

"Oh?" It was the undersecretary's turn to write a note, which he did on the back of one of his countless pages. "I hadn't thought of it that way. I was looking for an absence where the explanation might not hold up. You're saying something quite different."

"Yes, I am. Our man's better than that; there won't be any explanation. Don't look for someone missing; look for someone who wasn't there, who wasn't where he was supposed to be."

"Someone on assignment, then."

"It's a place to start," agreed Havelock, tearing off a second page. "The higher the profile, the better, incidentally. Remember, we're looking for a man who's got maximum clearance, and the more prominent the man the better the smoke screens work. Don't forget Kissinger's diarrhea in Tokyo; he was really in Peking."

"I'm beginning to understand your accomplishments."

"Considering the mistakes I've made," replied Michael, writing on the page he had just torn out of the notebook, "I wouldn't qualify for a code ring on the back of a cereal box." He got up, stepped around the coffee table to where Bradford was sitting, and held out the two pages. "This is the list. Do you want to look it over and see if there are any problems?"

"Sure." The undersecretary of State took the papers and settled back into the chair. "By the way, I'll have that drink now, if you don't mind. Bourbon on the rocks, please."

"I thought you'd never ask." Havelock looked at Jenna; she nodded. He took her glass from the coffee table and walked around the couch as Bradford spoke. "There are a couple of surprises here," he said, glancing up and frowning. "There's no problem with the Matthias material—the appointments, logs, itineraries—but why do you need all this stuff on the doctor in Maryland? Background, financial statements, employees, laboratories. We *were* thorough, believe me."

"I do believe you. Call it a throwback. I know a doctor in the South of France, and he's one hell of a surgeon. But he gets brain fever when he's near the tables; he's crashed a couple of times and had to get bailed out."

"There's no parallel here. Randolph hasn't had to work since his mother first saw him in the hospital. His family owns half the Eastern Shore, the richer half."

"But not the people who work for him," said Michael, pouring drinks. "They may not even own a sailboat."

Bradford's gaze again dropped to the page. "I see," he said, more bewilderment in his voice than conviction. "I'm not sure I understand this. You want the names of people in the Pentagon who form the Nuclear Contingency Committees."

"I read somewhere that there are three," added Havelock, carrying the drinks back. "They play war games, changing sides and cross-checking their strategies." He handed Bradford his bourbon, then sat down next to Jenna; she took her drink, her eyes on Michael.

"You think Matthias used them?" asked the undersecretary.

"I don't know. He had to use somebody."

"For what purpose? There's nothing in our arsenals he didn't know about, or have on file somewhere. He *had* to know; he negotiated."

"I just want to be thorough."

Bradford nodded with an embarrassed smile. "I've heard that before. Okay." He went back to the page, reading aloud. " 'List of negative-possibles going back ten years. Follow-ups on each. Sources: CIA, Cons Op, Army intelligence.' I don't know what this means."

"They will. There'll be dozens of them."

"What are 'they'?"

"Men and women who were priority targets for defection, but never came over."

"Well, if they didn't come over—"

"Moscow doesn't announce those who got out themselves," interrupted Havelock. "The computer follow-ups will clarify current statuses."

Bradford paused, then nodded again, reading silently.

Jenna touched Michael's arm; he looked at her. She spoke softly, her eyes questioning. *"Proč ne paminyatchik?"*

"Ne Ted'."

"I beg your pardon?" The undersecretary glanced up as he shifted the pages in his hands.

"Nothing," said Havelock. "She's hungry."

"I'll be finished in a minute, get back to Washington and leave you alone; the rest of this is routine. The D.C. psychiatrists' reports on Matthias will have to be signed over by the President and additional security put on here, but it can be done. I'm seeing him when I get back tonight."

"Why don't you just take me over to Bethesda?"

"Those records aren't there. They're down at Poole's Island locked away with the other psychiatric probings and very special. They're in a steel container and can't be removed without presidential clearance. I'll have to get them. I'll fly down tomorrow."

Bradford stopped reading and looked up, startled. "This last item ... Are you sure? What can they tell you? They couldn't tell *us* anything."

"Put it down as my own personal Freedom of Information Act."

"It could be very painful for you."

"What is it?" asked Jenna.

"He wants the results of his own twelve days in therapy," Bradford said.

They ate by candlelight in the country-elegant dining room, the scene somehow shifting from the deadly sublime to the faintly ridiculous. Adding to the contrast was a large, reticent man who was a surprisingly accomplished cook, but the bulge of a weapon beneath his white jacket did little to emphasize his talents in the kitchen. There was, however, nothing humorous about his eyes; he was a military guard and as accomplished with a gun as he was at preparing beef Wellington. Yet whenever he left the room after serving or clearing, Jenna and Michael looked across the table at each other, trying unsuccessfully not to laugh. But even these brief moments of laughter did not last; the unthinkable never left them.

"You trust Bradford," said Jenna, over coffee. "I know you do. I can tell when you trust a person."

"You're right, I do. He has a conscience, and I think he's paid for it. You can trust a man like that."

"Then why did you stop me from bringing up the *paminyatchiki*—the travelers?"

"Because he couldn't handle it and it can't help him. You heard him; he's the methodical man, one step at a time, each step exhaustingly analyzed. That's his value. With the *paminyatchiki* he's suddenly asked to question everything geometrically."

"I don't understand. Geometrically?"

"In a dozen different directions at once. Everyone's immediately suspect; he wouldn't be looking for one man, he'd be studying whole groups. I want him to concentrate on smoke screens, bore into every assignment on the fifth floor, whether eight blocks or eight hundred miles away from the State Department, until he finds someone who might not have been where he was supposed to be."

"You explained it very well."

"Thanks."

"You might have added the use of a puppet, however."

Havelock looked at her through the glow of the candles, a half-smile coming to his lips. She leveled her eyes with his, smiling also. "Damn it, you know you're absolutely right," he said, laughing softly.

"I wasn't making a list, you were. You can't be expected to think of everything."

"Thanks for the kindness. I'll bring it up in the morning. Incidentally, why didn't you? You weren't shy in there."

"That was asking questions, not giving orders or advice. There's a difference. I wouldn't care to give orders or advice to Bradford until he accepts me. And if I were forced to, it would be in the form of questions, leading to a suggestion."

"That's an odd thing to say. You're accepted; Bradford heard it from Berquist. There's no higher authority."

"I don't mean in that sense. I mean him. He's uncomfortable with women; impatient, perhaps. I don't envy his wife or his women; he's a deeply troubled man."

"He couldn't have more to be troubled about."

"Long before this, Mikhail. He reminds me of a brilliant, talented man whose brilliance and talent don't mix very well. I think he feels impotent, and that touches his women . . . all women, really."

"Am I with Sigmund again?"

"Limburský sýr!" Jenna laughed. "I watch people, you know I do. Do you remember the jeweler in Trieste, the bald-headed man whose shop was an M.I. Six drop? You said he was— What's the peculiar word you have? Like *houkačka?*"

"Horny. I said he was horny, that he walked around the women in his store with a spike in the middle of his trousers."

"And I said he was gay."

"And you were right, because you unbuttoned your blouse a few inches and the son of a bitch kept following me."

They both laughed, the laughter echoing off the veloured walls. Jenna reached over and touched his hand.

"It's good to laugh again, Mikhail."

"It's good to laugh with you. I don't know how often we'll be able to."

"We must make time for it. I think it's terribly important."

"I love you, Jenna."

"Then why don't we ask our gun-bearing Escoffier where we sleep? I don't want to appear *nevyspaný*, my darling, but I love you, too. I want to be close to you, not with a table between us."

"You figured I wasn't gay."

"Latent, perhaps. I'll take what I can get."

"Direct. I always said you were direct."

The gun-bearing Escoffier walked in. "More coffee?" he asked.

"No, thank you," said Havelock.

"Some brandy?"

"I think not," said Jenna.

"How about television?"

"How about the sleeping quarters?"

"The reception's lousy up there."

"We'll manage," said Michael.

He sat on the antique deacon's bench in front of the dying fire in the bedroom, stretching his neck and moving his shoulder in circles. He was sitting there under orders, Jenna's favors to be withheld for seven years or some such nonsense if he disobeyed. She had gone downstairs to find bandages, antiseptic, and no doubt whatever else she could lay her hands on in pursuit of her immediate medical aims.

Ten minutes ago they had walked into the room together, hands clasped, bodies touching, both laughing softly. When she leaned into him, Michael had suddenly winced from the pain in his shoulder, and she had looked into his eyes. She had then unbuttoned his shirt and studied the dressing underneath on his shoulder in the light of a table lamp. An accommodating guard had started the fire over an hour before; it was nearly out, but the coals were glowing, the stone hearth throwing off heat.

"Sit down here and stay warm," Jenna had said, leading him to the bench. "We never did pick up a Red Cross kit. They must have something downstairs."

"You'd better call it 'first-aid' or they'll think you're taking up a collection."

"Just be still, my darling. That shoulder's raw."

"I haven't thought about it, I haven't felt it," said Havelock, watching her go to the door and let herself out.

It was true; he had neither thought about the wound from Col des Moulinets nor, except for mild spasms, been aware of the pain. There had been no time. It hadn't been important enough to think about. Too much had been too overwhelming too quickly. He looked over at the large bedroom window, a window with the same thick beveled glass as the one below in the study. He could see the wash of floodlights beyond—distorted by the glass—and wondered briefly how many men prowled the grounds protecting the sanctity of Sterile Five. Then his eyes wandered back to the burning coals that were the end of the fire. So much . . . so overwhelming . . . so quickly. The mind had to catch up before it was drowned in the onrushing revelations released by floodgates no longer holding back unthinkable—*unbearable*—truths. If he was going to keep his sanity, he had to find time to think.

It's good to laugh with you. I don't know how often we'll be able to. We must make the time for it. I think it's terribly important.

Jenna was right. Laughter was not inconsequential. *Her* laugh was not; he suddenly wanted desperately to hear it. Where was she? How long did it take to find a roll of tape and a couple of bandages? Every sterile house was fully equipped with all manner of medical supplies; they went with the territory. Where *was* she?

He got up from the antique bench, suddenly alarmed. Perhaps other men—men not assigned to Sterile Five—were prowling the grounds outside. He had a certain expertise in such matters. Infiltration was made easier by a profusion of woods and underbrush, and Sterile Five was a country house, surrounded by trees and foliage—natural cover for unnatural experts bent on penetration. *He* could intrude, invade, undoubtedly take out opposition silently, and if he could, others could. *Where was she?*

Havelock walked rapidly to the window, realizing as he approached it that the thick glass which was impervious to bullets would also distort movement outside. It did; he turned swiftly and started for the door. Then he realized something else: he had no weapon!

The door opened before he reached it. He stopped, his breath cut short, relief sweeping through him as Jenna stood there with one hand on the knob and the other holding a plastic tray filled with bandages, scissors, tape and alcohol.

"Mikhail, what is it? What's the matter?"

"Nothing. I . . . I felt like getting up."

"Darling, you're perspiring," said Jenna, closing the door and coming to him; she touched his forehead, then his right temple. "What *is* it?"

"I'm sorry. My imagination went a little off the track. I . . . I thought you were gone longer than . . . I expected. I'm sorry."

"I was gone longer than *I* expected." Jenna took his arm and led him to the bench. "Let's get the shirt off," she said, placing the tray down and helping him.

"Just that?" asked Havelock, sitting down and looking at her while removing his arms from his sleeves. "Just longer than you expected? That's it?"

"Well, outside of two brief affairs under the staircase and a mild flirtation with the cook, I'd say it was sufficient. . . . Now, hold still while I take this off." Jenna carefully, expertly sliced through the borders of the dressing on his shoulder and peeled it back, then removed the bandage. "Actually, it's healing quite well, considering what you've put it through," she said as she stripped the tape and reached for the alcohol and cotton. "More irritation than anything else. The salt water probably prevented infection. . . . This will sting a bit."

"It *does*," said Michael, wincing, as Jenna swabbed the flesh around the wound, then stroked the residue of tape away. "Outside of that activity under the staircase, what the hell were you doing?" he asked while she placed squares of gauze over his skin.

"Concentrating on the mild flirtation," she replied, reeling out the surgical tape and strapping the clean dressing in place. "There. You won't feel any better, but you look better."

"And you're avoiding me."

"Don't you like surprises?"

"Never did."

"*Koláče!*" she said, drawing out the word, while laughing and pouring alcohol over his exposed skin. "In the morning we'll have *koláče*," she added, massaging his back.

"Sweet rolls? . . . You're crazy. You're positively out of your mind. We've spent twenty-four hours in a goddamned hell and you're talking about hot cross buns!"

"We must live, Mikhail," said Jenna, her voice suddenly soft beside him, the movement of her hands slowing to a halt. "I did speak with our armed-to-the-teeth cook, and I'm sure I flirted. In the morning he'll make sure we have apricots and dry yeast; nutmeg he has—and ground mace. He'll order it all tonight. In the morning, *koláče.*"

"I don't believe you—"

"Try and you'll see." She laughed again, and held his face in her hands. "In Prague you found a bakery that made *koláče.* You loved it and asked me to bake some for you."

"In Prague there was another set of problems, not what's facing us now."

"But it *is* us, Mikhail. *Us* once more, and we must have our moments. I lost you once, and now you're here, with me again. Let me have these moments, let *us* have them . . . even knowing what we know."

He reached for her, pulling her to him. "You have them. We have them."

"Thank you, my darling."

"I love to hear you laugh, have I told you that?"

"A number of times. You said I laughed like a small child watching a marionette show. Do you remember saying that?"

"I do, and I was right." Michael tilted her head back. "It fits, a child and sudden laughter . . . a nervous child sometimes. Broussac saw it too. She told me what happened in Milan, how you stripped that poor bastard, colored him red, and stole his clothes."

"As well as an enormous sum of money!" interrupted Jenna. "He was a dreadful man."

"Régine said you laughed about it like a small child remembering a joke or a prank or something like that."

"I suppose I did." Jenna glanced at the fire. "I was so frightened, hoping so much that she would help me, thinking she might not. I think I was holding on to a memory that amused me, that might calm me down. I don't know, but it's happened before."

"What do you mean?" asked Michael.

Jenna turned back to him, her wide eyes inches from his but not looking at him—instead, looking beyond, seeing images from the past. "When I ran away from Ostrava, when my brothers were killed, and I was marked by the anti-Dubčeks—when my life there was finished—I came into the world of Prague. It was a world filled with hatred, a world so violent that I thought at times I couldn't stand it anymore. But I knew what I had to do, I couldn't turn back to a life that wasn't mine any longer. . . . So I would remember things, relive the memories as if I were actually *there*, not in Prague, not in that world of fear. I was back in Ostrava, my adoring brothers taking me for rides, telling their sister outrageous stories to make me laugh. During those moments I was free, I wasn't afraid." She looked at him. "Those memories were hardly like Milan, were they? But I could laugh, I *did* laugh. . . . Enough! I'm not making sense."

"You're making sense," said Michael, pulling her to him again, his face against hers. "Thank you for that. Not much sense is being made these days. Anywhere."

"You're tired, my darling. More than tired, you're exhausted. Come on, let's go to bed."

"I always obey my doctors."

"You need rest, Mikhail."

"I always obey my doctors up to a point."

"*Zlomený,*" said Jenna, laughing softly against his ear.

Strands of her blond hair were layered over his face, her arm across his chest, but neither was asleep. The splendid, warm comfort of their lovemaking did not bring sleep; the unthinkable was too much with them. A soft shaft of light came from the partially closed bathroom door.

"You didn't tell me everything that happened to you on Poole's Island, did you?" said Jenna, her head next to his on the pillow. "You told Bradford that you did, but you didn't."

"Almost everything," replied Havelock, staring at the ceiling. "I'm still trying to figure it out."

Jenna took her arm away and, supporting herself on her elbow, faced him. "Can I help you?" she asked.

"I don't think anybody can. It's the bomb in my head."

"What is, my darling?"

"I know Parsifal."

"You *what* . . . ?"

"That's what Matthias said. He said I saw them all coming and going, the 'negotiators of the world,' he called them. But there was only one and I must have seen him. I must know him."

"That was the reason he did what he did to you? To us? Why he wanted you out?"

"He said I could never understand . . . the deadliest treaties were the only solution."

"And I was the sacrifice."

"Yes. What can I say? He's not sane; he wasn't when he ordered up the case against you. You were to die and I was to live, live and be watched." Michael shook his head in frustration. *"That's* what I can't understand."

"My death?"

"No, my *living."*

"Even in his insanity, he loved you."

"Not *him.* Parsifal. If I was a threat, why didn't Parsifal kill me? Why was it left to the mole to put out the order three months later?"

"Bradford explained that," said Jenna. "You'd seen me; you were reopening Costa Brava, and it could have led you back to the mole."

"It still doesn't explain Parsifal. He could have had me taken out twenty times over. He didn't. That's the gap. What kind of a man are we dealing with?"

"Certainly not rational. That's what's so terrifying."

Havelock turned his head and looked at her. "I wonder," he said.

The ringing was harsh, unexpected, reverberating throughout the room. He bolted up from a deep sleep, his hand reaching for a nonexistent weapon. It was the telephone, and Michael stared at it before picking it up from the bedside table. He glanced at his watch as he spoke. It was four-forty-five in the morning.

"Yes?"

"Havelock, it's Bradford."

"What's the matter? Where are you?"

"In my office. I've been here since eleven. Incidentally, I've had people working through the night. Everything you wanted will be at Sterile Five by ten o'clock, except the records at Poole's Island. There'll be a few hours' delay with those."

"You called at this hour to tell me that?"

"Of course not." Bradford paused, an intake of breath filling the moment. "I may have found him," he said rapidly. "I did as you suggested.

I looked for someone who might not have been where he was supposed to be. I won't know for certain until late this morning; that's the delay with Poole's Island. If it's true, it's incredible; his record is as clean as they come, his military service—"

"Don't say any more," ordered Michael.

"Your phone is as sterile as that house."

"Mine may be. Yours may not be. Or your office. Just listen to me."

"What is it?"

"Look for a puppet. He could be alive or dead."

"A what?"

"Someone filling in, the strings leading back to your man. Do you understand that?"

"Yes, I think so. As a matter of fact, I do. It's part of what I've found already."

"Call me when you know. From the street, from a booth. But don't close in, don't do anything." Havelock hung up and looked at Jenna. "Bradford may have found Ambiguity. If he has, you were right."

"Paminyatchik?"

"A traveler."

29

It was a morning Sterile Five had never experienced before and would probably never see again. A persuasive inmate had taken over the somber asylum. Despite the tension, despite the anticipated call from Bradford, by eight-thirty Jenna had commandeered the kitchen, the gun-bearing Escoffier relegated to the position of assistant. Ingredients were measured and mixed to the accompaniment of glances of approval and the gradual breaking down of culinary barriers; the armed cook began to smile. Pans were selected and the outsized oven was turned on; then two additional guards emerged on the scene as if their nostrils belonged to hounds and the kitchen had become a meat market.

"Please call me Jenna," said Jenna to the others, as Havelock was demoted to a corner table and dismissed with a newspaper.

First names were exchanged, wide grins appeared, and before long there was conversation interspersed with laughter. Hometowns were compared—bakeries the basis of comparison—and a kind of frivolity took over the kitchen at Sterile Five. It was as though no one had ever before dared lighten the oppressive atmosphere of the security-conscious compound. It was lightened now and Jenna was the bearer of that light. To say that the men—these professionals familiar with the deadly arts—were taken with her was too modest an observation. They were actually having fun, and fun was not normal at Sterile Five. The world was going to hell in a galactic basket and Jenna Karas was baking *koláče*.

At nine-fifty-five, however, after quantities of sweet rolls had been eaten in the kitchen and dispensed throughout the grounds, the serious air of the sterile house returned. Static on a dozen radios erupted, as inside bells and television monitors became operational. An armored van from the Department of State had entered the long, guarded drive from the highway. It was expected.

By ten-thirty Havelock and Jenna were back in the ornate study to examine the papers and photographs, which were separated by classification. There were six stacks, some thicker than others: four on the desk in front of Michael; two on the coffee table, where Jenna sat reading on the couch. Bradford had been thorough, and if more was more, his only error was in duplication. An hour and twenty minutes passed, the near-noon sun filling the windows; refracted in the bulletproof glass, the rays scattered across the walls. There was silence except for the turning of pages.

The approach they used was standard when dealing with such a mass of diverse information. They read everything rapidly, concentrating on the totality and not on specifics, trying first to get a feel for the landscape; they would get to the details later and relentlessly scrutinize them. Despite the concentration on reading, a comment was inevitable now and then.

"Ambassador Addison Brooks and General Malcolm Halyard," said Michael, reading a page that contained the names of all those involved —however remotely, with or without knowledge—with the Parsifal mosaic. "They're the President's backups if he's forced to expose Matthias."

"In what sense?" asked Jenna.

"After Anton, they're among the most respected men in the country. Berquist will need them."

Several minutes later Jenna spoke. "You're listed here."

"Where?"

"An entry in an early Matthias calendar."

"How early?"

"Eight—no, nine months ago. You were a house guest of his. It was when you were flown over for the Cons Op personnel evaluation, I think. We hadn't known each other very long."

"Long enough for me to want to get back to Prague as fast as I could. Those sessions were usually a monumental waste of time."

"You told me once they serve a purpose, that the field often has strange effects on certain men and they should be periodically checked."

"I wasn't one of them. Anyway, I said usually, not always. On occasion they'd pick out a . . . a gunslinger."

Jenna put the page down on her lap. "Mikhail, could it have been then? That visit with Matthias? Could you have seen Parsifal then?"

"Anton was himself nine months ago. There was no Parsifal."

"You said he was tired—'terribly tired' were the vords you used. You were worried about him."

"His health, not his sanity. He was sane."

"Still—"

"You think I haven't gone over every minute in my mind?" interrupted Havelock. "It was in Georgetown, and I was there two days, two nights, the length of the evaluation. We had dinner twice, both times alone. I didn't see anybody."

"Certainly people came to the house."

"They certainly did; they never gave him a moment's peace, day or night."

"Then you saw them."

"I'm afraid I didn't. You'd have to know that old place; it's a maze of small rooms in the front. There's a parlor to the right of the hallway, a library on the left that one goes through to get to his office. I think Anton liked it; he could keep people waiting who probably wouldn't see each other. Petitioners in stages, moved from one area to the next. He'd greet them in the parlor, then they'd be taken to the library and, finally, the sanctum sanctorum, his office."

"And you were never in those rooms."

"Not with anybody else. When he was interrupted at dinner, I remained in the dining room in the back. I even used a separate side entrance when coming or going from the house, never the front door. We had an understanding."

"Yes, I remember. You didn't care to be seen with him."

"I'd put it differently. I'd have been honored—I mean that, honored —to have been seen with him. It just wasn't a very good idea, for either of us."

"But if it wasn't during those two days, when was it? When *could* you have seen Parsifal?"

Michael looked at her, feeling helpless. "I'd have to go back over half a lifetime, that's part of the madness. In his fantasy, he sees me leaving a conference; that could be anything from a classroom to a seminar to a lecture hall. How many were there? Fifty, a hundred, a thousand? Postgraduate degrees take time. How many have I forgotten? Was it there, in one of those? Was Parsifal somewhere in that past?"

"If he was, you could hardly be considered a threat to him now." Jenna sat forward, recognition suddenly in her eyes. " 'He could have taken me out twenty times over but he didn't,' " she repeated. "Parsifal *didn't* try to kill you."

"Exactly."

"Then he could be someone you knew years ago."

"Or there's another possibility. I said he could have taken me out and he could have, but regardless of how careful or how removed a person is, there's always a risk in killing someone or contracting for a gun, no matter how slight. Maybe he can't tolerate even the hint of a risk. Maybe he's in a crowd of faces right in front of me and I can't pick him out. But if I knew who he is or what he looks like, I'd know where to find him. *I'd* know, but not necessarily too many others, probably no one in our line of work."

"The mole could supply you with both an identity and a description."

"Good hunting, Mr. Undersecretary," said Havelock. "And I wish to hell he'd *call!* . . . Anything else in there?" he added, going back to the material on the Maryland physician.

"I haven't gotten that far with the calendars. But there's something in the itineraries and it's repeated frequently. I'm not sure I understand. Why is the Shenandoah mentioned so often, Mikhail?"

Havelock looked up from the page as a dissonant chord echoed in the recesses of his brain.

Emory Bradford struggled to keep his eyes open. Except for brief catnaps, taken when he could no longer function, he had not slept in nearly thirty-six hours. Yet he *had* to stay awake; it was past noon. The newsreel tapes and photographs from New York would be arriving any minute, flown down by an accommodating network television station that had accepted an innocuous explanation in exchange for a new and confidential source at the Department of State. The undersecretary had ordered up the proper equipment; he could run the tapes within minutes after receiving them. And then he would know.

Incredible. Arthur Pierce! *Was* it Pierce, after all? The senior State Department official at the United Nations delegation, chief aide to the ambassador, a career officer with a service record to be envied by just about anyone working in the upper regions of the government, a record that fairly screamed "advancement." And prior to his arrival in Washington there was a superb military record. Had he stayed in the army he would have been on his way to the Joint Chiefs of Staff. Pierce had arrived in Southeast Asia as a second lieutenant out of the University of Michigan, summa cum laude, master's program, and Benning's OCS. Thereafter, for five voluntarily uninterrupted tours of duty he had risen to the rank of major, replete with decorations for bravery, citations for leadership and recommendations for further strategic studies. And before that, before Vietnam, there was a dossier that exemplified the young American achievement of a farm boy: church acolyte, Eagle Scout, high school valedictorian, college scholarship with academic honors—even member-ship in a 4-H club. As General Halyard had said, Arthur Pierce was flag, mother, apple pie and God. *Where* was the connection to Moscow?

Yet there was one if there was validity in Havelock's use of the term "smoke screen," and especially in his warning "Look for a puppet. He could be alive or dead." It was the initial suggestion, however, that had first caught Bradford's attention: *Look for a man who wasn't there, who wasn't where he was supposed to be.*

He had been studying routinely—too routinely, for the thought seemed too farfetched—the recommendations and positions taken by the Ameri-can delegation at the Security Council's meetings during the week of Costa Brava. These included the confidential discussions within the dele-gation, as summarized by an attaché named Carpenter. His superior, Pierce, the man second only to the ambassador, was mentioned fre-quently; his suggestions were concise, astute, very much in character. Then Bradford came upon a parenthetical abbreviated phrase deep in the text of that Thursday's meeting: *"(Del./F.C.)."*

It followed a strong and lengthy recommendation presented to the ambassador by Pierce. Bradford had not picked it up before, probably because of the unnecessarily complicated diplomatic verbiage, but seven hours ago he had looked hard at it. "(Del./F.C.) *Delivered by Franklyn Carpenter.*" Translation: Not offered by the ambassador's senior aide, Arthur Pierce, whose words they were, but relayed by a subordinate. Meaning: Pierce was not there, not where he was supposed to be.

Bradford had then studied every subsequent line in the delegation report. He'd found two additional bracketed *F.C.*'s for Thursday and three more for Friday. *Friday.* Then he had remembered the obvious and gone back to the beginning of the week. It had been the end of the year; the operation at Costa Brava had taken place on the night of January 4. Sunday. *A weekend.*

There had been no Security Council meeting that Wednesday because the majority of the delegations who were still on speaking terms were holding diplomatic receptions for New Year's Eve. On Thursday, the first day of the new year, as if to show the world the U.N. meant to greet it seriously, the council had resumed work, then again on Friday—but not Saturday or Sunday.

Therefore, if Arthur Pierce was not where he was supposed to be, and had instructed a subordinate to deliver his words, he could have left the country Tuesday evening, allowing five days for the Costa Brava. If, if . . . if. *Ambiguity?*

He had called Havelock, who told him what to look for next. The puppet.

The lateness of the hour was irrelevant. Bradford had raised an operator on the all-night tracing switchboard, and told him to reach one Franklyn Carpenter wherever he might be. Eight minutes later the operator had called back; Franklyn Carpenter had resigned from the Department of State almost four months ago. The number on file was useless; the telephone had been disconnected. Bradford had then given the name of the only other person listed at the American desk during that Thursday meeting of the Security Council, a lower-level attaché no doubt still in New York.

The tracing operator had called back at 5:15 A.M., the U.N. attaché on the line.

"This is Undersecretary of State Bradford. . . ."

The man's initial response had been one of astonishment mixed with the fuzziness of sleep, and more than a touch of fear. Bradford had spent several minutes reassuring him, trying to bring him back to those few days nearly four months ago.

"Can you remember them?"

"Reasonably, I suppose."

"Did anything strike you as unusual during the end of that week?"

"Nothing that comes to mind, no, sir."

"The American team for those sessions—and I'm mainly concerned with Thursday and Friday—consisted of the ambassador, the senior State Department official Arthur Pierce, yourself and a man named Carpenter, is that right?"

"I'd reverse the last two. I was low man on the totem pole then."

"Were all four of you there every day?"

"Well . . . I think so. It's hard to recall every day four months ago. The attendance rolls would tell you."

"Thursday was New Year's Day, does that help you?"

There was a pause before the attaché answered. When he did so, Bradford closed his eyes. "Yes," the aide said. "I *do* remember. I may have been listed at the desk, but I wasn't there. The White Flash had— Excuse me, I'm sorry, sir."

"I know who you mean. What did Undersecretary Pierce do?"

"He had me fly down to Washington to compile an analysis of the entire Middle East position. I spent damn near the whole weekend on it. Then, wouldn't you know, he didn't use it. Never has, to this day."

"I have a last question," Bradford said quietly, trying to control his voice. "When a team member's recommendations are given to the ambassador by someone else at the desk, what exactly does it signify?"

"That's easy. The senior members try to anticipate adversary proposals and write up strategies or counterproposals to block them. In the event he's out of the council room when a controversial proposal is brought up, his advice is there for the ambassador."

"Isn't that dangerous? Couldn't someone simply write up something under an official title and hand it to a member?"

"Oh, no, it doesn't work that way. You don't wing it in those deliveries. You've got to be on the premises, that's a must. Suppose the ambassador likes an argument, uses it, and gets hit with a counter he can't handle. He wants the man responsible back in session to get him away from the fan."

"Undersecretary Pierce gave a number of deliveries, as you call them, during the Thursday and Friday meetings."

"That's standard. He's out of that room as much as he's in it. He's terrific in the Diplomats' Lounge, I've got to say it. He's there a lot, buttonholing God knows who, but it works. I think he's as effective as anyone up here; I mean he's really impressive. Even the Soviets like him."

Yes, they do, Mr. Attaché. So much so that controversial proposals could be avoided by prearrangement, Bradford said to himself.

"I know I said a last question; may I have one more?"

"I'm not going to argue, sir."

"What happened to Carpenter?"

"I wish to hell I knew. I wish I could find him. I guess he just fell apart."

"What do you mean?"

"I guess you didn't know. His wife and kids were killed in an automobile accident a couple of days before Christmas. How'd you like to have three coffins in front of a Christmas tree with the presents unopened?"

"I'm sorry."

"He showed a lot of guts coming back as soon as he did. Of course, we all agreed it'd be the best thing for him. To be with people who cared, not alone."

"I imagine that Undersecretary Pierce concurred."

"Yes, sir. He was the one who persuaded him to come back."

"I see."

"Then one morning he just didn't show up. The next day a telegram arrived; it was his resignation, effective immediately."

"That was unusual, wasn't it? Actually improper, I believe."

"After what he'd been through, I don't think anyone wanted to pursue formalities."

"And again the undersecretary concurred."

"Yes, sir. It was Pierce's idea, Carpenter just disappeared. I hope he's all right."

He's dead, Mr. Attaché. The puppet is dead.

Bradford had continued until the sun was up, until his eyes ached from the strain. The next items he had examined were the time sheets for the night the Ambiguity code had been taken over, the "beyond salvage" sent to Rome. He saw what he expected to see: Arthur Pierce had been not in New York but in Washington, at his office on the fifth floor—and, naturally, he had checked out shortly after five o'clock in the evening, the time corresponding to a half-dozen others'. How simple it must have been to walk out in a crowd, sign the security sheet and go right back inside. He could have stayed there all night, signed in in the morning and no one would have known the difference. Just as he, Undersecretary Emory Bradford, could do the same thing *this* morning.

He had gone back to the military transcripts—a nonpareil army record —to the State Department dossier—an inventory of achievement—to an early life that read like an officially documented tribute to Jack Armstrong, All-American Boy. Where in God's name was the connection to Moscow?

By eight o'clock it had become impossible to concentrate, so he leaned back in his chair and slept. At eight-thirty-five he had been stirred awake by the hum of life beyond his office door. The day had begun for the Department of State. Coffee was made and poured, appointments checked, schedules set up as secretaries awaited the arrival of their crisp, starched superiors. There was an unwritten but understood dress code at State these days; frizzled hair, loud ties and unkempt beards were out. He had gotten up, walked outside and greeted his own middle-aged secretary, startling her by his appearance. At that moment he realized what an impression he must have made—tieless, in shirt sleeves, dark circles under his eyes, his hair rumpled and the black stubble of a beard on his face.

He had asked for coffee and headed for the men's room to relieve himself, wash, and straighten up as best he could. And as he walked through the large office, past desks and secretaries and arriving executives, he felt the stares leveled at him. If they only knew, he had thought to himself.

By ten o'clock, remembering Havelock's admonition, he had gone out to a public booth and made arrangements for the tapes and the photographs to be flown down from New York. He had been tempted to call the President. He did not; he spoke to no one.

Now he glanced at his watch. It was twenty-two minutes past twelve, three minutes later than it was when he last checked. The shuttle flights were every hour out of New York; which one was the shipment on?

His thoughts were interrupted by a quiet rapping on his door and a corresponding acceleration in his heartbeat. "Come in!"

It was his secretary, and she looked at him the way she had looked at him early in the morning, concern in her deep-set eyes. "I'm off to lunch, okay?"

"Sure, Liz."

"Can I get you anything?"

"No, thanks."

The woman stood awkwardly in the doorframe, pausing before she continued. "Are you feeling all right, Mr. Bradford?" she asked.

"Yes, I'm fine."

"Is there anything I can do?"

"Stop worrying about me and go to lunch," he said, attempting a smile; it was not successful.

"See you later, then."

If she only knew, he thought.

His telephone rang. It was lobby security; the unmarked delivery from New York had arrived. "Sign for it and send it up with a guard, please."

Seven minutes later the tape was inserted into the video recorder and an interior view of the Security Council of the United Nations appeared on the screen. On the bottom of the picture a date was flashed on: *Tues. December 30. 2:56 P.* The occasion was an address by the Saudi Arabian ambassador. A few minutes into the speech there was a reaction pan shot —first the Israeli delegation, then the Egyptian, followed by the American team. Bradford stopped the tape with the remote control and studied the picture. The four men were in place; the ambassador and his senior aide, Arthur Pierce, in front, two men seated behind. There was no point listening or watching further for Tuesday the thirtieth; Bradford resumed the movement, pulling the remote mechanism up in front of him to locate the forward button. He pressed it, and a rushing blur appeared on the screen. He released the button; the Saudi was still there. He was about to resume the forward motion when a quick-cut shot revealed the American delegation again. Arthur Pierce was not there.

Bradford pressed the reverse several times until he found the action that he was looking for, that he knew would be there. An official from State did not walk out on a friendly speech without at least some explanation. There it was. Pierce was looking at his watch as he rose, leaning first toward the ambassador and whispering, then to the man behind him, presumably the lower-level attaché, who nodded. A female announcer's voice came from the speaker: "We understand that a telephone call has been received by the United States delegation, quite possibly from the Secretary of State, who might care to have his comments registered for Ibn Kashani's most laudatory comments."

Bradford pressed the forward button again, and again, and once again. The address was over; many delegations rose in an ovation. Arthur Pierce had not returned to his chair.

Thurs. Jan. 1 10:43 A. The welcoming of the new year by the president of the Security Council. Pierce was not at the American desk. In his place was the man—presumably, Franklyn Carpenter—who had been seated behind the ambassador; he was beside him now, a sheaf of papers in his hands.

Fri. Jan. 2 4:10 P. A provocative speech by the P.R.C. delegate, necessitating the use of translation earphones. Pierce was not at the American desk.

Mon. Jan. 5 11:43 A. Arthur Pierce was absent.

Mon. Jan. 5 2:16 P. Arthur Pierce was absent.

Mon. Jan. 5 4:45 P. Arthur Pierce was in his chair, shaking his head in response to comments by the ambassador from Yemen.

Bradford turned off the videotape and looked at the manila envelope containing photographs of the New Year's Eve receptions. He did not really need them; he knew the undersecretary of the American delegation would appear in none.

He had been at the Costa Brava.

There was a final check, and with computer scanners it would take less than a minute. Bradford reached for his phone; he asked for transport backlog information, made his request and waited, rubbing his eyes, aware that a tremble had developed in his breathing. Forty-seven seconds later the reply came: "On Tuesday, December thirtieth, there were five flights out of New York to Madrid. Ten o'clock, twelve, one-fifteen, two-thirty and five-ten. . . . On Monday, January fifth, Spanish time, there were four flights from Barcelona routed through Madrid, starting at seven-thirty, A.M., arrival Kennedy Airport, E.S.T., twelve-twenty-one; nine-fifteen, A.M., arrival Kennedy, E.S.T., three o'clock—"

"Thank you," said Bradford, interrupting. "I have what I need."

He did. Pierce had taken the 5:10 Tuesday flight to Madrid, and had returned on the 9:15 Monday flight from Barcelona, permitting him to appear at the United Nations by 4:45, Eastern Standard Time. Somewhere in the manifests there would be a passenger whose name on a passport would in no way correspond to that of the undersecretary of the delegation.

Bradford pivoted in his chair, breathing deeply, staring out the large window at the tree-lined streets of Washington below. It was time to go out into one of those streets and find another telephone booth. Havelock had to know. He got up and walked around his desk toward his jacket and overcoat, both draped carelessly over a straight-backed chair against the wall.

The door opened without a knock, and the undersecretary of State froze, his every muscle paralyzed. Standing there, closing the door and leaning against the frame, was another undersecretary of State, a shock of white streaking through his dark hair. It was Pierce. He stood erect, his eyes level, cold, somehow weary, his voice flat as he said, "You look exhausted, Emory. You're also inexperienced. Exhaustion and inexperience are a bad combination; together they cause lapses. When you ask questions of subordinates, you should remember to demand confidentiality. That young man, the one who took Carpenter's place, was really quite excited this morning."

"You killed Carpenter," whispered Bradford, finding a part of his voice. "He didn't resign, you killed him."

"He was in great emotional pain."

"Oh, *Christ* . . . His wife and children, you did that, too!"

"You have to plan, create circumstances, foster need—dependence. You can accept that, can't you? Good Lord, in the old days you never gave it a thought. And how many did *you* kill? Before your celebrated conversion, that is. I was out there, Emory. I saw what you did."

"But you *were* there—"

"Hating every minute of it. Sickened by the waste, the body counts—on both sides—and the lies. Always the lies, out of Saigon and Washington. It was the slaughter of children, yours and theirs."

"Why *you?* There's nothing anywhere to *explain!* Why *you?*"

"Because it's what I was meant to do. We're on different sides, Emory, and I believe in mine far more than you believe in yours. That's understandable; you've seen what it's like here, and you can't do anything about it. I can and I will. There's a better way for this world than yours. We'll bring it about."

"*How?* By blowing it *up?* By plunging us all into a nuclear war that was never meant to be!"

Pierce stood motionless, his eyes boring into Bradford's. "It's true, then," he said quietly. "They did it."

"You didn't *know* . . . Oh, my *God!*"

"Don't blame yourself, we were close. We were told—*I* was told—that he was going mad, that he was creating a strategy so intolerable the world would be revolted, the United States would never be trusted again. When it was completed, and the documents were in our hands, we would have the ammunition to dictate or destroy, the option would be ours—in either case your system would be finished, wiped from the face of the earth you've raped."

"You're so *wrong* . . . so misguided." Bradford's voice was a whisper. "Great mistakes, yes! Massive errors of judgment, *yes!* . . . But we *face* them. At the end we always face them!"

"Only when you're caught. Because you haven't the courage to fail, and without that you can't win."

"You think suppression's the answer?" roared Bradford." "You think because you silence people they won't be *heard?*"

"Not where it matters; that's the practical answer. You've never understood us, anyway. You read our books but you don't grasp their meaning; you even choose to overlook specifics. Marx said it, Lenin reconfirmed it; but you didn't listen. Our system is in constant transition, phases to be passed through until change isn't needed any longer. One day our free-doms will be complete, not like yours. Not hollow."

"You're spoon-fed! No change? People *have* to change. Every day! According to the weather, to birth, to death . . . to needs! You can't turn them into automatons; they won't stand for it! That's what *you* can't understand. You're the ones who are afraid of failure. You won't let anybody argue with you!"

"Not those who would undo more than sixty years of hope, of progress. Our great scientists, the doctors, the engineers . . . the vast majority of their parents weren't able to read."

"So you taught the children and banned the books!"

"I thought you were better than that." Pierce took several steps for-ward, away from the door. "You can't find him, can you? He delivered his nuclear blueprints, then went underground. You don't know whom he's shown them to, or sold them to. You're in panic."

"You can't find him, either. You lost him."

"But we know who he is. We've studied his habits, his needs, his talents. Like all men with outstanding minds, he's complicated but pre-dictable. We'll find him. We know what to look for, you don't."

"He defected from you, didn't he?"

"A temporary condition. His quarrel was with the bureaucracy, with unimaginative superiors, not the objectives of the state. When he came to me, I could have taken him, but I chose not to; he offered me too high a price. You see, he believes in us, not you—certainly not you, *never* you. His grandfather was a tenant serf on the lands of Prince Voroshin. He was hanged by that grand nobleman for stealing a wild boar in winter to feed his family. He won't turn on us."

"Who's 'us'? Moscow doesn't acknowledge you, we've learned that much through Costa Brava. The KGB had nothing to *do* with Costa Brava; it was never sanctioned."

"Not by anyone you deal with. They're old and tired; they accommo-date. They've lost sight of our promise—our destiny, if you like. We haven't." Pierce looked at the television set and the video recorder be-neath it, then at the box on Bradford's desk. "A network film library—or is it archives? Images recorded, so they can be studied to settle disputes, or investigate death. Very good, Emory." The mole glanced up. "Or we could add a third *d.* Disappearance. Yes, those would tell you; that feeble excuse for a diplomat we call an ambassador certainly couldn't. He'd check his records, find that I'd given him the best arguments for those sessions, and swear I was there. It might amuse you to know that I frequently talk with my true associates in the lounge and tell them to go easy on him, let him win a few. He was heaven-sent for me."

"It doesn't amuse me."

Pierce approached Bradford, standing directly in front of him. "Havlíček's come back, hasn't he?"

"Who?"

"We prefer his real name. Mikhail Havlíček, son of Václav, an enemy of the state, and named for a grandfather from Rovno, across the Carpathians. Mikhail is a Russian name, you know. Not Czech. On the other hand, you probably *don't* know that; you put such little emphasis on heritage. Under different circumstances, he might be standing where I am at this moment. He's a talented man; I'm sorry he was so misguided. He's here, isn't he?"

"I don't know what you're talking about."

"Oh, come on, Emory. That outrageous newspaper story, that very opaque whitewash done so very badly out of State in response to the killing on Morningside Heights. That old Jew knew something, didn't he? And the pathological Havlíček shot his head off finding out what it was. Then you covered for him because he'd found *you* out, and no doubt found the girl as well. You need him now; he could blow you apart. You made your accommodation with him. You told him the truth, you had to. It all goes back to the Costa Brava, doesn't it?"

"*You* go back to the Costa Brava!"

"Certainly. We were on our way to the total compromise of one of the most powerful men in the Western world. We wanted to make sure it was done right. You didn't have the stomach for it. We did."

"But you didn't know why. You still *don't!*"

"It never mattered, can't you see that? He was going insane. You, with your extraordinary expectations, were driving him insane; he was a gifted man doing the work of twenty. The Georgian syndrome, Emory. Stalin was a babbling idiot when he was killed. All we had to do with Matthias was fuel his fantasies, gratify his every whim, grievance and suspicion—encourage his madness. Because that madness compromised this country into its own madness."

"There's no compromise now. Only annihilation. Extinction."

Pierce nodded his head slowly. "There's the risk, of course, but one can't be afraid to fail."

"Now *you're* the one who's insane!"

"Not at all. The extinction would be yours, the annihilation yours. That court of world opinion you whiningly appeal to so frequently would see to it. And right now, all that matters is that we find the man who single-handedly ushered Anton Matthias into his disintegration, and we want those documents. Don't worry about Havlíček; *you* were going to put him 'beyond salvage,' we weren't."

"You did. *You* did! You put him beyond salvage."

"At the time it was right to order his execution. It isn't now. Now he'll help us. I wasn't joking before; he's one of the most talented men you've ever fielded, a very accomplished hunter. With *his* expertise and what *we* know, we'll find the man who'll bring this government to its knees."

"I've told people who you are!" whispered Bradford. "*What* you are!"

"I'd have been followed at the airport—especially the airport—and I wasn't. You didn't tell anyone because you didn't know until a few minutes ago. I'm far too important a figure for such speculations from a man like you. You've made too many mistakes; you can't afford any more. This city doesn't like you, Mr. Undersecretary."

"Havelock will kill you on sight."

"I'm sure he would if he could see us, but that's his problem, isn't it. We *know* Havlíček; he doesn't know us; he doesn't know me. That puts him at quite a disadvantage. We'll just watch him; it's all we have to do."

"You'll never find him!" Bradford lurched to his left, instantly blocked by Pierce, who shoved him against the wall.

"Don't, Emory. You're tired and very weak. Before you could raise your voice you'd be dead. As for finding him, how many safe houses are there? Steriles One through Seventeen? And who wouldn't tell a man like me—a man involved with numerous diplomatic 'defections'—which ones are available? I've brought in several enviable catches—or presumed catches." Pierce took several steps, once again standing in front of Bradford. "Now, don't die. Tell me. Where is this catastrophic document? I assume it's a photostat. The original is held over your head, a nuclear sword hanging by a very thin thread."

"Where you could never find it."

"I believe you," said the traveler. "But you could."

"There's no way . . . could or would."

"Unfortunately, I believe that, too."

There was a brief snapping sound as Pierce suddenly thrust out his right hand, gripping Bradford's bare arm, pressing his palm into the flesh. With his left, the mole simultaneously reached up and clamped his fingers over

Bradford's mouth, twisting the undersecretary's body, arching him to the side. In seconds, Bradford's eyes widened, then closed as the choking sounds from his throat were muted. He collapsed to the floor as Pierce withdrew the palmed needle. The mole raced behind the desk and picked up the tape container; beneath it was a note on corporate stationery. He reached for the telephone, pressed the outside-line button and dialed.

"Federal Bureau of Investigation, New York Office," a voice answered.

"Internal Security, please. Field Agent Abrams."

"Abrams," said a male voice seconds later.

"Your travels went well, I hope."

"A smooth flight" was the reply. "Go ahead."

"There's a network executive," continued Pierce, reading the note, "an R. B. Denning at the Trans American News Division. He supplied library footage to the wrong man at State, an unbalanced man named Bradford, whose motives were offensive to the interests of the United States government. The tapes were destroyed by Bradford in a rage, but for the good of Trans Am's news department—the entire company, as well, of course—Denning's officially advised to say nothing. The Department of State feels it's mandatory to contain the embarrassment, et cetera, et cetera. This is a very green light."

"I'll reach him right away even if he's into his second martini."

"You could add that State might be reluctant to deal with Trans Am in the future, insofar as they delivered company materials without checking the source of the request through proper channels. However, if everyone cooperates for the good of the country—"

"The picture will be clear," interrupted the *paminyatchik* from New York. "I'll get on it."

Pierce hung up, walked to the television set, and carefully moved it back against the wall. He would have the video recorder taken away to another office. There would be no trace of the newsreel tapes or any way to trace them.

There was no prolonged, agonized scream, no cry of protest against offending gods or mortals—only the sound of shattering glass in the huge window as a body plummeted from the seventh floor of the State Department.

It was said by those who had seen him that morning that it was the way he had to go—in a moment of frenzy, of total despair, wanting it over with, not wanting to think any longer. The pressures had become overwhelming; he had never really recovered from those soul-searching days of the late sixties, everyone knew that. He was a man whose time had come and gone, and he had never reasoned out the role he had played in its arrival and departure. Substance had eluded him; at the end he was a voice in the shadows, a voice disturbing to many, but dismissed by many others because he couldn't *do* anything.

The press printed it all in the evening editions, the obituaries ranging from kind to cool, depending on the editorial stripe. But it should be noted that none was very long; no one really cared. Inconsistency was not compatible with that most desirable of political sins: typecasting. To change was to be weak. We want Jesus or the strong-jawed cowboy. Who the hell can be both?

Undersecretary of State Emory Bradford, committed hawk turned passionate dove, was dead. By his own hand, of course.

And there was no odd piece of equipment such as a video recorder in the stand beneath the television set. It had been delivered to the wrong office, a G-12 on the third floor confirming his original request. The set was rolled back against the wall. Apparently unused.

30

"You couldn't have prevented it," said Jenna firmly, standing in front of Havelock at the desk. "You're not permitted to go to the State Department and it's a condition you accept. If the mole saw you, he'd either kill you quietly and remain where he was, or bolt and run to Moscow. You want him, and your being seen isn't the way to find him."

"Maybe I couldn't have prevented it, but I might have let his death —his life—mean more than it did. He wanted to tell me and I told him not to say any more. He said this phone was as sterile as the house and I wouldn't accept that."

"That's *not* what you said. You told him *his* phone, *his* office, might not be sterile. From everything you've learned over the years, everything you've seen, you made the logical decision. And I still believe there are *paminyatchiki* in your State Department who would lie for this man, tap an office for him."

"You know, a paranoid named McCarthy said things like that and tore this country apart thirty years ago. Tore it apart with fear and frenzy."

"Perhaps he was one himself. Who could have done it better?"

"It's possible. The *paminyatchik* is the total patriot. He'll call for a loyalty oath every time because he has no compunction about signing one."

"That's what you have to look for now, Mikhail. A total patriot; a man with an unblemished record. He will be the mole."

"If I could find out what it was Bradford was waiting for yesterday, I think I'd have both. He said he wouldn't know until 'late morning.' That means he expected something that would tell him where a man wasn't, proof someone on the fifth floor wasn't where he was supposed to be. The security desk said Bradford received a package at twelve-twenty-five, but no one knows what it was, and, naturally, it wasn't there later."

"There was no return address or company name?"

"If there was, nobody noticed. It was delivered by messenger."

"Check the firms who provide those services. Certainly someone can recall the color of the uniform; that would narrow it down."

"She wasn't that kind of messenger. She wore a fur-collared tweed coat, and the only thing Security remembers is that she was pretty high-toned for delivering packages."

"High-toned?"

"Attractive, well-spoken, direct. I think that covers it."

"Someone's secretary."

"Yes, but whose? What sort of person would Bradford go to, what kind of proof?"

"What was the size of the package?"

"The guard who took it up said it was a large, padded envelope with a bulge on the bottom, and thick throughout. Papers and something else."

"Papers?" said Jenna. "Newspapers? Could he have gone to a newspaper?"

"He might have. Four-month-old clippings that would describe an event or events during that time. Or he could have pulled in data from the CIA; he had friends there. Something from the files that pertained to the evidence against you, or perhaps Costa Brava . . . something we've overlooked. Or he could have been checking hospitals, or ski lodges, or hometown, small-town neighborhoods or divorce-court dockets—representation in absentia—or Caribbean resort reservations—signatures on meal and bar checks, a maître d' or a beachboy who makes his money by remembering. All of it's possible because everything I've said pertains to someone in these records." Michael touched the sheaf of pages on the desk, running his thumb along the edge. "And a dozen other possibilities I haven't even thought about." Havelock leaned back in the chair, folding his hands under his chin. "Our man's good, Jenna. He'll cover himself with a layer of invisible paint."

"Then go on to something else."

"I am. A doctor in Maryland. Talbot County's most revered physician."

"Mikhail?"

"Yes?"

"Before . . . you were reading the reports of your own therapy at the clinic. After the Costa Brava."

"How did you know?"

"Every now and then you'd close your eyes. Those pages weren't easy for you."

"They weren't easy."

"Did they tell you anything?"

"No. Other than describing your execution and my reactions to it, nothing."

"May I see them?"

"I wish to Christ I could think of a reason to stop you. I can't."

"Your not wanting me to is reason enough."

"No, it's not. You were the one being killed; you have to know." He opened the drawer on his right, reached in and pulled out a thick, black-bordered manila envelope. He gave it to her, their eyes briefly locking. "I'm not proud of it," he said. "And I'll have to live with it for the rest of my life. I know what that means now."

"We'll help each other—for the rest of both our lives. I believed them too."

She carried the envelope to the couch, sat down, and opened it, removing the file folders inside. They were in sequence; she picked up the first and leaned slowly back, looking at the object in her hands as though it were some horrible yet holy thing. She opened the cover and began reading.

Havelock could not move, could not concentrate. He sat rigid in the chair, the papers in front of him blurred, dark lines without meaning. While Jenna read he relived that terrible night; images flashed across his inner vision and exploded inside his head. Just as he had watched her die, she was now witnessing the naked thoughts of a mind in chemical therapy—*his* mind, his deepest emotions—and was watching him die also.

The phrases—the screams—came back to him; she was hearing them too. She had to be, for it was she who now closed her eyes and held her breath, a tremor developing in her hands as she went on . . . and on. She finished the third folder, and he could feel her staring at him. It was a look he could not return. The screams were pounding in his ears, thunderbolts of intolerable violence, unforgivable errors. Betrayal.

Go quickly! Die quickly! Leave me quickly! You were never mine. You were a lie and I loved a lie but you were never part of me! . . . How can you be what you are, yet so much that you are not? Why did you do this to us? To me? You were the only thing I had and now you're my personal hell. . . . Die now, go now! . . . No! For God's sake, let me die with you! I want to die . . . but I won't die for you! . . . Only for myself, against myself! Never for you. You gave yourself to me but you gave me a whore and I took a whore . . . and I believed in the whore. A rotten slut of a whore! . . . Oh, Christ, she's hit! She's hit again. Go to her! For God's sake, go to her! Hold her! . . . No, never to her! It's over! It's all over and it's history and I won't listen to the lies any longer. Oh, Jesus, she's crawling, crawling in the sand like a cut-up, bleeding animal. She's alive! Go to her! Hold her! Lessen the final pain—with a bullet if you have to! No! . . . She's gone. There's no movement now, only blood on her hands and streaked through her hair. She's dead and a part of me is dead, too. Still, it's got to be history, as the early days are history. . . . Oh, my God, they're dragging her away, dragging the lanced, dead animal away. Who? Who are they? Have I seen . . . photographs, files . . . it doesn't matter. Do they know what they've done? Did she? Killer, slut, whore! . . . My once, my only love. It's history now, it has to be history. A killer is gone . . . love gone. A goddamned fool survives.

She had finished. She placed the last file on the coffee table in front of her and turned to him; she was crying silently. "So much love and so much hatred. Hatred and self-hatred. I wasn't forced to go through what you did; perhaps it was easier, if more bewildering, to be the victim. But when the bewilderment was replaced by anger, I *felt* the way you did. Hating you so very much, yet loathing myself for the hatred, never forgetting the love that I knew—I *knew*—had been there. It couldn't have been false, not so much, not all of it. The anger took over at the border and later at the airfield in Col des Moulinets when I thought you had come to finally kill me. Kill me with the violence you had shown that woman on the pier at Civitavecchia. I saw your face through the window of the plane and—if there's a God, may He forgive me—you were my enemy. My love was my enemy."

"I remember," said Michael. "I saw your eyes and I remember the hatred. I tried to shout, tried to tell you, but you couldn't hear me; I couldn't hear myself through the sound of the engines. But your eyes were weapons that night, more frightening than any I'd ever faced. I wouldn't have the courage to see them again, but I suppose in a way I always will."

"Only in your memory, Mikhail."

The telephone rang; Havelock let it ring again. He could not take his gaze off Jenna. Then he picked it up.

"Yes?"

"Havelock?"

"Mr. President."

"Did you get the information on Emory?" asked Berquist, the Minnesotan's voice laced with sadness and exhaustion, yet forcing an illusion of strength.

"Nowhere near what I need."

"What you need is a liaison. I'll pick someone here at the White House, someone with authority and a man I can trust. I'll have to bring him on board, but that can't be helped. Bradford's gone and you *do* need a funnel."

"Not yet, sir. And not anyone at the White House."

There was a pause from Washington. "Because of what Rostov told you in Athens?"

"Possibly. The percentages are minor, but I'd rather not test them. Not now."

"You *believed* him?"

"With all due respect, Mr. President, he was the only one who told me the truth. From the beginning."

"Why would he tell you a truth like that?"

"I'm not sure. On the other hand, why did he send Cons Op that cable? In both instances the information was sufficiently startling to force us all to pay attention. That's the first step in sending a signal."

"Addison Brooks said very much the same thing."

"He was talking diplomatically, and he was right. The Voennaya doesn't speak for Moscow."

"I understand. Bradford—" Berquist paused, as if he suddenly remembered he was referring to a dead man. "—Bradford explained it to me last night. So you really believe there's a Soviet agent operating inside the White House?"

"As I said, I'm not sure. But there may be—or more than likely, may have been. I don't think Rostov would have brought it up unless he could have substantiated the reality, present or past. He was probing, looking for responses. The truth provokes the most genuine answers in this business; he learned that when he brought up Costa Brava. In this case, I don't want to take the risk."

"All right, but then, how can you function? You can't be seen walking around questioning people."

"No, but I can question them without being seen. I can use the phone if it's set up properly. I know what I want to ask and I'll know what to listen for. From these conversations I'll refine whom I want to see and set up contacts. I'm experienced at this, Mr. President."

"I don't have to take your word for it. How is it set up—properly?"

"Give me a name, and call me an assistant counsel to the President, or something like that. It's not unusual for the Oval Office to make its own discreet inquiries into certain matters, is it?"

"Hell, no, I've got a staff for that, and it's not necessarily discreet. Hundreds of reports are sent to the White House every week. They have to be checked out, experts questioned, figures substantiated. Without it all, responsible decisions can't be made. In Lincoln's time he had two young men, and they took care of everything, including the drafting of letters. Now we have scores of aides and assistants to aides and secretaries to assistants and they can't half handle the volume. The answer is yes."

"What happens if someone is called by an aide or an assistant aide and that someone doubts the authority of the person questioning him?"

"It happens a lot, especially at the Pentagon; there's a simple solution. He's told to call the White House switchboard and ask to be connected to the aide's or the assistant's office. It works."

"It *will* work," said Michael. "Along with the lines already on this phone can you add another one, listing me in the White House index, the extension routed here?"

"Havelock, one of the more exotic pleasures in being President, or close to a President, is the trunkful of electronic gimmickery available on short notice. You'll be indexed and patched into the switchboard within the hour. What name do you want to use?"

"You'll have to choose one, sir. I might duplicate someone already there."

"I'll call you back."

"Mr. President, before you hang up—"

"What is it?"

"I'll need another one of those things that may not be in your lexicon. A context backup."

"It sure as hell isn't. What is it?"

"In the event someone calls the White House index and wants to know exactly what I do, there should be someone else there who can tell him."

Again there was the pause from Washington. "You were right, down on Poole's Island," said Berquist pensively. "The words say exactly what they mean, don't they? You need someone to back you up in the context of what you're presuming to do, or be."

"That's right, sir."

"Call you back."

"May I suggest something?" said Michael quickly.

"What?"

"Within the next few days—if we have a few days—someone is going to come up to that someone else in the White House and ask where my office is. When he or she does, hold him—or her—because whoever it is will bring us a step closer."

"If that happens," said Berquist angrily, "whoever it is may be strangled by a Minnesota farm boy before you get a chance to talk to him. Or her."

"I'm sure you don't mean that, Mr. President."

"I'm not going to throw a nuclear warhead on Leningrad, either. Call you back."

Havelock replaced the phone and looked over at Jenna. "We can begin narrowing down the names. We'll start calling in an hour."

"Your name is Cross. Robert Cross. Your title is Special Assistant to the President, and all inquiries as to your status and functions are to be directed to Mrs. Howell—she's counsel to White House internal affairs. She's been told what to do."

"What about my office?"

"You've got one."

"What?"

"You've even got an assistant. In the security area of E.O.B. You need a key to get in the main corridor over there, and your man is instructed to take into custody anyone who comes around looking for Mr. Cross. He's a member of the Secret Service detail and if anyone does show up asking for you, he'll alert you and bring that person down to Fairfax under guard. I assumed that's what you wanted."

"It is. What about the other offices in that area? Will the people in them be curious?"

"Unlikely. By and large those assignments are temporary, everyone working on his own quiet project. Curiosity's discouraged. And if it surfaces, you've got your man in place."

"It sounds tight."

"I think so. Where are you going to start? . . . Emory showed me the list of the items you wanted and assured me you'd have it all in the morning. Did you get everything?"

"Everything. Bradford's secretary is first, then the doctor in Maryland. MacKenzie's death."

"We were extremely thorough with him," said Berquist. "Under the circumstances, we were able to bring in the Central Intelligence Agency and those people were aggressive. What are you looking for?"

"I'm not sure. Someone who's not around anymore, perhaps. A puppet."

"I won't try to follow that."

"I may need your direct intervention in one area, however. You said before that the Pentagon frequently balks at being questioned by White House personnel."

"It goes with the uniforms; they're not worn over here. I expect you're referring to the Nuclear Contingency Committees. I saw them on your list."

"I am."

"They're touchy. Rightfully so, I'd say."

"I have to talk to every member of those three teams; that's fifteen senior officers. Can you get word to the chairman that you expect them all to cooperate with Mr. Cross? Not in the area of maximum restricted information, but in terms of—progress evaluation."

"One of those phrases again."

"It says it, Mr. President. It would help if you could work Matthias in."

"All right," said Berquist slowly. "I'll lay it on the great man. It's not in character, but he can hardly deny it. I'll have my military aide convey the word: the Secretary of State wants those committees to provide an in-depth progress report for the Oval Office. A simple memorandum ordering cooperation within the limits of maximum classification should do it. . . . They'll say there's a crossover, of course. You can't have one without violating the other."

"Then tell them to err on the side of classification. The final report's for your eyes only, anyway."

"Anything else?"

"The psychiatric file on Matthias. Bradford was to have gotten it for me."

"I'm going to Camp David tomorrow. I'll detour to Poole's Island and bring it back with me."

"One thing more. This Mrs. Howell; outside of calling in the Secret Service if anyone approaches her about me, what has she been told to say? About me, my functions?"

"Only that you're on a special assignment for the President."

"Can you change it?"

"To what?"

"Routine assignment. Researching old agendas so White House files can be completed on various matters."

"We have people doing that. It's basically political—how is this position defended, or why did that senator buck us and how do we stop him from doing it again."

"Put me in with the crowd."

"You're in it. Good luck . . . but then you'll need a great deal more than luck. This world needs more than luck. Sometimes I think we need a miracle to last another week. . . . Keep me informed; my orders are that whenever Mr. Cross calls, I'm to be interrupted."

Bradford's secretary, one Elizabeth Andrews, was at home, the sensational death of her superior having had its emotional impact. A number of newspaper people had telephoned her, and she had relayed the events of yesterday morning sadly but calmly, until a gossip-oriented reporter, noting Bradford's marital track record, hinted at a sexual entanglement.

"You sick bitch," Elizabeth had said, slamming down the phone.

Havelock's call came twenty minutes later, and Elizabeth Andrews was not inclined to tell the tale again. He suggested she call him back at the White House when she felt better; the ploy worked. The phone in the study in Fairfax rang six minutes after Michael had hung up.

"I'm sorry, Mr. Cross. It's been a very trying time and some very trying reporters."

"I'll be as brief as possible."

She recounted the morning's events, beginning with Bradford's sudden and unexpected emergence from his office shortly after she had arrived.

"He looked dreadful. He'd obviously been up all night and was exhausted, but there was something else. A kind of manic energy; he was excited about something. I've seen him like that lots of times, of course, but somehow yesterday it was different. He spoke louder than he usually did."

"That could have been the exhaustion," said Havelock. "It often works that way. A person compensates because he feels weak."

"Perhaps, but I don't think so, not with him, not yesterday morning. I know it sounds ghastly, but I think he'd made up his mind . . . that's a horrible thing to say, but I believe it. It was as though he were exhilarated, actually looking forward to the moment when it was going to happen. It's ghoulish, but he left the office shortly before ten, said he was going out for a few minutes, and I have this terrible picture of him out on the street, looking up at the window . . . and thinking to himself, Yes, this is it."

"Could there be another explanation? Could he have been going to see someone?"

"No, I don't think so. I asked him if he'd be in another office in case a call came for him and he said no, he was going out for some air."

"He never mentioned why he'd been there all night?"

"Only that he'd been working on a project that he'd fallen behind on. He'd been doing a fair amount of traveling recently—"

"Did you set up the transportation arrangements for him?" interrupted Havelock.

"No, he usually did that himself. As you probably know, he often . . . took someone with him. He was divorced, several times actually. He was a very private person, Mr. Cross. And so very unhappy."

"Why do you say that?"

Ms. Andrews paused, then spoke firmly. "Emory Bradford was a brilliant man, and they didn't pay attention to him. He was once very influential in this city until he told the truth—as he saw the truth—and as soon as the applause died down, they all ran away from him."

"You've been with him a long time."

"A long time. I saw it all happen."

"Could you give me examples of this running away from him?"

"Sure. To begin with, he was consistently overlooked when his experience, his expertise could have been of value. Then he'd frequently write position papers, correcting powerful men and women—senators, congressmen, secretaries of this and that—who had made stupid mistakes in interviews and press conferences, but if one out of ten ever responded or thanked him, I never knew about it, and I would have. He'd monitor the early-morning television programs, where the worst gaffes are made—just as he was doing yesterday, right up to the end—and dictate what he called clarifications. They were always gentle, even kind, never offensive, and, sure enough, 'clarifications' were usually issued, but never any thanks."

"He was watching television yesterday morning?"

"For a while . . . before it happened. At least, the set was rolled out to the front of his desk. He moved it back . . . before it happened. Right up until the end he couldn't break the habit. He wanted people to be better than they are; he wanted the government to be better."

"Were there any notes on his desk that could have told you whom he was watching?"

"No, nothing. It was like his final gesture, leaving this world tidier than he'd found it. I've never seen his desk so neat, so clean."

"I'm sure you haven't."

"I beg your pardon?"

"Nothing. I was agreeing with you. . . . I know you were at lunch, but were there any people in the vicinity of his office door who might have seen someone go in or out?"

"The police covered that, Mr. Cross. There are always people milling around; we all have different lunch breaks, depending on what's happening in what time zone, but no one saw anything unusual. Actually, our section was pretty much cleared out. We had a secretarial pool meeting at one-thirty, so most of us—"

"Who called that meeting, Miss Andrews?"

"This month's chairman—then, of course, he said he didn't, so we sat around drinking coffee."

"Didn't you get a memo about the meeting?"

"No, the word was just passed around that morning. It frequently is; that's standard."

"Thank you very much. You've been most helpful."

"It's all such a waste, Mr. Cross. Such a goddamned terrible waste."

"I know. Good-bye." Havelock hung up and spoke, his eyes still on the phone. "Our man *is* good," he said. "Invisible paint."

"She couldn't tell you anything?"

"Yes, she did. Bradford listened to me. He went outside to a booth and called for whatever it was he wanted. The number we need won't be found charged to his office phone; it's among a couple of million lost in the underground trunk lines."

"Nothing else?"

"Maybe something." Michael looked over at Jenna, a frown on his face, his eyes clouded. "See if you can find a copy of yesterday's paper around here, will you? I want to know the name of every senior official at State who was interviewed on the morning television programs. It's crazy. The last thing on Bradford's mind was television."

Jenna found the newspaper. No one from the Department of State had been on television that morning.

31

If Talbot County, Maryland, had an esteemed physician in Dr. Matthew Randolph, it also had an extremely unpleasant man. Born to Eastern Shore money, raised in the tradition of privilege, which included the finest schools and clubs, and possessing what amounted to unlimited funds, he nevertheless abused everyone and everything within these rarefied circles in the pursuit of medicine.

When he was thirty, having graduated magna cum laude from Johns Hopkins and completed pathological and surgical residencies at Massachusetts General and New York, he decided he could not function at his talented best within the stultifying, politicized confines of a normal hospital. The answer for him was simple: he virtually extorted monies from the legions of the Chesapeake privileged, threw in an initial two million dollars himself and opened his own fifty-bed medical center.

It was run his way, which amounted to a none too benevolent dictatorship. There was no exclusivity with regard to admission, but there was a rule-of-thumb policy: the rich were soaked outrageously for services rendered them, and the poor given financial consideration only after enduring the ignominy of disclosing overwhelming proof of poverty and listening to a lecture on the sin of indolence. Rich and poor alike, however, continued in growing numbers to put up with these insults, for over the years the Randolph Medical Center had established a reputation that was second to none. Its laboratory equipment was the finest money could buy; its generously paid staff physicians were the brightest graduates from the best schools and toughest residencies; the visiting surgical and pathological specialists were flown in from all over the globe, and the talents of the overpaid technicians and nursing corps were far in excess of normal hospital standards. In essence, treatment at Randolph was both medically superb and personally gratifying. The only way it might be improved upon, some said, would be to remove the abrasive personality of the sixty-eight-year-old Matthew Randolph. However, others pointed out that one way to cripple a smoothly running craft in rough waters was to tear out the throttle because the engine pitch was grating to the ears. And in Randolph's case, short of his own death—which seemed unlikely for several centuries—physically tearing him out was the only way to remove him.

Besides, who else could look down at a nephew of Emile du Pont just before an operation and ask, "How much is your life worth to you?"

In the du Pont case, it was a million-dollar-plus tie-in computer with four of the nation's leading research centers.

Havelock learned these details from CIA files as he researched the death of a black-operations officer named Steven MacKenzie, the "engineer" of Costa Brava. In Cagnes-sur-Mer, Henri Salanne had by implication questioned the veracity of the doctor who signed MacKenzie's death certificate. Michael in his own mind had gone further; he had considered altered laboratory reports, autopsy findings not consistent with the state of the corpse and—after the President had mentioned X-rays—the obvious switching of photographic plates. However, in light of the information on Randolph and his Medical Center, it was difficult to credit these possibilities. Everything connected to and with the official cause of death was processed through Randolph's personal on-site attendance and his own laboratories. The abrasive doctor might well be dictatorial, petulant, most definitely opinionated and unpleasant, but if ever there was a person who deserved to be called a man of integrity, it was Matthew Randolph. His Medical Center, too, was irreproachable. All things considered—*all* things—there was no reason on earth for either to be otherwise.

And for Havelock, that was the flaw. It was simply too symmetrical. Pieces rarely, if ever, fell into place—even negatively—so precisely. There were always caves to explore that might lead to hidden pools—whether they did or not was irrelevant, the caves were *there*. Here, there were none.

The first indication Michael had that there might be substance to his doubts was the fact that Matthew Randolph did not return his first call. In every other instance, including calls to eight senior officers of the Pentagon's Nuclear Contingency Committees, Bradford's secretary, CIA and NSC personnel, the phone in Fairfax had rung within minutes after he placed the contact call. One did not dismiss lightly a request to reach a presidential aide at the White House.

Dr. Matthew Randolph apparently felt no such compulsion. And so Havelock had phoned a second time, only to be told: "The doctor is extremely busy today. He said to say he'll get back to you, Mr. Cross, when he has the free time."

"Did you explain that I'm to be reached at the White House?"

"Yes, sir." The secretary had paused, embarrassment in her brief silence. "He said to tell you the Center's painted white, too," she added in a very soft voice. *"He* said that, Mr. Cross, *I* didn't."

"Then tell Genghis Khan for me that I'll either hear from him within the hour or he may find the sheriff of Talbot County escorting him to the D.C.–Maryland border, where a White House detail will pick him up and bring him down here."

Matthew Randolph returned the call, in fifty-eight minutes.

"Who the *hell* do you think you are, Cross?"

"An extremely overworked nonentity, Dr. Randolph."

"You threatened me! I don't like threats whether they come from the White House or a blue house or an outhouse! I trust you get my meaning."

"I'll convey your feelings to the President."

"Do that. He's not the worst, but I could think of better."

"You might even get along."

"I doubt it. Sincere politicians bore me. Sincerity and politics are diametrically opposed. What do you want? If it's any kind of endorsement, you can start with a healthy government research grant."

"I have an idea President Berquist would entertain that idea only if you openly opposed him."

Randolph paused. "Not bad," he said. "What do you want? We're busy here."

"I want to ask you several questions about a man—a dead man—named Steven MacKenzie."

Again the doctor paused, but it was a different silence. And when he resumed speaking, it was in a different tone. Previously his hostility had been genuine; now it was forced.

"Damn it, how many times do we have to go over that? MacKenzie died of stroke—a massive aortal hemorrhage, an aneurysm, to be precise. I turned over the pathology report and conferred with your spook doctors till hell froze over. They've got it all."

"*Spook* doctors?"

"They sure as hell weren't from Mary-General or Baltimore's Mother of Mercy, I can tell you. Nor did they claim to be." Randolph paused again; Michael did not fill the moment. He was listening with a trained ear, silences and audible breathing being a part of the abstract tonal picture he was trying to define. The doctor continued, his phrases too rushed, the edge of his voice too sharp; his previous confidence was waning, replaced by volume alone. "You want any information on Mac-Kenzie, you get it from them. We all concurred; there was never any doubt. Aortal hemorrhage, plain and simple, and I don't have the time to rehash this sort of thing. Do I make myself clear?"

"More than you know, Dr. Randolph." It was Havelock's turn to pause. He did so until he could see in his mind's eye a mouth that had dropped open and hear the aggressive breathing of a man with something to hide. "I'd find the time, if I were you. The file isn't closed here, Doctor, and for reasons of specific external pressures we can't shut it—as much as we'd like to. You see, we *want* to conclude it precisely the way you determined, but we have to cooperate with each other. Do *I* make myself clear?"

"The pathology was unequivocal, you all agree with that?"

"We *want* to. Please understand that. Be convinced of it."

"What do you mean 'external pressures'?" The doctor's confidence was returning, the question asked sincerely.

"Let's say in-house intelligence troublemakers. We'd like to shut them up."

Costa Brava was never far away. Even in deceit.

Randolph's final pause was brief. "Come up tomorrow," he said. "Be here at noon."

Havelock sat in the back seat of the nondescript, armor-plated sedan; three Secret Service men were his companions. Conversation was at a minimum. The two men in front and the pleasant but quiet agent beside Michael had obviously been ordered to make no direct inquiries.

The Randolph Medical Center was indeed painted white. It was a glistening white complex of three buildings connected by enclosed walkways set down in the middle of a generous acreage of lawns, paths and a central winding driveway. They parked in the nearest available space to the entrance labeled ADMISSIONS AND ADMINISTRATION. Michael got out of the car, walked up the smooth concrete path that led to the glass double doors and went inside; he was expected.

"Dr. Randolph's in his office, Mr. Cross," said a uniformed nurse behind the marble counter. "Take the first corridor to your right; his is the last door at the end of the hall. I'll tell his secretary you're on your way."

"Thank you."

As he walked down the spotless white corridor toward Randolph's office, Havelock considered the options available to him. How much he told the doctor depended upon how much Randolph already knew about Steven MacKenzie. If what he knew was little, Michael's words would be laced with security-conscious innuendo; if a great deal, there was no harm corroborating parts of the truth. However, what primarily concerned Havelock was the reason behind the doctor's extraordinary behavior. The man as much as admitted having twisted or concealed *some* aspect of MacKenzie's death, and regardless of whether he considered it minor or not, it was a dangerous act. Tampering with cause of death or withholding pertinent information was a criminal act. What had the physician done and why had he done it? Even to consider Matthew Randolph as part of an intelligence conspiracy was absurd, irrational. What *had* he done?

A stern-visaged secretary with disciplined angry hair pulled back and lashed into a bun rose from her chair. But her voice contradicted her appearance; it was the same voice that had relayed the doctor's comment about his Medical Center's being the same color as the White House. It was obvious that she had thrown up a wall to protect herself from the Randolph hurricane.

"He's very upset today, Mr. Cross," she said in that frail, intense tone. "You'll do better getting straight to your business. He hates to waste time."

"So do I," replied Michael as the woman escorted him to an ornate paneled door. She rapped twice—not once or three times, but precisely twice—standing rigidly with splendid posture, as though she were about to refuse a blindfold.

The cause of her stoicism was soon apparent. The door opened, revealing a tall, slender, angular man with a fringe of gray hair circling a bald head, the eyes behind the steel-rimmed glasses alive and impatient. Dr. Matthew Randolph was rich, American Gothic, with not a little of Savonarola thrown in, his long graceful hands somehow looking appropriate for holding a pitchfork, a torch or a scalpel. He looked past his secretary and barked; he did not speak.

"You Cross?"

"Yes."

"You're eight minutes late."

"Your watch is fast."

"Maybe. Come in." He now looked at his secretary, who had stepped aside. "No interruptions," he instructed.

"Yes, Dr. Randolph."

The physician closed the door and nodded at the chair in front of his large, cluttered desk. "Sit down," he said, "but before you do, I want to make damn sure you don't have one of those recording machines on you."

"You have my word."

"Is it any good?"

"Is yours?"

"You called me. I didn't call you."

Havelock shook his head. "I have no taping device on me for the simple reason that our conversation could be far more harmful to us than to you."

"Maybe," muttered Randolph, going behind the desk as Michael sat down. "Maybe not. We'll see."

"That's a promising beginning."

"Don't get smart-ass, young fella."

"I apologize if I sounded that way. I meant it. We have a problem and you could put it to rest."

"Meaning I didn't before."

"Let's say there are new questions and, frankly, they may be valid. Certainly they could be embarrassing, not only politically but in terms of morale in certain areas of the intelligence community. Someone might even care to go into print. That's our problem."

"That's what I want to hear." The physician nodded, adjusting his glasses so he could look over the steel rims. "Your problem. Spell it out."

Havelock understood. Randolph wanted an admission of guilt from the White House before he would implicate himself in any conceivable wrongdoing. Therefore, it was reasonable to assume that the more serious Havelock's first admission, the more latitude Randolph would permit himself regarding his own possible duplicity. Thieves in concert and conversation; who could go screaming to a judge?

"Do you know the kind of work MacKenzie was involved in?"

"I've known Mac and his family for over forty years. His parents were close friends of mine and his three children were born right here at the Center. I delivered them myself—probably delivered his wife, Midge, too."

"That doesn't answer my question."

"It should. I've been caring for the MacKenzies most of their lives, and that included young Steve, as well as the adult Steve—as far as you permitted him to live as an adult. Actually, to be more accurate, these past years I more or less double-checked whatever the doctors did at Walter Reed; by and large they were damned good. You could hardly tell from the scars that four of them were bullet wounds."

"Then you did know," said Michael, nodding.

"I told him to get out. My God, I told him that over and over again for the last five, six years now. The strain on him was something fierce —worse, I think, for Midge. Him flying all over the world, she never knowing whether he'd come back; not that he ever told her a hell of a lot, he wouldn't do that. . . . Yes, Mr. Cross, I knew what Steve did— not the specifics or his title or anything like that, but I knew it wasn't your everyday desk job."

"It's strange," mused Havelock, indeed sensing the strangeness. "I never thought of MacKenzie as having a wife and children, coming from a relatively normal background." *He was not a survivor. Why did he do it?*

"Maybe that's why he was so good. You looked at him and saw a pretty average successful executive—something like you, in fact. But underneath he had a fever because you bastards poisoned him."

The suddenness of the charge, its harshness, and the fact that it was delivered in a conversational tone was unnerving. "That's quite a statement," said Michael, his eyes roaming the doctor's face. "Would you care to explain it? To the best of my knowledge, no one held a gun to MacKenzie's head and told him to do whatever it was he was doing."

"You didn't have to, and you're damn right I care to explain it. I figure it's your blueprint for *narcotizing* a man so he turns away from a normal, productive, reasonably happy life to one where he wakes up in a cold sweat in the middle of the night because he probably hasn't had the luxury of sleeping for the past several weeks. Or if he does sleep, the first sharp sound sends him lunging for protection. Or a gun."

"You're very dramatic."

"It's what you did."

"How?"

"You fed him a diet of tension, excitement—even frenzy—with fair doses of blood to go with it."

"Now you're melodramatic."

"You know where it started for him?" Randolph went on, as if Havelock had not spoken. "Thirteen, fourteen years ago Mac was one of the best sailors on the Eastern Shore, probably the Atlantic coast and the Caribbean, too. He could sense a new wind and smell the currents. He could look at the stars in a dark sky and helm a craft—pot or sail—all through the night and take you within sight of where he said you'd be by dawn. It was a gift. . . . Then came the war in Vietnam and he was a naval officer. Well, it didn't take those brass boys long to spot a good thing. Before you could pronounce one of those unpronounceable places, he was ferrying men and supplies up the coast and the inland waterways. That's where it started. He was the best there was; he could read gook maps and get anybody anywhere."

"I'm not sure I understand."

"Then you're thick. He was taking assassination and sabotage teams behind enemy lines. Fleets of small craft were under his command; he was a secret navy all by himself. Then it happened."

"What?"

"One day he didn't just ferry those people, he became one of them."

"I see."

"I wonder if you do. It's where the fever first touched him. Men who were nothing more than cargo became friends he made plans with, fought beside, who died before his eyes. He did that for twenty-eight months until he was wounded and sent home. Midge was waiting for him; they got married and he headed back to finish law school. Only, he couldn't stand it. Before a year was up, he left, and began talking with people in Washington. A part of him missed that crazy—Christ, I don't know what you call it."

"It doesn't make any difference," said Havelock quietly. "I know what you mean."

The doctor looked hard at Michael. "Maybe you do. Maybe that's why you're here. . . . Like a lot of men, Mac came back from that war a different person; not on the surface, but underneath. There was an anger in him I'd never seen before, a need to compete—angrily—for the highest stakes he could find. He couldn't sit still for twenty minutes at a time, much less absorb the finer points of law. He had to keep moving."

"Yes, I know," interrupted Michael involuntarily.

"And you bastards in Washington knew just what to feed him. Get him back into the excitement, the tension. Promise him the best—or worst —competition *you* could find, and make the stakes so high no normal man would consider them. And all the while keep telling him he was the best, the best, the *best!* He thrived on it . . . and at the same time it was tearing him apart."

Havelock brought his hands together, gripping them, moved both to anger and understanding. It was no time, however, to betray either; he wanted information. "What should we—bastards in Washington—have done, then?" he asked calmly.

"That's such a stupid question only one of you sons of bitches would ask it."

"Would you mind answering?"

"Get him medical attention! Psychiatric care!"

"Why didn't you? You were his doctor."

"Damn it, I *tried!* I even tried to *stop* you!"

"I beg your pardon?"

"Somewhere in a number of old files there are letters from me to the Central Intelligence Agency describing—goddamn it, *diagnosing*—a troubled man, a disturbed man. Mac would come home and for a few weeks he'd cover it, driving back and forth to Langley like a regular commuter. Then you could see it happening; he'd go into a kind of depression, wouldn't talk very much, and when he did, he sure as hell wasn't listening. Then he'd become restless, impatient—his mind always somewhere else. You see, he was *waiting,* waiting for his next *fix!*"

"And we gave it to him," said Michael.

"Right on, as the youngsters say! You knew exactly how long he could take it. You were priming him, honing his machine until he'd either blow apart or get back into—whatever the hell you call it."

"The field," said Havelock.

"That's it, the goddamned *field!* Midge would come to me and tell me Mac was going to pieces, couldn't sleep, wouldn't communicate, and I'd write another letter. You know what I'd get back? A thank-you-for-your-interest, as though I'd suggested you bastards change your laundry service! Midge and those kids were going through hell, and you people thought your shirts had just the right amount of starch in 'em!"

Michael's eyes strayed to bare white wall behind Randolph. *How many buried letters were there in how many unopened files? How many MacKenzies . . . and Ogilvies . . . and Havelocks? What was the gunslinger count these days? Men primed, machines honed in the cause of futility. Deadly talents kept in the field because somewhere it was written they could do the job regardless of the mind and the body count . . . their own and others. Who profited?*

"I'm sorry," said Havelock. "With your permission, I'll report this conversation where it won't be overlooked."

"So far you've got my permission. Up to now."

"Up to now," agreed Michael.

The physician leaned back in his chair. "I've drawn a picture for you. It's not pretty, but I've got my reasons. Now, you draw one for me and we'll see where we stand."

"All right." Havelock crossed his legs, then spoke, choosing his words cautiously. "As I'm sure you're aware, most intelligence work is dull, pedestrian. It's routine digging for facts, reading newspapers, reports, scientific journals, and gathering information from a wide variety of other sources, the majority of which are reasonable people, perfectly amenable to imparting what they know because they see no reason to conceal it. Then, of course, there are others who are in the business of making a profit by selling the facts they've bought; buy low, sell higher, a time-honored principle. These people generally deal with a different kind of intelligence officer, one trained to distinguish between fact and fiction; the buy-low-sell-highers can be pretty imaginative." Michael paused, knowing that the timing of his delivery was vital. "Normally," he continued, "the combination of these sources and the sheer volume of the information they provide is sufficient for specialists to put together an accurate pattern of facts and events, like fitting the pieces of a puzzle together. That's an abused expression, but it says it." Again Havelock paused. What Randolph wanted—needed—to hear called for a silent introduction. Three seconds were enough. "Finally, there's a last category of potential information. It's the most difficult to obtain because it has to be extorted from sources who know they possess secrets that could cost them their lives if their superiors knew they had revealed them. These require an entirely different sort of intelligence officer, a specialist himself. He's trained to manipulate, to engineer situations in which individuals are convinced they have no choice but to take a specific course of action, in the end revealing secrets —or doing something—they would not previously have considered. Steven MacKenzie was that kind of specialist, and he *was* one of the best; no one had to convince him. But on his last, his final, assignment, someone intercepted and altered the situation MacKenzie had created. And in order for that original situation to remain the accepted one, he was marked for takeout."

"What the hell is that, a plate of spaghetti?"

"He was killed."

Randolph shot forward in his chair. "He was *what?*"

"Murdered. We might have prevented it if we'd taken the proper precautions. That's our problem, Doctor, and a growing number of people know it. Mac, as you call him, didn't die of a stroke on his sailboat, he was killed. We're aware of it, but we don't want to acknowledge it. . . . Now you can understand why I don't have any taping device concealed anywhere. The picture I just painted is uglier than yours."

"It sure as hell is—if it were true. But I'm afraid it isn't. We'll stick to the aortal hemorrhage because it works. You bastards couldn't be further off base. You blew it."

"What does that mean?"

"Steven MacKenzie committed suicide."

32

"That's impossible!" cried Havelock, rising to his feet. "You're *wrong!*"

"Am I? Are you a doctor, too, Mr. Cross?"

"I don't have to be. I know men like MacKenzie. *I* am one!"

"I figured as much, and that statement is about on a par with my assessment of the lot of you."

"No, don't mistake me," said Michael quickly, shaking his head emphatically. "It's no sophomoric generalization. I'm the first to admit that the thought of packing it in can become a recurrent fixation, obsessive, but not *this* way. Not alone on a boat. That doesn't work!"

"Sorry. The pathology—the evidence—is against you. I wish to Almighty God it weren't, but it is."

Havelock could not help himself; he leaned over Randolph's desk and shouted, "There was evidence against a woman very close to me and that evidence was a lie!"

"I don't know what that's got to do with the price of perfume in Alaska, but it doesn't change anything."

"In this case it does. There's a connection!"

"You're downright incoherent, young fella."

"*Please.* Listen to me. I'm not a 'young fella' and I'm not a raving idiot. Whatever you found you were *meant* to find."

"You don't even know what it was."

"I don't *have* to! Try to understand me, Doctor. A black-operations officer like MacKenzie—"

"A *what?* Mac was white!"

"Oh, Jesus! An engineer, a manipulator . . . a man in sanction, with the authority to bring about events in which people might be killed, usually *are* killed—because it has to be done. More often than I can tell you, men like this have very painful doubts, enormous feelings of guilt, feelings of . . . goddamn it, *futility!* Certainly, depression sets in; sure, they've considered blowing their brains out, but not *this* way! There are other ways that make sense, because if there's one thing ingrained in such men it's function, function, *function!* For Christ's sake, *take* yourself out, but *accomplish* something when you do it! And do it *right.*"

"That's subkindergarten psychobabble," protested Randolph.

"Call it whatever you like, but it's true. It's the first thing, the most *important* thing recruiters look for in a candidate. It's the single overriding factor. . . . You said it yourself. You said MacKenzie had to compete— angrily compete—for the highest stakes he could find."

"Ultimately, he did. Himself."

"No, that's waste! That's not even making a statement. . . . Look, I'm *not* a doctor, not a psychiatrist, and I probably can't convince you, but I know I'm right, so let it pass. Just tell me what you found, what you did."

"Mac gave himself a needle and let it all drift away."

"*Never.*"

"Sorry. He was damned smart about it too. He used a steroid compound of digitoxin combined with enough alcohol to float an elephant. The alcohol blood count overshadowed everything else, but the digitoxin blew the heart. It's one hell of a combination."

"Then the X-ray was valid?"

Randolph did not reply at first. Instead, he pursed his thin lips and fingered his glasses. Then he spoke. "No."

"You *did* switch the plates."

"Yes."

"Why?"

"To carry out what Mac intended. To make sure."

"Go back."

The doctor leaned forward. "He knew what he'd put Midge and the kids through all these years, and it was his way of trying to make up for it, make peace with himself. Midge had had about all she could take; she was finished pleading. She told him he had to get out of the Agency or get out of the house." Randolph stopped briefly, shaking his head. "Mac knew he couldn't do either, so he just decided to get out, period."

"You've skipped something."

"He had a whale of an insurance policy, and considering the work he did—work the insurance company didn't know a damned thing about—it was understandable. Those kinds of policies don't pay on suicide. I was going to be damned before Midge and those kids were cheated out of what they deserved. . . . That's the story, Mr. Cross. You made him what he was, and together, he and I made him better."

Havelock stared at the physician, then turned and sat down in the chair, his eyes still on Randolph. "Even if you were right," he began wearily, "and, believe me, you weren't then—you're not now—you could have spelled it out for the Agency and they'd have gone along with you; the last thing they want is for this sort of killing to get into print. Instead, you put everyone off, wasted valuable time and the damage you've done is incalculable."

"What in *hell!* Twenty minutes ago you said you *wanted* it my way! Yesterday on the phone you said you wanted to shut up some troublemakers!"

"I lied. Just as you lied. But at least I knew what I was doing; you didn't. If you'd told the truth—if only to one person—every minute of MacKenzie's day would have been examined; something might have turned up, somewhere a connection. . . . No one even bothered to go over the boat. Oh, *Christ!*"

"Maybe you didn't *hear* me!" shouted the physician, his eyes wild, his face apoplectic. "Midge MacKenzie had given her ultimatum! He was between a rock and a hard place. He couldn't, as you put it, *function* anymore! He fell apart!"

"That accounted for the alcohol, I don't doubt it."

"And when he was plastered, he made his final decision. It's all there!"

"It's not there," said Michael, feeling far older than the elderly doctor in front of him. "I don't expect you to accept this, but the last thing a man like MacKenzie would do is make a decision when he's drunk."

"Hogwash!"

"Let me ask you something. I assume you take a drink now and then, and when you do, you know when you've had a few."

"Certainly."

"Would you ever operate if you knew you were high?"

"Certainly not, but there's no parallel!"

"Yes, there is, Dr. Randolph. Because when men like MacKenzie or myself—twenty or thirty more I could mention—are in the field, *we're* surgeons. They even call most of the jobs we do 'operations.' It's hammered into us from our first day of school that every reflex, every observation, every reaction has to be as accurate and as fast and as clear as we can make them. We're primed—our machines are honed."

"You're playing with words—yours *and* mine! Mac wasn't in the field."

"If what you believe is true, he was, and the highest stakes were himself."

"*Goddamn* it, you're twisting everything I said!"

"No, I'm not. Because a lot of what you said was as perceptive as I've ever heard it expressed. I respect it. . . . Don't you *understand?* MacKenzie wouldn't have killed himself this way because—everything else aside—the digitoxin might not have *worked!* And that he *couldn't* accept. It was too much a part of him, had been for too many years. If it was going to be his final decision, the one thing he couldn't afford was a mistake! Can't you *see* that?"

It was as though Matthew Randolph had been struck. His eyes were wide and fixed, the muscles of his face taut, his mouth rigid. When he spoke, it was a whisper. "God *Almighty . . .*" he said, his voice drifting off into silence. Then softly, unexpectedly, he rose from his chair, and stood motionless, a helpless old man struggling with a massive error he did not want to confront. "Oh, my God," he added, taking off his glasses, breathing deeply.

Havelock watched him, moved to make things easier. "You did the right thing by your lights. Mine, too, if I'd been you. But at the wrong time, the wrong way. Still, we can go back over everything. We might find something."

"Shut up!"

It was the last thing Michael had expected to hear. "What?"

"I said, '*Shut up!*' "

"You're full of surprises."

"I may have a real one for you."

"MacKenzie?"

Randolph did not answer. Instead, he walked rapidly to a file cabinet against the wall; taking out a small chain of keys, he selected one and literally jammed it into the upper lock. "These are my private files, *very* private. A lot of broken marriages and altered wills could result if they were read. Mac's in here."

"What about him?"

"Not *him*. The staff pathologist who put it all together. Who worked with me to convince those fellas from Langley it was a cardiovascular, pure and simple."

"A question," interrupted Havelock. "The CIA report says everything was processed here. Your laboratories, your equipment—your staff. How come they didn't remove the body to Bethesda or Walter Reed?"

The physician turned, his hands in an open file drawer, his long fingers inserted between the folders. "Some pretty strong language on my part with the promise of a lot stronger from Midge MacKenzie if they tried. I told them she'd kick up a mess of feathers the like of which they haven't seen since the Bay of Pigs, that she hated their guts, figured the strain killed Mac and the least they could do was leave him in peace."

"Did they talk to her?"

"They tried to. She gave them five minutes, answered their questions, and told them to go to hell. They got the picture; they didn't want any loud trouble from her."

"I'll bet they didn't."

"Also," said Randolph, turning back to the files, "we've got a hell of a reputation here, treat some of the most important people in the country. Who's going to call us liars?"

"You counted on that, didn't you?"

"You're damn right   Here it is."

"What did your pathologist find that you think might help?"

"It's not what he found. Like I said, it's *him*. He was a temporary."

"A what?" Michael could feel a sudden, hollow suspension of breath in his chest.

"You heard me," Randolph continued, carrying the file back to his desk and sitting down. "He was a temporary replacement, took over for our regular man, who was out with a case of mono."

"Mononucleosis?"

"Herpesvirus. Easiest damn thing to transmit, if you've a mind to."

"You're losing me."

"Catch up," said the surgeon, turning the pages in the folder. "Several days before Mac's death our pathologist comes down with mono. Then, thank you very much, a highly qualified man shows up; he's in the middle of a transfer, has a month or so free, and is staying with a sister in Easton. Jesus, I grabbed him."

"And?"

"Mac's body's brought in; he does the initial work, and asks to see me in my office. I'll never forget it; the first thing he says to me is, 'How well did you know this MacKenzie?' "

Havelock nodded. "One thing led to another, and the bottom line was that MacKenzie's body couldn't stand an independent autopsy."

"He'd found minute traces of digitoxin," said Randolph.

"And a puncture wound, the position and angle indicating that it was probably self-inflicted," Havelock added.

"You got it."

"I'm sure he also inquired about MacKenzie's work, his mental state, his family—and, somewhere along the line, brought up the subject of insurance."

"He did. Oh, *Christ!*"

"Don't cut your throat, Doctor. These people do their homework like no one else on earth."

"What people?"

"If I'm right, they're called *paminyatchiki.*"

"Who?"

"Never mind. And don't bother looking for holes in there. He covered himself; he didn't tell you a single lie, that's his blanket. He simply knew it all in advance. You couldn't touch him without incriminating yourself and ruining your Center."

"I'm not looking for holes," said the doctor, rapidly scanning the pages.

"A sister in Easton? Forget it. She never was, and he's gone, and you won't find him."

"That's just it. I know where he is."

Michael bolted forward in the chair. "You *what?*"

"His name came up several weeks ago. I was talking to a salesman from a surgical supply house and he mentioned that he had to check our purchase orders because a pathologist wanted to duplicate a piece of equipment we had. I recognized the name, of course, but not the place. It wasn't where I thought he'd transferred to." Randolph stopped and looked up from the file. "I did an odd thing," he continued. "Childish, I suppose. It was as though I didn't want to acknowledge him, or think about what he and I had done . . . just wanted to keep tabs on him. I didn't tell my secretary—as I usually do—to list his current position in our personnel records. Instead, I came in here and wrote it in Mac's file. Somewhere." The doctor went back to the pages.

Stunned, Havelock sat rigidly on the edge of the chair. Over the years in his shadow world, he had learned that the most incredible turns of circumstance generally had the most credible reasons for happening. He barely found his voice as he explained. "Your pathologist kept the name because he knew that you of all people could never come after him. He had his hooks into you *with* the name, not without it. Believe me, Doctor, sooner or later he would have pulled you in, viciously and effectively."

"I've got it," said Randolph, raising his eyes and staring at Michael. "He still could, you know. Pull me in, I mean."

"So could I, but I won't unless you destroy the information on that page. It's not likely because I wouldn't give you the chance. On the other hand, he'll never come near you because I won't give *him* the chance. He's made the one mistake he can't afford to make in his very strange life. It's fatal. The name, please."

"Colin Shippers. Chief pathologist, the Regency Foundation. It's a private research center."

It's far more than that, Doctor. It's where a paminyatchik *can be found. The first concrete step toward Ambiguity. Toward Parsifal.*

"This is what I want you to do," said Havelock. "And I'm afraid you'll have to do it."

It was vital to operate not only once removed but almost blindly, and that was the most difficult thing in the world for Michael to do. The highly concentrated surveillance had to be left to others, something Havelock hated because his team was operating totally in the dark, told only to follow instructions, given no clear reason for the job they were doing. There were always built-in risks in such methods; responsibility without knowledge or authority led to resentment, and resentment was the first cousin to carelessness. That could *not* be permitted. Nor, unfortunately, could inquiries be made regarding routine habits, friends, medical associates, places frequented . . . all the minutiae that might help them were denied them.

For if MacKenzie's death linked Dr. Colin Shippers to the initial cover-up of Costa Brava—a cover-up that was no part of the White House strategy—he was at the Medical Center under orders from the mole at State, the *paminyatchik* who had assumed the Ambiguity code. And a *paminyatchik* in that position would never entrust an assignment as sensitive as the killing of a CIA black-operations officer to any but one of his own. Therefore they had to operate on the assumption that Shippers himself was a traveler, and that even the hint of an alarm would send him underground, severing the connection to Ambiguity, and, with it, any possibility of tracing the mole through the link. Sources of information were continuously covered by the travelers; personnel offices, bank and credit references, professional records—even FBI checks—all were assiduously scrutinized by informants—willing and unwilling, Russian plants and blackmailed clerks—who alerted these thoroughly Americanized Soviet agents that someone was interested in them. This practice, in concert with Amendments IV, V and VI of the Bill of Rights, made it virtually impossible to trap a *paminyatchik;* he was a citizen and entitled to the protection of the Constitution of the United States. By the time probable cause eliminated unreasonable search, or a grand jury returned a presentment or an indictment, and the accused was informed of the nature and cause of his possible crime the traveler had long since departed, only to surface in weeks or months with another identity, a wholly original résumé, and not infrequently a new face, courtesy of surgeons in Moscow.

However, as Rostov had pointed out in Athens, the irony of this long-range Soviet penetration was found in the practical results. Far too often the American "experience" served to undermine the Soviet commitment. During his rare but necessary trips to Moscow's Dzerzhinsky Square, the *paminyatchik* was made aware of the inevitable comparisons between the two countries. In the final analysis, the travelers were far less productive than the KGB felt it had a right to expect in light of the money and the effort it expended. Yet to threaten one was to court exposure of the whole program.

Futility was not always the province of those with God on their side, thought Havelock.

Yet, again, there were the exceptions, and exposure would never come from them. A mole called Ambiguity, who roamed the sacrosanct corridors of the State Department, and a bright, persuasive pathologist named Colin Shippers, who could grasshop from laboratory to laboratory—how often were these laboratories branches of United States intelligence?— these justified the expense and whatever manpower Moscow allotted to the *paminyatchik* operation. Ambiguity was obviously Shippers's superior, the on-site control, and without doubt a respected satellite in the KGB firmament—but he was not keeping his normal KGB channels informed of the present crisis. Costa Brava, and all the madness it represented, was not only disavowed by Dzerzhinsky Square, but what little they did know about it alarmed men like Pyotr Rostov.

It had to; events had taken place that could *not* have taken place without complicity in Moscow. A VKR officer had been trapped and wounded in Paris by the central figure at Costa Brava, and it took little imagination to know that the orders the officer followed were obfuscated so as to be untraceable within the complex machinery of Russian intelligence. Of course Rostov was alarmed; the specter of the fanatical VKR was enough to frighten the most dedicated Marxist, just as it frightened Havelock. For the unknown Ambiguity obviously sent routine dispatches to his controls in the KGB but reserved his most explosive information for his masters in the Voennaya.

Rostov sensed it, but he could not pin it down, much less expose it. It was the reason for his offer to a former counterpart in Consular Operations. *He says he's not your enemy any longer, but others are who may be his as well.*

If Rostov had any idea how valid his instincts were, he would risk a firing squad to make contact, thought Michael. But Rostov was wrong; the Russian *was* his enemy. Essentially neither could trust the other because neither Washington nor Moscow would permit such trust, and not even the horror of Parsifal could change that.

Futility in a world gone mad . . . as mad as its former savior, Anthony Matthias.

"How long do you think it will take?" asked Jenna, sitting across from Havelock in the small, sunlit alcove off the kitchen where they had their morning coffee.

"It's difficult to tell. It'll depend on how convincing Randolph is and how quickly Shippers suspects that an insurance company may be something else, something that alarms him. It could be today, tonight, tomorrow . . . the day after."

"I'd think you'd want Randolph to force him to react immediately. Can you afford the time?"

"I can't afford to lose him; he's the only link we've got. His name didn't appear in the laboratory report—which was easy for him to insist on in light of Randolph's decision to cover up what he thought was a suicide. Shippers knows the only way he could surface would be for Randolph to incriminate himself, which he'd never do. Beyond practical considerations, his ego wouldn't permit it."

"But swiftness is everything, Mikhail," objected Jenna. "I'm not sure I understand your strategy."

Havelock looked into her eyes, his own eyes questioning. "I'm not sure I do, either. I've always known that to make things work in this business —this so-called profession of ours—was to think as your enemy thinks, to *be* him, then do what you're convinced he doesn't expect. Now I'm asked to think like someone I can't possibly relate to, a man who literally has to be *two people.*" Michael sipped his coffee, staring now at the rim of the cup. "Think about it. An American childhood, adolescence—the Yankees, the Knicks, the Denver Broncos, the Lakers—friends at school and college; going out with girls, talking about yourself, confiding in people you really like. These are the years when secrets are for telling; it's against human nature to keep them to yourself—part of growing up is revealing yourself. So explain it to me. How does a man like this, a *paminyatchik,* keep the one secret he can never reveal so deep inside him."

"I don't know, but you've just described someone I do know very well."

"Who?"

"You, my darling."

"That's crazy." Havelock put his cup down. He was anxious to leave the table; that, too, was in his eyes.

"Is it?" Jenna reached over, putting her hand briefly over his. "How many friends at school and in college, how many girls and people you really liked did you tell about Mikhail Havlíček, and Lidice? How many knew about the agonies of Prague and a child who hid in the forests and carried secret messages and explosives strapped to his person? Tell me, how many?"

"It was pointless. It was history."

"I would never have known—*we* would never have known—except that our leaders insisted on a thorough background check. Your intelligence services have not always sent the best people into our part of Europe and we paid for the mistakes. But when the dossier of Havlíček and the Havlíček family was brought to us—all easily verified—it came sealed with a man from the highest office of your State Department, who took it away with him. It was apparent that your immediate superiors—our normal contacts—were not aware of your early days. For some reason they were concealed; for some reason—you were two people. Why, Mikhail?"

"I just told you. Matthias and I agreed; it was history."

"You didn't care to live with it, then. You wanted that part of your life to remain hidden, out of sight."

"That'll do."

"I was with you so many times when older people spoke of those days and you never said anything, never let on that you were there. Because if you had, it could have led to your secret, the years you didn't care to talk about."

"That's consistent."

"Like this Shippers, you'd been there and you were staying out of sight. You *were there* but your signature didn't appear anywhere."

"It's a farfetched parallel."

"Different, perhaps; not farfetched," insisted Jenna. "You can't make even the usual inquiries about Shippers because informants might alert him and he'd disappear, protecting his secret. You're waiting for him to consider Randolph's call; finally, perhaps—you hope—he'll decide that he should find out whether or not this insurance company is really— How do you say it?"

"Balking," offered Michael. "Asking last questions before agreeing to the final settlement on MacKenzie's policy. It's standard; they hate like hell paying money."

"Yes, you believe he'll do this. And when he discovers there *are* no questions, he'll be alarmed, then make his move to contact his control, again you hope, Ambiguity."

"I think that's the way he *will* behave. It's the best and the safest way I can come up with. Anything else would send him underground."

"And each hour he . . ." Jenna shook her head, searching for words.

"Thinks about it," said Havelock. "Concentrates."

"Yes, concentrates. Every moment is a lost moment, giving him time to spot his surveillance, the men who worry you because you don't know them and you can't give them the true background material on their subject."

"I don't like it, but it's been done before."

"Hardly under these conditions, never with such terrible consequences for error. Swiftness *is* everything, Mikhail."

"You're trying to tell me something and I don't know what it is."

"You're afraid of alarming Shippers, afraid he might disappear."

" 'Terrified' is a better word."

"Then don't go after *him*. Go after the man who was silent, who was at the Medical Center when MacKenzie died, but whose signature did not appear. As you were two men in Prague, he is two men here. Go after the one you *see* because you have no reason to believe he *is* two men, or has a secret to conceal."

Havelock touched his cup, his eyes fixed on Jenna's eyes. "Go after a laboratory pathologist," he said quietly. "On the assumption that someone had to be there with Randolph. . . . Corroboration. The insurance company insists on a corroborating physician."

"In my country five signatures are barely adequate for any one document."

"He'll refuse, of course."

"Can he? He *was there.*"

"He'll tell Randolph he can't support him, can't agree openly to the diagnosis of aneurysm leading to aortal hemorrhage."

"Then I think the doctor should be quite firm. If that's Shippers's medical position, why didn't he take it before?"

Michael smiled. "That's very good. Blackmail an extortionist with his own material."

"Why not? Randolph has—how do you say it?—the leverage. Age, reputation, wealth; who is this Shippers to oppose him?"

"And none of it makes a damn bit of difference, anyway. We're simply forcing him to move quickly. For his own protection—not as a traveler, but as a *doctor*—he'll have to determine how serious the insurance people are. Whether it's a routine measure or whether they mean it. Then he finds out there's nothing; he's got to move again."

"What's today's schedule?" asked Jenna.

"Initial surveillance will pick up Shippers when he leaves his apartment this morning. Secondary will take over inside the Regency buildings."

"How? . . . I'm sorry, I wasn't listening last night when you were on the phone."

"I know you weren't, I was watching you. Are you going to have something for me?"

"Later, perhaps. How did your men get inside the buildings?"

"The Regency Foundation's a private firm with its share of classified government contracts. That's obviously the reason Shippers went there; a lot of those contracts are defense-oriented. Regency was the company that first projected the radius burn-level of napalm. It's common for government technocrats and GAO personnel to be around there, shuffling papers and looking official. Starting this morning, there are two more."

"I hope no one asks them questions."

"They wouldn't answer if anyone did; that's standard. Also they've got briefcases and plastic ID's on their lapels that identify them. They're covered if anyone checks." Havelock looked at his watch as he got up from the table. "Randolph's making his call between ten and ten-thirty. Let's go. I'll reach him and give him the new word."

"If Shippers reacts," said Jenna, following Michael down the hall toward the paneled study, "he won't use his office phone."

"There are three mobile units in the streets, separated by blocks, everyone in radio contact, wrist cameras activated by arm movements. They can move out on foot or by car—cars alternating in traffic. If they're any good, they won't lose him."

"They *do* worry you, don't they?"

"They worry me." Havelock opened the door of the study, holding it for Jenna. "They'd worry me more if it wasn't for a fellow named Charley who wanted to put a bullet in my head down on Poole's Island."

"The one from Consular Operations?"

Michael nodded, going to the desk. "He flew up last night—my personal request, which didn't exactly thrill him. But he's good, he's thorough, and he knows that Shippers is involved with the Matthias crisis. That's enough to make him better than he ever was. He's in charge, and if he doesn't choke on the mobile phone he'll keep me posted, let me know if anything breaks."

Jenna had gone to her own desk—the couch; on the coffee table in front of it there were neat, narrow stacks of papers and several pages of handwritten notes. She sat down and picked up a bound typewritten report from the pile on the left. She spoke while reading, her voice indefinite, her concentration split. "Have you gotten in touch with the insurance company?"

"No, that's a risk I don't want to take," replied Havelock, sitting down at the desk and watching Jenna, but his interest was diverted. "MacKenzie's policy might be flagged."

"You're probably right."

"What have you got there? It's the same thing you were looking at last night."

"It's the report from your Central Intelligence Agency. The list of potential Soviet defectors over the past ten years, none of whom materialized."

"Look for a nuclear scientist or an armaments strategist who disappeared."

"Others disappeared too, Mikhail," said Jenna, reading and reaching for a pencil.

Havelock kept his eyes on her for several moments, then looked down at a sheet of paper on which were scribbled various telephone numbers. He checked one, picked up the phone, and dialed.

"He's a cold son of a bitch, I can tell you," snapped Dr. Matthew Randolph. "Once I laid it out for him, he clammed up, asked a couple of questions like a mortician settling with a family lawyer, and said he'd get back to me."

"How did you lay it out, and what were his questions?" asked Michael, putting down the page of Pentagon stationery on which were written the identities of the senior officers on the Nuclear Contingency Committees. He had circled a name. "Try to be as accurate as possible."

"I'll be *completely* accurate," objected the surgeon testily.

"I only meant in terms of the words, the phrases he used."

"It won't be hard; they were damned few and damned short. . . . Like you figured, he said I had no right to involve him, that was our understanding. He simply brought me his findings and how I altered them was my responsibility, not his. So *I* said I wasn't a goddamned lawyer, but if my memory for trivia served me, he was an accessory and there was no way around it and I was going to be fried in hell before Midge MacKenzie and those kids got screwed out of what was coming to them."

"So far very good. What was his response?"

"He didn't have any, so I blasted along. I told him he was a damned fool if he thought he was invisible around here four months ago and a bigger fool if he thought anyone on the staff would believe I'd spend hours in a pathology laboratory over the body of a friend all by myself."

"*Very* good."

"He had an answer to that. Like a talking piece of dry ice, he asked who specifically knew."

Havelock felt a sudden spasm in his chest, the specter of unnecessary executions rising. "What did you say? Did you mention anybody?"

"Hell, I said probably *everybody!*"

Michael relaxed. "You can get on the payroll, Doctor."

"You couldn't afford me, son."

"Please, go on."

"I backed down a bit, told him he was getting all worked up over nothing. I said the fella who came to see me from the insurance company said it was just a formality, that they required a second signature on the path report before sending the check. I even suggested he call Ben Jackson over at Talbot Insurance if he was worried, that Ben was an old friend—"

"You gave him a *name?*"

"Sure. Ben *is* an old friend; he set up Mac's policy. I figured if anyone phoned Ben, he'd call me and ask what the hell was going on."

"And what were *you* going to say?"

"That whoever it was got it backwards. *I* was the one who wanted the second signature for our own records."

"What did *Shippers* say?"

"Just a few words, spoken like a frozen computer. He asked whether I had told either Ben or the man from the insurance company who he was."

"And?"

"I said 'No, I didn't.' Fair was fair, and I guessed the best way was to handle it quietly. For him to get over here and sign the damned report without any fanfare."

"His response here?"

"Again, damned short and bloodless." Randolph paused, and spacing his words apart in a monotone, he continued, " 'Have you told me everything,' he wanted to know. I tell you he was a zombie."

"What did you say?"

"I said of course I had, what else was there? That's when he told me he'd call me back. Just like that, 'I'll call you back,' in that God-awful voice."

Havelock breathed deeply, his eyes dropping to the names on the Pentagon stationery, to one name in particular. "Doctor, either you've done a remarkable job or I'm going to have your inflated head."

"What the hell are you *talking* about?"

"If you'd done it my way, just using the insurance company alone, without any other name, Shippers would have assumed MacKenzie's death was being reexamined by a third party without telling you. Now, if he calls this Jackson he'll know you're lying."

"So what? Same result, isn't it?"

"Not for you, Doctor, and we can't ring in your friend; we can't take the risk. For your sake I hope he's gone fishing. And I mean it—if you've given me another complication, I'll see your head rolling down the street."

"Well, now, young fella, I've been doing some thinking about that. There could be a *couple* of heads rolling down a *two-* way street, couldn't there? Here you are, a muckamuck from the White House telling me the executive branch of our government is trying to cover up the brutal killing of a heroic veteran, an employee of the CIA, and I'm just a country doctor trying to protect the interests of his bereaved widow and fatherless orphans because they've suffered more than anyone had a right to ask them to suffer. You want to tangle with me, you bastard?"

"Please call me if you hear anything further, Dr. Randolph."

Special Detachment Officer Charles Loring, Consular Operations, late of Poole's Island, rubbed his eyes and raised the thermos of black coffee to his lips as he sat in the front seat of the gray sedan. The driver was for all intents and purposes a stranger; that is to say, Loring had not seen him before ten o'clock last night, when he had met the entire unit selected by Havelock from thirty-odd service records submitted by the Federal Bureau of Investigation at the Justice Department's request. The unit was now his responsibility, the assignment of continuity surveillance understood, the reasons behind it withheld—which was not the smartest thing to do when dealing with superior talent.

And regardless of Havelock's minor—very minor—attempt to stroke him, Charley Loring knew that the former Cons Op field man was getting some of his own back by claiming "reluctant privilege." The only clue Havelock gave him was that this Shippers was tied in with Poole's Island, and it was—with reluctance—enough for Charley. Havelock was a low-blow-dealing prick and he had made fools of Savannah, but if he was running some part of the Matthias show in Washington, he had more problems than they did. Loring would do what he could to help. There were times when likes and dislikes just did not mean very much; the catastrophe—the tragedy—of Poole's Island was such a time.

The unit had met at ten o'clock at Sterile Eleven down in Quantico, and had stayed up until four in the morning covering the variables of total surveillance—without knowing a damn thing about the subject. They had a photograph, but except for an inadequate description furnished by Randolph that was about all they had, and it, too, was inadequate. It was a blowup made at Sterile Eleven from a 1971 Jefferson Medical School yearbook that had been located by the FBI office in Philadelphia. No reason was given the agents who found it, only that they should observe complete secrecy. Actually, it had been stolen out of the university's library by an agent, who had concealed it under his coat. Examining the grainy blowup, the unit had to imagine a face considerably older than that in the photograph, and since no one they could speak with had seen Shippers in four months, the possibility of a beard or a moustache could not be discounted. And they could speak to no one about Dr. Colin Shippers, no one at all. Havelock's orders.

Initial surveillance had dispelled the conjecture about any hirsute additions to the subject's face; tinted glasses and a heavier frame were the essential differences between his appearance now and the yearbook photograph. The men inside the Regency Foundation had radioed out twice; they had picked up Shippers. One man was down the hall from the laboratory where the pathologist worked; the other covered his office on the floor below. The waiting had begun, thought Loring. But waiting for what?

The hours or the days would tell. All Charles Loring knew was that he had done everything he could to position the unit effectively: spaced apart and in contact to ensure maximum concealment. The cars were at one-way intersections, his own down the street and across from the research center with a full view of the entrance and the adjacent garage used for personnel parking.

A sharp, high-pitched hum came from the dashboard console; it was a signal from one of the men inside. Loring reached for the microphone, depressed the switch, and spoke. "S-Five. What is it?"

"S-Three. He just left the lab, seems in a hurry."

"Any clues?"

"I heard a telephone ring in there a few minutes ago. He's alone, so he could have talked, but that's spec. I wasn't able to overhear any conversation."

"It's good enough. Stay where you are and stay out of sight."

Loring replaced the microphone, only to hear a second jarring signal before he could lean back in the seat.

"S-Five."

"S-Two. Subject went into his office. From the way he walked—his general demeanor—he's agitated."

"Good description; it fits upstairs. We may be moving faster than any of us—"

"Hold it! Stay on the line," instructed Surveillance 2 as static filled the speaker. The man had concealed his radio under his clothing without breaking the open circuit. In seconds his voice was back. "Sorry. Subject came right back out and I had to spin. He chucked the white coat and is in his street clothes. Same tan raincoat, same soft, floppy hat. I guess he's yours."

"I guess he is. Out." Loring held the microphone in his hand and turned to the driver. "Get ready, the package is coming our way. If I have to go on foot, take over. I'll stay in touch." He reached under his jacket and took out the small compact hand-held radio, checking by habit the battery charge. He then pulled back his left sleeve, revealing the flat miniaturized high-speed camera attached to the underside of his wrist. He twisted his hand and heard the muted click; he was ready. "I wonder who this Shippers is," he said, watching the entrance of the Regency Foundation.

The telephone rang, breaking Havelock's concentration on his Pentagon notes. He picked it up.

"Yes?"

"Cross?"

Michael blinked, recognizing Randolph's strident voice. "Yes, Doctor?"

"Maybe we can both keep our heads. Ben Jackson just called, angrier than a Point Judith squall."

"What about?"

"Seems this lawyer phoned him asking why the final payment on MacKenzie's policy was being held up."

"Shippers," said Havelock.

"You got it, and Ben was madder'n hell. There *was* no final payment. The entire settlement was mailed to Midge's lawyer about eight weeks ago."

"Why did Jackson call you and not Mrs. MacKenzie's attorney?"

"Because Shippers—I figure it was Shippers or someone calling for him —got shook up and said there was some confusion over signatures on a medical report and did Ben know anything about it. Naturally, Ben said he didn't; the money was paid—processed through his agency—and that was that. He also added that he didn't appreciate his reputation—"

"Listen to me," interrupted Havelock. "I won't lose *my* head, but you may have blown yours away. I want you to stay in your office and don't see anybody until I can get a couple of men up there. If anyone tries to reach you, have the desk say you're operating."

"Forget it!" shot back Randolph. "A mealy-mouthed snot like Shippers doesn't worry me. He comes near here, I'll have one of the guards throw him into a padded cell."

"If he did and you could, I'd kiss your feet at this point, but it won't *be* Shippers. He may call you; that's as near as he'll come and it'd be the best thing that could happen to you. If he does, say you're sorry for the white lie, but after long consideration, you wanted to cover yourself on that report."

"He wouldn't believe it."

"Neither would I, but it's a stall. I'll have men up there within the hour."

"I don't want them!"

"You have no choice, Dr. Randolph," said Michael, hanging up and immediately centering the page of telephone numbers in front of him.

"Do you really think Shippers will go after him?" asked Jenna, standing by the window with the CIA report in her hand.

"He won't, but others'll be sent up there, not at first to kill him, but to take him. Take him and get him alone where they can press his head until they find out who he's dealing with, who he's lying for. Killing could be nicer." Havelock reached for the phone, his eyes on the page below.

"On the other hand," observed Jenna, "knowing Randolph lied, knowing he was involved, made Shippers move faster than we thought possible. How long ago was Loring's last call?"

"Over an hour. Shippers took a taxi downtown; they're with him on foot by now. We should be hearing soon." Michael dialed; the line answered quickly. "This is Sterile Five, Fairfax. Under that code name I was taken under escort up to the Randolph Medical Center yesterday. Talbot County, Maryland, Eastern Shore. Will you confirm, please?" While waiting, Havelock covered the phone and said to Jenna, "I just thought of something. With any luck we might turn a liability into an asset," then returned to the phone: ". . . Yes, that's right. Three-man team; departure was eleven hundred hours. Are you ready for instructions? . . . Return two men, up there immediately on a priority basis. Subject is Dr. Matthew Randolph; he's to be given protection, maximum visual contact, but there's a hook. I want the men to be part of the local scenery —orderlies or staff or whatever I can work out with Randolph. Tell them to get en route and call me on the mobile phone in twenty minutes; patch it through you." Michael paused again, looking again at Jenna as the Secret Service dispatcher checked schedules. "Randolph may have done us another favor at a risk to himself he'll never understand."

"If he cooperates."

"He hasn't got a choice, I meant that." The dispatcher returned; Havelock listened, then spoke. "No, that's fine. Actually, I prefer men who weren't up there yesterday. By the way, the code will be—" Michael stopped, his thoughts going back to the Palatine, to a dead man whose words had sent him to Maryland's Eastern Shore. "Apache," he said. "They were hunters. Tell Apache to call me in twenty minutes."

Dr. Matthew Randolph roared his objections to no avail. He would either cooperate, Havelock told him, or they could all take their chances *and* the fallout "tangling" with each other. "Mr. Cross" was prepared to press his suit to the limit even if it meant admitting the murder of a CIA operations officer named Steven MacKenzie. And Randolph, understanding that he was now between a rock and a hard place, entered into the dangerous charade with a fair degree of inventiveness. The Apache team would be two visiting cardiologists from California, complete with white jackets and stethoscopes.

Havelock's orders were explicit, no room for error. Whoever came for Matthew Randolph—and someone was bound to come—he or they were to be taken alive. Wounds were permitted, but only in the legs, the feet, nothing above the waist.

It was a Four Zero order, none more sacrosanct in the clandestine services.

"Havelock, it's Loring."

"How goes it?"

"My driver said he wasn't able to raise you."

"I was talking with an irascible doctor, but if there was an emergency, your man could have broken in. He knows that."

"It wasn't and it isn't. It's just weird." Loring stopped. The pause was uncomfortable.

"What's going down, Charley?"

"That's just it. Nothing. Shippers's taxi let him off in front of Garfinckle's Department Store. He went inside, made a call from one of the phones on the first floor, and for the past hour or so he's been wandering around the men's shop on the fifth. I'm calling from there; I've got him in sight."

"He's waiting for someone."

"If he is, it's an odd way of doing it quietly."

"What do you mean?"

"He's buying clothes like he was going on a cruise, trying on things and laughing with the clerks. He's a one-man gross for the day."

"It's not usual, but be patient. The main point is he made the call, made his first outside move. You're doing fine."

"Who the hell is he, Havelock?"

Michael reflected. Loring deserved to be told more than he had been; it was the moment to bring him nearer to the truth. So much depended on the sharp, plainspoken Cons Op officer.

"A deep-cover entry who's going to meet a man who could blow Poole's Island out of Savannah harbor. I'm glad you're there, Charley. We *have* to know who that man is."

"Good enough, and thanks. All the floors and exits here are covered, we're in contact and our cameras ready. If it's a question of choice, do we drop Shippers and stay with his contact?"

"You may not have to. You may recognize him. The others probably wouldn't, but you might."

"Jesus, from *State?*"

"That's right. My guess is fairly high-level, forty-five to middle fifties, and some kind of specialist. If you *do* recognize him, stay far back until they separate, then pick up Shippers and bring him down here. But when you close in, be very fast and very careful and check for capsules."

"Shippers is that deep? Christ, how do they do it?"

"Past tense, Charley. Did. A long time ago."

The waiting would have been intolerable had it not been for Havelock's growing fascination with a Lieutenant Commander Thomas Decker, Annapolis '61, former skipper of the submarine *Starfire,* and a member of the Pentagon's Nuclear Contingency Committees. Decker was a liar with no apparent reason for lying.

Michael had spoken with all fifteen NCC senior officers, calling several twice, a few three times, ostensibly to put together a clear picture of the committees' working methods for updated presidential comprehension. In most of the conversations the initial remarks were guarded—each, of course, demanding White House switchboard verification—but as the words flowed and the officers realized Havelock knew what he was talking about, they grew less wary and more specific within the bounds of maximum security. Hypothetical events were matched with theoretical responses, and beyond his fundamental reason for speaking to each man, Havelock was impressed. If the laws of physics determined that for every action there was an equal and opposite reaction, the NCC teams had come up with a better equation. For any nuclear action on the part of an enemy the reaction was anything but equal; it was devastatingly superior. Even Lieutenant Commander Decker's contributions were electric in this sense. He made it clear that a ring perimeter of undersea nuclear marauders could demolish all major enemy installations from the North Atlantic to the Black Sea and most points in between in a matter of minutes. In this area he did not lie; he did in another. He said he had never met Secretary of State Anthony Matthias.

His name had appeared on three separate telephone logs from Matthias's office, all within the past six months.

It was, of course, possible that Decker's statement *was* true, that he had not actually *met* Matthias, merely spoken with him on the phone. But if that was the case, why had he not volunteered the information? A man who was asked whether or not he knew a statesman of Matthias's stature did not deny it readily without quickly offering the qualification that he *did* know him by way of the telephone. It was not natural, actually contradictory for an obviously ambitious naval officer rising fast in the Pentagon who would typically clutch ferociously at the coattails of Anthony Matthias.

Thomas Decker, USN, had lied. He did know Matthias and, for obscure reasons, did not care to admit it.

It was time for the fourth call to Lieutenant Commander Decker.

"You know, Mr. Cross, I've given you about all I can or should in these matters. I'm sure you're aware that there are restrictions placed on me that can only be countered by the President himself—in his presence, I might add."

"I'm aware of that, Commander, but I'm confused by one of my notes. It probably has nothing to do with anything we've talked about, but the Secretary of State didn't understand it, either. You said you didn't know him, never met him."

Decker's pause was as electric as his data on undersea nuclear warfare. "That's the way he wanted it," he said quietly. "That's the way he said it had to be."

"Thank you, Commander. Incidentally, Secretary of State Matthias was trying to pinpoint it this morning. He couldn't recall where you and he last talked with each other."

"The lodge, of course. Sometime in August or September, I think."

"Of course. The lodge. The Shenandoah."

"That's where it was, where it always was. No one knew anything. It was just ourselves. How is it possible he can't remember?"

"Thank you, Commander. Good-bye."

The Shenandoah.

The bell was piercing, the ring unbroken; it was the switchboard's way of signaling emergency. Havelock had been pacing, thinking; he rushed across the room and grabbed the phone. It was Loring.

"You've got my tail on a plate and I'll start carving it for you! *Jesus,* I'm *sorry!*"

"You lost him," said Michael, drained, his throat dry.

"*Christ.* I'll turn in my cards! Every fucking one of them!"

"Calm down, Charley. What happened?"

"A switch. A *goddamned switch!* I . . . I just wasn't *looking* for it! I should have, but I *wasn't!*"

"Tell me what happened," repeated Michael, sitting down as Jenna got up from the couch and started toward the desk.

"Shippers paid for the stuff he bought, arranging for most of it to be delivered except for a couple of boxes he took with him. He went into the fitting room and came out dressed for the street, same raincoat, same soft hat, carrying the boxes."

"Held high," Havelock broke in wearily, again the sense of futility spreading through him.

"Naturally," agreed Loring. "I followed him to the elevator, staying several aisles away—frankly looking at every son of a bitch in the men's department, figuring one of them might be your man. One lousy son of a bitch who might have brushed up against Shippers and gotten something from him. The elevator door closed, and I raised the men on each floor, every stop covered, each man to head below and join the others at the outside exits the second that elevator passed his floor. My S-Nine picked him up at the Fourteenth Street entrance and followed him, radioing the rest of us his position; we spread out in cars and on foot. *Jesus!*"

"When did it happen?" asked Michael.

"On the corner of Eleventh, four minutes after I left the store, and I was the last one out. The man hailed a cab, threw the boxes inside and, just before he got in, took off his hat. It wasn't Shippers at all. It was some guy ten, fifteen years older and mostly bald."

"What did your Nine do?"

"The best he could. He tried to stop the cab, but he couldn't; it shot right through a break in traffic. He called us, spelling everything out, giving the cab's number and description. Five of us ran back to the store, covering what exits we could, but we all knew we'd lost him. S-Eleven and -Twelve went after the cab; I told them to stay with it if they had to break every traffic law on the books—since we'd lost the subject, we could still grab the plant. They picked it up six blocks west, and there was no one inside. Only the raincoat, the hat, and the two boxes lying on the floor."

"The driver?"

"He said some nut got in, took off his coat, gave him five dollars, and jumped out at the next light. The men are taking the boxes in for possible prints."

"They won't find any matching anything in the Bureau's computers."

"I'm *sorry*. Havelock, I'm really sorry. Shippers's whole act was a diversion, and I bought it. Of all the goddamned times to lose an instinct, I had to pick this one."

Michael shook his head as he spoke. "You didn't lose it, Charley, I pushed it out of your head. At least you sensed a break in the pattern and I told you to forget it. I told you to be patient and concentrate on a man who never intended to be there."

"You don't have to do this," said Loring. "I wouldn't if I were you."

"You don't know that. Besides, I need you. You're not off the hook, Charley, I want those instincts of yours. There's a naval officer at the Pentagon, a Lieutenant Commander Thomas Decker. Under a very thick screen, find out everything you can about him. Everything."

"An entry?"

"No. A liar."

Jenna supported herself on the desk at Michael's side, looking over his shoulder as he studied the names and brief summaries of the men she had selected from the CIA, Cons Op, and Army intelligence reports. Out of a hundred and thirty-five potential Soviet defectors who had not come over to the West and whose current whereabouts were unknown she had chosen eight for priority consideration.

Michael looked at the list, put it down and slowly turned to her. "This has been a rotten day. It's no time for jokes."

"I'm not joking, Mikhail," said Jenna.

"There's not an armaments expert or a high-ranking military man or even an atomic scientist here. These are doctors, specialists—old men now, none of whom was remotely connected with any sort of strategic planning or nuclear strike capabilities."

"Parsifal needs no such connections."

"Then maybe I wasn't clear about what those documents *say*," Havelock said. "They spell out a series of nuclear moves—first and second strikes, interceptor counterstrikes, territorial neutralization and automated reclamation—detailed strategies that could only be conceived and negotiated by experts."

"Matthias didn't carry around such details in his head, you've said as much."

"Of course not, which is why I'm going after the men on the Contingency Committees—one in particular. But Parsifal *did*. He had to have those projections available to him. They were chips, his bargaining points in their insane game."

"Then someone is missing," insisted Jenna, walking around the desk, then suddenly turning to face Havelock. "Who spoke for the People's Republic? Who bargained China's position? Who gave *its* projections, *its* strategic details? According to your theory, there has to be a *third* negotiator."

"No, there doesn't. Their combined sources would be enough to build a totally convincing case for a China strategy. It's common knowledge in intelligence circles that if U.S. and Soviet penetration of the PRC arsenals were linked up, we'd know more about China's nuclear capabilities than anyone in Peking."

"A convincing *case?*"

"Totally."

"*Combined* sources, Mikhail? Why?"

Havelock studied Jenna's face, gradually understanding what she was trying to say. "*One* source," he said quietly. "Why not?"

The telephone rang, its strident signal producing an abrupt tightness in Michael's throat. He reached for it; the President of the United States was on the line, his first words as ominous as any Havelock had ever heard.

"The Soviets know about Matthias. There's no way to tell their next move."

"Parsifal?" asked Michael, with no breath in him.

"They can smell him, and what they smell is flaring their nostrils. They're close to panic."

"How did you find out?"

"They reached one of our high diplomatic personnel. They told him that they were prepared to expose Matthias. The only hope we've got now is that the man they contacted is one of the best we've got. They respect him; he could be our single hope for containment. I'm bringing him on board; he's taking Bradford's place. He's got to be told everything, understand everything."

"Who is he?"

"A man named Pierce. Arthur Pierce."

33

The *paminyatchik* sat in the underground strategy room of the White House as the President of the United States and two of the nation's most influential men briefed him. The conference had taken precedence over all of Charles Berquist's prior appointments and obligations. It had so far lasted nearly three hours, the incredulous undersecretary of State for the U.N. delegation rapidly taking brief notes, his intelligent gray eyes conveying a deep awareness of impending catastrophe, yet behind that sense a mind that was obviously in complete control, seeking answers, avoiding panic.

The tension was electric, intermittently broken by expressions of courtesy and respect. Arthur Pierce could not be called a friend of either the President or Addison Brooks, but neither was he a stranger. He was a professional with whom both men had worked, and in whom both had confidence. They remembered with gratitude his penetrating analyses in previous crises. As for General Malcolm Halyard, "Tightrope" had met Major Pierce in Saigon years ago, and was so impressed with his performance there that he had cabled the Pentagon recommending that the War College make a serious appraisal of the major's potential for permanent, as opposed to reserve, status.

Despite these extremely favorable appraisals, the outstanding citizen-soldier had chosen civilian status, albeit government-oriented. And since, to its dismay, the military establishment was frequently part of the government, the word had gone out: an exceptional man was available and looking for challenging work; someone should come up with something before the corporate headhunters descended on him. Washington needed all the genuine talent it could find.

It had happened so easily, so logically in its arithmetic: one plus one plus one. People became steps and the steps led to a high place. An elderly career officer at State said he just happened to be at a dinner party in Alexandria where his military host mentioned Pierce to him. Naturally, the career officer felt compelled to mention Pierce's name at a conference attended by Addison Brooks. State was perpetually scouting for that rare man with proven abilities who also had the potential for further intellectual growth. Arthur Pierce was summoned for an interview, which evolved into a lengthy lunch with the aristocratic statesman. This, in turn, led to an offer of employment, an entirely feasible decision in light of the record.

The mole was in place. There had in fact been no dinner party in Alexandria, no host who had discussed in uniquely flattering terms an outstanding soldier from Saigon. It did not matter; others were discussing him; Brooks had verified that. A dozen corporations were about to make offers to the brilliant young man, so Addison Brooks spoke first.

As the years went by, the decision to recruit Arthur Pierce could only be applauded. He *was* an outstanding talent with an increasingly apparent ability to comprehend and counter Soviet maneuvers, especially in face-to-face confrontations. There were, of course, specialists who studied *Izvestia* and the various Russian journals and communiqués to interpret often obscure Soviet positions, but where Pierce was most effective was at the conference table, whether in Helsinki, Vienna or Geneva. At times his perceptions were uncanny; he frequently seemed to be ten steps ahead of the spokesmen sent by Moscow, preparing counterproposals before the Soviet position had even been made clear, thus giving the U.S. team the advantage of an immediate response. His presence was increasingly sought by upper-level diplomats until the inevitable took place: he was brought into Matthias's orbit, and the Secretary of State lost little time making Arthur Pierce an upper-level diplomat himself.

The *paminyatchik* had arrived. An infant, genetically selected in Moscow and sent covertly into the heartland of America, was in place after a lifetime of preparation, and at this moment he was being addressed by the President of the United States.

"You now have the whole ungodly picture, Mr. Undersecretary." Berquist stopped as a painful memory flooded his mind. "It's strange using that title," he continued softly. "Only days ago another undersecretary sat at this same dais."

"I hope I can contribute even a fraction of what he did," said Pierce, studying his notes. "The fact that he was killed is appalling. Emory was a friend of mine . . . he didn't have many friends."

"He said the same thing about himself," observed Addison Brooks. "And about you."

"Me?"

"That you were his friend."

"I'm flattered."

"You might not have been at the time," said General Halyard. "You were one of nineteen people he was looking into."

"In what way?"

"He was trying to find someone on the fifth floor of State who might have been out of the country, who might have been at the Costa Brava," explained the President.

"The man who later used the Ambiguity code?" asked Pierce, frowning.

"That's right."

"How did my name come up? Emory never told me, never called me."

"Under the circumstances," said the ambassador, "he couldn't. Several query responses between you and Washington during that week had been misplaced. I don't have to tell you what a shock it was to him at first. They were found, of course."

"Those misfilings are a constant irritant," said Pierce, going back to his notes, checking off items with his gold-plated ball-point pen. "I don't even know that there's a solution. The volume of traffic is simply too great and there are too few people cleared for the material at that level." The undersecretary circled a note, adding as an afterthought, "On the other hand, I'd rather put up with the irritation than take the chance that some of those confidential memoranda might get out."

"How much of what you've learned here in this room do you think the Soviets know?" Berquist asked, his Nordic face set, his eyes hard and level, the muscles in his jaws pulsating.

"Less than I've learned here in this room but probably more than we suspect. The Russians are so damned elliptical. What's more, they're working themselves up into a frenzy. I can't form a judgment until I've had a chance to study those—incredible documents."

"False documents," said Halyard emphatically. "Agreements between two madmen, that's what they are."

"I'm not sure either Moscow or Peking would believe that, General," said Pierce, shaking his head. "One of those madmen is Anthony Matthias, and the world isn't ready to accept him as insane."

"Because it doesn't want to," interrupted Brooks. "It's afraid to."

"That's right, sir," agreed the undersecretary of State. "But apart from Matthias, as the President has described these so-called nuclear aggression pacts, they contain extraordinary and extraordinarily classified information. Locations, megatonnage, detailed delivery capabilities, launching codes—even abort systems. From what I can gather, the gates of the arsenals of the two superpowers and their runner-up in China have been opened; the most secret hardware in each camp is there for anyone to see who reads the agreements." Pierce turned to the soldier. "What would be the Pentagon's recommendation if a similar Sino-Soviet pact against *us* were brought in by clandestine services, General?"

"Launch," answered Halyard flatly. "There'd be no alternative."

"Only if you were convinced it was authentic," interjected Brooks.

"I'd be convinced," said the general. "So would you be. Who else but men with access to that information could include it? Also, there are the projected dates. I'd be *damned* convinced."

"When you say the Soviets are elliptical," said the statesman, "I concur wholeheartedly, but how do you mean it in the current sense?"

"They threw phrases at me—disjointed non sequiturs—watching me to see if I'd pick up on any. We've been confronting each other for a number of years now, whether in Vienna or Bern or New York; you get to spot even concealed reactions."

"But they first told you they knew Matthias was insane," said Berquist. "That was their opening, wasn't it?"

"Yes, sir. I don't think I used the exact words before. I will now. I was in the Soviet ambassador's office at his request—summons, really—along with his senior aide. Frankly, I thought he'd asked to see me so we might work out a compromise on the Pan-Arab resolution, but instead he greeted me with a statement that could only refer to Matthias: 'We understand from a most reliable source that a holiday has been extended because the mental condition of the vacationer has deteriorated to a point beyond recovery.' "

"What was your reply?" asked Brooks. "The exact words, please."

" 'The Russian compulsion for brooding, self-serving fantasy is no different now from what it was when Dostoyevsky described it.' Those were my exact words."

"Provocative yet insouciant," said the statesman. "Very good."

"That's when the fireworks started. 'He's mad!' shouted the ambassador. 'Matthias is mad! He's done insane things, undermined what's left of détente.' Then his aide joined in, demanding to know where the next meetings were being held, which unstable governments Matthias had been in contact with, and whether they knew he was insane, or was a madman sending out secret communications, concealing his insanity from the people he was reaching? What frightens me, Mr. President, Mr. Ambassador, General Halyard, is that *they* described what you've described to *me*. If I understood correctly, Matthias has been doing just that for the past six months. Reaching unstable regimes, instant prime ministers, revolutionary juntas we shouldn't be touching."

"That's where the Soviets got their information, of course," said Berquist. "They think a demented Matthias is implementing a number of his well-known 'geopolitical realities.' Moving in on them."

"They think far more than that, sir," corrected Pierce. "They believe he may have funneled nuclear materials to extremist regimes and fanatic camps—Islamic, for example, or Afghan, or anti-Soviet Arab factions— we've all agreed shouldn't have them. They're paranoid about it. We can protect ourselves from each other by the sheer magnitude of our arsenals, but neither of us can protect ourselves from an irrational partisan junta or sect that possesses launch and nuclear capability. Actually, we're far safer; we're separated by oceans. Strategic Russia is part of the Euro-Asian land mass; its borders are vulnerable if only by proximity to potential enemies. If I read them correctly, it's these concerns that are pushing them toward the panic button."

"But not Parsifal," said Brooks. "In your judgment, the man we call Parsifal has *not* made contact with Moscow."

"I can't rule *anything* out," said Pierce. "There were so many phrases, threats, implications—as I said, elliptical references. For instance, they mentioned 'next meetings,' 'unstable governments,' 'nuclear materials.' All of these—again, if I understood correctly—are actually a part of these agreements. If I could study them I'd be able to spot parallels with the original texts." The undersecretary paused, then spoke quietly, firmly. "I think it's possible this Parsifal *has* made contact, delivering provocative hints, perhaps nothing more. And I think it's urgent that we know even this."

"He wants to blow us all up," said the President. "My God, that's all he wants to do."

"The sooner I can get to Poole's Island, Mr.—" Pierce was interrupted by the humming of the white telephone on the white dais, a red light flashing on its miniaturized console. Berquist picked it up. "Yes?"

The President listened in silence for nearly thirty seconds, then answered, nodding, "I understand. Let me know what happens as soon as it happens." He replaced the phone and turned to the others. "That was Havelock. He won't get here this afternoon."

"What *is* happening?" asked the general.

"Too many things for him to leave the phone."

"I'm sorry," said Arthur Pierce. "I wanted to meet him. I think it's vital we stay in touch. I can tell him what's going on with the Soviets and he can keep me up-to-date. I have to know when to press forward, when to back off."

"You'll be kept informed; he has his orders from me. . . . They lost the pathologist."

"*Damn!*" exploded the general.

"He either picked up the surveillance or, knowing things were out of control, decided to disappear."

"Or was ordered to disappear," added the statesman.

"That's what I can't understand," said Berquist, turning to the silent undersecretary of State. "The Russians gave you no indication that they were *aware* of any Soviet involvement in this whole damn thing? They didn't mention the Costa Brava or Rostov's cable to us?"

"No, sir. That may be the one advantage we have. We know, but they don't."

"*Rostov* knows," insisted the President.

"Then he's too frightened to act," replied Pierce. "It's often the case with entrenched KGB personnel; they're never sure whose toes they may be stepping on. Or if he is searching, he's not getting anywhere."

"You're talking as though we were speaking about two different Moscows," objected Halyard.

"I agree with Havelock," said the mole. "We are. And until the Moscow that wants to get its hands on Matthias's documents succeeds, the one I'm dealing with speaks for the Kremlin. That won't be the case otherwise. It's all the more reason why I've *got* to be kept current. If Havelock caught even one man we could trace to that other Moscow, it would be leverage. I could use it."

"He's already told us," interrupted Brooks. "A branch of Soviet intelligence known as the VKR. Rostov as much as admitted it."

Pierce looked bewildered. "I didn't hear that mentioned."

"Perhaps I overlooked it," said Berquist.

"In any event, it's too general. The VKR is a consolidation of many units. I'd need specifics. Which unit? Which directors?"

"You may get them."

"I beg your pardon, sir?" Pierce's gold-plated pen was suspended above his notes.

"It's one of the things that's keeping Havelock at Sterile Five."

"Sterile Five . . ."

"They may have lost this Shippers, but Havelock expects that whoever gave him orders will send men up to Maryland to find out who Matthew Randolph's been working with. He's got his own people in place with orders to wound and take. As I told you, the doctor lied about MacKenzie's death but for the wrong reasons."

"Yes, I know." Pierce looked down at his notes as he replaced the pen inside the coat of his dark pinstriped suit. "It helps me to write things out; I didn't expect to take these with me."

"I'm glad," said the President. "I wouldn't have let you. . . . You've got a lot to think about, Mr. Undersecretary, and not much time. How do you plan to handle the Soviets?"

"Cautiously," replied the mole. "With your permission, I'd like to substantiate a part of what they told me."

"You're out of your *mind,*" said Halyard.

"Please, General, only a very minor part. They obviously have a fairly accurate source, so to deny the whole would only make them more suspicious, more hostile. We can't afford that now. In the President's words, we have to contain them as much as possible for as long as possible."

"How do you think you can do it?" asked Berquist, his eyes wary.

"By admitting that Matthias collapsed from exhaustion. Everything else has been exaggerated way out of proportion to the medical diagnosis, which is of minor consequence. He's been ordered to rest for several weeks; that's all. The rest is rumor and wild gossip, the sort of thing that goes with a man like Matthias. Don't forget, they have their memories of Stalin; they can't dismiss them. By the time Stalin was dead most of Moscow believed he was certifiably insane."

"Excellent," interjected Ambassador Brooks.

"They can't dismiss the other sources," said Halyard, obviously wanting to agree but the strategist in him prohibiting it. "The leaks from unstable regimes—instant prime ministers, or whatever you called them. Matthias *reached* them."

"Then they have to be more specific with *me*. I think I can handle them case by case. At the least, they'd have to confer with Moscow, double-check the origins. Every case could buy us time." Pierce stopped, turning to Berquist. "And time, Mr. President, is what's on my mind now. I think the sooner I get back to New York and ask—no, demand—a meeting with the Soviet ambassador, the better chance I have of pushing their hands away from the buttons. I *do* believe they'll listen to me. I can't guarantee how long, but for a while—a few days, a week—they will."

"Which prompts the obvious question," said the statesman, his well-tailored elbows on the table, his slender hands folded beneath his chin. "Why do you think they contacted you and not the more direct, crisis-oriented channels in Washington?"

"I'd like to know that too," added Berquist. "There's a phone never more than fifty feet away from me for such contingencies."

Arthur Pierce did not reply at first, his eyes shifting back and forth between the President and the ambassador. "It's difficult for me to answer that without appearing arrogant or overly ambitious, and I don't believe I'm either."

"We'll accept that," said Berquist. "Just give us your opinion."

"With all due respect to our ambassador in New York—and I'm sincere; he has an extremely likable presence, which is terribly important, and he's had an outstanding career in government—"

"*Had,*" the President broke in. "He's a soft bush in a high wind, but the roots are deep. He's there because of his *lovable* presence, and the fact that he doesn't make a goddamn decision. We'll accept that, too. Go on."

"The Soviets know you appointed me—at Matthias's request—to be the State Department's spokesman. To be *your* spokesman, sir."

"And the spokesman for Anthony Matthias," said Brooks, nodding his head. "Which assumes a close relationship with our Secretary of State."

"I enjoyed such a relationship until a number of months ago—when, apparently, all relationships were terminated by his illness."

"But they think you still have it," observed Halyard. "And why the hell not? You're the closest thing we could have there *except* Matthias."

"Thank you, General. Basically, I think they came to me because they thought I'd know if there was any substance to the Matthias rumors. The madness."

"And if they thought you knew but were lying, what would be their response?"

"They'd disregard the hot line, Mr. President. They'd put the world on nuclear alert."

"Get back to New York and do what you can. I'll make the security arrangements for you to get down to Poole's Island. Study those agreements until you know them word for word."

The *paminyatchik* rose from the dais, leaving his unnecessary notes behind.

The limousine passed through the White House gates as Arthur Pierce shot forward in the seat, his hand gripping the strap, and, in a harsh voice, spoke to the driver assigned to him by the Department of State. "Get me to a phone booth as fast as you can."

"The mobile phone's in working order, sir. It's in the case in the center of the floor." The driver removed his right hand from the wheel and gestured at the black leather receptacle behind him. "Just pull up on the latch."

"I don't care to use this phone! A booth, please."

"Sorry, sir, just trying to be helpful."

The undersecretary checked himself. "I apologize. It's those mobile operators; they can take forever, and I'm in a great hurry."

"Yeah, I've heard that complaint before." The driver accelerated briefly, only to apply the brakes seconds later. "There's one, sir. On the corner."

Pierce got out of the car and walked rapidly to the glass booth, coins in his hand. Inside, he pulled the door shut, inserted a quarter and dialed. "Your trip?" he asked curtly.

"Smooth flight. Go ahead."

"Has the detail left for Maryland?"

"About fifteen minutes ago."

"*Stop* them!"

"How?"

The *paminyatchik* bit his lip. There could be no mobile phones for them, no system where numbers could be recorded. He had only one question left before issuing the order. "Is there any way you can reach them once they're on the premises? Any way at all?"

The initial silence was his answer. "Not the way it's orchestrated," was the quiet reply.

"Send a second detail immediately. Police vehicle, automatic weapons, silencers. Kill them; kill them all. No one must be left alive."

"You *sent* them!"

"It's a trap."

"Oh, *Christ* . . . Are you sure?"

"I've just left the White House."

A low whistle was the astonished response. "It really paid off, didn't it?"

"They had no choice. As we say over here, I had all the marbles and I was shooting from the top of the circle. I'm inside. There's also something else."

"What?"

"Reach Mother. Rostov's centered in on Victor. Find out how deep; elimination must be considered."

Loring walked down the steps of the Pentagon thinking about Lieutenant Commander Thomas Decker. He was not sure what Havelock was looking for, but he was fairly certain he did not have it. After having read Decker's complete service record, including endless evaluation and fitness reports over at the Department of the Navy, Charley had decided to pull in a few debts owed him at the Pentagon. On the pretext that the officer was being considered for a sensitive embassy position that required tact and a fair degree of personality, he called on several friends in Army intelligence and said he needed a few confidential interviews. Could they help and did they remember when he had helped them? They could and they did.

Five people—each held accountable for confidentiality—were brought separately to meet with him for informal, very-off-the-record conversations. There were three fellow naval officers who had served with Decker aboard the submarine *Starfire,* a secretary who had worked in his office for six months, and a marine who was on his Nuclear Committee team.

Havelock had said Decker was a liar. If he was, Loring had found no evidence to support this characterization. He was, if anything, something of a moralizer, who had run a tight ship on the basis of strict Judeo-Christian principles to the point where he read the Lessons at each weekly interdenominational religious service he insisted be part of the *Starfire*'s schedule. His reputation was that of a firm but fair skipper; like Solomon, he weighed all sides of an issue before rendering a decision, which he then proceeded to justify on the basis of what he had heard. As a fellow officer put it, one might disagree with a given course of action on Decker's part, but one understood how he had arrived at it. His "engineer's mind," said another, grasped the "blocks and tackles" of a complicated argument quicker than most, and he was adept at spotting fallacies. Yet he never, according to the third officer, used another man's honest error to assert his own superiority; he accepted others' mistakes compassionately, as long as they were the products of best efforts, which he made sure to determine that they had been. This, thought Loring, was not a liar's approach.

It was the secretary, however, who shed light on another side of Thomas Decker not readily perceived from his service record and the statements of his fellow naval officers. The lieutenant commander apparently went to great lengths to please and support his own superiors.

He was always so tactful, so generous in his appraisals of other people's work even when you knew he thought it wasn't very good. There was this admiral . . . Then the White House put out a directive that choked him, but still he . . . And he gave his full endorsement to a JCS position which he told me was really counterproductive. . . . You talk about tact—well, the commander is about the most diplomatic man I've ever known.

The last person to talk with Charley Loring was the marine, a major and a member of Decker's Nuclear Contingency Committee. He put his own assessment of his colleague somewhat more succinctly.

He kisses ass something fierce, but what the hell, he's damned good. Also, that's not exactly an unknown exercise around here. Tact? . . . Christ, yes, he's got tact, but he's not going to hang himself over something really important. I mean, he'll find ways of greasing an issue so the oil's all over the table.

Translation: Spread the responsibility for disagreement, preferably as high as it will flow, but if this attitude made for a dangerous liar, there were few truthful men at the Pentagon—or anywhere else, for that matter.

Loring reached his car in the side parking area, settled back in the seat, and pulled out the microphone from its cradle beneath the dashboard. He flipped the power switch and pressed the transmission button, making contact with the White House mobile operator.

"Patch me through to Sterile Five, please," he instructed. While everything was fresh in his mind he would relay it all to Havelock. For all the good it might do.

The Apache unit roamed the corridors of the Medical Center, one or the other of the two men keeping Dr. Matthew Randolph in sight wherever he went. Neither man approved of the arrangements and let Sterile Five know it; they were inadequate for this particular subject. Randolph was an aging jackrabbit who darted in and out of doors and hallways and outside exits with determined alacrity. Whatever had prompted the doctor to cooperate initially had evaporated as his contrariness reasserted itself. It was as though he were consciously trying to draw attention to himself, to *make* something happen, to challenge anyone who might be waiting for him in an empty room or darkened corner to show himself. Beyond the intrinsic difficulty of protecting such a person, the two men found it senselessly unsafe to be forced to show *themselves.* Professionals were, by training and nature, cautious, and Randolph was making them behave otherwise. Neither man relished the thought of being picked off by a sharpshooter a hundred-odd yards away as he followed the cantankerous doctor down a driveway or across a lawn. There was nothing amusing about the situation. Two men were not enough. Even one other man covering the outside would relieve the pressure; more than one, they understood, might defeat the purpose of the strategy by making the whole operation too obvious. One more, however, was mandatory.

Sterile Five accommodated. The emergency call from Apache had interrupted Loring's report to Havelock concerning Decker. Since Loring was free, he would be flown up by a Pentagon helicopter to within a few miles of the Medical Center, where a car would be waiting for him. He would be there in thirty-five to forty minutes.

"How will we know when he gets here?"

"Check the desk by an intercom phone. He'll come inside and ask directions to—Easton. Then he'll drive out and return on foot."

"Thank you, Sterile Five."

The sun was at the treetop mark in the western sky, bathing the Virginia countryside in soft bursts of yellow and gold. Havelock wearily got up from the desk, his hand still warm from clutching the ever-present telephone.

"The Agency will dig all night, cross-checking with Cons Op and G-Two. They've located two photographs; six are still missing."

"I'd think photographs would be the first consideration in these files," said Jenna, standing by the silver tray and pouring Michael a drink. "You can't bring over such people if you don't know what they look like."

He watched her as he repeated the words he had heard over the phone. "The men you chose were never considered that important," Havelock said. "They were marginal, to begin with; their value was limited."

"They were specialists."

"Psychiatrists, psychologists, and a couple of professors of philosophy. Old men who were permitted the privilege of expressing their views— some vaguely offensive, none earthshaking to the Kremlin."

"But they all questioned theories promoted by Soviet strategists. Their questions *were* relevant to everything you've learned about Anton Matthias."

"Yes, I know. We'll keep looking."

Jenna carried the short glass of straight whisky to the desk. "Here, you need this."

"Thanks." Havelock took the glass and walked slowly toward the window. "I want to pull in Decker," he said. "I've got to bring him down here. He'll never tell me over the phone. Not everything."

"You're convinced he's your man, then?"

"No question about it. I just had to understand why."

"Loring told you. He fawns on superiors, says he agrees with them even when he doesn't. Such a man would do Matthias's bidding."

"Strangely enough, that's only part of it," said Michael, shaking his head, then sipping his drink. "That description fits most ambitious men everywhere; the exceptions are rare. Too rare."

"Then what?"

Havelock stared out the window. "He makes a point of justifying everything he does," began Michael slowly. "He reads Lessons at services instituted at his command; he plays at being Solomon. Underneath that tactful, unctuous exterior there has to be a zealot. And only a zealot in his position would commit a crime for which—as Berquist says—he'd be summarily executed in most countries, and even here he would spend thirty years in prison. . . . It wouldn't surprise me if Lieutenant Commander Thomas Decker did it all. If I had my way, he'd be taken out and shot. For all the good it would do."

The sun had dropped below the trees, mottled orange rays, filtered by branches, spreading across the lawns and bouncing off the white walls of the Randolph Medical Center. Charles Loring crouched by the trunk of a tall oak at the far end of the parking area, the front entrance and rear emergency ramp in clear view, his radio in his hand. An ambulance had just brought in the victim of a traffic accident and his wife from U.S. 50. The injured man was being examined by Dr. Randolph and the Apache unit was in place in the corridor outside the examining room.

The Cons Op agent looked at his watch. He'd been at his post for nearly three-quarters of an hour—after a hastily arranged flight from the Pentagon helicopter pad to a private field on the outskirts of Denton, eight minutes away, where a car was waiting for him. He understood the Apache team's concerns. The man they were assigned to protect was making things difficult, but Charley would have handled it differently. He would have sat on this Randolph and told the doctor he didn't give a good goddamn whether he was chopped down or not, that the primary objective of the stakeout was to take even one of those coming after him, that *that* man's life was far more important than his. Such an explanation might have made Randolph more cooperative. And Loring might have been having a decent dinner somewhere, instead of waiting for God knew what on a cold, wet lawn in Maryland.

Charley looked up toward the intruding sound. A black-and-white patrol car swerved into the rear parking area, turned abruptly, and came to a sudden stop at the side of the emergency ramp. Two police officers got out quickly and raced up toward the doors, one leaping on the platform, both awkwardly holding their sides. Loring lifted the radio to his lips.

"Apache, this is Outside. A police car just drove up to the emergency dock in a hurry. Two cops are entering."

"We see them," came the reply, accompanied by static. "We'll let you know."

Charley looked again at the patrol car, and what he saw struck him as odd. Both doors were left open, something the police rarely did unless they intended to stay close to their vehicles. There was always the possibility that a radio might be tampered with, or a signal book stolen, or even concealed weapons . . .

The static erupted, words following. "Interesting, but no sweat," said an Apache as yet unseen by the Cons Op agent. "Seems the wreck on Highway Fifty was traced to a prominent member of a Baltimore family. Mafia all the way, wanted on a dozen counts. They've just been admitted for identification and any possible last statements."

"Okay. Out." Loring lowered the radio and considered a cigarette, deciding against it for fear the light would give him away. His eyes strayed again to the stationary patrol car, his mind wandering. Suddenly, there was something to think about, something immediate.

He had passed a police station on the road to the Medical Center, not five minutes away. He had noticed it at first not from the sign but by the cluster of three or four patrol cars in the side lot—not black-and-whites, but *red*-and-whites, the kind of bright color scheme often adopted by shore resort areas. And if a sought-after, major-league mafioso had been taken minutes ago to a local hospital after a collision, there certainly would be more than one patrol car covering the action.

Open doors, men racing, arms at their sides—concealed weapons. Oh, my *God!*

"Apache! Apache, come in!"

"What is it, Outside?"

"Are those police still in there?"

"They just *went* in."

"Go in after them! *Now!*"

"What?"

"Don't argue, just *do* it! With weapons!"

By the time the radio was in his pocket and the .38 in his hand, Charley was halfway across the parking lot, racing as fast as he could toward the emergency dock. He reached the platform and sprang up with one hand on it, legs scrambling, and lunged for the wide metal doors. He crashed them open and dashed past a startled nurse behind a glass-partitioned reception counter, his head turning in all directions, his eyes choosing the corridor straight ahead; it conformed to the Apaches' position, their immediate sighting of the policemen. He ran down to an intersecting hallway, staring first to his left, then his right. There it was, ten feet away! EXAMINING ROOM. The door was shut; it did not make sense.

Loring approached swiftly, silently, taking long cautious steps, his back pressed against the wall. Suddenly he heard two muted spits and the start of a terrible scream from behind the heavy steel door, and he knew his instincts had been as right as he now wished they had been wrong. He spun around the frame so as to give his left hand free access to the metal handle, then jammed the handle down and threw his shoulder against the panel, sending the door open, then turned back for the protection of the frame.

The shots came, exploding into the wall in front of him; they were high, the spits from deep inside the room, not close by. Charley crouched and dived, rolling as he hit the floor, and fired into a blue uniform. He fired low, bullets ricocheting off obstructing steel. *Legs, ankles, feet! Arms, if you have to, but not the chest, not the head! Keep him alive!*

The second blue uniform lunged over an examining table—a rushing blur of dark color—and Loring had no choice. He fired directly at the attacking man, who held a pipe-stock repeating weapon in his arms. The killer spun off the padded table, plummeting to the floor, his throat ripped open. Dead.

Keep the other alive, keep the other alive! The order kept screaming in his head as Charley kicked the door shut and lurched, rolling, firing at the ceiling and blowing out the bright overhead fluorescent tubes, leaving only the harsh glow of a small high-intensity lamp on a faraway table.

Three spits erupted from the shadows, the bullets embedding themselves in the plaster and wood above him. He rolled furiously to his left and collided with two lifeless bodies—were they Apaches? He could not tell; he only knew he could not let the man who was alive escape. And there were only two alive in that room—blood, shattered flesh, and corpses everywhere.

It had been a massacre.

A spitting burst of gunfire staccatoed across the floor, and he could feel the searing heat of the bullet that had punctured his stomach. But the pain did an odd thing to him, which he had no time to think about. He could only experience the reaction. His mind exploded in anger, but the anger was controlled, the fury directed. He had lost before. He could not lose again. He simply *could not!*

He sprang diagonally to his right, crashing into a stretcher table and sending it rolling toward the shadows where the staccato burst had come from; he heard the impact and rose swiftly, held his gun in both hands and aimed at another hand in the shadows. He fired as the screams swelled in the corridors beyond the closed door.

He had one last thing to do. And then he would not have lost.

34

Lieutenant Commander Thomas Decker walked into the study of Sterile Five, escorted by two men from the White House Secret Service. His angular face was set, and he looked both purposeful and anxious. The broad-shouldered frame under the well-tailored blue uniform was that of a man who kept in shape not from enjoyment but from compulsion; the body was too rigid, with too little fluidity in its movement. But it was the face that fascinated Havelock. It was a hard-shelled mask about to crack, and once that process started, it would shatter. Strength, purpose, and anxiety aside, Decker was petrified, and try as he might, he could not conceal his inner terror.

Michael spoke, addressing the Secret Service detail. "Thanks very much, gentlemen. The kitchen is outside to the right, at the end of the hallway. The cook will find you something to eat—beer, coffee, whatever you want. I'm sure I've interrupted your dinner break and I don't know when we'll be finished here. Make any phone calls you like, of course."

"Thank you, sir," said the man on Decker's left, nodding to his companion, as they both turned and started for the door.

"You've also interrupted *my* dinner, and I expect—"

"Shut up, Commander," broke in Havelock quietly.

The door closed, and Decker took several angry steps toward the desk, but the anger was too contrived, too forced. It had been summoned to replace the fear. "I have an engagement this evening with Admiral James at the Fifth Naval District!"

"He's been informed that pressing naval business precludes your being there."

"This is outrageous! I *demand* an explanation!"

"You're entitled to a firing squad." Havelock rose as Decker gasped. "I think you know why."

"*You!*" The officer's eyes grew wide; he swallowed as the color left his mask of a face. "You're the one who's been calling me, asking me those questions! Telling me . . . a very *great man* . . . doesn't remember! It's a *lie!*"

"It's the truth," said Michael simply. "But you can't understand, and it's been driving you up the wall. It's all you've been thinking about since I told you—because you know what you've done."

Decker became rigid again, brows arched, eyes clouded, a military man having given his serial number but refusing any subsequent interrogation despite impending torture. "I have nothing to say to you. Mr. Cross. It *is* Cross, isn't it?"

"It'll do," said Havelock, nodding once. "But you've got a great deal to say, and you *are* going to say it. Because if you don't, a presidential order will send you to the deepest cell in Leavenworth and the key will be thrown away. To put you on trial would be far too dangerous to the security of this country."

"No! . . . You *can't!* I did nothing wrong! I was right, *we* were right!"

"The Joint Chiefs and key members of the House and Senate will agree," continued Michael. "It'll be one of the few times when the umbrella of national security will be completely valid."

The mask cracked; the face shattered. Fear turned to desperation as Decker whispered, "What do they say I've done?"

"In violation of your oath as an officer and the codes of secrecy you've sworn to uphold, you reproduced dozens of the most sensitive documents in this country's military history and removed them from the Pentagon."

"And to *whom* did I deliver them? Answer me that."

"It doesn't matter."

"It *does!* It's everything!"

"You had no authorization."

"*That* man has all the authority he needs!" Decker's voice trembled as he tried to regain control. "I demand that you get Secretary of State Matthias on the phone."

Havelock walked away from the desk, away from the telephone. The movement was not lost on the naval officer. It was the moment to retreat slightly. "I've been given *my* orders, Commander," said Michael, permitting a degree of uncertainty in his own voice. "By the President and several of his closest advisers. The Secretary of State is not to be consulted in this matter under any circumstances whatsoever. He's not to be informed. I don't know why, but those are my orders."

Decker took a halting step, then another, zeal joining the desperation in his wide, frantic eyes. He began barely above a whisper, the words growing louder with a zealot's conviction. "The *President?* His *advisers . . . ?* For God's sake, can't you *see?* Of course they don't want him informed because he's right and they're *wrong.* They're afraid and he isn't! Do you think for a moment if I disappeared he wouldn't know what had happened? Do you think he wouldn't confront the President and his advisers and force a showdown? You talk about the Joint Chiefs, members of the House and the Senate. My God, do you think he couldn't call them together and show what a weak, ineffectual, *immoral* administration this really *is?* There'd *be* no administration! It would be repudiated, crippled, thrown out!"

"By whom, Commander?"

Decker straightened his broad-shouldered body, a condemned man knowing that ultimate justice would bring a pardon. "The people, Mr. Cross. The people of this nation recognize a giant. They won't turn their backs on him because a hack politician and his weak-kneed advisers say so. They won't stand for it! The world has lamented the loss of great leadership these past few decades. Well, we produced a great leader and the world knows it. And my advice to you is to get Anthony Matthias on the telephone. You don't have to say anything, I'll speak to him."

Havelock stood motionless, something more than uncertainty now in his voice. "You believe there could be a showdown? The President— impeached?"

"Look at Matthias. Can you doubt it? Where in the last thirty years has there been a man like him?"

Michael slowly walked back to the desk and lowered himself into the chair, glancing up at Decker. "Sit down, Commander," he said.

Decker quickly sat in the chair that Havelock had purposely placed in front of the desk. "We've used some harsh words with each other, and for my part I apologize. But you *must* understand. We *are* right."

"I need more than that," said Havelock. "We know you removed copies of detailed strategies developed by the Nuclear Contingency Committees, documents that spelled out everything in our own arsenals as well as the results of our deepest penetrations of both the Soviet and Chinese systems. You delivered these to Matthias over a period of months, but we've never understood why. If you could tell me, give me a reason. *Why?*"

"For the most obvious reason in the world! It goes back to the key word in the title of those committees. 'Contingency.' *Contingency*, Mr. Cross, always contingency! *Reaction*—reaction to *this*, reaction to *that!* Always replying, never *initiating!* We don't need contingencies. We can't let our enemies think we'll only *respond.* We need a master plan, let them know we have a master plan that will ensure their total destruction should they transgress. Our strength, our survival, can no longer be based on defense, Mr. Cross, it must be based on *offense!* Anthony Matthias understands this. The others are afraid to face it."

"And you helped him develop this—master plan?"

"I'm proud to say I contributed," said the officer, his words rushed—the pardon was in sight. "I sat with him hour after hour going over every conceivable nuclear option, every possible Soviet and Chinese response, not a single capability overlooked."

"When did you meet?"

"Every Sunday, for weeks on end." Decker lowered his voice, confidentiality joined now with zeal and desperation. "He impressed on me the highly classified nature of our relationship, so I'd drive out in a rented car to his lodge in West Virginia, to a cabin on the secondary road where we'd meet alone."

"The Woodshed," said Michael, the word escaping from him.

"You know it, then?"

"I've been there." Havelock briefly closed his eyes; he knew the Woodshed only too well. A small cabin retreat where Anton went to work on his projected memoirs—to talk out his thoughts, every phrase picked up by a voice-activated tape recorder. "Is there anything else? I want you to know I'm listening, Commander. You're very impressive—and I'm listening."

"He's such a truly *brilliant* man," continued Decker, his tone close to an awestruck whisper, his eyes gazing on some unseen holy light. "That probing mind, the depth of his every observation, his grasp of global realities—all *truly* remarkable. A statesman like Anthony Matthias can take this nation to its zenith, bring us to where we were meant to be in the eyes of man and God. Yes, I did what I did and I'd do it again, because I'm a patriot. I love this country as I love the Scriptures, and I would lay down my life for it, knowing that I would retain my honor. . . . There really is no choice, Mr. Cross. We *are* right. Pick up the phone and call Matthias, tell him I'm here. And *I'll* tell him the truth. Small men who worship graven images have crawled out of the ground and are trying to destroy him. He'll stamp them out—with our help."

Michael leaned back in the chair, the weariness, the futility, as complete as they had ever been. " 'With our help,' " he repeated in a voice so low he was barely aware he had spoken.

"Yes, of course!"

Havelock shook his head slowly back and forth. "You sanctimonious son of a bitch," he said.

"What?"

"You heard me. *You sanctimonious son of a bitch!*" Michael roared. Then he breathed deeply and continued quietly, rapidly, "You want me to call Matthias? I wish to hell I could, just to watch your goddamn face, to see your steely, self-righteous eyes grow wild when you learn the truth."

"What are you talking about?" whispered Decker.

"Matthias wouldn't know who you *are!* Any more than he knows who the President is, or his aides, or the undersecretaries, or the diplomats he works with every day—or *me,* who's known him for over twenty years, closer to him than any other person alive."

"No . . . no, you're wrong. *No!*"

"*Yes,* Commander! He broke. More precisely, *we broke him.* That mind is gone! It's shattered. He's insane. He couldn't take it any longer. And, by Christ, you did your part. You gave him his ultimate authority, his final responsibility. You stole the world's—yes, the *world's*—secrets and told him his genius could handle them. You took a thousand facts and a hundred theoretical strategies, mixed them up, and turned them into the most terrifying weapon this earth has ever known. A blueprint for global annihilation."

"That's *not* what I did!"

"Granted, not all by yourself, but you provided the—what the hell's that God-awful Pentagonese?—support structure, that's it. You provided the support structure for a fiction that's so real there's not a nuclear expert alive who wouldn't accept it as truth. *Gospel* truth, if you like, Commander."

"We only discussed, analyzed, tore apart options! The final plan was to be his; you can't *understand.* His grasp was brilliant! There was nothing he couldn't comprehend; it was incredible!"

"It was the act of a mind dying, on the edge of becoming a convoluted vegetable. He wanted you to believe, and he was still good enough to make you believe. He had to, and you wanted to."

"I did! So would *you!*"

"That's what I've been told by a better man than you'll ever be."

"I don't deserve that. He appealed to a truth I *do* believe in. We *must* be strong!"

"I don't know any sane person who would argue with that, but there are different kinds and degrees of strength. Some work—usually quietly; others don't, because they're swollen with bellicosity. The savage explodes from his own tension; he can't contain himself, he's got to flex. And somewhere along the line he blows up, setting in motion a dozen responses that are explosions themselves."

"Who *are* you? *What* are you?"

"A student of history who went astray. But I'm not the issue. You are. Everything you gave Matthias is within arm's reach of the Soviets, Commander. That master plan, which you're so convinced we must let the world know we have, may in all its details be on its way to Moscow. Because the man you gave it to is insane, was on his way to becoming insane when you delivered the materials to him."

Decker rose slowly from the chair. "I don't believe you," he said, his voice hollow, the words spoken in dread.

"Then why am I here? Why would I say it? Personal considerations aside, do you think anyone with the brains to get out of the rain wants to make that statement? Have you any idea what it means to this country to know that the mind of its Secretary of State has been destroyed? I'd like to remind you, Commander, that you don't have an exclusive claim on patriotism. None of us does."

Decker stared down at Havelock until he could no longer bear the contact. He turned away, the broad-shouldered body somehow shrinking beneath the tunic. "You tricked me. You made me say things I never would have said."

"It's my job."

"Everything's over for me. I'm finished."

"Maybe not. As of this moment, I'd guess you are the least likely candidate as a security risk in the Pentagon. You've been burned by a legend and it's a pain you'll never forget. Nobody knows better than I do how persuasive Matthias could be. . . . We need help, not prison sentences. Packing you off to Leavenworth would only raise questions no one wants raised. We're in a blind race; maybe you can help."

Decker turned, swallowing, his face ashen. "In any way I can. How?"

Michael got out of the chair and came around the desk to face the officer. "For starters, nothing I've told you can be repeated."

"My God, of *course* not."

"No, of course not. You'd be hanging yourself."

"I'd be hanging the country. I have no exclusivity on patriotism, but I am a patriot, Mr. Cross."

Havelock walked past the coffee table and the couch, and was reminded of Jenna's absence. Since they had agreed her presence would be inhibiting, she was upstairs; more accurately, she had insisted on not being there. He reached the wall, aimlessly studied a brass plaque, and spoke. "I'm going to guess again, Commander. There came a time when Matthias wouldn't see you anymore. Am I right?"

"Yes. I phoned repeatedly—not at State, of course—but he never returned my calls."

"Not at State?" asked Michael, turning. "But you *did* call there. It's how I found you."

"Only three times. Twice to say there were Sunday conferences at the Pentagon, and once to tell him I was going into the hospital for minor surgery on a Friday and expected to be there until Tuesday or Wednesday. He was very solicitous, but that was when he told me never again to reach him at the State Department."

"You called the lodge, then?"

"And his house in Georgetown."

"This was later?"

"Yes. I called night after night, but he wouldn't come to the phone. Try to understand, Mr. Cross. I was aware of what I'd done, of the enormity of the violation I'd committed. Mind you, until a few minutes ago I never regretted it; I can't change my beliefs, they're ingrained in me. But back then—five or six months ago—I was bewildered, frightened perhaps, I'm not sure. I'd been left stranded—"

"You were in withdrawal," interrupted Havelock. "You'd been on a high, on one of the most potent narcotics in the world. Anthony Matthias. Suddenly he wasn't there any longer."

"Yes, that's it. Those were heady days, magnificent memories. Then I don't know why, my connection to greatness ended. I thought perhaps it was something I'd done that displeased him, or information I'd brought him that was deficient, incomplete. I didn't know; I just knew that I'd been cut off, with no explanation."

"I understand," said Michael, remembering so clearly the night in Cagnes-sur-Mer when his *přítel* did not come to the telephone five thousand miles away. "I'm surprised you didn't force the issue, confront him somehow, somewhere. You were entitled to that explanation."

"I didn't have to. It was finally given to me."

"What?"

"One evening, after I'd tried to reach him again, to no avail again, a man called me back. A very strange man—"

The prolonged outburst of the phone shattered the moment, blowing apart the taut line of concentration. Havelock ran to the phone, to the sustained ring that signaled *Emergency.*

"It's Loring," said the strained voice in a half-whisper. "I'm hit. I'm okay, but I'm hit."

"Where are you?"

"A motel on Highway Three-seventeen, near Harrington. The Pheasant Run Motel. Cabin Twelve."

"I'll send a doctor."

"A very *special* doctor, Havelock. Use the field in Denton."

"What do you mean?"

"I had to get out of there. I grabbed a police car—"

"A police . . . ? *Why?"*

"I'll tell you later. Everything. . . . Special doctor with a bagful of needles."

"For Christ's sake, spell it *out,* Charley!"

"I've got one of those sons of bitches. He's strapped naked on the bed —no capsules, no razors. I've *got* one!"

Havelock stabbed the buttons on the Sterile Five telephone one after another, issuing orders one after another, as Lieutenant Commander Decker stood rigidly across the room, watching, listening, a helpless shell of a crusader whose cause had collapsed. The President was informed, and a very special doctor was being tracked down, to be sent to Maryland by helicopter, a Secret Service detail accompanying him. A second helicopter was prepared for takeoff, waiting for Michael at the field in Quantico six miles away; he would be driven there by the Secret Service escorts who had brought Decker to Sterile Five. The final call placed by Havelock was within the house itself. Upstairs. To Jenna Karas.

"I have to leave. It's Loring in Maryland. He's wounded, but he may have picked up a traveler—don't ask me how. And you were right. One source. He's here and has more to say; please come down and take it. I have to go. . . . Thanks."

Michael got up from the desk and addressed the frightened naval officer. "A lady's on her way here, and I'm ordering you—ordering you, Commander—to tell her everything you were going to tell me, and answer fully any questions she may ask. Your escort will be back in twenty minutes or so. When you're finished, and only if she agrees, you may go. But once you reach your house you're not to leave it for any reason whatsoever. You'll be watched."

"Yes, Mr. Cross."

Havelock grabbed his jacket off the back of the chair and started toward the door. He stopped and turned to Decker, his hand on the knob. "Incidentally, her name is Mrs. Cross."

All low-flying traffic was diverted as the two helicopters roared into the small private field in Denton, Maryland, the aircraft from the Bethesda Naval Hospital arriving eleven minutes before the chopper from Quantico. Havelock raced across the tarmac to the staff car sent over from Annapolis, the driver an ensign reputed to know the roads on the Eastern Shore of Chesapeake Bay. The ensign knew nothing else; no one did; not even the doctor whose orders were to take care of Charles Loring first, and not to administer anything to Loring's prisoner until Sterile Five was on the scene. Two state police patrol cars had been sent to the Pheasant Run Motel; they would be given their instructions by the Secret Service.

If the name Pheasant Run gave rise to images of squiredom and hunt country, it was misapplied to the sleazy motel's run-down cabins that stood in a row off the highway. Apparently, the motel's primary function was to serve as a place for assignations lasting an hour or so; cars were parked in small dirt lots at the rear, out of sight of the main road. The management catered to its clientele's idiosyncrasies, if not to their comforts, and Loring had used his head. A man in pain, concealing wounds, without luggage but with a prisoner he wanted to rush surreptitiously into hiding, could hardly hope to register at a brightly lit Howard Johnson's Motor Lodge.

Havelock thanked the ensign and told him to return to Annapolis, reminding him that the present emergency called for the utmost secrecy. Washington had his name, and his cooperation would not be overlooked. The young man, obviously impressed by the sight of searchlights and military helicopters at night, as well as by his own participation, replied in a monotone, "You may be assured of my silence, sir."

"Just say you went out for a beer, that's good enough. Better, maybe."

A government man, holding up an encased silver badge in his palm, intercepted Michael as he ran along the row of cabins looking for number twelve.

"Sterile Five," said Havelock, noticing for the first time the two state police cars parked in the shadows twenty feet apart to his left. Number twelve was nearby.

"This way," said the man, pocketing his badge, and led Michael between two cabins toward the rear of the motel's grounds. Beyond was a shorter row of cabins, which were not visible from the front. Loring had spent precious moments of pain and anxiety studying the motel's layout —again an indication that he was in control.

In the distance, at the rear of the cabin on the left, the hood of a stationary automobile could be seen, but it was not an ordinary car. A streak of white ending in an arrowhead was stenciled over the black chassis at midpoint. It was the patrol car Loring had stolen, the only indication that perhaps he had lost a part of the control that had served them all so well. Someone in Washington would have to reach a panicked Maryland police headquarters and call off the hunt.

"This is it," said the federal agent, pointing to the door of a cabin above a stoop of three steps. "I'll be out here," added the man. "Watch those steps; they're loose."

"Thanks," said Havelock, and quickly but cautiously went up to the door. He tried the knob; it was locked. In answer to his knock, someone inside asked, "Who is it?"

"Sterile Five," replied Michael.

The door was opened by a stocky, red-haired man in his middle thirties, his Celtic face freckled, his eyes wary, his sleeves rolled up. "Havelock?"

"That's right."

"Name's Taylor. Come on in, we've got to talk fast."

Michael walked inside the room with the soiled wallpaper; the doctor closed the door. On the bed was a naked man, spread-eagled, bloody hands and feet tied to the frame, belts around the wrists, torn sheets lashed to his ankles. His mouth was pulled taut by a striped blue tie to inhibit any loud sound, and his eyes were wide with anger and fear.

"Where's . . . ?"

Taylor gestured toward the far corner of the room. There on the floor, his head on a pillow and a blanket over him, was Charles Loring, his eyes only partially open; he was dazed or in shock. Havelock started across the filthy gray carpet but was stopped by the doctor's grip on his arm.

"That's what we have to talk about. I don't know what's going on here, but I do know I can't be responsible for that man's life unless we get him to a hospital an hour ago. Do I make myself clear?"

"As soon as we can, not right now," said Michael, shaking his head. "I've got to question him. He's the only person who can give me the information I need. Everyone else is dead."

"Maybe you didn't hear me. I said an hour ago."

"I heard you, but I know what I have to do. I'm sorry."

"I don't *like* you," said Taylor, staring at Havelock, removing his hand as if he had touched something loathsome.

"I wish that could concern me, Doctor, because I like *him.* I'll be as brief and as quiet as I can. He'd want it this way, take my word for it."

"I have to. I couldn't convince him he should get out of here ten minutes ago."

Michael walked over to Loring and knelt down, putting his face close to the wounded man's. "Charley, it's Havelock. Can you hear me?"

Loring opened his eyes wider, his lips trembling, struggling to form the words. Finally the whisper came. "Yes. Hear . . . you . . . fine."

"I'll tell you what I've learned, which is damned little. Nod your head if I'm on the track, shake it if I'm not. Don't waste words or breath. Okay?" The Cons Op agent nodded and Michael continued, "I spoke with police who are trying to put it together. As they tell it, an ambulance brought in a traffic accident with his wife, and Randolph, a staff doctor and a nurse were cleaning him up, checking the extent of injuries." Loring shook his head, but Havelock went on, "Let me finish, then we'll go back. They weren't in there five minutes when two state troopers came running in and spoke with our cardiologists. No one knows what was said, but they were admitted into the examining room." Again the Cons Op agent shook his head. "A couple of minutes later a third man—I assume that was you —crashed through emergency doors, and that's when everything went down." Loring nodded.

Havelock took a breath and continued softly, rapidly. "The staff heard gunshots, perhaps five or six, no one's sure. Most of them ran out of the building. The rest hid in the corridors and patients' rooms behind locked doors, everyone trying to reach a phone. When the gunfire stopped, someone outside saw you and one of the state police come running down the ramp—you were bent over with a gun in your hand, the officer was bleeding, limping and holding his arm. You forced him into the patrol car and got out of there. The police are trying to find out who the other trooper was, but identifications were taken off some of the bodies, not all." Loring shook his head violently. Michael touched his shoulder and said, "Take it easy; we'll go back. I don't have to tell you the body count was full. Randolph, the staff doctor, the nurse, the accident victim and his wife and our Apache unit. Two automatic weapons equipped with silencers were found; they're still counting the shells. Yours was the gunfire that was heard; they're tracing the weapons, matching prints. Beyond what I've told you, no one knows what happened. Now, let's go back." Havelock squinted, remembering. "The traffic accident."

Loring shook his head, whispering, "No accident."

"Why not?"

"They *weren't* troopers."

Michael looked up at the naked man strapped to the bed, and at the uniform rumpled on the floor. "Of course they weren't. And the patrol car was a mock-up; they've got the money for that kind of thing. I should have known; you wouldn't have taken it otherwise."

The wounded agent nodded, his hand emerging from under the blanket, gesturing for Havelock to lean closer. "The man and the woman . . . from the ambulance . . . the accident. Any ID's?"

"No."

"Same with the troopers . . . right?"

"Right."

"The accident," whispered Loring, stopping for breath. "Too easy. Man hurt . . . a woman who won't leave his side. They get in . . . to a room . . . doctor, nurse . . . Randolph. They got him."

"How could they know Randolph would be there?"

"Doesn't matter. They'd tell the doctor . . . or the nurse to call for him . . . under a gun. Probably did. They *got* him. Too easy."

"And the troopers?"

"In a hurry . . . running like hell. They were sent to break it up, break it *all* up . . . in a hurry."

"How did you figure that?"

"They left the doors open, ran funny . . . heavy weapons under their coats. The pattern wasn't normal, wasn't right. . . . Apache said the accident was a big-balled mafioso the cops came to question. If he was, there'd be ten vehicles there, not one." Loring expelled his breath, coughing; blood trickled out of the corners of his mouth. He gasped, and resumed breathing. The doctor was now behind Havelock.

"For Christ's sake," said Taylor quietly but with angry intensity. "Why don't you just put a bullet in his head?"

"Why don't I put one in yours?" Michael leaned back toward Loring. "*Why*, Charley? Why do you think they were sent in to break it up?"

"I'm not sure. Maybe I was spotted . . . maybe I blew it again."

"I don't believe that."

"Don't be so goddamn nice, I can't stand it. . . . I probably did blow it. . . . I'm getting old."

"Then just pass on your instincts, Methuselah, we need them. You didn't blow anything. You brought us one, you *brought* us one, Charley."

Loring tried to raise his shoulders, Michael gently holding him down. "Tell me something, Havelock. You said this morning . . . about Shippers. 'A long time ago.' You said he was programmed a long time ago. Tell me. Is that son of a bitch over there a . . . a traveler?"

"I think he is."

"Goddamn . . . maybe I'm not so old."

Michael got to his feet and turned to the doctor behind him. "All right, Taylor, he's yours. Get him over to the field and have him taken to the best facilities at Bethesda. And you get on the phone and tell those mothers the White House wants the finest team of surgeons you've got ready and waiting for this man."

"Yes, *sir*," said the doctor sardonically. "Anything else, *sir?*"

"Oh, yes, physician. Prepare your bag of magic. You're about to go to work."

Loring was carried out on a stretcher by two paramedics who had been standing by; they were given firm instructions by the doctor as they took away the wounded Cons Op agent.

Taylor turned to Havelock. "Do we start now?"

"What about the wounds?" asked Michael, looking down at the naked man's taped, blood-streaked right arm and left foot.

"Your friend put tourniquets where they were needed, and I added adhesive; the bleeding's arrested. Also, he was damned accurate. Bone was shattered, but beyond the pain, nothing'll drain him. Naturally, I gave him a couple of locals to ease him, keep his head clearer."

"Will they interfere with the chemicals?"

"I wouldn't have administered them if they did."

"Then shoot him up, Doctor. I can't waste time."

Taylor went to his large black leather case, which was open and on a table next to the window under the glow of a lamp. He studied the contents for several moments, took out three vials and three cased syringes, and placed them on the edge of the bed next to the naked man's thigh. The prisoner raised his head, his features contorted, his eyes glazed, frenzied; he was close to hysterics. Suddenly he began to writhe furiously, and muffled animallike howls came from his throat. He stopped, overwhelmed by the pain in his right arm, and gasping for breath, he stared at the ceiling. Then abruptly he stopped breathing, holding the air in his lungs, his face becoming redder by the second, eyes now bulging.

"What the hell is he—?"

"Get out of my *way!*" shouted Havelock, pushing the doctor aside and crashing his clenched fist down on the killer's bare stomach. The breath exploded out of the traveler's bound mouth, and the eyes and flesh tone began returning to normal.

"*Jesus,*" said Taylor, rushing forward to steady the vials, which were about to roll off the edge of the bed. "What was *that?*"

"You're dealing with something you may never have dealt with before, Doctor. They're programmed like robots, killing whomever they're told to kill—without any feeling at all, without the slightest concern. Not even for themselves."

"Then he won't negotiate. I thought maybe if he saw these things, he might."

"No way. He'd stall us, throw us off with every plausible lie in the books, and they know them all. They're masters of the craft. Let's go, Doctor."

"How do you want to progress? In stages, which will bring him back one step at a time, or do you want to chance a maximum? It's the fastest, but there's a risk."

"What's the worst with it?"

"Incoherence. Disjointed rambling, no logical pattern."

"No logical . . . ? That's it. I'll chance the incoherence; just get him away from any patterns that might trigger programmed responses."

"It doesn't work quite that way. The flow becomes formless; dissociation is the first reaction. The key is to hit certain words—"

"You're saying everything I want to hear, Doctor, and you're also wasting time."

"You think so?" With the swiftness of a surgeon stemming a sudden internal eruption, Taylor broke off a vial's tiny glass casing, inserted the syringe, withdrew it, and plunged it into the traveler's thigh before the bound man knew it was happening. The killer writhed violently, yanking at the belts and the torn sheets in an effort to break them, rolling from side to side as muffled cries filled the room. "The more he does that, the quicker it'll take effect," added Taylor, pressing his hand on the side of the stretched, whipping neck. "Only a minute or so."

Michael watched, fascinated and revolted, as he always was when observing the effect of these chemicals on a human being. He had to remind himself that this killer had brutally taken the lives of men and women less than three hours ago—his own people and others, the guilty and the totally innocent. How many would mourn for them and never understand? And how many were laid at the feet of one Michael Havelock, courtesy of Anton Matthias? Two career officers, a young staff doctor, a younger nurse, a man named Randolph, whose only crime was to try to right a terrible wrong.

Futility.

"He's about ready now," said Taylor, studying the filmy, partially closed eyes of the prisoner, whose movements had contracted into slow, weaving motions, accompanied by moans.

"You must be happy in your work, Doctor."

"I was always a nosy kid," answered the red-haired man, gently removing the striped tie from the traveler's mouth. "Besides, someone's got to do it, and Big Uncle paid for my medical degree. My old man couldn't swing a bucket of suds in Paddy O'Rourke's saloon. I'll pay my debt and get out."

Havelock could not think of a reply any less tasteless than his comment, so he leaned over the bed as Taylor backed away. "May I begin?" he asked.

"Talk, he's your crossword puzzle."

"Orders," began Michael, his hand on the headboard, his lips near the traveler's ear, his voice firm, steady, low. "Orders, orders, *orders.* None of us can move without our *orders!* But we have to be certain, we can't make a mistake. Who can clear our *orders,* clear our orders *now?"*

The prisoner's head moved back and forth, his mouth alternately opening and closing, stretching the bruised flesh. But no sound came.

"It's an emergency," continued Havelock. "Everybody *knows* it's an emergency . . . an *emergency.* We've got to hurry, hurry . . . hurry up."

"Hurry . . . hurry *up."* The whisper emerged, tentative, uncertain.

"But how can we be *sure?"* Michael raced on. "We have to be *certain."*

"The flight . . . the flight was *smooth.* We heard it twice. That's all we have to know. The flight . . . *smooth."*

"Of course. A *smooth flight*. We're all right now. We can hurry. . . . Now, let's float back . . . before the emergency. Relax. Sleep."

"Very good," said the doctor from across the dimly lit, squalid room. "You centered him as quickly as I've ever seen it done. That was a response."

"It wasn't difficult," replied Havelock, rising from the bed and studying the traveler. "Since he was given his orders he's had three things on his mind. Emergency, speed and clearance. His instructions were to kill—an extreme order, also a dangerous one—so clearance was vital. You heard him, he had to hear it twice."

"The code was a 'smooth flight.' He gave it to you, and now you'll give it back to him. You're closer."

"And you're no amateur, Doctor. Get me a chair, will you? I've also got speed and emergency on my mind. Things may get rough." Taylor brought a straight-backed chair over to the bed; Michael sat down; the chair was unsteady but serviceable. He leaned forward, arms on the edge of the bed, and spoke again to the bound man. "We have a smooth flight . . . a smooth flight . . . a *very smooth flight! Now,* kill your partner!"

The traveler whipped his head to the right, his clouded eyes blinking, lips moving—protest without sound.

"You heard me!" shouted Havelock. "We have a smooth flight, so *kill him!*"

"What . . . ? *Why?*" The whispered words were guttural.

"Are you married? Tell me, since we're on a smooth flight, are you *married?*"

"Yes . . . yes, married."

"Kill your *wife!*"

"Why?"

"We're on a *smooth flight!* How can you *refuse?*"

"Why . . . *why?*"

"Kill your partner! Kill your wife! Do you have children?"

"No!" The traveler's eyes widened, the glaze within on fire. "You could never ask . . . *never!*"

"I do! A smooth flight! What more do you need?"

"Clearance. I demand clearance! I . . . must have it!"

"From where? From whom? I've already told you. We're on a smooth flight! That's *it!*"

"Please . . . ! Me, kill *me.* I'm . . . confused!"

"Why are you confused? You heard my orders, just as you heard the orders for today. Did I give you those orders?"

"No."

"*No?* You don't remember? If not me, *who?*"

"The trip . . . the smooth flight. The . . . control."

"The *control?*"

"The source."

"The source control! *Your* source control. I *am* your source control! Kill your partner! Kill your wife! *Kill the children! All* the children!"

"I . . . *I.* You can't ask me . . . please don't ask me."

"I don't ask. I demand, I give orders! Do you want to sleep?"

"Yes."

"You *can't* sleep!" Michael turned his head and spoke to Taylor, his voice soft, barely audible. "How long will the dose last?"

"The way you're eating it up, half the normal time. Another ten minutes, tops."

"Prepare another. I'm taking him up."

"It'll blow him into space."

"He'll come down."

"You're the doctor," said the doctor.

"*I* am your source control!" shouted Havelock, getting out of the chair, leaning over the traveler's face. "You have no one else, *paminyatchik!* You will do as I tell you, and *only* what I tell you! Now, your *partner,* your *wife,* the *children* . . ."

"*Ahhhh* . . . !" The scream was prolonged, a cry beyond helplessness.

"I've only *begun* . . ."

The bound, narcotized killer strained against the leather and the cloth, body and features twisted, his mind in a labyrinth of terror, with sacrifice demanded upon sacrifice, pain upon pain, no way out of the impossible maze.

"*Now,*" said Havelock to the doctor beside him.

Taylor plunged the hypodermic needle into the traveler's arm; the reaction was there in moments, drug accelerating drug. The screams turned into animal screeches, saliva flowing from the killer's mouth—violence the only answer to violence.

"*Give* it to me!" yelled Michael. "*Prove* it to me! Or be killed with everyone else! Partner, wife, children . . . you all die unless you can *prove* yourself to me. Right now, this moment! . . . *What is the code for your source control?*"

"*Hammer-zero-two!* You *know* it!"

"Yes, I know it. Now tell me, where can I be reached—don't *lie!*"

"Don't know . . . don't *know!* I'm called . . . we're all called."

"When you want clearance! When you have information to deliver. How do you reach me when you want clearance, when you have information that has to be relayed."

"Tell them . . . need it. We all do. Everyone."

"Who?"

"Orphan. Reach . . . Orphan."

"Orphan?"

"Ninety-six."

"Orphan-ninety-six? Where is he? *Where?*"

"O . . . r . . . p . . . h . . . ." The final scream was shattering. The traveler thrashed his full strength and weight against the belts and broke one, which freed his left arm, as he lunged up, then arched his back in a spasm and fell unconscious over the far side of the bed.

"He's had it," said Taylor, reaching across Havelock and holding the prisoner's wrist in his fingers. "His pulse is a jackhammer; it'll be eight hours before he can sustain another jolt. Sorry—Doctor."

"It's all right, Doctor," said Michael, walking away from the bed and reaching into his pocket for a pack of cigarettes. "We could have done worse. You're a hell of a good chemist."

"I don't consider it my life's work."

"If it weren't right now, you might not have—" Havelock stopped to light a cigarette.

"What?"

"Nothing. I meant *you* might not have time for a drink, but I do."

"Sure, I do. I'll get Boris here down to a clinic."

"Boris? . . . You know?"

"Enough to know he's not a Boy Scout."

"That's the funny thing. He probably was."

"Tell me," asked the red-haired doctor, "would a source control order him to do that? Kill his wife and kids, people that close to him?"

"Never. Moscow wouldn't risk it. These people are like robots, but it's blood inside, not oil. They're monitored continuously, and if the KGB wants them taken out, an execution squad is sent in to do it. A normal family is part of the cover; it's also a powerful secondary hook. If a man's ever tempted, he knows what will happen."

"You used it the same way, didn't you? Only in reverse."

"I'm not wildly proud of the accomplishment, but yes."

"Jesus, Mary and Paddy O'Rourke," muttered the doctor.

Michael watched as Taylor reached for the bedside phone to issue his
instructions through Bethesda Central. The *telephone. Orphan-96.*
"Wait a minute!" Michael cried suddenly.

"What's the matter?"

"Let me use that phone!" Havelock rushed to the table, picked up the
telephone and dialed, saying aloud as he did so, "O–r–p–h–a–n . . .
nine–six."

"Operator," said the female voice on the line.

"What?"

"Is this a collect call, billed to a credit card, or to another number?"

"Credit card." Michael stared at the wall to remember his untraceable,
State-assigned number. He gave it to the operator and heard the subsequent ringing.

"Good evening and thank you for calling the Voyagers Emporium,
luggage for the sophisticated globe-trotter. If you'll state the numbered
item or items from our catalog you wish to purchase, you will be connected to the proper representative in our twenty-four-hour service department."

Havelock replaced the phone. He needed another code; it would be
found in a clinic. It *had* to be found. . . . *We all do. Everyone* . . .
Ambiguity was at the end of that code.

"Anything?" asked the bewildered Taylor.

"That'll be up to you, Doctor. Ever heard of the Voyagers Emporium?
I don't know it, but then, for years I've bought most of my stuff in
Europe."

"The Voyagers? Sure, they've got branches all over the place. They're
the Tiffany of the luggage business. My wife bought one of those carry-on
bags, and I swear to God when I got the bill I thought she'd picked up
a car. They're first-class."

"They're also a KGB proprietary. That's what you're going to work on.
Whatever your schedule is, scratch it. I want you down at the clinic with
our globe-trotter here. We need another series of numbers. Just one more
set."

There was a sound of heavy footsteps outside the cabin, followed by a
harsh rapping on the door.

"What is it?" asked Havelock, loud enough to be heard outside.

"Sterile Five, you're wanted. Urgent call over the state police radio.
You're to be taken to the airfield pronto."

"On my way." Havelock turned to Taylor. "Make your arrangements.
Stay with it—with *him.* I'll be in touch. Sorry about the drink."

"So's Paddy O'Rourke."

"Who the hell is Paddy O'Rourke?"

"A little man who sits on my shoulder and tells me not to think too much."

Michael climbed into the marine helicopter as the giant overhead blades thundered and the pilot beckoned him forward to the flight deck.

"There's a patch phone back there!" shouted the pilot. "It'll be quieter when the hatch is closed. We'll put your call through."

"Who is it?"

"We'll never know!" yelled the radioman, turning from his console against the bulkhead. "Our link is filtered. We're bypassed."

The heavy metal door was electronically swung into place, shutting out the spill of the airfield's searchlights and reducing the thunder of the rotors to a muffled roar. Havelock crouched in the flashing darkness and gripped the phone, holding it to his right ear, his free hand covering the other. The voice that came last on the line was that of the President of the United States.

"You're being flown directly to Andrews Air Force Base to meet with Arthur Pierce."

"What's happened, sir?"

"He's on his way to Poole's Island with the vault specialist, but wants to talk with you first. He's a frightened man, and I don't think he frightens easily."

"The Soviets?"

"Yes. He can't tell whether they bought his story or not. They listened to him in silence, nodded and showed him the door. He has an idea that during the past eighteen hours they've learned something major, something they won't talk about—something that could blow everything apart. He warned them not to make any precipitous moves without communication at the highest levels."

"What was their response?"

"Deadly. 'Look to yourselves,' they said."

"They've got something. Pierce knows his enemy."

"In the last extremity, we'll be forced to parade Matthias—hoping to deter a launch, no guarantee that it will. I don't have to tell you what it will mean—we'll be a government of lepers, never trusted again. If we're on the map."

"What can I do? What does Pierce want?"

"All you've got, everything you've learned. He's trying to find something, *anything,* he can use as a lever. Every hour he can present a countercharge and prevent escalation, every day he can buy us, is a day for you. You *are* making progress?"

"Yes. We know the Ambiguity connection now, where he sends and receives. By midmorning we should learn just how he does it, through whom. When we do we'll find him."

"Then you *could* be a step away from Parsifal."

"I think so."

"I don't want to hear that! I want to hear '*yes.*' "

"Yes, Mr. President." Havelock paused, thinking about the few, brief words they needed to break the Voyagers code. They would be heard and recorded in a clinic. "I believe it."

"You wouldn't say it otherwise, thank *God.* Get down to Pierce. Give him everything you've got. *Help* him!"

35

The intersecting runways were lined with amber airstrip lamps, and the beams of searchlights crisscrossed and penetrated the dense cloud cover as routine patrols and check-out flights soared off into the night sky and swooped down from the darkness onto the floodlit open field. Andrews was a vast, guarded military city unto itself. The activity was intense both on the field and off. As headquarters of the U.S. Air Force Systems Command, it had responsibilities as far-ranging as they were endless. For thousands there was no such thing as day or night—merely duty hours and assignments. Banks of computers in a dozen buildings coexisted with the constant flow of expertise from the human interpreters, all forming judgments that affected NORAD, CONAD, the DEW line stations and SAC. The base occupied some forty-four hundred acres east of the Potomac and west of Chesapeake Bay, but its interests circled the globe, its purpose being the defense of the North American continent.

The marine helicopter was given clearance to enter a low-altitude pattern and set down on a pad north of the main field. Searchlights caught them a quarter of a mile away from ground zero as radar, radio and a pilot's sharp eyes eased them into the threshold from which they could make the vertical descent. Among the instructions radioed from the control tower was a message for Sterile Five. A jeep would be standing by to take Havelock to a runway on the south perimeter. It would wait there until his business was concluded and return him to the helicopter.

Havelock climbed out of the hatch and jumped to the ground. The damp chill of the air was accentuated by the rushing wash of the decelerating rotors, and as he walked rapidly away from it he pulled the lapels of his topcoat around his throat, wishing he had worn a hat—but then he remembered that the only hat he owned at the moment was a ragged knit cap that he'd left somewhere down on Poole's Island.

"Sir! *Sir!*" The shout came from Michael's left, beyond the tail assembly of the helicopter. It was the driver of the jeep, the vehicle itself barely visible in the shadows between the blinding, arcing lights of the pad.

Havelock ran over as the sergeant behind the wheel started to get out as a gesture of courtesy. "Forget it," said Michael, approaching the side panel, his hand on the windshield frame. "I didn't see you," he added, stepping over and lowering himself into the seat.

"Those were my instructions," explained the air force noncom. "Stay out of sight as much as possible."

"Why?"

"You'll have to ask the man who gives the orders, sir. I'd say he's careful, and since nobody's got a name, I don't ask questions."

The jeep shot forward, expertly maneuvered by the driver onto a narrow asphalt road fifty yards east of the helicopter pad. He turned left and accelerated; the road virtually circled the massive field, passing lighted buildings and enormous parking lots—flickering black structures and dark, spacious blurs—interspersed with the glare of onrushing headlights; everything at Andrews was seemingly always at triple time. The wind whipped through the open vehicle, the slapping damp air penetrating through Michael's coat and making him tense his muscles against the cold.

"I don't care if he calls himself Little Bo Peep," said Havelock, as much for conversation as for anything else. "So long as there's heat wherever we're going."

The sergeant glanced briefly at Michael. "Sorry, again," he replied, "but the man doesn't have it that way. My instructions are to take you to a runway on the south perimeter. I'm afraid that's it. A runway."

Havelock folded his arms and kept his eyes on the road ahead, wondering why the undersecretary of State was being so cautious within a military compound. Then his thoughts dwelt briefly on the man himself and he found part of the answer—the blind part, but nevertheless intrinsic: there had to *be* a reason. From what he had read about Arthur Pierce in the State Department dossier, coupled with what he had known from a distance, the undersecretary was a bright, persuasive spokesman for American interests at the United Nations, as well as around the international conference tables, with an avowed profound mistrust of the Soviets. This mistrust, however, was couched in a swift, aggressive wit, and woven into deceptively pleasant frontal assaults that drove the Russians up their Byzantine walls, for they had no matching counterattacks, except for bluster and defiance, and thus were frequently outmaneuvered in the open forums. Perhaps Pierce's outstanding credential was that he had been handpicked by Matthias himself when Anton was at the height of his intellectual powers. But the characteristic that stood out in Havelock's mind while racing down the dark airfield road was the highly regarded self-discipline attributed to Arthur Pierce by just about everybody who had contributed to his service dossier. He was never known to say anything unless he had something to say. By extension, thought Michael, he would not do something unless there was a reason for doing it.

And he had chosen to meet on a runway.

The driver swung left into an intersecting road that ran the distance of a huge maintenance hangar, then turned right onto the border of a deserted airstrip. In the distance, silhouetted in the glare of the headlights, was the figure of a man standing alone. Behind him, perhaps five hundred feet beyond and off the strip, was a small propjet with interior and exterior lights on and a fuel truck alongside it.

"There's the man," said the sergeant, slowing down. "I'll drop you off and wait back by the junk shop."

"The what?"

"The maintenance hangar. Just shout when you want me."

The jeep came to a stop thirty feet from Arthur Pierce. Havelock got out and saw the undersecretary of State starting toward him—a tall, slender man in a dark overcoat and hat, his stride long and energetic. Protocol was obviously unimportant to Pierce; there were too many with his title in the State Department who, regardless of the crisis, would expect a mere foreign service officer to approach *them.* Michael began walking, noticing that Pierce was removing the glove from his right hand.

"Mr. Havelock?" said the diplomat, hand extended, as the jeep sped away.

"Mr. Undersecretary?"

"But of course it's you," continued Pierce, his grip firm and genuine.

"I've seen your photograph. Frankly, I've read everything I could get my hands on about you. Now, I suppose I should get this over with."

"What?"

"Well, I guess I'm a little awestruck, which is a pretty silly thing for a grown man to say. But your accomplishments in a world I don't claim to understand are *very* impressive." The undersecretary paused, looking embarrassed. "I imagine the exotic nature of your work evokes this kind of reaction quite a lot."

"I wish it would; you make me feel terrific. Especially considering the mistakes I've made—especially during the last few months."

"The mistakes weren't yours."

"I should also tell you," Michael went on, overlooking the comment, "I've read a great deal about you, too. There aren't many people in your league at State. Anthony Matthias knew what he was doing—when he knew what he was doing—when he pulled you out of the pack and put you where you are."

"That's one thing we have in common, isn't it? Anthony Matthias. You far more than me in depth, and I'd never pretend otherwise. But the privilege, the goddamn *privilege*—there's no other way I can put it—of having known him the way I knew him makes the years, the tensions, the sweat worthwhile. It was a time of my life when everything jelled for me; he made it come together."

"I think we both feel the same way."

"When I read the material on you, you have no idea how I envied you. I was close to him, but I could never be what you were to him. What an extraordinary experience those years must have been."

"It was—they were. But nothing's there for either of us any longer."

"I know. It's unbelievable."

"Believe. I saw him."

"I wonder if they'll let me see him. I'm on my way to Poole's Island, you know."

"Do yourself a favor. Don't. It sounds trite, but remember him—especially him—the way he was, not the way he is."

"Which brings us to now." Pierce shook his head while staring at Havelock in the chiaroscuro of the runway. "It's not good. I don't think I really described to the President how close we are to the edge."

"He understood. He told me what they said to you when you warned them. 'Look to yourselves,' wasn't that it?"

"Yes. When they get that simple, that direct, I shake. They'll strike out at shadows; one violent shove and we're over. I'm a fair debater and not bad at negotiations, but you know the Soviets better than I do. How do you read it?"

"The same as you. Understatement isn't their way, bombast is. When they don't bother to threaten, they're threatening. Moves will take the place of words."

"That's what frightens me. The only thing I cling to is that I really don't believe they've brought in the men who push the buttons. Not yet. They know they have to be absolutely accurate. If they have concrete proof, not just hints, that Matthias entered into nuclear aggression pacts against the U.S.S.R. and if they even smell China, they won't hesitate to push the decision up where it won't be theirs any longer. That's when we can all start digging into the ground."

"Nuclear aggression . . . ?" Havelock paused, alarmed more than he would have thought possible. "You think they've assumed *that* much?"

"They're close to it. It's what's working them up into a frenzy. Pacts negotiated by a maniac—with other maniacs."

"And now the frenzy's gone. They keep quiet and show you the door. You warn them and they tell you we should look to ourselves. I'm frightened too, Mr. Undersecretary."

"You know what I'm thinking, then?"

"Parsifal."

"Yes."

"Berquist said you thought the Soviets had learned something during the past eighteen hours. Is this it?"

"I'm not sure," said Pierce. "I'm not even sure I'm working the right side of the street, but *something's* happened. It's why I wanted to see you. You're the only one who knows what's going on hour by hour. If I could pick something out, piece it together with something they said or reacted to, I might find a connection. What I'm looking for is a person or an event, anything that I can use to interdict them, to bring up before they do, and deflect them. *Anything* to keep them from alarming the warlords in the Presidium."

"They're not fools, they know those men. They'd know what they were delivering."

"I don't think that would stop them." Pierce hesitated, as if debating with himself whether or not to cite an example, then decided to speak. "You know General Halyard?"

"I've never met him. Or Ambassador Brooks. I was supposed to meet them both this afternoon. What about him?"

"I consider him one of the most thoughtful, *skeptical* military men in this country."

"Agreed. Not only from his reputation; I was given his dossier. And?"

"I asked him this afternoon what he thought the reaction would be—his included—if our clandestine services unearthed a Sino-Soviet pact against us, one that projected attack dates within forty-five days, and contained the kind of information found in those documents on Poole's Island. His reply was one word: 'Launch.' If he can say that, what about lesser, far more insecure men?"

Arthur Pierce did not dramatize the question but asked it calmly, and the chill Michael felt was now only partially due to the damp, cold air. Forces were closing in; time was running out. "The President said to help you," he began. "I don't know if I can, but I'll try. You say you're looking for something to deflect them; I may have it. There's a long-standing KGB operation that goes back to the days of the NKVD—to the thirties. It's called *Operatsiya Paminyatchik*—"

"Sorry," interrupted the man from State. "My Russian's not very good without an interpreter."

"It doesn't matter; an interpreter wouldn't know it. It's a code name. It stands for a strategy that calls for young children, even infants, selected by doctors and brought over here. They're placed with specific families —deep-cover Marxists—and grow up as Americans, in every superficial way normal, the more successful the better. But all through the years they're being trained—programmed, if you like—for their adult assignments, which are dependent on their given skills and development. It comes down to infiltration—again, the higher the better."

"Good *Lord,*" said Pierce quietly. "I'd think there'd be enormous risks in such a strategy. Such people have to be instilled with extraordinary belief."

"Oh, they believe, it's the essential part of their programming. They're also monitored; the slightest deviation, and they're either eliminated or brought back to Mother Russia, where they're reeducated while training others at the American compounds in the Urals and in Novgorod. The main point is that we've never really been able to crack the operation; the few we've taken are the least competent and so low on the ladder they haven't been able to shed any light. But we may have cracked it now. We've got ourselves an honest-to-God *paminyatchik* who's sanctioned for killing, as part of an execution unit. His kind has access—*must* have access —to clearance centers and source controls. There's too much risk in killing, too many possibilities for overreaction, to say nothing of being caught. Orders have to be rechecked, authorization confirmed."

"You've *got* such a man? My God, where?"

"He's being flown now to Bethesda—he's wounded—and, later tonight, will be transferred to a clinic in Virginia."

"Don't *lose* him! Is there a doctor with him? A good one?"

"I think so. He's a clinic specialist named Taylor; he'll stay with him."

"Then by morning you think you'll be able to give me something I can use with the Soviets? This could be the deflection I need. I counter their attacks with an attack of my own. I accuse—"

"I can give it to you now," interrupted Havelock, "but you can't use it until I tell you. Tomorrow night at the earliest. Can you stall that long?"

"I think so. What is it?"

"We put him under chemicals an hour ago. I don't know how the right people are reached, but I know the cover identity of their clearing center. Also the code name for the *paminyatchik* source control for this area— which I have to assume includes the Washington operation, the most vital in the U.S."

Arthur Pierce shook his head in astonishment and admiration. "You floor me," he said, with respect in his quiet voice. "I told you I was a little awestruck. Well, I take it back, I'm a *lot* awestruck. What can I use?"

"Whatever you have to. After tomorrow I'll trade off the whole *Operatsiya Paminyatchik* for another few days."

"'The President told me a few minutes ago—he called after reaching you. You think you're that close to Parsifal?"

"We'll be closer still when we get Taylor's patient down to the clinic. With a few words he can put us within arm's reach of the man we call Ambiguity. And unless everything that we've projected—that Bradford projected—is wrong—and I don't think it is, it *can't* be—once we have Ambiguity we'll know who Parsifal is. *I'll* know."

"Christ, *how?*"

"Matthias as much as told me I know him. Are you familiar with a company, a chain of stores, called the Voyagers Emporium?"

"Most of my luggage is, I regret to say. At least, my bank account regrets it."

"Somewhere inside, in a department or a section, that's the KGB clearing center. Ambiguity has to stay in touch; it's where he gets his orders, transmits information. We'll break it quietly—*very* quietly—tear it apart and find him. We don't need much; we know where he's located."

"Right where you see him every day," said Pierce, nodding. "What about the code name for the source control?"

"Hammer-zero-two. It doesn't mean anything to us, and it can be changed by the network overnight, but the fact that we broke it, broke the *paminyatchik* circle so decisively, has got to make someone sweat inside the Kremlin." Michael paused, then added, "When I give you the go-ahead, use what you need, all of it or any part. It's basically a diversion, what you call deflection, but I think it's a strong one. Create a diplomatic rhubarb, cause a storm of cables between Moscow and New York. Just buy us time."

"You're sure?"

"I'm sure we don't have a choice. We *need* time."

"You could lose the source control."

"Then we'll lose him. We can live with a source control—we've all got them in more than sixty countries. We can't live with Parsifal. Any of us."

"I'll wait for your call." The undersecretary of State glanced at his watch, squinting in the dim light to read the radium dial. "I still have a few minutes before we leave. The vault specialist had to be flown in from Los Alamos; he's meeting with one of the men from his company who brought him the internal diagrams. . . . There're so many things I want to ask, so much I need to know."

"I'm here as long as you are; when you leave, I leave. I heard it from the President."

"I like him. I haven't always liked presidents."

"Because you know he doesn't give a damn whether you do or not—not while he's in the Oval Office. That's the way I read him. I like him too, and I have every reason in the book not to."

"Costa Brava? They told me everything."

"It's history. Let's get current. What else can I tell you that may help?"

"The obvious," said Pierce, his voice descending to a hollow sound. "If Parsifal *has* reached the Soviets, what can I say—if I'm given the chance to say it? If he's hinted at the China factor, or at the vulnerabilities in their own counterstrike capabilities, how can I explain it? Where did he *get* it all? Exposing Matthias is only part of the answer. Frankly, it's not enough, and I think you know that."

"I know it." Havelock tried to collect his thoughts, to be as clear and concise as possible. "What's in those so-called agreements is a mix of a thousand moves in a triple-sided chess game, the anchor player being us. Our penetration of the Russian and Chinese systems is far deeper than we've ever hinted at, and there are strategy committees set up to study

and evaluate every conceivable option in the event some goddamn fool
—on *any* side—gives the order to launch."

"Such committees, I'm sure, exist in Moscow and Peking."

"But neither Moscow nor Peking could produce an Anthony Matthias,
the man with geopolitical panaceas, respected, even worshiped—no one
on either side of the world like him."

Pierce nodded. "The Soviets treat him as a valued go-between, not as
an adversary. The Chinese throw banquets for him and call him a vision-
ary."

"And when he began to fall apart, he still had the imagination to
conceive of the ultimate nuclear chess game."

"But *how?*"

"He found a zealot. A naval officer on one of the Pentagon committees
who's up to his eyeballs in overkill theories. He gave Matthias everything.
He made copies of all the strategies and counterstrategies the three
committees exchanged with one another. They contained authentic data
—they *had* to contain it; those war games are very real on paper. Everything can be checked by computers—the extent of megaton damage
inflicted, damage sustained, the limits of punishment before the ground
is useless. It was all there, and Matthias put it together. Matthias and the
man who's got us by the throat. Parsifal."

"I'd say that naval officer is scheduled to begin a long period of confine-
ment."

"I'm not sure what that would accomplish. At any rate, I'm not finished
with him; he's still got more to give—may have given it by now."

"Just a minute," said the undersecretary of State, his face suddenly
alive. "Could *he* be Parsifal?"

"No, not possible."

"Why not?"

"Because in his own misguided way he believed in what he was doing.
He has a permanent love affair with his uniform and his country; he'd
neither allow the possibility of compromise nor give the Russians an ounce
of ammunition. Decker's not an original, but he's genuine. I doubt the
Lubyanka could break him."

"Decker . . . You've got him put away, don't you?"

"He's not going anywhere. He's at home with an escort unit outside."

Pierce shook his head while reaching into his pocket. "It's all so insane!" he said as he pulled out a pack of cigarettes and matches. "Care
for one?" he asked, proferring the pack.

"No, thanks. I've had my quota of five hundred for the day."

The man from State struck a match, holding the flame under the cigarette. Without the protection of a second hand, it was extinguished by the wind. He struck another, left palm up, and inhaled, the smoke from his mouth mingling with the vapor of his breath. "At the meeting this afternoon, Ambassador Brooks brought up something I didn't understand. He said an intelligence officer from the KGB had made contact with you and speculated on the identity of the faction in Moscow who'd worked with Matthias at Costa Brava."

"He meant with Parsifal; Matthias was being led by then. And Rostov —his name's Rostov—didn't speculate. He knew. They're a collection of fanatics in a branch called the VKR, the Voennaya. They make even our Deckers look like flower children. He's trying to break it open and I wish him luck. It's crazy, but a dedicated enemy may be one of our hopes."

"What do you mean, 'break it open'?"

"Get names, find out who did what and let the saner people deal with them. Rostov's good; he may do it, and if he does, he'll somehow get word to me."

"He *will?*"

"He's already offered me a white contact. It happened at Kennedy Airport when I flew in from Paris."

There was the sound of a gunning engine in the distance. Pierce threw down his cigarette and crushed it under his foot as he spoke. "What more do you think this Decker can give you?"

"He may have spoken to Parsifal but doesn't know it. Or someone calling for Parsifal. In either case, he was reached at home, which means that somewhere in a couple of hundred thousand long-distance records is a specific call made to a specific number at a specific time."

"Why not a couple of million records?"

"Not if we've got a general location."

"*Do* you?"

"I'll know more by tomorrow. When you get back—"

"Mr. Undersecretary! *Mr. Undersecretary!*" The shouting was accompanied by the roar of the jeep's motor and the screeching of its tires as it came to a stop only a few feet from them. "Undersecretary Pierce?" said the driver.

"Who gave you my name?" asked Pierce icily.

"There's an urgent telephone call for you, sir. They said it was your office at the United Nations and they have to speak to you."

"The Soviets," said Pierce under his breath to Havelock; his alarm was apparent. "Please, wait for me."

The undersecretary of State swung himself rapidly into the air force jeep and nodded to the driver; his eyes were on the lights of the maintenance hangar. Michael pulled his coat around him, his attention drawn to the small propjet aircraft several hundred feet away in the opposite direction. The left engine had been started, and the pilot was revving it; the right coughed into operation seconds later. Then Havelock saw another jeep; it had taken the place of the fuel truck next to the plane. The vault specialist had arrived; the departure for Poole's Island was imminent.

Arthur Pierce returned six minutes later, climbed out of the open vehicle and dismissed the driver. "It *was* the Soviets," he said, approaching Michael. "They wanted an unrecorded, unlogged meeting tomorrow morning; that means an emergency. I reached the senior aide of the delegation and told him I had called my own emergency conference tomorrow on the strength of their reactions late this afternoon. I also suggested I might have information for them that would necessitate a storm of cables—I used your phrase—between New York, their embassy in Washington and Moscow. I hinted that perhaps the pounding shoe was in another hand." The undersecretary stopped, hearing the preliminary warm-up of the jets from the plane in the distance; the jeep was leaving the area. "That's my signal; the vault specialist's here. You know, it's going to take at least three hours to break into that room. Walk over with me, will you?"

"Sure. What was the Soviets' reaction?"

"Very negative, of course. They know me; they sense a deflection, a diversion—to use your word. We agreed to meet tomorrow evening." Pierce paused and turned to Havelock. "For God's sake, give me the green light, then. I'll need every argument, every weapon I can have. Among them a medical report diagnosing exhaustion for Matthias . . . God knows, not the psychiatric file I'm bringing back to you."

"I forgot. The President was to have gotten it to me yesterday—today."

"I'm bringing it up." Pierce started walking again as Michael kept pace. "I can see how it happens."

"What happens?"

"The days melding into one another. Yesterday, today . . . tomorrow, if there is a tomorrow. One long, unending, sleepless night."

"Yes," said Havelock, feeling no need to amplify.

"How many weeks have you been living it?"

"More than a few."

"*Jesus.*" The roar of the combined engines grew louder as they drew nearer the plane. "I suppose this is actually the safest place to talk," said

Pierce, raising his voice to be heard. "No device could filter that noise."

"Is that why you wanted to meet on the runway?" asked Michael.

"You probably think I'm paranoid, but yes, it is. I wouldn't care if we were in the control room of a NORAD base, I'd want the walls swept before having a conversation like the one we just had. You probably *do* think I'm paranoid. After all, this is Andrews—"

"I don't think you're paranoid at all," interrupted Havelock. "I think I should have thought of it."

The door of the small aircraft was open, the metal steps in place. The pilot signaled from his lighted window; Pierce waved back, nodding affirmatively. Michael walked with the undersecretary to within ten feet of the door where the wash of the propellers was strong and growing stronger.

"You said something about having a general location in mind regarding that call to Decker," shouted Pierce. "Where is it?"

"Somewhere in the Shenandoah," yelled Havelock. "It's only speculation, but Decker delivered the materials there."

"I see."

The engines roared a sudden crescendo, and the wind from the propeller blades reached gale force, whipping the hat from Arthur Pierce's head. Michael crouched, scrambling after it through the powerful wash. He stopped it with his foot and carried it back to the undersecretary of State.

"Thanks very much!" shouted Pierce.

Havelock stared at the face in front of him, at the streak of white that sprang up from the forehead and shot through the mass of wavy dark hair.

36

It was an hour and forty-five minutes before he saw the floodlights that marked the entrance to the drive at Sterile Five. The flight from Andrews to Quantico and the trip by car to Fairfax had been oddly disturbing, and he did not know why. It was as though a part of his mind were refusing to function; he was conscious of a gap in his own thought process but was blocked by a compulsion not to probe. It was like a drunk's refusal to face the gross embarrassments of the night before: something not remembered did not exist. And he was incapable of doing anything about it; he did not know what it was, only that it was not, and therefore, it was.

One long, unending, sleepless night. Perhaps that was it. He needed sleep . . . he needed Jenna. But there was no time for sleep, no time for them to be together in the way they wanted to be together. No time for anything or anyone but Parsifal.

What was it? Why had a part of him suddenly died?

The marine sedan pulled up in front of the ornate entrance of the estate. He got out, thanked the driver and the armed guard, and walked up to the door. He thought as he stood there, with a finger on the bell, that like so many other doors in so many other houses he had entered, he had no key with which to open it. Would he ever have a key to a house that was his—theirs—and be able to open it as so many millions opened theirs every day? It was a silly thought, foolishly pondered. Where was the significance of a house and a key? Still, the thought—the need, perhaps —persisted.

The door abruptly opened and Jenna brought him back to the urgent present, her striking, lovely face taut, her eyes burning into his.

"Thank *God!*" she cried, clutching him and pulling him inside. "You're *back!* I was going out of my mind!"

"What is it?"

"Mikhail, come with me. Quickly!" She gripped his hand as they walked rapidly down the foyer past the staircase to the study, which she had left open. Going to the desk, she picked up a note and said, "You must call the Bethesda hospital. Extension six-seven-one. But first you have to know what happened!"

"What—?"

"The *paminyatchik* is dead."

"Oh, *Christ!*" Michael grabbed the phone that Jenna held out for him. He dialed, his hand trembling. "When?" he shouted. *"How?"*

"An execution," she replied as he waited for Bethesda to answer. "Less than an hour ago. Two men. They took out the guard with a knife, got in the room and killed the traveler while he was sedated. Four shots in the head. The doctor's beside himself."

"Six-seven-one! *Hurry,* please!"

"I couldn't stand it," whispered Jenna, staring at him, touching his face. "I thought you were there . . . outside somewhere . . . seen, perhaps. They said you weren't, but I didn't know whether to believe them or not."

"Taylor? How did it *happen?"*

As Havelock listened to the doctor a numbing pain spread through him, stealing his breath. Taylor was still in shock and spoke disjointedly; Jenna's brief description had been clearer, and there was nothing further to learn. Two killers in the uniforms of naval officers had come to the sixth floor, found Taylor's patient, and proceeded professionally with the execution, killing a marine guard in the process.

"We've lost Ambiguity," said Michael, hanging up, his hand so heavy the phone fell into the cradle, clapping into place. *"How?* That's what I can't understand! We had maximum security, military transport, every precaution!" He looked helplessly at Jenna.

"Was it all highly visible?" she asked. "Could the precautions and the transport have drawn attention?"

Havelock nodded wearily. "Yes. Yes, of course. We commandeered an airfield, flew in and out of there like a commando unit, diverting the other traffic."

"And not that far from the Medical Center," said Jenna. "Someone alerted to the disturbance would be drawn to the scene. He would see what you didn't want him to see. In this case, a stretcher would be enough."

Michael slipped off his topcoat and listlessly dropped it on a chair. "But that doesn't explain what happened at the Medical Center itself. An execution team was sent in to abort a trap, to kill their own people, so there'd be no chance that anyone would be taken alive."

"*Paminyatchiki,*" said Jenna. "It's happened before."

"But how did their controls *know* it was a trap? I spoke only to the Apache unit and to Loring. *No one* else! How *could* they? How could they have been so sure that they would risk sending in sanctioned killers? The risk was enormous!" Havelock walked around the desk, looking at the scattered papers, hating them, hating the terror they evoked. "Loring told me that he was probably spotted, that it was his fault, but I don't believe it. That mocked-up patrol car didn't just emerge from around the block; it was sent from somewhere by someone in authority who had made the most dangerous decision he could make. He wouldn't have made it on the strength of one man seen in a parking lot—that man, incidentally, was too damned experienced to show himself so obviously."

"It doesn't seem logical," agreed Jenna. "Unless the others were spotted earlier."

"Even if the cardiologist cover was blown, at best they'd be considered protection. No, the control *knew* it was a trap, knew that the primary objective—let's face it, the sole objective—was to take even one of them alive. . . . Goddamn it, *how?*" Michael leaned over the desk, his hands gripping the edge, his head pounding. He pushed himself away and walked toward the wide, dark windows with the thick, beveled glass. And then he heard the words, spoken softly by Jenna: "Mikhail, you did speak to someone else. You spoke to the President."

"Of *course,* but . . ." He stopped, staring at the distorted image of his face in the window, but slowly *not* seeing his face . . . seeing, instead, the formless outline of another. Then the night mist that had rolled in through the trees and over the lawns outside became another mist, from another time. The crashing of waves suddenly filled his ears, thundering, deafening, unbearable. Lightning shattered across the luminous, unseen screen in his mind, and then the sharp cracks came, one after another until they grew into ear-splitting explosions, blowing him into a frenzied galaxy of flashing lights . . . and *dread.*

Costa Brava. He was *back* at the *Costa Brava!*

And the face in the mirror took on form . . . distant form . . . unmistakable form. And the shock of white hair sprang up from that face, surrounded by waves of black, framed, isolated . . . an image unto itself.

"No . . . *no!"* He heard himself screaming; he could feel Jenna's hands on his arms, then his face . . . but *not* his face! The face in the window! The face with the sharp path of white in the hair . . . his hair, but *not* his hair, his face but *not* his face! Yet both were the faces of *killers,* his and the one he had seen that night on the Costa Brava!

A fisherman's cap had suddenly been blown away in the ocean wind; a hat had been whipped off the head of a man by the sudden wash of propellers. On a runway . . . in a shadowed light . . . two hours ago!

The same man? Was it *possible?* Even *conceivable?*

"Mikhail!" Jenna held his face in her hands. "Mikhail, what *is* it? What's wrong?"

"It's *not* possible!" he screamed. "It can't be!"

"What, my darling? *What* can't be?"

"Jesus. I'm losing my mind!"

"Darling, *stop it!"* shouted Jenna, shaking him, holding him.

"No . . . no, I'll be all right. Let me alone. Let me *alone!"* He spun away from her and raced to the desk. "Where is it? Where the *hell is it?"*

"Where is what?" asked Jenna calmly, now beside him.

"The file."

"What file?"

"My file!" He yanked the top right-hand drawer open, rummaging furiously among the papers until he found the black-bordered folder. He pulled it out, slammed it on the desk and opened it; breathing with difficulty, he leafed through the pages, eyes and fingers working maniacally.

"What's troubling you, Mikhail? Tell me. Let me help you. What started this? What's making you go back? . . . We agreed not to punish each other!"

"Not me! *Him!"*

"Who?"

"I can't make a mistake! I *can't!"* Havelock found the page he was looking for. He scanned the lines, using his index finger, his eyes riveted on the page. He read in a flat voice: " 'They're killing her. Oh, my God, he's killed her and I can't bear the screams. Go to her, stop them . . . stop them. No, not me, never me. Oh, Christ, they're pulling her away . . . she's bleeding so, but not in pain now. She's gone. Oh, my God, she's gone, my love is gone. . . . The wind is strong, it's blown his cap away. . . . The face? Do I know the face? A photograph somewhere? A dossier? The dossier of a killer. . . . No, it's the hair. The streak of white in the hair.' " Michael stood up and looked at Jenna; he was perspiring. "A streak . . . of . . . white," he said slowly, desperately trying to enunciate the words clearly. "It *could be him!*"

Jenna leaned into him and held his shoulders. "You must take hold of yourself, my darling. You're not being rational; you're in some kind of shock. Can you understand me?"

"No time," he said, removing her hands and reaching for the phone. "I'm okay, and you're right. I am in shock, but only because it's so incredible. *Incredible!*" He dialed, breathed deeply, and spoke: "I want to be connected to the main switchboard of Andrews Air Force Base, and I want you to give instructions to the duty officer to comply with any requests I make with regard to information."

Jenna watched him, then backed away to the table with the decanters. She poured him some brandy and handed it to him. "You're pale," she said. "I've never seen you so pale."

Havelock waited, listening as the head of the White House Secret Service gave his instructions to Andrews and, conversely, the electronic verification check made by the colonel in charge of field communications. The incredible was always rooted in the credible, he thought. For the most credible reasons on earth he had been on that beach at the Costa Brava that night, observing the extraordinary, and a mere gust of wind had blown a man's cap away. Now he had to know if there was substance in the observation. *Both* observations.

"There are calls from New York constantly," said the colonel in answer to his question.

"I'm talking about those five to ten minutes," countered Michael. "Transferred to a maintenance hangar on the south perimeter. It was less than two hours ago; someone has to remember. Check every operator on the boards. *Now!*"

"Christ, take it easy."

"You take it fast!"

No operator at Andrews Air Force Base had transferred a call to a maintenance hangar on the south perimeter.

"There was a sergeant driving a jeep, ordered to pick up cargo labeled Sterile Five, marine equipment. Are you with me?"

"I'm aware of the Sterile classification and of the flight. Helicopter, north pad."

"What's his name?"

"The driver?"

"Yes."

The colonel paused, obviously concerned as he answered, "We understand the original driver was replaced. Another relieved him on verbal orders."

"Whose?"

"We haven't traced it."

"What was the second driver's name?"

"We don't know."

"Thank you, Colonel."

Paminyatchik!

"Find me the dossier on Pierce," said Havelock, looking up at Jenna, his hand on the telephone button.

"Arthur Pierce?" asked Jenna, astonished.

"As quickly as you can." Michael dialed again, and said, "I can't make a mistake, I *can't make a mistake.* Not here, not *now.*" Then: "Mr. President? It's Havelock. I've been with Pierce and tried to help him. . . . Yes, sir, he's bright, very bright and very good. We'd like a point clarified; it's minor but it would clear something up for both of us. He had a lot on his mind, a lot to absorb. At the meeting this afternoon, after I called you, did you bring up the Apache operation at the Randolph Medical Center? . . . Then everyone's current. Thank you, Mr. President." Michael replaced the phone as Jenna handed him a dark-brown file folder.

"Here's Pierce's dossier."

Havelock opened it and immediately turned to the synopsis of personal characteristics.

The subject drinks moderately at social occasions, and has never been known to abuse alcohol. He does not use any form of tobacco.

The match, the open flame unprotected, extinguished by the wind . . . A second flame, the flare of light prolonged, unmistakable. The sequence as odd and unmistakable as the cigarette smoke emerging solely from the mouth and mingling with the curling vapor of breath, a non-smoker's exhalation. A *signal.* Followed moments later by an unknown driver delivering an urgent message, using a name he was not supposed to know, angering the man he was addressing. Every sequence had been detailed, timed, reactions considered. Arthur Pierce had not been called to the phone, he had been *making* a call.

Or had he? There could be *no* mistake, not now. Had an operator transferring rapidly incoming calls throughout the vast expanse of an air force base forgotten one among so many? And how often did soldiers take over innocuous assignments for friends without informing their superiors? How frequently did highly visible men appear to be on the side of the avenging medical angels by never smoking in public but in a crisis pulling out a concealed pack of cigarettes, a habit they were sincerely trying to kick, the act of smoking actually awkward? . . . How many men had streaks of premature white in their hair?

No mistakes. Once the accusation was made it could not be taken back, and if it could not be sustained, trust at the highest level would be eroded, possibly destroyed; the very people who *had* to communicate with one another would be guarded, wary, commanders in silent conflict. Where was the ultimate proof?

Moscow?

There is first the KGB; all else follows. A man may gravitate to the VKR, but first he must have sprung from the KGB. Rostov. Athens.

He says he is not your enemy . . . but others are who may be his as well. A Soviet agent. Kennedy Airport.

"I can see it in your eyes, Mikhail." Jenna touched his shoulder, forcing him to look at her. "Call the President."

"I have to be absolutely certain. Pierce said it would take at least three hours for the vault to be opened, another two to sort out the documents. I've got some time. If he's Ambiguity, he's trapped."

"How can you be absolutely certain about a *paminyatchik?*"

"At the source. Moscow."

"Rostov?"

"I can try. He may be as desperate as I am, but if he isn't, I'll tell him he should be. We've got our maniacs, and he's got his." Havelock picked up the phone and dialed the three digits for the White House switchboard. "Please get me the Russian consulate in New York. I'm afraid I don't know the number. . . . No, I'll hold on." Michael covered the mouthpiece, speaking to Jenna. "Go over Pierce's file. Look for something we can trace. Parents, if they're alive."

"A wife," said Jenna.

"He's not married."

"Convenient. Lovers, then."

"He's discreet."

"Naturally." Jenna picked up the file from the desk.

"Dobriy vyehchyer," said Havelock into the phone, his hand removed. *"Ja khochu govorit's nachal' nikom okhrany."* Every operator at every Soviet embassy and consulate understood when a caller asked to be connected to the director of street security. A deep male voice got on the line, acknowledging merely that he had picked up the phone. Michael continued in Russian: "My name is Havelock and I have to assume I'm speaking to the right person, the one who can put me in touch with the man I'm trying to reach."

"Who might that be, sir?"

"I'm afraid I didn't get his name, but he knows mine. As I'm quite sure you do."

"That's not much help, Mr. Havelock."

"I think it's enough. The man met me at Kennedy Airport and we had a lengthy conversation, including the means I might employ to reach him again; a forty-eight-hour time span and the New York Public Library figured prominently among them. There was also some discussion about a missing Graz-Burya automatic, a splendid weapon, I think you'll agree. It's urgent I speak with that man—as urgent as his message was for me."

"Perhaps if you could recall the message, it might be more helpful, sir."

"An offer of sanctuary from the director of External Strategies, Pyotr Rostov, KGB, Moscow. And I wouldn't say those words if I were taping this. *You* can, but I can't afford it."

"There is always the possibility of a reverse order of events."

"Take the chance, comrade. You can't afford not to."

"Then why not talk with me . . . comrade?"

"Because I don't know you." Michael looked down at the list of the direct, unlisted numbers he had been assigned; he repeated one to the Russian. "I'll be here for the next five minutes." He hung up and reached for the brandy.

"Will he call back, do you think?" asked Jenna, sitting in the chair in front of the desk, the Pierce file in her hand.

"Why not? He doesn't have to say anything, just listen. . . . Anything there we can use?"

"The mother died in 1968. The father disappeared eight months later and has never been seen since. He wrote his son in Vietnam that he 'didn't care to go on without his wife, that he'd join her with God.' "

"Naturally. But no suicide, no body. Just a Christian fade-out."

"Naturally. *Paminyatchik.* He had too much to offer in Novgorod."

The telephone rang, the lighted button corresponding to the number he had given the Soviet consulate in New York.

"You understand, Mr. Havelock," began the singsong voice in English unmistakably belonging to the Soviet agent from Kennedy Airport, "that the message delivered to you was offered in the spirit of compassion for the great injustice done by those in your government who called for the execution of a man of peace—"

"If you're doing this," interrupted Havelock, "for the benefit of any recording on this end, forget it. And if you're auditioning for the consulate's, do it later. I haven't got time. I'm accepting a part of Rostov's offer."

"I was not aware that it was divided into parts."

"I'm assuming prior communication."

"I assume that's reasonable," said the Russian. "Under extremely limited circumstances."

"Any circumstances you like, just use this telephone number and have him get back to me within the hour." Michael looked at his watch. "It's not quite seven o'clock in the morning in Moscow. Reach him."

"I don't believe those circumstances are acceptable."

"They've got to be. Tell him I may have found the enemy. *Our* enemy, the word temporary, of course, assuming again there's a future for either of us."

"I really don't think—"

"Don't think. Reach him. Because if you don't, I'll try myself and that could be acutely embarrassing—to you, comrade, not to me. I don't care anymore. I'm the *prize.* " Havelock replaced the phone, aware of the beads of perspiration that had broken out on his forehead.

"What can Rostov actually tell you?" Jenna got up from the chair and placed Pierce's dossier on the desk. "There's nothing here, incidentally. Just a brilliant, modest hero of the republic."

"Naturally." Michael wiped his forehead with the back of his hand and leaned forward, supporting himself on his elbows. "Rostov told me in

Athens that one of his sources for Costa Brava was a mole operating out of the White House. I didn't believe him; it's the kind of shock treatment that makes you listen harder. But suppose he was telling me the truth— a past truth—because he knew the mole was out and untraceable. The perfect traveler."

Jenna raised her hand, pointing to the dossier on the desk. "Pierce was assigned to the National Security Council. He had an office in the White House for several months."

"Yes. And Rostov meant what he said; he couldn't understand, and what you can't understand in this business is cause for alarm. Everything he had learned about Costa Brava—which I confirmed—told him it couldn't have taken place without the cooperation of someone in Moscow. But *who?* These operations are under his direct control, but he didn't have anything to do with it, knew nothing about it. So he tested me, thinking I could tell him something, bringing in the mole for credibility, knowing that we both accepted a mole's information as being reliable. The truth—as he was told the truth—except it was a lie."

"Told by a KGB officer, a *paminyatchik* mole, who had transferred his allegiance from the KGB to the Voennaya," said Jenna. "He throws off his former superiors for his new ones."

"Then proceeds to intercept and take over Costa Brava. *If* he was at Costa Brava. If . . . *if.*"

"How will you handle Rostov? He'll be taped; he'll be monitored."

"It'll be light. He is, after all, director of External Strategies. I'll play on the power struggle. KGB versus VKR. He'll understand."

"He won't talk about the *paminyatchik* operation over the telephone, you know that. He can't."

"I won't ask him to. I'll name the name and listen. He'll tell me somehow. We've both been around a long time—too long—and the words we use have never been written to mean what we say they mean, the silences we use never understood except by people like us. He wants what I have—if I have it—as much as I want what he can confirm. It'll work. Somehow. He'll tell me if Arthur Pierce is the mole—if he's convinced the mole has gone around his back and joined the maniacs."

Jenna walked to the coffee table, picked up a note pad, and sat down in the leather armchair. "While you're waiting, do you want to talk about Commander Decker?"

"Christ!" Havelock's right hand shot out for the phone, his left centering the list of numbers in front of him. He dialed as he spoke, his voice

strained: "I mentioned him to Pierce. Oh, *God,* did I mention him! . . . Raise the Decker escort, please. *Hurry.*"

"Naval escort. In position."

The words over the radiophone were clear, and the sudden throbbing in Michael's temples began to subside. "This is Sterile Five. We have reason to believe there could be hostile activity in your area."

"No signs of it" was the reply. "Everything's quiet, and the street's well lighted."

"Nevertheless, I'd like additional personnel."

"We're stretched pretty thin at Sixteen Hundred, Sterile Five. Why not call in the locals? They don't have to know any more than we do, and we don't know a damn thing."

"Can you do it?"

"Sure. We'll label it diplomatic and they'll get overtime. By the way, how do you read the activity?"

"Abduction. Neutering you first, then taking Decker."

"Thanks for the warning. We'll get right on it. Out."

Havelock leaned back in the chair, his neck stretched over the back, and stared at the ceiling. "Now that we know there still *is* a Commander Decker, what did he tell you?"

"Where did you leave off? I went back over everything."

Michael closed his eyes, remembering. "A phone call," he said slowly. "It was later, after their Sunday meetings at the lodge. He tried for days, weeks, to get in touch with Matthias, but Anton wouldn't talk to him. Then someone called him . . . with an explanation. That was it, he said it was an explanation."

Jenna flipped through her notes, stopping at a page, then going back two. "A man with a strange voice, an odd accent—'clipped and rushed' was the way Decker described it. I asked him to recall as thoroughly as possible every word the man said. Fortunately, that call was very important to him; he remembered nearly everything, I think. I wrote it down."

"Read it, will you?"

Jenna rolled the page over. "The man identified himself as a colleague of the Secretary of State, and asked Decker several questions about his naval career, obviously to make sure it *was* Decker. . . . Then here it begins —I tried to write it down as though I'd heard it myself. 'Secretary Matthias appreciates everything you've done, and wants you to know that you will be mentioned prominently and frequently in his memoirs. But you must understand the rules, the rules can't be broken. For the Secretary's global strategy to be effective, it must be developed in total secrecy; the element of surprise is paramount; no one *in* or *out* of government—' " Jenna paused. "The emphases were Decker's," she added. " '—*in* or *out* of government aware that a master plan has been created.' " Again Jenna stopped and looked up. "Here Decker wasn't precise; the man's reasons for excluding people in government were apparently based on the assumption that there were too many who couldn't be trusted, who might divulge secrets regardless of their clearance."

"Of course he wasn't precise. He was talking about himself and it was a painful reference."

"I agree. . . . This last part I'm sure was accurate, probably word for word. 'The Secretary of State wants you to know that when the time comes you will be summoned and made his chief executive officer, all controls in your hands. But because of your superb reputation in the field of nuclear tactics, there can't be even a hint of any association between you. If anyone ever asks you if you know the Secretary of State, you must say you do not. That's also part of the rules.' " Jenna put the note pad down on her lap. "That's it. Decker's ego was thoroughly flattered, and by his lights his place in history was assured."

"Nothing else was needed," said Havelock, straightening himself up in the chair. "Did you write that out so I can read it?"

"I write more clearly in English than I do in Czech. Why?"

"Because I want to study it—over and over and over again. The man who spoke those words is Parsifal, and somewhere in the past I've heard that man speak before."

"Go back over the years, Mikhail," said Jenna, sitting forward, raising the note pad and flipping the pages. "I'll go back with you. *Now!* It's not impossible. A Russian who speaks English rapidly, clipping his words. It's *there.* That's what Decker said. 'Clipped and rushed,' those were his words. How many such men can you have known?"

"Let's do it." Havelock got up from the desk as Jenna tore off the two pages that contained her notes on the call to Thomas Decker. Michael came around and took them from her. "Men I *know* who've met Matthias. We'll start with this year and work backwards. Write down every name I come up with."

"Why not do it geographically? City by city. You can eliminate some quickly, concentrate on the others."

"Association," he added. "We scratch Barcelona and Madrid; we never touched the Soviets. . . . Belgrade—a river warehouse on the Sava, the attaché from the Russian consulate, Vasili Yankovitch. He was with Anton in Paris."

"Yankovitch," said Jenna, writing.

"And Ilitch Borin, visiting professor at the University of Belgrade; we had drinks, dinner. He knew Matthias from the cultural exchange conferences."

"Borin."

"No one else in Belgrade. . . . Prague. There must be at least a dozen men in Prague. The Soviets are crawling in Prague."

"Their names? Start alphabetically."

The names came, some rapidly, others slowly, some striking chords of possibility, others completely improbable. Nevertheless, Jenna wrote them all down, prodding Michael, forcing him to jolt his memory, one name leading to another.

Krakow. Vienna. Paris. London. New York. Washington.

The months became a year, then two, and finally three. The list grew as Havelock probed, pushing his conscious, permitting the free association of his subconscious, digging, straining, forcing his mind to function as if it were a finely tuned instrument. And again the sweat broke out on his forehead, his pulse oddly quickening as he reached the end of his energies.

"God, I'm tired," said Michael quietly, staring at the beveled windowpane where over an hour ago two faces had appeared, one replacing the other, both killers, both from the Costa Brava. Or were they?

"You have thirty-nine names," said Jenna, coming to him, touching the back of his neck, massaging it gently. "Sit down and study them, study the telephone conversation. Find Parsifal, Mikhail."

"Do any match the names on your list? I thought of that when I mentioned Ilitch Borin; he's a doctor of philosophy. Is there anyone?"

"No."

"I'm sorry."

"So am I."

"He hasn't called. Rostov hasn't called."

"I know."

"I said an hour, the deadline was an hour." Havelock looked at his watch. "It's thirty-four minutes past the deadline."

"There could be mechanical troubles in Moscow. It would be nothing new."

"Not for him. He's pulled in the white contact; he doesn't want to acknowledge."

"How often have you stretched a deadline? Waiting until the one who expected your call was filled with anxiety, his defenses eroded."

"He knows my dossier too well for that." Michael turned to her. "I have to make a decision. If I'm right, Pierce can't be allowed off that island. If I'm wrong they'll think I've crashed, gone over the edge. Berquist won't have any choice, he'll have to remove me."

"Not necessarily."

"Of course necessarily. I'm seeing monsters in dark closets, wasting valuable hours on delusions. That's not a man you want giving orders. My God, Arthur Pierce! The most valuable asset we have—if we have him."

"Only you know what you *did* see."

"It was night, a night that was racking me. Look through that clinic file. Is that a rational man talking or thinking? What *was* he seeing? . . . I need one word, one sentence from Rostov."

"Wait, Mikhail," said Jenna, touching his arm and urging him back to the armchair. "You still have time. Study the list of names, the words spoken to Decker. It may happen for you. A name, a voice, a phrase. It could happen."

Scholars. Soldiers. Lawyers. Doctors. Attachés. Diplomats. . . . Defectors. All Soviets who at one time or another had direct contact with Anthony Matthias. Havelock pictured each man, each face, his inner ear hearing dozens of voices speaking in English, matching the voices with the faces, listening for phrases that were spoken rapidly, words that were clipped, consonants harsh. It was maddening, faces and voices intermingling, lips moving, suddenly no sound followed by shouts. *You will be mentioned prominently and frequently.* Did *he* say that, *would* he say that? *You will be summoned* . . . how many times had that phrase been used? So many. But who used it? *Who?*

An hour passed, then most of another and a second pack of cigarettes with it. The expired deadline for Moscow was approaching the final deadline for Poole's Island. A decision—*the* decision—would have to be made. Nothing was forgotten, only submerged, eyes straying to watches as the inner search for Parsifal reached a frightening level of intensity.

"I can't find him!" cried Michael, pounding his hand on the coffee table. "He's here, the *words* are here, but I can't find him!"

The telephone rang. *Rostov?* Havelock shot up from the chair, staring at it, motionless. He was drained, and the thought of finding the resources to fence verbally with the Soviet intelligence officer eight thousand miles away drained him further. The abrasive bell sounded again. He went to the phone and picked it up as Jenna watched him.

"Yes?" he said quietly, marshaling his thoughts for the opening moves on both sides.

"It is your friend from Kennedy Airport who no longer has his weapon—"

"Where's Rostov? I gave you a deadline."

"It was met. Listen to me carefully. I'm calling from a phone booth on Eighth Avenue and must keep my eyes on the street. The call came through a half hour ago. Fortunately, I took it, as my superior had an engagement for the evening. He will expect to find me when he returns."

"What are you driving at?"

"Rostov is dead. He was found at nine-thirty in the morning, Moscow time, after repeated calls failed to rouse him."

"How did he *die?*"

"Four bullets in the head."

"Oh, *Christ!* Have they any idea who killed him?"

"The rumor is Voennaya Kontra Razvedka, and I, for one, believe it. There have been many such rumors lately, and if a man like Rostov can be taken out, then I am too old, and must call from a phone booth. You are fools here, but it's better to live with fools than lie among jackals who will rip your throat open if they don't care for the way you laugh or drink."

At the meeting this afternoon . . . something I didn't understand . . . An intelligence officer from the KGB made contact . . . speculated on the identity . . . Arthur Pierce, while awkwardly smoking a cigarette on a deserted runway.

Rostov didn't speculate. He knew. A collection of fanatics in a branch called the VKR, the Voennaya . . . He'll break it open . . . A fellow killer from the Costa Brava.

Had Pierce's call encompassed more than the death of a *paminyatchik?* Had he demanded the execution of a man in Moscow? Four bullets in the head. It had cost Rostov's life, but it could be the proof he needed. Was it conclusive? Could anything be conclusive?

"Code name Hammer-zero-two," said Michael, thinking, reaching. "Does it mean anything to you?"

"A part of it possibly, not all of it."

"What *part?*"

"The 'hammer.' It was used years ago, and was restricted. Then it was abandoned, I believe. Hammarskjöld, Dag Hammarskjöld. The United Nations."

"*Jesus!* . . . Zero, zero . . . two. A zero is a circle . . . a circle. A council! Two . . . double, twice, *second.* The second voice in the delegation! That's it!"

"As you gather," interrupted the Russian, "I must cross over."

"Call the New York office of the FBI. Go there. I'll get word to them."

"That is one place I will *not* go. It is one of the things I can tell you."

"Then keep moving and call me back in thirty minutes. I have to move quickly."

"Fools or jackals. Where is the choice?"

Havelock pressed the adjacent button on the phone, disconnecting the line. He looked up at Jenna. "It's Pierce. Hammer-zero-two. I told him —we all told him—about Rostov closing in on the Voennaya. He had Rostov killed. It's *him.*"

"He's trapped," said Jenna. "You've got him."

"I've got him. I've got Ambiguity, the man who called us dead at Col des Moulinets. . . . And when I get him to a clinic I'll shoot him into space. Whatever he knows I'll know." Michael dialed quickly. "The President, please. Mr. Cross calling."

"You must be very quiet, Mikhail," said Jenna, approaching the desk. "Very quiet and precise. Remember, it will be an extraordinary shock to him and, above all, he must believe you."

Havelock nodded. "That's the hardest part. Thanks. I was about to plunge in with conclusions first. You're right. Take him up slowly. . . . Mr. President?"

"What is it?" asked Berquist anxiously. "What's happened?"

"I have something to tell you, sir. It will take a few minutes, and I want you to listen very closely to what I've got to say."

"All right. Let me get on another phone; there are people in the next room. . . . By the way, did Pierce reach you?"

"What?"

"Arthur Pierce. Did he call you?"

"What *about* Pierce?"

"He telephoned about an hour ago; he needed a second clearance. I told him about your call to me, that you both wanted to know if I'd brought up the Randolph Medical Center business—lousy goddamned mess—and I said I had, that we all knew about it."

"*Please,* Mr. President! Go back. What, *exactly,* did you say?"

"What's the matter with you?"

"What did he say to you?"

"About what?"

"Just *tell* me! First, what you said to him!"

"Now, just a minute, Havelock—"

"*Tell* me! You don't have time, *none* of us has time! What did you say?"

The urgency was telegraphed. Berquist paused, then answered calmly, a leader aware of a subordinate's alarm, not understanding it but willing to respect its source. "I said that you'd phoned me and specifically asked if I had brought up the Randolph Medical Center at the meeting this afternoon. I said that I had, and that you seemed relieved that everyone knew about it."

"What did *he* say?"

"He seemed confused, frankly. I think he said 'I see,' then asked me if you'd given any reason for wanting to know."

"Know *what?*"

"About the Medical— What *is* wrong with you?"

"What did you *say?*"

"That I understood you were both concerned, although I wasn't sure why."

"What was his reply?"

"I don't think he had one. . . . Oh, yes. He asked if you'd made any progress with the man you've got at Bethesda."

"Which wasn't until tomorrow and he knew it!"

"What?"

"Mr. President, I don't have time to explain and you can't lose a moment. Has Pierce gotten into that vault, that room?"

"I don't know."

"Stop him! He's the mole!"

"You're *insane!*"

"Goddamn it, Berquist, you can have me shot, but right now I'm *telling* you! He's got cameras you don't know about! In rings, watches, cuff links! Stop him! Take him! Strip him and check for capsules, *cyanide!* I can't give that order but you can! You *have* to! *Now!*"

"Stay by the phone," said the President of the United States. "I *may* have you shot."

Havelock got out of the chair, if for no other reason than the need to move, to keep in motion. The dark mists were closing in again; he had to get out from under them. He looked at Jenna, and her eyes told him she understood.

"Pierce found me. I found him, and he found me."

"He's trapped."

"I could have killed him at Costa Brava. I wanted to kill him, but I wouldn't listen. I wouldn't listen to myself."

"Don't go back. You've got him. You're within the time span."

Michael walked away from the desk, away from the dark mists that pursued him. "I don't pray," he whispered. "I don't believe. I'm praying now, to what I don't know."

The telephone rang and he lunged for it. "Yes?"

"He's gone. He ordered the patrol boat to take him back to Savannah."

"Did he get into that *room?*"

"No."

"Thank Christ!"

"He's got something else," said the President in a voice that was barely audible.

"What?"

"The complete psychiatric file on Matthias. It says everything."

37

The police swept through the streets of Savannah, patrol cars roaring out to the airport and screeching into bus and train stations. Car-rental agencies were checked throughout the city and roadblocks set up on the major highways and backcountry routes—north to Augusta, south to Saint Marys, west to Macon and Valdosta. The man's description was radioed to all units—municipal, county, state—and the word spread down through the ranks from the highest levels of authority: *Find him. Find the man with the streak of white in his hair. If seen, approach with extreme caution, weapons drawn. If movements are unexpected, shoot. Shoot to kill.*

The manhunt was unparalleled in numbers and intensity, the federal government assuring the state, the cities and townships that all costs would be borne by Washington. Men off duty were called in by precincts and station houses; vehicles in for minor repairs were put back on the streets, and private cars belonging to police personnel were issued magnetic, circling roof lamps and sent out to prowl the dark country roads. Everywhere automobiles and pedestrians were stopped; anyone even vaguely approaching the man's description was politely requested to remove his hat if he was wearing one, and flashlights roamed over faces and hairlines, searching for a hastily, imperfectly dyed streak of white hair rising above a forehead. Hotels, motels and rural inns were descended upon; registers were checked for late arrivals, desk clerks questioned, the interrogators alert to the possibility of evasion or deception. Farmhouses where lights remained on were entered—courteously, to be sure—but the intruders were aware that the inhabitants could be hostages, that an unseen child or wife might be held captive somewhere on the premises by the man with the streak of white in his hair. Rooms and barns and silos were searched, nothing left to speculation.

Morning came, and weary thousands reported back to points of dispatch, angry, frustrated, bewildered by the government's ineffectual methods. For no photographs or sketches were issued; the only name given was "Mr. Smith." The alarm was still out, but the blitzkrieg search was essentially over, and the professionals knew it. The man with the streak of white in his hair had slipped through the net. He could be blond or bald or gray by now, limping with a cane or a crutch, and dressed in tattered clothes, or in the uniform of the police or the military, without a vestige of his former appearance.

The newspapers carrying early-morning stories of the strange, massive hunt abruptly called off their reporters. Owners and editors had been reached by respected men in government who claimed no special knowledge of the situation but had profound trust in those higher up who had appealed to them, *Play it down, let the story die.* In second editions the search was relegated to a few lines near the back pages, and those papers with third editions carried no mention of it at all.

And an odd thing happened at a telephone exchange beginning with the digits 0-7742. Since midnight it had not functioned, and by 8:00 A.M., when service was suddenly, inexplicably, resumed, telephone "repairmen" were in the building of the Voyagers Emporium annex, where orders were received, and every incoming call was monitored and taped, all tapes *under* fifteen seconds in length played instantly over the phone to Sterile Five. The brevity reduced the number to a very few.

International airports were infiltrated by federal agents with sophisticated X-ray equipment that scanned briefcases and hand luggage; they were looking for a two-inch-thick metal case with a combination lock on the side. There were two assumptions: one, the devastating file would not be entrusted to a cargo hold; and, two, it would remain in its original government container for authenticity. If container and file were separated, either shape was sufficient cause for examination. By 11:30 A.M.

over twenty-seven hundred attaché cases had been opened and searched, from Kennedy to Atlanta to Miami International.

"Thanks very much," said Havelock into the phone, forcing energy into his voice, feeling the effects of the sleepless night. He hung up and looked over at Jenna, who was pouring coffee. "They can't understand and I can't tell them. Pierce wouldn't call Orphan-ninety-six unless he thought he could get his message across with a very few words, spoken quickly. He knows I've got the place wired and manned by now."

"You've done everything you can," said Jenna, carrying the coffee to the desk. "All the airports are covered—"

"Not for him," Michael broke in. "He wouldn't risk it, and besides, he doesn't want to leave. He wants what I want. Parsifal. . . . It's that *file!* One small single-engine plane crossing the Mexican border, or a fishing boat meeting another between here and Cuba, or out of Galveston toward Matamoros, and that file's on its way to Moscow, into the hands of the overkill specialists in the Voennaya. And there's not a damn thing I can do about it."

"The Mexican border is being patrolled, the agents doubled. The piers and marinas are watched both here and in the Gulf, all boats tracked, stopped if directions are in question. You insisted on these things and the President issued the orders."

"It's a long border, and those are large bodies of water."

"Get some rest, Mikhail. You can't function if you're exhausted—it's one of your rules, remember."

"One of the rules . . . ?" Havelock brought both hands to the sides of his head, massaging his temples with his fingers. "Yes, that's one of the rules, part of the rules."

"Lie down on the couch and close your eyes. I can take the calls, let you know what they are. I slept for a while, you didn't."

"When did you sleep?" asked Michael, looking up, doubting.

"I rested before the sun was up. You were talking to your Coast Guard."

"It doesn't belong to me," said Havelock wearily, pushing himself up. "Maybe I will lie down . . . just for a few minutes. It's part of the rules." He walked around the desk, then stopped; his eyes roamed the elegant study strewn with papers, notebooks and file folders. "God, I hate this room!" he said, heading for the couch. "Thanks for the coffee, but no thanks."

The telephone rang, and Michael steeled himself, wondering if the bell would stop before a second ring or whether it would remain unbroken, the signal of an emergency. It stopped, then resumed ringing.

Havelock lowered himself down on the couch as Jenna answered, speaking calmly. "This is Sterile Five. . . . Who's calling?" She listened, then covered the phone and looked over at Michael. "It's the State Department, New York City, Division of Security. Your man's come in from the Soviet consulate."

Havelock rose unsteadily, briefly finding it necessary to center his balance. "I've got to talk to him," he said, walking toward the desk. "I thought he'd be there hours ago." Michael took the phone from Jenna and, after peremptory identifications, made his request. "Let me have the candidate, please." The Russian got on the line. "Where the hell have you been?"

"Apparently, it is considered in poor taste over here to defect except during business hours," began the Russian in a weary, singsong voice. "I arrived down here at the Federal Plaza at four o'clock this morning, after having survived an attempted mugging on the subway, only to be told by one of the night guards that there was nothing he could do until the *office* opened! I explained my somewhat precarious position, and the kind, vacuous idiot offered to buy me a cup of coffee—in a public diner. Finally getting into the building myself—your security is ludicrous—I waited in a dark, drafty hallway until nine o'clock, when your militia arrived. I then presented myself and the imbeciles wanted to call the *police!* They wanted to have me *arrested* for breaking and entering and the possible destruction of government property!"

"All right, you're there now—"

"I'm not *fin-nished!*" yelled the Russian. "Since that auspicious beginning I have been filling out uncountable forms—with Russian nursery rhymes, incidentally—and repeatedly giving your number, asking to be put in touch with you. What *is* it with you people? Do you limit *toll calls?*"

"We're in touch now—"

"Not *fin-nished!* This past hour I have been sitting alone in a room so poorly wired I was tempted to lower my trousers and fart into the microphones. And I have *just* been given additional forms to fill out, including one inquiring about my hobbies and favorite recreational pastimes! Are you sending me to *camp,* perhaps?"

Michael smiled, grateful beyond words for a momentary break in the tension. "Only where you'll be safe," he said. "Consider the source. We're fools, remember, not jackals. You made the right choice."

The Russian sighed audibly. "Why do I work myself up? The *fruktovyje golovy* are no better in the Dzerzhinsky—why not admit it? They're worse. Your Albert Einstein would be on his way to Siberia, assigned to pull mules in a gulag. Where is the sense in it all?"

"There's very little," said Havelock softly. "Except to survive. All of us."

"A premise I subscribe to."

"So did Rostov."

"I remember the words he sent you. 'He's not my enemy any longer, but others are who may be mine as well.' They are ominous words, Havelock."

"The Voennaya."

"Maniacs!" was the guttural reply. "In their heads they march with the Third Reich."

"How operational are they here?"

"Who knows? They have their own councils, their own methods of recruitment. They touch too many you can't see."

"The *paminyatchiki?* You can't see them."

"Believe me when I tell you I was trusted but never that trusted. However, one can speculate—on rumors. There are always rumors, aren't there? You might say the speculation has convinced me that I should take the action I've taken." The Russian paused. "I *will* be treated as a valuable asset, will I not?"

"Guarded and housed as a treasure. What's the speculation?"

"In recent months certain men have left our ranks—unexpected retirements to well-earned dachas, untimely illnesses—disappearances. None so crudely as Rostov, but perhaps there was no time to be clever. Nevertheless, it seems there is a disturbing sameness about the departed. They were generally categorized as quiet realists, men who sought solutions and knew when to pull back from confrontation. Pyotr Rostov exemplified this group; he was in fact their spokesman in a way. Make no mistake, you were his enemy, he despised your system—too much for the few, too little for the many—but he understood there was a point where enemies could no longer push forward. Or there was nothing. He knew time was on our side, not bombs."

"Are you saying those who replaced the Rostovs think otherwise?"

"That is the rumor."

"The Voennaya?"

"That is the speculation. And should they take over the power centers of the KGB, can leadership of the Kremlin be far behind? This cannot happen. If it does . . ." The Russian did not finish the statement.

"There'll be nothing?" offered Havelock.

"That is the judgment. You see, they think *you'll* do nothing. They believe they can chew you up, first in one area, then in another."

"That's nothing new."

"With tactical nuclear weapons?"

"That's very new."

"It's insane," said the man from the KGB. "You'll *have* to react, the world will demand it."

"How can we stop the VKR?"

"By giving them little or no ammunition."

"What do you mean, 'ammunition'?"

"Knowledge of provocative or inflammatory actions on your part they can use to threaten the tired old men in the Presidium. The same as over here; you have your jackals. Beribboned generals and wild-eyed colonels closeting themselves with overweight, overaged senators and congressmen, making pronouncements of disaster if you don't strike first. The wisest men do not always prevail; actually, you're better at that than we are. Your controls are better."

"I hope so," said Michael, thinking fleetingly of men like Lieutenant Commander Thomas Decker. "But you say the Voennaya has filtered into your ranks, into the KGB."

"Speculation."

"If it's true, it means that at least several of them could be walking around the embassy here or the consulate in New York."

"I'm not even sure of my own superior."

"And a *paminyatchik* outside would know them, could reach them, make a delivery."

"You assume I know something. I don't. What delivery?"

Havelock paused, trying to still the throbbing in his temples. "Suppose I were to tell you that just such ammunition as you describe was stolen last night by a mole so deep and entrenched he had access to information released only by executive order. He disappeared."

"Willing to give up his entrenched position?"

"He was found out. You were instrumental; you told me about Rostov's death and the VKR. He belongs to the Voennaya. He's the enemy."

"Then look for the sudden diplomatic departure of a low-level attaché, a street security man, or a communications officer. If there is a VKR recruit, he would be among these. Intercept if you can; hold up the plane if you have to. Claim stolen property, espionage, go to the limit. Don't let them have that ammunition."

"If we're too late—"

"What can I tell you without knowing the nature of the delivery?"

"The worst."

"Can you deny?"

"It's beyond deniability. Part of it's false—the worst part—but it will be accepted as the truth—by the beribboned generals and the wild-eyed colonels."

The Russian was silent, then replied quietly, "You must speak with others much higher, much wiser. We have, as you say here, a rule of thumb when dealing with such matters. Go to substantial men in the Party between the ages of sixty and seventy who went through Operation Barbarossa and Stalingrad. Their memories are acute; they may help you. I'm afraid I can't."

"You have. We know what to watch for at the embassy and the consulate. . . . You'll be brought down here for debriefing, you understand that."

"I understand. Will I be permitted to see American films—on the television, perhaps? After the interrogation sessions, of course."

"I'm sure something can be arranged."

"I do so like the Westerns. . . . Havelock, stop the delivery to Moscow. You don't know the Voennaya."

"I'm afraid I do know it," said Michael, rounding the desk and sinking once again into the chair. "And I'm afraid," he added, hanging up.

There was no rest for the next three hours, coffee, aspirin and cold-water compresses serving to keep him awake and numb the piercing ache that pounded through his head. Every department in every intelligence and investigatory agency that had information on or access to the Soviet embassy or the consulate in New York was contacted and ordered to divulge whatever Sterile Five requested. The schedules for Aeroflot, LOT Airlines, Czechoslovak Airlines—CSA—and all the carriers to the Eastern bloc were studied, their manifests checked for diplomatic passengers. The cameras were doubled on both Soviet buildings in Washington and New York, personnel leaving the premises placed under surveillance, the units told to keep their subjects in sight even at the risk of being seen themselves. Everything was designed to inhibit contact, to cut off the delivery on its way to Moscow, and nothing could achieve this more effectively than a VKR agent knowing he might expose the fugitive if he kept a rendezvous, or Pierce realizing he might be caught if he made one.

Helicopters crisscrossed along the Mexican border by the scores, following small aircraft; radio checks were constant, and planes with unsatisfactory replies were ordered to return and searched. Off the coasts of Florida, Georgia and the Carolinas, navy jets soared low over the water, tracking boats that veered too far southeast; radios were used here, too, and unless explanations were satisfactory, directions were altered. Out of Corpus Christi, other jets and Coast Guard patrols spotted and intercepted fishing and pleasure craft on their way toward Mexican waters; fortunately, inclement weather in the western Gulf had reduced their number. None made contact with other boats; none went beyond Port Isabel or Brazos Island.

It was a quarter to four when Havelock, exhausted, returned to the couch. "We're holding," he said. "Unless we've missed something, we're holding. But we may have . . ." He fell onto the pillows. "I've got to go back to the names. He's there. Parsifal's *there* and I have to find him! Berquist says we can't go beyond tonight, he can't take the chance. The *world* can't take the chance."

"But Pierce never got into that room," protested Jenna. "He never saw the agreements."

"The psychiatric file on Matthias spells them out—in all their insanity. In some ways it's worse. A diagnosed madman running the foreign policy of the most powerful, most feared country on earth. We're lepers . . . Berquist said we'll be lepers. If we're alive."

The telephone rang; Michael expelled his breath and buried his head. The mists were closing in again, now enveloping him, suffocating him.

"Yes, thank you very much," said Jenna into the phone across the room.

"What is it?" asked Havelock, opening his eyes, staring at the floor.

"The Central Intelligence Agency unearthed five more photographs. That leaves only one, and that man they're quite sure is dead. Others may be also, of course."

"Photographs? Of what, whom?"

"The old men on *my* list."

"Oh?" Michael turned over; his eyes, fixed on the ceiling, were closing rapidly. "Old men," he whispered. "Why?"

"Sleep, Mikhail. You *must* sleep. You're no good to yourself or anyone else this way." Jenna walked to the couch and knelt beside him. She pressed her lips lightly against his check. "Sleep, my darling."

Jenna sat at the desk, and each time the phone began to ring she pounced on it like a breathless cat protecting its lair from predators. The calls came from everywhere—progress reports issued by men who were following orders blindly.

They were holding.

The handsome couple in riding breeches, boots and emblazoned red jackets galloped across the field on their hunters—the horses straining, nostrils flared, long legs pounding the hard earth and plunging through the tall grass. In the distance to their right was a split-rail fence signifying the property line of an adjacent estate, and beyond it was another field that disappeared into a wall of giant maples and oaks. The man gestured at the fence, laughing and nodding his head. The woman at first feigned surprise and maidenly reluctance, then suddenly whipped her mount to the right and raced ahead of her companion, high in the saddle as she approached the fence. She soared over it, followed by the man only yards behind and to her left; they rode swiftly toward the edge of the woods, where both reined in their horses. The woman grimaced as she came to a stop.

"*Damn!*" she shouted. "I pulled the muscle in my calf! It's screaming!"

"Get off and walk around. Don't sit on it."

The woman dismounted as the man reached over for the reins of her horse. His companion walked in circles, her limp pronounced, swearing under her breath.

"Good God, where are we?" she asked, half shouting.

"I think it's the Heffernans' place. How's the leg?"

"Murder, absolute murder! *Christ!*"

"You can't ride on it."

"I can hardly walk on it, you damn fool."

"Temper, temper. Come on, let's find a phone." The man and woman started through the edge of trees, the man leading both horses, threading them around several thick trunks. "Here," he said, reaching for a low branch on a thick bush. "I can tie them up here and come back for them; they won't go anywhere."

"Then you can help me. This really is excruciating."

The horses tied and grazing, the couple began to walk. Through the trees they could see the outlines of the wide semicircular drive at the front entrance of the large house. They also saw the figure of a man who seemed to emerge out of nowhere. He was in a gabardine topcoat, with both hands in his pockets. They met and the man in the topcoat spoke. "May I help you? This is private property."

"I trust we *all* have private property, old man," replied the sportsman supporting the woman. "My wife pulled a muscle over our last jump. She can't ride."

"What?"

"Horses, sport. Our horses are tied up back there. We were doing a little pre-hunt work over the course before Saturday's meet, and I'm afraid we came a cropper, as they say. Take us to a phone, please."

"Well, I . . . I . . ."

"This *is* the Heffernans' house, isn't it?" demanded the husband.

"Yes, but Mr. and Mrs. Heffernan are not here, sir. Our orders are to allow no one inside."

"Oh, shit!" exploded the wife. "How tacky can you be? My leg hurts, you ass! I need a ride back to the club."

"One of the men will be happy to drive you, ma'am."

"And my chauffeur can bloody well come and pick me up! Really, just who *are* these Heffernans? Are they members, darling?"

"I don't think so, Buff. Look, the man has his orders, and tacky as they are, it's not his fault. You go along and I'll take the horses back."

"They'd better not try to *become* members," said the wife as the two men helped her across the drive to an automobile.

The man walked back through the woods to the horses, untied them, and led them across the field, where he lowered the rails and prodded them through into the tall grass. He replaced the rails, mounted his hunter and, with the woman's horse in tow, trotted south over the course of Saturday's hunt—as he understood the course to be from his first and only study of the charts as a guest of the club.

He reached under his saddle and pulled out a powerful hand-held radio; he pressed a switch and raised the instrument to his lips.

"There are two cars," he said into the radio. "A black Lincoln, license plate seven-four-zero, MRL; and a dark green Buick, license one-three-seven, GMJ. The place is ringed with guards, and there are no rear exit roads. The windows are thick; you'd need a cannon to blow through them, and we were picked up by density infrareds."

"Got it" was the reply, amplified over the tiny speaker. "We're mainly interested in the vehicles. . . . By the way, I can see the Buick now."

The man with the various saws clipped to and dangling from his wide leather belt was high up in the tall pine tree bordering the road, his safety strap around it and clamped to his harness. He shoved the hand-held radio into its holster and adjusted the binoculars to his eyes, looking diagonally down through the branches, focusing on the automobile coming out of the tree-lined drive.

The view was clean, all angles covered. No cars could enter or leave the premises of Sterile Five without being seen—even at night; the capabilities of infrared applied to lenses as well as trip lights.

The man whistled; the door of the truck far below opened, and on its panel were the words HIGH TOP TREE SURGEONS. A second man stepped out and looked up.

"Take off," said the man above, loud enough to be heard. "Relieve me in two hours."

The driver of the truck headed north for a mile and a half to the first intersection. There was a gas station on the right; the doors of its repair shop were open, and an automobile was inside, off the ground on a hydraulic lift, facing front. The driver reached for the switch and snapped his headlights on and off. Instantly, within the garage's shop the headlights of the car on the lift flashed on and off—the signal had been acknowledged, the vehicle was in position. The station's owner believed he was cooperating—confidentially—with the narcotics division of the state police. It was the least a citizen could do.

The driver swung to his right, then immediately to the left, making a U-turn between the converging roads; he headed south. Three minutes later he passed the pine tree that concealed his companion beyond the branches near the top. Under different circumstances he might have touched his horn; he couldn't now. There could be no sound, no sight that marked in any way that area of the road. Instead, he accelerated and in fifty seconds came to another intersection, the first south of Sterile Five.

Diagonally across on the left was a small country inn, miniature antebellum in design—a large dollhouse built to bring back memories of an old plantation. In the back was a black asphalt parking lot, where perhaps a dozen cars were lined up, like large brightly colored toys. Except one, the fourth from the end, with a clear view of the intersection and swift access to the exit. Facing front, it was layered with dirt, a poor relation in the company of its shiny, expensive cousins.

Again the driver leaned forward and flicked his headlights on and off. The dirty automobile—with an engine more powerful than any other in the lot—did the same. Another signal was acknowledged. Whatever emerged from Sterile Five could be picked up in either direction.

Arthur Pierce studied his face in the mirror of the run-down motel on the outskirts of Falls Church, Virginia; he was satisfied with what he saw. The fringe of gray circling his shaved head was in concert with the rimless glasses and the shabby brown cardigan sweater worn over the soiled white shirt with the frayed collar. He was the image of the loser, whose minor talents and lack of illusion kept him securely, if barely, above the poverty level. Nothing was ventured because it was useless. Why bother? No one stopped such men on the street; they walked too slowly; they were inconsequential.

Pierce turned from the mirror and walked across the room to the road map spread out under the light of a plastic lamp on the cheap, stained desk against the wall. On the right, holding the map in place, was a gray metal container with the emblem of the United States Navy stamped on the top, the medical insignia below it, and a brass, built-in combination lock on the side. In it was a document as lethal as any in history. The psychiatric diagnosis of a statesman the world revered, a diagnosis labeling that man as insane—as having *been* insane while functioning as the international voice of one of the two most powerful nations on earth. And the nation that permitted this intolerable condition to exist could no longer serve as the leader of the cause it espoused. A madman had betrayed not only his own government but the world—lying, deceiving, misleading, forging alliances with enemies, scheming against supposed allies. No matter that he was insane, it had happened. It was all there.

The steel container contained an incredible weapon, but for it to be used with devastating effect it had to reach the proper hands in Moscow. Not the tired old compromisers, but the visionaries with the strength and the will to move swiftly to bring the corrupt, incompetent giant to its knees. The possibility that the Matthias file might fall into soft, wrinkled hands in Moscow was insufferable; it would be bartered, *negotiated*, finally thrown away by weak men frightened of the very people they controlled. No, thought Arthur Pierce, this metal container belonged to the VKR. Only to the Voennaya.

He could afford no risks, and several phone calls had convinced him that there *was* risk in channeling it out with the few he could trust. As expected, embassy and consulate personnel were under heavy surveillance; all international flights were monitored, and hand and cargo luggage X-rayed. Too much risk.

He would bring it out himself, along with the ultimate weapon, the terminal weapon, documents that called for successive nuclear strikes against Soviet Russia and the People's Republic of China—agreements signed by the great American Secretary of State. They were nuclear fantasies conceived by an insane genius, working with one of the most brilliant minds ever produced by the Soviet Union. Fantasies so real that the tired old men in the Kremlin would run for their dachas and their vodka, leaving decisions to those who could cope, to the men of the Voennaya.

Where *was* the brilliant mind that had made it all possible? The man who had turned on his homeland only to learn the truth—that he had been wrong. *So wrong!* Where was Parsifal? Where was Alexei Kalyazin?

With these thoughts Pierce turned to the map again. The inept—and not so inept—Havelock had mentioned the Shenandoah—that the man they called Parsifal was somewhere in the Shenandoah area, by implication within a reasonable distance of Matthias's country home. The implied reasonable distance, however, was the variable quotient. The Shenandoah Valley was more than a hundred miles long, over twenty miles wide, from the Allegheny to the Blue Ridge Mountains. What might be considered reasonable? There was no reasonable answer, so the solution was to be found in the opposite direction. In the plodding mind of Michael Havelock—Mikhail Havliček, son of Václav, named for a Russian grandfather from Rovno—a man whose talents lay in persistence and a degree of imagination, not brilliance. Havelock would reduce the arc, put in use a hundred computers to trace a single telephone call made at a specific time to a specific place to a man he called a zealot. Havelock would do the work and a *paminyatchik* would reap the benefits. Lieutenant Commander Decker would be left alone; he was a key that might well unlock a door.

Pierce bent over the map, his index finger shifting from one line to another. The arc, the semicircle that blanketed the Shenandoah from Sterile Five, was covered, with men and vehicles in position. From Harpers Ferry to the Valley Pike, Highways 11 and 66, Routes 7, 50, 15, 17, 29, and 33, all were manned, waiting for word that a specific car was approaching at a specific time heading for a specific place. That place was to be determined and reported; nothing else was required of the men in those vehicles. They were hirelings, not participants, their time paid for in money, not purpose or destiny.

Arthur Pierce, born Nikolai Petrovich Malyekov in the village of Ramenskoye, Union of Soviet Socialist Republics, suddenly thought about that destiny, and the years that had led to his own electrifying part in it. He had never wavered, never forgotten who he was or why he had been given the supreme opportunity to serve the ultimate cause, a cause so meaningful and so necessary for a world where the relative few tyrannized the many, where millions upon millions lived on the edge of despair or in hopeless poverty so that the capitalist manipulators could laugh over global balance sheets while their armies burned pajama-clad children in faraway lands. This was fact, not provocative propaganda. He had seen it all for himself—from the burning villages in Southeast Asia to the corporate dining rooms where offers of employment were accompanied by grins and winks and promises of stock options that were the first steps toward wealth, to the inner corridors of government power where hypocrites and incompetents encouraged more hypocrisy and incompetence. *God,* he hated it all! Hated the corruption and the greed and the sanctimonious liars who deceived the masses to whom they were responsible, abusing the powers given them, lining their pockets and the pockets of their own. . . . There *was* a better way. There was *commitment.* There was the Voennaya.

He had been thirteen years old when he was told by the loving couple he called Mother and Father. They explained while holding him and gazing into his eyes to let him see their love. He was theirs, they said, but he was also not theirs. He had been born to a chosen couple thousands of miles away who loved him so much they gave him to the State, to a cause that would make a better world for generations to come. And as his "mother" and "father" spoke, so many things in Arthur Pierce's young memory began to fall into place. All the discussions—not only with his "mother" and "father," but with the scores of visitors who came so frequently to the farmhouse—discussions that told of suffering and oppression and of a despotic form of government that would be replaced by a government dedicated to the people—*all* the people.

He was to be a part of that change. Over the early years certain other visitors had come and had given him games to play, puzzles to work, exercises to read—tests that graded his capabilities. And one day when he was thirteen he was pronounced extraordinary; on that same day he was told his real name. He was ready to join the cause.

It would not be easy, his "mother" and "father" had said, but he was to remember when pressures seemed overwhelming that *they* were there, *always* there. And should anything happen to them, others would take their place to help him, encourage him, guide him, knowing that still others were watching. He was to be the best in all things; he was to be *American*—kind, generous and, above all, seemingly fair; he was to use his gifts to rise as far as he was capable of rising. But he was never to forget who and what he was or the cause that gave him the gift of life and the opportunity to help make the world better than it was.

Things after that auspicious day were not as difficult as his "mother" and "father" had predicted. Through his high school years and college, his secret served to prod him—because it was *his* secret and he *was* extraordinary. They were years of exhilaration: each new prize and award was proof of his superiority. He found it easy to be liked; as though in a never-ending popularity contest, the crown was always his. Yet there was self-denial, too, and it served to remind him of his commitment. He had many friends but no deep friendships, no relationships. Men liked him but accepted his basic distance, ascribing it usually to his having to find jobs to pay his way through school. Women he used only for sexual release and formed no attachments whatsoever, generally meeting them miles away from wherever he was living.

During his postgraduate studies at Michigan he was contacted by Moscow and told his new life was about to begin. The meeting was not without amusement, the contact a recruitment executive from a large conservative corporation who had supposedly read the graduate student files and wanted to meet one Arthur Pierce. But there was nothing amusing in his news; it was deadly serious—and exhilarating.

He was to join the army, where certain opportunities would be found leading to advancement, and further advancement, and contact with civilian and military authorities. He would serve out an appropriate amount of time and return not to the Midwest but to Washington, where word of his record and talents would be spread. Companies would be lined up, anxious to employ him, but the government would step in. He was to accept.

But first the army—and he was to give it everything he had, he was to continue to be the *best.* His "father" and "mother" had thrown him a farewell party on the farm, and invited all his friends, including most of the old Boy Scout Troop 37. And it *was* a farewell party in more than one sense. His "father" and "mother" told him at the end of the night that they would not see him again. They were getting old and they had done their job: him. And he would make them proud. Besides, their talents were needed elsewhere. He understood; the cause was everything.

For the first time since he was thirteen, he had cried that night. But it was permitted—and, besides, they were tears of joy.

All those years, thought Arthur Pierce, glancing in the cheap motel mirror at the fringe of gray and the frayed collar around his neck. They had been worth it; the proof would be found in the next few hours.

The waiting had begun. The reward would be a place in history.

Michael opened his eyes, a sea of dark brown leather confronting him, moisture everywhere, the heat oppressive. He turned over and raised his head, suddenly aware that it was not sunlight but the glow of a distant lamp that washed the room. He was drenched with sweat. It was night, and he was not ready for night. What had *happened?*

"*Dobrý den.*" The greeting floated over to him.

"What time is it?" he asked, sitting up on the couch.

"Ten past seven," said Jenna, who was sitting at the desk. "You slept a little over three hours. How do you feel?"

"I don't know. Left out, I think. What's going on?"

"Not a great deal. As you said, we're holding. Did you know that the lights on these buttons actually go on before the telephone rings? Only a split-second, but they do."

"It's not comforting. Who called?"

"Very serious, bewildered men reporting nothing, reporting that they had nothing to report. Several asked how long they were to keep up what they referred to as their 'reconnaissance.' I said until they were told otherwise."

"That says it."

"The photographs arrived."

"What . . . ? Oh, your list."

"They're on the coffee table. Look at them."

Havelock focused on the row of five grainy faces staring at him. He rubbed his eyes and wiped the perspiration from his hairline, blinking repeatedly as he tried to concentrate. He began with the face on the far left; it meant nothing to him. Then the next, and the next, and the . . . next.

"Him," he said, not knowing why he said it.

"Who?"

"The fourth one. Who is he?"

Jenna glanced down at a paper in front of her. "It's a very old picture, taken in 1948. The only one they could find. It's over thirty years old."

"Who is he? Who was he?"

"A man named Kalyazin. Alexei Kalyazin. Do you recognize him?" Jenna got up from the desk.

"Yes . . . no. I don't know."

"It's an *old* photograph, Mikhail. *Look* at it. *Study* it. The eyes, the chin, the shape of the mouth. Where? *Who?*"

"I don't know. It's there . . . and it's not there. What did he do?"

"He was a clinical psychotherapist," said Jenna, reading. "He wrote definitive studies evaluating the effects on men of the stress of combat or prolonged periods of enduring unnatural conditions. His expertise was used by the KGB; he became what you call here a strategist, but with a difference. He screened information sent in to the KGB by people in the field, looking for deviations that might reveal either double agents or men no longer capable of functioning in their jobs."

"An evaluator. A flake with a penchant for overlooking the obvious."

"I don't understand you."

"Gunslingers. They never spot the gunslingers."

"I still don't know what you're talking about."

"I don't know him. It's a face like so many other faces, so many dossiers. God, the *faces!*"

"But there's *something!*"

"Maybe, I'm not sure."

"Keep looking at it. *Concentrate.*"

"Coffee. Is there any coffee?"

"I forgot," said Jenna. "The first rule upon waking is coffee. Black and too strong. You *are* Czech, Mikhail." She went to the table behind the couch, where an accommodating guard had plugged in the silver pot.

"The first rule," repeated Havelock, suddenly disturbed. "The first *rule?*"

"What?"

"Where are your notes on Decker's telephone call?"

"You had them."

"Where *are* they?"

"Down there. On the table."

"Where?"

"Under the last photograph. On the right."

Get yourself a drink. You know the rules.

Michael threw the photograph of an unknown face off the table, and gripped the two notebook pages. He stared at them, shifting them back and forth.

"Oh, my *God!* The rules, the goddamned *rules!"*

Havelock got up and lurched toward the desk, his legs unsteady, his balance fragile.

"What is it?" asked Jenna, alarmed, the cup in her hand.

"Decker!" shouted Michael. "Where are the notes on *Decker?"*

"Right there. On the left. The pad."

Havelock riffled through the pages, his hand trembling again, his eyes seeing and not seeing, looking for the words. He found them.

" 'An odd accent,' " he whispered. " 'An *odd* accent,' but *what* accent?"

He grabbed the phone, barely able to control his finger as he dialed. "Get me Lieutenant Commander Decker, you've got his number on your index."

"Mikhail, get hold of yourself."

"Shut *up!"* The elongated buzz signified the ring; the wait was intolerable.

"Hello?" said the tentative voice of a woman.

"Commander Decker, please."

"I'm . . . terribly sorry, he's not here."

"He's there to *me!* This is Mr. Cross calling. Get him on the phone."

Twenty seconds elapsed, and Michael thought his head would explode.

"What is it, Mr. Cross?" Decker asked.

"You said an 'odd accent.' What did you mean?"

"I beg your pardon?"

"The call! The call you got from Matthias, from the one who said he was speaking for Matthias! When you said he had an odd accent, did you mean foreign, Russian?"

"No, not at all. It was high-pitched and very Anglicized. Almost British, but not British."

"Good night, Commander," said Michael, hanging up.

Pour yourself a drink . . . you know the rules here. . . . Come now, we're both out. Freshen yours and do mine while you're at it. That's also part of the rules, remember?

Havelock picked up the phone again, pulling the list of numbers in front of him. He dialed. The waiting was almost a pleasure, but it was too short; he needed time to adjust. Poole's Island!

"This is Mr. Cross. Let me have Security, please."

Two short hums were heard, and the officer on duty answered, "Checkpoint."

"This is Cross. Executive order, priority-zero. Please confirm."

"Start counting," said the voice.

"One, two, three, four, five, six—"

"Okay. Scanners match. What is it, Mr. Cross?"

"Who was the officer who took an emergency leave approximately six weeks ago?"

The silence was interminable; when the reply came, it was a matter-of-fact response by a knowledgeable man. "Your information's incorrect, Mr. Cross. There's been no request for an emergency leave from the officer corps or anyone else. No one's left the island."

"Thank you, Security."

Alexander the Great . . . *Raymond Alexander!*

Fox Hollow!

38

"It's him," said Michael, leaning over the desk, his hand still gripping the phone. "He's Parsifal. Raymond Alexander."

"Alexander?" Jenna took several steps away from the table and stared at Havelock, shaking her head slowly.

"It *has* to be! It's in the words—'the *rules.'* 'One of the rules, part of the rules.' Always rules; his life is a series of unbreakable rules! The odd accent wasn't foreign, *wasn't* Russian. It was thirties Harvard with Alexander's pretentious emphasis. He's used it in a thousand lecture halls, hundreds of debates. Points made quickly, retorts thrown in unexpectedly, thrust and parry. That's Alexander!"

"As you've described him," said Jenna calmly but firmly, "there's an enormous contradiction I don't think you can explain. Are you prepared to accuse him of knowing the identity of a Soviet mole and doing nothing about it? Especially one so dangerous as an undersecretary of State?"

"No, I *can't* explain it, but he can. He will. He sent me to Poole's Island, telling me a bullshit story about an army officer on an emergency leave who let it slip to his wife. There wasn't any such person; no emergency leaves were taken."

"Perhaps he was protecting another source."

"Then why the elaborate lie? Why not a simple refusal to disclose? No, he wanted me to believe it, made me give my word to protect him—knowing I *would* protect him!"

"For what *purpose?*" said Jenna, coming to the desk. "Why did he tell you in the first place? To have you *killed?*"

"Let him answer that." Havelock picked up the phone, pressing the house intercom button. "I want a car and an escort to follow me. It's about an hour's drive from here. Right away." He replaced the phone and, for a moment, looked at it, then shook his head. "No," he said.

"The President?" asked Jenna.

"I'm not going to call him. Not yet. The state he's in he'd send in a battalion of commandos. We won't learn the truth that way. Cornered like that, Alexander might blow his brains out."

"If you're right, what more is there to learn?"

"*Why!*" said Michael furiously, opening the top drawer and taking out the Llama automatic. "And how," he added, checking the magazine and cracking it back in place. "That large contradiction you mentioned. His beloved republic."

"I'm going with you."

"No."

"*Yes!* This time you have no right to refuse me. My life is in this room —my death as well. I have a right to *be* there."

"You may have a right but you're not going. That son of a bitch set you up, he marked you for extinction."

"I have to know *why.*"

"I'll tell you." Michael started to leave.

"Suppose you can't!" cried Jenna, blocking him. "Yes, Mikhail, look at me! Suppose you do not come back—it's possible, you know. Would you finally rob me of my sanity?"

"We've been out there. There are no alarms, no dogs or guards. Besides, he doesn't expect me. I'll come back—with *him!* . . . What the hell do you mean, your 'sanity'?"

"I lost you once—I loved you and lost you! Do you think I can take even the risk of losing you again and never knowing *why?* How much do you *want* from me?"

"I want you to live."

"I can't live, I *won't* live unless you're with me! I've tried it—it simply doesn't appeal to me. Whatever's out there is for both of us, not you alone. It's not fair, Mikhail, and you know it."

"I don't give a damn about being fair!" He reached for her and pulled her into his arms, aware of the gun in his hand, wishing they were somewhere else where there were no guns—*ever.* "I only care about you. I know what you've been through, what I *did* to you. I want you here, where I'll know you're all right. I can't risk you, don't you understand?"

"Because you love me?"

"So much . . . so very much."

"Then respect me!" cried Jenna, whipping her head back, her blond hair swirling over her shoulders. "Damn you, Mikhail, *respect* me!"

Havelock looked at her, at the anger and the pleading in her eyes. *So much to make up for.* "Come on," he said. "Let's get our coats. Let's go."

Jenna turned and went to the coffee table, where she picked up the photographs, including the one on the floor. "All right," she said.

"Why?" asked Michael, gesturing at the pictures.

"Why not?" she replied.

The man concealed high up in the darkness of the tall pine drove his spikes deeper into the trunk, adjusting his harness to relax the pressure of the straps. Suddenly, in the distance far below, he saw the beams of headlights streaking out of the tree-lined drive at Sterile Five. He raised the infrared binoculars to his eyes with his right hand as his left pulled out the radio from its holster. He brought it to his lips and pressed the switch.

"Activity," he said. "Stay alert. Respond."

"North in touch" came the first reply.

"South also" was the second.

Pushing the open-channel radio into the leather collar around his throat, the man focused the binoculars on the car emerging from the drive. It was the Buick; he refined the focus, and the images beyond the windshield sharpened.

"It's our man and the woman," he said. "Turning north. It's yours, North."

"We're ready."

"South, take off and assume your alternate position."

"Leaving now. North, keep us posted. Let us know when you want relief."

"Will do."

"*Hold* it! There's a second car. . . . It's the Lincoln, two federals in the front; I can't see in back. . . . Now I can. No one else."

"It's an escort," said one of the two men in the automobile a mile and a half north. "We'll wait till he passes."

"Give him plenty of room," ordered the man in the tree. "They're curious people."

"Don't worry."

The Buick reached the intersection and turned left, the Lincoln Continental several hundred feet behind and following, a prowling behemoth protecting its young. Both vehicles headed west.

Inside the dark repair shop of the gas station, a hissing sound accompanied the lowering of the hydraulic lift; the engine of the descending car was turned on and gunned. The driver raised his radio and spoke.

"South, they've taken the B route. Head west on the parallel road and pick us up six miles down."

"Heading across into west parallel," was the reply.

"Hurry," said North. "They are."

The white fence that marked the start of Alexander's property shone in the glare of the headlights. Seconds later the floodlights beaming on the trees scattered throughout the immense front acreage could be seen on the left, the wood and stone house beyond. Havelock then saw what he hoped he would see. There were no cars in the circular drive, very few lights in the windows. He slowed down and pulled the microphone from its dashboard recess.

"Escort, this is it," he said, depressing the transmission switch. "Stay up here on the road. There are no visitors and I want the man we're seeing to think we're alone."

"Suppose you need us?" asked Escort.

"I won't."

"That's not good enough. Sorry, sir."

"All right, you'll hear me. I'm not shy; I'll fire a couple of shots."

"That's good enough, as long as we're down there at the house."

"I want you up here on the road."

"Sorry, again. We'll leave the Abraham up here, but we'll be down there, right outside. On foot."

Michael shrugged, replacing the microphone; it was pointless to argue. He snapped off the headlights and turned into the drive, idled the engine, and let the Buick glide to within thirty feet of the entrance. The car came to a stop and he looked at Jenna. "Ready?"

"I think more than my life. Or death. He wanted both." She slipped the photographs under her coat. "Ready," she said.

They got out, closed the doors quietly, and walked up the broad steps to the huge paneled oak door. Havelock rang the bell; again the waiting was unbearable. The door opened and the uniformed maid stood there, startled.

"Good evening. It's Enid, isn't it?"

"Yes, sir. Good evening, sir. I didn't know Mr. Alexander was expecting guests."

"We're old friends," said Michael, his hand on Jenna's arm, as both stepped inside. "Invitations aren't required. It's part of the rules."

"I've never heard that one."

"It's fairly new. Is Mr. Alexander where he usually is at this hour? In his library?"

"Yes, sir. I'll tell him you're here. The name again, please?"

There was a sudden hollow echo preceding the voice that filled the large hall. "It won't be necessary, Enid." It was the clipped, high-pitched voice of Raymond Alexander pouring out of an unseen speaker. "And I *have* been expecting Mr. Havelock."

Michael's eyes darted about the walls, his hand now gripping Jenna's arm. "Is this another rule, Raymond? Make sure the guest is who he says he is?"

"It's fairly new," replied the voice.

Havelock walked with Jenna through the elegant living room, filled with antiques from the far corners of the earth, to the hand-carved door of the library. He guided her to his left, beyond the frame; she understood. He reached under his jacket for the Llama automatic and held it at his side before turning the heavy brass knob. He shoved the door open, his back pressed against the wall, his weapon ready.

"Is that really necessary, Michael?"

Havelock moved slowly into the frame, quickly adjusting his eyes to the shadowy indirect lighting of the library. The source was two lamps: one fringed and on the large desk at the far end of the room; the other a floor lamp, above the soft leather armchair, shining down on the wild, unkempt head of Raymond Alexander. The old warhorse sat motionless, and in his bloated, pale white hands was a brandy glass, held in front of his deep-red velvet smoking jacket.

"Come in," he said, turning to a small boxlike device on the side table. He pressed a button, and somewhere overhead, on the wall above the door, the dim glow of a television monitor faded away. "Miss Karas is a handsome woman. Very lovely. . . . Come in, my dear."

Jenna appeared, standing next to Michael. "You're a monster," she said simply.

"Far worse."

"You wanted to kill us both," she continued. "Why?"

"Not him, never him. Not—*Mikhail.*" Alexander raised his glass and drank. "Your life—or death—was never really considered one way or the other. It was out of our hands."

"I could kill you for that," said Havelock.

"I repeat. Out of our hands. Frankly, we thought she'd be retired, returned to Prague, and eventually cleared. Don't you see, Michael, she wasn't important. Only you; you were the only one that mattered. You had to go, and we knew they'd never let you, you were too valuable. You had to do it yourself, insist on it yourself. Your revulsion had to be so deep, so painful that there was no other way for you. It worked. You left. It was necessary."

"Because I knew you," said Havelock. "I knew the man who led a sick, disintegrating friend down the road of insanity, turning him into some kind of grotesque thing—Belial with his finger on the nuclear switch. I knew the man who did this to Anton Matthias. I knew Parsifal."

"Is that the name they've given? Parsifal? Exquisite irony. No healing wounds with this fellow, only tearing them apart. Everywhere."

"It's why you did what you did, isn't it? I knew who you were."

Alexander shook his head, the unkempt hair a thousand coiled springs in motion, his green eyes, under the full, arched brows, briefly closing. "I wasn't important, either. Anton insisted; you became an obsession with him. You were what was left of his failing integrity, his decaying conscience."

"But you knew how to do it. You knew a Soviet double agent so high in the government he could have been made Secretary of State. Would have been if he hadn't been there on that beach at the Costa Brava. You knew where he was, you knew his name, you *reached* him!"

"We had no part of the Costa Brava! I learned of it only after inquiring about you. We couldn't understand, we were shocked."

"Not Matthias. He was beyond being shocked."

"It was when we knew everything was out of control."

"Not we! *You!*"

The old journalist again stopped all movement, his hands gripping the glass. He locked his eyes with Michael's and answered, "Yes. Me. I knew."

"So you sent me to Poole's Island, expecting me to be killed, and once dead I was guilty by reason of silence."

"No!" Alexander shook his head, now violently. "I never thought you'd *go* there, never thought you'd be *permitted* to go there."

"That very convincing story about a soldier's wife you met and what she told you. It was all a lie. There've been no emergency leaves, no one's left that island. But I believed you, gave you my word I'd protect the source. Protect *you.* I never said anything, not even to Bradford."

"Yes, yes, I wanted to convince you, but not *that* way. I wanted you to go up the ladder, using your regular channels, confront them, make them tell you the truth. . . . And once you learned the truth, the *entire* truth, you might see, you might understand. You might be able to stop it. . . . Without me."

"How? For Christ's sake, *how?*"

"I think I know, Mikhail," said Jenna, touching Havelock's arm as she stared down at Alexander. "He did mean 'we.' Not 'I.' This man is not Parsifal. His servant, perhaps, but not Parsifal."

"Is that true?" asked Havelock.

"Pour yourself and Miss Karas a drink, Michael. You know the rules. I have a story to tell you."

"No drinks. Your rules don't apply any longer."

"At least sit down, and put that gun away. You have nothing to fear here. Not from me. Not any longer."

Havelock looked at Jenna; he nodded, leading them both to adjacent chairs across from Alexander. They sat down, Jenna removing the photographs from her coat and placing them on her lap. Michael shoved the weapon into his pocket. "Go on," he said curtly.

"A number of years ago," began the journalist, staring at the glass in his hands, "Anton and I committed a crime. In our minds it was far more serious than any punishment for it might indicate, and the punishment would have been severe in the extreme. We were fooled . . . 'gulled' is the innocuous word, 'deceived' more appropriate, 'betrayed' more appropriate still. But the fact that it could have happened to us—two pragmatic intellectuals, as we believed we were—was intolerable to us. Still, it had happened." Alexander drained his glass and placed it on the table next to his chair. He folded his puffed, delicate hands and continued. "Whether it was because of my friendship with Matthias, or for whatever standing I might have had in this city, a man called me from Toronto saying he had obtained a false passport and was flying to Washington. He was a Soviet citizen, an educated man in his early sixties, and an employee in a reasonably high position in the Soviet government. His intention was to defect, and he asked if I could put him in touch with Anthony Matthias." The journalist paused and leaned forward, gripping the arms of the chair. "You see, in those days everyone knew Anton was about to be tapped for extraordinary things; his influence was growing with every article he wrote, every trip to Washington. I arranged a meeting; it took place in this room." Alexander leaned back and kept his eyes on the floor. "That man had remarkable insights to offer, a wide knowledge of internal Soviet affairs. A month later he was working for the State Department. Three years after that Matthias was special assistant to the President, and two years later, Secretary of State. The man from Russia, by way of Toronto, was still in the department, his talents so appreciated that by then he was processing highly classified information as the director of Eastern bloc debriefings and reports."

"When did you find out?" asked Havelock.

The journalist looked up, and said quietly, "Four years ago. Again, in this room. The defector asked to meet with us both; he said that what he had to say was urgent and our schedules for that very night must be cleared—there could be no delays. He sat where Miss Karas is sitting now and told us the truth. He was a Soviet agent and had been continuously funneling the most sensitive information to Moscow for the past six years. But something had happened and he could no longer function in his role. He felt old and worn-out, the pressures were too great. He wanted to disappear."

"And since you and Anton—the pragmatic intellectuals—had been responsible for six years of infiltration, he had you exactly where he wanted you," Michael said sharply. "God forbid the great men should be tarnished."

"That was part of it, surely, but then, there was a certain justification. Anthony Matthias was at his zenith, reshaping global policies, reaching secure accommodations and détente, making the world somewhat safer than it was before him. Such a revelation would have been politically disastrous; it would have destroyed him—and the good he was doing. I myself presented this argument strongly."

"I'm sure it didn't take long to convince him," said Havelock.

"Longer than you think, perhaps," replied Alexander, a trace of weary anger in his voice. "You seem to have forgotten what he was."

"Perhaps I never really knew."

"You say this was part of it," interrupted Jenna. "What was the other part?"

The journalist shifted his gaze to rest on Jenna before he spoke. "That man was given an order with which he could not—would not—comply. He was told to be prepared for a series of shocking Eastern bloc reports, which he was to shape in such a way as to force Anton to request a naval blockade of Cuba along with a presidential Red Alert."

"Nuclear?"

"Yes, Miss Karas. A replay of the '62 missile crisis, but far more provocative. These startling reports would corroborate photographic 'evidence' purporting to show the jungles and southern coastal regions of Cuba ringed with offensive nuclear weapons, the first bridge of an imminent attack."

"For what *purpose?*" asked Jenna.

"A geopolitical trap," said Michael. "He walks into it, he's finished."

"Precisely," agreed Alexander. "Anton brings the full military might of the United States to the brink of war, and suddenly the gates of Cuba are opened and inspection teams from the world over are invited to see for themselves. There is nothing, and Anthony Matthias is humiliated, portrayed as a hysterical alarmist—the one thing he never was—all his brilliant negotiations thrown away. The healing with them, I might add."

"But this Soviet agent," said Jenna, bewildered, "this man who had for six years fed Moscow secrets, was a professional, if nothing else; he refused. Did he say why?"

"Quite movingly, I thought. He said Anton Matthias was too valuable to be sacrificed to a cabal of hotheads in Moscow."

"The Voennaya," said Havelock.

"Those shocking reports came in and they were ignored. No crisis ever took place."

"Would Matthias have accepted them as authentic if he hadn't known?" asked Michael.

"Somebody would have forced him to. Perfectly conscientious men and women in the section would have become alarmed, would possibly have come to someone like me—if they hadn't been told in advance what to expect, what the intemperate strategy was. Anton called in the Soviet ambassador for a long confidential talk. Men were replaced in Moscow."

"They've come back," said Havelock.

The journalist blinked; he did not understand, nor did he pretend to.

He continued. "The man who had deceived us, but who ultimately would not betray some voice inside himself, disappeared. Anton made it possible. He was given a new identity, a new life, beyond those who would have had him killed."

"He came back too," said Michael.

"He never really went away. But yes, he came back. A little over a year ago, without calling, without warning, he came to see me and said we had to talk. But not in this room; he wouldn't talk in here and I think I appreciated that. I remembered too well that night when he told us what we'd done. It was late afternoon, and we walked along the ridge above the ravine—two old men making their way slowly, cautiously over the ground, one profoundly frightened, the other curiously intense . . . in a quiet way, possessed." Alexander paused. "I'd like some more brandy; this isn't easy for me."

"I'm not interested," said Michael.

"Where is it?" asked Jenna, getting up and going to the table, reaching for the glass.

"The copper bar," said the old man, looking up at her. "Against the wall, my dear."

"Go on," said Havelock impatiently. "She can hear you; we can both hear you."

"I meant what I said. I *need* the brandy. . . . You don't look well, Michael. You look tired; you're unshaven and there are dark circles under your eyes. You should take better care of yourself."

"I'll make a note of it."

Jenna returned. "Here you are," she said, handing Alexander his drink and going to her chair.

It was the first time Havelock noticed that Raymond's hand shook. It was why he held the glass in both hands, gripping it to reduce the tremble. " 'In a quiet way, possessed.' That's where you were."

"Yes, I remember." Alexander drank, then looked at Jenna. "Thank you," he said.

She nodded. "Please, go on."

"Yes, of course. . . . We walked along the ridge, we two old men that late afternoon, when suddenly he stopped and said to me, 'You must do as I ask, for we have an opportunity that will never be presented to the world again.' I replied that I was not in the habit of acceding to such requests without knowing what was being asked of me. He said it was not a request but a demand, that if I refused he would reveal the roles

Matthias and I had played in his espionage activities. He would expose us both, destroy us both. It was what I feared most—for both of us, Anton more than myself, of course. But still myself, I can't say otherwise."

"What did he want you to do?" asked Havelock.

"I was to be the Boswell and my journals were to record the deterioration and collapse of a man with such power that he could plunge the world into the insanity that was down the road for him. My Samuel Johnson was, of course, Anthony Matthias, and the message to mankind was to be a sobering one: 'This must not be allowed to happen again; no one man should ever again be elevated to such heights.' "

" 'We made him a god,' " said Michael, recalling Berquist's words, " 'when we didn't own the heavens.' "

"Well put." The journalist nodded his head. "I wish I'd written it. But then, to borrow from Wilde, I probably will, if I ever get the chance."

"This man, this Russian," said Jenna, "told you that afternoon what was happening to Matthias?"

"Yes. He'd seen him, been with him, knew the signs. Sudden tirades, followed by weeping, constant self-justification, false humility that only served to point up his accomplishments . . . growing suspicions about everyone around him; yet in public there was always the façade of normalcy. Then there were the lapses of memory—in the main, concerning failures and, when prodded, the necessity to blame others for those failures. . . . I came to see it all, write it all. I'd drive to the Shenandoah every week or so—"

"On Sundays?" broke in Havelock.

"Sundays, yes."

"Decker?"

"Oh, yes, Commander Decker. By then, you see, the man you call Parsifal had convinced a deteriorating Anton that all his policies, all his visions would find their ultimate justification in total strength. The Master Plan, they called it . . . and they found the man who could provide them with what they needed."

"For the ultimate chess game," said Michael.

"Yes. Decker would use the back road and meet with Matthias in the cabin he used when he wanted to be alone."

"The Woodshed," said Havelock. "A voice-activated tape system."

"It never failed," agreed Alexander, in a voice barely above a whisper. "Never. Even afterwards, when Matthias and . . . Parsifal played their dreadful game, it was all the more terrifying because Matthias was one of the players. It was frightening in another aspect, too, for Anton would become the warlord statesman, the brilliant negotiator, not seeing the man you call Parsifal but seeing others, addressing others. Russian generals and scientists who weren't there, Chinese army commanders and commissars halfway across the globe. During those moments he *saw* them, they were *there*. It was a running pattern of self-induced séances, therapy of the most destructive kind. And each time he came out of it he was a little bit worse, his eyes guarded by those tortoiseshell glasses a little less focused. He was a man who'd been on some sort of drug trip, his mind a touch less clear for it. It was progressive, but he could still function in both worlds. . . . I saw it all, wrote it all."

"When did I come up?" asked Havelock. "Why me?"

"You were there all the time, photographs of you were on his desk, his bureau . . . in the Woodshed. An album of the two of you on a camping trip through the Canadian far west."

"I'd forgotten," said Michael. "It was so long ago. I was in graduate school, Anton was my adviser."

"Far more than that. You were the son he never had, speaking to him in his native language, recalling another place, another time." Alexander raised his head from the cradle of his chest, riveting his eyes on Havelock. "Above all, you were the son who refused to believe that his visions, his solutions for the world, were the right ones. He couldn't convince you. Your voice kept telling him he was wrong, and he couldn't stand that. He couldn't stand being told he was wrong, especially by you."

"He was. He knew I'd tell him."

"His eyes would stray to your pictures, and suddenly he would see you and be talking with you, tormented by your arguments, your anger. He was afraid of you, really . . . and the work would stop."

"So I had to be put out of reach."

"Where you could no longer judge him, I think. You were part of his everyday reality, the Department of State. You had to be separated from that reality. It began to consume him; he couldn't tolerate your interference. You had to go; he wouldn't have it any other way."

"And Parsifal knew how to do it," said Michael bitterly. "He knew the mole at State. He reached him and told him what to do."

"I had no part of that. I knew it was being done, but I didn't know how. . . . You had spoken to Anton about Miss Karas. About your devotion to her and how after the long years of your own inner turmoil—going back to your childhood—you were ready to come out. With her. Getting out was very important to you. Your decision had been made."

"You thought I'd come out *without* her? Why?"

"Because Parsifal was experienced in such matters," said Jenna. She selected one of the photographs and handed it to Michael. "A clinical psychologist attached to the KGB. A man named Alexei Kalyazin—the face that struck a chord with you."

"I don't *know* him!" shouted Havelock, getting out of the chair and turning to Raymond Alexander. "Who *is* he?"

"Don't ask me to say the name," whispered the journalist, shaking his head and pulling back into the chair. "Don't ask me. I can't be involved."

"Goddamn you, you *are* involved!" yelled Michael, throwing the photograph on Alexander's lap. "You're the *Boswell!* . . . Wait a minute!" Michael looked at Jenna and said, "He was a defector. Forget the fact that he was a plant, he was a *defector.* He had to be listed!"

"All references to the defection of Alexei Kalyazin were expurgated," said Alexander quietly. "All files were removed; a man with another name simply disappeared."

"Naturally. So the great man couldn't possibly be tarnished!" Havelock approached Alexander's chair; he reached down and, gripping the lapels of the journalist's jacket, yanked him up. "Who *is* he? *Tell* me!"

"Look at the photograph." Alexander's body was trembling. "Look at it. Remove much of the hair, the eyebrows as well. Give him many lines around his face, his eyes . . . a small white beard, speckled with gray."

Michael grabbed the photograph and stared at it. "Zelienski—Leon *Zelienski!*"

"I thought you'd see, I thought you'd understand. Without me. The ultimate chess game . . . the finest chess player Anton knew."

"He isn't Russian, he's a Pole! A retired professor of history from Berkeley . . . brought over here years ago from the University of Warsaw!"

"A new identity, a new life, papers in place and locations obscured. Living on a backcountry road less than two miles from Matthias. Anton always knew where he was."

Havelock brought his hands to his temples, trying to contain the racking pain in his head. "You . . . you and Zelienski. Two *demented old men!* Do you know what you've *done?*"

"It's out of control. Everything's out of control."

"You never had it *in* control! The instant Zelienski reached the mole, you lost! We all lost! Couldn't you see what was happening? Did you think it would end with a goddamn *message?* Couldn't you *stop* him? You knew Matthias was at Poole's Island . . . *how* did you know?"

"A source. One of the doctors—he's frightened."

"Then you knew he'd been diagnosed insane! How could you let it go on?"

"You just said it. I couldn't stop him. He wouldn't listen to me—he *won't* listen to me. I *can't stop him!* He's as crazed as Anton now. He has a Christ complex—his is the only light, the only way."

"And you traded your holy name in print so he could have it! What the *hell* are you made of?"

"Leave me something, Michael. He had me caged. Zelienski told me that if I went to anyone, if anyone came for him, a telephone call that he made daily from various phone booths would *not* be made, and those so-called nuclear agreements—*signed* by Anthony Matthias—would be on their way to Moscow and Peking."

Havelock watched the uneasy green eyes of the old journalist, and looked at the bloated hands gripping the arms of the chair. "No, Raymond, that's only part of it. You couldn't stand being exposed, being wrong. You're like Anton—frightened by the truth of your own mistakes. The blind but omniscient Tiresias, seeing things others can't see, the myth to be sustained whatever the cost."

"*Look* at me!" shouted Alexander suddenly, his whole body shaking. "I've lived with this—*through* this—for nearly a year! What would *you* have done?"

"God help me, I don't know. I can only hope better than you . . . but I don't know. Pour yourself a lot of brandy, Raymond. Maintain the myth; keep saying to yourself over and over again that you're infallible. It may help. It also may not make any difference anymore. Go out with a grin on that pompous face of yours. Just go." Michael turned to Jenna. "Let's get out of here," he said. "We've got a long drive."

"South to North, come in."

"North in touch. What is it?"

"Get to a phone and call Victor. There's movement. Our people came out fast and spoke with the escort; they were on the grounds. Both cars raced out of here a few moments ago, heading west, pedals to the floor."

"Don't lose them."

"No chance. The escort left the Lincoln up on the road and we placed a directional homer under the trunk. An earthquake couldn't move it. We've got them tracked up to twenty miles and down to a hundred yards. We've got them."

39

The night sky was oddly divided—clear moonlight behind, a ceiling of darkness ahead. The two automobiles raced over the country roads, the men in the Lincoln committed to protection without understanding, and Michael and Jenna understanding too well and afraid.

"There are no rules now," said Michael. "The book hasn't been written."

"He's capable of change, that's all you really know. He was sent here for one purpose and walked over to the other side."

"Or did he stumble? Alexander said Zelienski—Kalyazin—told them he felt old and worn-out, the pressures too great. Maybe he just gave up and walked into sanctuary."

"Until he found another commitment and accepted an entirely different set of pressures," said Jenna. "Exhilarating pressures for a man of his age, I imagine. He's over seventy, isn't he?"

"Around there, I'd guess."

"Think of it. The end may not come for a long time but, still, it's in sight. And as you approach it you suddenly find you've discovered an extraordinary solution you believe the world needs desperately, a lesson it has to be taught. What do you do?"

Havelock glanced at her. "That's what frightens me. Why should you move off center? How can I make him move?"

"I wish I could answer that." Jenna looked up at the windshield—at the myriad globules of water forming over the glass. "We're heading into the rain," she said.

"Unless there's another solution," said Michael quietly, switching on the wipers. "Exchange one lesson for another."

"What?"

"I'm not sure, I don't know. There aren't any rules." Havelock reached for the microphone and pulled it to his lips. "Escort, are you with me?"

"About four hundred feet behind, Sterile Five."

"Slow down and make it at least a mile and a half. We're getting into the area, and to a lot of people you're an obvious government vehicle. I don't want any connection between us or any startled eyes. If the man I'm making contact with gets even a hint of you, I don't want to think about the consequences."

"We don't like the distance," said the escort.

"Sorry to offend, but it's an order. Stay out of sight. You know the destination; just take the mountain road as I described it. Seneca something or other. Go up about half a mile. We'll be there."

"Would you mind repeating the order, sir?"

Michael did so. "Is that clear?"

"Yes, Sterile Five. It's also on tape."

The dirt-layered car met the blanket of rain, dust and mud dissolving under the downpour. The driver swung into a long curve as the red signal light on the powerful radio amplifier suddenly glowed.

"We're on a different frequency," said the man in the passenger seat as he reached for the microphone. He pressed the scanner for contact. "Yes?" he said.

"South?"

"We're here."

"It's Victor. I'm approaching Warrenton on Sixty-six. Where are you?"

The man with the microphone studied the map on his lap with a pencil light. "North on Seventeen, heading into Marshall. You can pick it up in Warrenton."

"Status?"

"Normal. We figure once they reach Marshall, they'll either continue north on Seventeen or head west on the Front Royal Road. The turns are getting hairy; we're going into the mountains."

"We've got men covering both routes up there. I want to know which road they take and the distance between Sterile Five and his escort. Use this channel. I should catch up with you in ten to fifteen minutes."

"What flight plan?"

"My own."

The blond man sitting in the brown sedan in front of the Blue Ridge Diner slumped back in the seat, the microphone in his hand, his eyes on the road. He depressed the button. "It's the Front Royal Road," he said as the Buick coupe rushed by in the rain. "Right on time and in a hurry."

"How far behind is the Lincoln?" asked the voice from the speaker.

"No sign of it yet."

"You're sure?"

"No headlights, and anyone damn fool enough to drive up here in this mess isn't going to roll in the dark."

"It's not normal. I'll be right back."

"It's your equipment."

The blond man lowered the microphone and reached for the cigarettes on the seat beside him. He jerked one out of the pack, put it to his lips, and snapped his butane lighter. Thirty seconds went by and still the Lincoln Continental had not come into view; nothing was in view but sheets of rain. Forty-five seconds. Nothing. A minute, and the voice, accompanied by static, burst out of the speaker. "Front Royal, where are you?"

"Here and waiting. You said you'd be right back, remember?"

"The escort. Has it gone by?"

"Nope. If it had, I would have rung you up, pal. . . . Wait. Stay there. We may have it." A stream of light came out of the curve, and seconds later the long, dark car roared by in the downpour. "He just went by, old buddy. I'll roll now." The blond man sat up and eased the sedan out into the road.

"I'll be right back," said the voice.

"You keep repeating yourself, pal," said the blond man, stepping on the accelerator. Gathering speed while watching the rain-soaked road closely, he saw the red taillights of the Lincoln flickering in the distance through the downpour. He breathed easier.

"Front Royal," erupted the voice from the speaker.

"Right here, li'l darlin'."

"Scan to seventeen-twenty megahertz for separate instructions."

"Scanning now." The blond man reached down and pressed the metal button; the digital readouts appeared on the narrow horizontal strip above the radio's dials. "Front Royal in position," he said.

"This is the man you don't know, Front Royal."

"Nice not to know you, old buddy."

"How much are you being paid for tonight?" asked the new voice.

"Since you're the man I don't know, I figure you ought to know how much."

"How good are you?"

"Very. How good's your money?"

"You've been paid."

"Not for what you want now."

"You're perceptive."

"You're kind of obvious."

"That big fellow up ahead. He knows where the little fellow's going, wouldn't you agree?"

"Sure would. There's a lot of space between them, 'specially for a night like this."

"Do you think you could get between them?"

"Can do. Then what?"

"A bonus."

"For what?"

"The little fellow's going to stop somewhere. After he does, I don't want the big fellow around him any longer."

"You're talking about a pretty big bonus, Mr. No-Name. That car's an Abraham."

"Six figures," said the voice. "A reckless driver. Very reckless and very accurate."

"You're on, li'l darlin'."

Arthur Pierce nodded through the window and the rain as he passed the old car four miles down the Front Royal Road. He lifted the microphone and spoke on the 1720 frequency.

"All right, South, here's the manual. You stay with me, everyone else is dismissed. Thank them all for their time and say we'll be in touch."

"What about North? They travel."

"I want them back with the naval contingent. It's theirs now; they can alternate. Sooner or later—tonight, tomorrow, the next day—they'll let him out. When they do, terminate. We don't want to hear his voice."

Havelock stopped the car and lowered the window; he peered through the rain at the sign nailed to the tree, feeling certain it was the one. It was:

SENECA'S NOTCH
DEAD END

He had driven Leon Zelienski home twice, once in the afternoon when the old man's car would not start, and then several years later on a night like tonight when Matthias was worried that Leon might get stuck in the mud. Zelienski had not gotten stuck, but Michael had; it had been a long, wet walk back to Anton's house. He remembered the roads.

He had taken Leon Zelienski home; he was coming after Alexei Kalyazin. Parsifal.

"Here we go," said Havelock, turning up into the rock-hewn road with only remnants of long-eroded tarring on its surface. "If we stay in the center we should make it."

"Stay in the center," said Jenna.

They lurched and skidded up the narrow road, drenched darkness all around them, tires spinning, hurling loose rock behind and up into the metal fenders. The jarring ride did nothing to steady their nerves or set the tone for awesome negotiations. Michael had been brutal with Raymond Alexander, knowing he was right, but only partly right. He began to understand the other aspect of the journalist's profound fear, fear that was driving him to the edge of hysteria. Zelienski's threat was clear and terrifying: should Alexander betray the Russian or interfere in any way, the daily telephone call that Zelienski placed from various booths would not be made. The silence would be the signal for the nuclear agreements to be sent to Moscow and Peking.

And chemicals could not be used to force Zelienski to reveal the number that he was calling; there was too great a risk with a man of his age. One cubic centimeter of excess dosage and his heart could blow apart, and the number would be lost with the internal explosion. There were only words. What *were* the words one found for a man who would save the world with a blueprint for its annihilation? There was no reason in such a mind, nothing but its own distorted vision.

The small house came into view above them on the right; it was hardly larger than a cabin, square in design and made of heavy stone. A sloping dirt driveway ended in a carport, where a nondescript automobile stood motionless, protected from the downpour. A single light shone through a bay window, which was oddly out of place in the small dwelling.

Havelock switched off the headlights and turned to Jenna. "It all began here," he said. "In the mind of the man up there. All of it. From the Costa Brava to Poole's Island, from Col de Moulinets to Sterile Five; it started here."

"Can we end it here, Mikhail?"

"Let's try. Let's go."

They got out of the car and walked through the rain up the wet, soft mud of the driveway, rivulets of water racing down around their feet. They reached the carport; there was a door centered under the attached roof with a concrete step below. Havelock walked to the door; he looked briefly at Jenna and then knocked.

Moments later the door opened, and a slight, stooped old man with only a few strands of hair and a small white beard peppered with gray stood in the open space. As he stared at Havelock his eyes grew wide and his mouth parted, lips trembling.

"Mikhail," he whispered.

"Hello, Leon. I bring you Anton's affection."

The blond man had seen the sign. The only part meaningful to him were the words *Dead End.* It was all he had to know. With his headlights still extinguished, he maneuvered the brown sedan several hundred feet down the smooth wet road and stopped on the far right, motor idling. He turned the headlights back on and reached under his coat to remove a large automatic with a silencer attached. He understood Mr. No-Name's instructions; they were in sequence. The Lincoln would be along any moment now.

There it was! Two hundred yards away at the mouth of the road that branched off the highway. The blond man released the brake and began coasting, spinning the wheel back and forth, weaving—the unmistakable sign of a drunken, reckless driver. Cautiously the limousine slowed down, pulling as far to the right as possible. The blond man accelerated, and the weaving became more violent as the Lincoln's horn roared through the torrents of rain. When he was within thirty feet, the blond man suddenly pressed the accelerator to the floor and swung to the right before making a sharp turn to the left.

The impact came, the sedan's grille ramming the left rear door of the Lincoln. The sedan skidded and crashed into the entire side of the other car, pinning the driver's door.

"Goddamn you sons of *bitches!*" screamed the blond man through the open window, slurring his words, his head swaying back and forth. "Holy *Christ,* I'm bleeding! My whole stomach's *bleeding!*"

The two men lurched out of the limousine from the other side. As they came running around the hood in the blinding glare of the headlights the blond man leaned out the window and fired twice. Accurately.

"Do I call you Leon or Alexei?"

"I can't *believe* you!" cried the old Russian, sitting in front of the fire, his eyes rheumy and blinking, riveted on Havelock. "It was degenerative, irreversible. There was no *hope.*"

"There are very few minds, very few wills like Anton's. Whether he'll ever regain his full capacities no one can tell, but he's come back a long way. Drugs helped, electrotherapy as well; he's cognizant now. And appalled at what he did." Havelock sat down in the straight-backed chair opposite Zelienski-Kalyazin. Jenna remained standing by the door that led to the small kitchen.

"It's never *happened!*"

"There's never been a man like Matthias, either. He asked for me; they sent me to Poole's Island and he told me everything. Only me."

"Poole's Island?"

"It's where he's being treated. Is it Leon or Alexei, old friend?"

Kalyazin shook his head. "Not Leon, it's never been Leon. Always Alexei."

"You had good years as Leon Zelienski."

"Enforced sanctuary, Mikhail. I am a Russian, nothing else. Sanctuary."

Havelock and Jenna exchanged glances, her eyes telling him that she approved—approved with enormous admiration—the course he had suddenly chosen.

"You came over to us . . . Alexei."

"I did not come over to you. I fled others. Men who would corrupt the soul of my homeland, who went beyond the bounds of our convictions, who killed needlessly, wantonly, seeking only power for its own sake. I believe in our system, Mikhail, not yours. But these men did not; they would have changed words into weapons and then no one would have been proven right. We'd all be gone."

"Jackals," said Havelock, repeating the word he had heard only hours ago, "fanatics who in their heads marched with the Third Reich. Who didn't believe time was on your side, only bombs."

"That will suffice."

"The Voennaya."

Kalyazin's head snapped up. "I never told Matthias that!"

"I never told him, either. I've been in the field for sixteen years. Do you think I don't know the VKR?"

"They do not speak for Russia, not *our* Russia! . . . Anton and I would argue until the early hours of the morning. He couldn't understand; he came from a background of brilliance and respectability, money and a full table. Over here none of you will ever understand, except the black people, perhaps. We had nothing and were told to expect nothing, not in this world. Books, schools, simple reading—these were not for us, the millions of us. We were placed on this earth as the earth's cattle, worked and disposed of by our 'betters'—decreed by God. . . . My grandfather was hanged by a Voroshin prince for stealing game. Stealing *game!* . . . All that was changed—by the millions of us, led by prophets who had no use for a God who decreed human cattle." An odd smile appeared on Kalyazin's thin white lips. "They call us atheistic Communists. What would they have us be? We *knew* what it was like under the *Holy Church!* A God who threatens eternal fires if one rises up against a living hell is no God for nine-tenths of mankind. He can and should be replaced, dismissed for incompetence and unwarranted partiality."

"That argument is hardly restricted to prerevolutionary Russia," said Michael.

"Certainly not, but it's symptomatic . . . and we were *there!* It's why you'll lose one day. Not in this decade or the next—perhaps not for many, many years, but you'll lose. Too many tables are bare, too many stomachs swollen, and you care too little."

"If that proves to be true, then we deserve to lose. I don't think it is." Havelock leaned forward, elbows on his knees, and looked into the old Russian's eyes. "Are you telling me you were given sanctuary but you gave nothing in return?"

"Not of my country's secrets, nor did Anton ever ask me a second time. I think he considered the work I did—the work you did before you resigned—to be in the main quite pointless. Our decisions counted for very little; our accomplishments were not important at the summits. I did, however, give you a gift that served us both, served the world as well. I gave you Anthony Matthias. I saved him from the Cuban trap; it would have driven him from office. I did so because I believed in him, and not in the madmen who temporarily had far too much control of my government."

"Yes, he told me. He would have been destroyed, his influence finished. . . . It's on that basis—your belief in him—that he asked me to come and see you. It's got to stop, Leon—excuse me—Alexei. He knows why you did what you did, but it's got to *stop.*"

Kalyazin's gaze strayed to Jenna. "Where is the hatred in your eyes, young lady? Surely, it must be there."

"I won't lie to you, it's close to my thoughts. I'm trying to understand."

"It had to be done; there was no other way. Anton had to be rid of the specter of Mikhail. He had to know he was far away from the government, with other interests, other pursuits. He was so afraid his . . . his son . . . would learn of his work and come to stop him." Kalyazin turned to Havelock. "He couldn't get you out of his mind."

"He approved of what you did?" asked Michael.

"He looked away, I think, a part of him revolted by himself, another part crying to survive. He was failing rapidly by then, his sanity pleading to be left intact whatever the cost. Miss Karas became the price."

"He never asked you how you did it? How you reached men in Moscow to provide what you needed?"

"Never. That, too, was part of the price. Remember, the world you and I lived in was very unimportant to him. Then, of course, everything became chaos . . ."

"Out of control?" suggested Jenna.

"Yes, young lady. The things we heard were so unbelievable, so horrible. A woman killed on a beach . . ."

"What did you expect?" asked Havelock, controlling himself and not finding it easy. *Two . . . three demented old men.*

"Not that. We weren't killers. Anton had given orders that she was to be sent back to Prague and watched, her contacts observed, and eventually her innocence was to be established."

"Those orders were intercepted, changed."

"By then he could do nothing. You had disappeared and he finally went completely, totally mad."

"Disappeared? *I* disappeared?"

"That's what he was told. And when they told him he collapsed, his mind went. He thought he'd killed you, too. It was the final pressure he could not withstand."

"How do you know this?" pressed Michael.

Kalyazin balked, his rheumy eyes blinking. "There was someone else. He had sources, a doctor. He found out."

"Raymond Alexander," said Havelock.

"Anton told you, then?"

"Boswell."

"Yes, our Boswell."

"You mentioned him when I called you from Europe."

"I was frightened. I thought you might speak to someone who had seen him at Anton's house; he was there so often. I wanted to give you a perfectly acceptable reason for his visits, to keep you away from him."

"Why?"

"Because Alexander the Great has become Alexander the Diseased. You've been away, you don't know. He rarely writes anymore. He drinks all day and most of the night; he can't stand the strain. Fortunately, for his public, there's the death of his wife to blame it on."

"Matthias told me you had a wife," said Michael, his ear picking up something in Kalyazin's voice. "In California. She died and he persuaded you to come here to the Shenandoah."

"I had a wife, Mikhail. In Moscow. And she was killed by the soldiers of Stalin. A man I helped destroy, a man who came from the Voennaya."

"I'm sorry."

A brief rattling somewhere in the small house was louder than the pounding rain outside. Jenna looked at Havelock.

"It's nothing," said Kalyazin. "There's a piece of wood, a wedge, I place in that old door on windy nights. The sight of you made me forget." The old man leaned back in his chair and brought his thin, veined hands to his chin. "You must be very clear with me, Mikhail, and you must give me time to think. It's why I did not answer you a few moments ago."

"About Anton?"

"Yes. Does he really know why I did what I did? Why I took him through those terrible nights? Auto and external suggestion, swelling him up until he performed like the genius he was, debating with men who weren't there. Does he *really* understand?"

"Yes, he does," replied Havelock, feeling a thousand pounds on the back of his neck. He was so close, but a wrong response would send this Parsifal back into self-imposed, unbreakable silence. Alexander was right, after all; Kalyazin had a Christ complex. Beneath the old Russian's mild speech was a commitment forged in steel. He knew he was right. "No single man," said Michael, "should be given such power and the strains of that power ever again. He begs you, pleads with you on the strength of all the talks you and he had before his illness, to give me those incredible agreements you both created and whatever copies exist. Let me burn them."

"He understands, then, but is it enough? Do the others? Have *they* learned?"

"Who?"

"The men who allocate such power, who permit the canonization of would-be saints only to find that their heroes are only mortals, broken by swollen egos, and by the demands made on them."

"They're terrified. What more do you want?"

"I want them to know what they've done, how this world can be set on fire by a single brilliant mind caught in the vortex of unbearable pressures. The madness is contagious; it does not stop with a broken saint."

"They understand. Above all, the one man most people consider the most powerful on earth, he understands. He told me they had created an emperor, a god, and they had no right to do either. They took him up too high; he was blinded."

"And Icarus fell to the sea," said Kalyazin. "Berquist is a decent man, hard but decent. He's also in an impossible job, but he handles it better than most."

"There's no one I'd rather see there now."

"I'm inclined to agree."

"You're killing him," said Havelock. "Let him go. Free him. The lesson's been taught, and it won't be forgotten. Let him get back to that impossible job and do the best he can."

Kalyazin looked at the glowing embers of the fire. "Twenty-seven pages, each document, each agreement. I typed them myself, using the form employed by Bismarck in the treaties of Schleswig-Holstein. It so appealed to Anton. . . . I was never interested in the money, they know that, don't they?"

"They know that. He knows it."

"Only the lesson."

"Yes."

The old man turned back to Michael. "There are no copies except the one I sent to President Berquist in an envelope from the State Department, from Matthias's office, with the word *Restricted* stamped across the front. It was marked, of course, for his eyes only."

Havelock tensed, recalling so clearly Raymond Alexander's statement that Kalyazin had "caged" him, that if a telephone call was not made, the documents would be sent to Moscow and Peking. The numbers added up to four, not two. "No other copies at all, Alexei?"

"None."

"I would think," remarked Jenna unexpectedly, taking hesitant steps toward the frail old Russian, "that Raymond Alexander, your Boswell, would have insisted on one. It's the core of his writing."

"It's the core of his fear, young lady. I control him by telling him that if he divulges anything to anyone, copies will be sent to your enemies. That was never my intention—on the contrary, the furthest thought from my mind. It would bring about the very cataclysm I pray will be avoided."

"Pray, Alexei?"

"Not to any god you know, Mikhail. Only to a collective conscience. Not to a Holy Church with a biased Almighty."

"May I have the documents?"

Kalyazin nodded. "Yes," he said, drawing out the word. "But not in the sense of possession. We will burn them together."

"Why?"

"You know the reason; we were both in the same profession. The men who allow the Matthiases of this world to soar so high they're blinded by the sun, those men will never know. Did an old man lie? I deceived them before. Am I deceiving them again? *Are* there copies?"

"Are there?"

"No, but they won't know that." Kalyazin struggled out of the chair; he stood up and breathed deeply, planting his feet firmly on the floor. "Come with me, Mikhail. They're buried in the woods along the path to the Notch. I pass them every afternoon, seventy-three steps to a dogwood tree, the only one in Seneca's burial ground. I often wonder how it got there. . . . Come, let's get it over with. We will dig in the rain and get terribly wet and return with the weapons of Armageddon. Perhaps Miss Karas might make us some tea. Also, glasses of vodka . . . with buffalo grass, always buffalo grass. Then we shall burn the evidence and rekindle the fire."

The door to the kitchen crashed open like a sudden explosion of thunder, and a tall man with a fringe of gray around his bald head stood there, a gun in his hand.

"They lie to you, Alexei. They *always* lie and you never know it. *Don't move*, Havelock!" Arthur Pierce reached out, gripped Jenna's elbow and yanked her to him, lashing his left arm around her neck, the automatic pressed against her head. "I'm going to count to five," he said to Michael. "By which time you will have removed your weapon with two fingers and thrown it on the floor, or you will see this woman's skull blown into the wall. *One, two, three—*"

Havelock unbuttoned his coat, spreading it open, and, using two fingers as pincers, took out the Llama from its holster. He dropped it on the floor.

"Kick it over!" yelled the traveler.

Michael did so. "I don't know how you got here, but you can't get out," he said quietly.

"Really?" Pierce released Jenna, shoving her toward the astonished old Russian. "Then I should tell you that your Abraham was cut down by an ungrateful Ishmael. *You* can't get out."

"Others know where we are."

"I doubt that. There'd be a hidden army out there on that road if they did. Oh, no, you went in solo—"

"*You?*" cried Kalyazin, shaking, then nodding his trembling head. "It *is* you!"

"Glad you're with us, Alexei. You're slowing down in your old age. You don't hear lies when you're told them."

"What lies? How did you *find* me?"

"By following a persistent man. Let's talk about the lies."

"What *lies?*"

"Matthias recovering. That's the biggest lie of all. There's a metal case in my car the contents of which will make remarkable reading all over the world. It shows Anthony Matthias for what he is. A screaming, hollow shell, a maniac, violent and paranoid, who has no working concept of reality. He builds delusions out of images, fantasies out of abstractions— he can be programmed like a deranged robot, reenacting his crimes and offenses. He's insane and getting worse."

"That can't be true!" Kalyazin looked at Michael. "The things he told me . . . only Anton would know them, recall them."

"Another lie. Your convincing friend failed to mention that he's just driven down from the village of Fox Hollow, the residence and dateline of a well-known commentator. One Raymond Alexander— What did Miss Karas just call him? Your Boswell, I think. I'll visit him. He can add to our collection."

"*Mikhail?* Why? Why did you say these things? Why did you lie to me?"

"I had to. I was afraid you wouldn't listen to me. And because I believe that the Anton we both knew once would have wanted me to."

"Still another lie," said Pierce, lowering himself cautiously, his gun extended as he picked up the Llama from the floor and shoved it into his belt. "All they want are those papers so business can go on as usual. So their nuclear committees can go on designing new ways to blow the godless out of existence. That's what they call us, Alexci. Godless. Perhaps they'll make Commander Decker the next Secretary of State. His type is very much in vogue; ambitious zealots are the order of the day."

"That couldn't happen and you know it, Traveler."

Pierce looked at Havelock, studying him. "Yes, a traveler. How did you do it? How did you find me?"

"You'll never know that. Or how deeply we've penetrated the *paminyatchik* operation. That's right. Penetrated."

The traveler stared at Michael. "I don't believe you."

"That doesn't matter."

"It won't make any difference. We'll have the documents. All the options will be ours, nothing left to you. *Nothing.* Except burning cities if you make a wrong turn, a wrong judgment. The world won't tolerate you any longer." Pierce stabbed the air with his gun. "Let's go, all of you. You're going to dig them up for me, Havelock. 'Seventy-three steps to a dogwood tree.' "

"There are a dozen paths up to the Notch," said Michael quickly. "You don't know which one."

"Alexei will show me. When it comes down to it, he chooses us, not you. Never you. Not business as usual, conducted by liars. He'll tell me."

"Don't do it, Kalyazin."

"You lied to me, Mikhail. If there must be ultimate weapons—even on paper—they can't be yours."

"I told you why I lied, but there's a final reason. *Him.* You came over to us not because you believed in us but because you couldn't believe in *them.* They've come back. He was the man at the Costa Brava—he killed at the Costa Brava."

"I carried out what you only pretended! You had the stomach only for pretense. It had to be *done,* not faked!"

"No, it didn't. But where there's a choice, you kill. You killed the man who set up the operation, an operation where *no* one's death was called for."

"I did exactly what you would have done but with far more finesse and inventiveness. His death had to be credible, accepted for what it appeared to be. MacKenzie was the only one who could retrace the events that night, who knew his personnel."

"Also killed!"

"Inevitable."

"And Bradford? Inevitable, too?"

"Of course. He'd found me."

"You see the pattern, Alexei?" shouted Havelock, his eyes on Pierce. "Kill, kill, *kill!* . . . Do you remember Rostov, Alexei?"

"Yes, I remember him."

"He was my enemy, but he was a decent man. They killed him, too. Only hours ago. They've come back and they're marching."

"Who?" asked the old Russian haltingly, memories stirred.

"The *Voennaya*. The maniacs of the VKR!"

"*Not* maniacs," said Pierce firmly, quietly. "Dedicated men who understand the nature of your hatred, your mendacity. Men who will not compromise the principles of the Soviet Union only to watch you spread your sanctimonious lies, turning the world against us. . . . Our time has come, Alexei. You'll be with us."

Kalyazin blinked, his watery eyes staring at Arthur Pierce. Slowly he shook his head and whispered, "No . . . no, I will never be a part of you."

"What?"

"You do not speak for Russia," said the old man, his voice growing until it filled the room. "You kill too easily—you killed someone very dear to me. Your words are measured and there's truth in what you say, but not in what you *do* or the *way* you *do it!* You are *animals!*" Without the slightest warning, Kalyazin lunged at Pierce, hurling his frail body at the traveler, his gaunt hands gripping the weapon. *"Mikhail,* run! *Run,* Mikhail!" There was a muffled roar as the gun exploded into the old man's stomach. Still he would not let go. *"Run . . . !"* The whisper was a final command.

Havelock spun around and propelled Jenna toward the open kitchen door. He turned, prepared to throw himself on Pierce, but stopped, holding himself in check, for what he saw caused him to make an instantaneous decision. The dying Kalyazin held on fiercely, but the bloody gun was coming free; in an instant it would be aimed at him, fired into his head.

He lurched for the kitchen door and slammed it shut as he raced inside, colliding with Jenna. She held two kitchen knives in her hand; Michael grabbed the shorter blade, and they ran for the outside door.

"The woods!" he shouted, in the carport. "Kalyazin can't hold him. Hurry up! You go to the right, I'll head left!" he cried as they ran across the grass in the downpour. "We'll converge a couple of hundred yards inside!"

"Where is the path? Which is it?"

"I don't know!"

"He'll be looking for it!"

"I know."

Five gunshots exploded, but not from a single gun; there were two. They separated, Michael zigzagging toward the darkness of the trees on his left, spinning quickly to look behind him. Three men. Pierce was shouting orders to two others who had raced up the muddy drive. They ran from the carport, fanning out, flashlights on, weapons ready.

He reached the edge of the tall grass and plunged into the protective cover of the woods; he removed his coat and scrambled to his right, diving for the thickest underbrush. He crawled forward, his eyes on the field, on the beam of the middle flashlight, and worked his way back toward the edge. His body was soaked; mud and wet foliage were everywhere. The border of the grass was his battle line; the downpour was loud enough to drown out the pound of quick movements. The man would come swiftly, then be stopped both by the overgrowth and by his own caution.

As the beam approached, Havelock inched toward the last bank of tangled bush; he waited, crouching. The man slowed down, sweeping the area with light. Then he entered the woods quickly, the beam moving up and down as he used his arm to open a path through the thick brush.

Now. Michael rolled out on the grass and rushed ahead; he was directly behind the traveler. He sprang, the knife gripped in his hand. As he plunged the blade into the killer's back, his left hand yanked back the man's neck and clamped his mouth. Both fell into mud and brush, and Michael worked the blade brutally until there was no movement beneath him. He yanked the head up as he ripped the gun from the lifeless hand; it was not Arthur Pierce. He lunged for the flashlight and snapped it off.

Jenna raced into the dark, narrow alleyway cut through the trees and the foliage. Was this *it?* she wondered. Was it the path to Seneca's Notch: "seventy-three steps to a dogwood tree"? If it was, it was her responsibility. No one could be allowed to pass through, and the surest way of preventing it was as distasteful as it was frightening.

Yet she had done it before, always terrified by the prospect, sickened with the results, but there was no time to think of such things. She looked behind her; the flashlight beam was veering to its left, toward the path! She let out a short cry loud enough to be heard through the pounding rain. The flashlight halted, and was briefly immobile before shifting, now focusing directly on the entrance of the path. The man rushed into it.

Jenna lurched into the tangled branches on the border and crouched, holding the long blade of the kitchen knife rigid, diagonally up from her knees. The oscillating beam of the flashlight drew nearer, the figure behind it running hard, slipping on the mud, his concentration up ahead on the path, a killer racing after the remembered cry of an unarmed woman.

Ten feet, five . . . now!

Jenna lunged up through the brush with her eyes and blade centered on the body directly behind the light. The contact was sickening: a rush of blood erupted as the long blade sank into the flesh, impaling the body that had raced into it.

The man screamed, the terrible scream filling the woods and for a long moment drowning out the downpour.

Jenna lay gasping for air beside the dead man, rubbing her blood-soaked hand in the soft mud. She grabbed the flashlight and switched it off. Then she rolled to the border of the path and vomited.

Havelock heard the sudden scream, and closed his eyes—then opened them, grateful beyond life itself to realize it was a man's scream. Jenna had done it; she had taken out the man whose orders were to kill her. And that man was not Pierce. He knew it. He had seen the positions in the carport. Pierce had been on the left, closest to the door, the angles consistent when the chase had begun.

Arthur Pierce was somewhere between the middle ground and the road beyond Kalyazin's house, an acre of forest drenched by the rain surging downward, dripping everywhere from the imperfect roof of the treetops.

Where was the last beam of light? It was not there—of course it was not there! Light was a target and Pierce was no fool. They were two animals now, two predators stalking each other in the waterlogged darkness. But one had the advantage, and Michael knew it instinctively, felt it strongly: the forests had been good to Mikhail Havlíček; they were his friend and sanctuary. He did not fear the webbed darkness, for it had saved him too often, protected him from uniformed hunters who would shoot a child because of his father.

He crawled swiftly through underbrush, eyes straining, ears alert, trying to pick up sounds that were not part of the rain and the creaking weight of drenched limbs above. He semicircled the area, noting among a thousand other intuitively gathered bits of information that there were no paths, no breaks in the forest leading to Seneca's Notch. Inside the house he had said there were a dozen such paths to confuse Pierce, not knowing whether there were any, never having been beyond Zelienski-Kalyazin's front door.

He swept the arc again, closing it, snaking through the overgrowth; the trunks of trees were his intermittent fortress walls—he used them like parapets as he peered around them.

Movement! The sound of suction, not weight. A foot or a knee pressing into and rising from the mud.

Light was a target . . . light *was* a target.

He crawled out of the arc, fifteen, twenty, thirty, forty feet beyond the perimeter, knowing what he was looking for, feeling for—a branch. He found it.

A sapling—strong, supple, no more than four feet high, its roots deep, clawing the earth beneath.

Havelock reached into his belt and pulled out the flashlight he had taken from the dead traveler. He placed it on the ground and removed his shirt, spreading it in front of him and moving the flashlight to the center of the cloth.

Thirty seconds later the flashlight was securely tied and wrapped in the shirt, the sleeves wound around it, with sufficient cloth remaining for the final attachment. He knelt next to the small tree and lashed the flashlight laterally against the thin shaft of the trunk; he crisscrossed what remained of the sleeves so it was held firmly in place. He pulled the trunk back and let it go, testing it.

He snapped on the light and pulled the trunk back for the last time, then raced into the woods to his right. He spun around a thick tree and waited, watching the beam of light as it eerily swept back and forth over the ground. He leveled the traveler's gun, steadying it against the bark.

His ears picked up the sound of suction again, footsteps coming through the rain. Then the figure emerged, looming grotesquely through the webbed branches.

Pierce crouched, trying to avoid the light, and fired his automatic; the ear-shattering explosions echoed throughout the dripping forest.

"You lose," said Michael as he pulled the trigger and watched the killer of Costa Brava reeling backwards, screaming. He fired again, and the man from the Voennaya fell to the ground motionless, silent. Dead. "You didn't know the woods," said Michael. "I learned them from people like you."

"Jenna! *Jenna!*" he yelled, lurching through the trees toward the open grass. "It's *over!* The field, the *field!*"

"Mikhail? *Mikhail!*"

He saw her walking slowly, unsteadily in the distance through the sheets of the downpour. Seeing him, she quickened her pace and broke into a run. He, too, raced over the wet grass, wanting—needing—the distance between them to vanish.

They held each other; the world for a few brief moments was no part of them. The cold rain on his bare skin was only cool water, warmed by her embrace, her face against his face.

"Were there other paths?" she asked, breathless.

"None."

"Then I found it. Come, Mikhail. *Hurry!*"

They stood in Kalyazin's house, where the old Russian's body was covered with a blanket, his tortured face mercifully hidden. Havelock walked to the telephone. "It's time," he said, dialing.

"What's *happened?*" asked the President of the United States, his voice tense. "I've been trying to reach you all night!"

"It's over," said Michael. "Parsifal's dead. We've got the documents. I'll write a report telling you what I think you'll have to know."

There was a stunned silence over the line; then Berquist whispered simply, "I know you wouldn't lie."

"I would, but not about this."

"What *you* think *I* have to know?" said Berquist, finding a part of his voice.

"Yes. I'll leave out nothing that's essential to you, for that impossible job you're in."

"Where are you? I'll send an army for you—just get those documents here."

"No, Mr. President. We have a last stop to make, to a man they called Boswell. But before we leave, I'm going to burn them. There's only one set and I'm burning it. The psychiatric file as well."

"You've—?"

"It'll be in the report. . . . There's a practical reason for my doing what I'm doing. I don't know what's out there—I think I know, but I can't be certain. It started here and it's going to end here."

"I see." Berquist paused. "I can't change your mind and I can't stop you."

"That's true."

"Very well, I won't try. I like to think I'm a judge of men. You have to be to sit in this office—at least, you should be. . . . What can a grateful nation, a very grateful President do for you?"

"Leave me alone, sir. Leave us alone."

"Havelock?"

"Yes?"

"How can I be certain? The burning?"

"Parsifal didn't want you to be. You see, he never wanted it to happen again. No more Matthiases. Superstars are out. He never wanted you to be absolutely sure."

"I'll have to think about that, won't I?"

"It'd be a good idea."

"Matthias died this evening. It's why I tried to call you."

"He died a long time ago, Mr. President."

EPILOGUE

Autumn. New Hampshire alternately chilled into gray submission by the gathering arctic winds and then warmed by the vibrant colors of fall, the persistent sun giving life to the fields and refusing to submit to the slow approach of winter.

Havelock hung up the phone in the enclosed porch that Jenna had insisted should be his study. She had seen him, had watched his eyes, as he had walked through the living-room door of the old house and stood there, mesmerized by the expanse of glass and the framed countryside beyond. A desk, bookshelves against the inner brick wall, and an odd assortment of comfortable furniture had transformed the bare porch into an airy room protected by transparent walls that allowed a spacious view of the fields and the woods that meant so much to him. She had understood, and he loved her for understanding. What he could see from that very unusual place was not what others would see, not simply the tall grass and vastly taller trees in the distance but an ever-changing landscape of sanctuary.

And memories of tension and survival, they were there, too, suddenly welling up until he had to move—physically—to overcome them, to suppress them. It would take time; normality was not to be found in a matter of weeks, even months.

Underneath he had a fever because you bastards poisoned him. You fed him a diet of . . . frenzy. He needed his fix! Dr. Matthew Randolph, dead man, talking about another dead man . . . and so many others.

They had discussed it, Jenna and he, and defined the fever that gripped him every now and then, and she was the only doctor he needed. They would take long walks; sudden bursts of running frequently became necessary for him, until the sweat came and his chest pounded. But the fever would pass, the explosions in his head dissolve—the guns would be stilled.

Sleep came easier these days, and his fits of restlessness caused him to reach only for her and not for a weapon. There were no weapons in the house. There never would be in any house they would ever live in.

"Mikhail?" The cheerful shout was accompanied by the opening and closing of the door beyond the living room.

"In here!" He turned in the leather swivel chair that was her last addition to his study.

Jenna walked into the sun-drenched room, the light catching her long blond hair that fell from beneath a dark wool cap, her tweed coat buttoned to ward off the autumn chill outside. She lowered a canvas bag to the floor and kissed him lightly on the lips. "There are the books you wanted. Anybody call?" she asked, taking off her coat. "They put me on the student foreign exchange committee and I think I'm supposed to be at a meeting tonight."

"You are. Eight o'clock, Dean Crane's place."

"Good."

"You enjoy it, don't you?"

"I can help, I *do* help. Not only because of the languages, but mainly with the government papers. All those years falsifying documents does give one an advantage. At times I find it terribly difficult to be so honest. As if I'm doing something wrong."

They both laughed. Havelock reached for her hand. "Someone else called."

"Who?"

"Berquist."

Jenna stiffened. "He hasn't tried to reach you since you sent in your report."

"He honored my request. I told him to leave us alone."

"Then why call you now? What does he want?"

"He doesn't want anything. He thought I should be brought up to date."

"About what?"

"Loring's all right, but he'll never get back in the field again."

"I'm glad. On both counts."

"I hope he can handle it."

"He will. They'll make him a strategist."

"That's what I suggested."

"I thought you would."

Michael released her hand. "Decker didn't make it."

"What?"

"It happened months ago, but they covered it up. It was the most generous thing they could do. He walked out of his house the morning after Seneca's Notch and was caught in the cross hairs. The guards moved in on the killer's car—the one sent by Pierce—and so did Decker. He just kept walking into the fire, so help me God, singing 'The Battle Hymn of the Republic.' He wanted to die."

"The death of a zealot."

"Futility. He'd learned; in his twisted way he had a lot to offer."

"It's history, Mikhail."

"History," agreed Havelock.

Jenna walked back to the canvas bag and took out the books. "I had coffee with Harry Lewis. I think he's working up the courage to tell you."

"Birchtree?" Michael smiled. "It'll be something he can tell his grandchildren. Professor Harry Lewis, undercover man, complete with a code name."

"I don't think he's terribly proud of it."

"Why not? He didn't do anything wrong, and he did it better than most. Besides, he got me a job I happen to like very much. . . . Let's have Harry and his wife to dinner, and when the phone rings—believe me, it'll ring—I'll say it's for Birchtree."

"You're outrageous," said Jenna, laughing.

Havelock stopped smiling. "I'm restless," he said.

"It was the call."

"I get so goddamned . . . *restless.* " He looked at her.

"Let's take a walk."

They climbed the steep hill several miles west of the house where the high grass bent with the breezes; the earth was hard, sun-baked, the sky an eloquent blue, speckled with the tassels of windswept clouds. Below to the north was a winding stream, the waters curling gently around the bends, flirting with the low-hanging branches and heading south with a purpose on the other side of the hill.

"We had a picnic in Prague," said Michael, looking down. "Remember? The Moldau was below then."

"We'll have a picnic here," said Jenna, watching him closely. "Chilled wine, salad—those dreadful sandwiches you like so much."

"Ham and cheese, with celery, onions and mustard."

"Yes," she said, smiling. "Unfortunately, I remember."

"If I were famous, they'd name it after me. It'd sweep the country, be on every menu."

"Then keep a low profile, my darling."

His smile waned. "You're stronger than I am, Jenna."

"If you want to believe that, fine, but it isn't true."

"It keeps coming back . . . the restlessness."

"Depression, Mikhail. And less and less, we both know that."

"Still, it comes back and I turn to you. You don't have to turn to me."

"But I do."

"Not this way."

"I never went through what you did for the length of time you did. And there's something else. It was always your responsibility, not mine. Every decision you made had to cost you a part of yourself. It was yours, you were there. I could hide—behind you. I couldn't have done what you did. Quite simply, I don't have the strength."

"That's not true."

"Stamina, then, and that *is* true. All those weeks I was running, every now and then I had to stop, stay where I was and do nothing, think of nothing. I couldn't go on, not during those moments, and I didn't question myself. I just knew I couldn't. You did; you could. As a child and as a man, and a price has to be paid for what you did—what was done to you. It will pass; it *is* passing."

"A child," said Havelock, glancing at the stream below. "I see him, I feel him, but I don't really know him. But I remember him. When he was frightened or awfully hungry or tired and afraid to sleep, he'd climb a tree at daybreak and check for patrols. If there were none, he'd climb down and run through the fields as fast as he could, faster and faster and *faster.* After a while he felt good again, somehow—confident. Then he'd find a trench in a ravine or a deserted, bombed-out barn and sleep. A six-year-old getting a shot of whisky, all that oxygen in his lungs. It worked, and that was the only thing that mattered. The fever went down."

Jenna touched his arm, studying his face, and began to smile. "Run *now,* Mikhail. Run down the hill and wait for me, but run by yourself. Go on, you lazy thing! *Run!*"

He ran, his legs scissoring the air, his feet pounding the earth, the wind whipping his face and cooling his body, taking the breath from him, replacing it with new breath. He reached the bottom of the hill far below, his chest expanding with each gasp, quiet laughter coming from his throat. The fever was passing; soon it would be gone. Again.

He looked up at Jenna, the sun behind her, the blue sky above. He shouted between swallows of air, "Come *on*, you lazy *thing!* I'll race you back to the house. *Our* house!"

"I'll trip you at the last moment!" yelled Jenna, coming down the hill rapidly but not running. "You know I can do it!"

"It won't do you any good!" Michael took out a bright metal object from his pocket. "I've got the key to the door. *Our* door!"

"Silly!" Jenna shouted, breaking into a run. "You didn't lock it! We've *never* locked it!"

She came to him and they held each other.

"We don't have to," he said. "Not any longer."

ABOUT THE AUTHOR

ROBERT LUDLUM, whose work has been published in seventeen countries and twenty-three languages, is the author of *The Scarlatti Inheritance, The Osterman Weekend, The Matlock Paper, The Rhinemann Exchange, The Gemini Contenders, The Chancellor Manuscript, The Holcroft Covenant, The Matarese Circle* and *The Bourne Identity*. He lives with his wife in Connecticut.